FAE
GUARDIANS

SEASON
OF THE
WOLF
TRILOGY

LANA PECHERCZYK

PRINT ISBN: 978-1-922989-31-4

Season of the Wolf Trilogy features the first three books in the Fae Guardian Series.
The Longing of Lone Wolves
The Solace of Sharp Claws
Of Kisses and Wishes Novella (bonus novella)
The Dreams of Broken Kings

www.lanapecherczyk.com

CONTENTS

ELP
WINTER COURT
ACONITE CITY
ICE WITCH
ACONITE SEA
THE ICE FOREST
HUMAN TERRITORY
UNSEELIE KINGDOM
SEELIE KINGDOM
CRYSTAL CITY
RUSH'S CABIN
MEANDERING WOODS
WHISPERING WOODS
CRESCENT HOLLOW

NE
OBSIDIAN MINE
OBSCENDIA
CLAW BASIN
IE ORDER UTPOST
AUTUMN COURT
RUBRUM CITY
CORNUCOPIA TRADE CITY
FENRYSFIELD
THE CEREMONIAL LAKE
THE ORDER OF THE WELL
DELPHINIUM CITY
SPRING COURT
HELIANTHUS CITY
SUMMER COURT

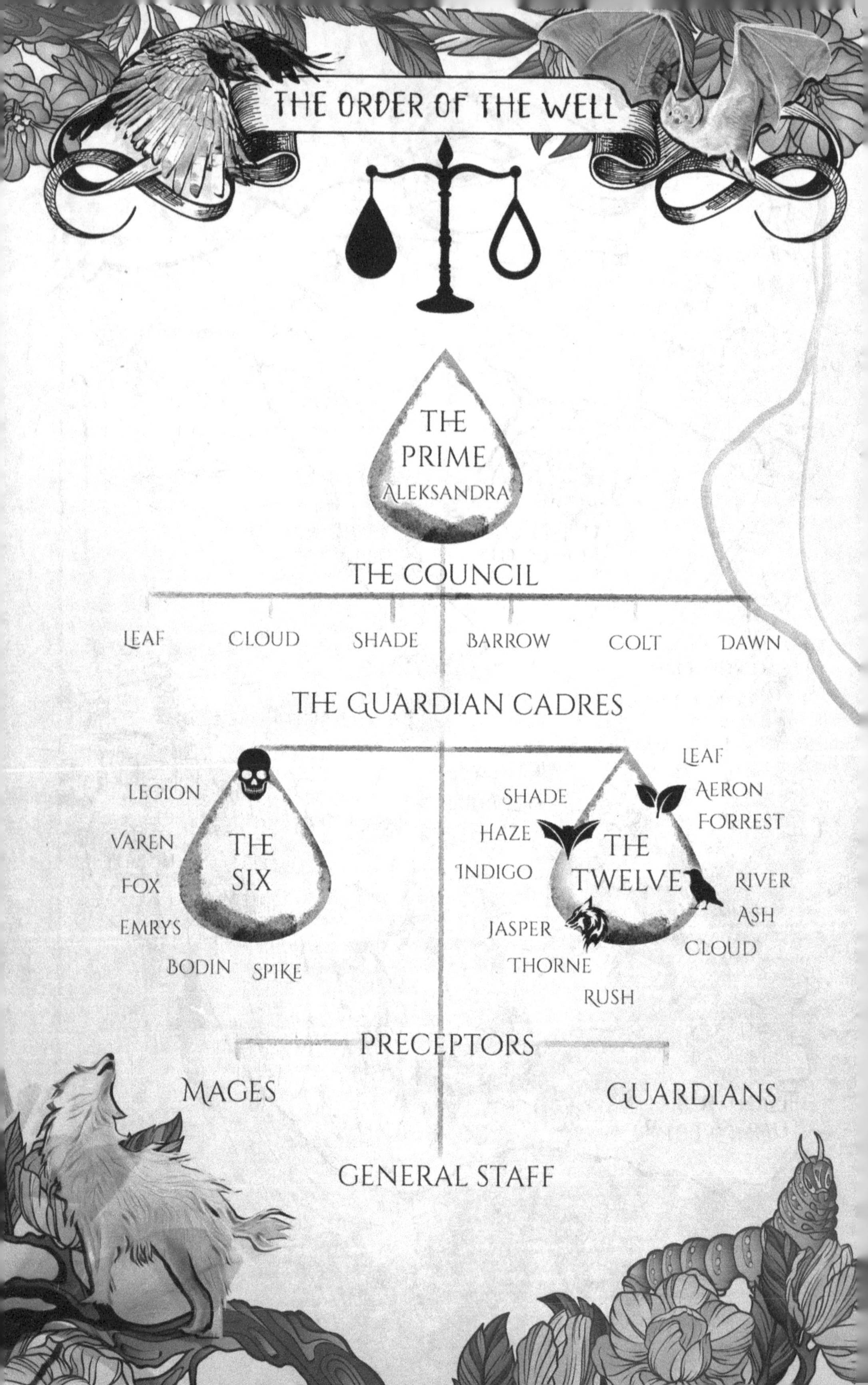
THE ORDER OF THE WELL
THE PRIME
ALEKSANDRA
THE COUNCIL
LEAF
CLOUD
SHADE
BARROW
COLT
DAWN
THE GUARDIAN CADRES
LEGION
VAREN
FOX
EMRYS
THE SIX
BODIN
SPIKE
SHADE
HAZE
INDIGO
JASPER
THORNE
RUSH
THE TWELVE
LEAF
AERON
FORREST
RIVER
ASH
CLOUD
PRECEPTORS
MAGES
GUARDIANS
GENERAL STAFF

THE LONGING OF LONE WOLVES

FAE GUARDIANS BOOK 1

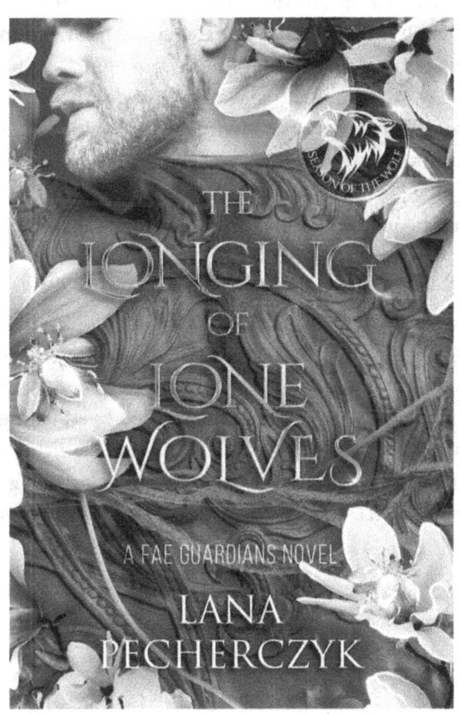

BLURB

Rush is a Fae Guardian, a wolf-shifter whose enhanced abilities have made him a ruthless protector of Elphyne. His job is to protect the realm from the human enemy, and to ensure the sins of the past never come to pass again lest magic die forever. But one night of weakness resulted in a curse worse than death – exile. Now he spends his lonely time longing to be part of the living, once again protecting them from monsters... until one mysteriously washes up on the shores of his lake.

Clarke is human. She's beautiful, feisty, and fierce. She's also the only person who can see him, speak to him, and touch him.

If he hands her over to the Order, she's his ticket to having his curse removed. Unable to resist the opportunity, he tricks her into a bargain of obedience, never once suspecting his world is about to be turned upside down. The more he learns about this human enemy, the more he realizes she's not the monster he's been trained to believe. In fact, she's capable of inciting passion he'd never dreamed possible again. But Clarke has a message from the past... sins are already repeating. This time, if they don't stop the coming evil, it won't just be magic that dies. It will be everything.

THE
LONGING
OF
LONE
WOLVES

CHAPTER
ONE

Clarke O'Leary woke up yawning. Then the tang of sulfur burned her nose and she sneezed, jolting with a splash.

A splash?

She opened her eyes and blinked until everything came into focus. She lay in shallow warm water. Icy air bit her nose. Tall snow-tipped fir trees crowded her on one side, and on the other, clear blue sky. *Blue* sky. The shock of it slammed through her.

Where the hell am I?

Because it wasn't Vegas. At least not the one she knew with the scorched sky and nuclear winter. *That* Vegas had been quarantined, half-underground and isolated in the futile hope of avoiding radiation drifting across the continent.

Clarke jackknifed up and grasped her head at the giddy onslaught. Her stomach revolted and she leaned to the side to vomit something thick, dark and sluggish. *Gross.* Moving her eyes hurt. God, everything hurt.

Shifting away from her mess, her fingers hit something rough underwater. Smooth and curved. She pulled out an oxidized Coke can. The letter "C" had been carved into the aluminum. It was just like the can she had drunk from last night... but old. And in water. In the middle of nowhere.

A growing sense of doom settled in her stomach. She noticed more odd things. The metal on her watch had deteriorated and a network of rust covered her bracelet's brittle charms. She fumbled about the shore, searching for more evidence of... of what, she wasn't sure... but all she came across was more mud, more strange sulfur smelling water, and more throat-tightening panic.

Where was she?

Why was she there?

She jammed the heels of her palms into her eye sockets.

Calm down, Clarke. Think.

Scrambling back in time, she tried to conjure the last thing she remembered—the long sleep, waking in water—but her brain was as sluggish as the surrounding lake. Tiny warm waves lapped against her legs in a soothing way, as if to say, "It's okay. Don't stress. You are where you're meant to be."

Think.

She had to reach further back than that. Back to *before* the sleep. To yesterday. To the end of the world.

She had been in a one room apartment, watching apocalyptic news on a tiny television, drinking soda with two girlfriends—Ada and Laurel—wondering if it would be her last. *Knowing* it would be her last. The memory solidified in her mind. Laurel wouldn't stop switching channels, looking for more up-to-date news. Ada had paced beside the couch. And Clarke had scratched her initials into the Coke can. But that was yesterday... wasn't it?

Chilly air brushed her face and nipped at her skin. This wasn't her apartment. And she wasn't in war-torn Vegas. But she was alive.

Clarke checked down the shore. The lake stretched for miles. She glimpsed a cabin hiding in the snow-capped fir trees some distance away. Smoke curled from the chimney until it disappeared in a lazy dance. It looked like something out of a fairytale.

But this was real. Down in the water, her reflection still belonged to the same freckle-faced redheaded grifter. Flushed cheeks. Fever-bright blue eyes. Purple lips and chattering teeth despite the warm water. It was her, Clarke O'Leary, petty thief. Sometimes psychic, sometimes fake. Always a dreamer.

Think, Clarke. Breathe. Remember.

The world had gone crazy. She'd just come home from the casino. With her precognition skills, she could usually feel out when the cards would play her way. Usually. But this particular night, she'd gone home early. The casino had been closed.

Why had the casino been closed?

Because of the war. They'd thought they were safe, that the bombs hadn't hit Vegas, but it was the fallout they should have worried about. The war came for everyone, and for those it missed, the scorched sky took care of them. Weather patterns changed. Crops wouldn't grow. Nuclear plants went into meltdown. Around the world tectonic plate movements tore buildings down as the land shifted. They'd tried to continue with normal life for as long as possible, hoping they'd be safe. Until they weren't.

A wave drew back from her legs like a blanket, exposing threadbare jeans and previously white tennis shoes, now brown and full of holes. She tapped her watch. Dead. Her rusty charm bracelet tinkled, and the matching earrings rocked at her ears. Her father had given her the jewelry. A gift for every important event in her life. A candle charm for her sweet sixteenth. An ice-cream charm for her graduation. The watch when her mother walked out on them. Her father had died just before her eighteenth birthday. Heart attack.

But that was years ago. She shook off the memories and picked at her disintegrating clothes. If this was the outfit she wore yesterday, then why was it falling apart? Why was her bracelet so rusted? And the weird vomit...

Something landed on her lashes and she blinked. Another thing got in her eye. She pushed wet hair from her cheek and trapped it around her ear. The unmistakable flurry of snow floated down to dust her face. Wonder warmed her, and then the memory hit.

She'd stepped outside the apartment because it had been snowing. In Vegas. That was the last thing she remembered.

CHAPTER
TWO

Fifty years of hunting rogue humans had brought Rush to this—peeping at a woman while she bathed in the hot springs of a lake. *His* lake. He scrubbed his face at the absurdity and stepped out of the forest to see better, but couldn't keep the scorn from his mind. Him, an ex-Guardian, leering like a teenager.

"What do you think," he grumbled to the gray wolf next to him. "Does she look good enough to eat?"

For much of the past decade, the scrappy old wolf had been Rush's constant companion. Him and his pack of snow wolves currently hunting in the surrounding forest. Even though Rush had not shifted into wolf form for decades, the locals still scented him as a kindred spirit and bowed to his energy.

Rush winced. He may not be with the original Nightstalk family, but he'd made a new family. A new pack.

Gray growled and licked his teeth, eyes never leaving the woman, his prize. *Their* prize. Rush's curse forbade him to touch another living being, but the wolf at his side was free. The pack helped Rush hunt wayward humans roving into their territory. They were how Rush continued to keep the realm of Elphyne safe, even if his job as a Guardian was finished.

The woman had overlong russet hair. Pale, creamy skin. A delicate neck that drew the eye down to plump breasts stretching her top. She was a beauty like no other, but she would forever be out of reach for someone like him. He tugged at the neck of his fur-lined cape. Despite the snow surrounding him, he cooked.

"Possibly a nymph, playing in the water?" he murmured.

Gray snorted.

Maybe.

She couldn't see Rush. No one could. The curse took care of that too. So he studied her openly.

She wore strange tattered clothes in a fashion he'd not seen before. Rush had traveled all over Elphyne, even beyond into the forbidden Crystal City where humans killed fae on sight... if they'd been able to see him. But this woman, her clothes were strange. She tugged at her shoes.

A snarl ripped from his throat as a shard of light hit his eyes.

"Metal," he hissed to Gray. "She's wearing metal on her wrist."

His hand moved to his belt and hovered over the bone knife, still bloody from his recent hunt. The knife almost sang as his palm hit the hilt. It wanted out again, and when the woman tucked long red hair behind a small round ear, Rush gave the knife what it wanted. He pulled it out.

She's human.

Through clenched teeth, he ordered Gray, "Go back to the pack. Wait for the word."

Gray snuffled in protest.

Damn it. He should have brought his sword *Starcleaver*. At least with that, he'd have less of a chance at touching her and triggering the pain that came with the curse. Another order was on the tip of his tongue, and then movement near the lake caught his attention. Multiple bodies crept toward the woman from the sides. Two, three... six. Six fae. And—Rush sniffed the air with a throaty snarl—someone he hated more than anything in the world. Thaddeus. His uncle. And now alpha of the Crescent Hollow wolf-shifter pack.

Fabulous
VEGAS

THREE

The howl of a wolf snapped Clarke's attention to the shadows of the woods. The hairs on her arms lifted. She crawled out further onto the bank, leaving the warm water behind. A feeling wrapped around her chest. The familiar buzzing of premonition. And then... *caution.* Someone or something watched from the darkness of the woods. The sense of it creeped up her spine and then *she knew.* Something was hunting her. It was the same as all her premonitions. Good or bad, the sensation she felt in the square of her chest predicted her own future when she saw everyone else's in full color motion pictures.

Another howl.

Breath caught in her throat, her pulse picked up speed, and she squinted to scan the area for the source of danger.

She found it.

But not in the woods as she'd thought. Crouching, hostile shadows closed in on her. Two, maybe three from each side. To the right, muscular men with long, white hair crept toward her. Others encroached from the left. The buzzing in her chest grated with slick bad vibes, just like it had every time Clarke had been around an evil person in her past. These men fit the mold. All of them held weapons—swords, axes, hammers. None were metal, but still looked dangerously fierce. Wooden handles with creamy white blades. She swallowed. Bone. They were made from bone.

Run.

Run!

The only escape was the forest ahead. Ignoring the protest of her stiff body, she bolted. Her feet flew across the sodden shore. Hair whipped behind her, and the wind whispered in its place. *"Run faster. They're coming for you. They'll eat you alive. Run."*

And then she heard it.

Thudding footsteps behind her. Every step, every clouded breath, was echoed by a deeper, heavier one. Guttural. Powerful. Getting closer. Closer. Almost... Terror filled her, gushing from within. Something brushed against her back, causing her to stagger. She let out a scream. Her cry shook the trees and echoed across the water. Birds took to the air in fright.

A hit between her shoulder blades blasted air from her lungs. She launched forward onto hard snow, only inches from the forest's edge. Hidden sharp things dug into her cold palms as she slid across the ground like she was on a sled. Her hands hit something smooth under the snow and she tried to grasp it, but couldn't gain purchase. When she stopped, what she saw beneath the snow didn't make sense. The familiar pattern printed on shiny perspex didn't belong here. Red. Yellow. Blue. White. It couldn't be. But it was. One second, that's all it took, and then her brain clicked. She'd fallen on the *Welcome to Las Vegas Sign*, cracked and deteriorated.

Old.

Ancient.

Something heavy landed on her back and jarred her out of her shock. It pressed down with a beastly warning snarl that breathed heat on her neck. Her face squashed into the sign until her nose hurt. She whimpered, struggling and bucking frantically, but the thing on her back was too heavy, too strong. And then she felt it snuffling into her wet hair, breathing her scent in. Clarke froze, petrified. *What the hell?*

Something soft yet rough explored the ridge of her curved ear, running from top to bottom. Outraged, she pushed the last of her stamina into her limbs, but she only convulsed beneath the immense pressure. She hit her chin. Dizziness blurred her vision.

A deep male voice bloomed hot in her ear. "Don't move, filthy human."

A man. Not a monster. Men were made of flesh and blood, not beings of terror and dreams. Men could be fought. Men could be defeated.

"I should kill you right now," he said and pressed something cold and hard against her neck. It was a knife. She was sure of it. "But I think my soldiers are hungry."

A chorus of male snickering and boots crunching announced more attackers. The hungry he spoke of wasn't food. She could almost feel their hostile energy surround her like a living thing. Every instinct in her body screamed that they would hurt her, claim her, destroy her.

Never.

She'd never let Bishop's boss take her. And she wouldn't let these men. Clarke gritted her teeth, kicked out and scrambled forward, clawing at the edge of the forest, grasping the dirt and leafy debris for something to hold. Just a little further. Just an inch.

Find a rock. A stone. A piece of the sign.

The male behind her cursed, gripped her ankles and dragged her back with a grunt. She dug into the ground, gouging for purchase, but it was no use. He was strong, and when he flipped her body so she was on her back, she knew why. Her nightmare was real.

A man loomed over her, almost seven foot high. Fur-lined cape. Long silver-white hair tied at the nape. A puckered scar across the hollow of his cheek. He looked to be in his mid-thirties, but the menace in his eyes told another story. It was full of age-old cruelty, and when he sneered with salacious knowing, her skin crawled.

"What have we got here?" he drawled.

Shadows pressed in around her. Stag horns protruded from the head of a stocky man with a longbow strapped over his shoulders. Two men had ram horns curling in their dark, oily hair. They also had cloven feet. And when her gaze shifted back to her captor, she realized one thing linked them all.

Pointed ears.

Tipped with a light dusting of fur.

Was this a costume party? Some kind of weird anime cosplay convention? Even though it was illogical, some part of her mind still tried to send her back to Vegas, to any excuse that made this a dream. But the sign beneath her body told another story. The old can in the lake. Her rusted jewelry...

The scarred one's ears flattened. He bared vicious teeth that belonged on a wild animal.

Clarke's fingers curled around snowy dirt, and she threw it in his eyes.

He dodged with a smile that never hit his cold eyes.

The stag-man, sucked his teeth loudly. "I don't think you should let 'er get away with that, Faddeus."

"It's Thaddeus, you imbecile. Th-th-*th*. Crimson, save me." Her captor rolled his eyes, but then his mood changed in an instant. He was on her, flattening her with his powerful body, gripping her chin painfully, forcing her lips to squish like a fish. He made her look into his yellow gaze. "You'll pay for that, human wench."

Then his weight was off her. He barked to his men, "String her up."

Hands of steel gripped her from all sides and carried her toward a tree. They pushed her back against it and tied her wrists to the tree.

"Get off me, you pointy-eared beasts!" She kicked out.

But they only laughed and dodged. Excitement rolled off them as much as fear convoluted inside Clarke. One of them struck her across the cheek until her eyes blurred. Pain numbed her mind and she retched, nauseated.

More cruel laughter.

Thaddeus, seemingly their leader, stalked up to her with a curious glint in his eye. His bone sword dragged lazily in the snow behind him. He used its tip to lift the tattered hem of her shirt and dipped his gaze to take a cheeky look beneath. Then the sword lifted, shredding her shirt in two, exposing her dirty bra.

That bone was sharp. It would cut deep.

Whistles of encouragement spurred Thaddeus on and he puffed out his chest. He grazed the sword tip up to her chin, then gently pushed her hair out of the way to inspect her ear again. For a moment, his eyes narrowed and turned thoughtful.

"Red hair," he murmured softly. "Red wasn't on the list. That means you're mine."

The point of his blade caught on her earring, and he ripped it from her lobe. Agony exploded. Gulping, she repeated a mantra in her head. *Don't show weakness. You are not a victim. You are a survivor.*

At her lack of reaction, he gave a disappointed sigh. "And to think I was going to keep you for my own pleasure. With your face, I almost mistook you for an elf. Almost. Oh well. I guess all that is left to do with your kind is use you for sport." He leaned in close, his stale breath on her cheek. "My crew have been hunting for days. We're not allowed to play with the other humans we found, but you're not on the list. It means you're mine."

Clarke spat in his face.

A backhand to her cheek sent her face careening to the side. The rope tugged sharply at her wrists, keeping her upright.

But then something odd happened. Through blurred eyes, she saw a tall, well-built stranger casually wander into the group and lean against a tree. One of them, but... not. Where the others triggered sickly vibrations in her chest, this one provoked good tingles. Fluttering. There was no other way to explain it. All the pain, fear, and terror in her body emptied as she locked eyes with the golden-eyed man. No... not man. Male. Like the others, he was the male of some new species. Silver shoulder-length hair was pulled back to reveal fur-tipped and pointed ears. A short beard peppered a sharp jaw. Unbridled curiosity played across his handsome face. The fact he took no part in her ridicule showed he had nothing to prove. He was already aware of his own strength.

Just as tall as Thaddeus, just as muscular, but a world apart in sophistication.

"Help," she croaked.

Dark brows lifted, and he checked over his shoulder, as if she spoke to someone else.

Her attackers continued to paw at her. The forced removal of her shoe demanded her attention, but she refused to accept what it meant. Already she felt her consciousness try to leave the physical constraints of her body, to distance herself from what was about to happen, but she wouldn't take her eyes from the golden-eyed stranger. He pushed off the tree and prowled toward her, wending through those watching the show, intense eyes always on Clarke. No one else saw him, but they shifted out of the way as though they felt the wind and parted for the storm.

There was power in that man. It licked against her skin.

The others made no move to suggest they knew of his presence. They continued to rib and pat each other on the back for their delicious find, a bonus considering they weren't allowed to play with their earlier hunt.

"You can see me," the stranger stated, voice deep like rolling thunder.

"Am I not supposed to?"

Another shoe came off. More raucous male laughter. And then a ram-horned man came up with a lascivious look on his face. His thick, stubby fingers dug into her jeans and tugged down. He had hair on his knuckles.

Clarke let out a cry of resistance and kicked out. But they liked that. Another took hold of an ankle, and a third took the other. Someone sucked her toe. There were too many hands. Too many faces. Four, five of them? Thaddeus watched from a few paces back, enjoying every moment as he picked his nails with a knife.

"Come on!" Tears burned Clarke's eyes as she turned to the stranger. Why wouldn't he help? "Don't be an ass. Do something."

"Oh yes, you'll beg," Thaddeus laughed. "You'll beg right up until the end. Humans always do." He turned to his crew, rested a boot on a rock, and then leaned on his knee. "Isn't that right? Humans and their disgusting *mana*-less lives. You'd think they'd love to end their pitiful existence sooner, but they always want to be spared. And for what?"

His men stopped pawing her to grumble, scrunching their faces in confusion.

"Humans have nothing," Thaddeus elaborated. "It's why they want *our* land. The land we earned through blood, sweat and tears. The land we fostered back to life, now so full of plenty and magic. While they live between cold walls, we have this!" He gestured at the greenery bursting from beneath the snow.

Clarke looked too. Truth be told, it was greener than she'd expected wildlife to be in a cold territory. When the nuclear winter had settled, Vegas heat made way for ice. All plant-life had suffered. Nothing much grew as bountiful as it did here.

The men shouted their agreement to something Thaddeus had declared. Clarke tuned into the tail end of it.

"... it's why I'm the alpha of Crescent Hollow. Your Lord. I'm the only Nightstalk who can protect you from both fae *and* human threats. I'm the only one who can play both sides of the game and win. I'm the only Nightstalk who will reward you like this." He gestured at Clarke, to the three touching and groping her.

They cheered.

A look of disgust ghosted the stranger's features. He met Clarke's eyes coolly.

"I'll help you."

"Thank you," she murmured.

Thaddeus laughed. "Thank you? Are you insane? Never say thank you to a fae. It means you are in our debt."

Clarke slid her eyes back to the stranger. Was this true?

He gave a curt nod. "I need something in return. A bargain."

Are you fucking kidding me? "Fine. Whatever. I'll do whatever you want."

Her attackers broke out into glee-filled laughter.

"Hear that? Line up, fae," one of them said. "No need to turn into heathens. We can share."

A long, peaked tongue ran up the side of her face and she shuddered in revulsion. Another wet tongue hit the skin of her stomach.

"What," she whispered. "What do you need me to say?"

"Say you want more, wench," one of her attackers said and then laughed.

She gritted her teeth. Why couldn't they see the stranger? Or hear him?

The stranger tossed one side of his cape over a shoulder and then rolled up his sleeve to reveal a corded forearm covered in blue glowing glyphs.

"You can be heard when I cannot," he explained. "So you will be my voice where I cannot speak. You will be my hands, where I cannot touch. Do you understand?"

"Yes. For crying out loud," she shouted at him. "Just do it already." Whatever he was about to do. *Do it now.*

The men surrounding her started to look oddly at each other.

"Never had a willing participant before, boss," noted a ram-horned one.

Thaddeus, still picking his nails with the tip of a small bone knife, only shrugged. "You learn something new every day."

Clarke scowled at the handsome stranger.

"I need you to do these things for me," he added. "Do you accept?"

"I already said yes."

"Just making sure." His lips curved in a slow, wicked smile. Clarke's heart skipped a beat, and for a moment, she thought the good vibrations she'd picked up from him were wrong, but he slammed his palm onto hers. A deep electric shock made her fingers spasm and shot heat down her arm.

His eyes widened. "I can touch you."

So intimately close, his lashes lowered on her with awe. A strange blue teardrop tattoo glittered under his eye. Clarke had no time to wonder what it meant, and then the electricity intensified at their joined hands. Energy and light rippled between their touch, casting the area into blue relief.

"Then we are bound," he rasped, letting go.

The light flared only for a moment, just long enough for Clarke's attackers to jump back with shock.

"Witch," someone shouted.

Thaddeus answered calmly, "Impossible. She's human. She's forsaken by the Well."

"Hurry!" Clarke shouted at her supposed savior. The idiot still stared at his palm, proud as punch.

Snapping out of his daze, he winked at her—*the bastard winked!*—and then let loose a shrill whistle. Wincing, Clarke shut her eyes and turned to the side, waiting for something to happen. Nothing.

She opened her eyes to see her attackers gathering themselves. They hadn't heard the whistle. Not one of them. Maybe this was all a dream, a delusion. Maybe she still lay in the frozen yard in Vegas, and she'd seen that sign before she'd passed out. It made better sense than the evidence she'd been presented with... that she had awoken in a time long since past hers.

But then the first haunting howl of a wolf sounded in the distance.

And then another.

And another.

Each time, the sound grew louder.

"*Damn it,*" spat Thaddeus. He pointed his knife to the stag-antlered man. "Take the left." He pointed at the rams. "To the right." Then to the remaining men, "You wolves with me."

Wolves? They looked like normal men with unusual ears. Clarke glanced at her savior. His ears perked as though he'd caught the mouse, and then he flashed her a grin. He had the kind of smile that transformed a face. It created double brackets next to his mouth, crinkles besides his eyes and infectious mirth in Clarke's own body. Words vacated her mind.

Only for an instant.

Then shock slammed everything out as a pack of snarling wolves emerged from the trees. One by one, the wild animals prowled closer, baring teeth beneath trembling lips. A gray wolf locked onto Thaddeus with single-minded focus.

Thaddeus strode into the center of the small clearing and tossed a placating look at his crew. Something like, *I got this*. And then he crouched into an attack stance and snarled back at the gray wolf.

Energy burst in the clearing. It made Clarke feel like she should turn tail and run for the trees, but the gray wolf wouldn't back down. It stepped toward Thaddeus, strengthening the power of its snarl.

Shocked, and a little confused, Thaddeus blinked. He gave a short, impotent laugh, and then seemed to gather himself. Cracking his neck, he refocused on the wolf and shook out his fists. This time when he snarled, it transformed his body. Energy rippled from him. Claws protruded from his fingers. His nose elongated. His canines lengthened over his bottom lip, and the deep alpha snarl that came from the base of his throat froze every movement within Clarke's body. He was more wolf than man. Every inclination within wanted her to lie on the floor and submit.

The gray wolf paused. It stopped snarling and whined. It too felt the driving force of the alpha's growl.

With a smug toothy smile, Thaddeus advanced.

"Gray," her savior warned.

But the wolf rolled to show its belly.

A curse ripped out of her savior's mouth. He tossed a concerned glance at Clarke, clearly grappling with a decision he didn't want to make. Then he refocused on the wolves.

"Attack," he ordered, voice as gravelly as Thaddeus's had been during the change. Power exploded from him. Clarke could feel it against her skin as though she'd come too close to a fire.

The pack of wolves changed. Submission gave way to dominance. They launched at Clarke's attackers, ferociously biting down on whatever piece of skin they could find. The stench of fresh blood filled the air, and she swooned. Memories from her past hit her squarely between the eyes. Stumbling into an alley to find Bishop and his men executing someone. A gunshot. Blood. Brains. The blurry video of a man watching it all from a smart phone. The sour burn of a Tequila Sunrise as it regurgitated up her throat.

A wave of dizziness drove Clarke to the side to puke. Something like mud came out again. She groaned. So gross. Heat and sweat prickled her skin. She only had time to register Thaddeus give the order to retreat when blackness crowded her vision.

Everything went fuzzy. No.

No no no.

Not now. Don't—

FOUR

Thrashing in sleep, Clarke's dreams took her back to her past.

She shivered as she ducked inside the Bellagio lobby. She lifted her chin and pretended she had the right to be there, despite the rain drenched outfit she wore. Squelching along the tiled lobby, she headed straight toward the casino. The electronic pings and ca-chings covered her grumbling stomach. Those sounds meant food. They meant survival.

Armed security eyed her as she entered, but she pushed past as though she had somewhere to be. For all they knew, she was on her way through the casino, to the hotel access on the other side. This was the third casino she'd tried today. Each time security had strongly encouraged her to leave. Word must be getting around about her card reading skills. Still... a girl had to eat.

Knowing her face was most likely on a watchlist wall somewhere, Clarke decided today she would try her luck at the slot machines. She squeezed water from her ponytail and wiped her face as she trolled the slot machine aisles, listening to that little feeling in her chest that fluttered when she neared a lucky machine. It took a few laps. When an old man wearing a Baker Boy cap vacated a quarter slot machine, she took his place.

The seat was still warm.

He sat down next to her with a frown cast her way. Probably wasn't a polite thing to do when he'd been working the machine for hours. But she was hungry. She put a quarter in, and pulled the lever. Tension rode her body as she waited for the slots to line up. Two stars and a cherry. Not this time. She popped another quarter in, and held her breath as she pulled the lever. It shouldn't be long now. The fluttering was worse.

The slots whirled in a dizzying blur of motion. Then slowly... each slot stopped with a blip.

Cherry.

Cherry.

Cherry.

The alarm bell went off and money poured from the collection tray. Shit, she'd forgotten to get a cup. Next to her, the old man pulled his cap off and handed it to her. "Got more luck than me, girl."

Her heart tugged. "Thank you."

She collected the coins, took out enough for a meal, and then handed the cap back to the man with a smile. "You warmed the machine up for me," she said.

His mouth opened in protest, but she didn't stick around. She turned and left. Just as she approached the exit, she bumped face-first into a security guard. The big beefy guy glared at her and then at the coins in her hands.

"I know you did something to fix the machine."

She lifted her chin. "You can't prove anything."

"We've been watching you, red. Give the coins back, or you're done in this town."

Begrudgingly, she handed him the money she was going to use for dinner. There was no way to prove she'd cheated, but she didn't want to draw attention. Not if she wanted to keep using this town as her paycheck. She'd have to lay low for a while until her face came down from the watchlist.

Cold and shivering, she trumped out of the casino and went to stand before the fountain. The jets burst and danced to a Celine Dion tune. She wanted to hate it, but couldn't. Vegas was home.

A man sidled up next to her.

"Beat it," she snapped. "I got no money."

"Neat trick you did in there," he replied.

Fuck. She groaned and turned, but it wasn't security. It was a man in his thirties, smiling at her all charming and winsome as the breeze lifted his short brown hair.

"I don't know what you mean." She looked away.

"Sure you do." He held out his hand. "The name's Bishop."

"As if I care."

His laugh was hearty and infectious. "You might if you hear what I have to say."

"What?"

"My boss will pay top dollar for someone like you. Come work with me and I'll show you how to use that gift to earn more than a few quarters. I'll make sure you're never taken for granted again."

His hand still hovered between them. She eyed it warily.

And she wasn't sure why she did it. Maybe Celine Dion knew how to serenade. Maybe it was his smile. Maybe she was sick of living day to day. It certainly wasn't the fluttering in her chest because that had made way for the harsh buzzing premonition of dread. But when she put her hand in his, she found she didn't care.

He took her hand and, thinking about her hungry stomach, she let him. But it wasn't a restaurant he took her to. It was through a void.

The dream became a nightmare.

· · ·

FIRE AND DEATH SURROUNDED HER. Wails and screams compounded in her ears. Thunder shook the ground and she thought she might fall through.

Smoke.

Blood.

Brimstone.

Was this hell?

No.

This was the end.

CLARKE SCREAMED AWAKE. Her eyes stung with the remnants of the nightmare still making her heart gallop. *The fire. The terror.* She cried out again, but her voice lost power as it carried away.

Breathing deep lungfuls of air, it took her a moment to get the charred smell out, but eventually the scent of cedar and bergamot filled her nose. Calmer, she shut her eyes. *The nightmares were back.* Strangely, hope flared in her chest. Maybe it was all a dream—the lake, the pointed-eared men who attacked her, the other wolfish man who'd saved her—she opened her eyes.

"Nope. Not a dream," she groaned.

No longer near the woods, she was inside a one-room log cabin. A cozy wood fire blazed in the hearth opposite her. To her right, a window, and on the left, a long kitchen counter. Over it hung a collection of utensils, ceramic pots, and wooden crockery. An unusually large potted plant was in the corner, its leaves weaving up a spindly trunk to branch out like an umbrella near the roof. The foliage fanned halfway across the ceiling. She'd never seen that kind of plant before. Its leaves seemed almost blue. It gave the illusion of living under a forest canopy.

Pinned to the walls on all sides of the cabin were remnants of someone's life. Knickknacks, papers with sketches, and little glass jars filled with odd biological samples. Stones. Leaves. Wooden carvings of little wolves and people. Nothing looked valuable. Nothing worth selling or stealing for later use.

Shelves overflowed with old books. A chest of drawers and trunk stood at the end of the bed she lay in. An old leather battle jacket with segmented pauldrons hung limp on a hook behind the door. Faded blue and black, the jacket belonged in a medieval war zone.

A flurry of white drew Clarke's attention to the window. Through it was a winter wonderland of towering trees around a small, semi-frozen lake. She wasn't far from where she woke up. Nerves bundled in her stomach. She tried to sit for a better look, but bindings halted her. Her hands were tied to the wooden bed frame on either side of her body. The woolen blanket previously pulled up to her neck had fallen to her lap. Split down the middle, her shredded top showed her bra. The grazes on her hands were cleaned.

"What the hell?"

The restraints wouldn't budge. Clarke twisted and pulled until, exhausted, her heavy head fell back on the pillow. A musky, male scent bloomed. She tensed. It smelled good. Homey. Comforting. She turned and inhaled, eyes fluttering closed. God, it was so good. She missed the smell of a man in her bed. There was nothing like two powerful arms surrounding her to chase the nightmares away. That and a good round of physical, muscle-aching love-making was the perfect recipe for a peaceful night's sleep. But she hadn't had a man for at least half a year, about the same time the war had started. The same time she'd realized the depth of Bishop's insanity.

Six months.

That's all it had taken for things to go too far, for panic to grip humanity, for the weather to change and then for the inevitable chaos and death that followed. She bit her lip and wondered what had happened to her friends. Laurel and Ada had helped Clarke leave Bishop and his manipulating ways.

Thumping on the porch warned her before the door opened. In came the tall and broad-shouldered stranger, still as imposing as the first moment she'd laid eyes on him. That restrained strength. That silver-white hair. That dangerous expression. She gulped.

This must be his home.

This must be his bed.

She had smelled him. And *liked* it.

Disgusted with herself, she blurted, "We had a bargain. Let me go."

He dominated the open doorway. Fingers twitched at his side, but he didn't falter. He just stared at her as though she were made of something foreign. Then he kicked his boots on the doorframe to shake the snow and stepped inside. He removed his cape and hung it next to the battle uniform on the hook. Try as she might, she couldn't stop staring. The breadth of his shoulders, flat stomach, and aura of strength, completely captured her attention. He was simply magnetic.

Maybe it was just her brain trying to force this all into being a dream again. She'd been blinded by the charm of a man once, but she'd never do it again. Pity she would have to pull one over this guy and escape. Once Clarke shifted her mindset into grifter mode, she could be callous with her mark's feelings. It was that or live on the streets. She'd chosen her own survival.

Clarke forced her feelings back to the clear and present danger—her captor who was taking a moment to trace a reverent finger down the leather jacket's collar. He tossed a frown Clarke's way, and then reached outside to collect a small, skinned carcass. Maybe a squirrel. He waved in a scruffy looking wolf and then kicked the door closed. It slammed shut with a finality that unnerved her more than she wanted to admit.

That was the same wolf who'd led the pack that ripped into her attackers. And now it padded to a mat before the fire to watch her with golden eyes... the same kind of eyes as her captor. Who looked similar to the man who had turned into a half-wolf. Did that mean her captor was capable of the same terror?

He dumped his catch on the kitchen bench and unhooked a pot. After placing it on the counter, he pushed back the sleeves of his sweater to bare forearms covered with strange blue glowing marks. Clarke stared at his hands for way too long, trying to gauge how much strength was in that grip. How much power would she need to get out of it?

A lot.

Better to use her wit, mind and clever knack for reading people. Plus, she could always shiv him when he wasn't looking. She just needed to find a shiv.

Knowing she stared, he turned the full force of his glower her way. She sunk a little lower on the bed and then realized she was still half naked.

"Are you going to leave me like this?" she muttered. "It's humiliating."

"You *were* covered."

"So this predicament is my fault?" She raised a brow. "Untie me."

"The bargain"—he planted his hands on the bench and leaned toward her—"was for you to be my voice and hands. I never agreed to anything about your *predicament*."

Clarke gasped.

He continued to slice, unperturbed. The fire crackled in their silence. Vegetables tinkled as they hit the pan.

"Hey!" Clarke shouted, irritation heating her neck.

His knife paused mid-slice, but then he continued to work.

This was insane.

What happened to the cheeky, mischievous attitude she'd seen before in the woods? That wild and reckless grin he'd tossed her way before whistling for his wolves. Forget about trying to swindle him. She was getting downright pissed off.

"If you don't untie me, give me some decent clothes and... well if you don't, then you're no better than the men you saved me from."

His face darkened. He growled in warning.

At the fire, the gray wolf's ears perked up.

"I am nothing like that bastard."

"So prove it."

He slammed the knife down and came over. It took all of Clarke's resolve not to cower, but he only tugged the blanket up to her chin and then strode back.

"Oh yeah," Clarke said. "Real mature. I'm still tied up."

"You're a human in fae territory. You don't have rights," he grumbled, and then carried on with his work.

Clarke swallowed a retort because another part of her mind was shouting at her to pay attention to his words. *Fae territory.*

She narrowed her eyes. Didn't the scarred man say something about fae as well? What was his name... Thaddeus?

For the millionth time, she wondered how the hell she'd found herself in the future. Only one possibility kept circling her mind. Could she have been frozen and slept for so long that the world had changed? Evolved into something else? So why the hell wasn't she freaking out?

It was that fluttering *knowing* lodged between her breasts. She explored the premonition further. It was stronger than the fancies her mother hated her having.

"Mind your fancies today, Clarke. We don't want the congregation thinking you're a nit-wit."

Her mother had left because she was afraid of Clarke's premonitions. As a child, Clarke had told her on more than one occasion that the world would end, and when some of Clarke's smaller predictions rang true, her mother walked out. But not before calling her the devil's spawn.

Clarke cleared her throat and sent her awareness around her body, thought about the large fae now stirring a pot at the hearth, of how he'd saved her from being attacked —at his own leisure and gain—and of how she was tied to his bed. He was definitely linked to the fluttering in her chest.

She should be freaked out, but she wasn't. For Christ's sake, she swooned at his scent on the pillow.

Over by the fire, he whittled with a bone knife, turning the wood with aggravated care. Clarke thought the irritation was aimed at her, but when she saw the carving more clearly, she recognized a man with the face of a wolf, like Thaddeus. He was carving memories.

He stared long and hard at the figurehead and then ditched it into the fire. Sparks caught. Shadows moved in the flames, almost making them come alive. Tense and concentrating, he went back to the pot like it held the world's answers. He refused to acknowledge her, but every so often when she looked his way, he must have sensed it. His wolfish ears flattened.

And then it came to her—*he* was the one freaking out. He'd tied her not only to stop her escaping, but because she confused him as much as he did her.

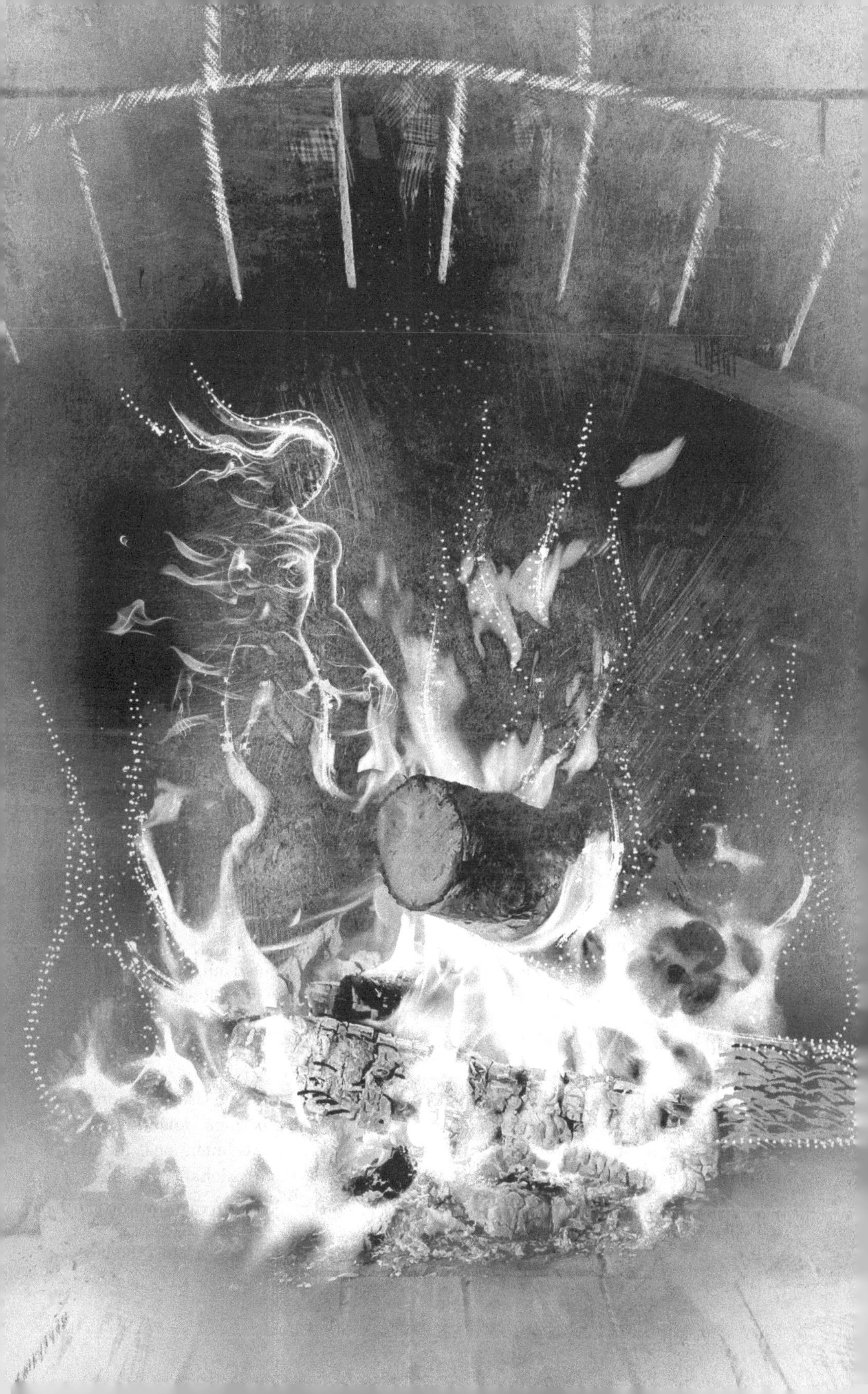

FIVE

Damned woman.

Crackling flames warmed Rush's face as he stirred stew in the pot. Two fire sprites watched in avid fascination from a log. But Rush's attention was elsewhere. Despite the hum of awareness down his body, he refused to look at the female in his bed, or think about the night she'd spent there. The *human* female, he reminded himself.

He could smell her from where he sat.

The next time he slept, her scent would be in his sheets, invading his space with her sweet musk, reminding him of what a selfish asshole he was because he'd put her there for that very reason. A part of him wanted that smell. He'd come home with her unconscious in his arms. Her soft, fragile body curled into his... and he'd felt so big. He'd felt needed. She'd just been attacked, and all he could think was that he didn't want that feeling to go.

Lock her up and never let her leave.

The wolf inside him agreed. It was tired of being caged. It wanted out, and it wanted to be useful again. The rescue had sparked something deep within Rush, and for a moment, he'd forgotten his place.

He shut his eyes, inhaled, held his breath and let it out slowly.

Decades.

It had been decades since he'd touched... *anyone* without suffering. Usually, upon a touch, his curse made them disoriented and forgetful while he became violently ill. It prevented him from communicating by clamping down on his intentions. Small animals had a lesser effect, and like Gray, he got away with the occasional pat of affection before feeling sick.

But with her, no sickness had come. At all.

It would do Rush well to remember that she was the enemy. It was against the law for his kind to mix with hers. They had zero affinity with magic of the Well—*mana*—and held zero capacity for storing mana within. Their love affair with metals and plastics had taken care of that. Mana refused to exist where those resources were present.

He'd taken both plastic items and metal from her body when he'd found her. The wrist item had proved most curious, and he would be sure to ask her about it later. It was like nothing he'd seen in the human city. Their craftsmanship was not so advanced. Not anymore.

None of that mattered anyway. Regaining control of the pack used up much of his mana reserves. One more burst of power, or one shift to wolf, and there would be nothing left to hold the curse at bay. Soon he would look and feel the one hundred and seventy-eight years he'd lived. He would die within minutes.

Unless he found a Well-blessed mate.

May as well get *Starcleaver* and hunt down the mythical dual tusk el'fant. He scoffed. A mate was hard enough to find in this violent and cruel world, but a Well-blessed mate, someone with whom the cosmic divine spirit of the planet deemed worthy enough to share his power. Someone whose magic called to his own. What a fucking joke. There hadn't been a Well-blessed union in centuries. No one expected Rush to break his curse. They never had. And a union between a human and a fae? Impossible. She had no magic.

When the Prime from The Order of the Well had cursed him, she expected him to die a long, lonely death, suffering for the recklessness of unsanctioned breeding in a finite world like theirs.

Shifting awkwardly, Rush tried to ignore the sense that she watched him. She had more demands than a princess. But that wasn't the only thing odd about the woman. He'd not seen a human this far east on their own, let alone a female in tattered clothes. Everyone knew the dangers of being in the Elphyne wilderness without protection. The humans knew. Thaddeus's hunting party was tame compared to the creatures and monsters further inland. Even fae rarely dared leave the safety of numbers for what lived in the wild.

A tingle in Rush's palm reminded him of the cost of the bond he'd made with the woman. A blue glowing glyph had appeared right there, a symbol that his time was ending. Soon all his skin would be covered, and all his mana would be gone. The amount he'd spent today to control the pack had been borderline brainless.

It will be worth it.

He'd failed to help his sister Kyra in Crescent Hollow. He'd failed to protect the female who'd borne his child, and he'd failed to protect that child. But with this human to help him, he wouldn't go to his deathbed without speaking to his son Thorne for the very first time.

Afterwards, he'd have to kill the human.

To protect the Well, our eternal souls, and the future of our planet.

He shut his eyes at The Order's mantra and reminded himself what they taught the young Guardians during training. At the first sign of rot, a plant must be pruned swiftly and without mercy to stop the infection from spreading. One human this far into Elphyne signified more would come, perhaps try to reclaim the land they destroyed.

The woman in his bed might be the harbinger of war, and Rush owed it to the Order to let them know.

"You built this house," she declared.

He tensed. "What?"

"It feels like you've built it yourself. Am I right?"

His breath hitched at her white irises. The blue had washed out. He'd only ever seen that color in the eyes of a Mage of the Well—one blessed with foresight. A Seer. Then the white dissolved to color and the human scowled at him.

"Not that I should give you advice for the way you've treated me, but you shouldn't stand so close to the fire," she quipped. "It might spark and catch you in the eye."

A rumble of dissent vibrated in his throat, and he turned back to the fire. But when he glanced at the sprites dancing, toying with a charred whittled piece of wood, unease tickled his gut. The sprite couple had moved in recently. They kept the place heated and warm while he was out, and he gave them somewhere to live on this frozen, Well-forsaken mountain. But they were irresponsible, wild, and needed to be tamed. There had been accidents on more than one occasion.

Rush rubbed his beard.

The human's eyes had been white.

Like a Seer.

He removed the pot from the flames early. It was ready, anyhow. Time to dish up and see to feeding her. The moment he crossed to the kitchen, the fire sparked, and an ember shot out. Wide-eyed, he watched it arc high into the air, and then descend to smolder on his wooden floor.

A tittering of laughter filtered out from the fire.

He bared his teeth at the flames, and the laughter stopped. Gray joined in, his lip curling with warning.

"Get out." Rush waved at the sprites. Enough. "Shoo."

He strode to the door, opened it wide and stood there waiting with a crinkled forehead aimed at the hearth. Frigid air rushed in, but he wanted those little cretins to know he meant business.

A high-pitched whine shot back at him.

"I told you if you set fire to my house, you're out," Rush ground out.

The male squeaked a challenge, but a piece of fire in the shape of a woman broke loose, jumped to the floor and picked up the smoldering ember before returning to the flames. An almost inaudible voice piped up.

Rush put his hand to his ear. His hearing was excellent, but he wanted to prove a point.

"What was that?" he prompted.

"See? All fixed," the female sprite squeaked.

"Don't do it again." He booted the door shut and then rounded on the human in his bed. "How did you know that would happen?"

"I didn't," she mumbled. "I mean... what the hell? Did you see those things? They were real, right?" She squeezed her eyes shut. "Honestly, if this is a dream, it's the best one I've had."

"I can assure you, it's not a dream, and I'm very real. Now, answer my question."

"Lucky guess, I suppose."

He wasn't convinced.

But how could a human use mana? Could they somehow steal it from a fae and use the power for themselves? Even though they held no capacity for holding it?

None of these questions seemed logical, but in his unseen trips into Crystal City, he'd seen things that defied logic. Giant metal machines billowing smoke and soot. Boxes that carried humans inside and moved on their own accord through the streets. But in all his trips, he'd not once seen any evidence of mana being used. He'd only seen their filthy war machines.

A coldness ran through him at the memory. One day, the humans would use them on the fae, and there would be no turning back for this planet.

He rubbed his jaw again. "But the cabin. How did you know I built it? Have you been spying on me?"

"I only just got here!" Her eyes flew wide.

He filled a bowl with stew and walked over to the bed. Sitting down next to her, he braced himself for the contact-sickness. Old habits died hard. Even though there had been no evidence of it with her, he had to be wary.

He held a spoonful near her mouth, but she clamped those plump lips shut.

"Eat," he ordered, ears twitching.

"I'd rather you untie me so I can feed myself."

A surge of irritation boiled under his skin. Infuriating woman. He was doing her a favor. She'd *thanked* him. She owed him a boon for saving her from assault, mutilation, and who-knew-what by his uncle.

Thaddeus.

The name beat against his mind with unfurling hatred. The bastard uncle. Him being so close to Rush's home was disconcerting, and with a hunting party no less.

I'm the only Nightstalk who can protect you, Rush mocked in his mind.

Thaddeus couldn't protect his crew from the wind.

"I refuse to be treated like a prisoner," she insisted. "We made a deal."

"Fine," he shouted. "Don't eat. Starve." He stood up so fast, hot liquid sloshed out of the bowl and landed on her arm.

She hissed in pain.

Damn it. This was too much.

He strode back to the kitchen and tossed the bowl on the bench. More liquid spilled, but he couldn't care less. With his hands braced on the counter, his knuckles white, he barked over his shoulder, "Well I'd rather not have a filthy Well-damned human in my house, but here we are."

"If I'm human, what does that make you?"

CHAPTER
SIX

The human's gumption astounded Rush. Could she not see who was in charge here? How could she not know? Maybe she didn't. Some humans in Crystal City had been ignorant to what went on beyond their walls.

He faced her with slitted eyes. "I'm fae. Or as you Untouched like to call us, a Changeling."

"A fae changeling," she laughed. "Like when the fairies would swap human babies with a cursed one of their own?"

"Have your people been locked away in your Crystal City so long that you've forgotten?"

"I'm still not following." The mirth in her eyes died, and she bit her bottom lip and then took a deep breath. "I'm sorry if this is rude, but okay, here goes. Why do you have pointed ears? Can you do what that other... fae did? Make your face extend like a werewolf and have claws come out of your hand?"

A werewolf? The wolf in him howled indignantly at the insult. He was a full-blooded shifter, not some mythological creature that only half-turned on a full moon. He was more than that. Before his curse, his mana capacity allowed him to transform five times the size of a normal shifter. That's what being a Guardian of the Well gave him. Being the alpha heir apparent to the Crescent Hollow pack also gave him a great capacity to hold mana, and an even faster rate of replenishing from the cosmic mana that existed in nature.

If the curse hadn't blocked him from refilling his internal mana stores, he'd never have needed to rely on the pack to take Thaddeus down. He would have done it on his own. And none of them would be left standing.

But Rush was cursed. And he couldn't replenish his mana stores. His wolf was a part of him, the darker, more primal part, but still him. Even though he didn't have enough mana to shift, it still howled inside his heart, yearning to be let out.

"Okay," she continued. "Untouched by what? Changed by what?"

Had the humans forgotten their conjoined history?

"Untouched by the magic of the Well," he confirmed. "I'm changed from what you puritans called the superior race. All fae descended from both human and animal. I'm fire-fae. I shift into a wolf through the grace of the magic of the Well. Being connected to the animal species gives us a greater appreciation for the land that feeds us. It is why we are blessed with this glorious power. It gives us the means to defend the land from monsters like you."

"I take offense to being called a monster."

"I don't care. The magic of the Well doesn't care."

"Magic. Shyeah, right." She snorted. "And I'm Mrs. Claus."

"All right, Mrs. Claus." At least they were getting somewhere.

She grimaced. "It was a joke. That's not my name. My name is Clarke."

Clarke. He tested the word in his mind. It rolled off the tongue nicely.

"This is where you tell me your name," she prompted. "Or should I call you Wolfie?"

"I don't have a name." Gritting his teeth, he collected the bowl and went back to the bed. The moment they had cursed him, he lost his Guardian name, D'arn Rush. Then the moment he rose from the ceremonial lake to initiate into the Order, he'd lost the name he was born with, Kaden Nightstalk. As far as his loved ones were concerned, he was a ghost.

A brief image of his proud sister and her long white braid tucked over her shoulder, came to mind.

"Eat," he grumbled and shoved a spoonful toward Clarke's mouth.

She would either have to part her lips, or deal with a disaster down her front, which was already becoming bare with each movement she made. That damned blanket kept sliding down, giving him a tantalizing peek at her odd, but not entirely unwelcome undergarment.

She opened her mouth, took the spoon inside and seemed to melt from the pleasure of it. A little husky moan of appreciation escaped her lips.

"*Crimson*, woman. When was the last time you ate?"

She made an incomprehensible sound and then begged for more, eyes bright and glued to the bowl. He gave her another mouthful, which she devoured with equal relish. Rush's mouth dried and he couldn't take his eyes from the wetness as she licked every morsel from her lips.

"Mm," she moaned. "Goddamn, the fae can cook. Could use a touch more salt."

He raised a brow. "Any more demands, princess?"

She mashed her lips to hold a smile.

It took him a long, pained minute before he could ladle another spoonful of stew and feed her again. This time, she took it silently, watching him watching her. Something primal reared up inside him at the action of feeding her. It was the wolf's longing. Its nature. Provide. Feed. Protect.

Or maybe it was his own.

Seeing her devour something he'd hunted, made, and now hand fed... it wound everything tight.

This was torture.

This was a sacred act reserved for loved ones.

By the time he scraped the bowl clean, and she gave her last feminine moan of appreciation, a very uncomfortable stiffness grew between his legs. He went back to the kitchen bench and ladled himself some stew. With his back to her, he ate it until the evidence of his inconvenient arousal was gone.

Crimson.

She didn't know how she sounded. How she looked. That blanket had fallen too far down her front, and he'd ignored it knowing that it was there. Maybe he had spent too much time watching humans. His body responded as if it didn't care. Heat flushed up his neck, hitting his ears.

Time to get out of this house. He cleared his throat and collected his cape from the hook on the door. He tossed it on the bed, along with a linen tunic he'd pulled from his clothing trunk.

"You'll put those on," he demanded, then found a pair of boots and added them to the heap. "Those too."

"Why?"

"Because you'll perish out there in the cold if you wear improper clothing. You're worth more to me alive than dead."

He untied her and waited for an attack or an attempt at escape, but nothing. She only stood tall and proud, chest and chin out. Not a care in the world for the state of her underclothes. None that she let him see, anyway. She made no move for the tunic splayed on the bed, so Rush picked it up and tugged it over her head. A frustrated sound came from beneath the linen, and she wrested it out of his hands.

"You'll pull all my hair out if you continue doing that," she huffed, and stuck her head through the neck hole. "Plus my old shirt needs to go first."

Not wanting to seem indecent, he averted his gaze and folded his arms. He stared out the window as if it were about to move.

"They're too big," she announced. "Whatever your name is."

Too big?

Unsure of the state he'd find her, Rush gingerly looked over his shoulder and relaxed. The tunic was on, and she held a big boot in her hand.

"Then you can walk barefoot," he replied. "Through the snow."

Her jaw flexed, but after darting a look outside, she fitted them on.

He gathered the rope to retie around her wrists. His bargain would control her movements, but his curse could keep her invisible, like him—only if he touched her, or her by extension.

Rush took Clarke's wrists. The heat of her touch sparked. Her eyes clashed with his, as though she'd felt the jolt too. A moment of blissful connection coursed through his starved emotions, bringing to life urges he'd long since denied. For a long forgotten minute, she wasn't the enemy. She was just a female with startling blue eyes. Touching him.

He reached into his pocket to grasp the strange object he'd found on the lake shore while she'd slept in his bed. Made of two strips of plastic, and one square piece of glass, he'd sensed that it belonged to her. That it might be important. But like the metal jewelry he'd removed from her body, it was just more proof of her blasphemy. And it helped him to stamp down the wicked hope flaring in his chest. He bared his teeth in distaste at the realization a human was the first person to see him in decades.

It could have been a pix, an orc, or even a royal. Hell, he'd take a manticore. But a human?

He looked to the lake through the window. There were two ways a fae could replenish his personal stores of mana. One was to let it seep back into his body from the cosmic mana present in the world around him. Depending on the strength of the fae, this replenishment could take a night, or a week... or a few hours for a Guardian. The other option was to find a source of power, like the hot springs in his lake. It was rife with rejuvenating mana. When he'd built the cabin, he'd liked the idea that if he could break his curse, he'd be able to simply walk into the warm waters and replenish his stores fast. Then he could shift and run in the woods with the pack.

If he had a red coin for every fantasy he'd had while cursed, he'd be a rich man.

He tugged the rope tight, ignoring Clarke's wince. Leaving a long length so he could use it as a lead, he pulled until she staggered out the door and onto the porch where he secured her to a patio pole. Like an obedient soldier, Gray watched her while he went back into the cabin.

The morning air was still cold, but the temperature further down the mountain would be warmer. Rush had given his only cape to Clarke, and he couldn't shift to keep warm because he saved the last of his mana for emergencies. He had no other option than to use his old Guardian uniform.

An errant thrill tripped in his stomach.

With trembling fingers, he lifted the Kingfisher blue and black garment from the hook and shook it out. Blooms of dust clouded the air, and somehow the blue seemed brighter. He slipped it on, flexing his fists as they emerged, as though coming alive for the first time in decades. Perhaps he was. The jacket fit him like a painful embrace. The last time he'd worn it, they had stripped him of his ability to replenish from the Well. He'd not run on four paws since.

That was half a century ago.

As if sensing his yearning, Gray whined from outside.

Rush smoothed his touch down the front bone buttons as he did them up. Next was his sword, Starcleaver. He collected it from beneath his bed and inched the beast from its sheath. Spanning four feet, the steel blade was always clean, as was the edge sharp. No other fae in the realm could use metal and still access their mana. No other fae, but Guardians. The Well had blessed him through a life-threatening initiation. But having this dual ability—to use the very item the rest were forbidden to touch—it was priceless, especially when eradicating magic born monsters. Metal nullified magic.

Two thousand years ago, the humans destroyed the planet. The fae rebuilt it, but at a cost. Magic had an inky side, just like the darkest depths of the ocean, it harbored things and creatures no one had predicted. Every so often, one of these things emerged, ravenous for anything that held mana in its body. Born out of necessity, a Guardian's job was to protect the realm from such creatures, and to preserve the integrity of the Well. Without magic, fae would become mortal like the humans, and they wouldn't be able to foster the frigid land back to life.

Tempted to draw Starcleaver and get reacquainted, he gritted his teeth and resisted, settling for admiring the Elven glyphs on the exposed pommel. He shoved it back into the scabbard and strapped it to rest between his shoulder blades as though it had never left. The sword would provide an additional level of protection through the Whispering Woods.

After he packed, he strode to the hearth and kicked ash over the flames until nothing was left but the two sprites.

"Light this while I'm gone," he warned, "and you'll have nowhere to live when I get back. Understood?"

The female sat on the smoldering log and rested her head in her hands. Her male partner flared blue with rage, but a stern squeak from his female set him straight. He joined her on the log and lifted his glowing hands in surrender.

Good.

Rush slung the rucksack over a shoulder, locked up and joined Clarke on the porch.

He waited for her to comment, to tremble in fear from the sight of the blue, to piss her pants or faint in a swoon. It was often said in omen, if you happened across the flight of the Kingfisher, it would be the last thing you'd see. But the woman watched him with curious eyes, taking in everything from the pommel peeking over his shoulders, to the logo stamped on his breast pocket—a set of scales with a drop of water on each side. No sour scent of fear bloomed in the air, only her infallible sweetness that had confounded him from the moment he'd captured her.

He exhaled sharply through his nose to get her scent out.

"Let's go," he growled and untied her from the pole, then tugged her down the steps and through the shallow snow. She'd better pick up the pace. He wanted to be down the mountain before dark, and it was at least a four day walk to Crescent Hollow.

To his surprise, after a few minutes, she trotted up and overtook him until she walked as far ahead as the lead allowed. Suddenly, she became the one dragging him.

He almost smiled at her tenacity.

Once again, the oddness of her behavior struck him. If she truly knew what he was, she'd never have let him walk behind her. In all his time as a Guardian, he'd never come across a prisoner who'd run headfirst into their doom.

Fear of Guardians kept the humans locked behind their crystal wall.

Not knowing what else to do, Rush examined her from behind as they walked. Scratching his beard, he looked first to the round shell of her ear. He'd have to cover that before they got to Crescent Hollow. The law said a fae must either have their ears visible or be prepared to show them on request on pain of incarceration. With his mana stores so low, and without access to the Well, he couldn't cast a glamour to make her ears look pointed. He'd have to keep the hood of the cape up and hope no one stopped her.

As if she felt his gaze, she tossed a glance over her shoulder. Their eyes met, and that jolt of awareness speared him again. Growling and yanking on the lead, he glared until she remembered her place and returned her attention to the front. The set of her narrow shoulders tensed. She kept walking, but slowed down.

"Tell me more about this place," she said. "I mean, if I'm to help you, I need to know about it."

"Where are you from?" he asked.

"Vegas."

He gave a sound of acknowledgment, as though he knew where this human city was, but he didn't. There was only one human city. One.

"It's been a long time since any human ventured this far from the Crystal City fortress," he added.

"Oh? How long?"

"Since... you don't know?"

She gave an exasperated sigh. "Let's just assume that I know nothing about this world. Remind me of everything."

"Since the fae killed your queen and the brief trade routes were closed."

"Oh. Yeah, that sounds like that would do it."

He narrowed his eyes.

She skipped a rock. "Tell me more."

"You next. Where is Vegas?" He didn't expect her to answer.

"In Nevada. America."

He halted, jerking her to a stop. Gray yipped behind him.

America.

He'd not heard that word since he was a pup. History told of the ancient custodians of this world. No matter the continent they lived, they'd pillaged it for minerals and treated every living thing with disrespect, infecting its surface with metal and plastic, ensuring magic from the earth could not flourish. And then they destroyed it all with their war machines. It was a story all fae children learned from the moment they understood speech. Of course, like cockroaches, some ancient humans had survived. They'd hidden themselves underground, quarantined from the change that blended human DNA with animal until centuries later, they emerged and took their place in the new world.

Greedy humans were never happily contained on their insignificant piece of desecrated land. No. They wanted more. They wanted to harvest the abundant life growing anew—the life the fae had fostered in harmony with the Well. These humans—the Untouched—they were long past reasoning with. Their queen had ordered the invasion of Elphyne, but the fae wouldn't stand for it. After the fae executed their queen, humans used reviled steel, iron and filthy metals to slaughter thousands of fae in retaliation. Decimation continued on both sides until the humans had run out of weapons and retreated behind the high walls of their city like the filthy sacrilegious cowards they were.

The queen's death was centuries ago, before Rush was cursed, before he was exiled from the Order, before... he forced the painful thought from his mind and focused on the human and what she represented.

The Order of the Well would pay dearly to have one such as her in their grasp. Maybe even enough to lift his curse, maybe even enough to reinstate him as a Guardian. And if they didn't, then he had her as his voice. Yes, he could use the woman.

<h1 style="text-align:center">CHAPTER
SEVEN</h1>

The trek down the mountain had taken hours. Clarke's captor only allowed her to stop for a quick toilet break behind a bush, still linked to the lead. She'd tried cajoling him into removing the shackles, but no dice. The fae was rock solid with his decree to keep her tied.

His wolf trotted behind Clarke's heels, yipping when she slowed too much. Her initial drive to lead the way had waned with each passing mile they walked. It would have been laughable if she weren't feeling a little afraid. And tired.

The snow-capped mountain range they descended separated fae territory from human, but all Clarke saw was the lush green forest down the side they walked on. Eventually they wound down to a plateau that showed a one-eighty view from both sides of the mountain, and it was true, on the other side was nothing but white wasteland.

Her captor forced her to stop. Her grateful feet sighed in relief. He pulled out a waterskin from his rucksack and fiddled with the ceramic nozzle while he watched her with intense eyes.

Whatever.

Sometimes working a mark took time. You had to get them in your confidence and trick them into complacency. At least she was alive, fed, and relatively unharmed. The fae hadn't once made a move to assault her the way the others had, in fact, he'd attempted to keep her dignity intact. He wasn't truly bad, he just needed her for something, and as soon as she found out what it was, she could use it to weasel her way out of his bargain.

And then she'd take his jeweled bone knife. Or better yet, his sword. Either would go a long way to help her protect herself. The jewels on that knife would fetch a price... wherever things were sold in this world.

Clarke walked to the edge of the natural viewing platform and shielded her eyes with bound hands. Wind rushed up to greet her. It smelled fresh. Unpolluted. So unlike the air that had been in Vegas at the end. That had been dusty and dank. This was amazing, pure and restorative. To one side was the vast tundra. Not much grew there. Turning, she took in the other side of the mountain where a lush forest thrived.

Magnificent.

Anticipation thrummed when she faced in the forest's direction. She pointed. "So what's down there? That's where we're headed, right?"

The fae studied her while playing with his waterskin.

When he didn't answer, she pursed her lips. "Fine. I'll guess it on my own."

His cocky snort of disbelief made Clarke want to prove him wrong. She drew on the gift that had served her well over her life. It surged to the surface, as though waiting for her call. The longer she spent in this time, the stronger her instinct got. It responded to her call like a living thing. Unnervingly, she could *feel* it growing inside her.

She focused on the unknown land and let the *fancies* come. Images of golden people, laughing and dancing swam before her eyes. "I think that way is... well, down south a little further is a kingdom where the sun shines more than the shadows hide, and beings come from far and wide to bask in the warmth. I can see them sunbathing on the stone near the water. They dance. They have parties. And a queen—no, a king— with golden hair crowned with glass rules over them all. He's beautiful. But... something is wrong in his mind." She slid her captor a glance. "How did I do?"

His handsome, rugged face had turned to stone.

"Your eyes went white again," he eventually noted.

"What?" She touched her lashes. "What do you mean?"

"Your irises turned white when you spoke those words."

"That's weird."

He barked a laugh. "No. It's a sign of magic flowing through you."

She enjoyed seeing his smile. He frowned too much. Then what he said sank in. It was her turn to laugh. "Again with the magic. Right."

But the instant the words came out, she felt in her gut that he was right. How else could she explain her premonitions? She'd always been psychic and, since waking, it had become stronger. Had her years of lying hidden in the earth exposed her to this cosmic mana that he'd proclaimed existed, or was it something else?

A profound sense of home settled in her bones. It was as if her entire life she'd been waiting to be here, to come to this world where her idiosyncrasies weren't exploited. Where she wasn't forced to use her gift to cheat for others, but where her gift was accepted and lauded.

If only she weren't tied and bound. But she was working on that.

"Was I right?" she prompted, a smile forming on her own lips.

He gave a stiff nod and pointed far south-east. "The Summer Court is a new addition to our realm. The thaw in Elphyne only began a few centuries ago. Until then, life had survived as best it could in this harsh, icy realm. Whether Seelie or Unseelie, all fae races existed in the Winter Court. But then Summer came. Summer is an unfamiliar concept to us all, and it's a drug to many." His gaze turned wistful. "It's like our bodies remember what was once here in this world, even after all this time."

"And how much time is that?" Clarke asked warily.

An eyebrow shot up. "Two thousand years, give or take. No one knows for sure. Maybe the humans with their record keeping, but out here, we only began tracking the passage of time when Jackson Crimson discovered the link between the magic of the Well and the treatment of the land. No magic flows where metals and plastics are used."

Her fingers moved to touch the watch on her wrist and found it was gone. She missed being able to tell the time. And the convenience of having a smart watch. She'd have called a cab already.

Clarke had worn metal her entire life. If what the fae said was true, then it could have been blocking her from reaching her true psychic potential. It could be the reason she felt it moving inside her now.

"Tell me more about the summer kingdom," she said.

The frown smoothed from his brow as he gazed out at the land. "I remember first hearing the story of when King Mithras broke from the winter lands and created the glass throne in the sun. After he did that, the Spring elves broke away and started the Spring Court, and the Autumn Court followed. I was only young, and the Summer King was a wolf—just like me. There had been a sense of pride amongst my entire pack because it was one of our kind who had created the magnificent glass palace. But I was more interested in joining the Guardians." He tapped to the logo of scales over his breast pocket.

When he was young? Didn't he just say the thaw began centuries ago?

"How old are you?" she blurted.

"One-seventy-eight."

"Years." She blanched. Surely she heard him wrong.

He nodded. "I was only a child when the Seelie Court was made."

"Seelie?"

"Fae races are divided into two. Those that prefer to live in the light—the Seelie— and those that like the dark—the Unseelie."

"Got it."

"Before the Seelie Court existed, there was only one kingdom in the winter lands, and all manner of fae, whether Seelie or Unseelie were under its rule. But the pull of the sun proved too much for many, and it split in two. Then it split into four. The Spring and Summer Courts are part of the Seelie Kingdom, and the Autumn and Winter are part of the Unseelie."

"Sounds incredible. I'd love to visit one day."

It was the wrong thing to say. Her captor narrowed his eyes on her. "I've spoken too much."

She shrugged. "What am I going to do with that information? Look at me. I'm tied up and dragged around by you. I'm surprised you haven't gagged me."

"Now that's an interesting idea."

His laughter turned her scowl into a smile. It couldn't be helped. It was those lips of his. The double brackets and mirth twinkling in his eyes. The way it lit up his otherwise downcast face. And she'd helped put it there.

But he was the mark. She was being friendly to get under his skin. She had to remember that.

He thought for a long time, then said, "Why are you using magic? How?"

Clarke shifted her gaze back to the summer kingdom. "I guess I've always had a bit in me. Since before this time."

"What do you mean, before this time?"

Here goes. "I think I've been frozen beneath the ice since my kind went to war what seems like many, many years ago."

"But you're human. And you use magic."

"If you call this magic, then I guess not all of us were lost to it. I can feel it growing inside me."

He grunted, deep in thought and murmured, almost to himself, "Now that I have removed the metals from your body."

She lifted her fingers to her ears. One was still raw from where Thaddeus had ripped the ring out. The other was bare.

"So... Vegas is gone?" she added.

"Your America is gone. This land you see to either side is all that is left. But it's not the same. The earth has shifted. Where there are hills, there might have been valleys. Some ruins remain."

Clarke's throat tightened. Tears burned her eyes. It was stupid. She'd *known* the truth, deep down inside, but still she hoped for this all to be a dream. It wasn't. Maybe she was the last of her kind. From a time long forgotten. That part of her life was gone.

As if the turn of her thoughts brought it on, dread gripped her throat and spread through her body. Panic engulfed her. She knew this feeling. It was the one she woke up with after nightmares. But it was the middle of the day... darkness crowded her vision and she dropped to the ground.

"No no no," she muttered.

"What's wrong?" The fae's voice came at her from a distance.

"I can't stop it. It's happening."

"What..."

"The nightmare."

Laurel's scream rent the air.

"Stop!" Clarke tugged at the ties binding her to a chair. "Just leave her alone. She's done nothing to you."

But the mercenary who had Clarke's friend under his grip, cared little. He took Laurel's bloody hand, caught the only intact nail in a pair of pliers, and cast Clarke a warning look. "Last chance, Clarke. Give us the numbers."

Laurel's short black bob was plastered to her face. Her light-brown skin had paled. She looked about to pass out, but she refused to show defeat to the shadowed face on the cell phone video. The Void, Clarke had named him because she'd never seen his face, just a shadow that seemed to suck the life out of everyone. He was Bishop's boss.

Bishop stood to the side, arms folded. Clarke was the one tied to a chair, yet he glared at her as though *she* embarrassed *him*. "Just tell them, Clarke."

"Fuck you," Laurel spat.

"Move to her teeth next," said the Void.

No!

"Fine," Clarke cried.

"No," Laurel blurted. "They want it this bad, Clarke. It's not good."

"She's right," said the Void. "The numbers are the nuclear codes. I need them to stop the war."

"He's telling the truth, Clarke," Bishop added.

They're lying. Clarke knew because of the sensation buzzing in her chest. It grated like nails down a blackboard. Panic engulfed her. Tears burned her eyes. She couldn't let her friend suffer.

Laurel's scream shattered the dream.

Clarke whirled away... out of her memory and into another. This time, she was the voyeur in a room, listening to a group of faceless people talking. But one voice she recognized. The Void. Only this time he wasn't so faceless. Tall. Dark. Grayed streaks at his temples. Clearer, but still far away, still emanating the sickly dark vibes. She had to strain to hear what he said.

Leaning over a map, the Void pointed at a spot. "There," he said. "That's where we find the copper deposit." He pointed at another spot. "And there is the tungsten."

"It's too deep into their territory," replied his companion. The mercenary.

"So we bleed it out."

Clarke only had enough time to look at the map and register a familiar word. Elphyne. She gasped. And then the Void looked up. His eyes clashed with Clarke's.

She was booted out of the vision and into never ending inky water.

She couldn't breathe.

She was drowning.

Elphyne.

Whirling in darkness, she repeated the word, as if she could return there like Dorothy in Oz. Elphyne. Her new home. Maybe if she repeated it enough, she'd leave this nightmare.

Elphyne.

The darkness gave way to light, and she found herself soaring over the magnificent green forests of Elphyne. A spark of red caught her eye, and she dived. The closer she got, the larger the spark grew until it became a campfire.

Clarke saw smiling faces of men... not men, fae. Males of different fae species, all surrounding a campfire, laughing with shared camaraderie. Warmth flooded through her. They were enjoying themselves. A drink or two, a clap on the back.

Every male was made from thick muscle and broad strength. Ruthless eyes, scarred hands. Swords leaning by their sides. Bows. Axes. Other strange weapons she'd not seen before. Every single one wore a blue coat. Kingfisher blue.

Guardians.

Safe. Somehow she knew she was safe with them.

One by one, their pointed ears pricked up. Each male turned their face in the same direction, toward the darkness Clarke's sight couldn't pierce, and then the incredible roar of an explosion decimated her eardrums.

Fire. Destruction.

The land of Elphyne was burning. Water wasn't safe. Ice wasn't safe.

All gone.

In a heartbeat.

And then....

A mocking laughter echoed in the dark.

Emptiness. A Void.

CHAPTER
EIGHT

Clarke came out of her vision, throat raw and eyes burning. She looked into the face of the fae, his brow crimped with worry. Her head rested on his lap, and his warm hands steadied her face. The wolf whined at their side.

"Are you well?" he asked.

And it was that small act of concern that broke the banks of her emotion.

"He's coming," she whispered, silently sobbing.

"Who's coming?"

But she couldn't voice it. Not yet. For long moments they stared at each other. In his golden reflection, she saw herself. Not the woman she used to be, but a new one. The person she wanted to be. None of her past transgressions were a part of this world, nothing was stopping her from being a different person... one who used her gift for good, not selfish gain. She could take control of her life. She could be stronger.

The gift in her body surged, as though in agreement.

And then she remembered the first part of her nightmare. Those "lotto numbers" weren't lotto numbers at all. They were the nuclear codes that started the destruction of the world.

Oh, God, she felt sick.

"What's wrong. What did you see?" He seemed to stare right through her facade and into the tragic truth wrapping itself around her heart.

She twisted off him and landed on her hands and knees. Nausea rolled in her gut. Guilt. Bone crushing guilt.

"I can't breathe," she wheezed, and tried to loosen the cape's neck tie with trembling fingers. The war was her fault. When she'd used her gift to feel out the numbers of the codes, she'd known what they were for. He said he was going to stop a war. But he created it.

Her fault.

All because she'd failed to listen to herself.

She squeezed her eyes shut. She'd always had a choice on some level. Behind her eyelids, the sins of the past flashed and morphed with the images from her vision. The Void was pointing at a map of Elphyne. But that was in *this* time. At first she'd thought it was a repeat of what happened in her time, but... that other vision. With the fire and explosions. Those were fae she'd seen.

Unless she did something about it.

A darkness clouded Rush's expression as he grasped her shoulders. "What did you see?"

"Doesn't matter."

"You're lying."

His wolf snarled at her. She clamped her lips shut. How could she make a difference if people saw her as evil? She was already battling against a preconceived notion that humans were the enemy.

"*Tell me*," he ordered.

This time, the fae's words seemed to reach within her body, grip her voice box and demand it work. A tingling force compelled her to move her lips. She blurted her shame before she could stop. "I saw my past. I saw the moment I helped them uncover the nuclear codes that armed weapons that ended the world. And I saw the same fiery destruction in this time."

A darkness like she'd never seen before washed over the fae. Every muscle in his body tensed. Nostrils flared. Jaw clenched. "You are the one responsible for annihilating the old world? *Tell me.*"

Alarm skated up her spine. As before, the words blurted out in an uncontrollable flood. "Yes. But he made me do it."

As if that excused her. The end of the world came. Laurel died anyway.

He stilled. "Someone forced you?"

"Yes." Fingers going to her throat, she tried to stop her words with actions. What the hell was happening?

"Who forced you? Who used you?"

"My boyfriend. His boss. Another mercenary called Bones." Fear clogged her throat. "What are you doing to me?"

"I'm compelling you through our bargain."

"You're *making* me speak?"

"I can make you move, too."

The horror of it hit her. This whole time he'd lulled her into a pretense of complacency. The bindings were a ruse. He could *make* her do anything.

"You asshole." She jerked out of his hold. "You had no right to force that out of me."

"It's a good thing that I did. I had no idea the woman I'd captured."

"I had no idea the jerk I'd bargained with to save my life."

"Tell me about this person who forced you."

"And are you going to tell me about your deepest, darkest shame? Those blue glyphs are there for a reason. One you don't like. I've seen you glaring at them. You're not perfect."

He folded his arms, pushing out his biceps and returned her glare. "Do I have to compel you?"

She sighed, suddenly feeling exhausted. What was the point in trying to hide things? She stared out into the forests of Elphyne.

"You ever heard the story of the boy who cried wolf?" she asked.

His lip twitched, but he shook his head.

"It's about a child who used to shepherd his family's flock of sheep. He found it so boring on his own, that he would pretend a wolf hunted in the paddock and run screaming for his parents to come and have a look. Every time they went down to check, there was nothing there but the boy laughing. One day, an actual wolf wandered into his paddock, but when he called for help, no one came. The boy got eaten."

Clarke turned to the wasteland side of the mountain and took in the lack of life.

"My entire life I had these visions," she said. "Some turned into reality, but many didn't. As a child, I had no way of telling which dreams were real and which weren't. My mother's answer was to walk out. She couldn't handle a daughter with issues. My father was there for me. He helped me as much as he could, but he never believed me.

"I saw his death. I saw that it was from his unhealthy lifestyle, but he didn't believe me, all because I'd grown up telling many lies with the truths. My psychic powers weren't always reliable, and sometimes I made things up for attention."

She wiped her eyes. "One person always believed me. He turned my small little quirks into an empire. And then he sold my skills to someone worse. By the time I had the nerve, or the support to get out of there, it was too late. The damage had been done."

If it weren't for Ada and Laurel, and their friendship, Clarke would never have left Bishop. She depended on him. Thinking of her two friends sent an ache through her body. She missed them. So much.

The big fae at her side squinted into the distance, zeroing in on something.

She'd not noticed it before, but could now see a structure reaching into the sky. It looked faded and purple from the haze that separated them, but it was an unmistakable city. Tall skyscrapers in the middle, and a dull wall of crystal surrounding them.

"Is that..." But she knew. The rightness of her next words just made them come out. "It's the human city."

He nodded.

"But"—she focused harder—"what is that over the top of the tall buildings, something strung between?"

"It's barbed wire. It prevents winged fae from entering the city from above. Or rather, if they get in, it stops them from flying out."

"So... they use the wire to cut winged fae down?"

He nodded grimly. "And by electrocuting them, then keeping and dissecting their bodies for research."

She frowned. "But that would also harm any winged creature who dropped into the city, right?"

A meeting of their eyes said it all. Yes, all animals were harmed, and yes, she understood how vile humans could be. She was one of them, and yet, it was a hard pill to swallow.

She might not be one, but she knew good people. Her friends Laurel and Ada were good. Ada rescued abused animals and rehabilitated them for the wild. Laurel ran a fitness empire and donated self-defense lessons to victims of domestic abuse. It still baffled Clarke that the two of them wanted to be her friend.

"There are good people out there," she declared. Surely some still existed.

"And there are bad," Rush answered. "But the Well cares not. This land cares not. It only wants to survive and flourish. We don't choose the rules of life, but if we don't follow them, we're destined for nothing."

His words were an echo of the emptiness in her nightmare. They shattered her nerves. There was nothing left to say. They went back to staring at Crystal City in the distance until some time had passed, and he began talking.

"Apart from myself, only one fae escaped that city intact. A crow shifter. He'd been a curious thief in his teens who'd flown down on a dare. He'd been in crow form when he'd dropped through the gaps in the barbed wire. The fool didn't realize the same wire made it impossible for him to fly out, and because that place is desecrated land, you cannot draw from the Well there. They've tampered too much with the natural order of things. For all we know he'd depleted his personal mana stores and was trapped there as a crow for all that time, unable to shift."

"And if he'd had some left?"

"Then he might have had one or two shifts in him."

"You don't know?"

"One day he reappeared in Elphyne as a crow. It took him a while to shift back, and it took him even longer to think and speak coherently again. He never spoke of the horrors he endured… if he could remember them at all. When he got out, he joined the Guardians. He's one of the most ruthless we've ever had."

"I'm sorry."

"What for?" he asked, surprised.

"I guess for everything."

"We don't need your pity." He reached into his pocket and gripped something. His face hardened, and then he took hold of the lead. "Let's go."

For the rest of the journey down the mountain, Clarke forced herself to come to terms with her new reality. She wasn't near Vegas. Vegas was gone. She was in the future. In an unfamiliar world where magic desperately wanted to bloom, but the withering greed of humans still wanted to reign. But not all humans were evil. Many, in fact, were not. She'd pick-pocketed and conned people, but that was to survive. She'd never stolen from people she didn't get bad vibes from. She never considered herself an amoral person.

But was she good?

A good person wouldn't use their powers of premonition to steal at all. A good person would try to stop the evil of her dreams from eventuating, no matter the cost. She'd been given a second chance at life. This world had been given a second chance. She had to at least try to make it worth it.

All she knew for sure was that this fae holding her captive knew her darkest shame, and yet he wasn't looking at her with disgust. Perhaps his darkest shame was worse than hers.

As CLARKE WENDED DOWN rocky terrain, the snow melted and revealed fresh dirt and abundant nature. The more they descended, the grumpier she got. Something shifted inside when she saw how the world had changed because of the way she'd lived her old life. Death had been on one side of the mountain and life on the other. Even though she'd had a part, she didn't want to be lumped in with humans who'd intentionally destroyed the world.

The fae's words came back to her. *"We don't choose the rules of life, but if we don't follow them, we're destined for nothing."*

"You know," she said as she dodged a divot in the path. "We've been walking for hours and you still haven't told me your name."

She was also tired, itchy, and hungry.

The fae nudged her between the shoulder blades. She almost lost her footing.

He may have a giant sword, scary mother-fucking teeth, and a powerful body she was sure could snap her in two, but her instinct just wasn't feeling the fear. He had the ability to control her words and her actions, yet he'd only just used the power. She rounded on him.

"Take these off me," she demanded. "Free me."

He looked down his nose and flicked his gaze to the restraints. Her breath stuck in her throat and, for a moment, she thought her instincts needed a serious talking to. But then he moved toward her. *Fast.*

With a speed that left her breathless, and a flick of his powerful hand, his bone knife sliced through her restraints. Clarke's fists dropped to her sides.

He leaned forward, his menacing presence only inches from her face. And then he sniffed, nostrils flaring as he trailed his nose along her cheek, jaw and neck. Where he stayed. Hot air puffed out as he exhaled, and goosebumps erupted over her flesh. The tattoo under his eye flared, casting an eerie blue glow as he bared sharp teeth and bit the air, snapping with an audible click.

Clarke squeaked. A tremble of fear skated up her spine.

He raised a brow. "It matters not if you are free. You will not run."

"And why not? Because you'll compel me to stay?"

"Because, woman," he growled, mouth curving into a wild, wicked grin, "I am the reason for those goosebumps on your skin. I am the reason children have nightmares, and in there"—he pointed into the shadowed woods only a few hundred feet away—"there are far worse things than nightmares. I am the reason you will live to breathe another day."

"So I need a monster to fight a monster, is that it?"

Stupid woman. Stop provoking the beast.

His eyes narrowed and held her gaze.

An unearthly howl came from deep within the woods. At least, Clarke thought it was a howl. It could be any manner of creature in this foreign place. His pet wolf stiffened and raised his hackles.

Watching the woods, the fae stilled in a way that was wholly inhuman. He reached for his sword. Fingers locked tight around the hilt. Knuckles whitened. His ears pricked up straight.

Leaves rustled and trees whispered that night was falling. Then the tension left his shoulders and he let go of the sword. He tossed a self-righteous look at her, and then swaggered away, continuing toward the very forest that had caused him concern only moments before.

Goddamn it. She wanted to stomp her feet.

Smug, smug bastard.

She should leave just to spite him. But where would she go? To the human city that brutalized fae and animals through a barbed wire ceiling? The one the source of her dread came from? No thanks. She had to face facts. She was in a strange place and on her own. There were dangers out there in the night, and her gut said to go with the fae. He had the upper hand.

She hurried to catch up, for she knew something he didn't. She could make friends with nightmares. She'd had practice.

CHAPTER
NINE

C larke thudded along the path behind the fae. He continued toward the darkening woods as if it didn't scare him, as if the gnarled trees didn't cause every bone in his body to quake. He stopped at where the trees grew thickest and looked at the darkening sky.

"We'll camp here for the night," he announced and dropped his heavy rucksack.

He shuffled debris, stones and leaves out of a ten-foot diameter area, and then busied himself with pulling out six yardsticks from his pack.

Her stomach rumbled. Her skin itched. Her boots rubbed. She could use a good bath. *I'm so over this.*

With a sigh, she said, "Can you *please* tell me your name? I'll stop asking only when you tell me."

She had to get him to trust her and first names were everything.

The uncertainty in his eyes gave her a chill. There was more to this than he let on. It made her think, perhaps, he could be on the run from the law, if there were such a thing in this place. He'd called himself a Guardian, but maybe that logo on his jacket wasn't from a friendly place.

She ducked her head to where he faced. He couldn't avoid her, or the question.

He gave an annoyed grunt. "Like I said, I have no name. I am a ghost."

He continued to stake each yardstick into the dirt until he made the shape of a circle.

A Ghost.

Okay. They'd made progress. But it still wasn't enough.

"And what does that mean? You look pretty real to me."

He stabbed the last yardstick and rounded on her. "None of your Well-damn business."

"Shall I guess it?" Why not? Her guesses had been right lately. She didn't need some sort of compulsion on her side. She already had an inbuilt lie detector.

Something like fear flashed in his eyes, and then he clamped down hard. "Fine. Call me Rush."

She tried to hide her smile, but failed. *Finally.*

Her smile threw him off. He did a double-take, paused long enough for her to know she'd caused discomfort, and then kneeled. Looking into his wolf's eyes, he calmly said, "You should go back. I need you to protect the cabin and your pack needs you."

The wolf whined, but Rush gave it an affectionate scrub between the ears, stood and made a shooing motion. The wolf trotted back the way they had come, gave one last look over his shoulder at Rush, and then kept going.

Clarke didn't miss the way Rush winced after the wolf had gone. Once the wolf was out of earshot, he mumbled to himself, "These woods aren't suitable for an old wolf like him. He's better off on his own."

He finished checking the perimeter of stakes and then sat toward the center of the secure circle and pulled out a wrapped package of dried meat and nuts. He took his fill, and then begrudgingly handed her a few morsels. While Clarke ate, he shoved his rucksack behind his head and sprawled his long legs out. Without a word, he closed his eyes, shimmied to get comfortable, and then relaxed.

Seriously?

After a minute or two, when she was sure he'd think she'd just given up and gone to sleep, she chewed loudly and asked, "What are those sticks for?"

Silence.

She asked again. "You know, the sticks around us?"

He gave a grunt and rolled away from her.

"Rush."

The tension in his shoulders revealed he regretted telling her his name.

An incredible urge to get a rise out of him washed through her, but she used the self-control of a god, and kept it inside. She ended up resting her elbows on her legs, head in hands, and leaned forward. Staring.

If he fell asleep, she might be able to rifle through the rucksack. Find some money. Something to help her when she managed to get away from him. With each breath he took, his chest moved and the knife at his belt tilted, catching the dying light of the sun. Jewels were embedded in the pommel. Jewels were as good as cash in any time.

It didn't take long for him to open an eye. Then another. His attention dipped to her chest and lingered long enough to let her know her shirt must be gaping. The tunic he'd given her was too big. That heated linger caused her nipples to contract.

He lifted his gaze to her lips, then her eyes where they locked and heated with a sensual challenge. A dark eyebrow lifted. The message was clear. *"I'm game if you are."*

She'd never used her femininity to get what she wanted, but couldn't deny it was useful. Regardless of whether she was human or fae, he was attracted to her, and that gave her a little power.

The memory of the two sides of the mountain came back to her. One dead. One living. She'd sworn this time, she'd do things differently. No more manipulating, sneaking, or lying. Her darkest truth was out there, and the world hadn't crumbled. This fae hadn't looked at her with bone deep scorn, and if she did this... use her body to get what she wanted... then she was back to old tricks.

For a single insane moment, she wished she could see her own future, then she would know exactly what was in store between her and the fae. But as usual, nothing stronger than a flutter or buzz vibes influenced her own life. Warnings. That was all. And she got nothing where he was concerned. That should be a good thing, she supposed.

He thought she was his enemy, but he wasn't hers.

"I want to know about the stakes," she pushed, and gestured to the sticks.

Tension diffused, he closed his eyes again. "You seem to know it all. Guess."

She glanced around. Okay. A test. Maybe she wanted the same thing. So she took a deep breath and focused on the sticks. They had stones wrapped to the tops with a leather cord. She'd not noticed in the light, but now the sun had dipped beyond the horizon, the stones resonated with luminescence.

"Solar powered lights?" she asked, but the moment the words came out, she knew they were wrong. Like a lightning strike that turned her thoughts to dreams and dreams into reality, she knew the answer. "No. They're more than that. They're for protection. From what?"

He opened one eye and then closed it. "Get some rest, human. The nights are brief in this part of the woods." He paused, his breath evening out as he slipped deeper into relaxation. Just before she thought he was asleep, he mumbled, "And don't listen to the wind."

"Why not?"

"It listens back."

Shit. She cast a wary glance into the darkness beyond the bracket of trees. Things seemed to stare back at her. Things she couldn't see, only sense. Shivering, she wrapped his borrowed cape around her shoulders and laid down in the cramped space provided by the luminescent stakes. She tried to ignore the buzzing bugs in the air, and the phantom itches up her sleeves and legs. But no matter how hard she tried, she couldn't shake the feeling of being watched, and when the wind whispered inaudible words, she shuffled closer to her sleeping captor, irritated that he knew this would happen and that's why he'd cut the binds on her hands. She needed his protection. Even knowing all this, she was fast becoming accustomed to the notion he wasn't the monster he made himself out to be.

She shuffled closer.

TEN

A snuffling and scratching to Clarke's right made her snap awake. The silhouette of a man back-lit by dawn hovered over her. She blinked and recognized Rush's face, inches from hers. Was he coming in for a morning cuddle? Her languid body didn't object to that, even if some still waking part of her mind did. He smelled good. Like comfort. She held her breath and smiled tentatively. But then...

Amusement flashed in his eyes. "I'd love to play, princess, but a warada is about to eat you."

He kept moving. She held up her hands for protection, but he sailed right over her body and stabbed something to her right. A shrill squawking filled the air, grinding her nerves.

Oh, my God. What is that?

Scrubbing her face, she blinked and then felt sick when she saw what squirmed beneath Rush's sword. His biceps bulged through his jacket, straining to pin a hog-like beast to the ground. The wild, writhing animal was only a foot from where Clarke had lain. With sharp teeth, mandibles and leathery black skin, the animal was a cross between a boar and an insect. It had a barrel chest, sharp claws and six legs. If that thing had gotten to her...

Rush had saved her life.

The creature still writhed and screamed beneath Rush's sword. Its cries grated down Clarke's bones. Rush twisted his sword to anchor it to the ground. She tried not to look at the ominous stain blooming beneath the beast. If she closed her eyes, it sounded like a normal animal in pain. Maybe it was.

"Hold this." Rush shoved a glass container into her hands. "Catch the manabeeze when they release. Get as many as you can."

"The what?" she gasped, still hazy and disorientated.

"The manabeeze." He snatched the glass cylinder from her hands and twisted it at the halfway mark. It opened. He then showed a sweeping motion, as if he were catching air. Then he closed the container.

"I'm not stupid," Clarke groused. "I know how to close a container."

His lip curled in a one-sided smirk. "Someone isn't a morning person."

She couldn't say the same for him. He'd woken looking just as handsome as he did going to sleep. Hair brushed back as though he'd run his hands through it. Beard looking a touch thicker but not messy. Laughing eyes watching her. Her body hummed in the most delicious way and she remembered her first thought when seeing him upon wakening. She'd liked the idea of a morning cuddle. It was stupid. She shouldn't even be thinking about that, but she was half asleep. Her guard was down. And she was lonely.

She didn't want to be thousands of years from anyone she'd ever known. She didn't want the nightmares to be her only friend. She blurted, "Yeah, well, you wouldn't be a morning person either if you were always dreaming about fire and death."

Liar. Her dreams last night had been nightmare free. That only happened when she was around someone she felt safe with.

"You are a confusing woman, Clarke." He used his knife to gesture urgently at the glass container in her hands. "Use it to catch the manabeeze."

She opened her mouth to explain, again, that she knew nothing about manabeeze, but shut it when he gripped the creature's head and held it to make the neck taut. Every line in his body tensed and strained as though it hurt to touch the little beastie. "You ready?"

"I—"

He lowered his voice and closed his eyes, muttering a prayer of respect. He sliced the neck, killing it, and then said, "Now."

She jolted, and then the strangest thing happened. Little white balls of light buzzed out of the animal's body and hovered in a swarm.

"Catch them!" Rush barked. He retrieved another container from his rucksack.

Jumping to her feet, Clarke opened the glass container and tried to scoop as many balls of light—*manabeeze*—as she could. Restless energy rippled through her body. She released a yip of excitement. It was like catching fireflies. She chased the damned things around the circle as they swarmed in lazy patterns, getting faster and flying higher with each lap around her. One brushed her face, tickling like an electric caress. She giggled. There was something so pure about the light.

Twirling around like a school girl in a yard, grinning from ear to ear. She stopped just in time to see a single manabee buzz drunkenly and come straight for her.

Rush saw it at the same time. "Don't let—"

It hit her sternum and soaked into her being, spreading warmth.

"—it go through you." Rush's shoulders slumped.

Clarke felt woozy. Who moved the ground? Stumbling, she barely held upright and tumbled into Rush's arms. "Wha... What's wrong with me?"

He shook his head and set her straight. "You shouldn't have let it go through you. Now you will pay."

"Do you accept Visa?" She giggled then clapped her hand over her mouth. Why was she laughing? Because it was funny! She felt funny too. The world around her became hyper-focused and yet soft at the same time.

Rush rescued the glowing glass canister filled with buzzing manabeeze from her hands. Her knees buckled, and she landed hard on her butt, blinking lazily at the sky swirling pink and yellow with a new day. But she felt... a fizzing through her body. From the tip of her toes to the end of her hair. Which was totally weird. Hair had no feelings.

She laughed again.

"I feel great." She shot him a goofy grin.

He stowed his prize. "You're lucky it was only one, and it was from a warada."

"A warada?"

"Doesn't matter. Point is this stuff is potent. If you ingested mana from a stronger being, you'd be hallucinating the memories of their life right now... among other things."

She blinked. Wow. "So this... this stuff is like a drug."

"This *stuff* is sacred. It's the last remaining mana left in one's body before you die. It has many uses, all of which are lucrative."

"What happens if you just leave it?"

"It rejoins the Well—the cosmic mana of the planet."

Clarke sighed. "That sounds so nice. Cosmic. Say it again and let me watch your lips move. Coz-mik."

He rolled his eyes, but couldn't hide his humor. "Here we go."

"Hey, you know you're pretty cool, right? You're not nearly as scary as you pretend to be."

His smile dropped and he raised a brow. "Cool."

"Yeah, I mean," she continued, "I once dated this guy who used to make me tell him the lotto numbers every week. And then he sold me to this scary dude who pulled my friend's fingernails out so I'd tell him those other numbers." Her voice turned soft. "Can't believe I dated him."

Rush stared at her. "He sounds like a floater."

"Don't know what that means, but don't worry, he got what he deserved." That man, along with everyone else she knew, had died with her old world. His greed had given him nothing in the end.

A shiver ran up her spine when she remembered that she'd seen two of them pouring over a map of Elphyne. Maybe he wasn't dead.

"No." She shook her head. "Only good vibes, please."

Rush looked at her long and hard, then went to the warada and lifted it to inspect the spiky tail. Even with the permanent grimace, he was much nicer to think about than jerk-face Bishop. Or his evil friends. Enough with those floaters.

She giggled. What a weird phrase.

But Rush. If it weren't for the fact he was trying to use her, she might have liked him.

"You're also pretty cute when you frown." She rested her chin on her hand. "If you stop forcing me to do things, we could be friends, you know."

ELEVEN

Rush froze at Clarke's words.

We could be friends.

The problem was, he'd been holding the warada when he froze, and the contact sickness hit. Like a jolt of anti-adrenaline, the curse dragged his energy down, just like it always did when he touched another creature. *Stupid.* He knew he'd felt off when he'd sliced its throat but ignored the warning, just like he did when he gave Gray a scratch or tickle. It was stupid to get distracted, but her talk of a man who extorted her powers made him angry and he'd neglected to pay attention to the sickness creeping up on him. He knew better.

His hand snapped open and the carcass fell to the ground as the nausea hit. The second wave of the curse was always worse. It took all his restraint to hold the pain in, hoping Clarke wouldn't notice in her state of disarray. Sweat itched beneath his beard and above his brow. Taking deep, even breaths, he concentrated on the thing that triggered his curse.

The warada was reckless to come so close to the perimeter stakes. Usually the magic stone deterrent was enough to send all creatures skittering away, even the larger monsters. They were only at the start of the woods. It would be a few more days until they got through. Perhaps something spooked the creature and made it desperate.

Biting through the waning pain, Rush reminded himself that he had to be watchful. A cursed reaction from an animal the warada's size was bearable. A bigger creature, not so much.

He looked at the forest and groaned inwardly. If they were attacked, he'd better be careful not to touch, or he would be incapacitated in hostile territory for Crimson-knew how long.

Damned curse. He was over it. Fifty damned years and he was completely over it. The sooner they got through the Whispering Woods, the sooner they got to Crescent

Hollow, and the sooner they found a portal stone to take them to the Order. Without a stone, the journey would take weeks on foot.

Rush removed Starcleaver from the beast, wiped the blade on the body, and then sheathed it over his shoulder.

A glance at Clarke showed she'd already forgotten about him and studied the way her hand looked before the sky. But her words still rattled in his mind.

If you stop forcing me...

He tapped his thigh, deep in thought. The woman had been forced to do a despicable thing. He was under no illusion that she was perfect, that she deserved his pity, but he also wasn't the kind of male who forced a woman to bend to his will... not like the way his uncle did. He was nothing like Thaddeus, and the fact that Rush had to use magic to compel Clarke didn't sit well with him.

He turned to face her, ready to corral the town drunk, but found she studied him.

"What?" he demanded.

Her still-glazed eyes dropped to his right ear. With a sway and pout of plump lips, she said, "I want to touch them."

"Oh no. No, you don't." Rush backed up, but she advanced on him. Two pale hands outstretched and grasped air, aiming for his head.

"Woman." He dodged and weaved out of her reach. Putting his back to her and shaking his head, he finished packing away the canisters. "The manabee effect will wear off soon. Just sit down and don't hurt yourself."

He shouldn't have assumed. She came up behind him and touched.

Every aching bone in his body stiffened, expecting the sickness to hit again. Shutting his eyes, he tensed, but the only pain was bittersweet. A woman's touch. A tender sweep of fingers over the arch of his ears. A slide of blissful agony as she pressed under the lobe. And a stroke over the furred tips, then back down again.

Every nerve in his body sang at the connection. Ears were erogenous for fae. A tremble wracked through him. His eyes fluttered. His limbs loosened. The bastard he was, he pushed into her hand, nudging his head into her touch like a bleedin' scrappy pup.

Touch there.

"Feels so good," she murmured, dusting the furred tip of his second ear. "It tingles my skin."

A wave of need washed down him. Arousal became a tight, hot weight beneath his skin and he remembered how she'd looked when she leaned toward him the night before, all feminine curves and temptation. He rounded on her. "Stop," he croaked.

Wide, naïve eyes met his. "Why?"

Rush's response lodged in his throat.

Because I want to tear off your clothes and feel you from the inside.

She had no idea how long he'd waited to sink into the tight, wet center of a female, and he was afraid of the lines he'd cross to make it happen. But he wasn't the deviant his uncle had made him out to be. Even if his family would never know, *he'd* know.

Why indeed. "We have to keep moving."

Disappointed, she dropped her hands to her sides. "I need a drink."

"Anything else, princess?" He handed her the waterskin.

She flattened her lips. "If we're being honest, I'd like my watch back."

"Your watch?"

"The thing you took from my wrist. It tells the time." She pouted. "I hate not knowing what the time is. I feel as though, if I do, then I'll know where I am. It's stupid."

She shook her head.

Rush wasn't giving her the plastic and metal watch. He put the protection stakes away and willed his body to forget the way she'd made him feel. Less isolated. Less forgotten. And less in control of his urges. He wasn't wrong when he'd called her a confusing woman. Shouldn't he hate her for who she was?

But he knew as well as anyone, that one thoughtless act made in the heat of the moment could have dire consequences.

Growling in frustration, he collected his rucksack and stalked into the woods where the thickest trees thinned suddenly from a wending path between. The trees bowed toward him and shifted in the wind, their leaves rustling in greeting or warning. He could never decide.

While he waited for her to follow, he willed his arousal away, but his hormones didn't care if she was human. They didn't care if his time on this earth was coming to an end. They didn't even care that he was about to enter a dangerous place. He'd screw her anywhere if he could.

Fuck.

He scrubbed his face.

No, he wouldn't.

From the sound of her thudding feet, she followed. So he set off.

TWELVE

Another two days of endless walking passed.

Rush set an unforgiving pace. He was used to it, even though Clarke wasn't. In Elphyne, they had no moving metal boxes, like the human city had. They had to walk, or use portals. Since he had no access to the Well, he couldn't create one. He had to find a mana-imbued stone instead. Crescent Hollow was the nearest market he could find a portal stone.

Each day they made camp when the sun set, and rose with the dawn. Determined not to put himself in a position of arousal again, he kept his distance, and refused to engage in conversation, despite her babbling and questions about Elphyne.

Every night, she shuffled closer when she thought he was asleep. And every night she made these little sounds of feminine exhaustion. Sighs and moans that reminded him of fantasies he'd dreamed in his loneliest moments. In the middle of the night, he'd caught himself reaching for her. He woke each morning with hard steel between his legs, and the wolf inside him closer to the surface, howling for a taste of her.

Damned woman.

Until she'd come along, he didn't think he would miss the quiet solitude of his curse. His words came less frequently when no one talked back. Being cut off from the Well meant the past few years had been blessedly silent. Until her.

She got under his skin in a way he wasn't entirely certain he wanted to end. An itch at his palm—at their bargain site—punctuated the thought. He shook out his fist and concentrated on the path ahead.

The last time he'd visited Crescent Hollow was just after his son, Thorne, had been shipped off to the Order at the tender age of twelve. That was forty years ago. Destiny was a cruel, hungry beast that kept devouring long after death. It ate Rush's father, it ate Rush, and it still went for his son. It was for his son that Rush needed to lift the curse. Rage rose swiftly in him at the memory, at the panic riding his system when the alpha, his uncle Thaddeus, had announced Rush's son would be the pack's yearly tribute to the Order.

Thorne needed to know that he didn't need to live the life of a Guardian, despite being forced into it.

Rush should have been the alpha. He should never have messed up his father's life by wanting to join the Order, but he could never say he'd regretted becoming a Guardian. Only what came before and after because of it.

"So, like, where are we headed again?" Clarke asked.

Rush bared his teeth and snapped at her. Should have known the blessed silence wouldn't last.

She should have been afraid. Should have jumped back. But she only blinked at Rush, waiting. Must be losing his touch.

With a grunt, he trudged onward, ignoring her and the wind whispering sweet things into his ears. *Stay awhile, Rush.* He shut out the voices until nothing but the dirt leaf-littered path and the occasional earth sprite skittering behind the trees held his attention. He found them more reliable for news of danger than the wind. If the sprites weren't bothered, then the road was clear.

Onward he plodded. The light from the sun waned. It was only mid-morning, but the woods were thickening and the grim life held inside seemed to stretch its shadowy touch across everything. As though walking through a barrier to another world, the greenery and chittering birds turned to death and eerie silence. The temperature dropped.

They were here. The last leg of their journey. If they took this route, they'd be in Crescent Hollow by nightfall. He withdrew Starcleaver. Just ahead was a fork in the path. Down one, the limbs of trees bent to connect with the other side to create a gloomy tunnel. Reaching into the rucksack, he retrieved a jar of manabeeze, still buzzing and giving off light.

He handed it to Clarke. "Hold that."

Her eyes darted between the two paths, clearly seeing that the one with the most light wasn't the direction they were headed.

"No." She shook her head and pointed down the dark path. "We're not going down there."

"We have to. It will only take a few hours. The alternative route will take days."

Clamping her lips, she shook her head again. "No. There's something bad down there. I can feel it."

Crimson save him. It was times like these he truly missed the ability to shift. All he used to do was shred his human skin, let the beast out, and the very air would quake with fear.

"Woman." He clenched his jaw. "I will keep us from harm."

He couldn't say the same for when they arrived at the Order, though. But as long as he got to his son, whatever happened to her after that wasn't his concern.

A tightness constricted his chest, and he frowned at his own callousness. When had he become so cruel as to discard the safety of a female? Even a human one. The rogue humans he'd hunted over the years were all men, all scouts from Crystal City. It was easy to kill them. They were as monstrous as the magic-warped creatures he exterminated when he worked for the Order.

"I'm not sure you can," she said. "No offense."

He planted Starcleaver's tip into the ground and leaned on it with a sigh. "If you had any idea what a Guardian is, you wouldn't be saying that."

"So tell me."

Rush raised a brow. She was serious.

"And then tell me why you are no longer one," she added.

He had a mind to not tell her anything. They had to keep moving. A sitting duck was dinner in these parts.

"A Guardian has gone through a special initiation where their hearts and courage are tested by the Well. When they emerge, if they emerge, they have a deeper capacity for holding mana within their bodies. They can also draw from the Well at any location, as long as they are connected with the land in some way. Most others can only replenish slowly over time, or from a location of power. Like the lake you woke up in. When I shift into wolf form, I'm larger than most other wolves. If I concentrate, I can control the elements too."

He preferred to use his mana to shift. Elements were unstable and the domain of Mages or elves who lacked the ability to shift.

She swallowed. "What happens during the initiation?"

Flashes of Rush's hit him, as fresh as the day it happened. Drowning. Water. Suffocating. Sinking to the bottom, then, just as his lungs were bursting for air...

"Rush?"

He met her eyes. "You don't need to know. Only that the strong survive, and those weak in heart and courage drown in their own fear."

His father had not made it. He'd not intended to enter the ceremonial lake. He'd thought Rush had, and went to rescue him. The thing was, his father was an alpha, the strongest Nightstalk that had lived in centuries. He was neither weak-willed nor a coward, yet the Well hadn't chosen him. It had spit him out until his bloated body floated on the surface for all to see his shame.

Rush still remembered the day Thaddeus told him that his father had died because he'd thought Rush had snuck off to the lake. The shame and the guilt in his youthful mind had been all consuming. And so, at twelve, the official age allowed for initiation, Rush followed his father. He didn't expect to come out of the lake a Guardian. Not when his father, the fae he'd looked up to, had been rejected. Floated.

Before that, Rush had an unhealthy obsession with the powerful Guardians in Kingfisher blue. Every time they came through his village, most sneered in disgust. Many only saw the tax they paid for the protection the Guardians provided, but Rush knew their job went beyond prohibition of metals and plastic. They fought monsters. They bled to keep chaos out and harmony in. They gave their lives to preserve the integrity of the Well. For the future of fae kind.

"Every year," he began, "There is a mass offering from around the realm to the Order. When Guardians die, only Guardians can replace them. Metal is needed to kill magical monsters, and only Guardians can use metal without diluting their mana.

When fae realized the initiation ceremony lost more than it approved, they stopped wanting to become Guardians. So once a year tributes have to be made." He ground his teeth. "And sometimes they are taken from the age of twelve."

The terror on Thorne's young face, his eyes squeezed shut as they pushed him toward that jetty edge. Rush had tried to stop it. He'd stabbed a few fae with Starcleaver, but soon they caught onto what happened. Rush couldn't get to Thorne without touching anyone and then the sickness took over.

"Old enough to remember, but young enough to be molded." Her touch on Rush's arm shook him out of his thoughts. "I'm so sorry."

"How do you keep doing that?" he whispered, searching her attentive eyes. Did she see all the way into his heart? Into the black pit of guilt. His father. His lover. His son... Rush couldn't protect any of them.

"I just know things." She tapped between her breasts. "In here. It's worse now than before. Or better, I suppose, if you want to look at it that way." Her eyes turned wistful. "I don't suppose I can convince you to take the lighter path?"

"No."

Her brows lowered. "I just finished telling you I *know* things, and you're ignoring me. Why?"

Infernal woman. "I should just kill you and be done with you."

She gasped and took a step back. Fear was an acrid scent in the air.

Rush growled, "But I need you. I need you as payment for lifting my curse. I'm tired of being a ghost. I want people to see me again. And not only are you human, but you have magic, and seeing as you're related to how this world came to be in its state, you're also important. Now you know how desperate I am, and you know there is no escape for you. Unless you want me to force you..." He pointed his sword at her neck despite the bitter taste his words left. "Move."

"No." She planted her feet. "I refuse to be the person no one listens to. My nightmares are real. I saw things. Elphyne is in danger, and I refuse to be the person who does nothing to stop them. Not this time."

The fire in her eyes was admirable.

"You say you're a Guardian. You wear the coat. But you're a coward, Rush."

"You're walking on shaky ground, human."

"Yeah that's right. I'm human. The most despicable creature you can think of in your world and guess what? I'm the only one trying to save it. So, go figure. You know what? I don't care. Kill me then. Be done with it. At least I'll know I went down swinging."

"Go float yourself, Clarke," he snapped.

"I would if I knew what that meant!"

"It means you're not worthy of the Well. If you'd gone through the initiation, you would have been rejected, floated and bloated."

She gasped. "You, sir, are the one who can go float himself!"

With a frustrated, drawn out grumble, he gripped her wrist and yanked her down the path. It took him a good few strides before the truth of her words hit him in the chest. All this time he'd been consumed with the selfish need to have his curse lifted and see his son, but he'd failed to remember what had drawn him to become a Guardian in the first place.

He wanted to protect.

Instead of floating during initiation, against all odds, he'd sunk and been blessed by the Well. He'd emerged more powerful than before and blessed with the responsibility of being able to hold metal and mana at the same time. The Well chose him to be its protector. And it took a human to remind him of that.

CHAPTER
THIRTEEN

Clarke clutched the jar of manabeeze to her chest as though it could protect her from the unnamed terror she felt coming. Like the imprint of a future memory, the psychic backlash already affected her. But without seeing it, she had nothing to tell Rush, and the stubborn fae refused to acknowledge she was right. His mood had soured with every mile they traipsed.

Onward they walked. Every so often a skittering and scuttling sounded from deep within the darkness behind the branches.

She flinched.

He didn't. Calm as the center of the storm, he strode.

Goddamn you, Rush.

But when she thought about it, Clarke was more angry at herself than him. Why should she expect this fae to be any different to the man who'd manipulated her most of her adult life? Right before she'd taken Bishop's hand that day at the Bellagio fountains, she'd felt his bad intentions. But then the bad vibes had disappeared. It took her a long time to realize it was because Bishop's fate had been entwined with hers, and she couldn't see her own future, so how could she see the parts of his overlapping hers? Maybe that was why she sensed nothing from Rush that went beyond the initial fluttering when he was around. His fate was linked with hers.

He could be just as bad as the worst, and she had no idea. He could be taking her to her doom. Glancing down at his knife again, she reminded herself to be vigilant. First moment she had, she'd take it and escape.

A sound to her right didn't belong. Clarke stopped, heart pounding in her throat, and listened.

A heartbeat echoed hers.

Thud-thud. Thud-thud.

She swallowed and hugged the jar. The area darkened from the cover of her hands. She forced herself to relax and let more light through her fingers.

Rush's gaze collided with hers. "What is it?"

"Did you hear that?"

He cocked his head, ears pricked.

Thud-thud. Thud-thud.

"I hear nothing," he said.

"But it's there. It's another heartbeat. I swear."

"Unless you have the hearing of a wolf, I'm right."

"But—" Something was watching them.

"Hurry up."

That feeling of ominous dread wouldn't leave. It tightened her skin. Clarke quickened her pace, trotting to catch up to Rush.

Every step she made, she heard an echo. Every breath, another just behind her. Every heartbeat, it reflected.

After another hour of walking at a brisk pace, the ground grew soft and wet. It squelched underfoot. The sound of her own, and a shadow's.

She blurted, "How can you not hear that?"

"It's probably still a side effect of the manabee going through you." Frowning, he stopped and focused on her and lowered his voice with serious intent. "I would hear anything that tried to get close to us."

"Would you? What about something masked with magic? That can happen, right?"

He paused.

"I want a knife," she added.

"No."

Screw him. She reached and made a grab for the one at his belt. He caught her hand.

"Why can't you just admit that I might be right?" she hissed.

"Because—" His words bit off.

A woman's keening wail cut through the air. Clarke jumped closer to Rush. His nostrils flared, and he turned in a three-sixty rotation until he sourced the direction it came from and then scented the air. He peered into the darkness, eyes scanning for danger.

After a breath, he murmured, "Let's go."

He pulled her by the wrist. His long legs ate up the muddy floor. Clarke jogged, splashing brown mess out with every step.

"Almost there," he said, breathing hard. "Just another few minutes."

But that hollow wail echoed through the trees like a siren's song. And that heartbeat. It followed. It quickened in time with Clarke's.

Thud-thud. Thud-thud.

They broke out of the tunnel and into a clearing where the sun failed to break through thick bracken overhead. Gray mist hung low over a muddy bog separating them from the safety of the path on the other side where green willow trees grew. It was either head back down the gloomy tunnel of trees, or wade through the mud. Trees without leaves looked like dead spindly limbs weaving in and out of the bog. Stress gripped Clarke's heart. She wasn't sure how much of this she could take. That woman's cry wouldn't stop.

"Well, this is new." Rush rubbed his beard.

"What do you mean?"

"Never used to be a bog here, but I guess it's been a while since I've passed this way."

"We have to keep going," she said, glancing back over her shoulder with a shiver.

During the walk, Starcleaver had never left Rush's hand, but now he sheathed it in the scabbard between his shoulder blades. He tested the strength of a long thin branch jutting out of the ground. It snapped off. He used the length to test the depth of the mud.

"About a yard," he noted. "That's not bad."

"Here, but what about in the middle?" she replied.

"Then we go around the perimeter."

The eerie feminine wail turned soft, like a song. Like she was cooing and coaxing. But what? Who? Coaxing them, or someone else? The obvious answer knocked at the edges of her mind, but she refused to let it in.

"Hurry," Clarke said.

"Don't let your fear take hold of you," he added, retrieving the manabeeze from her. "No one can see me, so I won't be the target. As long as you ignore the White Woman's song, you'll be safe. And if you get caught in her web, I'll be here to drag you out. Just follow me and do what I say."

The White Woman? Web? "That makes me feel so much better."

He pursed his lips at her sarcasm and then repacked the glowing jar before adjusting his rucksack over his shoulder. The fae moved as though this was a regular occurrence for him—the surprise danger—with swift and efficient actions. If she wasn't so shit-scared, she might be impressed with his confidence. He made sure the knife at his hip released and then sized up which side of the bog was easiest for them to traverse.

The eerie song picked up speed and intensity, and suddenly Clarke knew what the danger was. Her voice... it was like a drug. Soft chords melting her insides, and making her want to get closer to hear more. She shook her head.

"That's right," Rush said. "Don't listen. Ignore it."

"Why doesn't it bother you?"

"I've had training."

Clarke tried to move forward, but she couldn't. Terror had taken control of her senses.

"This way," he said and gestured for her to hold his hand. "If it makes you feel safer, hold my hand. I won't let go."

His unwavering confidence gave her the strength to take his hand and move forward under his guidance. The moment her feet hit mud, she sank to calf-high, but his hold kept her from lowering too far. The cape behind her lifted and floated. It stank. It stuck.

"Dear God, I will need a bath after this," she murmured.

"Your God doesn't exist anymore. I would pray to the Well for guidance instead."

"And where has that gotten you?"

A sharp look made her blanch. Fine. Whatever.

"Dear Well," she started. "Please find me a bath after this."

He snorted in a half-laugh but continued without breaking his pace.

"With lavender soap," she added, to keep her mind occupied. "And a nice hot fire."

Her voice trailed off as she concentrated. They got half-way around the bog when the woman's song became too hard to ignore. Clarke needed a distraction.

"Tell me what happened to my world," she said. Maybe if they talked, she wouldn't hear the woman.

A breathy grunt. "Not sure you should hear that."

"I know about the war. The sky being scorched. The nuclear winter... but is everything gone? Across the oceans too?"

Rush's grip tightened around her hand, but he continued to drive them through the mud. "I think nothing survived. Our Seers have seen no evidence of life beyond Elphyne. This is the last remaining pocket of life on the planet."

Sadness filled Clarke. "And I'm the first to wake up from my time?"

"You're the only I've heard of."

But she wasn't the only one.

"And my watch... there's no hope of getting that back I suppose?" Not that it would work.

"It was metal. It's been destroyed."

"It was a gift from my father."

Silence. "That is unfortunate."

She bumped into his broad back. He'd stopped.

"What is it?" she whispered, but his gaze locked on the center of the bog.

A beautiful woman was perilously stuck, flailing. She hadn't been there a moment ago. The area around her seemed less viscous, like a brown lake. Little dark streaks slashed across her pale skin. Muddy water glued her white dress indecently to her skin, giving them both unrestricted view of her naked breasts. Black hair floated behind her and dragged on the surface. Two large brown eyes implored them.

"Help me," she breathed. "Please."

Clarke frowned. This was too... convenient. And she wore white.

This thing was the source of her dread. The moment she understood, the woman's appearance shattered like a broken reflection. Gone was the stunning female, and in its place stood a humanoid bug-like creature. Enormous brown eyes that belonged on a praying mantis blinked at Clarke, as though she were its prey. It cocked its triangular head. Its frothing mouth ticked. Black hair fell from its head in stringy streaks. Folded forelegs pawed at the mud as though it drowned.

Gross.

"You are *so* not drowning," Clarke said and shook her head.

Focus, Clarke. Ignore her.

It was surely a her. The breasts were real. The white tattered dress was real. But the rest... it was a warped mess of human and insect. A monster, like the ones Rush said he fought. Clarke turned her attention back to the task at hand, getting around the bog. But Rush's gaze was fixed on the creature.

"I have to help her," he said. He let go of her hand and waded out.

"No!" Clarke reached out. "Stop!"

But it was too late. She missed him by a hair. He only had eyes for the thing.

"Rush!" Clarke's eyes burned. Panic gripped her throat. "It's not real. It's not the woman. It's a monster!"

He paused and glanced at Clarke.

The cooing and singing picked up in strength and speed. It may not see Rush, but maybe its magic did. It focused on Clarke, but Rush was caught in the snare of its magic web.

"Don't you see?" she shouted. "It can't see you, but its spell can affect you. If you continue, it will catch you anyway. Come back!"

He didn't. He kept wading toward the monster's pawing forelegs. The further he went, the deeper he got. The muddy water came up to his armpits. Any second, the creature's arms would hit him and then it wouldn't matter if Rush's curse kept him invisible. It would *feel* him.

A rising sensation took control of her body. Panic. Desperation. The need to help him. Her instinct moved inside her, bubbled up her throat, and she let it out with a tremendous scream. All that buzzing and fluttering in her chest pushed out with her emotion.

"You need to see the truth!" she shouted.

The power of her voice pushed air from her body. It was more than her voice. It was power... magic. Waves rippled, branches rustled. And Rush stopped wading. Slowly, both beings turned to each other, seeing the truth for the first time.

Rush saw the monster.

The monster saw him.

Understanding scorched through both of them. A breath. That's all it took. And then they attacked.

The monster's mandibles screeched wide. It dragged itself out of the muddy water to reach for him.

"Good God," Clarke murmured. The body hidden in the water was half human, half bug. Four legs, two arms. Six limbs. All splashing and thrashing. It was like something from a horror movie, a science experiment gone wrong. It paralyzed her, but Rush... he exploded into action.

He withdrew his sword and swung, aiming for the monster's head. It dodged with otherworldly speed, but it wasn't fast enough. Rush's blade lodged in the space between the monster's shoulder and neck. Rush strained, his muscles extending, veins in his temples popping. He pushed the blade down and down.

Bones cracked.

An almighty screech rent the air.

Clarke covered her ears and winced. When she looked, Rush waded back to her with a grim look on his face and the blade was back in its scabbard. Behind him, the monster sank.

FOURTEEN

Rush had let his guard down, and it was unforgivable.

How the White Woman had caught him in her web, he couldn't say, but he knew with absolute certainty that the woman he waded back to had broken the spell. Unlike any human he'd ever seen, this one had the capacity for magic. And she knew little about how to use it.

She was a recipe for disaster.

He could deny it no longer. This changed everything.

She reached out and helped draw him close. He searched her blue eyes. The only way to know how powerful she was would be to test her at the Order.

She jutted out her chin and straightened her shoulders, but the contrary tremble of hands told Rush she barely held it together. This would all seem strange to her.

"How did you do that?" he asked cautiously.

"What?"

"You know what I'm talking about. Peeling back the glamour the creature had cast. That was you."

"I meant, what, no thanks? No—oh, hey Clarke. You saved my life. Awesome." Her lips flattened. She let go of his hand.

He raised a cocky eyebrow. "Were you the one in there with the sword?"

"You're incredible. And I don't mean that as a compliment."

"And you're avoiding the question. How did you break the spell?"

"I, um..." She looked to the center of the bog where the monster had disappeared. Thick viscous bubbles popped on the surface. Clarke's delicate neck bobbed with a swallow as she dragged her gaze back to him. "I don't know. One minute, she was this woman in need of help, but then I saw through it. I saw the truth, but you couldn't. And then I wanted you to see it. I didn't want you to die. Something broke out of me... and..." Her eyes glistened. "What's happening to me?"

He wasn't sure, so gestured in the direction they were headed. "We need to keep going."

The hairs on Rush's arms lifted. His ears pricked. Ice slid down his spine.

Something was wrong.

The monster burst out of the muddy water, its sharp forelegs aiming for Clarke, snagging her cape. It happened so quickly. She was there, and then she wasn't.

"Clarke!"

He dove into the bog, aiming for where she'd submerged. *The bargain's bond.* He concentrated on it. Like the red string of fate, it bound his hand to hers. All he had to do was follow it through the thick, viscous mud. She couldn't be far. His fingers grazed something.

Soft skin.

The monster's had been rough and segmented.

He grasped. He yanked.

Her scream rose with bubbles and he hoped he hadn't ripped her arm from its socket, but she broke free. They hit the surface, gasping for air. Both covered in mud and sludge and bits of forest debris.

"Go." He pushed her.

Spluttering, crying, she didn't think twice. She used her arms to windmill through the swamp, but the cape was caught. The monster. He used his dagger to cut the neck tie and then free her. He shoved her toward the shallows.

"Get to the edge and out of the bog."

With his eyes still on her, something hit his right arm, tearing through his jacket. Fury unleashed, and he twisted, dagger in hand, aiming for its eye.

But it had touched him. The sickness triggered. His arm became heavy, his weapon weighted. The dagger should have gone through its socket, right to the brain. It didn't. It lodged halfway to the hilt. That's when he saw it—blue glittering glyphs on the side of the creature's neck. It was cursed, just like him.

But who would track down a White Woman and curse her? For what purpose?

There was no time to unsheathe Starcleaver. Gritting his teeth, fighting the blurriness dragging him under, he yanked the knife and stabbed again. Two things happened at once. His knife entered the creature's throat, sinking to his fist, spurting fiery blood over his hand. And a burning slice of pain clamped his shoulder as a mandible chomped down. His energy waned. He only had time for one more blow. It had better be good.

But the knife hilt got stuck on the collarbone. With his fist still lodged inside its body, his other hand held its pincers at bay. Defeat battered at the edge of his will, waiting for him to falter.

The voice of his uncle rose to the surface, as clear as it had been the day he'd been cursed. *You can't even protect yourself.*

Fuck you, Thaddeus.

One more push.

He could draw on the last of his mana.

He could ask Clarke for help.

He could force her.

No.

Instead, he clenched his teeth and took a chance. He released the dagger, let go of the pincer clamping onto his shoulder with the force of a hunting trap, and gripped either side of the monster's head. Agony screamed down from its bite. If this didn't work...

He twisted. Heard a crack. And exhaled.

The monster was dead, floating on its back. The muddy water slowly reclaimed its body, but he gripped onto it, refusing to let it go. Those curse marks needed to be investigated.

Too late.

With no energy left in his body, he slipped. He searched through his haze for the shock of red hair that signaled Clarke. He found her. Near the exit path lined with Willows. She crouched on solid ground, watching him with a furrowed brow.

"Clarke," he rasped, reaching.

Why was she just watching him?

She stood up and shook her head, resignation in her eyes. "When I was in peril, instead of helping me, you made a bargain that put me in your servitude. Then you kept me tied up and forced me to reveal my darkest shame."

His eyes fluttered. His consciousness drifted. But he wouldn't release her from their bargain. He needed her to act as his proxy. He gritted his teeth and shook his head.

"Then why don't you compel me to save you?"

Body going limp, floppy, the mud enveloped his shoulders.

Maybe this was how it ended. After all that.

The gray around his vision turned black, and the last thing he remembered was a muttered, "Stubborn bastard," before his face dropped into the bog.

RUSH WALKED along the dirt path that led to his old clan compound at Crescent Hollow. The fortress was nestled between the foot of a mountain range and the Whispering Woods. Only fools would try to invade based on location alone. But despite this, the buildings were made from thick stone. A high wall ran around the outside to protect the ten-thousand-plus residents inside.

A heavy pat on Rush's back jolted him forward. He turned to the grinning face of his Guardian comrade, D'arn Jasper. A tall and athletic black-wolf of the Mithras line, Jasper had shoulder-length brown hair tipped in black, and a pretty-boy face he hated being known for. It was the same as the king's. To combat the similarities, the wolf had tattooed his body, but it wasn't enough. His pretty face was something no Guardian let him live down.

But there was a darker reason Jasper had joined the Guardians. Whilst he'd never spoken about it, they all knew he needed to escape the rumored culling of Mithras descendants by the Seelie King. For centuries King Mithras had ruled the glass palace. Hell, he'd built it. He was The King. The High King of the Seelie, including both Summer and Spring Courts. But with each offspring he bore, more paranoia crept into his mind, and when a powerful Seer foretold that one of his own would dethrone him, he executed them all.

"Good to be back, yeah?" Jasper said, black brows quirking. "Even if we're covered in monster guts."

Rush looked down at the black gunk covering him from head to toe. Jasper was the same, yet he somehow still looked presentable. That stiff royal spine was always present, no matter how much he tried to deny it. Rush growled low. "You know I hate this place."

"Hate. Love. Same thing." Jasper clapped him on the back. "Last time you were here was what, nigh on a year ago?"

Rush flicked monster brain from his shoulder. "Bit less than that."

He preferred not to take jobs there, but when he had to, he did his duty and then spent the rest of time at the tavern, usually balls deep in some nameless female until he forgot about the haunting memories around every Crescent Hollow corner. The sound of his sister's feminine war cry still echoed in his mind as she chased him through the fox-tail fields. And then there were their dares to get as close to the Whispering Woods as possible without caving to the call of the forest.

"And so how much tax are we to ask for again?" Jasper asked.

A heavy weight descended on Rush's shoulders. He hated this kind of call out. "Shouldn't you know this? You're the senior Guardian."

"I may be older in age, but younger at heart." He shot Rush an incorrigible grin.

Damned joker.

"It's two red coin," Rush said.

"Balls," Jasper muttered. "I hate these."

"The law is the law."

"Yeah, yeah." Jasper waved him down. "We exterminate the magical monsters. They pay for their gratitude. Pity none of them actually give a shit."

Rush gave a casual shrug. "When the monsters eat the children, they will."

"Maybe that's where we've gone wrong. Should let a few of them get taken first." Jasper broke off a piece of jerky he'd retrieved from his pocket and handed some to Rush. "Want some?"

Rush screwed up his face. "After it's been in your monster gut filled pocket? No thanks."

"Suit yourself." Jasper popped it into his mouth with a wink. "All I know is that I'll need the energy if I see that tavern wench again."

"It's been months. What makes you think she'll remember you."

Jasper blinked. "Everyone remembers this face."

With a snort, Rush turned back to the Crescent Hollow compound. Just outside the gate, a pregnant female was tied to a pole, strung up, and treated like a criminal all because a child grew in her belly. She must be in labor. Two midwives stood by, ready to take the child after she expelled it.

Rush's gaze darkened at the sight.

Jasper spat out a masticated mess, then straightened his Kingfisher blue coat. "Looks like an unsanctioned breeding."

The two of them strode forward. With every heavy step Rush took, tension increased in his body. He knew the captive female. Intimately. Long silver hair, cherry cheekbones, round face.

One night of passion, many moons ago.

A glance down at her protracted belly was all the clue he needed to know the child was his. The timing fit, and he could sense it in her shifting scent. She smelled like kin. The rightness of it hummed across his skin. The child was his. Alarmed, he checked to see if his fellow Guardian recognized her, but he didn't. Jasper just looked as undignified as the female most likely felt. No Guardian enjoyed seeing this kind of punishment, but with resources scarce, population had to remain in check. Well, that's what the king told them.

It had never sat right on Rush's shoulders, but...

"Not magic. Not our problem," Jasper mumbled under his breath.

Jasper didn't recognize the female. He had been with Rush at the Laughing Den when they'd met, but he'd been upstairs, face between another female's thighs at the time. Rush couldn't even remember her name, he realized with shame.

The two midwives sneered at the Guardians as they neared.

"Relax," Jasper drawled. "We're not here for you."

A stout female wearing a scarf around her neck folded her arms and gave him the side-eye. "But you're here to take our coin, no doubt."

Jasper shrugged, and Rush saw how callous it was for the first time. It was all callous. He looked at his hands, at his jacket... what was he doing with his life to be part of a system that brushed away a pregnant female's plight like this.

Why?

Because the Prime said their resources were already spread thin. Because the magic of the Well was more important than caring about the affairs of the every day fae.

The stout midwife gave the captive female a worried glance and then tugged her friend. "Let's leave. The pup won't come yet. We have time." She gave the captive a gentle pat on the shoulder. "We'll be back. Don't worry, love."

Then the midwives scurried away.

Rush's ex-lover lifted her weary gaze and widened her eyes.

"Find the alpha," Rush ordered Jasper.

Sensing something was off, Jasper's ears twitched, but he nodded. The moment Jasper moved out of earshot, Rush turned on the female.

"Why?" he asked. "Why didn't you tell me?"

He could have helped her. Could have done something!

Guilt splashed over her face. "Because you would have told me to get rid of him."

Darkness unfolded within Rush. No he wouldn't have. Then a single word in her sentence stood out.

"It's a boy?" Rush's throat clogged.

She nodded grimly.

After joining the Guardians—a group of fae who rarely mated—Rush had given up on ever having his own family.

"But you and I..."

"Véda," she offered with a small, defeated smile. "My name is Véda. Although I'm not even sure we exchanged those. I've always known where to find you but thought I could get away with saying I was... forced."

Blood drained from Rush's face. "But I never."

"Not by you. Just someone I never saw. I thought they would let me go. I didn't want you to

know." She squeezed her eyes shut as a contraction came over her. A keening cry of pain ripped from her lips. Rush tried to hold her upright, so she didn't pull too much on her bindings.

When it was done, she kept her eyes closed as she spoke. "It was my decision to keep the child. And I needed to know that if I was found out, at least one of his parents would be around to care for him. If no one knew it was you, then a Guardian would be the perfect protector—"

"So the father is revealed."

Rush whirled to see his uncle, Thaddeus.

Jasper stood by with a shocked, but stoic look on his face. He knew what this meant, what he'd have to do to both Rush and Véda. There was no way Thaddeus would let this go.

A slow, slithering smile curved up Thaddeus's mouth. "You can't even protect yourself, let alone this wench."

Rush turned to Jasper who only flinched and said, "The law is the law."

"Wake up."

A slap on Rush's face drew him out of the past.

He blinked until his vision cleared. But the pain of his curse still crippled him. He could barely lift his head from the soil as air dragged in and out of his lungs.

Clarke crouched before him, beautiful face crumpled with worry.

A wash of emotions hit him—surprise, relief, disbelief.

"You saved me," he croaked. "Why?"

Was it the bond? But he never compelled her.

So why help him?

"I've been asking myself the same thing," she admitted. "The thought crossed my mind to steal your belongings and continue on by myself, but I didn't. And the only reason I can come up with is that despite what happened to this world because of a mistake I made, I'm not a killer. I'm not a cruel person. Unlike you, I can't stand by idly and watch another person suffer. You saved my life, and instead of forcing me to save yours through your despicable bargain, you didn't. So I saved you anyway. I'm making the choice to be a better person."

Her words cut straight to the core of his guilt. His inability to do anything when Véda had died but watch her suffer. The way she'd accepted her fate was the bravest thing he'd ever seen. All for the life she grew inside of her. And Rush? He'd been a coward.

This human was worth more than him.

She stood, checked one direction of the path they were on, then the other. She dusted her hands and tugged her shredded shirt closed. And then she clenched her jaw with determination before locking eyes with him.

"Why are you cursed, Rush?" He wished her away, but she kept talking. "I could guess, I suppose. You think I haven't noticed that touching other things hurts you, but I have. You were surprised that first time we touched. You wince in reflex, as though you think it will hurt. And you looked in pain with the warada, and here you are in pain again."

He said nothing.

"Fine. Don't share. I mean, I'll get close enough to the truth eventually, but once again, I'm not like you. I'll never force someone's darkest shame out without their consent. I'd rather you share it with me yourself."

"I saved your life three times," he breathed.

She sneered. "It's all a currency in this world, isn't it? Say thank you, and you're in debt. Do a good deed, get one back. Doesn't anyone do anything because it's the right thing?"

He had no answer to that. She was right.

"See you around, Rush."

His bones were heavier than iron. All he could do was watch her walk away and know that this was what he deserved. He couldn't save Véda. He couldn't protect his son. And Clarke? She was the one who'd forced him to see the truth.

He closed his eyes. Letting his guard down wasn't so bad. It was keeping it up that hurt.

CHAPTER

FIFTEEN

Clarke strode with determination down the path leading from the bog.

It was fine that she left Rush there. Completely fine. She'd pulled him out. She'd stopped him from drowning. She didn't even steal his belongings. She didn't need him.

Surely she could get by in this new world without him. How different could it be? The urge to stay must be wrong because it was simply cruel to side with a fae who cared little about her dignity and more about whatever secret drove his need to hold her to their bargain.

But he let her walk away.

"There's work to do, damn it." Her voice rang clear and lonely on the path ahead. "I have work to do."

Lives to save. Evil was coming. No. It was already in this world. Memory of the Void was a constant companion, pushing her forward. The certainty of it filled her mind. *This* was her purpose. Save this small scrap of habitable earth from annihilation. It wouldn't make up for what had happened to her world, but it would help this one.

So why did that ache in her chest get worse with each passing step? Why did her mind keep traveling back to the nice things Rush had done? Feeding her. Clothing her. Letting her explore those incredible ears even though it caused him great discomfort. Holding her hand to cross the bog. Diving headfirst into murky water to rescue her.

He could have forced her to save him. But he didn't.

Her whole life she'd been forced to use her powers for other people's gain. Bishop couldn't have cared less if he'd forced her to save himself. In fact, he'd done it frequently.

"Tell me my future, babe."

"You're going to die."

Bishop laughed. "Then tell me how to cheat death."

Leaving Bishop before the world froze didn't feel like this. Leaving Rush hurt like her soul was being ripped in two, and half was back with him. Why?

Clarke stopped. She clenched her fists and rubbed them over her sternum. And then she screamed her frustration, letting the sky and the air know how she felt. With every fiber of her being, she told the world, *This isn't fair.*

For once, she would like just a little free will. Just a little.

Those days grifting in the casino, only worrying about her next meal, were looking like a dream.

The last note of her cry left her breathing hard and her stomach stinging. With a wince, Clarke glanced down. Red welts ran down her front. She poked around but saw no worrying damage. The monster's claws had just scraped the first layer of flesh. She'd been lucky.

She wanted to hate Rush. He was a grade-A stubborn fae. But he needed her, even if he wouldn't admit it. One of them had to be mature about this. If she ignored her intuition, then she was no better than him, no better than the fools who ignored her warnings and destroyed her world.

She used to think her ex was the fool. By the time she'd caught on to his greed and callousness, he was already knee deep in messing with all the wrong people. The Void and the man who did his dirty work for him. His name was Bones. A mercenary with sharp angles.

She heard an echo of Laurel's scream as Bones pulled her nails out.

"These numbers will only bring death and destruction," she'd warned Bones.

Clarke slammed the heel of her palms into her eye sockets, hoping to shove the memories away. But they were as sharp as the day she'd made them. She should have done more. She should have done *something* instead of walking away, but all she could think of was that she'd not expected them to actually release Clarke and Laurel. And when they had, they didn't look back. If they had, the Void might have changed his mind.

But was it worth it?

Was Laurel's life worth it?

She dropped her palms and lifted her gaze to stare at the sky through the branches. And what was she doing right now? Walking away from the tug of destiny. Her instincts weren't telling her to run forward, they were telling her to go back.

Spinning on her heels, she stomped back to the bog.

And found Rush on the ground, still as the dead under the branches of a willow tree. Hatred fled, leaving her cold and empty. This was the result of saving her. Like a crocodile in a death roll, that monster had dragged her down, but Rush had fearlessly come after her. There weren't men like him in her time. None that she'd known anyway.

Rush had known touching the monster would make him sick, yet he'd done it. He was just too stubborn to admit it. She refused to believe it was because of some bargain he'd made with her when he wouldn't even use the bargain to ensure his survival. His pride may have stopped him from reneging on their deal, but this... there must be more to his story.

He remained unmoving, face pale and pinched.

Clarke went to him and landed on her knees. She touched his hot skin and then felt for a pulse at his neck. He jerked, gold eyes opening to lock on her with turbulence. Fury and hurt and shame shone back at her. She could see it in every line of his strained face.

"Get away," he growled and tried to shift his big, linebacker body but he managed nothing more than an inch, a drag in the dirt.

"No," she replied.

An anguished frown scored his forehead.

"Why?" he whispered.

Why did she come back?

Firming her lips, she squeezed his hand. His reason must be strong enough to think he didn't deserve to live. Clarke knew that feeling. A single tear ran down her cheek, and he looked away.

"Rush," she whispered and smoothed hair from his face. "I don't know how this is happening to me. I keep coming back to you and I can't think of why, only that maybe I've been brought to this time for a reason, and you're part of it. Your god, your Well of Life, or whatever you want to call it, put me on your doorstep. It thawed me in your lake. I guess together we are stronger. Alone, we are nothing."

Denial flashed in his eyes, and he looked away.

She bit her lip. "I hate the way you forced me into your bargain, but I can't deny the pull between us. You feel it too. I know it."

The breath that left him was shaky. He gathered enough strength to push himself to sitting. "When they cursed me, they made me invisible to everyone that mattered to me. And when no one can see you, they forget. You... disappear. I lost my purpose."

"Now you have a new one."

"What, to protect you on some divine mission to save the world?"

"That sarcasm is uncalled for. You're a Guardian. You tell me. What about me seems normal?"

He scrutinized her. "You have magic."

"I know."

"But you're human."

"I know."

"I'm supposed to kill your kind."

"Again... I know."

Was this his way of apology? She couldn't say his prejudice against her kind was unfounded, but she wouldn't mind a little regret.

"You made me see the White Woman's true appearance, simply by willing it."

"I think you should call her evil bug-woman, but..." Her breath caught on a sigh. "Yeah. I think I did. For the record, this is just as disturbing for me as it is for you. Trusting someone is hard when I've been used before. But I'm trying. By the way, that was a good segue for you to apologize for using me."

"Fae don't apologize."

"You don't apologize. You don't say thanks." She rolled her eyes. "What else don't you do?"

"Lie." And then closed his eyes with a wince.

Her eyes widened. They couldn't lie?

But they could withhold the truth. Maybe if she could force the monster to see the truth, she could force him to speak it. But that would make her as bad as him. She would never do it. Not unless survival was on the line.

She bit her lip. The wind picked up and gusted her hair. She turned and hugged her knees, staring at the trodden leaves and sticks on the floor. An insect that reminded her of a dung beetle crawled up the base of a branch opposite her. She fixated on it, grateful for something familiar in this place because this power inside her was frighteningly foreign. The visions were getting stronger, and the new ability—she'd *seen* the evidence of her energy explode outward from her body. It still moved and rolled inside her, waiting for the next time she needed it.

The touch of his hand hit between her shoulder blades. She scrunched her burning eyes closed.

"Learning to trust is new for me too, but... I'll keep you safe. Fae don't lie." The baritone of his deep voice rumbled through her like rolling thunder. Bit by bit, she relaxed. It wasn't just his words, it was the *knowing* inside. Her chest fluttered. He told the truth.

"As to your purpose here?" he continued. "Only the Order can confirm that."

"And that's where we're going?"

He nodded.

"What if they think I'm lying? I'm human, right? I can lie."

"After what I've seen, I find that hard to believe. It's clear you have the magic of the Well running through your veins." He rubbed his bottom lip, eyes shrewd on her. "I don't know how, or why, but the Order will know."

"So what now?"

"I believe I owe you a bath."

A laugh barked out of her. "I *believe* I prayed to God for that, not you."

He lifted a haughty shoulder, more energized. "Your god is a being with magical powers. So... same thing."

"Right."

They shared a smile. It was good to see the light back in his eyes, even for a moment. But already his expression turned somber as he angled toward the bog. "That thing should never have caught me in its spell. The White Woman is a malevolent member of the Unseelie Court, yet she shouldn't even be this far south. It's either the thaw, or..."

"Or what?"

He pushed to his knees. "I think I can stand now."

She lifted him by the elbow, and helped him get to his feet.

Out of breath, he waited a moment with his hands on his hips before unbuckling the baldric keeping his sword strapped on. "You can't go into town with that torn shirt."

"What are you doing?" She kept a cautious eye on him as he removed his outer layer.

"Giving you something to wear." He handed her the mud-covered jacket and reached over his neck with a wince to draw his shirt off.

"You're injured. You need it." An angry slash scored his neck.

"No one can see me. And I've had worse. When we get there, I will find us fresh clothes while you clean up at the inn."

With his shirt removed, blue light flashed and Clarke squinted at the piercing glow. Shimmering glyphs covered his entire frame, sparkling like the tiny tear drop under his eye. Her cheeks flamed as she scanned his sculpted abs and perfect torso, his muscular physique flexing and rolling. Thoughts fled. She'd never be able to unsee it. He wasn't so animal after all. He was pure, hot blooded male.

"Get a good look," he said. "Once the curse ends, I'll be shriveled and old."

Bitterness laced his joke. And she didn't care. Her hand was on him in an instant, tracing the shape of the glyphs, fascinated and wondering what they meant. He took a sharp breath, but she couldn't stop. With every turn of her touch, glimpses in her mind's eye showed someone painting them, and then watching the glyphs sink into his flesh.

"They weren't always like this," she murmured.

"The more that appear, the closer I am to the end." His voice was dark honey near her ear.

The markings tingled against her palm. Every time she shifted her touch, a slow burn built inside her, making every feminine instinct aware of his state of undress. She lost her clinical demeanor and enjoyed the heat of his touch. She watched, enthralled, as his skin went taut in response to the press of her fingers. A stillness came over him, as though he held his breath.

He watched her.

She knew.

Co-awareness bounced between them. Lifting her lashes, she met his gaze. An eternity passed as they stared into each other's eyes. She wanted—needed—to know more about him. Everything. Starting with his body.

Why that jagged scar from beneath his rib cage to his hip? Why the wolf tattoo over his pec? It was dark and liquid, throwing colors as though oil spilled in water. Maybe it wasn't even a tattoo. Shifting her touch, her thumb grazed his Adam's apple. It bobbed on a swallow. She stroked his beard... along to his pointed ears.

"You need to stop now," he rasped.

"Why?"

"Because you're turning me on, and it's been"—he licked his lips, a sight that had her stifling a moan—"it's been a long time. Fae can be... relentless in their lovemaking. You are a fragile human."

"But I'm not that human, am I?"

"You won't like me when I lose control."

"So make me stop."

He didn't. Her brazen fingers glided back down his front, bumping over abdominals, aiming for the top of his breeches. She couldn't stop. Desire took control of her function. He'd said *lovemaking* and *relentless,* and now she couldn't get it out of her mind. Two sweaty bodies, naked and tangled with primal need. A mindless craving pushed her every action. Her fingers dipped into the private space beneath his waistband, teasing the coarse hair there. His skin was so hot. She moaned, low and hoarse. He halted her movement with a hand. A warning growl escaped his throat.

"I find I cannot stop," she murmured, eyes lowering to watch her hands, still alive with sensation. Veins popped on the flesh of his hard lower belly. His heady scent called to her, and it was everything she wanted. Right there. Right then. She needed to see more and... she licked her lips. "Let me—"

"Stop touching me." His words compelled her, and her hands snapped to her side, forced by the bargain binding them.

Agape, she stood back.

He stared as though a tempest raged in his mind, as though he wanted to devour her and fought hard not to. As though he hated himself for wanting her. He ran trembling fingers through his silver hair, downcast eyes on her.

God, moving like that, lifting his arms and popping biceps... he made it worse. Clarke shivered. Her cool hands flew to pat her hot cheeks. "I'm so sorry. I don't know what's come over me."

It was a desire like she'd never felt before. It wracked her body and hummed along her skin. His hot gaze dipped to her lips, lowered to her bra, and then went to where the need was strongest. Nostrils flared as though he could scent her arousal. His attention caressed her body, lighting her up.

In two quick strides, he was in her space, bringing her lips to his. But then he paused. Hesitated. Their breaths mingled. Was that her heart beating, or his... or...

She didn't care. She needed it. Wanted it. Expected it.

Mine, her mind growled possessively. But he didn't ravage her like she wanted, like he'd promised. He lowered his lips and touched hers with tenderness. The softness of pillowed skin. The scratch of his beard. Then the gentle, shy push of his tongue requesting access. He nibbled her bottom lip, savoring a moment before thrusting through her parted lips and devouring with a guttural growl of need.

Heady. Salty. His taste smashed right through her restraint. She gripped his neck and pulled him flush against her body. The feel of his long drawn-out moan against her chest turned her liquid. They kissed and licked and tongued. God, she needed him.

It was only when her spine hit the spindly trunk of a tree did she realize he'd pushed her backward. Pressed hard against the bark, he took her mouth as though she was his. Lost in his arms, his taste, and his complete devotion, Clarke sank into the moment. No inner alarm screamed for her to run the other way. It was all him. His hard body, his warmth, his roving mouth.

She pushed his hand down to her breast and arched into him. "Rush, touch me."

He jumped back, chest heaving with ragged breath.

"Clarke." He shook his head, a pained look in his eyes. "I can't."

She blinked and hugged herself. What just happened?

"You sure look like you can." Was it really this human versus fae thing? "Never mind. I get it."

His brows lifted in the middle. "I let desire cloud my judgement once, and someone died for it. I can't..."

Someone had died?

"I understand."

She removed the torn tunic and replaced it with his shirt. The muddy and wet thing came down to her thighs, but it was whole.

He put on his jacket and left it unbuttoned as if he were too hot to close it. A flush had ruddied his complexion too. He retrieved his rucksack and then finally buttoned the jacket before putting the baldric and sword back on.

Everything had shifted between them, and yet nothing had. He'd not reneged on his bargain. He wasn't ready to let go of his prejudices, but his perception was changing. For the first time since waking in this strange version of her world, she was on the right track.

That kiss had felt good, damn it. She wanted him. Not because her powers told her to, or this mystical Well, but because he was hot, sexy, desirable. He made her want. And he made her feel safe. Knowing it, and taking ownership of it made her feel good.

Clearing her throat, she gave him a smile that said they weren't done yet and moved, but he got in her way. A solid wall of fae blocked her. She met his gaze and saw something different. No more hate. No. This darkness was more like the need she felt. Like the want. Her chest warmed with hope.

"Clarke." His velvet-storm voice slid over her in a wave. She held her breath, waiting, wishing. But he only tugged her muddy hair over her ears. "Keep your ears hidden."

SIXTEEN

They emerged from the Whispering Woods into a field painted gold by the setting sun. Rush's original plan had been to make a quick trip beyond the border walls of Crescent Hollow and steal a portal stone from the markets. Back then, he couldn't give a fee-lion's whiskers about her state of dress. Now he wouldn't let her stay covered in mud. He owed her that act of kindness. Plus, with the late hour, it might take some time to locate a portal stone. Without one, the journey to the Order involved a trip across the Seelie Sea, or further up river via Cornucopia, the trade city.

So to an inn it was.

The thought of sharing a room with Clarke sent a tug straight to his balls. Rush didn't trust himself alone with her, not with the way she looked at him, and not with the way she'd kissed him. After all these years, she was a temptation he couldn't succumb to, especially since she wasn't his Well-blessed mate, and more so because he was beginning to not care.

He still remembered the look of disappointment on his sister's face when she found out he was an unsanctioned breeder. It was one thing to dip your wick, but they expected you to take proper precautions. The elves brewed a certain elixir for these exact purposes. But Rush had not planned. It was a mistake that ended in death for an innocent woman.

He was a disgrace to his father's legacy. Not only had their father died trying to save Rush from drowning in a ritual he'd yet to take, but his mother had followed his father into death not long after. Kyra had lasted as long as she could in Crescent Hollow. She'd cared for Thorne, but after he was the tribute to the Well, she'd had nothing left for her at the Hollow. Thaddeus was cruel to her, so she left.

He should have found a way to help Kyra more. He'd followed her around for a few months, making sure she settled into her job at Cornucopia. He'd found a way to drop coin to help her finances, but in the end, it wasn't enough. It was never enough.

But they were here. At Crescent Hollow. Rush had Clarke to speak for him. There was something he could do now. Maybe if he couldn't get to Thorne, he'd get to Kyra. At least then he'd know what to say.

With Thorne... he was at a loss for words.

"I'm thirsty," Clarke said.

"Yes, princess."

The compound came into sight and they regrouped. Rush handed Clarke a last swig from the waterskin. She took a mouthful and then sprayed it out when her eyes caught on the walls of his old town, just across the field. "*That's* where you grew up?"

He nodded. "Not much to look at, but it kept us safe."

Clarke wiped her mouth. "Um. I'm pretty sure the word you're looking for is castle. Or fortress. With a village inside the walls."

He forced himself to look at it as though for the first time. It was no castle. Village, yes. A small community of about ten thousand.

"More like a fort," he agreed.

"What's on those banners flying over the gate?"

"The Nightstalk Crest." He tapped his chest, where his own family crest had been tattooed on. "You've seen the emblem on my skin."

"And you were the heir?" She returned the waterskin.

"Alpha heir apparent."

"What does that mean?"

"It means I'm strong enough take over the leadership of the pack from my father without being challenged. We wolves call him the alpha, but the king calls him a lord. Lord Nightstalk."

She raised a dark eyebrow. "And you gave that up to join the Guardians?"

He narrowed his eyes at her. "I didn't give it up. More so encouraged to do so after my father died."

Her plump bottom lip disappeared between her teeth. "That sucks."

He shrugged, eyes stuck on those lips of hers.

"If you had the chance, would you want it back?"

He rubbed his chest. No one had asked him that before. Even if he did somehow break his curse, the Order would have to let him go. He'd have to be accepted back into the Nightstalk pack. Then he'd have to challenge Thaddeus.

"Even if I had a future there," he replied. "I'm a Guardian."

"But they cursed you."

"They own me. Even if I get them to lift my curse."

"That... well, that sucks."

He shrugged. "Giving your life over to the service of the Well for enhanced abilities isn't something you can take back. Come on. It's getting dark."

The dirt and grass they were on turned into a red gravel path that crunched when they walked. On either side of them stretched fields of dandelions and fox-tail weeds. They'd only walked half a mile when something lying in the middle of the path caught their attention. Little fee-lions hopped about, prancing and playing. The mischievous creatures were often a sign of irreverence.

"Are those cats?" Clarke asked, shielding her eyes from the sunset.

"They're pests."

"Oh, come on. They can't be that bad. Look at how cute their faces are, all smooshy and those tails swishing about, all agitated. Wait. What are they doing?"

The little beasts lifted their heads. One sniff of his inner wolf and they scampered off with a chitter.

"Don't." He put a palm to her chest, holding her back. He caught a scent on the wind. Sour, rotting flesh. "It's a body."

Which in itself wasn't that unusual. Between the different fae racial clans, a dead body frequently turned up. Guardians didn't solve squabbles between clans or courts. They were better than that. The kings and queens that ruled Elphyne had their own military to keep their subjects in line, but there was often a gap. The poor and smaller races could be overlooked.

"I'll check it out," he warned. With a glance her way, he found her unworried, just curious. "Stay there."

She nodded but tried to see around his body. "Something's not right."

Rush strode toward the dead fae and strained his senses. No heartbeat. Definitely putrefying flesh. It was a satyr. Part man, part goat, the fae's horns had been shorn off. The puncture marks in its neck signaled a vampire's bite, but the corpse wasn't exsanguinated. Perhaps one of the Unseelie had gotten a little rough while eating, a little too far from their territory. But to dump the body here in full view of a Seelie compound. Something smelled off.

It wasn't the first time on this journey something had smelled wrong. The White Woman was far from her usual northern haunt. And she had been cursed, perhaps forced into moving south. That made two Unseelie causing inexplicable harm in Seelie territory.

He went to wave Clarke onward, but she was already behind him.

"What happened?" she asked.

"Vamp got overzealous."

"Why am I not surprised you have vampires?" She frowned down at the body. "Shouldn't he look a little less, I don't know, full of blood?"

"Vamps don't drain to feed. They like to relish one meal over days and usually their meals walk away." Rush took another look at the satyr. His tanned cheeks were rather plump. The hooves sticking out from beneath his nicely creased trousers were shoed with precious stone. So he was well-off, perhaps one of the Seelie gentry. Rush kneeled down and touched the face with the back of his hand. His curse didn't work on dead things.

The satyr had warm skin.

"Recently dead," he murmured. "And vamps rarely travel during the day."

Not unless they had been conditioned, like those in the Order.

"Something about it just doesn't feel right," Clarke added.

Rush agreed. He met her eyes. "You *seeing* something?"

"No. But... maybe..." She patted her sternum and scanned the body. "Maybe check under his shirt."

He lifted it. The lightly fuzzed torso had scorch marks consistent with a mana related attack. Except the pattern was wrong. Instead of a darker ring on the inside with an explosion of striations, the marking was uniform. Not a direct hit to the middle and the visual effect of the blow. This was more like a water stain. Or a mana stain. As though the magical life-force had been ripped from his body, not thrust into it or allowed to naturally escape upon death. He sniffed again and caught a slight metallic scent coming from the body, but when he checked the pockets, there was no metal to be found. Could someone have forcibly taken the mana while he was alive? Rush dropped the shirt and took Clarke's elbow.

"Let's keep moving."

"Why?" She jogged along next to him, hurrying to keep his pace.

"Because someone used magic to kill that fae, and they tried to make it look like a vampire did it." He flexed his jaw with the understanding. "Vampires are Unseelie, yet we are in Seelie territory. With the White Woman far out from her home, it looks like the precarious peace between the two kingdoms is about to break."

"Shit, that's not good."

"Dead bodies are never good. But it's not my business." It was best they stay out of it and stay on course. The last thing he needed was for Clarke to get caught up in something like this. "We should get into the inn and be out tomorrow as early as we can."

SEVENTEEN

Clarke tugged the hair covering her ears. Coming up to the gate of the compound, it was clear the two sentinels standing beneath the stone portcullis could only see her and not the big brooding fae stalking next to her. He wasn't happy coming back to this place, and it had little to do with the two heavyset guards wearing dirty white uniforms, strapped with weapons. A longbow flashed over their broad shoulders and the scarred faces and broken noses gave her no reason to believe she'd ever be able to escape if they deemed her a threat. Not to mention the lethal wolven fangs pressing into their bottom lips.

No turning back now.

Still fifty feet away, she forced each step closer to remain steady and tried not to look at the strange vines hanging over the walls of the compound. She tried to ignore the way they swayed and shifted, or how tendrils unfurled with predatory focus when a butterfly got too close. But she couldn't ignore the suspended wooden cage on each side of the gate. In one was a wolf. In the other, a petite female fae with prismatic dragonfly wings. Short disheveled, blue hair stuck to her face. Pearlescent tear tracks smeared down her dirty cheeks. She slept, or was passed out, on the base of the cage. A dainty hand dangled through the bars as though she'd tried to reach the wolf on the other side.

Clarke looked at Rush.

"Eyes forward," he reminded.

"Sorry." She did as was told and continued walking.

"They're being punished," Rush explained. "By raising a fae from the ground, it cuts them from the source of the Well. Not being able to replenish your spent mana is akin to a hangover you can't escape from. It's torture. And of course, it stops you from shifting as the shift expends a lot of mana. They have trapped the shifter in his animal form until they lower him to the ground."

"You say that like you've experienced it."

He lifted a shoulder. "They tried it on me once. That's when they learned even metal bars can't keep a Guardian from accessing the mana in the earth. It's why they had to resort to a curse." His gaze darted to the female. "My guess is the pix already belonged to a harem, and the lord in charge here has dispensed local reprimands to avoid starting political unrest with the pix clan."

"Harem," she mumbled under her breath. How horrible. "She's being forced into being a sex slave?"

Rush laughed wryly. "So you don't know everything."

She clenched her fists and spoke through her teeth. "Why are you laughing?"

"Because, naïve little princess, for each pixie female, there are at least three male partners and protectors. I've seen some harems reach up to twelve males for one female. She's not being forced into anything. They treat their females like queens."

Clarke's jaw dropped to the ground. "Three men weren't enough for her?"

"Well, you know what they say." He gave her a salacious, toothy grin. "Once you go pack, you never go back."

She blanked. Then got it. "Oh, you're real hilarious, Wolfie."

Pure male smugness rolled off him. "It's not a joke."

"Whatever." Her mood darkened. "It's still wrong to dictate who you can and cannot fall in love with."

She must have hit a sore spot because he gave her a dark sideways glance and compelled her. "*Stop talking.*"

Her lips clamped shut on their own accord. Irritation hit just before the two sentinels hailed her down.

"You. Female." A brutish fae broke away from his friend and stepped toward her. His bruiser face accentuated a stocky body. Bushy eyebrows and hair gave him an unhinged vibe. "State your business."

"Tell them you're just here to get cleaned up after a lengthy journey and that you'll be on your way in the morning."

Before Clarke processed Rush's words, they tumbled from her mouth. Alarm pricked through her. She couldn't stop them. Rush's demand was her compulsion.

The words of the deal came back to haunt her. *You will be my voice where I cannot speak. You will be my hands, where I cannot touch.*

Goddamn him. She had thought they were past this. Pain burned hotly from her nails digging into her palms.

The guard leered at her. "I knock off in five minutes. There's plenty of room at my place. If you need a hand cleaning up... well, I'm real good at using my tongue." He licked his lips.

Ew.

The other guard snickered. From the corner of Clarke's eyes, Rush reddened with fury.

"No thanks," she said of her own accord.

The guard looked her up and down. He lifted his nose and flared his nostrils. "You're not a wolf. What manner of fae are you?"

"Say you're Elven," Rush ordered.

"I'm Elven." She smiled weakly.

"Far away for an elf." The guard still under the shadows of the gate stepped forward, eyes narrowing. He held a drumstick of some animal in one hand, complete with blue and purple feathers still sporadically attached.

Rush nodded to the cage. "The pix is far away too. Is that a crime?"

Clarke was compelled to repeat his words. The two guards looked at her, and then the stocky one laughed.

"The pix's crime is that she fornicated outside her clan."

"Nah," said the other with a chortle. "She's there because she denied Lord Nightstalk."

"If Thaddeus hears you talking like that, you'll be next."

Clarke's blood turned to ice. Thaddeus?

Rush grumbled something under his breath. Unwilling to look at him, Clarke had to assume he knew well that Thaddeus was here. And from memory, Rush said something about an alpha running this place. Which meant only one thing. Clarke was about to step into the territory ruled by the fae who'd tried to assault her.

The guard sniffed and wiped his nose, then motioned for Clarke to enter the compound.

Still fuming at herself for failing to see Thaddeus's connection to this place, and Rush's inability to tell her the truth, she stormed inside a good few feet before taking in the place.

She stopped and gaped. Cobblestone roads. Townhouses with terracotta tiled roofs. Ivy over archways. Moss and lichen painted a patina across the limestone steps and walls. It was quaint, inviting, and it smelled like mouthwatering cooked onions, garlic, and something else she couldn't place. But it was delicious.

Many fae bustled down the streets. From those who looked virtually human, to others with wings or horns. There were no modern amenities... at least none that she saw. From her point of view, it looked like she'd stepped through a looking glass and into the Middle Ages. No cars. No electric lights.

The wonder must have shown on her face because Rush leaned toward her to say, "Wait until you see Cornucopia. That place has fae from all over Elphyne. Or even better, wait until you see the Summer or Winter Court. One castle is made from glass, the other from obsidian. The Spring and Autumn Courts aren't bad either. The summer solstice festival is one you won't want to miss, at any of the Courts."

His words stole her breath, and then she remembered she was furious with him. Her brows slammed down, and she strode forward into the unknown. Following the scent of cooked onions seemed a marvelous idea.

Rush jogged to catch up. "I should have told you Thaddeus was the lord here."

"You think that's the only reason I'm angry?" she replied, then smiled at a gray-haired woman with jaw tusks who looked at her strange for speaking to the air.

"Why else?"

Typical. Males of any species were all the same. "You forced me to speak for you. Again."

He put his hands in his pockets. His expression turned distant, then he nodded up ahead. "Next right. The Laughing Den is where we can stay."

He put something cold in her hand. She looked down and opened her fingers to see two coins made from red glass. Light hit an embellished letter M suspended in the middle of each coin. She lifted it to the sky and turned to marvel at the intricate refractions inside.

"M," she murmured.

"For King Mithras. Good in the Seelie Kingdom and the neutral ground of Cornucopia. That will pay for a room, food and a meal," said Rush. "It's also enough that they'll look the other way."

She desperately needed to bathe, so strode onward until she came to the small narrow street he motioned to turn down. It wasn't so much as a street, but a set of higgledy piggledy stone steps leading upward to a mezzanine with a wooden door and a sign dangling overhead. A laughing wolf carved into the wood meant she was at the right place. Stomping up the steps, she considered asking whether he would force her to speak for him again, or if she was safe to do so herself.

The door burst open and a bodybuilder type came barreling out. Stag horns protruding from his head knocked on a support beam and he jimmied his head a few times to get loose.

Clarke tugged on her hair to hide her face. The stag was from Thaddeus's hunting party. And he was drunk. Rush bared his teeth and pulled Clarke to his side. She narrowly missed the stag as he tumbled down the steps, belching disgustingly. She stood frozen until he made it to the bottom and tracked out of sight.

Rush stared after him. Clarke had to tug him back to attention. Fiery eyes clashed with hers. He'd been close to chasing after the stag.

"What's wrong with you?" she whispered.

He bared lethal fangs. "The wolf in me wants out."

Christ. That's just what she needed. "Keep it in your pants. You can't chase him. You'll get sick, and I don't have time to wait on you. I need a bath, a meal, and a nap."

The primal fire in his eyes turned soft when he dragged his gaze down to her. He gave a curt nod.

She tugged open the door and went in.

The foyer filtered into a raucous tavern. The smell of onion was stronger. Her stomach rumbled.

"I'm going to order everything on the menu," she joked.

"Make that two."

"Done."

His lip curved, and he waved toward the back of the tavern. "Take the coin to the bar."

Clarke paid no attention to the curiosity thrown her way by tavern patrons. She knew she must look a sight with mud in her hair, on her face and all over her clothes. Rush looked worse. With his fierce gaze roaming the room, and the battered Guardian jacket barely holding his pumped muscles, she knew many patrons would run the other direction if they could see him. Not to mention the enormous sword angled over his shoulder.

Dodging the sweaty males and occasional scantily clad female, Clarke wondered if the inn was just a magnet for testosterone, or if all drinking establishments were the same, no matter what the era. A female sitting on the lap of a ruddy cheeked male giggled. He moaned. The jimmy of her hand under the table made Clarke blush.

Just exactly what kind of inn was this place?

Finally getting to the bar, Clarke hailed down the barmaid, grateful she seemed normal and not some madame who might wrangle service from her. The brunette had larger than normal arched ears and smooth chocolate skin. A bead dangled down her cheek from a leather headband. It bobbed every time she moved. Black coal rimmed her eyes in a fifties cats-eye fashion. On second glance, the black rims appeared part of the barmaid's physiology, perhaps part of the animal she evolved from. Dusted black, the tip of her nose scrunched as she approached Clarke.

"What," she snapped. "Do I have something on my face?"

Movement low behind the barmaid drew Clarke's attention. Wow. She had a bushy wolf's tail sticking out of her pants. Clarke opened her mouth to speak, but nothing came out.

Rush compelled her to talk.

"I need a room with a bath drawn," she said.

"Put the coin on the bench," Rush instructed.

Her hand whipped out jerkily and slammed money onto the wooden surface. It was as though she were a puppet, and Rush the master.

"Now ask her for two steins of the house ale, cheese, bread and some beef and gravy to be brought up to the room."

The request blurted out of Clarke's mouth.

The barmaid wiped her palms down her black apron and eyed the money. "That's a lot of red coin for those things."

"Throw in some lavender soap," she replied on Rush's command. "And then I want to be left alone."

"Fair enough." The barmaid swiped the coin and put them in the front pocket of her apron. "Two of everything? You expecting someone?"

"I'm hungry."

"Right. Well, I'll put you in the room with the big bed. Just in case." She winked at Clarke. "I'll get the boy onto getting a room and bath prepared."

Rush touched his mouth and then arched his hand low and out. "Repeat that action as a sign of gratitude."

She copied him, touching her fingers to her lips and then out. It was like she blew a kiss but without the blow.

She nodded and then reached under the bench and withdrew a key, which she placed in Clarke's palm. "The name's Anise. You need anything. You come see me."

Clarke nodded, was about to say thank you and then clamped her lips shut. She did the action.

Anise tipped her chin toward the far right of the bar. "Up those steps and second door to the left. Give us ten to get the room and meal ready, and then head up." Anise grabbed Clarke's wrist and lowered her voice. "Make sure you bolt the door before you retire for the night."

Another small nod, and then Clarke went with Rush to wait in the shadows at the base of the stairs. The floor was sticky with spilled ale. Every step met resistance beneath her boots. God, she hoped it was ale.

This bath couldn't come sooner. Honestly. When she got into that water, she wasn't coming out until it was cold. At the stairs, she faced the tavern and ignored the fae at her side.

"Clarke," he whispered, remorse lacing his voice.

She held up her palm.

He'd taken control of her body as if it were his own, and to be frank, she felt violated. She couldn't speak with him now. Not with a room full of drunk and disorderly fae who may or may not include members of Thaddeus's hunting party. The stag hadn't recognized her, but someone else might. Being alert and focused on her ability might be the only thing keeping them safe. She also needed to know more about this world if she wanted to survive here.

Clarke let her gaze wander the room and tried to relax, to let her instincts talk to her. Most of the patrons seemed to be wolf shifters. Except that guy. Her eyes roved toward a table near the blazing hearth where one of the biggest fae she'd ever seen sat, joking loudly with his companions. Even sitting at the table, his head towered over the others. He was hard to miss with the big mop of shaggy hair, beard and horns coming down from either side of his forehead to bow outward near his pink-tinged cheeks. Jovial eyes danced as he listened intently to a hooded figure she couldn't identify. Must be a story. Within seconds, a roaring laugh came out of him and he thumped the table, sending every stein and jug soaring half a foot into the air before crashing back down.

"Again!" he shouted to the cowled figure.

A small smile echoed on Clarke's lips.

"He's a muskox shifter," Rush murmured. "Turns into a bull."

Clarke folded her arms. She didn't want to talk to Rush, but who else would translate this place? "Tell me about this village."

He sighed heavily. She didn't know what he was brooding about. He was the one using her as a puppet. He should be fine.

"My uncle is the alpha, or the lord, as the rest of Elphyne call him. Mainly snow wolves live here. We're at the edge of Elphyne, so not much west except the human wasteland." He lifted his shoulders half-heartedly. "Most people here want to get as far away from society as they can. Not sure what else you want to know."

"Do you have family here?"

He stilled. "Mother and father are dead. Sister is... not here."

"I'm sorry to hear about your parents." When she looked at him, he appeared lost. "Have you seen your sister since they cursed you?"

"Not for many years."

"Do you want to?"

"I owe her gratitude."

A male dressed like the soldiers at the gate, and a female in a sheer flowing skirt, bustled passed. No top on. Her breasts bounced far too close to Clarke, and she had to duck out of the way as the soldier chased her up the stairs. The female squealed when he grabbed her rear. He trapped her against the wall, halfway up and gave her an open mouthed kiss.

"Was there no better inn than this?" Clarke murmured.

"This is nothing compared to Cornucopia. It's also the only inn which won't question a female traveling alone." He lowered his lashes, amused. "And I wouldn't go pulling that face on the professional females. They sacrificed their wombs to work here. And they make good coin for it."

She gaped. "Sacrificed their wombs?"

"For the prospect of earning a very good living. None of them have been forced."

She supposed she could understand that. It was a choice, whether in her time or this. But getting rid of your womb. Surely that was extreme.

A gangly youth of about fifteen descended the steps. He stopped halfway, spotted Clarke and said with a breaking voice, "You room six?"

She checked her key and nodded.

"It's ready."

CHAPTER

EIGHTEEN

R ush followed Clarke into their small allotted room and placed his rucksack against the wall near the door. He sniffed about and resisted marking his territory. The overwhelming urge had been all-consuming since arriving at the Hollow. Thaddeus's scent was everywhere. The wolf inside Rush wanted to obliterate it with his own. It would be satisfying to know his uncle would smell him all over the village. But he couldn't risk Clarke's safety. Rush's fresh scent would only draw unwanted attention.

He took stock of the room. It was about twenty-five feet across, with a double bed and window overlooking the street. The long red velvet drapes matched the comforter on the bed and the rug on the floor. Extra pillows and a fire blazing on a hearth felt cozy. No sprites. Thank the Well. A long wooden tub had been dragged in and steamed with water heated by mana stones at the base. A small round table for two was the last piece of furniture by the hearth, and it was laden with food. They'd been given the best room red coin could buy. It was clean. It would do.

He could ignore the moaning and thumping coming from the next room across. Sure.

Clarke groaned upon entering. The husky sound was a bolt of heat straight to his groin.

"I don't know what to do first," she sighed. "A four day hike is the longest I've ever been on. This seems like heaven."

Rush broke off some bread and dipped it in gravy. He shoved it in his mouth and then took a chunk of cheese, curiously watching her choose food. She made more tiny feminine sounds of satisfaction when she ate.

Her lips mesmerized him. He could watch her eat in a timeless loop.

It had been so long since he'd been like this with a female, he'd forgotten the minor things that brought him pleasure—the brightness in her eyes, the flush in her cheeks, the relish as she chewed. This was a different kind of intimacy he missed. The kind he'd always longed for with a mate. Small, domestic moments in which they would sit, complacent and content. She could sleep, and he could keep watch, protecting. Doing what he was born to do. But those longings had been pushed to the side the moment he became a ghost.

He was a fool. Guardians rarely mated anyway.

And he had no time for such indulgences. There were things to do before they left. He couldn't do it in his torn jacket. Since it was easier to leave it than to carry it around while he sourced clean clothes, he unbuttoned his baldric and removed his sword. Then he did the same for his jacket and tossed it against the back of a chair. He took a swig of ale and then another mouthful of cheese.

Clarke flinched and hesitated.

"What's wrong?" he asked.

"Oh nothing," she cooed with a hint of sarcasm, then she narrowed her eyes. "Nothing beyond waiting to see if you'll compel me to strip, or something equally humiliating."

He almost spat out his cheese. "You think I'd command you to…" His voice trailed off as he took in the tub, the bed, and his discarded jacket. She also grumbled about the type of establishment it was. He swallowed the painful lump and then strode to her with a growl. "Never put me in the same category as Thaddeus and his men. I'm leaving the jacket because I can't carry it around with me. It's torn and dirty, but it is a crime to leave it in public as someone could steal it and impersonate a Guardian."

"I thought it was invisible." She lifted her chin.

"Only when I touch it."

A contrite blush tinted her cheeks, but challenge danced in her eyes. He didn't think she realized what that did to a wolf like him. It made him want to dominate her. To take her. He tossed the rest of his cheese on the platter and headed to the door.

"Where are you going?" she demanded.

"I'm leaving you to your privacy. Bolt the door and don't go anywhere." He opened the door and slammed it behind him, shoulders pressed against the wood until he heard the satisfying thud of the bolt falling into place. If she refused to let him back in, he could either use the window or compel her. Until then, he had work to do.

There was only one place he could use to clean himself up. The abandoned family home passed down to Thorne. Hopefully, it might still hold some items of clothing. Kyra hadn't been back to the family home since Thorne's initiation to the Order.

A FEW HOURS LATER, Rush returned to the inn, bathed, cleaned and in borrowed buckskin breeches and a woolen sweater. Before he entered the Den, he stood outside on the street, and let the fresh night air cool his skin.

The family home had been clean, but clearly not visited in years. Thorne had probably only taken the apartment because it was the one thing that had been left for him after Rush's sentence. Thaddeus had run Kyra out of town, but the Order of the Well had power over the Crown and its lords. They wouldn't have let the house be taken from a Guardian.

Rush had sat too long in the house, wondering what his son thought of him, wondering what he would say to him if they ever got to meet. It was always the same questions running through his mind, but since Thorne had been forced to join the Guardians, Rush had seen little of him. Going back to the Order had been too painful.

Thorne was the same size as Rush, albeit a little smaller in the chest, so finding something to wear had been no issue. Clarke's clothes, on the other hand, Rush had to break into the neighbor's house and pilfer from the closet. He now had a pair of leather pants, a blouse, a thick-waisted belt, and a pair of lace-up boots that might actually fit her.

He dropped some coin to pay for the clothes. Long ago Rush had learned that if he accidentally dropped coin, the curse didn't think he was trying to communicate. The loophole had served him well when he'd helped his sister establish herself in Cornucopia after her exodus from the Hollow.

But he still needed to locate a portal stone. He figured he would drop the outfit off and then head out again. Better than letting Clarke sit on the bed naked.

Heat crept up his neck at the thought, and his mind kept returning to the kiss they had shared in the woods. Her lips were so soft it maddened him. At the time, he'd lost all sense of logic. He'd reasoned that if he let himself have that one moment, he could use it to... he didn't know what... take the edge off his loneliness? Something like that. And the tortured bastard he was, he let himself replay the scene over in his head, relishing in the touch and feel of her against him. That scent of hers... It had only made things worse. He couldn't stop thinking of her. His mind stalled when he got to the part where she'd taken his hand and demanded he touch her.

He went to tug his collar and realized he had none. The jacket wasn't on, and the sweater had a low V-neck. Crimson save him. Tonight would be difficult. Maybe he'd take the floor... or even sleep in the drained tub. Maybe he could sleep outside in the hall and just hope no one tripped over him.

Time to go in.

He strode into the tavern, took his time going up the stairs, and then got to their room and knocked.

A shuffle came from within.

A scraping sound came when the bolt lifted. Not sure what state to expect her in, he cleared his throat and froze when the door swung open. He almost forgot his purpose for being there. She was... beautiful. Red hair, cleaned and brightened to match the flames in the hearth. Milky white skin glowed and smelled like the lavender soap he'd compelled her to order. The one she'd fantasized about having when she rambled while they'd crossed the bog. Now he fantasized about that lavender on her body.

Bright blue eyes flashed defiantly, and for a moment, he failed to understand why. Then his gaze dropped to her cover. His Guardian jacket. Washed clean, virtually dried, and with the rip at the shoulder mended. Too big and heavy for her, it hung off one shoulder, giving him a tantalizing taste of décolletage.

Had she mended the jacket? For him?

A swollen sense of pride hummed at the sight. A Guardian let no one wear his jacket. Ever. But on her... it was perfect. *Both belong to me.* The thought came out of nowhere, but once it had, the wolf inside him howled. *Mine.*

His fingers clenched so tight on the package in his hands that he feared he'd rip the items in two.

She stepped aside to allow him entry. "You took your sweet-ass time."

He couldn't move. His stillness was the only thing keeping his raw instincts from reaching out and claiming her, biting, and marking her as his. His tongue thickened and dried. His chest heaved with ragged breath. And he couldn't stop staring at the rosy bottom lip caught between her teeth.

This was insane.

She was human. He, a cursed fae. This would never work.

"What?" Her brows puckered. "I cleaned and fixed it before I put it on. There was a small sewing kit in a drawer. My jeans were ruined, and your tunic was too cold."

He shoved the package into her arms. It gave him the excuse to get close, drop his nose to her hair, and inhale deeply. He lived for that moment. Would battle a horde for that moment. But when it was done, he left the room and slammed the door closed behind him. He leaned back on the wood. Again. This was the second time he'd found himself speechless and leaning against this door. Curse him again.

His wolf wanted her with a savage intensity he'd not felt in all his years. It claimed her as his. What did this mean?

Mind whirling in confusion, he took the stairs two at a time until he burst through the exit. He broke into a jog, heading for the markets and hoped he crossed paths with that stag... or any of his uncle's hunting party. But if he didn't, he'd find a way to release this pressure of need inside him, even if that meant he was crippled with pain afterwards because the truth battering his defenses was too difficult to accept.

That he'd found a mate.

But not one blessed by the Well, or they would have instantly received an identical blue mana-marking along their arms, a mirror of the other. The marking signaled the Well—nature—approved. It would link them in mind and spirit.

But if they weren't blessed, then the curse wouldn't be broken.

What cruel world would taunt him with happiness so close to his death?

CHAPTER
NINETEEN

Clarke had to burn her bra and jeans due to severe deterioration and disgustingness, but was pleased with the outfit Rush had brought her. It could have been worse. It could have been one of the stuffy medieval type dresses some ladies had worn in the streets. Or one of the flimsy sheer skirts and strips of fabric covering the working women downstairs. Instead, she ended up in soft brown leather pants, a gray linen blouse, and a thick belt that went around her middle, almost like a corset. With the blouse tucked, the folds gathered around her roving breasts, holding them in place.

Did Rush know how this would look on her when he chose the outfit? Curves accentuated, bust amplified... She touched her lips at the memory of their kiss. He'd left so suddenly after giving her the clothes. He'd looked nervous.

In the black glass mirror behind the door, her reflection showed no evidence of the person she used to be. Clarke smoothed her hands down her hips. Everything fit, even the calf-high boots. Rush had purposefully sourced an outfit similar to what she had already worn. Knowing the big brooding fae had been thinking about her made her stomach do a little flip. She tried to suppress the flutter by putting her hand to her stomach. Her dreams were still filled with nightmares, but more often than not, her instincts kept veering toward Rush. She realized he used to be an honorable fae. His past and curse had changed him, but she didn't believe that part of him was completely gone. Still, it wouldn't hurt Clarke to start thinking about a plan B. Trusting a man had steered Clarke down dark paths before. Trusting herself was a better option.

The woman staring back at her was someone she didn't recognize. A different person. Something about Rush empowered her to speak her mind. To stand her ground. He was a big bad wolf, yet she'd snapped at him, shouted at him, and even saved his life. And that part had been hard. Dragging his heavy body out of the swamp. There had been a moment or two when she'd thought it was too much, but she did it.

Purpose and resolve hardened within her. She would find a way to warn the right person about what she'd seen in her nightmare. Maybe it was the king. Maybe it was someone else. If Rush would not help her, then she'd find someone who would.

Either way, she was learning that making her own decisions felt a hell of a lot better than having someone make them for her.

The memory of the barmaid's pretty face came to mind. Clarke would go down to the tavern, have a drink at the bar, and speak with her. Barmaids in any time would be useful sources of information, and Clarke was good at talking.

Clarke fluffed her hair to ensure her ears were well and truly covered, and then on second thought, tore off a strip from the bottom of Rush's old tunic. She wrapped it around her head to keep her ears from sticking out. Once satisfied her look was solid, she rustled around in the rucksack for more coin. She found a collection of different colored glass discs in a bag. Red, blue, yellow and clear. From the way the barmaid had reacted, the red was worth more. But to be safe, she took a variety of each and pocketed them. Rush wouldn't miss them, and if he did, she didn't care.

She also found a curious little wooden carving, just like at Rush's cabin. Picking it up, she let the figurine roll in her fingers. It was a wolf. Deciding she liked it, she shoved it in her pocket next to the coins.

Feeling more upbeat already, Clarke paused at the open door and pushed out with her senses to feel for any bad vibes filtering back from the tavern downstairs. Biting her lip, she concentrated hard on her instincts. After a moment, nothing echoed back but continual joy and merriment. A smile tickled her lips. Perfect.

Down in the tavern, the place had become crowded. The line at the bar went two people thick, and new bartenders fielded the drinks. Disappointment swamped Clarke, but then an urge pulled her gaze to the right. On a small table near the fireplace, Anise sat sharing a meal with the largely muscled muskox fae she'd noticed earlier. As though sensing her attention, Anise looked up and met Clarke's eyes. Her lips curved, she leaned toward the fae at her side and spoke. His gaze flicked Clarke's way, and then he grinned. An enormous hand lifted into the air, high over others' heads, and waved for Clarke to come over.

This could be the opportunity she'd been waiting for, and the wherewithal to proceed on her own in this world. If Rush continued to push her to uncomfortable limits with this bargain of his, then it mattered not if she thought he was honorable. She needed a better escape plan.

She straightened her blouse, smoothed her hands over her hips and strode forward as though she belonged there. She had to sidestep an energetic arm wrestle by two rotund looking fae, but she made it otherwise intact.

"Hi," she said upon arrival and smiled.

"Take a seat." The big fae's voice was a deep, slurred rumble. If he'd been drinking since she'd arrived, he'd be quite drunk. He pulled a stool out for her to sit and then hit his chest with a fist. "I'm Caraway."

"Nice to meet you, Caraway. I'm Clarke." She held out her hand over the chipped table for a shake.

He looked at her hovered hand and chuckled heartily. "What do I do with that?"

"Sorry." Probably not a custom observed in this time. She wiped her palm on her pants. "It's something we elves do."

Clarke sat down in a rush and noticed Caraway had a blue teardrop tattoo under his eye.

"You're a Guardian!" she exclaimed, excited that she knew something of worth.

He stiffened. Anise looked at her with shrewd eyes. "That's not a problem, is it?"

"No." Clarke held up her palms. "I meant no offense."

"Well, I'm off duty," Caraway mumbled.

She sensed anguish lacing the big mountain-man's soul. It was the same suppressed melancholy she'd felt in Rush. Something in the way he laughed, but it didn't quite hit his eyes. Maybe all Guardians had it. Their jobs were brutal, unforgiving, and often went unappreciated. When Anise's tail swished in agitation, Clarke realized she was staring.

"Elf, hey?" Anise asked as she tore into the cooked leg of an animal. "What brings you this far west?"

"Oh. Um." Shit. What had Rush said? Nothing? Clarke scrambled with her instincts, looking for something to say, but Anise saved her from embarrassment.

"It's the secret beau, right?" She gave Clarke a wink.

"Uh. Yeah. Sorry, I didn't want to mention before."

"Thought so." Anise turned to Caraway. "Pay up, big boy."

His cheeks pinked, and he pulled a clear coin from his pocket. After giving him a smug once over, Anise shifted her stein toward Clarke. "You want it? I have to get back to the bar in a minute."

Clarke lifted the stein to her lips. The ale tasted like sour cherries.

"This is good," she declared.

"Probably not the same quality as you're used to, but I make it myself." Anise's eyes lit up with a sudden thought. "If you're wanting something a little more up your alley, I have a few Elven elixirs under the bar."

"Oh? That sounds interesting."

"I'll bring some over after I go back." She waggled her brows. "I'll even bring something you can use later."

Clarke smiled over the lip of her stein as if she knew what Anise meant. "That sounds great."

Caraway and Anise shared a conspiring look that led Clarke to believe the elixir was something either completely disgusting, or very good and perhaps illicit. Either way, if it led the two to trust her, then all the better.

CHAPTER
TWENTY

Sitting across from Clarke on a chipped wooden table, Caraway's cheeks were pink. His eyes sloped down at the sides like a puppy. Anise glanced often at him from beneath her lashes. It was clear the two of them were hyper-aware of the other's presence.

"So, Caraway," Clarke started. "Do you mind if I ask you a question?"

"I'm all ears." His low muskox ears twitched out. And then he boomed a belly laugh at his own joke.

She smiled. "If I wanted an appointment with someone important at the Order of the Well, how would I go about getting one?"

He looked at her strangely, and Clarke knew this must be a very obvious answer to all fae.

Caraway scratched his beard. His deep voice rumbled, "You mean like the Prime? Or one of the Council?"

She nodded. Sure. That would do.

A loud burst of male voices cut through the room, and then a hush followed as the front door opened. In came three tall, haughty fae. All wore red embroidered coats and had jeweled bone-weapons strapped to their bodies.

"What are they doing here?" Anise grumbled.

"Don't know. Don't care." Caraway lifted his stein and drank.

"You might not have to serve the king, but I do."

Caraway turned ruminative and something unsaid passed between Anise and he. A lick of tension sizzled, and Clarke didn't need to be psychic to know this was a bone of contention between the two. Anise looked at him. Her lips pressed together as though she was holding in a tirade of words.

Clarke slid her gaze over to the serving bar to see most people in the tavern had given the guards a wide berth. And it was exactly what they liked. She didn't get the sense they were soldiers. They looked too pretty and too clean. From the polished, filed finger nails to the trimmed facial hair.

"They look like they're insta-famous assholes," Clarke said under her breath.

"Like what?" Anise asked.

"Oh." Heat hit Clarke's cheeks. She kept forgetting no one here knew a thing about Instagram, Facebook, or anything technically advanced. "Nothing."

Anise just rolled her eyes. "They look like they were born in a bed of red coin, that's what."

"They wouldn't know how to use those swords if they fell on them," Caraway grumbled.

"So why do you let them run around and cause so much trouble when they're here?"

"Because it's none of my business. Not magic, not my problem."

Oh. Here we go. This was the source of their contention.

Anise's eyes lit up with anger. "You keep spouting that bullshit, and I swear I'll—" She bit her words off.

Caraway's brows lowered. His voice rumbled. "You'll what?"

They stared at each other. And then Anise answered. "Being a Guardian is your job, Caraway. Not your life." Anise stood and shook herself from head to toe. "I'd better go before my pay gets docked. I'll bring back some of that elixir," she added to Clarke, and then strode off.

Caraway's droopy doe-eyes watched her rear the entire way, and from the extra swagger in Anise's step, she knew it. Clarke hid her smile behind the stein and pretended not to notice.

Caraway turned back to Clarke with a brooding scowl. "She's wrong. Being a Guardian is my life. And sticking my nose into local politics isn't in my job description." He slammed his fist on the table. "Right. Where were we?"

Clarke jolted with the sudden turn of conversation. "You were about to tell me how to get an audience with the Prime."

"Yes. Good." He rubbed his thick beard. "Helps if you know a Guardian or a Mage of the Order, and it just so happens, you're in luck." He tapped the tattoo under his eye. "I know both."

"You're both Mage and Guardian?"

A booming belly laugh came out of him. Clarke wanted to join in.

"No," he replied. "I'm barely one. But I know plenty. When you get there, ask for Thorne and tell him Caraway sent you—he's an honorable Nightstalk wolf. Or if you want a fellow elf, ask for Leaf. He can be a right warada's tail sometimes, but he's on the council. Stay away from Cloud."

"Right. Thorne—wolf. Leaf—elf. Er, stay away from Cloud. Got it. Th—" She took another a sip of ale to hide her thanks. Damn it. She needed to watch that. The last thing she needed was to be in debt to another Guardian. She remembered the action Rush had taught her. She touched her fingers to her lips and pushed out.

"Don't mention it," Caraway chuckled.

A burst of mocking laughter drew Caraway's attention to the bar. His expression darkened, his shoulders tensed, and his gaze moved as though following someone. Anise headed back their way. Her ears drooped and her bottom lip disappeared between her teeth as though she were trying to stop it trembling.

She put the two steins of cherry ale on the table and stood there, fingers clenched around the handles, eyes squeezed shut. "I hate those floaters."

Caraway's eyes softened. His hand moved to cover hers. "Neese..."

"Don't," she snapped and took her hand away. Water pooled at the black rims of her eyes. "You don't get to give sympathy when you refuse to do something about those cretins."

He drew his hand back, and for the first time, Clarke saw a flash of the lethal Guardian flickering beneath his casual demeanor. Those horns spilling from his head suddenly seemed extra pointy and hard.

"What did they want?"

"Nothing," she mumbled. "Some drivel about a dead body outside the gates. Apparently a vamp is hunting in the area."

"That's... odd." Caraway frowned, but then shrugged. "Guess it got overzealous."

Anise dipped her hand into her apron pocket and pulled out two little vials of glowing liquid. She placed them on the table before Clarke.

Caraway stiffened and glanced around. His gaze went specifically toward the red-coated guards loitering at the bar. "You know I don't like you dealing that shit in public, Neese."

Anise rolled her eyes at him. "Fuck them. They're not even looking. Besides, I like to know at least someone will get slippy tonight."

From Caraway's blush, Clarke guessed "get slippy" meant sex. And then Clarke blushed.

Anise sat down and pointed to the blue bottle. Her husky voice came out rushed. "This will give you and your beau stamina to last the night long." She pointed to the diluted pink water. "This will ensure you avoid an execution warrant."

Yep. Definitely sex. Wait. Clarke blinked. "Execution?"

"Unsanctioned breeding," Anise elaborated with a "duh" tone to her voice. "If you ask me, the law is archaic. They sit in their castle with mountains of food enough to feed Elphyne ten times over, yet they still insist on keeping control of who can have children and how many."

Caraway grumbled something under his breath.

"Yeah I get it," Anise snapped at him. "None of your business. But what if it was someone you knew or cared about? Oh, sorry. I forgot. You lot don't care about anyone but yourself."

"Low shot, Anise."

She raised her brows in challenge but said nothing.

Caraway took the bait anyway. "Need I remind you that Thorne's parents were both on the receiving end of that law. I know exactly how it affects the lives of those left behind."

"So why don't you do something about it?"

"The law is the law."

"The Guardians are above the law."

"Not that one."

"Ugh," Anise groused and turned her back on Caraway to face Clarke. "I'm over Guardians."

"Shh." Caraway cast a wary eye at the people surrounding them and waved her down. "Enough."

Anise lifted her eyes to the ceiling and took a breath, then refocused on Clarke. "Okay, well, because of that stupid law, don't use the blue one for a good time unless you're using the first elixir. Pink generally works within a few hours. Blue works in a few minutes. I'm not sure how the elves dose it in Delphinium, but don't take more than one drop of the blue, otherwise neither of you will be able to sit down for days, if you know what I mean." She winked mischievously.

Clarke sat there for a moment letting Anise's explanation sink in. One elixir was an aphrodisiac and one was contraception.

"So crude," Caraway said into his stein, but the brightness in his eyes told another story. He was into it. Perhaps had even tried the aphrodisiac. Maybe even with Anise.

"How much do I owe you?" Clarke asked, not wanting to be rude and turn it away.

"Nothing," Anise replied. "The two red coin you gave for the room will still cover it."

Caraway spurted ale out and then tried to wipe his front. "*Two* red coin? What on earth do you do for a living?"

Clarke decided something closest to the truth would be best. "I'm a Seer."

He raised a dark eyebrow. "Must be good if you earn red coin."

She shrugged. "I do okay."

"Do me." He waved a hand her way. "Read my fortune."

"Okay," Clarke laughed. "But nothing comes free."

"What do you want?"

"Information," she replied.

"Already done."

"Ooh, you drive a hard bargain." Clarke smiled. "But maybe you can give me a little more?"

He nodded. "Double done."

She did this sort of thing all the time back in Vegas. Before Bishop. Usually it was a bunch of fumbled guesses based on a combination of vibes she sensed, body language, and her vague instincts. But she managed well enough to score a quick buck and to feed herself. Sometimes she even swiped a watch from the wrist of a customer. Caraway had no valuables in easy reach, and she was trying to turn a new leaf, damn it.

Stop thinking about stealing.

Clarke took his hand and tipped it palm up. Making a show of smoothing his calloused fingers until he relaxed, she sent Anise a quick sideways glance to see if she watched. She did. Avidly.

Interesting.

She cleared her throat and concentrated on the Guardian's palm. "Very curious," she murmured.

"What?" He shuffled in his seat.

"See this line here? It's the life line. Very long and unbroken. That's good."

He snorted. "That's not unusual. Fae live long."

"But this line." She traced down another wrinkle on his palm. "This is the fate line. It twists and turns and links into your life and love line. Looks like you'll find your love from a pool of people you've spent much of your life with and will continue to do so."

"You mean I'll find a mate?" He blinked. "But I'm a Guardian."

She shrugged. "I can only tell you what your lines show. And there's a powerful link between them. Also this bit here." She pointed to a crease in his little finger. "This means you look excellent in buckskin breeches."

He blanked.

So did Anise.

Then the two of them burst out laughing. Clarke's own smile warmed her face, and she hoped she'd planted a few seeds to give the two of them a push in the right direction. Anyone who argued like they did, and stole glances at each other the way they did, must harbor hidden romantic feelings. Sometimes they just needed a nudge to get there.

She squeezed Caraway's hand, intending to let go, but a sudden spark of electricity zapped into Clarke's palm and she jolted. As the tingling intensified, her sight darkened around the edges. The sounds of the tavern filtered away to be replaced by a nightjar calling as a vision took hold of her.

Sun shone brightly in her eyes, and she lifted her hand to shield. When she took her hand away, it wasn't the sun, but a bright ring sparking with lightning and warping the vision inside. Through the ring, three dark human sized silhouettes formed. It was like she stared at something from a fantasy movie. A portal. Silhouettes stepped through. A shudder ran through Clarke's body when she recognized Thaddeus. Her vision swung to the side and landed on the stout soldier from the gate. He made a disgruntled face before he threw his feathered drumstick down.

Then Clarke was back in the tavern, blinking at both Caraway and Anise, who in turn looked at her with wary surprise.

"Your eyes went white," Anise murmured. "You truly are a Seer."

"It was a true-dream, wasn't it?" Caraway added, eyes dark and stern. "What did you see?"

"Um. I think the Lord of Crescent Hollow has returned. I should go." She shoved the blue vial his way. "Here. It's a gift. For when you meet that longtime friend."

His complete mortification took Clarke by surprise. Caraway darted a glance to Anise and then made a hasty exit with his stein. He didn't even say goodbye. He rejoined his ragtag group of male fae, still arm wrestling, and belched loud enough to cover the laughter. Then he made some crude comment. They all raucously cheered and lifted their steins.

Clarke looked to Anise. "What did I do wrong?"

She only laughed until tears glistened in her eyes. "You insulted his masculinity, you numb-nuts. Elves might be a bit liberal with their use of elixirs, but it's still a secret stimulant everywhere else... or maybe a private agreement. Also some use it when they're having trouble between the sheets, if you know what I mean. It's not exactly encouraged considering the laws about breeding."

"Oh." This conversation wasn't going so well.

Anise's humor dropped. "I'd keep the blue vial out of view if I were you. He wasn't wrong with not wanting to do this in public. If word gets around to the alpha that I'm dealing under the bar..." She bit her lip. "But with the taxes here, a wolf has to do what a wolf has to do."

"Say no more." Clarke swiped the tiny vials and tucked them down her blouse and wedged them under the pressure of the belt. She would find a way to get rid of them later... well, her cheeks heated, maybe she would keep the contraception elixir. That unsanctioned breeding law was savage.

Clarke looked at Caraway with a frown. "He left before giving me that extra information."

Anise collected an empty stein and wiped the wooden table with a rag. "What do you need? Maybe I can help."

"I think I've *Seen* something." Once again, a side of the truth was always the best lie. "I think it could endanger everyone and I'm not sure who to go to with it. Caraway gave me a few names from the Order, but now..." Clarke fumbled with a tie on her belt.

"You think they won't stick their noses into business that isn't theirs?" Anise finished for her.

Clarke nodded.

"Well," Anise continued. "If what you saw has to do with magic, then they'll help, no doubt about it. If not..." Anise glanced back to the bar where the red-coats still made trouble. "I don't know who else to suggest. I'm sorry. How will you get there?"

"To the Order? I guess I'll walk."

"It's a long way. Seems you could afford a decent portal stone."

A portal. Of course. "And where do I get one of those at this hour?"

"Just so happens I have a friend who sells them. Ask for Peytr at the markets. His stall is the one with the blue pix on the sign. If he's closed, just go around the back. He lives behind."

Clarke made the "thank you" hand sign just as someone shouted Anise's name from the bar.

"I need to go," she said. "Nice to meet you, Clarke."

"You too, Anise."

It was time for Clarke to leave. The vision she'd had worried her. It was hard to tell from the vision, but the soldier had been the same one she'd seen at the gate. Thaddeus was either in town, or he would be soon. And then he'd probably find her at the inn. She needed to track Rush down and alert him, or better yet, secure herself a portal stone. If it did what the name suggested, then it could be her ticket out of there and to safety.

CHAPTER
TWENTY-ONE

Rush whittled the finishing touches on a small carving as he stood quietly in a corner of a room at the barracks, watching a clandestine meeting take place. The meditative act of his hands cast his mind into the past, and the changes he'd gone through since his curse.

It had taken him most of his life to realize the benefit of understatement. From a young age he'd been enraptured with the power of the Guardians, the strength of his father, the alpha, or the glitz and glamour of the Seelie King in his castle of glass. To a young wolf, this attention and power had meant dominance. Worth. Righteousness. But it wasn't until Rush's identity was stripped from him did he realize the magic of being overlooked. No pressure to perform. No heightened ridicule. No gilded cage of expectation. For the first time, he'd been free.

The joy of it had lasted only a short while, and then he'd started learning things. Secrets. Lies. Manipulations. He'd seen the true colors of the fae he'd dedicated his life to protecting, and not all of it was pretty. He'd learned how much stock the castle kept in their cellars. Money, food, health elixirs. Enough to feed an army and more. Enough to supply their entire realm. The Winter Queen—the High Queen of the Unseelie— hoarded in the same way. The irony wasn't lost on him. Fae believed they were the better race because they had survived the ravaged world the original humans had left behind. But the thing was, fae were descended from humans. They'd inherited the same intrinsic desire for war and that driving urge to be on top of the food chain, no matter what the cost. Greed ran in the veins of both races.

So what made one better than the other?

Nothing.

Rush had to become a ghost to learn the fact. He'd seen inside the human city, how they acted and followed their leaders... exactly the same way fae did in Elphyne. Shadow copies of each other. Fae weren't the better race. They were the lucky race.

Through no fault of their own did fae evolve from mixed human and animal DNA. It was a freak skip in evolution, possibly brought about through the nuclear cataclysm that saw the extinction of most other beings. But it also involved the magic of the Well. The planet didn't want to die, and it needed someone to fight for it, so the fae were born, and they were given magic. And now they thrived. An undercurrent ran in the collective minds of complacent fae: they were the real gods. They were on top of the food chain. And they deserved to say who lived, who died, and how they went about doing it.

They talked a lot of shit.

It wasn't until Clarke came along that Rush was reminded not all were the reflection of their label. That he didn't have to stay indoctrinated to the beliefs forced onto him. That he could think for himself.

And right now, he was staring at a mislabeled mistake, thinking some terrible things. Thaddeus. Supposedly the town's protector, their alpha... their wannabe lord. Bullshit. Here he was having secret talks with three other underhanded fae: the Captain of King Mithras's Royal Guard; a dishonored Dark Mage of the Order; and a vampire of the Unseelie gentry. From what Rush gathered, they waited on a human.

Here were the most depraved beings on this land he could conjure, and that included the monsters he fought in the wild. Rush couldn't even say he was surprised by their collusion.

It made sense they'd picked this location. Crescent Hollow was the last fae settlement this far west, and it sat isolated between a mountain range and a dangerous forest. The barracks were near the gate. No one came down to these dank and shoddy stone buildings except for the sentinels and Nightstalk militia.

"I'm not willing to stake my reputation on the promises of a human who can't even turn up on time," the vampire said, folding his wiry arms across his chest.

"What reputation?" Rush scoffed aloud. "You can't even keep your shirt free from meal stains, let alone keep your colony safe."

This was the only part of his curse he enjoyed. He could mouth off to anyone, to their face, and they knew nothing. As a Guardian, he'd had to hold his peace on more than one occasion, especially when it involved opinions of kings and queens.

Rush snorted and gave the vamp a scathing once over. From his luxurious clothing, the vampire was clearly a lord of some kind. The vampires in the Order were brutal and lethal, but this one... he smelled weak willed. He looked entitled. He was nothing but a sleep-feeder, preying on the helpless and docile for his sustenance.

If Clarke were there, she'd probably tell him she had bad vibes about the fae.

A slight smile lifted Rush's lips when he thought of Clarke in his Guardian jacket, and how she'd mended it. For him.

He scrubbed his hand over his face. His world was turning upside down, and the worst part was that he was finally in a position to be smart enough to know which things needed changing, and that maybe Clarke was right, and he did want to do something about it, but his time was running out. Soon he wouldn't be changing anything, and the world he was leaving for his son was on the same path of destruction as the one that was destroyed millennia ago.

Casting his gaze around the small barracks room, Rush tried to commit their appearances to memory. This illicit meeting clearly had undertones of subterfuge. Every single person in this tiny room was a traitor to the Well, and potentially to the Elphyne as a whole.

Next to the vampire stood the Dark Mage. Once a member of the Order, he was now banished and exiled for using mana in twisted and unnatural ways. Like a drug, mana could take hold of one's logic and convince them their underhanded ways were acceptable. The wings peeking from beneath the Mage's long robe were skeletal-thin, just like his body. If there had been feathers there once, there weren't now. Rush would be surprised if those wings flew at all. Mana-addiction had a tendency to drain the body of all other nutrition, and the user often forgot to sustain themself. It's why the monsters they hunted were so ferocious. Many of them hunted to eat mana and nothing else. Malnutrition gave the Mage's long hook nose a more sinister appearance. He was probably striking once.

Shifting his gaze to the right, Rush surveyed the other two fae. A red-coated captain of the Seelie Royal Guard, and Thaddeus looking smug and content with his arms folded as he leaned against a small desk.

"I agree," the captain said, his one ear twitching. "I don't enjoy waiting, Thaddeus. You said this human would be here, and he's not."

"Relax," Thaddeus replied. He flicked a piece of lint from his navy woolen coat. "We didn't go to the effort of staging a murder just to get you out here for a game of three-stroke cards. He's on his way."

Rush's ears pricked up. So he had been right. The murdered satyr was a pretense for subterfuge.

"And the rest?" the captain asked.

"We've deployed a handful of monsters around this realm. Soon word will get out that the Winter Queen is encouraging her subjects to take up residence in Seelie land. King Mithras will take the bait."

"Good."

Disgust simmered beneath Rush's skin. He'd always known Thaddeus was underhanded, but he'd never believed he would commit treason. And to hear he was the reason for the White Woman. Clarke had almost died. Again. Everything about this situation was off.

Including, he realized with a start, that he cared whether Clarke lived or died. But once his mind had gone there, the feeling lodged with certainty in his gut. No. He wasn't prepared to put her in harm's way again. So... where did that leave them?

The door opened. A dark hooded silhouette stood in the threshold, his face hidden within the recess of the cowl.

"Ah," Thaddeus said. "Come in. We've been waiting for you."

The hooded figure walked in. From the breadth of the shoulders and the sheer size of him, Rush knew it was a man. And—he sniffed—the bastard had metal on him, in thick and heavy quantities. Forbidden weapons. War machines.

Two shifters walked in behind the human. Rush recognized them from Thaddeus's hunting party. And then Rush looked ten feet beyond the two fae, to further down the street. A familiar face made his heart stop. Pale skin. Beautiful red hair. Clarke stood in the alley outside the door, looking just as surprised as he. What the hell was she doing here?

No one seemed to notice she was there. He threw his gaze back to Thaddeus who had gone still, like a predator stalking its prey, eyes locked on the distance—outside the open door.

No.

Thaddeus turned to the hooded human. "Did you bring someone with you?"

The hood shook his head.

"Not a female? A woman with red hair?"

"No," came the gruff voice from inside the shadow of the cowl. "I came alone."

"Stay here," Thaddeus ordered his crew, and then flicked his right hand out until claws protracted from his fingers. He gave a low warning snarl. "Out of my way."

He moved, shouldering through his two wolf shifters. Rush stood no chance of getting between Thaddeus and Clarke. He pursued all the same. The moment he entered the dark stone cobbled lane, Rush caught a whiff of lavender soap and Clarke's unique musk on the wind. Dread unfurled in his gut. She'd just signed her own death warrant. There would be nowhere she could hide. Not now that Thaddeus had her scent a second time. It was too unique.

"Did you dress up for me?" Thaddeus's voice had a wicked lilt as he prowled toward Clarke.

Her eyes widened. She glanced at Rush helplessly, then spun on her heels and ran. Red hair streamed behind her.

She got a few doors down and then Thaddeus launched, pushing her up against the stone wall of an adjacent building.

"Well-damn it." Rush put on a burst of speed.

Thaddeus's claws went for Clarke's throat, but Rush reached around him and took her wrist. He yanked her body to him and found another piece of bare skin to put his other hand on—her sternum. With Clarke in his arms, Rush backed up cautiously until his own back hit a wall, praying to the Well that his curse would extend to blanket her temporarily as it did all things he touched.

Thaddeus shook his head as if clearing it. He blinked at Clarke, head cocking, eyes flaring. With every breath Thaddeus took, it was clear he fought the curse trying to cloud his mind. Rush wanted to laugh in his scarred face. The very punishment that Thaddeus had called down on Rush was now working against him.

Except the curse wasn't strong enough. Rush's bond with Clarke wasn't strong enough. She was a living thing, not an object.

Thaddeus's hands went to his head. He shook it, and refocused on the woman in Rush's arms with a growl. "I've been hunting your kind for years. You won't get away this time."

Clarke struggled in Rush's arms. "We need to run."

"Trust me," he said, gritting his teeth. "Don't move."

She stilled until it was only her chest heaving beneath his touch.

This would work. It had to. But their connection needed to be stronger. Only one other bond he knew of linked a female and a male so completely—the mating bond. Rush sank his teeth into the tender flesh between Clarke's neck and shoulder, just enough to mark and trigger the mating ritual. Scent glands around his body swelled and released pheromones to coat her, marking her.

The wolf inside him unfurled from its long slumber. It sniffed the air, caught Clarke's scent and battered itself against the cage of Rush's body. *Mine.*

Thaddeus twirled around, dazed. His yellow eyes darted about the street. If the curse worked, he saw an empty street. Most had retired for the night, or were safely ensconced indoors. Rush kept his teeth and grip on Clarke, willing his curse to hold and ignoring the painful urge to complete the mating ritual and take something she hadn't made the choice to give. She must have guessed a little of what he was doing because she leaned back into him and gripped his forearm over her sternum.

A haunting howl of frustration tore out of Thaddeus, and he paced the area before them.

They were standing not five feet away, yet Thaddeus couldn't see them. He couldn't scent them, and he couldn't remember them, but a part of him knew he'd been robbed. Shaking his head with a growl, Thaddeus stalked back to the room near the gate. The fae inside looked out, but Thaddeus only shook his head. He took one look back out at the street and then went in, closing the door behind him.

If the curse did its job properly, none of them would remember.

But now Rush had another problem. With immediate danger gone, his mating instincts were taking over, becoming all consuming. Once triggered they were hard to stop. *Mine.* His jaw tightened, teeth still on Clarke's flesh. He pressed down with the undeniable urge to deepen his mark on her because if he'd done this a long time ago, she'd have never disobeyed him and left the inn. She would have been safe.

Stay.

That's what he'd said.

Stay in the room until he came back for her. Any wolf would bow under the will of an alpha's energy like his. But she was frustratingly not wolf. Not pack. And not the kind who enjoyed submitting. She was a strong-willed woman who would make the perfect mate for an alpha like him. A partner. A matriarch of their own pack. The mindless primal instincts of his inner wolf battled with human logic inside his mind.

Take her. Make her submit.

She won't submit. She's loyal. Feisty. Fierce.

She's everything you want in a mate. Claim her.

She has a will of her own.

I like it.

She is soft beneath your hands. Feminine. Juicy.

I need it.

"You're hurting me," she whimpered.

Keeping his lips on her, he unlocked his jaw and smelled fresh blood. He'd broken skin. His musk was all over her. Anyone scenting her now would know she belonged to him, that she was under his protection. This was a wolf village. They'd all know. Pain and regret hit him hard in the chest. He hadn't meant to mark so deep. He shouldn't have gone so far, so irrevocably without conscience, yet he couldn't let go of her, couldn't bring himself to lift his lips from her.

"I'm sorry," he whispered against her skin. "I'm so sorry."

He was sorry because the pain he'd just inflicted on her flesh was nothing to how she'd feel when his curse broke down and he inevitably died. He'd essentially ruined her chances of mating again. His scent would take months, maybe years to completely come off. No male would want her with the scent of an alpha on her.

A part of him didn't care.

She was his, and he was hers.

He liked it.

He wanted her.

He was a sick, selfish bastard.

No denying it now. There it was, his mark, his bite, glistening under the light of the moon, clear in the night as it would be during the day. His inner wolf couldn't be prouder, even though deep down inside he knew it wasn't the blue marking of a Well-blessed union. That his curse would never lift. That he'd ruined her.

But even as the destructive thoughts hammered against his skull, blood heated in his veins, and desire mounted in his heart. A deep inhale of her intoxicating scent and he forgot where they were. His tongue darted out and lapped her wound. He laved and cared for the injury he'd made, the only one she'd ever suffer by his hands, teeth, or words.

She stiffened. "What are you doing?"

"I'm sorry." *I'm not sorry.* He kept repeating the words against her skin, licking and laving while his hands moved to bind her stomach and pull her against him, to grind the sweet curve of her ass against the aching need between his legs.

"Rush," she protested, squirming. "Let me move. What's going on? We should be out of here."

"No one can see us," he murmured. "You're safe now."

He growled and reversed their positions, flattening the length of his body against hers. Pushed against the wall, she had nowhere to go. And since they were still touching, flesh against flesh, neither of them were visible to any passersby who dared leave their dwellings after dark. Just as well, Rush couldn't take his eyes from the bountiful breasts bound by the tightness of her blouse. Lowering his lashes, he had trouble resisting. If he didn't get her home soon, he would take her against the wall. But she deserved better. He'd give her good memories, not hurried.

"*Touch me*, Clarke," he compelled, blind with desire.

Her hand lifted to his chest, to stroke his pecs through the woolen sweater, and then... she shoved him. Hard. He didn't budge, but it was enough to get his attention, to snap him out of the mating haze gripping his senses. She stomped on his foot.

"Get off me." Her cry came out strangled and thick.

Still inches apart, their gazes clashed. To his horror, he found hers glistening with tears.

"You're my mate." He frowned, as if that explained everything.

"What does that even mean? And..." She pushed again, but he wouldn't budge. "It doesn't give you the right to come onto me like this... here. To force me... Right after..."

A slap stung Rush's cheek, and he stood back, shocked. Putting his palm to the burning side of his face, he blinked at her.

"And you bit me!" she hissed, hand covering the mark on her neck. Her bottom lip trembled, but she lifted her chin. "Why did you bite me?"

"Shh," he hissed. "People can hear you now."

There was no one around, but wolf shifters had very good hearing. Thaddeus might have forgotten their previous interaction due to the curse, but there was always the possibility of new interactions.

"I don't care," she hissed back, but she lowered her voice. "Why did you bite me?"

"That bite saved your life."

"It's more than that, you arrogant pig." Her nostrils flared as she took him in, and Rush hated it—the look in her eyes—she acted like she didn't know him. "You look like you want to eat me."

His lashes lowered. Yes, he did. He stepped toward her again with a lazy grin curling his lips.

"Stop," she warned, a palm to his chest. "What's gotten into you?"

And oh, how it burned. Her imprint scorched through to his hammering heart, making itself a permanent fixture. His inner wolf howled in frustration. It wanted to claw its way to her. Couldn't she see?

"I'll never stop hungering for you, Clarke. Even in my death, I'll be thinking of you."

"Is this what all wolves are like?" The shake in her voice gave him pause. "Is this why you have a law against unsanctioned breeding?"

"What?" Coldness seeped in. The light leached from the night sky.

The fire in her eyes had become twisted. "Unsanctioned breeding. That's what they told me at the tavern. A crime punishable by death. They made it sound like a survival thing, but I'm not so sure anymore. This world is insane. Unsanctioned breeding, my ass. It's just another term for a woman being forced."

His world closed in. His mouth dried. "I didn't. I'm not..."

He backed up.

She's not wolf. She didn't understand. She thought he was as beastly as his uncle. Thaddeus may never have been caught for unsanctioned breeding, but that was because he killed everyone he screwed. Clarke thought Rush was the same, and that's why he was cursed. Clarke, who could see the truth in everyone. This was his heart laid bare, and she believed it was made of the same inky substance as his uncle's.

"If I didn't need to keep you safe," he murmured. "I would never have started the mating process with you."

He realized his mistake the moment her brows lifted.

"Clarke," he held his hand out. "I didn't mean it like that."

"Oh really? I don't know what to believe. Because you've said since the start that I'm a filthy human and you should just kill me and be done with it. How was it Thaddeus put it, humans are only good enough to use for sport, isn't that right?"

"I am *not* my uncle." His fingers balled into fists. "And you need to stop comparing me to him."

"You're not explaining anything! How else am I going to take it?"

"Obviously I want you." He gestured to the still present bulge in his pants. "Regardless of the shape of your ears."

"The shape of my ears?" she scoffed. "Yeah. Real nice. Well, I hope you die from blue balls. You deserve it." She walked away, paused and then turned back to him. "And for the record, I was only coming to find you because I had a vision about Thaddeus being in town. Stupid me for thinking you needed my help."

"Yes, stupid you. I don't need help. No one can see me."

"That's what you said right before the White Woman took you," she said and then continued away.

"Stop." He launched at her, took her wrist and jerked her back to him. He forced her to hold his hand. "I release you from our bargain, Clarke."

A tingling zipped from his palm to his elbow, and then an emptiness haunted his hand. One more sliver of mana had been expended, and another set of blue glyphs appeared. The itch of it crept up his neck. His curse shifted. The veil thinned. Death waited for him, just outside the periphery of his control. But none of it compared to the loss he felt, the ache in his chest when she simply removed her hand from his and glared with disappointed eyes. Then she walked away.

TWENTY-TWO

Clarke strode two steps, and then spun back with another harsh word on the tip of her tongue. She stopped. Rush was gone. In a blink, he'd blended into the shadows and disappeared in a way she'd not thought possible for one with such bright hair. Her hand went to her neck, to where he'd bitten her. It was tender, but strangely not painful. And she felt... she wasn't sure what she felt, only that she had an inexplicable urge to find him.

She took a few more steps toward where she saw him last. She willed her movements to quieten as she came back to the barracks building Thaddeus had disappeared into. And then she stopped, listened and watched. She ducked beneath a wall of overhanging jasmine and hoped they weren't the same kind of vine that ate butterflies. When nothing reached out and took hold of her, she narrowed her focus on the room to see if she could feel out whether Rush had gone back in, but all she sensed beyond the big wooden door was ill omens. Nothing good existed there.

The buzzing feeling in her chest was the opposite of how Rush made her feel, when he wasn't being a pushy jerk. Even then, her emotions clogged her throat with confusion. Being in this world, in this foreign time, became suddenly overwhelming.

Why did he have to ruin the budding friendship they'd carved out? Was the biting a claiming of some kind? Did it come with proprietary rights to her body? Was that how they did things in this time? The modern woman in her revolted, but then maybe it had nothing to do with modernity. Maybe it was the fact the last time she'd been "claimed" by a man, she'd allowed him to distort her life. All because she was afraid to be alone. Afraid that, like her mother had thought, there was something truly wrong with her.

Her stomach fluttered in confusion. She liked Rush. Was attracted to him. So much. The fae wouldn't get out of her head. But she'd be damned if another man, male, whatever this world had, demanded her body in a way she wasn't ready to give. Maybe it had been stupid to come down to the gate and see for herself if Thaddeus had arrived, but she *had* to see. To make sure it was real, and not a fancy.

Anxiety and yearning tugged a knot in her heart. Both emotions at once. He'd bitten her—that *hurt*—but then he'd released her from the bargain, and that *relieved*. The glow of his curse creeped up his neck, and that had alarmed her. The moment she'd turned and lost sight of him, her anger had waned. For some reason he'd needed her help so much that he bargained her free will for it. He was ashamed of his behavior. There were things he wasn't telling her, and it was high time he did.

He said fae couldn't lie.

Deciding to confront him, once and for all about his motivations, Clarke crossed to the other side of the street and kept to the shadows as she passed the barracks. With one eye in the direction the bad vibes came from, and one eye ahead, she almost missed the familiar face through the barracks window. She took two steps before it registered. She stopped. Tensed. And cranked her neck back to face the window.

There, through the glass pane and deep in conversation with other fae, was an unforgettable man from her time. A long face and small jaw, he had always reminded her of some kind of bird. She'd made the mistake of dismissing him as unimportant once and lived to regret it. Bones. That man was a sadist for sale. He worked for the Void. And now he was here, in this time, speaking with the vilest fae Clarke had met.

More of a conversation she'd had came back to her. She was sitting in that warehouse room with the nuclear codes before her. Bones was at another chair, holding Laurel's fingers. And Bishop was laughing.

"Tell me my future, babe," he'd said.

"You're going to die."

Bishop laughed. "Then tell me how to cheat death."

The part she'd forgotten was Bones' mumbled, *"We already know."*

Cold ice grew in the pit of her stomach. She'd never forget that face as long as she lived. And there he was, just like her, a thawed remnant of the past. Her nightmare had been a true vision. But if he was there, then Bishop could be there. Worse, the Void could be there. Everyone who had a hand in the apocalypse could be back. And just like her, they could have developed magical abilities.

Jolting into action, Clarke ran, fear nipping at her heels. She had to get back to the inn. She had to tell Rush.

But would he be there when she arrived?

Panic gripped her throat as she charged into the inn. She raced through the tavern, up the stairs and skidded to a halt as she crested the final step. Rush sat with his back against the door, long legs bent, and head in his hands. His gaze lifted, met hers, and held.

"I wasn't sure if you'd still be here," she admitted.

A flash of something washed over his expression, too brief to catch the meaning. His voice came out gravelly. "I can't leave you now, even if I wanted to."

Clarke wanted to say the same thing, but he already knew. She'd tried to leave him. The frustrating fae had kidnapped, tricked, and compelled her to do his bidding, and yet she still couldn't find it in her to walk the other way.

"What's wrong with us?" she whispered. "Why can't we leave each other?"

A look from his eyes to her neck said it all. They were mated. Whatever that meant. Maybe it happened long before he put his mark there. A link had always existed between them. She would find out what it meant, but first...

"There's something I need to tell you." She pulled the key from her pants pocket and nudged him with her boot to move. "Come inside and we'll talk."

He tensed, but didn't move. He stared up at her with a challenge in his eyes as though he spoiled for a fight.

"You're so stubborn, Rush. Just shift aside and let me in."

Eventually, he swallowed and got to his feet until he stood with his hands in his pockets, big body looming next to her.

Clarke opened the door and went inside. Casting the key onto the table near the fire, she noted the bath had been removed while she was out, and a complimentary bottle of liquor, hard cheese and dried fruit was left on the small round table. She put her hands on her hips and began pacing the small length of the opulent room.

"I saw someone from my time. A very *not nice* someone." She bit her nails. "He's here, thawed, just like me. And he worked for an awful man. I saw the same awful man in my nightmare that day out on the path."

She expected Rush to take a seat, but he didn't. He bolted the door and dipped his hand in his breeches pocket. He handed something to her.

"It's the portal stone. You should take it and head to the Order. They'll want to know."

She eyed it warily. "You're coming with me. I thought you need me to talk for you."

Although, he still hadn't revealed why.

His jaw clenched and he shook his head. "It doesn't matter anymore."

"And where will you go then?" she demanded.

He only lowered his gaze. "I don't know. Maybe back to the cabin."

"No."

"No?"

"You heard me. I don't think you're leaving. We've both admitted it. Neither of us can deny this thing between us. It was there before you bit me. It's been there from the moment I laid eyes on you in the woods."

He flinched.

"And for the record," she continued, "I'm well aware there is something driving you to behave the way you do, and when I ask, you give me half-truths and avoidance. I want answers. So sit." She pointed at the armchair facing the fire, still glowing with embers warm enough to keep the cool night air at bay.

The fight seemed to leave him, and he went to the chair. Clarke poured both of them a small glass of liquor from the decanter and handed Rush a glass. He swirled the amber liquid and stared while Clarke kept the advantage of height and stayed standing. She tapped her finger on her glass, eyes glued to the harsh lines of the fae's flawless profile as he grappled with words warring in his mind.

"This is where you tell me why you are cursed," she prompted.

With a sigh, he shot back the drink and then sprawled low in the chair, stretching his long legs out toward the fire. He watched the tiny flames dance. Clarke replaced the glass he held with her hand. Just like she had with Caraway, she smoothed the lines made by the passage of time and tried to ease his nerves. Through it all he watched her intently.

They shared an identical pattern on their fate lines. She pressed her smaller palm onto his larger one and marked the difference in size. He was so much bigger than her. Her fingers laced through his and squeezed.

"What is it you're afraid to tell me?" she asked.

He frowned and then pulled away. "It's not that I'm afraid. It's that I'm... ashamed."

Clarke's heart reached out to him. Whatever his secret was, it hurt. Deeply. She took the chair opposite him, next to the fireplace. The only light in the room came from low lit oil lamps in sconces around the room and the dying embers before them. Rush's hard features seemed to soften in the glow. His white hair colored. And his cheeks looked flushed. For a moment, Clarke forgot he was a magical fae, part wolf, and just saw an ordinary man relaxing before a fire.

"I fathered a child."

"Okay."

Maybe he expected something more from her because he glanced at her. She did her best to keep her features schooled to encourage him further.

"I... uh... I didn't know about the pregnancy until it was too late," he said. "I'd long since given up my claim to be a breeding male, and was with the Guardians, at any point. I know I couldn't save the mother, but I still feel as though I failed her."

"Did you know her long? The mother?"

He shrugged. "It was a one time thing. Her name was Véda. She was there and willing when I came in after a hunt. I left the next day and didn't come back until months later when I found her about to give birth, tied to an execution pole."

"*Jesus.*"

"She confessed her plan had been to make it seem like a stranger had forced her. She thought that if I didn't know, then nobody could hunt me down and punish me too. They'd either let her go because she was forced, or one of us would be there to care for the child. I suppose it was a good enough plan."

"What happened?"

"Thaddeus overheard us talking. He called the Royal Guard. The Guardian I was with refused to get involved. The breeding law is something the Courts enforce. It has nothing to do with magic, and so nothing to do with the Order. When Thaddeus called for my head, the Prime had found out, and convinced them that death would be too kind." He pushed back the sleeves of his sweater. Blue lights flashed and glittered in his living tattoo. "She stepped in at the end. Just not the way I wanted."

"But you didn't know about the pregnancy!"

"It didn't matter. I clearly wasn't careful enough to avoid it. Véda had told the entire village for months that she was forced. They all believed it to be true. According to them, because I couldn't keep control of my desire, a woman would lose her life and a child would be born parentless."

"I'm so sorry." Tears stung Clarke's eyes, and she reached out to him, but he tensed. Her hand fisted in the air and came back to her side.

"She gave birth right there outside the gate. Her arms were bound to a pole the entire time." His jaw clenched. He shook his head. "They refused to let me hold the newborn before they took him away. And then the Royal Guard slaughtered her before my eyes. Thaddeus laughed as they took me away. The bastard laughed. I should have ripped his throat out then."

The arms on the chair creaked from the force of his grip and suddenly it all became clear.

"You want to speak with your son," she whispered. "He's at the Order, isn't he?"

He gave a curt nod. "I have no excuses. I just want to speak to him. I don't even know what I would say."

He poured himself another big drink, and chugged it before sitting back down.

"Hey, Thorne," he said to the fire. "It's your dad. Sorry about your mother. But hey... couldn't keep it in my pants. Sorry I wasn't there to stop them from making you the tribute for the Well, but remember about those random acolytes who suddenly fell in the water at your initiation? Yeah that was me poking them with my useless sword."

"You're being too harsh on yourself."

"It's the truth."

For a long while, they both stared into the fire listening to the crackle made by tiny flames. Clarke didn't know what to say. He'd been given a raw deal. But could she forgive him for...

"Tell me about the mating and the marking," she urged.

He sighed. "It was the only way to keep you safe."

"I understand this. And I also understand that I'm very unprepared to live in a world like this. Not yet, anyway. But why did the mating make you behave the way you did? Why did you get so... aggressive and... it was almost like you were lost in a dream."

His fiery gaze snapped to hers. "Because you *are* a dream, Clarke. Never in my wildest imagination did I imagine a female like you coming into my life. Before you came, I'd given up. Even when you saw me at my vilest, you didn't leave. I have been cruel to you, and for that I will never be sorry enough. But you came back." His gaze softened. "The wolf inside me recognized that loyalty before me. You haven't met him, but he knows you. When I marked you as mine, it was all the permission my wolf needed. Nature can make me do things I wouldn't normally do. Sometimes the wolf is closer to the surface than I like to admit."

"Is it going to bite me as well?"

He laughed softly and shook his head. "I forget how human you are sometimes. No. It just wants to know you."

She rubbed between her breasts, hoping to ease the ache, but her fist hit something hard. The two vials Anise had given her were still there. It seemed so long ago now.

"You still haven't answered my question," she continued. "Not fully. I don't understand what mating means?"

"It's the fae version of marriage."

She narrowed her eyes. "We're married."

He had the decency to look repentant. "It's a little more than that."

"What can be more than marriage?"

"When we mate, it's a bond that goes beyond the natural order. My scent on you will make us hard to be around if any other males are interested in you." He scrunched his nose. "A Well-blessed mating lets us sense each other's emotions. For a union like that, a sacred blue light springs from the land to envelope the couple and leaves a visible marking. Then the couple share not only their thoughts and hearts, but their mana. I could borrow from you, and you could borrow from me. Our hearts would be open to each other. If we were blessed. Which we are not."

"You sound disappointed."

"A Well-blessed mating would break my curse."

"Oh." She bit her lip, surprised at the disappointment rising in her chest. "Then if I can't break it, we will make the Order remove the curse," she decreed.

"It's impossible."

"We have to try. It wasn't your fault. You shouldn't be in this situation. It's wrong. I know bad people, and you're not one of them."

Slowly, he lifted his gaze to hers. He stood, shifted his hand to his rear and pulled a small package from his pocket. He held it in his hands and turned the item over, unwrapping the teal patterned cloth to reveal something made from wood. Upon seeing it, Clarke shot to her feet and the two of them met before the fire. She held her breath as she looked down.

"You keep saying you wish you knew the time. So I made you this."

It was a carved sundial.

XII
I
II
III
IIII
X
IX
VIII
VII
VI
Sunrise-Sunset

TWENTY-THREE

Clarke hadn't received a gift like the one in Rush's hands for... she blinked, trying to remember. It hadn't been since her father had given her the charm bracelet and the watch.

He'd carved it himself.

"When did you have time to do this?" she asked.

"To be honest"—he scratched his head—"I started when we were walking here. I just didn't know what it was until earlier tonight."

Her finger traced over the intricate pattern around the dial. Roses and willow branches. "You're very talented."

He touched his fingers to his lips and hand-signed his thanks.

She shifted toward the fire to see the palm sized sundial better, trying hard to hold in her emotion, but her brows knitted together with the effort.

"You don't like it?"

She turned, eyes watering. "I love it. I... I'm speechless. Why?"

A pink tinge stained his cheeks and he dipped his gaze. "I don't know. I think... I think I just wanted to give you something you needed. Something that could help you, even after I'm gone."

His words hit the deepest part of her soul. Never before had anyone thought about her needs before his. Twice now. He'd saved her life at the bog. And now this? Suddenly, she no longer felt like a foreigner in a strange land. She felt like her old life was a dream, and this was her new reality. She crossed the floor, intending to thank him, but he stepped back and lifted his palms out.

"I don't want you to think I did this to manipulate you, or..."

To force her, he meant. The alarm in his eyes hurt to see. It shot straight to her heart and stabbed deep.

"Rush." She swallowed. "But I do like you. You haven't forced me. You've done quite the opposite. You made every attempt to make me hate you, yet... here I am. Wanting you."

His lips parted, eyes wide. He didn't believe her.

She flattened her lips and pulled the vials from beneath her shirt. "Look." She handed them to him, speaking fast and bumbling. "I intended to use these on you, or with you, or whatever. Anise sold them to me. She's the barmaid downstairs. Apparently elves love their elixirs. Do you know what they are?"

His gaze narrowed on the pink and blue vial and then sharpened with recognition. He growled and threw the blue into the fire. Flames burst as though gasoline had been thrown. Still agitated, he braced his hands on the mantle, head bowed. Every muscle in his back rippled with restraint as he took a moment to calm himself.

"Jeeze," she blurted. "You fae are sensitive with your masculinity."

He whipped around, eyes blazing. "I don't need any help being aroused for my mate."

Clarkes eyes dipped to below his belt and saw the evidence tenting there. She had to bite her cheek to hold back a smile. "Nope. No you don't."

Anguish stifled his expression. He turned back to the fire. "You think this is funny?"

He wanted her. Now he knew she wanted him. So why was he avoiding her? Had she not been clear enough? She wasn't ready before. But now she was. Knowledge had been exchanged and the power balance had shifted. She was more than willing. Her gaze ran down his body. God, he was hot. Sexy. Broad shoulders tapered to a small waist, an ass made by the gods, and thick, muscled thighs possibly double the width of hers. She imagined running her hands over his naked skin. The heat. The soft unyielding strength.

Heat speared between her legs. She bit back a groan.

Something was holding him back. Clarke's mind shifted back to his earlier confession and she stepped forward. Maybe this reluctance was more than his curse. Maybe he'd been cut deeper than he admitted. His sexual gratification had ruined lives.

"Rush." She dropped her palm onto his back. He shuddered beneath her touch. "You're not a bad person for wanting this, you know. You shouldn't feel guilty about your desire."

He tensed as if he wished her away, as if he wished his feelings away.

There was only one way to make her position clear. She stepped back until her thighs hit the edge of the bed and then unlaced her belt. Straightening her spine, she rolled up the belt length and threw it at the wall above his head. It bounced and landed on his shoulders.

He turned, confused eyes colliding with hers. But then his attention dipped and studied her from top to toe. With every inch he covered, heat smoldered in his eyes until his gaze snagged upon the motion of her fingers on the top pearl button of her blouse. She fingered it open, daring him with her eyes.

"I want this," she said, voice thick. "You're not forcing me. I've already had a drop of the pink elixir. I'm prepared." It was true. She'd taken some the moment she left the tavern. "No lives will be ruined if you let yourself go tonight."

Her finger plucked the button. He growled in warning.

"It's not bad to want a little comfort in each other's arms." She popped another button. "You chase my nightmares away, Rush."

"Stop."

"I want to feel your body against mine."

"I said, *stop.*"

She paused. "Why?"

He licked his lips, eyes still caught on her fingers, and then a yearning so deep and open flashed across his face. His voice dropped low. "Because I want to do it."

Clarke's heart almost soared out of her chest. Slowly, her hands drifted to her side. She lifted her chin, a dare in her eyes. *Come and get me.*

He pushed off the mantle and stalked forward, golden eyes never leaving her face. His arousal pushed against his breeches, giving her a dark outline of his shape. Seeing it only made her pulse thud faster with anticipation. His intensity, his predatory focus, gave her insight to his animal side and she knew that when he finally graced her with his shift, she'd be in awe. His wolf would be majestic.

The toe of his boot hit hers and he stopped, all brooding energy and thunderous scrutiny. Inches away, his eyes were wild, proud, and lit with some savage desire. First, his gaze landed on her breasts, to where her nipples strained against the fabric of her blouse. Then his hand went there, capturing the weight. Her lips parted. The touch rasped against the fabric and sent tingles zipping through her body. He squeezed and kneaded, taking his time in learning her shape, never removing his intense stare from her face as though he cataloged every reaction she gave him.

She closed her eyes, enjoying his simple yet consuming caress melting her from the inside. Two hands now, both toying and rolling each breast with skill and reverence.

"Playing with your food, wolf?" she teased.

He gave a guttural grunt, and then the weight at her front was gone. Her eyes snapped open to find him lifting trembling hands to cup her face. The rough pad of each thumb stroked along her cheeks. Golden eyes heated with a mix of wonder and adoration. It was so open, so raw, that she felt the tug down to her core. She pushed into his touch and smiled. This felt right. This is what her instinct had been trying to tell her. This was where it all pointed. To be in his arms. They were stronger together.

"Clarke..."

"Shut up and kiss me."

His eyes widened, and then he took her mouth in a consuming kiss. No more reservations. Nothing between them. Clarke sank into his heat, into the soft lips and bristle of beard, into the hardness of his chest. His tongue tangled with hers. It was a hot, heady kiss that wrenched a moan from deep in her lungs. She felt wanted. Needed. She couldn't get enough.

"I'm going to put my mouth here next," he murmured and touched her breast again.

"Oh God, yes."

"And then I will show you how I play."

He traced his lips on her jaw, nipped and nibbled and licked his way down her neck, leaving a trail of fire everywhere he touched. One powerful hand splayed on the small of her back, holding her up, the other worked at the buttons on her blouse until she was laid bare to him. Air hit her skin, sending goosebumps pebbling all over. He stepped back, eyes hooded, and then said, "I changed my mind. I want you to take the rest off while I watch."

Clarke lifted her brow. "And what about you?"

Something like amusement mixed with curiosity flashed over his features, and then his expression hardened with intent. He gripped the back of his sweater and dragged it over his head. His hair became disheveled in an altogether come-hither way that almost unraveled her.

"You're taking too long." He gave a pointed look at her pants.

But she didn't care about herself. He'd already unbuttoned his breeches, giving her a taste of the wicked delights beneath. Flexing abdominals, dark gray fuzz dusted with silver, the top of that hard length... and his thumbs were hooked on the waistband, ready to pull down. The blue glyphs covering his body only increased his preternatural physique. She wanted to trace her tongue around every blue line.

Clarke barely registered that she'd sat on the edge of the bed. Maybe she got one or two buttons on her pants open, but then she'd stopped, eyes glued to his undress. He slid those pants over his hips and ass, the arch of his thick thighs, and then completely down. Enraptured, her mouth dried.

Naked, the fae was a study in male beauty. Every minute move he made flexed muscles and tendons she never knew existed. The only time she saw a body like this in her time, was on the cover of a sports magazine. Or one of those calendars you bought to raise money for charity. But in this time, the people had to work to survive. The fact his shape was carved out of necessity made it even more desirable.

He was strong. A protector. A provider.

Her eyes dropped to below his waistline, to his desire jutting eagerly between his legs. An impatient snarl of need burst from her throat. She didn't care if she sounded like an animal. She suddenly knew how he'd felt out there in the alley. She had to have him. Now.

"When you look at me like that..." he murmured.

"Come here."

He wrapped his fingers around his arousal and stepped closer until the tip came before her face. She licked her lips and looked up to find raw anguish in his expression. Holding his gaze, she unwrapped his fingers and replaced them with her own. From his reluctance, he wasn't used to conceding, and even less used to being touched. But she got what she wanted. With long, smooth strokes, she let him see what she could do for him. The immediate defocus of his eyes made every feminine intuition scream with triumph. Locking eyes, she lowered her lips to his blunt tip and teased the sensitive ending with her breath. She intended to hold his gaze, but the moment her tongue darted out and tasted, her eyes fluttered closed with a groan. She took him inside and swirled and flicked with her tongue.

A shaky breath escaped him—a muttered curse as he threaded trembling fingers into her hair and let her take control, never once demanding something she wasn't ready to give. She licked and sucked and loved. She took pleasure with his body until she could feel him going taut, until the veins bulged at his abdomen, until his breath quickened and he twitched, fingers spasming in her hair.

He pulled out suddenly. He gripped her chin and angled it so she stared into his eyes, open with need. She felt like she was falling. Every line on his face was taut with need and the very sight sent hot tingles rippling through her body. No words came out to explain his thoughts, just a dark look of passion that twisted his features into something so breathtaking nothing else existed.

Rush crouched, tugged her pants off, and then his hard body was atop her. Lips landed on her skin and tasted every inch as though a starved man. He kissed and laved the marking on her neck with reverence. He grazed teeth along tendons and caressed with his fingers. It all heated her eagerly, sending her soaring after her fall. Up, up, up. While his mouth was busy, his fingers explored. Over breasts, nipples, stomach... lower... and then he found her wet.

A snarl tore out of him. He used his knee to pry her legs apart and he plunged a finger into the heat of her core. She arched into him greedily, holding his gaze, but he retreated down her body. He widened her thighs for a better view and traced fingers through her center. Then lifted them to his mouth and licked with a throaty growl of satisfaction.

"*This* is playing with my food, princess."

"You're cruel." She arched into him, begging for more, but he held her down.

She threw her head back onto the pillow with frustration.

"Tell me how you like it," he demanded.

"Whatever you want is how I like it."

The tickle of his beard on her thighs was the only warning before a long, torturous lick straight down her center sent her back bowing, and her hips driving into him. She pulled a pillow over her mouth and let loose a long strangled and drawn out moan.

TWENTY-FOUR

The mating need had never left Rush. Not since the moment he'd sunk his teeth into Clarke and coated her with his scent. Before they'd entered the room, he'd smelled himself on her body and it made every instinct within him howl with possessive pride. The way she'd taken him into her mouth... it had made him weak for her touch. And now he had her at his mouth while he feasted and probed and swirled. Her taste was drugging, and the way she responded to his every touch sent his mind spiraling, falling and crashing. He would turn into a beast of need if he couldn't keep her roving hands off him. She pushed him to a new urgent pace. The woman knew what she wanted, and she wasn't afraid to ask for it. Assertively, she took his head and guided the direction of his tongue to where she wanted it. He pulled back with a growl of restraint.

She looked down her body, cheeks flush. "Don't stop."

"You said whatever I want," he reminded.

She nodded.

"So I want to take my time."

A frustrated sound mewled out of her and she dropped her head to the pillow. "I don't know if I can wait that long."

"I've waited decades for this. I won't be rushed." He stroked her thighs. "You will wait."

"So bossy." But she said it with a bright-eyed smile.

She was the elemental divine made flesh. Silken flames flowed around her shoulders. The color also dusted her sex. He never wanted it to end, and she was eager for it to go faster. He wasn't playing. He was avoiding because if he let her have her way, he feared his resolve to make it last.

And it needed to last.

He hadn't been wrong when he told her she was a dream turned real for him. Any time he'd fantasized about being with a female, he'd imagined the flesh, the carnal act, but not the deep satisfaction filling the aching hollow of his chest. This connection went beyond gratification. It was like she'd said, there had been something between them from the start, something waiting for them to acknowledge, and now that they had, it was there to stay. With her, he never felt alone. She saw him. She saw *into* him.

The whisper of her voice floated back, *"You're not a bad person for wanting this."*

He only wished *this* wasn't so close to the end of his curse.

He shook the thought away. There was no place for that here. Right now he had to make himself last. His eyes tracked again to the torn tunic wrapped around her head.

"Clarke," he said, voice hoarse with an idea. It deepened. "Princess."

She drew her fevered gaze back to his.

"Do you trust me?" he asked.

No hesitation. She nodded. Her complete and utter submission sucked the air from his lungs. She trusted. Knowing this clicked something inside him. He would prove her trust founded. He would give her the best of him.

He gave an affectionate goodbye kiss at the apex of her thighs, just for now, and then prowled up the length of her body. He tugged off the torn strip and enjoyed splaying her red tresses around the pillow. She watched him, eyes dancing with humor. It would get messed up soon, but that wasn't the point. The point was she allowed him the moment to learn another intimate piece of her identity, an act reserved for loved ones. Tonight he would find many more of these brief moments with her.

"Do you have a thing for tying me up?" she teased.

"Only when you test my resolve."

"So this is my fault."

He bared his teeth. "The fault is my lack of restraint at the want of your touch."

She snorted, but gave him her hands.

With one knee on either side of her hips, he gathered her wrists and gently tied them together. As he lifted her bound arms over her head and leaned toward the bedhead, the tip of his cock grazed and tickled her abdomen, sending fire scooting up his spine. He cursed. Tensed. He was so close to the edge. All it took was a trace of her skin and he was almost over. Satisfied she couldn't reach out to him, he came back down to her, surprised to find her eying his member with heat.

He took himself in hand and squeezed. "Do you want this in your mouth again?"

She nodded, licking her lips.

He pumped until the aching need abated a little and then whispered low and rough in her ears. "First, I want to take my time giving you every pleasure I've fantasized about for decades."

"You torture me," she moaned. "I'm going to die."

"You'll die happy."

"Rush," she pleaded.

His lips curved up one side, and then his amusement dropped. "If it's too much, tell me." He eyed the wrist bindings warily. "You tell me. Understand?"

She licked her lip and nodded. "What... what did you fantasize about?"

His gaze lingered on the way her breasts lifted with her quickening breath. Tight, hard and aroused. She was more than his fantasy. He captured a pebbled nipple in his mouth and swirled his tongue, sucking and groaning around the peak. "This," he murmured, and then did the same to the other. "And this." He moved down her center, stopping and studying every inch as though it was his only chance. His last. Because tomorrow he might wake with the last of his mana expended. If Thaddeus came for them in the night, he would use any and every tool in his arsenal to protect Clarke. One more shift into wolf, one more slip of control, and he would be done. He was well aware that he could lose his hold even now. At least he'd have this moment, this small taste of honey. Frowning once again at the direction of his thoughts, he moved down her stomach until he reached the red patch of hair and nuzzled between her legs. He licked. She made little whimpering sounds. Then he opened her wide and blew a jet of air right where it mattered most.

Her writhing cry of abandon brought a smile to his lips.

"You like that?" he asked, then laved and did it again.

She tensed in response, and so he ran his finger around her heat, teasing the outside before finally slipping in. A deep, inarticulate sound came out of him when he found her ready.

"You really want this."

"God, yes." She lifted to him.

He increased his pace, dipping to explore with his tongue, taking more insistent strokes until his own need churned within restlessness. Every mewling sound she made, every bow of her back and small thrust of her hips delighted him to no end. He slid his hand beneath her pelvis and lifted her to him, increasing the pressure of his tongue. Her thighs clenched, coiling her tight. He gave more until her scream of ecstasy filled the room and she went languid beneath him.

Drawing back, he took pleasure in the way she panted to catch her breath, the sated expression on her face, and most importantly, the way she watched him, the way she saw him—with complete carnal belonging—it was the way he felt about her. He untied her hands and gently rubbed her wrists, giving each a reverent kiss on the inside.

"Thank you," he said. "For giving me that pleasure."

She arched a brow. "I think you have it all wrong, baby. It should be the other way around."

"Baby." A short laugh burst out. "Why do you call me a babe?"

She huffed, chagrinned. "It's a term of endearment in my time."

"Did I act like a mewling newborn?"

"No, sir, you most definitely did not."

His gaze darkened. "Maybe I thanked you because I want to be in your debt."

"I'm sure I can arrange something." She shimmied down the bed and hooked her legs around his waist, nudging him closer to her center. Her eyes fluttered closed and he scolded her.

"Keep them open, princess. I want you to see me when I fill you. I want you to always remember it is me bringing you to this bliss."

"God, you say the most arrogant things."

He angled himself at her entrance and in small teasing movements, sheathed himself to the hilt. The shear electric buzz of it curled his toes. She fit him, perfectly. Holding his position until he could function, he lowered his lips to hers and murmured, "You can touch me now."

A wicked gleam flashed in her eyes. "Maybe I'll tie you up."

He circled his hips. She whimpered.

"Nope," she breathed. "I'm... I can't. Oh God, do that again."

He dragged out and in, enjoying the way she went boneless beneath him. He did it again. And again. Each time he watched her reaction, finding something new to revel in. A lick or bite of her lips. A euphoric roll of her eyes. A slight frown of concentration. It was all a reaction to *him*, to the genuine moment they shared. He was alive. He was seen.

Each time she revealed herself, it carved out a little piece of his heart, making space for her to crawl in and occupy. He knew, without a doubt, that no matter what happened next, even if she didn't stay with him, or if these were his last moments, that space would still be there. It would follow him into the next life.

Clarke's breath caught, and then she let out a shuddering moan, bowing her back. His mark on her neck had never been more on display. Desire broke the banks of his control and he kissed her with hunger, swallowing the remnants of her bliss. His movements turned frantic, and it was all she could do to hold on. Tension rode his system. Every bone, muscle and tendon retracted from too much sensation. But he was powerless to stop. He thrust and pounded, kissed and nipped, faster and harder until the headboard crashed against the wall, and sweet heat sizzled up his spine. Until he planted himself and shuddered through his release with a deep, rumbling growl of satisfaction.

He stayed inside her, holding her in his arms. The oil in the lamps was almost spent, and the fire was almost out. Her breathing seemed to even out and he pulled out, jolting her awake.

"We're not done."

"What?" Her eyes flew open.

"We have all night."

She gave him a listless smile. "We have to sleep at some point."

"Yes." He dragged his teeth along her jaw. "At some point."

"I'm kinda hungry too."

Another swell of warmth hit him in the chest. He shifted off the bed and found a cloth at the wash basin to clean her, and then he filled a glass with liquor and broke off a chunk of hard cheese. Through it all, she studied him with one hand propped behind her head.

"You're glowing," she noted. "It's covering more of you now."

He settled on the bed and lifted a piece of cheese to her lips. "It's close to the end," he admitted.

"How much time is left?"

"Maybe a few weeks. Months at most."

She ate and sat up with a frown, chewing. Before she could speak, he lifted the glass of liquor to her lips. She drank, swallowed, but then scowled. "What's with the feeding?"

"I like knowing I'm providing for you." For now. He winced.

Her gaze softened and dropped to the glyphs. "Rush," she whispered, forlorn.

"Don't speak about it. Let's have tonight." He used his thumb to wipe a drop from the corner of her mouth. "And it's only just begun. I have more fantasies for you to fulfill."

TWENTY-FIVE

Clarke woke from a deep, dreamless sleep and instantly knew the warm weight over her body was Rush's arm and leg. Naked and cocooned in his arms, she didn't want to move and drifted lazily listening to the sounds of the inn waking up below them. Someone emptied water in the alley. Birds tweeted nearby. Banging sounds thudded on the wooden floors elsewhere in the establishment. The smell of fresh-baked bread wafted in and her stomach grumbled.

It was no wonder she was hungry. They'd stayed up half the night enjoying each other's company. Rush wasn't wrong when he'd said he needed no elixir to keep aroused around his mate. Clarke stretched languidly, feeling the pleasant pull of their lovemaking in every aching part of her body. The fae was a machine with endless stamina. Clarke was the one who had called it a night because she simply couldn't keep her eyes open any longer. Rush didn't complain. He'd tucked her smaller body into his larger one and surrounded her until she drifted away.

Not a single nightmare plagued her sleep.

Clarke rolled from her back toward the window to see if she could ascertain the time of day by the amount of light peeking through the cracks in the drapes, but Rush grumbled and placed his teeth on her shoulder in warning. He did that a lot—teeth on the neck or shoulder—to let her know without words what his feelings were. In this instance, it was not to ruin his deep comfort. It was never a sharp bite like it had been the time in the alley, but only a light pressure that eased off and grazed along her skin more often than not. She smiled, realizing she liked learning all these little pieces of him.

He tightened his grip and tugged across her middle so her rear fit nicely into his lap. A growing hardness pressed into her behind.

"Are you even awake?" she chuckled.

He made a throaty sound and kissed, or licked, the back of her neck, then tucked her in tight and rested his head back on the pillow. The sound of his soft breath evened out.

She remained content to spend her time tracing a finger up and down his forearm resting between her breasts and wondered what was going to happen next. Not knowing how her own future would unfold was an ever-increasing irritation. The bare hints she'd gleaned weren't enough. How was it fair that she could see into anyone else's future but hers?

Thaddeus hadn't come breaking down the door, so the curse must have worked to confuse him as to her presence. And then there was Bones. An involuntary shiver traveled through her. That man was despicable.

The glow of Rush's curse glanced off the furniture in the low lit room and amplified her anxiety. They'd have to get going to the Order after they had something to eat. A gnawing sensation of... something... tried to break through her reverie. Fear.

He'd said his curse was nearing its end. When it was done, he'd die. Just like that. Months. Maybe weeks were all he had left. She couldn't imagine a life without him. Since she couldn't see his future, she had to have faith that it was entwined with hers, but it didn't assuage her worry. His future may be with hers, but he could still die tomorrow... just with her at his side.

A knot formed in her belly. When she got to the Order, she would find a way to somehow trigger her psychic visions on demand. The way they just popped up was very inconvenient. Then she would learn how to lift the curse. If she couldn't work it out on her own, she didn't care if she used her abilities to exploit the people there. She'd done worse for greed. This was for Rush's benefit.

Wasn't it?

"You are fretting." His voice was still thick with sleep as he nuzzled into her hair.

"How can you tell?"

He took a deep breath and moved in a way that felt like a shrug. "Let me make you happy again."

He began a slow path down her front, hand splaying at her pelvis and holding her firm against his hips. She rolled to face him and found his gaze full of wicked intent.

"We didn't get much chance to talk last night," she said.

"We talked."

She frowned. "Okay, fine. Yes we did. But there's more. Remember that person I recognized at the barracks?"

He sat up. "The human?"

She hugged herself. "He was a very violent man. He tortured my friend to convince me to work for him."

"Then he is breathing his last. Tomorrow, I will—"

"No." Clarke touched his jaw gently, eyes soft. He hated not being able to protect her. She didn't want to remind him of his limitations, so steered the conversation. "We can't rush into anything. He could lead us to someone worse, and we're vastly unprepared. You were at Crystal City. Did you ever see him there?"

Rush threaded his fingers over his chest and stared at the ceiling. "When I visited, there was a new king. From what I gathered from the people, they were both equally awed and fearful of him. I never saw his face."

Clarke tugged on her hair. "I just think we need more information before doing anything. And hopefully we'll get some answers at the Order."

"I trust you and your visions. If you think this person is linked to a threat to Elphyne, then that's good enough for me."

Tension rode her body. She plucked a few strands out.

His hand covered hers, stopping the action. "You're fretting again."

"Maybe that's because I'm not sure if I can trust myself." She bit her lip and inhaled deeply. Here goes. "My mother abandoned me because of my visions. She thought I was demon spawn. My father ignored them. Bishop used them. I just... I don't know."

He kissed her on the shoulder. "I do."

"You shouldn't. I wasn't exactly a good person. I used to steal."

"I steal."

"But you do it out of necessity."

"Isn't that what you did?"

She lifted a shoulder. "Maybe."

"Then enough talking."

He lifted the blanket to cover his head and disappeared with a mischievous glint in his eye. The moving bulk of his body slid down the bed, and within moments, he pushed apart her knees. Another moment later she forgot her troubles.

"So," Clarke said, "to be clear, you want stew for breakfast, and some ale? But it's so early." She scrunched her nose as she tugged on her boot. "That's gross."

Being the only one others could see, ordering was Clarke's job. They'd made the decision to get dressed so they could head straight out after their meal. He'd conceded and was coming with her to the Order. It hadn't been hard to convince him when she said they could continue with his long list of fantasies the following night.

"The ale here is delicious," Rush replied. Now fully clothed, back in his worn Guardian jacket, he rustled through his rucksack with a mumbled, "I could have sworn I had more coin than this."

She made an awkward face. It was probably still in her pants from when she'd stolen it yesterday. She dug her fingers into the pocket and found not only the coins, but one of his little wolf carvings. She pulled both out.

"I think I have some," she said.

He tensed. "Where did you get that?"

"The wolf?" She bit her lip. "I took it from your bag."

A dark look flashed over his face. "It's not for you."

"Sorry. Here, have it back." She held it out.

"I... no, it is me who should apologize. I didn't mean to snap. I carved it for my son when he was younger." He picked it up and twirled it in his fingers. "I used to make them and drop them in his room. I hoped he'd see the resemblance and know his father was looking out for him." He handed it back to her. "He's an adult now. I don't know why I brought it. You have it."

"I think it's beautiful. It reminds me of you."

He returned her smile and opened the door. "Head down to the bar. I'll finish packing and readying the portal stone."

Clarke made her way down to the tavern level of the inn. Already filling with patrons, the room had mainly fae she guessed were overnight guests. Some lone travelers. Some couples. None of the provocative females she'd seen were anywhere in sight. From the sounds she'd heard last night, they were probably all worn out. Bit like her.

She tested the position of the torn strip around her ears and couldn't help the smile that lifted her lips. There would never be a time she failed to think about Rush when she touched that piece of fabric. How things had changed since the last time she'd worn it.

Buoyed by her emotions, she walked up to the bar and found it empty. No servers around, but the smell of freshly cooked food wafted from the kitchen behind it. Some clanking noises clashed with a loud male curse. She walked along the length of the bar until she came to the spot where she could see through the kitchen door. Beyond was an old style scullery. It was still odd for her to see something so normally heavy with metal in her time, now so stripped bare of it. Instead of stainless steel counters, there was wood. Instead of iron stoves, a long stone hearth with ceramic pots bubbled away. A tall, but rotund, fae with wolfish ears muttered to himself as he briskly stirred a pot. He must have sensed her there, because he immediately lifted his head and paused. He had golden eyes, streaky short gray hair, and a crooked nose which he lifted her way as though he tried to scent her. His eyes narrowed and he put the pot down.

Wiping his hands on his apron, he came out of the kitchen. "You need something?"

"Hi." She put some coin on the bench. "I'd like to order some food and have it sent up to our room please."

The fae's gaze narrowed even more. Clarke thought he might tell her to go away, but instead, he gave a big belly shout. "Anise! You're needed."

Then he returned to the kitchen.

Strange.

Not long after, Anise emerged. She wore similar attire to the previous night and looked drained.

"Morning," Clarke said. "You been here all night?"

"Just got in." Anise's gaze dipped to Clarke's neck and then gave her a knowing smile. "You're looking mighty chirpy. Took advantage of the elixir, I see."

"Um." Clarke's hand went to Rush's mark, still visible on her neck. "Actually. We did fine without it. But thank you anyway."

"Right," Anise laugh. "Well, you smell like you've been drowning in its aftereffects. No wonder Angus wouldn't take your order."

Angus must be the cook. "What does that mean?"

"The wolf who claimed you did it good. Any male sniffing around you like this will be in for trouble when your mate comes around."

"But the cook was just going to take my order."

Anise shrugged. "You're not around wolves much, are you?"

"I guess not."

"We're a territorial lot. I'm surprised he didn't accompany you down here. I want to meet the guy."

"You know, I truly wish you could, but he's getting our things ready. We have to leave soon."

"What's he look like?" Anise waggled her brows. "With that sated look on your face, I'm imagining some big alpha type. Although, a real alpha wouldn't let his mate come down and collect the meal. You're making me very curious." She whined a little at Clarke's closed mouth. "Come on. Tell me. I've got nothing else to live for but endless work hours."

Clarke pinched her lips, but couldn't resist sharing. It was nice to have a girl to talk to. "He's tall. Longish silver hair. Beard. Total"—she couldn't come up with the right words to explain Rush's physique and flexed her hands in front of her shoulders—"he's like…"

"That good, huh?"

She laughed and nodded. He was everything.

"Maybe if I bring the food, I'll get a peek."

"I wish you could see him." Her mood dropped because it was true. Wanting Rush to be visible and free of his curse was starting to dig a hole into her chest.

Nervous, she tucked hair behind her ear. It was such a habitual move that she'd not noticed she'd pushed aside the torn fabric keeping her ears hidden until Anise stiffened.

Alarm prickled through Clarke. Their eyes locked.

Neither knew what the other would do.

Anise made the first move.

"What are you doing?" She leaned over the counter and tugged the strap down. "Keep that hidden. If Thaddeus gets wind of your kind being here, you'll be gone before you can take a new breath."

"Sorry."

They went back to staring at the other, not knowing what to say.

"You're a Seer," Anise stated.

"Yes."

"But you're not an elf."

"No."

"And you're not fae." Anise lowered her voice.

Clarke shook her head cautiously. She waited for Anise to raise the alarm, or to look at her differently, but she only checked over her shoulder and then leaned over the bench to get closer to Clarke.

"Is there even a hot alpha in your room?"

"Definitely, that part is true."

"You know," Anise said, "I've always had a leaning toward the psychic. It's why I waved you over in the first place. Now I see why. We'll meet again, Clarke. Mark my words." She eased her weight to one side. "Now, what would you like to eat?"

With a nod of appreciation, Clarke gave her order and headed back up to the room. She liked Anise, and now seeing that she wouldn't betray someone like her on sight, she liked her even more.

She arrived at the room and found the fire had been stoked back to life. Rush looked a little flushed. She first thought that perhaps it was the activity of restarting the fire, but then she caught the guilty gleam in his eyes. Her nerves jangled.

"What did you do?" she asked warily.

He scratched the back of his neck. "I got bored waiting."

"What the hell does that mean?"

"It means I left a little gift around the main streets. I marked my territory."

"Like a... wolf?"

Rush gave her a toothy grin and lifted his hands playfully. "It's in my nature."

A nervous tension crept up her spine. "I wish you waited until after we ate before you announced to all the town that you're here."

Rush prowled up to her, his playful grin still lighting up his face. "And where would the fun be in that?"

Clarke went over to the window and pulled the drape to peer outside. Down in the street, life was beginning for the town's folk. Fae were bustling about. But no sign of his uncle. She let the drapes fall back into place.

"I thought you didn't want to rule this town."

"Doesn't mean I don't like fucking with his head."

She laughed. His finger hooked on her belt and tugged her close. The way he peered down at her, all mischief and joy, it was hard to stay angry. This was the side of him she'd seen when they'd first met. The same side that had attracted her to him in the first place. It was the real Rush. And she'd helped bring it out. How could she be cross with that?

"Just promise me we can get out of here on a moment's notice."

He nodded, dark lashes lowering as he closed the gap between their faces. "I have it all under control."

She sank into his kiss, running her hands around his waist, wishing that his Guardian jacket wasn't so thick.

A knock came at the door, interrupting them. Rush opened it with his goofy grin still stretching his lips. Neither of them expected Anise to see him, but as the door opened, and Anise came into view, her eyes widened to big saucers and her jaw dropped open. Her gaze ping-ponged between Clarke and Rush.

Holy shit. She could see him.

Anise clicked her jaw shut and gave Rush a cordial smile, then quickly entered the room and placed the tray on the small table near the hearth. On her way back to the door, she gave Clarke a secret flare of her eyes and whispered, "I see what you mean."

She shut the door on the way out, leaving both Clarke and Rush speechless.

He pointed at the door. "What just happened?"

"I don't know. I guess she saw you. Right?"

Rush strode to the door and stared at it. He rubbed his beard. "Did you speak to her downstairs?"

"Yes. She's the server who sold me the elixirs. We chatted a bit last night too. I like her."

He met her eyes. "Did you say anything about wanting her to see the truth?"

Clarke thought about it. "I guess I did mention something about wishing she could see what you look like."

He gave a grunt of understanding, mumbled something about her doing that with the White Woman.

Ushering her over to the table, he motioned for her to sit, and then proceeded to dish up her meal. He even tried to hand feed her again, but she took the spoon away from him, much to his displeasure.

"I think I can feed myself, big guy."

A scowl marred his face as he ate his own meal.

"You wolves are an interesting lot. Anise said something about being an alpha and wanting to provide for your mate. The cook down there also backed off once he smelled your special wolf cologne on me. Anise said he wouldn't go near a newly mated alpha's female."

Rush's jaw flexed. "It's not right that no one sees me by your side."

"Well," she squeezed his wrist, "perhaps soon that will change. I've done something already. First the bug-lady—"

"The White Woman."

"Yeah, that thing. Then Anise. Clearly I'm making something happen. Maybe the Order can help me the rest of the way."

As they ate their meal in silence, one unsaid thought hung over their heads. She could make someone see him, cut through the glamour that kept him hidden, but that had little to do with the rest of his curse.

Clarke was halfway through eating the last bit of fresh bread dipped in honey when a feeling of urgency rose swiftly and without mercy. Harsh buzzing exploded in her chest. The bread dropped on her plate.

"We have to go," she said.

He straightened. "Now?"

"Yes... something is—"

The door burst open, swinging on its hinges. Both Clarke and Rush jumped to their feet. He stood in front of her.

Standing in the doorway was a white wolf, snarling and baring its teeth. It took a step into the room, and then the air shimmered around it. Like a shifting mirage, the wolf became humanoid. It became Thaddeus, naked and pumped with fury. Behind him was a figure with a dark hooded cloak. And pushing through was Bones, also in a cloak. All three turned their heads her way.

None of them saw Rush, or the feral snarl curling his lips.

Thaddeus arched a brow and looked to Bones. "Is she the one?"

Bones' thin lips stretched into a smile as he took her in. "Yes. He will be pleased."

"I expect a bonus in the next shipment."

"Done." Bones' eyes never left Clarke, and a coldness settled into her stomach.

Who was the "He" Bones referenced? Someone who wanted her? Someone who knew her? The faceless Void loomed into her mind.

Bones dipped his finger into his jacket pocket and pulled out a red rose. He sniffed it, then tossed it into the room. It landed at her feet, rolled, and lost a petal. Clarke's heart stopped. The Void had always worn a red rose in the pocket of his suit.

Rush calmly slipped on his baldric and then secured his sword. No one noticed him.

That's what she thought.

The hooded figure behind Bones and Thaddeus faced Rush, and panic tightened Clarke's throat. He knew. He could either see Rush, or could sense him. Frozen, unable to move in case she alerted the rest of them to Rush's whereabouts, she didn't know what to do. Her gaze kept darting to Rush to check on his progress.

And then everything seemed to happen at once.

Thaddeus and Bones both caught her eyeing a seemingly empty corner of the room. They noticed the two cups on the table. Thaddeus sniffed the air and growled.

"He's here."

And then they were crowding into the room, Rush took hold of her arm, and a bright pop of light blinded them. She opened her eyes and wasn't in the room at the inn, but outdoors. Rush held her tightly. In his hand, a stone sizzled with smoke. He dropped it onto the grass.

"Well, that's spent," he muttered.

"What the hell happened?"

He nudged the stone. "I used the portal stone. We're at the Order."

CHAPTER

TWENTY-SIX

Rush held Clarke in his arms as she recovered from the effects of using the portal stone. The first time was never easy and the further you traveled, the greater the feeling of displacement. Her skin had taken on a greenish hue, and she clung to him. Any minute now, she might lose the contents of her stomach.

He helped her to her knees and pulled her hair back as she leaned forward.

"Take deep breaths," he instructed. "It will pass."

"Goddamned lack of cars." She made a gagging sound. "How come you don't feel sick?"

"Using portal stones is second nature for me. Some Mages and Guardians can create portals without the stones."

"Show-off." She retched again but covered her mouth.

Rush stayed with her while she crouched on the floor staring at the grass. It had been a risk to use the portal stone in close quarters. Many things could have happened. The energy rift in reality could have sliced through furniture and people too close. It was what he counted on. If Thaddeus and his men were smart, they would have jumped out of range to avoid being sliced in two by the rift. He'd closed the portal the instant he and Clarke were through. And if one of them tried to trace the portal, it would only lead them here.

To the Order.

His ears perked at the sounds of battle training coming from the distance. He squinted to scope their surroundings. As planned, the portal stone had brought them within walking distance of the Order grounds. Built like a fortress, a high stone wall and dense poisonous forest surrounded the grounds. Both kept the compound from prying eyes. Deep into the forest lay the ceremonial lake, an enormous turquoise body of water that fed into the Order academy buildings in small underground rivers. The lake seemed to have sprung from nowhere and was a source of power. There was no

146

mountain range nearby, no sea, and they weren't particularly below sea level, but the water was aplenty and sacred. In all of Elphyne, it was where the connection to the Well was the greatest.

"Okay," Clarke grumbled. "I think I'm good. No puke. Winning, right?"

He helped her up but caught sight of a wolpertinger hopping cautiously toward Clarke. At first glance, the creature was benign, but the pest was known to turn on its victims. With the wings of a pheasant, the body of a rabbit, and the horns of a deer, the wolpertinger's blended traits from multiple species was the epitome of haphazard evolution in the new world. But if it came sniffing around, then it believed Clarke to be single, despite his scent on her. It was a sign that his curse still held, even in this magical territory where glamour was prohibited unless for training purposes.

He frowned. He'd have to make sure his scent was stronger next time. He wanted no one, even a little pesky fire-fae, thinking it had the right to Clarke.

Clarke saw the creature and cooed. "Oh, aren't you a cute little thing?"

"She's taken," Rush hissed and stomped his boot. "Begone."

Not understanding where the vibrations came from, the furry and feathered animal snarled, showed its fangs to Clarke, and then bounded off.

"Why did you do that? Surely you're not jealous of a little winged rabbit?"

"Wolpertingers target single females because they're the weakest. The easiest way to get rid of one is to let him know you're taken. Be careful what you deem cute, Clarke," Rush grumbled and offered his hand.

She took it and stood. "It had fangs."

"And a mean bite." He raised a brow. "It's also fire-fae."

"Meaning... it can shift?"

He nodded.

"Into what?"

"Into something that targets single females."

She shivered. "Are all animals to be feared here?"

"No." He glanced at the Order gate and unlinked their hands. "It's better you remain visible now."

Uncertain whether the bond leached his mana, he had to be cautious. Now that he had her, he wanted to make the little time he had left last. He wanted that timeline to be months, not weeks.

She scanned the area and the fortress. "In there?"

He nodded, then shrugged on the rucksack.

"So I just walk up to the gate?" Clarke asked.

"Chances are they know you're coming and they haven't deemed you a threat."

"Why do you say that?"

He shot her a sideways glance. "You're still alive."

Together they walked down the path of trodden sweet grass. A buzzing tingle hit his nose and then passed him as they crossed the magical protection wards set in place. If they didn't know Clarke was there before, they did now.

⚖

"HALT," shouted a Guardian from atop the gate tower. Made from reinforced leather, his helmet sat snuggly over his head so it wasn't easy to determine what kind of fae he was. Rush liked knowing his opponents' strengths and weaknesses before heading in. The guard lifted the visor to see better, and all became clear.

The olive skin was a dead giveaway for vamp. That he worked the day shift must be either punishment or part of his rigorous conditioning. Probably a rookie. No matter what fae race, a Guardian had to be equally reliable in all conditions. Night fae had to be conditioned to function in the sun. Day fae had to get used to seeing in the dark. Nobody enjoyed working on their weaknesses, but the Well had chosen them, so they had no choice.

The vampires in the Guardian cadres could operate at any time of day.

Clarke darted a nervous glance at Rush. "I want to hold your hand," she whispered.

"You'll do fine. Tell them your name and that you're here to see the Prime."

With a lift of her chin, she repeated his words to the guard.

The vamp surveyed her, scrutinized her hair, and then nodded. "We've been expecting you."

Clarke relaxed.

But Rush didn't. This was the first time he'd been back to the place that had been his home for most of his life. When Thaddeus had called for Rush's punishment, the Prime failed to stand up for him. And Jasper, his partner, hadn't stepped in at all. He thought he knew Jasper better than that. That the more seasoned wolf wouldn't bow to the Prime's wishes if she decreed something so heinous. Rush had reasoned away Jasper's reluctance because he knew Jasper avoided any involvement with the Crown due to his heritage. But a part of Rush had always wondered. Maybe they weren't good friends after all. It had done more to deflate his courage than seeing his uncle call for his execution. Jasper's betrayal cut deeper than his thirst for vengeance against his uncle.

It was because the Cadre of Twelve were his family.

The Order was his home.

"Please step through the gate and wait immediately inside." The heavily perspiring guard tugged the collar of his blue coat. It wasn't snowing here, but it also wasn't hot. He was probably at his limits for daytime exposure. The rookie pulled a lever. "I'll be right down."

The arched wooden gate dwarfed them. At least thrice their size, it creaked open on stiff hinges.

Following Clarke through, Rush tried to keep his surreal emotions in check. He saw the campus as though for the first time. Stone buildings with deep red-tiled roofs and high arches were scattered around. Academy on the left, Mage dormitories to the academy's right. Straight ahead, the Guardian barracks housed the soldiers, and to the right, the armory and training fields bustled with activity. Majestically high at the back, lording over the entire campus, stood a moss-covered stone temple sparkling with glistening rivulets of water cascading down from the roof on rain chains.

Landscaped with lush green exotic plants and flowers, the campus was a beautiful sight. Rush could have happily stayed within the grounds most of his life. Many did, preferring the solitude of the library or engagement of the classrooms.

An almighty roar and gust of wind came from the training field. Instead of staying where she was told, as she should have, Clarke's eyes widened in awe and she trotted over to the lawn field surrounded by box hedges.

Two experienced Guardians were in the midst of sparring under the watchful gaze of a group of spectators near the infirmary. A semi-naked crow in angel form and a larger than normal white wolf circled each other. Rush's heart lodged in his throat. The wolf was his son, Thorne. Both had blood streaming down parts of their bodies. Rush narrowed his eyes. The dark-haired, tattooed crow-shifter had a wry smile on his face. One of Rush's old cadre. The wind gust had come from him, either from his wings beating behind his body, or a shot of mana induced air. He half-paced, half-flew around the unnaturally large wolf and twirled his dagger in his hand. Cloud wasn't known for honorable tactics, and the wolf seemed to like it.

Did he have a death wish?

The thought churned in Rush's gut. If Thorne fought Cloud, then he'd joined the ranks of the cadre. Perhaps he'd been promoted to replace the position Rush had left empty.

"Who are they?" Clarke asked, nodding at the couple fighting.

He cleared his throat and folded his arms. "The wolf is... my son."

"Wow."

"His opponent is the crow I told you about who was trapped in Crystal City for a decade in his youth."

"The thief?"

"Now the Order's best assassin."

"He's very..." She lifted her brows, assessing.

"Cruel. Reprobate. Deviant," was Rush's immediate response. Cloud had never done as he was told. He was the unit's nightmare. But he got the job done, and the Well had chosen him. They were stuck with him.

"I was going to say roguishly handsome, but okay, let's go with that. Rep-ro-bate." She made the word roll off her tongue.

A small rumble of possessiveness started in the base of Rush's throat. His inner wolf scratched at the surface of his control. He had been restless since the mating. Normally when a wolf mates another of his kind, the two spend not only days together privately, but time running in the wild. That primitive part of him still wanted out. It wanted to get to know its mate, feed her and play with her. Another rumble of dissent came out of him.

"Oh, settle down," Clarke chuckled softly. "I'm just observing."

"Observe me."

"Tonight." She gave him a placating pat on the arm.

Flexing his fists at his side, he forced his instincts to calm. He would have happily stayed within that room at the inn for days. They needed more time together and until they did, his restlessness wouldn't end.

Where was that damned Prime?

"That wolf is your son." She whistled through her teeth as though impressed. "He's certainly tenacious."

Rush shifted his gaze back to the battle. The wolf had his sharp teeth locked around a black feathered wing. As the wolf tore through it, a collective gasp rippled through the spectators. Black feathers scattered everywhere as though a pillow had burst. Red coated the wolf's jaw, and dribbled down his fur, but Cloud barely reacted. In one smooth motion, he twisted and shifted. For a blink, he wasn't a dark avenging angel, but a crow, flapping and cawing in the air, dagger in its claws.

The leather pants he'd been wearing drifted to the floor.

Rush snorted. "Show off."

"Why?" Clarke asked, eyes wide and fascinated.

"He's shifting without being connected to the land. He's showing the spectators, and his opponent, that his mana stores are high enough, he's confident he doesn't need to be connected to the land to shift back. Most fae need to be physically connected, but some of us Guardians can draw power from the Well from a few feet in the air. It seems the winged fae are best at this."

The crow circled around the wolf and then nose-dived. Just before hitting, the air shimmered around Cloud, and he elongated into fae form, and plunged the dagger into Thorne's white furry spine.

Clarke's hand flew to her mouth.

She soon found panic was not needed. Wolves were quick. Guardians were faster. Thorne had sensed the attack at his rear and rolled on the grassed floor, narrowly evading the blade as it embedded into the ground. Just like Cloud, Thorne shifted back to fae form and used the advantage of his hands to tackle and block his opponent. Both male bodies tumbled, grunted, and wrestled. Cloud could use his air-magic to blast Thorne off him, but he didn't. If memory served correct, Cloud was also adept with lightning. Perhaps he'd spent his cache of mana and hadn't replenished. Or he could be saving it for later. The battle was a display of strategy, of untamed strength and a struggle for domination. Naked and covered in dirt, grass and blood, neither fae gave a damn about spectators watching them in a state of undress. Shifters rarely cared about such human sensitivities.

"Oh my sweet Lord, if Laurel could see this now." Clarke whistled through her teeth. Then she tensed. Her eyes went white. "Rush," she whispered. "I see... I see my friend." She met Rush's stare, her eyes bleeding back to blue. Then she darted a glance to the battlefield. "Laurel is destined for one of them."

"Another like you will come?"

"I think... yes. Not just one, but many more."

They both turned back to the sparring match. Thorne had inherited his parents' silver hair, but unlike them, he wore it buzzed at the sides and a few inches at the top. With the battle, and the recent shift, the leather cord that held the hair out of his eyes had fallen. This was something Cloud was planning on taking advantage of—Rush could see it in the way his dark eyes kept darting to the strands catching the wind.

Cloud, who had short black curls barely long enough to grasp, wasn't beyond using dirty tactics to win.

Did Thorne see this intent in the crow?

A band constricted around Rush's chest. He'd missed so much. It was a regret that thickened his throat every time he thought about it. All he'd wanted over the past few years was to get here, to this point, where he had the means to talk to his son. And now that he was here... he didn't know what to say.

"Miss O'Leary." The gate guard came running up, his hand holding the too big helmet on his head as it drooped to one side. "I told you to wait at the gate."

She waved at the match. "There was something far better to do."

"Be that as it may, the Prime is expecting you."

"Can't I just watch for two more minutes? Please?"

While Clarke engaged in negotiation, Rush continued to scope the spectators. The team leader and a healer usually oversaw a sparring session this brutal. But then again, the Twelve had done whatever they wanted with training. In front of the infirmary, Leaf, the golden-haired and golden-skinned elf stood chatting with a tall, blue-robed male healer with underdeveloped goat's horns on his head.

So Leaf was still the team leader, Rush mused.

Continuing his search, he found another group watching from near the armory. And yet another group watched from near the forge on the opposite side of the field. The only of its kind in all of Elphyne, the forge produced the metal weapons the Guardians used to eliminate errant magical beasts. Among the watching fae, Rush recognized a good handful of his old cadre. The three Unseelie vampires, Shade, Haze and Indigo stood with their black leathery wings half out and their heads together. Knowing Indigo, he probably took bets on which Guardian would win the sparring match. Indi had only joined the Guardians because he thought it would be a grand adventure. Haze was the muscle of the group. With a shoulder span wider than brownies were tall, he'd joined the Order because he felt the incurable need to protect and he was quietly open with his mission. Obviously the Well had thought the same. Shade wanted power. Pure and simple. Rush was surprised Leaf hadn't fallen afoul of some training accident that relinquished him of his team leading duties. But vamps were good at lying in wait.

The hairs on the back of Rush's neck stood up, and every muscle in his body tensed in warning. A lack of sound came from the sparring match. The battle was done. He turned back to the field just in time to see Thorne lift his nose and scent the air in Rush's direction. No, the battle wasn't done, but interrupted. Thorne's sharp gaze snapped their way, but it wasn't Rush he locked his eyes onto. It was Clarke.

CHAPTER
TWENTY-SEVEN

Clarke only had time to register Rush's shout of warning when a large, white-haired and flesh toned *thing* collided with her, taking her to the ground. The wind knocked out of her lungs. Enormous snarling teeth snapped in her face and Clarke could smell the fresh blood on his breath. For the first time since arriving, true terror overwhelmed her.

The muscle-packed, heavy and very naked Viking lookalike pinned her down by the shoulders. Icy blue eyes glowed with adrenaline as he growled through clenched teeth, "Why do you smell like kin?"

But it wasn't the fury from Thorne that terrified Clarke, it was the reaction in Rush. She'd never seen him so close in appearance to his wolf. His eyes turned animalistic, his teeth elongated, and he reached toward Thorne with claw tipped fingers. The blue glyphs on Rush's face sparkled from the expense of his precious mana.

"Stop, Rush!" she shouted, tears in her eyes at what might happen. "You'll hurt yourself."

Please, don't let him use up his reserves. Not on her. Not like this.

"I'm okay. He's not hurting me. I'm okay." She held her palm out toward Rush.

Thorne jerked as though pulled, but it wasn't Rush who'd touched him. It was Clarke's words. Rush barely held onto his restraint.

"Who are you talking to, human?"

"It's him. It's Rush. Your father."

Surprise hit his eyes for a split-second, then he snapped at her and fisted the fabric at her chest. "My father is dead."

She squeezed her eyes shut and wished with all her might. *Please see Rush. Please see him.*

"You had better come up with an explanation, human, or you're—"

"Fuck me," someone said.

She opened her eyes. A group of powerful fae loomed over her, including the one who'd sparred with Thorne. He'd redressed in his leather breeches but stood back with unmistakable hatred in his eyes. The vampire guard looked green and panicked. A golden-haired fae skidded to a halt next to Clarke, wary eyes on Rush.

They could see him! Whatever she had done worked.

"Get off my mate," Rush snarled, eyes on Thorne.

Shit. This was not how Clarke had wanted this meeting to go. "Thorne," she said softly and patted his solid chest. "Please... this will all go much better if you get off me."

Thorne's wild gaze darted from Clarke to Rush, and then to the surrounding crowd. A collection of three winged fae in Guardian uniforms flew in on a dark cloud. Air gusted as they landed. All with similar toned skin and varying shades of dark hair, the trio circled around Rush, prowling for a fight.

As Thorne's grip eased off Clarke, she marked the similarities to his father. They were so alike it was uncanny. They both had a hard edge to their jaw, and a darkness to their eyes that told of untold heartache. But Thorne's eyes were blue, and Rush's were gold. Rush's beard was full, where Thorne's was trimmed close enough for her to see the dimples in his cheeks.

A lick of the unknown in the air had everyone looking to each other, and then at Rush with uncertainty.

"Ah," came a confident female voice from somewhere beyond the male heads. "There you are, Clarke O'Leary. I've been waiting for you. Do get off the lady, D'arn Thorne. She's our guest, and likely to stay for a while."

Thorne's face screwed up with malice. He shot Rush a dark look and then shoved off Clarke. It was hard not to see the clear anguish on Rush's face as he bent to help Clarke up. Choosing between a son and a mate wouldn't be fun. Nor was holding in his instincts when he just wanted to fight.

"I'm sorry," he whispered. "I can't protect you."

"Because there was no need," she answered firmly. "I'm fine. And... they can see you."

Rush wouldn't accept her words as an excuse and ignored those surrounding him, as though he'd mentally shut them out. Every hard line of his body betrayed his struggle. Tension in his shoulders. Jaw pressed hard. Fingers flexing at his sides. Finally, he looked at the fae. God, this must be hard for him. She wanted to reach out to him but didn't want to make him look weak.

A brown-skinned woman with white feathered wings pushed through the circle of Guardians. Ringlets of never ending silver hair flowed around her shoulders. Her Kingfisher blue dress draped from the empire line at her bust all the way to dust the ground as she walked with grace. The white, the brown, and blue came together in such a striking way that Clarke had to pick her jaw off the ground. The fae was beautiful, commanding, and regal all at once. Round face, dark plump lips, large eyes, and a long, slender nose. She gave the appearance of looking down at you without actually doing so.

"You—" Clarke pointed. "You have round ears too."

"Yes," she replied matter-of-factly. "Not all fae have ears like the elves. But most of us have other defining features that distinguish us apart from human. I'm sure you have many more questions about this time." She inclined her head. "We will endeavor to answer all of them." She then turned to Thorne. "You're dismissed. I'll leave it up to your team leader to allocate a suitable penalty for your reproachable behavior here today." She arched a brow at the golden-haired elf who had been watching, as stunned as the rest of them. His Guardian jacket was more embellished than the others in a way that gave him an altogether distinguished appearance. If it weren't for his formal attire, the golden tresses and tanned skin made him look like he belonged on a beach with a surfboard in his hands. "I meant you, D'arn Leaf," the female added. "And then be quick about the council meeting."

"Yes, Prime." He stared at Rush one last time and then gestured at Thorne. A gust of wind came from his hand and propelled Thorne back to the training field. *Magic.* Thorne stumbled, but tried to hold his position against the force of air. Leaf arched a brow. "I think you need to cool down first, Thorne," Leaf said and then nodded at Rush. "You can talk with him later."

From the look in Thorne's eyes, he didn't want to talk with either Rush nor Leaf. He turned and walked away.

The Prime snapped at the rest of them. "Show's over." She clicked her fingers at the rookie guard. "Get back to your post." Then she flapped her wings in irritation. "The rest of you, back to training. And you vampires, enough with the gambling on sparring matches."

The last of them trickled off. She laced her fingers and met Clarke's curious stare. "Right. Let's get on with it then. Follow me."

As the Prime spun, her wings dragged a crescent shape in the sand and left sparkling dust. She strode onward, not looking back to see if Clarke followed or not.

Clarke turned to Rush. "She's not used to people saying no to her, is she?"

He shook his head.

"Do you think I should say no? Just to see what happens?"

She was trying to weasel a smile out of Rush, but he only flattened his lips.

"I wouldn't advise it. She may only be an owl-shifter, and a Seelie, but she didn't get to be Prime by falling there. Her talons are sharp."

CHAPTER
TWENTY-EIGHT

Leaving the training fields behind, Clarke followed the Prime through the campus. With Rush at her side, she attempted to regroup and went over everything she had just learned. So the Prime had been aware of Clarke... She'd even used Clarke's surname and mentioned they'd been waiting for her. Considering it wasn't out of the ordinary to be psychic here, Clarke wondered what these people knew of her shameful past.

Seeing her lover's full-grown son transform into an actual wolf also took some getting used to. Four paws, claws, snarling teeth with blood dripping down his front. An involuntary shudder moved through her. Thaddeus had also been a wolf. These fae were part animal. Even those fae with the black leathery wings. Vampires, but clearly a little different from human mythology.

Wringing her hands, she forced herself to emulate Rush's ever watchful gaze, scanning for potential threats. But the architecture, gardens and citizens demanded attention. Small culverts of flowing turquoise water ran alongside every path. The trickling sound soothed her nerves like a spiritual retreat. Sizable buildings that reminded her of the Byzantine Cathedrals were to her left. Manicured lawns and fountains took up the space between smaller red-roofed buildings. Noticing the direction of her attention, Rush leaned over. "That's the academy and Mage classrooms. All those fae you see wandering the grounds in blue robes are Mages."

"Right." She nodded, then pointed to another set of close and cramped, one-story buildings. "And those?"

"The general barracks where the Guardians sleep. You'll recognize the Guardian uniform on most of those. The two big houses to the back are where the Cadres sleep. The Six are in the dark house. The Twelve are in the light—where the Guardians you saw today live." He cleared his throat. "Where I used to live."

"And where is she taking us?"

"Most likely to the temple for testing, or to her quarters nearby. It's only another few minutes walk. She said *we've* been waiting for you, so I believe other preceptors and council members will also arrive."

Clarke was all out of questions. Her intuition hadn't sparked in warning, so she kept following the Prime. It was a big campus, and the path wove in and out of outbuildings, a mess hall, and a library. The occasional blue-robed female or male walked by and stared oddly but said nothing.

A stone staircase rose up two levels from where Clarke stood at its base. At the top of the stairs, she saw a flat, red roof.

The Prime stopped and eyed Clarke's surroundings as though she were looking for something, or someone.

The Prime narrowed her white-tipped lashes on Clarke. "Has he gone, or is your hold on your mana slipping?"

"I don't understand. You mean Rush?" She glanced at him standing next to her. "He's right there. Can't you see him anymore?"

The Prime replied, "If he was visible earlier, but not now, your hold on your mana slipped. We can teach you to keep hold of the spell you wove to make Rush visible. First, you must prove to the others you are what we think you are."

"And what is that? You've told me nothing."

The Prime pinched the bridge of her nose and took a deep breath before responding.

"There have been Seers since the dawn of Elphyne who have predicted your arrival Clarke O'Leary. We have been waiting for you for a very long time. For some, too long, and they need a little convincing that you are who you say you are, and that the prophecies are real."

Prophecies?

"I'm sorry," Clarke said. "But—again—who, or what, do you think I am?"

"Both the destroyer and the savior. The darkness and the light. Chaos and order. You, my dear, are the first Well-blessed human to exist. Only you can lead us to more of your kind."

The shiver started slight. It began as an icy finger trailing up Clarke's spine, then a scrape, until it became a full drop in body temperature. Goosebumps broke out on her skin and she hugged herself.

"I..." She didn't know what to say. Hearing it laid out like that made it sound so important. So real. So dangerous. But what else had she been trying to do all this time? There was no going back. She came here to stop the Void from repeating what he did in her time.

"Look," she started, then paused, and tried to come up with a better way to say what she needed. But there was no sugar coating it. "Yes, I had an unfortunate hand in destroying the old world. I never intended it to happen. I admit to having a certain culpability. But I'm not a savior. I came here to tell you what I know about some bad people who may also have awoken from my time. I came to tell you, so you can help stop the evil man. I had a vision about him invading Elphyne for resources. Metals I know are used to make weapons. I'll help you fight him. Do you understand?"

The Prime stilled in a way that was more telling than if she'd revealed some sort of expressional twist of the features.

"What I understand is that this is a lot for you to take in. You have been preserved in ice for a long time, yet the Well has deemed now is the time for your awakening. There is a reason you awoke. Events are in play. And we need your help. This world is vastly changed from yours, and you need training to understand your gifts."

"You don't know me."

"We know more than you think."

Clarke clenched her jaw. Helplessness was just a sliver away from her resolve. It was like her composure dangled at the base of a thin frayed thread, and one more tug would send her falling. She didn't want this woman to think she was weak. She wasn't. It was just... sometimes... she feared being taken advantage of. She needed to investigate these people, to assess them, and then to make an informed decision. They had done nothing to aid her at the moment.

"I want you to lift Rush's curse," Clarke stated.

The Prime's gaze turned downcast. "We cannot lift his curse, I'm afraid."

"What?" Clarke sputtered. "You can. *You* put the curse on him. It wasn't his fault."

"Clarke," Rush intoned and then shook his head.

But she wasn't giving up. "In what world does it make sense for a good man to be punished because of a moment of oversight?"

The Prime's white brows rose. "You tell me, Clarke. What world do you know where a moment of oversight that causes devastating effects can go unpunished?"

The damned female knew exactly how that comment would cut deep. It wasn't Clarke who had paid the price. It was everyone else.

The Prime's poker face did nothing to convince Clarke of her integrity. She pointed at the Prime. "You're lying."

She held out her hand as an offering. "Take it and ask me again if you must."

Clarke strode closer, gripped the woman's warm, silken hand in hers and asked, "Tell me how to break Rush's curse."

"The only way to break it is for his Well-blessed union to snap into place."

Clarke looked into the Prime's large eyes and concentrated. Nothing came through her gift. The Prime spoke the truth. Clarke dropped her hand.

"I refuse to believe that you people, who made the curse, have no other way of breaking it."

"I regret you feel that way, Clarke."

Rush said nothing. He was probably used to more disappointment, but she wasn't. She would find a way, even if that meant scouring that extensive library she'd seen, talking to every single fae in this place, or forcing someone to tell her. She would see Rush freed.

"Now, if you don't mind." The Prime gestured up the steps. "The council have gathered and are waiting."

The Prime hiked her blue dress at the knees and slipped off her sandals. Giving Clarke's boots a pointed look, she then added, "Please instruct your beau to do the same. I'm sure he hasn't been away so long he's forgotten proper temple etiquette."

Rush rolled his eyes and tugged his boots off. He laid them next to the Prime's sandals. The moment he let go of them, the Prime looked down.

"Ah. Now I can see them."

Clarke added her own shoes next to the pair. She was careful not to place it too close to the running water falling down the steps and disappearing into a grate.

She followed the owl-shifter up the steps and couldn't help the curl of her lip. She should feel better than this, but the knot of tension in her stomach wouldn't leave. She'd thought these fae would help Rush, but it was sounding more like they would use her. And the sheer lack of empathy really grated on her.

She glanced at Rush. Sometimes he acted as though he cared, other times she thought he acted without empathy—like when he'd brushed off the two fae stuck in the cages. Was it because he didn't want to get involved in politics so he had closed that part of himself off? Anise had accused Caraway of the same thing.

But maybe it had to do with years lived on this earth. Maybe the Prime was many years older than him. As usual, with the thought came the swell of rightness sitting in her chest. Yes, the Prime was old. Older than Rush.

It had been two thousand years since Clarke's time. That was a long time to live. One could get emotionally weary from living that long.

They crested the top of the stairs and found a stone courtyard. Split into quadrants, each corner held a small colored pond with a pike coming out of the center. And in the middle of the courtyard was a larger pool, about two yards in diameter. The stone obelisk coming out of it had etchings similar in shape and size to Rush's blue glyphs.

Water dribbled down rain chains into the courtyard culverts, which then fed into the small ponds, which then fed into the streams running down the steps. It was all rather intricate, serene, and magical.

Six figures emerged from the temple doors. Three of the figures wore the blue robes of Mages, two female and one male. The other three were Guardians Clarke recognized. The golden one the Prime had called Leaf stood with his arms folded and a stiff posture. Next to him stood a vampire with black leathery wings. His short brown hair looked cover model ready and matched his soulful eyes. Sensual yet commanding. As if to prove status, he snapped his wings closed, and then they disappeared. His smug smile revealed short fangs.

The third Guardian was Cloud, the crow-shifter who had sparred with Thorne. The same jacket stretching across his shoulders looked extra wicked. Maybe it was because of the dark, oil slick tattoos gracing parts of his neck and hands, or maybe it was because the jacket was worn and cultivated, as though it had seen its fair share of torment, and dished out plenty. He stood leaning against the waist-high stone vase filled with pink blossoms, looking rather put out. She could almost feel his disgust roll onto her.

If this Guardian was treated poorly in the human city, then Clarke didn't blame him for having preconceived emotions towards her race. She may very well be the first human he'd associated with since.

"Clarke," the Prime started. "This is the Council of the Order of the Well."

"Try saying that five times real fast," Clarke joked.

It was the crow who snorted in amusement. The rest of them glared at Clarke.

"Sorry," she whispered. Temples weren't made for jokes, but religion had never been her strong suit. And she was nervous. "I guess, nice to meet you all. I'm Clarke O'Leary."

"Where is Jasper?" Rush asked suddenly. He went to the lip of the courtyard and looked down at the view of the grounds. Fae still swarmed about.

"Who's Jasper?" she asked him.

But one of the Mages answered. "Jasper has not been with us for a few years."

The Mage's robe was stained with green and brown bits. Twigs and leaves were stuck in his streaky long hair. His fae race was indeterminate, but he reminded Clarke of a wizard. He was the first fae she'd seen with some wrinkles around his eyes.

"He's missing," Leaf clarified.

Rush turned back sharply and locked eyes on Leaf. "For how long?"

"Wait. I'll translate in a minute." Clarke put up her finger to Rush. "Who is Jasper?"

Rush didn't answer. He began circling the room, scrutinizing the council members. They knew she'd spoken with him, but they couldn't see him, so stood awkwardly awaiting Clarke's signal that she'd received her answer. Rush began to poke and flick lint from their shoulders. He was clearly enjoying being invisible, so she didn't try to make him seen.

The Prime tugged on her ear lobe, irritated. "Enough. It's time to have you tested, Clarke."

"She must be initiated first." One of the female Mages stepped forward. Like the Prime, her skin was brown but her long curly hair was prismatic like a rainbow, as were her dormant dragonfly wings. Even her skin held a metallic sheen. "Anyone who steps into the sacred water must be initiated first."

"Dawn?" The Prime turned to the third and final fae Clarke hadn't heard speak. This one was not only quiet but seemed a world away. A jade butterfly clip held her short hair back from her eyes. Short, stocky, and with curling horns coming out of her head, she reminded Clarke of the same ilk as one of Thaddeus's hunters. Except where that one couldn't pronounce his name correctly, this female looked wise beyond her years. There was a reason the Prime asked for her opinion.

Dawn blinked and stared at the Prime. "Please repeat."

"Colt has suggested Clarke submit to the initiation ritual before she is tested. Your thoughts?"

Dawn's short fingers lifted to touch the butterfly clip and her eyes faded from blue to a glossy white. With a start, Clarke realized she was a Seer. The clip looked like a focusing tool.

"She's already been initiated." Dawn released the pin.

"Impossible."

"Can't be."

More dissent rumbled through the council. The Prime lifted a casual palm. "Please explain, Dawn."

"Her time underground has served as exposure to the Well. There is no point to initiate her in the lake. She's been in a permanent initiation ceremony for… millennia. You will see once we test her."

"Very well." The Prime motioned to the center pool with the obelisk. "You may enter now."

"Like, step into it?" She looked to Rush for clarification, but he was peeking inside the robe pocket of the male Mage.

Okay, then. She guessed she would just step into the pond. What was the worse that could happen?

She padded over barefoot to the pool. The icy water looked about a foot deep, so she rolled up the hem of her pants and then stepped in. Shock-waves of shivers wracked her body. She raised a brow and looked at the Prime.

"Now what?"

"Now touch the obelisk."

Clarke found the stone warm. Within seconds of touching, her will was ripped from her. A zing sizzled up her arm and held her in place. A bright light exploded, blinding Clarke and everyone nearby. It was white, hot and celestial. It felt alive. Light and heat invaded her body, getting to know her in a way that she had yet to give permission. It burned her nerves raw. A voice came from a distance, almost like a whisper.

"You can let go now."

She pulled away from the obelisk. The light dimmed. It took her a while for her eyes to adjust to the courtyard ambience. Even though swathed in daylight, the obelisk luminosity made the courtyard now seem dark.

"What did you say?" she asked.

Slowly her surroundings came into focus. Their expressions were no longer filled with disgust or thinly veiled wariness. Now they feared her.

"What's going on?"

"How long were you touching the obelisk, Clarke?" the Prime asked.

"A couple of seconds? Why?"

The Prime looked around. "It is late afternoon. If you didn't come out of your trance soon, your mate was readying to tear down the temple."

Clarke's eyes gravitated to Rush. Standing to her right, with one foot in the pool, he had dark circles under his eyes. "Are you okay?" she asked.

"I would ask you the same thing."

"He alludes to your extended period in stasis," the Prime added. "And yes, I can see him, although he appears to be fading. The illumination you cast upon touching the obelisk was the light of truth. I imagine that once you test yourself for elemental affinities, you'll be very heavily geared towards the spiritual energies. I dare say that one day you'll be able to use truth as a weapon."

"Lady, you're speaking in tongues to me." Clarke rubbed her eyes again. The weight of the event was dragging her down. How could she have been standing there for so long… hours it had seemed. "What was the point of touching that thing?"

She accepted Rush's hand and stepped out of the pond. For a brief moment, everyone lost sight of her and she considered running away with Rush. But then he let go, and his curse pulled away from her, casting her into the light.

"It proved what your capacity for holding mana is."

"And?"

"And if you weren't Well-blessed, you'd hardly trigger a glow."

"I made it go nuclear." The word left a bitter taste in her mouth. "Why was it so bright?"

"Because you are very strong in your gift. Perhaps the strongest we have ever encountered, even among the fae. You may be able to go days at full strength without having to replenish. Weeks. Months."

"At full strength. So not like how Rush is using the minimum to stay alive."

"That's right. If you conserve your mana, you could perhaps last centuries."

"How is that fair?" Cloud snapped. No longer leaning against the stone vase, he was sitting reclined against it. "She's human. The Well doesn't reward greed. She must have stolen it."

"Just because you like the five-finger discount, Cloud, doesn't mean everyone else does," the vampire drawled.

"I don't steal mana, ass-face."

Ha! Clarke almost laughed out loud. It was good to see some things, like cursing out your friends, never went out of style. And it amused her to no end that, in a way, Cloud was right. She had spent most of her life as a petty thief. So, apparently, was he.

"It is not for us to decide who gains power from the Well." Leaf strode over and gestured at both vampire and crow. "We would have chosen better on more than one occasion."

Shade's and Cloud's wings snapped out and hovered. Tension vibrated in the air as all three Guardians faced off. It seemed a common occurrence. The Mages sighed, and the Prime pressed her lips. Rush stood with his arms folded, and a wistful smile, as if this were something he missed.

But Clarke was over it. Her muscles ached from standing in one position for too long. She rubbed her temples and turned to the Prime. "Are we finished here?"

The Prime glanced at the four other pools and a sinking feeling settled in Clarke. She thought she might have to do the same in all of them, but the Prime nodded.

"Tomorrow," the Prime said, "We will begin your training at first light and test for affinity to the elements. For tonight, D'arn Leaf will take you to your room. I'm sure D'arn Rush can take care of giving you a tour of the grounds and point out the mess hall for future meals. You are dismissed."

CHAPTER
TWENTY-NINE

Many thoughts coalesced as Rush followed Clarke to the Guardian barracks. From the moment the curse glyphs had covered half his body a few years ago, his mental state had shifted. No longer content to ride out his exile finding new adventures to occupy his time, he'd been consumed with thoughts of his legacy, and at that point, there had been nothing to be proud of. His curse had prevented him from teaching his son to be the best possible fae he could be, and it stopped him from so many other things. He'd always thought he'd be the kind of parent to make his own proud, but from the start, he never had the chance.

Clarke was the glaring symbol of a reward he didn't feel he deserved. What had he done to merit the little slice of happiness she'd given him?

Rush's top lip lifted at the thought of how the Prime had reacted to meeting Clarke. Every protective instinct flared to life at the proprietary glint in the Prime's eyes. She had stared openly while they lost Clarke to the obelisk, and those big cynical eyes had seen everything. The future. The past. She calculated like a god. He knew it because he knew the Prime. She'd been the same when he was at the Order. It hadn't escaped his attention that she'd referred to Rush as D'arn, the same as she'd done with Leaf. It was their official Guardian title.

After all this time, why would she make the move to include him as one of the group? As though she'd never insisted he be cursed into exile. The female was up to something, and Clarke and he were in the middle of it. They were pawns in her game against the humans, or even potentially just within the realm. He intended to find out how far this plan of hers stretched, because he was under no illusion that if they weren't careful, neither Clarke nor Rush would come out of it intact.

Because he was lost in his thoughts, Rush failed to notice Leaf had bypassed the barracks and gone straight to the cadre house until they were upon the doorstep. The two-story behemoth had twelve private suites, a separate kitchen, and rooms for entertainment. The Twelve had earned their privacy through blood, sweat and kills.

Leaf took them inside and up the flight of stairs. He veered left down a red-carpeted corridor and stopped at the last door. Suspicion and disbelief coursed through him. This was his old quarters. He'd spent a century beyond that door. He put his palm to the wood and felt the memories: the proud day he'd arrived after being promoted at age forty-nine; the time Jasper had given him his first taste of mana-weed, and then the day after spent sleeping with a headache. As punishment for his tardiness, they had forced him to wash every window of the house. Jasper had laughed the entire time. But he'd also pitched in at the end.

"This is Rush's old room," Leaf said to Clarke. "I don't know if he's listening, but you can tell him we kept it untouched since he left." He paused, then added, "Upon orders of the Prime."

"Thank you," Clarke murmured.

Leaf pushed open the door. "There should be refreshments waiting for you. Someone will collect you at sunup."

"Am I a prisoner?" she asked.

"Not at all. But your tour will have to wait for another time, and exploring the grounds without a guide can be dangerous. You never know what concoctions the Mages have created." He scanned her up and down. "And if you come across any of the Six, run in the opposite direction."

"Who?"

"They're the cadre next door. All members are Sluagh and were part of the horde that led the Wild Hunt. Some say they still kidnap humans, so... stay away."

Leaf left and Rush followed Clarke inside. He shut the door behind them.

"He shouldn't scare you like that," Rush murmured.

"I can take it."

He smiled at her and then took in the room. Time reversed and his breath lodged in his throat with every memory his gaze landed on. *There* was Starcleaver's carved slice in the wall—an accident upon being gifted it for the first time. *There* was the stain on the carpet when he'd spilled mally-root wine. And *there* was the king-sized bed, made with its blue quilt and soft velvet pillows and most likely still complete with the squeak in the frame. Never in his wildest dreams had he imagined being back there, let-alone with a woman, a mate. It wasn't as though Guardians were forbidden to mate, it was just discouraged. They lived a dangerous life. Short dalliances were encouraged.

"I'm sorry about what the Prime said."

"What?"

"About your curse." Clarke frowned. "I wish I could have... I don't know, made her tell another truth. I wish what she said was different." Her face hardened. Rush had never seen such fire light up in her eyes. "I can promise you this, Rush. I will find a way. I'll stake my life on it. She might think she's my boss, but she's not."

The kiss he gave was everything he couldn't say. He wanted that to be true, but no one argued with fate. Fate was the tie that bound... and bound... and bound until it choked you in your own misery.

Her eyes had glazed and he let go of her, satisfied with the smile he'd left on her lips. He turned to inspect the room.

"Oh my sweet lord," Clarke murmured, and rushed over to a tray of food left near the settee on the opposite side of the room near the window. She began shoveling morsels into her mouth as though this was her last chance. A smile touched his lips. She ate with as much passion as she loved, making murmurs of appreciation with every taste.

"Hungry?"

She nodded and replied through a mouthful, "If I don't eat, I'm going to faint."

He left her devouring and paced around the sleeping chambers, getting reacquainted with the place. He ran his finger across the fireplace mantle. No dust. The bed had no residual scent, meaning no one had slept in it for a long time. He moved onto the bathing chambers. Clean and polished. A fresh bouquet of jasmine flowers was in a glass vase by the sink. The large tub and toilet were spotless and scentless. Maybe a hint of ginger and lemongrass beyond the jasmine. The house brownies still used the same products. Moving into the sitting room, he sat on the claw foot sofa and tested the cushion. The seat creaked, just like his bed.

He smiled.

Nothing had changed.

One last place in his suite to check. The storeroom. Before, it was filled with his clothes and weapons. He'd taken nothing into exile. Nothing except what he wore, including the Guardian jacket and Starcleaver. He pushed open the door and found everything was as he left it. No... not quite. He pushed aside the hanging jackets and found new female garments that smelled like lavender. Tension pulled across his shoulders. The clothes were like the style Clarke preferred to wear. No dresses. Just blouses and pants.

Gravity shifted. Horror dawned on him.

They knew Rush and Clarke would arrive back here one day. They knew what she would wear, and what perfume she preferred. The Prime had mentioned she'd been waiting for Clarke to arrive for a very long time. Perhaps even longer than Rush was cursed.

He slammed the jackets back into place and left the storeroom. Like a rising storm, every muscle and vein in his body filled with pressure. He couldn't see straight. His teeth hurt. And his fists sought something to punch.

He entered his room and found Clarke curled into a ball on the bed. He stopped still. The storm whisked away. Clarke. She was his calm. The very scent and sight of her so pure and vulnerable in his bed, heated his heart and filled it once more. She opened one eye and squinted at him. With a moan, she said, "I ate too fast and now I feel sick."

A rush of endorphins crashed through him. How could he tell this woman that since her arrival in this time she'd been a pawn in someone else's game? This fierce woman who insisted on doing things her way had been played, just like him. How much of their relationship was real? How much had been calculated and manipulated? Forcing himself to exhale and reveal nothing of his revelation, he strode to the bed. He brushed his knuckles across her cheekbones and then gently tugged the torn strap from her hair. "You won't need to hide your ears here."

She nodded and closed her eyes.

"Do you need anything, princess?" he asked.

She shook her head and then burrowed her face into the pillow. "It doesn't smell like you," she murmured.

"It's been a long time since I slept in this bed." He tugged down the duvet and shifted her so she was underneath. Then he covered her and tucked her in. Unable to resist, he brushed the hair from her face.

She caught his hand and tugged him down to her. "Sleep with me now."

His body moved before he'd allowed it, and he knew she'd always have this effect on him. He would do anything she asked. And that was dangerous.

He laid down behind her and flattened a hand against her stomach. She rolled to face him and lifted her nose to his neck. Inhaling deeply, she sighed on the exhale and then hugged him close. "Much better."

"Yes."

Much better. But only if he ignored the blue glow glancing off her face.

CHAPTER

THIRTY

While Rush laid next to his mate, feeling the soft push of breath on his face, he could only think of what he'd learned.

Everything.

The Prime's talons had been in *every* part of his life since birth. Scheming, shifting, rearranging. As Clarke softened and drifted to sleep, Rush's resolve hardened into an unbending desire for retribution. The Prime wouldn't get away with this. He'd dedicated his life to the preservation of the Well, to staying out of fae politics and to using his enhanced abilities for her prerogative only. This was the thanks he got.

He wasn't so expendable that they could throw him away. He would show her he was made of something more than trash. More than a second thought. More than a death sentence.

Rush waited until Clarke fell asleep and then left her in his bed.

Stalking down the hallway out of the house, he heard hushed voices in one of the entertaining rooms. Usually the cadre congregated at the end of a long day. They unwound with some ale, some wine, and the occasional misfit Mage in their lap.

He came up to the wooden doorframe of the games room and paused. It was cracked open. Obviously they weren't smart enough to keep it closed. If he wanted to, he could enter, and they'd forget they'd seen the door open, but he didn't want to risk the off chance that one of them remembered.

"I think if the Well chose her, then what more is there to say?" said a husky male voice he didn't recognize. Probably a new member of the Twelve since his time. Or one he'd forgotten.

"If the Well told you to jump off a cliff, would you do it?" This voice Rush knew well. Cloud.

"Now you're being overly dramatic." Shade's drawl was unmistakable. It surprised

Rush that he wasn't out securing his meal. The vamps hunted at night, and like all living creatures, needed to feed daily.

"What do you think, Thorne," Leaf said. "You're the one closest to this."

Rush's ears perked up.

"How so?" came the gruff response. "The only link I have to that wolf is my blood. There is nothing else that binds us."

Rush's ears went down and he fixated on a chip in the wooden doorframe.

"Blood is strong," said Shade. "And there is fate."

"Fuck fate," Thorne replied. "Fate tells us that Jasper's disappearance is part of some divine plan. It's not a coincidence he's missing. I say we find him. At least we'd be doing something."

Leaf grumbled. "No. We don't get involved. If Jasper is gone, it's the king's doing. We stay out of it."

A thump sounded as though something was hit. "How can you say that? He's one of us."

Silence, and then another whispered. "I can't say that seeing Rush today was an unwelcome sight."

Rush strained his ears and tried to place the voice. Someone he knew. But who? Indigo?

"That Well-damned bastard is still wearing a beard as though it makes him look tougher."

"Yeah. It was good to see him."

A few of them chuckled, but it was a warm laugh, not teasing. Rush rubbed his beard self-consciously. That's not why he grew it. It kept his jaw warm. The mountains were cold.

That familiar voice spoke again. "You may not be happy with your father, Thorne, but he is just the unfortunate victim of the same fate you hate so much. Dare I say he feels the same way."

It was Haze. The big vampire who'd been with Shade at the sparring match. Rush never expected him of all people to stick up for him. Haze was quiet, he kept to himself, and he rarely opened his mouth to voice an opinion. But in retrospect, it was always Haze who stepped in quietly to do the right thing. Perhaps the last fifty years had brought him out of his shell.

"Yeah, well, even unfortunate victims of fate can still take control."

"That's not exactly fair—" Leaf started, but Rush heard the stomp of booted feet approach the door. He jumped out of the way just in time to see Thorne storm off down the hall and disappear into his suites.

A coldness ran through Rush like a knife. Thorne had been right. Rush had been around. He wasn't dead. He'd seen it all go down. Thorne's mistreatment. Kyra being run out of the Hollow by Thaddeus. If Rush hadn't been so stuck in his self-pity, maybe he could have come up with a way to help keep Kyra in her home town. Maybe even put her up as the new alpha. She was strong enough.

He didn't need to hear anymore. It wasn't Thorne or anyone else who held his quarrel. It was the Prime.

THE EYRIE WAS cold and dark when Rush arrived. The Prime's house was grand, majestic and three levels high. It also had a platform on the roof where she took flight, either in her owl form, or her preferred angel.

With Starcleaver unsheathed, Rush stepped up to the front stained-glass door and tested the knob. Unlocked. Was she so confident in her status that she believed she was untouchable? Rush knew one thing about winged fae. The higher they flew, the harder they fell.

He opened the door and went in, locking it behind.

He cared little for the ancient artifacts Cloud had procured for her. From the porcelain statues of little gnomes with red hats, to the glass picture frames holding a smiling old-world family inside. Once, the entrance foyer used to be awe-inspiring. Not anymore.

He failed to even give her a blink of respect. This female was about to have her comeuppance.

Sniffing her out, he followed the rose and ash scent to find her sitting in her office, in the dark, tapping her finger on a stack of papers.

The moment he stepped in the room, she lifted her head and stared right at him. "It's about time you came to see me."

CHAPTER
THIRTY-ONE

Clarke awoke the following morning with a start. She pushed her hand out of the sheets and found no warm body. And then she realized she'd dreamed, she knew Rush was not there. Sweeping the room with her gaze, she found him sitting on the settee, asleep but holding Starcleaver unsheathed and balanced on his lap as though he expected trouble.

A knock pounded at the door, and a male voice filtered through. "Rise and shine, human."

Her eyebrow lifted with a wry tug. She'd bet that was the crow.

"I'm up!" she shouted, in case he burst through the door and woke the sleeping wolf, not even understanding she'd just done the very same thing.

She slapped her palm on her face. It was too early to make decisions. Rush's eyes popped open.

"Sorry," she said. "Didn't mean to wake you."

"You have fifteen minutes and then you're expected for training," said the crow through the door.

"Got it!" She threw off the duvet and padded over to the tray with the food. God, she was hungry all the time since arriving at the Order.

Rush rubbed his eyes. Registering he held his sword, he casually sheathed it in the baldric he still wore, and then joined her at the table. Every nerve ending in her body pinged with his arrival, and her hormones were very aware of the hard, flat torso in the vicinity as he reached past her and plucked a grape from the half-eaten bunch. His brows puckered as he looked at the seemingly perfect grape.

"Is everything okay?" she asked.

The scowl on his face wasn't there when he'd woken.

The only way she could describe his expression was shell-shocked. "Rush? What's wrong?"

"Nothing. Sweet fuck all, in fact."

She laughed. "I swear hearing you say that word cracks me up. Some things never change."

"What do you mean?"

"The curse words."

"Same as in your time?"

"Shit. Fuck. Asshole. Most of the big ones are the same."

"Huh. I guess we like them." He popped the grape into his mouth and then lifted his arms and stretched grandiosely. She pretended to eat, but watched from beneath her lashes. She enjoyed seeing the way his skin played over the tendons in his neck, and the way his Adam's apple bobbed when he swallowed. He caught her looking at him on the down stretch, and a slow smile curved his lips.

"I'm hungry," she announced stupidly.

"I can see."

She blushed. "I mean... you know what I mean. Jeeze. Okay. I meant that too, and if I'm being honest, I don't care if you know it. I was too tired for round two last night, but just you wait, Wolfie. You wait for tonight."

He gathered her into his arms and looked down at her with amusement. "Tonight you will be even more tired. And the next night. And the next. Training is brutal, even for Mages."

"Is that what they want me to be?" She scrunched her nose. "They don't own me. I make my own rules."

Something flickered in his expression and the last of the ease with which he'd awoken dissipated. Gone was the sleeping wolf, and in its place, a hunter. The determined set of his jaw and distance in his eyes told her he kept secrets, but she didn't push him. They may be none of her business. If they were, they would come to her eventually, whether on their own, or from his mouth. She'd find out.

She had plenty to think about. Like, how to get information about the curse. Who did it? Who designed it? And who had the power to break it. Whatever the Prime had said, Clarke refused to believe. Something had been playing on her mind since her conversation with her the previous day. She'd said the Well had chosen Clarke. That because she had been kept in a frozen state, she was imbued with more magic than others in this time. Clarke knew other evil people who'd awoken from her time.

Did that mean the Well had chosen them too? Or was it all chaotic bullshit?

There were only two feasible explanations as far as she understood. One was that the Well was not the sentient deity or cosmic know-all they believed. It wasn't a God who picked. It was pure, simple, random shit. Perhaps it was even steeped in science, something the people in this time seemed to lack. For all she knew, the reason people were "Well-blessed" was because of some genetic anomaly.

If that were true, then how did she explain her own psychic abilities?

Taking a grape and eating, she thought of the second possibility for Bones to be awake in this time. Cheating. He and his boss, the Void—she shivered—had orchestrated their preservation from their time until now. Perhaps it was their plan all along. The world was too big back then for domination. Those mana stains on the dead satyr body outside Crescent Hollow came to mind. Rush had said it looked like mana had been wrenched from his body.

There were too many unanswered questions in her head, and she had to investigate. One thing was certain, she would not have her story written by someone else's pen. She'd done enough of that in her time.

"There are extra clothes for you in the storeroom." Rush moved to another room. He came back with an outfit on a wooden hanger.

Clarke smoothed her touch over the softness of the blue blouse and then stroked the navy linen pants. "Did you get this last night for me? Was that why you'd left the bed?"

He gave her a tight-lipped smile.

"You're so sweet." She kissed him on the cheek, and then took the outfit with her to the bathroom. Once dressed and relieved, she joined him in the main room to find he'd done the same. Gone was his worn and beaten Guardian jacket, in was a long-sleeved navy sweater that hugged his frame, and a pair of leather pants that did equal justice to his behind. More of his blue markings were visible. It didn't escape Clarke's notice that he'd discarded the old jacket in the hearth. But he said nothing about it as he slipped the baldric over his shoulder and strapped it to his torso.

"We'll find you more food downstairs," he said.

She was almost out the door when she remembered something forgotten on the nightstand next to the bed. Hurrying over, she collected the scrap of torn fabric she'd used as a headband. She wrapped it around her wrist. She may not need to cover her ears there, but she still liked to think of him every time she looked at it. Lastly, she took the sundial and tried to jimmy it into her pockets.

"I'll find a leather cord so you can wear that around your neck," Rush said.

"I'd love that." She signed her thanks.

He shot her an amused look and then guided her out the door.

In the kitchen, two shirtless Guardians ate breakfast at the center bench. Leaf, and a rather tall, dark and buff fae. As big in frame as Caraway, he would have made a good bodybuilder in her time. He could lift a car with those biceps and thick thighs. Buzzed hair. Tiny bone studs pierced the lobe of a pointed ear. Intricate tattoos down one side of his torso curved in and out of the line of his anatomy as though they were a part of him.

Irritation vibrated off Rush. His gaze darkened upon seeing their state of undress. Quickly, she nabbed a small round piece of fruit off the counter, and then bit into it. Juicy, sweet, and a little tart. Almost like water, but not. She chewed loudly and looked at the two fae, now staring at her with uneasy hesitation.

"If I had known the dress code was tits out, I would have worn something else," she said.

Rush rolled his eyes. But her joke had done the trick. It distracted him.

The large fae scratched his lower stomach in a way only a male could get away with. He studied her with curiosity. His deep baritone almost rattled her ribcage. "We've not met, human."

"It's Clarke. Not *human*. I'd appreciate it if you just called me that. Please."

He gave a grunt. "I'm Haze."

"Nice to meet you, Haze."

He bared his fangs in a way she supposed was a smile. "Long night. I'm off to bed."

Leaf nodded and then eyed Clarke. "Cloud will be back soon to escort you to the academy."

"Right," she said. "Training. And what exactly am I training for?"

The fae shrugged. "That's a question for the Prime."

"Okay. When will I see her? I have many questions."

Leaf grabbed another piece of fruit and shrugged. "No one has seen her since last night. She's probably out."

Rush made a sound that drew Clarke's attention, but by the time she looked his way, his face was expressionless.

"Out?" Clarke prompted.

"The Prime answers only to herself and the Well. I have known her to disappear for weeks on end, especially when she seeks answers and wants to consult the Well. With your arrival yesterday, I'm not surprised she's gone."

"Where does one go to consult the Well?" she asked.

"Ceremonial lake."

"Excuse me, coming through." A high-pitched feminine voice was the only warning before Clarke got jostled to the side by a waist high figure. Another holding a full tray of food was immediately behind her. Clarke bopped out of the way with a squeak.

Her eyes widened at the two... small fae. They looked like someone put little old ladies into an oven and shrink-wrapped them. Small, leathery and wrinkly, but with smile lines around their lips and eyes. Fuzzy hair grew on their skin in the most random places. Tufts out of their ears. Whiskers besides their noses. Their knuckles were big and their nails were long. Both wore a luxurious silk ribbon in their long braids. One was red, the other yellow.

Seeing her gaping maw, Rush explained, "House brownies."

"Almost done with the jobs," clipped the yellow-ribboned one, all business like, as she pushed the tray of food onto the center kitchen bench. The other paused and looked at Clarke with a scowl.

"What are you looking at, human?"

"I... um."

Leaf jumped in rather frantically. "She means no offense, Jocinda. She's never seen brownies as beautiful as you and your sister. I'm afraid you've left her rather speechless."

He gave Clarke a warning flair of his eyes.

"Um. Yes, I'm so sorry if I was rude. I love the ribbons in your hair. Stunning." She showed them the scrap around her wrist. "Mine's nowhere near as beautiful."

The brownie's hand fluttered to her braid, and she gave a grunt of approval, then finished busying herself with removing the old food and tidying the kitchen. Then the two of them left.

Leaf waited a full minute before turning to Clarke. "Don't offend the brownies unless you'd like to clean the house on your own. I find a well-timed compliment puts them at ease."

"Are they insecure?"

"It's common courtesy."

Then he nabbed a bread roll, filled it with some meat and then left.

Clarke found Rush eating and trying to hold in a laugh.

"What?" she said. "How was I supposed to know?"

"I could have warned you, but where's the fun in that?"

She threw her remaining fruit at him, which he dodged and then eyed the mess on the floor. "Don't let the brownies see you making a mess."

"Shut up." She cleaned it up and tossed the pip into the trash can by the stove when Cloud came in, dragging his feet.

Today he didn't have his wings out. He appeared to be a normal, every day fae. One with a dangerous glint in his eye and angry tattoos and scars on his hands.

They stared. And stared. But damn her if she blinked first.

"I suppose we should get this over with," he grumbled, and then walked away.

She trailed behind him down the hall and noticed his particular Guardian jacket wasn't the same as Rush's. At first glance, yes. But on closer inspection, the back panel was made of the same leather with Kingfisher blue piping. The panels weren't stitched together at the seams. Slots, she realized. Slots for his wings to push through if he deemed them necessary.

On their way out, they passed the darkened living room where another vampire—the model type from the council—sat on a couch, legs sprawled and hands on the hips of a top-naked female sitting on his lap as she necked him and grounded her hips against his. He leaned his head back on the couch and slid his lazy, hooded gaze to Clarke as she walked by. Parting his sensual lips, he licked an errant drop from his blood-stained fangs. His tongue was very pointy.

Desire was a heady bouquet in the air. It pulsed at Clarke from across the room, quickening her breath as though she'd walked straight into a sex dream. The Mage's moans of pleasure increased as she rocked against Shade. Still watching Clarke, the vampire lowered his lips to the Mage's neck. He lapped with erotic gratification at a wound Clarke barely noticed. His eyes twinkled as though he knew exactly what heated reaction his feeding triggered in Clarke.

Suddenly Clarke caught a face full of brooding snow-wolf shifter. Rush scowled down at her. His ears twitched in irritation. "It's rude to watch a vampire feed."

"Well he shouldn't do it in clear view, should he?" she hissed and then jogged out the front door feeling as flustered as if she'd been the one on Shade's lap.

Shade's laughter echoed behind her.

Hot on Cloud's trail, Clarke followed the brisk pace he set as they crossed the dewy field in front of the Twelve's house. The sun peeked over the boundary wall, and the air was crisp. She rubbed her arms. *Should have brought a cape.* This field looked similar to the training field on the opposite side of the grounds, except perhaps more informal. She'd bet that the Guardians would mess about and rough-house there. She could almost see them playing the way college boys congregated and kicked the ball around in their free time.

Another big house stood next door. When she looked at it, shivers ran down her spine. Seeing as Cloud was doing his best to ignore her, she turned and asked Rush, "That's the other cadre house?"

"The Six. We don't talk to them."

"Why?"

"They don't play well with others."

Overhearing Clarke's half of the conversation, Cloud turned back and gestured at the house. "Horde. Blah blah. Kidnap humans. Blah blah. Don't go there."

Then he continued walking.

Now she was curious. Before she followed, Clarke tried to spy any fae within, but branches draped over the windows with drawn black curtains.

Down from the cadre houses, they slotted through a thin alley which bordered on an enormous mess hall. The delicious scent of food wafted out. Clanks of productivity came from within. On her way past, a gaggle of novitiate Mages and rookie Guardians almost crashed into her as they burst out of the swinging glass doors. Upon seeing who she followed, they gave her a wide berth. But once they were five feet away, she heard the muttered "*Human*" from more than one mouth. Try as she might, she couldn't stop her shoulders from slumping.

She thought it wouldn't bother her, this name calling and segregation, but it did. It wore her down, even more so because they were right. She should be despised for the hand she'd played in the near oblivion of the entire planet. There were a lot of wrongs to right and it was all beginning to feel a little overwhelming, but she wouldn't give up. She could do this. Screw anyone who said otherwise.

"Don't worry about them," Rush mumbled. "Bunch of mewling litter box sniffers."

The novitiates followed her. It was cautious curiosity at first, but it gave way to hurled insults under their breath. Soon other things were thrown. A small piece of meat landed in her hair. She didn't flinch. She just pretended they weren't there, because if she turned around, she'd do something stupid and Rush would probably burst into protective beast mode. As it was, his hand rested on the pommel of the dagger clipped to his belt. Aware of her slowed pace, Cloud glanced over his shoulder. Catching sight of the group on her tail, his gaze darkened.

Black feathered wings snapped out and flared wide with a smacking whoosh. Air gusted in Clarke's face. Gone was the leather clad, brooding fae, and in his place was a dark avenging angel. Electricity and air whipped around his body, circling up his legs, torso, and crackling in his gaze.

That's all he did.

Stand. And stare. And electrify.

The group of novitiates evaporated. One minute they were there, and the next, scattered across the quad courtyard that separated the Mage buildings. One male Mage even backed into the three-tiered fountain at the center.

"I appreciate it," Clarke said to Cloud.

"Read nothing into it." He powered down and then resumed his stride across the quad.

"Next time," Rush growled. "You use your gift to show them I'm here. Understood?"

"So you can have a pissing contest with Cloud, or make yourself sick? No thanks."

His face screwed with fury, and he punched the glass window to the mess hall. The pane exploded as though a bullet had gone through it. Shattered slivers tinkled to the ground. The fae eating at a bench before the window all gaped. Rush shot Clarke a fiery gaze and then stormed off.

"Where are you going?" she shouted, but he didn't respond.

Cloud sighed dramatically. "What the fuck happened?"

"What do you think?" She threw her hands up.

It took Cloud a moment to blink the confusion of the curse away, then it dawned on him. "Rush did it. Lover's spat?"

"You don't think he's going after them, do you?"

"Who the fuck cares?" Cloud squinted the way the novitiates went and then shook his head. "He's not stupid."

At least there was that. "I guess we know where Thorne gets his temper from."

At the academy, Clarke couldn't help drawing the comparison with a fancy college. Made from a mix of wood, glass, and different types of stone, the architecture was old school Oxford mixed with a dash of Byzantine. Extensive mosaic decoration glittered on the outer walls, and a heightened limestone dome dominated in the middle. An overload of archways at every window or door made her feel a little inadequate.

Waiting for them at the base of the steps was the pixie who'd been part of the Council. While she was small in stature, she was large in attitude. With her dragonfly wings half fluttering, little swaths of prismatic light reflected against the cobbled walls and set to amplify her annoyance.

"You're late," she clipped.

"Whatever," Cloud grunted and gave Clarke a mock salute. "Colt will take it from here."

Colt did *not* want to take it from here. Clarke didn't need to be psychic to know that. The female looked sharply down her nose at Clarke, lifted her brows and sighed judgmentally. "It still makes no sense to me."

"Yeah, well, lady, I'm what you've got, so get used to it."

Colt's wings snapped shut and tucked in close to her body, but they didn't disappear like the shifters' did. Pixies must always be in winged form. It made sense.

She gestured at Clarke. "We'll visit the temple pools and find out what your elemental affinity is first. My guess is you're all spirit and chaos, no fire or ice. Then we'll work on your ability to draw on your mana. Then there's mana theory and uses with council member Barrow. Then Dawn will take you for specific training in Seeing. You won't get to the defensive and offensive arts until we're certain you can control your ridiculous abundance of mana. Crimson help us all that someone like you is the chosen one."

A surge of defiance stabbed through Clarke. "I'm not the only chosen one," she said. "More will come. More have already arrived."

Whether they were all set to be chosen, and for what remained to be seen.

"All the more reason for you to understand that I will not hold your hand through this. There are only a few preceptors around. Which leads me to another thing. You will address me as Preceptress Colt. You will address Barrow as Preceptor Barrow. Do you understand? Male teachers are Preceptor. Female are Preceptress."

"How ever will I know the difference?" The sarcasm dripped from Clarke's tongue.

Colt pursed her lips. "You're not one for respect, are you? Were they all like you in your time?"

She shrugged.

"Well. I guess we all have something to look forward to, don't we? Right. Another thing. Where the Guardians have a tear under their eye, we Mages have one on our bottom lip." She tapped her finger on the pillow of her lip. "If none are wearing uniform, then that's how you can tell us apart, even out and about in Elphyne."

Clarke narrowed her focus to see the tiny symbol etched there. The point of the teardrop started near the mouth and the heavy part of the drop ended where her lip joined her chin. "What does it mean?"

Colt straightened her spine. "With the Guardians, they shed a tear for each soul sent back to the Well. For the Mages, it symbolizes the Well is sustenance. We must be careful not to deplete our mana lest we become parched. We must remember to use restraint. Understood?"

Not really. "Okay. Got it."

"You don't. Mana can be like a drug, it can destroy. Or it can be like food and nourish."

"Like ingesting manabeeze."

Colt's lip twitched, and thoughts collided behind her eyes. "Yes. Too much and you can go mad. Especially if you draw from the inky side of the Well."

Eventually Colt nodded and waved Clarke into the academy. Inside, more glass mosaics depicted many romanticized scenes Clarke could only imagine were the dawning of the understanding of magic. Robed in red, one figure moved from scene to scene in various states of repose, investigation, and spell casting.

"That is Jackson Crimson," Colt explained. "He is the first fae who discovered the link between the Well of life inherent in the world, and the mana we hold within ourselves. He founded the Order. I suggest you visit the library on your way home tonight and collect some books on our history. Since you will be living in this time, and defending this time, it's imperative you're all caught up."

Clarke bit her nail. "And where would I go to look up, oh, I don't know... let's say... how to cast and break curses?"

Colt whirled around, her robes, wings and curly prism hair swishing with her. "I beg your pardon?"

"Um. Curses? Where can I find out more about them."

"If you're referring to your mate's predicament, I believe the Prime has told you there's nothing more to be done about it. If I were you, I'd leave sleeping wolves lie."

"But you're not me," she replied. "And I won't ever stop trying to free him. So, you can either help me or you can hinder me."

"Why would I help you do something the Prime has directly forbidden?"

Clarke stopped. Stilled. And narrowed her eyes. "What did you say?"

Colt's eyes widened. "I meant that it's an impossible venture. If you want to waste time searching the archives, then knock yourself out."

That was the last word until they reached an empty classroom that housed about six desks and a chalkboard at the front. While Colt unlocked the room, Clarke's gaze wandered into the classroom on the opposite side of the hall. Set up like a laboratory, students sat at benches with scientific instruments. A Mage with pink hair leaned over the shoulder of another smaller fae, who in turn growled at her for spying. Glowing jars of buzzing balls of light were set up next to them. Each student experimented with individual recipes. Perhaps it was a test.

Barrow, who was at the head of the class, noticed her staring and walked over to the glass window and drew the drapes closed.

Yep. They were doing an exam. Goddamned college idiosyncrasies. Clarke rolled her eyes. "I'm too old for this shit."

"How old are you?" Colt asked.

"Twenty-nine."

A tinkling laugh burst out of Colt. "You're but a babe."

"And how old are you?"

Colt lifted a brow. "One never asks a pixie her age. But... fine. You're the all powerful Seer. You tell me. This can be your first lesson."

Okay. Clarke shook her hands at her side like a boxer. She could do this. Guess the lady's age. Got it. Squinting and scrutinizing, she looked for clues on her face. No lines beside her eyes like Barrow. No laugh lines next to her mouth. The skin on her neck was elastic. Going by Rush's age, and his appearance... damn. Who was she kidding? She had no clue.

"Stop looking with your eyes and start feeling with your gut." She tapped Clarke's stomach with her hand.

Clarke scratched beneath her ear and looked at Barrow's classroom window.

Fingers snapped in her face. "Pay attention."

"This is harder than it looks."

"Because you're untrained. It's like teaching a donkey how to fish."

"Oh-*kay*."

"I meant no offense. It's just the truth. I'm two-hundred-and-fifty-nine years."

Clarke bit her cheek to stop herself saying something derogatory. Apart from the Prime, Colt was the oldest fae she'd come across. And she didn't look a day over thirty. She probably had a lot to teach.

Clarke followed Colt into the classroom. Set up exactly like one from her time, the familiarities set her at ease. It also disgusted her to be in a learning environment again. Her life had been about education on the fly. Street smarts, not book smarts. She'd earned her meal ticket every day. That was until Bishop got his hands on her. Then it was ignore the fact she felt the bad vibes in her gut because at least she didn't have to work so hard for a meal.

"Where did you go, just now?" the preceptress asked.

"Just thinking about some poor decisions I made, despite the bad vibes in my gut warning me."

"Bad vibes. Vibrations?" Colt tapped her finger on her lip. "They say the connection to the Well is like another brain thinking in your stomach."

"It can feel like a flutter for something good, or a bad buzzing for something bad."

"Good. I believe this is a solid foundation for your training."

This was going to be rough.

Through a long window on one side, students and Mages gathered around the quad courtyard and three-tier fountain. The one who'd fallen in when Cloud had frightened them stood to the side, wringing his robe. Another smaller female with blue hair tried to use some sort of magic to air-dry it. Steam curled into the air.

"Take a seat. There is a lot to go through, and Preceptress Dawn says you only have four weeks," Colt said and gestured to a wooden desk.

It was nice and smooth. Perfect surface for carving a "C" into. Huh. Maybe Clarke would enjoy this lesson, after all.

She took a seat and then jolted. "Four weeks? Why?"

"You'll have to ask her. Okay, so we'll start with recognizing the sensations of replenishing from the Well, how to compare it to drawing on your own internal stores, and then again how to distinguish it from the feelings you'll get when your gift is trying to warn you..." Colt droned on. Clarke knew she should pay attention, but she couldn't help the worry creeping up her spine.

It hadn't escaped her notice that Colt had let it slip the Prime had ordered everyone not to help her break Rush's curse. Looking out the window, she wondered where Rush had gone. And if he would come back.

THIRTY-TWO

Cloud had escorted Clarke to the academy for eight days of training.

In those days, she'd been grilled, drilled and turned into a pumpkin. Well, that last one wasn't true, but she'd felt like it. Rush hadn't been wrong when he'd said she'd be exhausted after each day's lessons. She was the walking dead.

They kept her busy. Too busy. She'd not had time to research the curse.

On the ninth day, when the knock came at their door in the morning, Clarke and Rush were both surprised to hear the deep voice barking through, "Be ready in five."

Already half dressed, Clarke tugged on her boots and raised her brows at Rush.

Still in the bed, tangled gloriously in a sheet, he shrugged.

The voice had belonged to Thorne.

While Rush slipped on breeches, Clarke gathered the two books she'd borrowed from the library on elemental magic, and tucked them into a sling bag. She'd learned she had a small capacity for all the elements, but her strengths were in the spirit and chaos department... which was the psychic and the truth manipulation part of her magical canon. The teachers hypothesized she could one day learn to flip the truth on people, and make them think something was happening, when it wasn't. Like a mirage. But apparently that could take decades to learn.

And still, none of it revolved around breaking Rush's curse.

"Right," she said. "I'm ready."

Rush had been unusually quiet since their first day, and she put it down to the fact they'd not spoken to Thorne yet.

"I think today is the day," she said.

"For what?" He checked his appearance in a black mirror on the wall, and brushed his hair back.

"For telling Thorne whatever you needed to tell him."

He paused. And he slid her a look.

"Come on." She went up to him and hugged him from behind. With a sigh, she rested her cheek on his back. "It's been over a week. You wanted to speak to him so badly that you bargained with me, remember?"

The hard muscle under her face spasmed. "It seems like a long time ago."

Another rap at the door and Thorne shouted. "Let's go."

Clarke patted Rush's back and collected her bag.

Thorne waited in the hallway. At least he wasn't walking around naked today. The Guardian had on his uniform, and rested against the wall with his arms folded. He stared at her. The brooding animosity she'd felt on the first day was still there. Initially she had been offended, but then she came to see he was like that with everyone. The chip on his shoulder must be heavy.

"You know," she started, "I haven't had a chance to tell you that another Guardian told me to look you up. His name is Caraway. Do you know him?"

Thorne narrowed his eyes, but said nothing.

Okay, then. "Well, he said you're honorable. So... yeah."

He gave no sign that he cared.

What a tough crowd. She gestured down the hall. "After you."

Rush followed Clarke as they left the building. He never stayed with her at the academy, but he always joined the escort. It took her a few days to realize they weren't shadowing her because she was a prisoner, but because they were her bodyguards.

Passing the house of the Six, Clarke tried once again to spy inside the windows. She saw nothing but the twitch of a dark curtain. The Sluagh who lived inside were border-line evil, Rush had told her. Fallen angels, some said. Disgruntled fae spirits, others named them. During the Wild Hunt years ago, when the first war between human and the fae-folk happened, the Sluagh were sent by the Winter Queen to kidnap the humans. The Sluagh apparently developed a taste for them. They were rumored to fly to Crystal City and take humans into their horde. The humans were never seen again. But their cries were heard.

Rumors, Clarke decided. She'd make up her own mind. She just wanted one look inside the house. That was all.

These particular six Sluagh were Guardians, which meant the Well deemed them worthy of holding the extra power... they couldn't be that bad. Right?

Clarke shifted her gaze back to Thorne as he took brisk strides across the informal Guardian training ground. She glanced sideways at Rush, also taking brisk strides. They might not get another chance to speak and she was done waiting for their stubborn wills to concede. She stopped on the dewy lawn before the cadre houses.

"Wait."

Both Nightstalks stopped.

She fiddled with her bag. She swallowed.

"Rush. I think you want to say something to Thorne. Now's the time."

Thorne started walking again.

Clarke's irritation swiftly rose.

Rush gestured in the direction of the academy. "I still don't know what to say. Let's just go."

"No." She put her foot down. "Rush, you've been tying yourself up in knots about this. It's the least he can do to hear you out. I'm not leaving this lawn until he does."

Thorne checked over his shoulder, cast a wary glance at the house of the Six and came back. "Fine. Hurry up."

You're a jerk. "Good."

She tugged on her gift, and felt the movement in her soul. The past eight days had only worked to help strengthen the skills she'd fumbled across all her life. The rest was a work in progress. She looked at Rush, then at Thorne. *"Let Thorne see the truth."*

She sent her intentions out to him. Energy rippled from her body with the wind. To Clarke, nothing else happened. But Thorne's gaze suddenly shifted to take in Rush standing to his right.

Neither of them spoke.

Silence.

The breeze blew.

She was sure she heard a cry coming from the house of the Six. She shivered. And then shook it off.

Five minutes later, the two wolves still stared. It was getting ridiculous.

And then Rush cleared his throat.

"I regret..." He cupped the back of his neck. "I regret the way things went down with your mother. And I'm sorry I didn't do more to help you and your aunt at the Hollow."

Thorne narrowed his gaze. "You just apologized."

"Yes."

"You're admitting to owing me a debt."

"Correct."

Thorne's harsh blue gaze whipped to Clarke. "You know he'll leave you."

"I'm working on the curse." She patted her bag. Tonight she would hit the library stacks again. Surely someone could point her in the direction of tomes on curses. She just needed to garner a little more information.

"He'll leave you before the curse," Thorne added. "It's what he does."

Something snapped within Clarke. "I don't think any of us expected you to welcome your father with open arms, but this attitude of yours just sucks. Shit happens, buddy. Grow up."

A low, defensive growl shot out of Thorne. Clarke stepped back at the wild animalistic flash in his eyes.

"You were right about Jasper," Rush blurted, stepping between them.

Thorne's gaze snapped to his. "What?"

"He's not on hiatus, despite what the Prime said. She's not to be trusted."

Thorne shuffled his feet. "Why?"

"How long has Jasper been missing?"

"About a decade."

Rush straightened his spine. "I may not be able to do much in this state, but I can watch. I can learn secrets. And I followed many of you around for years. Some time ago, I saw Jasper at the Summer Court, having a discussion with King Mithras."

"About?"

"I'm not sure what Jasper told you about his heritage, but he's the king's bastard. There's a prophecy that the king's son will dethrone him, so any descendent was killed. But since Jasper is a Guardian, the king couldn't touch him. It's a point Jasper always liked to rub in Mithras's face."

"He's a Guardian. He can't claim rights to the throne. The king shouldn't see Jasper as a threat," Thorne replied.

Rush shrugged. "I can only tell you that I saw them together and I agree with you. I think Jasper is in danger."

Thoughts clashed behind Thorne's eyes. Then looked back in the direction they came. Clarke tried to stay silent and invisible. This was the most the two had spoken. If they didn't notice she was there, maybe there would be more. But Thorne continued toward the academy.

When they arrived on the doorstep, he shot Rush a contemplative look, and then left.

"I suppose that went well," Clarke said.

"I don't know what else to do."

"Well, I don't know if this is worth anything, but from a person whose mother abandoned her, the best thing you can do is to keep showing up. He'll get the picture soon."

Rush's smile never reached his eyes. He gave Clarke a quick kiss on the cheek. "See you tonight."

And then he left too.

Clarke jogged inside the building and hurried to her class with apprehension. She was beginning to understand these lessons were a ruse to keep her distracted from discovering more about the curse. Learning the skills to harness her power could take decades, and since she apparently lived in harmony with the Well, she would live as many years as the fae. Since she'd learned the fact from Colt, Clarke did nothing but think about a possible long life spanning before her. A life without Rush.

When she arrived at Barrow's classroom, she stalled. Taking a peek inside, she saw students preparing their lab stations. She wanted nothing more than to walk the other way.

With a start, she realized that feeling was her intuition. *So walk the other way, Clarke.*

Ducking her head, she carried on down the hall and followed her gut feeling until she ended up at the library. Before heading in, she took a deep breath. If anyone said she wasn't meant to be there, she could just say she was returning the books in her bags.

She strode in with her chin held high. The smell of old books hit her nose and tension ebbed from her posture. Out of everywhere she'd been in Elphyne, this library reminded her most of her own time. And she wasn't even a studious person. It was that smell. And the familiar shape of the leather-bound books as they lined the walls of shelves. It was the hushed tones used when students whispered to each other. And it was the atmosphere of respect. Of ideas. Here, she felt anything was possible.

A senior Mage sat behind a reception desk made from a dark cherry wood. His bushy brows lifted as his eyes met hers, and then he settled back to his work with obvious disinterest.

If the Prime had truly asked all the senior staff to avoid helping her with Rush's curse, she knew the senior Mage wouldn't reveal the answers she sought. Rush would probably know where to look, but he refused to come into the academy.

Scanning the floor, she let her gaze pass over each desk the students and scholars studied at. She let her intuition do the talking. There was definitely something here. She could feel it in her bones.

Her gaze landed on a table near the window. There was a tall, gangly Mage studying a large open book. He looked like a good place to start. Not too old. Not too new.

She shuffled along the carpeted floor and sat down next to him with a smile.

Completely taken with his book, he failed to look up. Now that she was closer, she took in more details of his body. The fae had a rather round head and golden skin with brown striations like a piece of french polished wood. A cow-lick of golden hair stuck up at the crown of his skull. He licked his long finger and turned the page, eyebrows lifting with avid fascination at whatever he was reading.

Clarke snuck a look at the text.

Cultivating new growth from frigid landscapes using a combination of...

Her eyes blurred with boredom. Yep. Not her thing.

"Hi," she said.

He craned his neck and blinked at her. Then his eyes went to her ears with a squeak. Little green leaves sprouted at his nose. His brown eyes went cross-eyed at the leaves and an incredible red blush hit his cheeks. When his gaze met hers, she caught genuine fear.

"I'm not here to hurt you," she whispered. "I promise."

"You're human." His voice broke like a teenager. "I... um."

"Yeah, I guess I get that a lot." She used her fist to make a circle over her chest. It was the sign for sorry. "I didn't mean to startle you."

"It's okay. It's just." He brushed his nose leaves away. They fluttered to the table. "I don't see many humans. Us Oak Men don't really get along... yeah. Humans kind of cut us down for wood. So we don't... yeah."

He shrunk away from Clarke.

Oak Men. Wow. And those leaves coming out of his nose. He was the first fae she had met who was blended from both human and plant. All others had some sort of animal or insect origin.

She offered another smile. "I can promise you I'm not here to cut you down."

"If you say so."

"Scout's honor." She crossed her chest. "Cross my heart and hope to die."

The Oak Man frowned. "Don't do that."

The senior Mage at the reception desk shushed Clarke.

She made the sorry sign again and lowered her voice to the Oak Man. "I'm Clarke."

He tapped his chest and whispered, "Frello."

Okay. They were getting somewhere.

"I'm hoping you could tell me if there are books on curses here," she asked.

He eyed her warily. "Why do you want those?"

"It's to help a friend."

His eyes widened. "Oh. The Wolf Guardian. Yes, I've heard about him." This knowledge seemed to relax him. He pointed down to the east end of the library. "They're next to the culinary section."

Elation lifted her clean off the seat.

And then she was forced back down when a hand clamped on her shoulder. She cranked her head to find Barrow's bushy wizard eyebrows scowling down at her.

Guess she would start her research tonight.

CHAPTER

THIRTY-THREE

Three weeks later, on one of her nightly visits to the library, novitiates and scholars still filled the study area, and lined desks. Every so often, she heard the distinct sound of a page turning, and it drilled her insecurities in deeper.

She sat in the back, between two stacks of floor-to-ceiling shelves, surrounded by a collection of littered books. Some of them were ancient, glued together scraps of fabric, bark, or leather. Others were newer paper and wood. All were about curses, but none indicated how to perform one, or how to break one.

The Oak Man had pointed her in the right direction, but the books that existed here were more like a warning to those stupid enough to dabble in the forbidden art. None of them used the glyphs present on Rush's body. She was fast coming under the impression that the Prime had orchestrated the fact that nothing of actual use was available to the public, or there was a hidden section somewhere. A place where tomes on the inky side of the Well were kept. A place as dark as the depths of said Well.

She cleared her mind, crossed her legs and concentrated on her intuition. The idea was to nudge that gut feeling to look for something that didn't want to be found. The secret library must be here somewhere.

But thoughts of her failings kept coming to the forefront of her mind. She couldn't find this connection to the cosmic Well. She couldn't spark a flame. She couldn't create a breeze with her gift. It was hard to stay positive when they'd all said she was this powerful person. *Ooh, I'm the chosen one.*

Whatever.

There came a point where her teachers had stopped looking at her with a mix of trepidation and awe and looked at her as though she was a fraud.

Rush had also been busy and hard to nail down. With what? She couldn't say. Only that he crawled into bed with her each night and when morning came, she'd find him sitting on the settee, either awake or half-asleep, staring out the window with Starcleaver in his hands, expecting trouble.

It felt like he avoided her.

Something had happened that first night they'd arrived, and he refused to talk about it. Perhaps it was the fact that Thorne continued to keep his distance, even after their brief talk, or that the Prime was still absent and the Council was beginning to worry.

The ticking time bomb that was Rush's curse made her feel sick. She'd even asked Preceptress Dawn how to See into her own future, or to his, so she could help him. Dawn had only replied with, "Well-blessed mates can sense the other's emotions down the bond."

Clarke had snapped something back at Dawn which hadn't been polite. She was tired of hearing about this grand other union Rush could potentially have and how it could save him, while Clarke couldn't. Her. This great, strong, chosen one. But not strong enough. Not good enough.

Clarke had wrung one good piece of advice from Dawn. She'd said, "When looking for your own future, don't look to the stone falling into the pond, look to the ripples it creates."

All these thoughts and more crowded her mind and stopped her from being able to meditate properly.

"Okay, Clarke. You can do this," she murmured, and thought about the books surrounding her, and the books she wanted to find. "They're like that... but they'd feel... darker. More chaotic. More..."

The hairs on the back of her neck lifted as someone sat behind her. For anyone else, that sensation would trigger a warning, but now... it melted her. She smiled.

"I knew I'd find you here." Rush swept hair from her shoulders and brushed his lips across her neck.

He shifted so his legs sprawled on either side of her body. Two warm hands circled her stomach. Clarke melted a little more.

"But where have you been?" She tensed, waiting for an answer.

"Around."

She released a breath. Not even reactions to her prying these days held the spark of defiance from him. It was almost like he'd... her throat closed up, refusing to acknowledge the thought. Instead, she leaned forward and picked up a book. It was a cook book, but she'd noted similarities in recipes to some information Preceptor Barrow had relinquished about how rare ingredients were needed to make a curse. She picked up a second book. It listed ingredients from the oil-slick tattoos she'd seen on several Guardians. These, she'd confirmed, enhanced abilities. Cloud was covered in them.

Rush's knuckles grazed down her arms. His big fingers closed over hers on each book, and then he pried them away.

"It's late. Come to bed."

Normally, she'd jump at the chance, but since the moment she'd woken that morning, a knot of tension had been ever present in her gut. It had distracted her to no end.

She huffed. "I can't."

Time was running out.

"Baby," he breathed and nibbled her ear lobe. It sent delicious shivers down her spine and heated her pleasantly. Hearing him use her own endearment was, well, endearing. He wanted to connect with her, to be closer. Because he'd been pulling away.

Unshed tears burned her eyes. She wasn't ready to let go of him.

She cleared her throat. "I have work to do."

"Forget about the curse," he said, voice all honey and spice. "You won't solve it by looking in the library."

"Where, then?"

She felt, more than heard, the sigh come out of him. "In dark places it's not safe to visit."

"I *knew* it."

"Of course you did."

"How do we get there?"

"We can't."

She craned her neck to look him in the eyes. Sadness pooled in the depths of his golden gaze.

"There's always a way."

"Not this time. You heard the Prime. Well-blessed mate only."

"Fuck your magical curse-breaking mate. *I'm* the one." She poked him in the chest. "I'm *your* one."

She knew it in the deepest parts of her soul.

His lips curved and he held her chin there as he sank into a kiss full of promises, need, and those wicked things she'd seen flashing in his eyes. A rumble of satisfaction rolled through him as she returned his heat, feeling every bit as beholden to his desires as her own.

"Let's go to bed," he insisted again, lips against hers.

"Rush..." She pulled away. "I can't even light a candle with my mana."

The truth hurt to say aloud. She knew all the theory to go with it, but still couldn't distinguish between the instinct that gave her vibes, and the sensation that supposedly connected her to the Well. It was all instinct to her, but it was something all fae inherently grew up with. She had a lifetime of bad habits to unpack.

"I've meditated so deep and long that I feel like I know every part of my body, but I still can't find the part that draws on the Well."

"It's not something you can find, Clarke. It finds you."

"Yeah, well how is that supposed to help me?"

She must have spoken louder than she realized because a hissed "Shhh" came from somewhere else in the library. She wanted to throw a book at them.

This was why she never went to college. It was filled with a bunch of pompous, stuffy do-gooders. Where were the party frat boys or sorority girls? Not here, that's for sure.

He sat back on his hands and considered her brooding face. She tried very hard not to think about the hard muscles slabbed beneath that deep burgundy sweater with the tantalizing V-neck he favored so much. The tailor or seamstress who made it didn't account for his broad shoulders and tapered waist. It was tight everywhere, except where it gathered with excess fabric around his abdomen. She tried to still her beating heart when he licked his lower lip. His beard had been trimmed short, making the angle of his jaw sharper than before. His silver hair had been brushed over as though he'd run fingers through it and shoved it to one side in agitation... or stifled passion. He still wore his weapons, even though it had become clear weeks ago that no other fae did within this compound unless specifically training. The Sluagh were overrated. She'd not seen a peep out of them. To everyone else, this was supposed to be a safe place.

Not for Rush.

He caught her frown and misconstrued it. "I can help you."

"What do you mean?"

Another shush filtered through the stacks and she shot the end of the aisle a disgruntled glare.

Rush's leather pants creaked as he stood and then strode down the aisle, disappearing around the corner. He came back with a lit half-melted candle stuck on a single pottery holder. He used a boot to irreverently shift her books aside and placed the candle down before her. Then he returned to sit behind her and spread his legs on either side. Two warm hands gripped her shoulders.

"Face the front. I will teach you how to blow it out with your power, and then how to light it."

She slid him a sideways stare. "I didn't know you could manipulate elements."

"All Guardians can. For shifters, we prefer to use our mana for the shift, but sometimes we resort to the elements for help. Some elements are stronger than others."

"So... those who can't shift, like Leaf, he's—"

"Basically just a Mage who fights."

She huffed a laugh. "Don't tell him you said that."

"Oh, don't worry. We made it our business to tell the elves about their shortcomings every day."

The humor in his voice brought a welcome surge of joy to her heart. This part of him she wanted to see more. It was the part that still acted like he was a member of the family here, not the part that existed on the outskirts. It was the part that still held hope.

She focused on the flickering candle. "Okay," she said. "So... just access my mana and blow it out. No biggie. It's not like I've been trying to do this for weeks."

"Relax." Rush's thumbs pushed into sore spots on her shoulders and massaged in circles.

Her eyes rolled with pleasure, and her posture softened. A groan slipped out.

His lips touched her ear, breath hot on her neck. "The act of accessing the mana within your internal Well is something so intrinsic, it's like moving your legs. You've been trying to run before you can walk. Relax and let nature take over."

"I can access the mana that makes me psychic, but not the other elements they tested me for. Easier said than done."

"I've done it."

"Shut up," she mumbled.

She felt his husky laugh down her spine. Every nerve in her body sang in his presence. She tried to think un-sexy thoughts, because if she didn't, fantasies about his clever fingers invaded her mind. Before her eyes rolled completely out of her head, she forced her lids to stay open and focused on the flickering candle flame.

"Air is breath." He blew gently on her ear.

She laughed. "You're so corny."

"Corny." He tested the word. "That's a new one." He massaged more, dug low on her back, knuckled down her spine, and just when she was about to fall back into him, he added, "Take a deep breath, hold it, feel it work in your lungs, and then let it go."

She shut her eyes, let the last of the tension out of her body and focused deeply.

"Breathe in," he murmured. "Breathe out."

For long moments, that was all she did. He stopped massaging, but she kept breathing. Air came into her lungs cold, filled her up, gave her life, and then left her lips in a warm rush.

"Good," Rush intoned. "Now open your eyes and push all that awareness to the candle."

Slowly her lashes lifted and, with a smooth exhale, she urged it onward with a sliver of her energy. She urged the flame to feel the wind enter cold, and then to fill it up. The flame flickered, guttered, and then died.

Silence. Dead silence. And then Clarke stifled a squeal. She twisted and climbed on Rush to plant a kiss on his face. He laughed, a deep chesty laugh, and then forced her off him.

"Don't get cocky," he warned. "You still have to light it up."

She waved. "No problem."

Then turned back to the candle, set herself up the same way and pushed that part of her conscience back to the wick, and urged it to light.

Nothing.

She cleared her throat and did it again.

Still nothing. Nothing but the echo of her stupid words coming back to haunt her. A frustrated growl tore out. She wanted to scream. Every day of her damned infernal training came back to tease her. For hours at a time Colt had forced her to do the same thing. No amount of meditating or lessons could give her the understanding. Her brain just couldn't click.

"I'm too human."

"Shh," Rush whispered. "You'll get it."

She mashed her lips together and took a deep breath. "It's not working. I'm doing the same thing as I did with the air."

"But is fire the same as air?" His hands moved down to her hips and tugged her backward until she was flush against his chest. Warmth soaked into her back.

Clarke eyed the dead candle. "I guess not."

"So think about fire."

"Great. Sure. Said no one ever."

"Think about heat." His voice lowered with intention. The pad of his rough fingers traced along the join where her blouse met her waistband. He repeated the motion, teasing her.

Okay. She squirmed. This was different. He stroked over her clothes, sparking sensation. Her nipples contracted. A flood of heat gathered between her legs. She sucked in a breath.

"Wrong element," he chided, and tugged her blouse from the confines of her pants. "Heat. Think heat."

"Rush..." She darted a glance to the end of the aisle and heard someone sniffle, then a murmur.

"No one can see us now." He found skin. Lazy fingers circled her stomach, massaging gently until he sighed pleasantly and flattened his palm, tugging her closer. Tingles zipped everywhere, and a deep husky moan wrenched from her throat. He murmured, "Still wrong element."

How could she not focus on her quickening breath when his splayed hand flexed under her breasts, thumb touching the under-pillow, little finger dipping into her pants. Hot lips landed on her neck, on the mark he always gravitated toward. She glanced again down the aisle.

He clicked his tongue. "Don't think about being caught. Think about..."

The hand at her stomach lifted to band around her chest. His thumb grazed a bare nipple. She arched into him. Whimpered. His other hand ventured where his little finger had been, but kept going, over the fabric of her pants to rub along the seam. Her blood ignited and she ground into him with an almighty moan of submission.

He bit down on her shoulder when he found her damp through her clothes. She became a coalescence of sensation. The fingers down there. The ones up higher. The hardness at her back, pushing into her. The circles, the rubs, the *heat*. He owned her. Consumed her. Her heart thudded in her ears with each urgent stroke he made. Knowing she was safe against his chest, she threw her head back and pulled his hair in a desperate grip, sinking into the sensation of his tongue at her earlobe and his fingers on her body.

She didn't know what this would prove. But she hoped he wouldn't stop.

"Tell me how it feels," he snarled, breath ragged against her ear.

"It feels—"

His hand dipped into her pants. Fingers down the middle. On the point she'd silently begged for.

She gasped. Sparks crackled. *More.*

"Clarke." He swore. Swallowed. "Tell me."

She could only whimper and thrust into him.

His finger slid down her center and plunged into her core. He cursed at her readiness. Paused. Tensed. Another swallow behind her, as though he schooled himself to restrain his own desire. Impatiently, she worked herself on his hand. He muttered under his breath, but then resumed his game of exploration. In. Out. Around. Press down. Dip in. Slide. It was too much. She cried out and arched into him. He plumped her breast, rolling her nipple, reading her mind.

"Clarke," he growled low. "Tell me how it feels."

"Great. Amazing. Fucking… insan… hha… God, yes. Rush. Yes. There."

He increased the pace of his fingers between her legs. "Tight. So tight."

Her eyes fluttered. She lifted her hips to meet his hand. "Tight."

"Wet."

"Hot."

So hot. She was burning up. It was as though every stroke he made, every squeeze or twirl, was another drop of fuel to the flame. It all coiled tight, flamed brighter, burned darker until she simply combusted. A harsh cry of release tore from her lips. He brought her mouth to his in a punishing kiss. His long, guttural groan of satisfaction fed into her.

"Was it hot?" he asked, voice guttural, fingers still lazily circling, drawing out her pleasure.

"Mm-hm." So hot.

"Send it to the candle." He pressed his thumb on her sensitized bud, sending aftershocks rippling through her. "*Feel* the heat."

Her slumberous gaze locked onto the candle.

"Or do I need to start the demonstration again." His voice held a wicked, cruel lilt, and it was everything.

"I'm tempted."

He smiled against her skin at her neck. "It's now or never. Don't think about it. Don't analyze. Just do it."

She pushed the heat still simmering in her body toward the candle. Energy hummed and burned through the resistance of her skin. Power ripped out of her.

It wasn't the candle that set alight. It was the books. The wood. The carpet. Little flickering flames danced and skipped over every surface, rapidly spreading outward.

"Shit!" she shouted and shot forward, trying to smother the sparks with her hands and body.

"Clarke," he barked, and lifted her from the floor as though she weighed nothing.

He tugged her back to him and patted her smoldering front, smothering the flames. "Never do that to me again. You gave me a heart attack. Fire is… unpredictable."

A balding Mage in a blue robe came barreling into the aisle. His hand shot out, fingers splayed, and water doused them all. Covered from head to toe in a dripping waterfall that had conjured from nowhere, Clark gaped.

Not seeing Rush, the Mage had missed him entirely with the burst of water.

Rush roared with laughter.

"You practice your elemental fire elsewhere!" the Mage said. "What's gotten into you —and how did that candle get in here?" He grabbed his head and tugged what was left of his hair.

Clarke couldn't suppress the laugh. Guess she knew why he was going bald.

Rush took her hand, and the curse must have enveloped them, because the Mage began twirling in confusion, wondering what had just happened.

They ran all the way back across campus to the Guardian quarters. And when they got to their room, Rush made love to her in a way he'd never done before. At first, she thought it was the bright shine of hope burning through his passion, but as she drifted off to sleep and he crawled out of bed to sit on the settee, she knew in her gut that it was not hope.

Forget about the curse.

The memory of his words brought tears to her eyes.

He was different that night because this was good bye.

THIRTY-FOUR

Without Rush by her side, Clarke's sleep was fitful and full of nightmares. Dreams within dreams. Meanings turned inside and out.

She saw people frozen in the ice. She saw them thaw. She saw the darkness shroud them and the horror as they rejoined the living. And she saw them die. Every time it was a new person, a new life, a new death. From a stab in the back, to a slice across the throat, to a sword in the heat of battle. Fae. Human. Something in between. It was all order and then chaos until she landed in front of a shadowy figure she knew well. The Void.

Never had she seen his face. Never his skin nor eyes nor mouth, but always she knew it was him. There was a distinct feel to his soul. Because that's what she saw... the dark void of his soul. That's why he was a faceless black shadow. A black hole that devoured all life. He didn't care about the natural order.

And he was coming for them. For her.

Panicked, she wished herself away.

The dream suddenly shifted, and she was at the academy, watching Preceptor Barrow instruct his class as they poured some concoction of liquid into a bowl. With tweezers and goggles, they lowered a glowing ball of mana into the water, and then they added a dull stone. Ripples formed in the water.

Preceptress Dawn's voice floated into her head. *"Don't look for the stone dropping in the water, look for the ripples it creates."*

So Clarke shifted gears.

She took a step back from the nightmares and watched from the outskirts. To find the ripples affecting her life, she had to look to those she knew.

Clarke dreamed she was a bird.

Under a moonlit sky, she soared through the clouds above the rooftops of an unknown city. Coasting and taking her time, she circled above a particular house and landed on a branch near an open window. She hooted. Once. Twice.

A tall stately figure arrived at the open window. He was tall, golden haired and gorgeous. Square jaw, sensuous lips, and honey-colored eyes that echoed a cold entity inside. Clarke saw the opposite of a void. She saw the chaos of life as it sparked with electricity. Tightness contracted her lungs as he stared at her. His attention suffocated her. Then his lips stretched into a wicked smile, and he stepped back, allowing her entry.

Flapping her wings, she landed gracefully on the red-stained glass floor. The cool surface sent a shock as her talons changed to feet. The hands held before her face were brown-skinned, and so were her feet... and her naked body full of curves. She walked to the golden fae and stroked his unimpressed face. He took her breast in hand and squeezed.

"Prime," he said, voice smooth like silk.

"King," she replied, and took hold of his crotch through his pants.

He squeezed her flesh tighter. She wrenched her grip. Neither made a twitch of expression on their stony faces. Then he lowered his lips and slanted them over hers, letting her feel his wolven fangs on her lips.

She pushed him back and squeezed his jaw. "I want the bastard back."

Fire flashed in his darkening gaze. He cupped her between the legs. "Regret is not a pretty color on you, owl."

"It is not regret. It is a change of plans, wolf."

"We made a bargain. I keep the breeding law in place. You give me the bastard."

"We never said for how long."

He clicked his tongue with derision. "You made me wait *four* decades before you handed him over, and now you want him back after a measly one?" He scoffed. "You still owe me another three."

The king's jaw hardened and he shifted his hand intimately. He tried to kiss her again. Her talons grew until they pierced the brocade fabric of his pants. He sucked in a breath and studied her face, finally whispering, "You dare threaten me?"

"You are the one with your fingers where they don't belong."

He growled and let go. She held on for a second longer, then let go too.

"Where is he?" the Prime asked. "Where have you put Jasper?"

"I'll have no bastard of mine impede my plans."

"And I'll have no green king impede..."

The Prime's voice suddenly filtered away, and the sounds of a crowd became a deafening roar. She saw nothing but darkness. She was blind. Clarke couldn't understand where she was. It felt like the rhythmic beat of a stadium. Roars. Cheers. Shouts. Boos. Stomping on the stadium seating floor. It was the symphony of her broken life. In the never-ending darkness, the symphony was all that kept her company. That and pain.

"Ripples... look for the ripples," Preceptress Dawn said.

Clarke looked down again and her hands were no longer the talons of a bird, but human. At first she thought it was herself, but then she was being pushed into a cage. A tiny, cramped, ugly smelling and feeling cage she didn't recognize. She struggled against the bars, trying not to let them push her in, but the force at her back was too strong. It was like death in there, but it was worse outside. Choking on her panic, she tried to scream. She thrashed about.

The dream shifted again.

Clarke wasn't in the cage, but out of it. Two cages this time, one on either side of a familiar portcullis in Crescent Hollow. She looked further down the wall. Three cages. Four. Five. But who occupied the cages? The pixie? Her lover? No... it was... a tail swished in irritation from behind the body of a female and Clarke stepped closer... or her spectral body, or whatever she was.

"Water," Anise rasped.

The guard rapped on the wooden bars with his bow. "Not your time yet, she-wolf."

"It's been so long."

"That's what you get for harboring a human."

Clarke screamed awake.

"Anise!" she shouted into the darkness.

THIRTY-FIVE

The room was gloomy when Clarke opened her eyes. She looked to the settee for Rush but found it empty. Unease dropped in her stomach like a stone. She'd always assumed he moved there after she fell asleep, but never considered he'd left the room altogether.

Throwing the covers off, she swung her legs over the side and fumbled with her feet until she found her slippers.

An inexplicable feeling of impending doom pulled her skin tight and quickened her pulse. *Where was he?* Scanning the room, it was clear he wasn't there.

She had to find him. Had to find *someone*. So many weird things she'd dreamed, but the one thing that wasn't murky or hard to decipher was Anise being in trouble. She'd been locked in one of those dastardly cages... all because she'd helped Clarke.

"It's been so long..."

Anise's voice was a puncture to Clarke's heart.

"That's what you get for harboring a human."

She'd probably been held captive for weeks.

Thaddeus must have needed to cast blame after he'd come bursting into the inn, narrowly missing Clarke and Rush as they went through the portal. She recalled him asking for more in the next shipment from the human, meaning Clarke had undercut some profit he'd hoped to make. She'd evaded him again. She—a despicable human. He would have assumed Anise knew, or even if she didn't, he wouldn't have cared. As long as someone remained locked and suspended in a cage, suffering for his humiliation, then the joke wasn't on him.

Bastard.

She blinked.

That was another word she recalled from her dream. The Prime had asked for the bastard. Jasper. At first, she'd thought the Prime didn't like Jasper, but it was more than that. Jasper was the king's illegitimate son.

God, there was so much of the dream to decipher.

Using her gift, Clarke sent heat to the oil lamps. Or she tried.

"Come on, damn you. Light." She forced the power welling in her body to spread out and touch the candle, but it wouldn't light. "No dice," she mumbled.

Damn it.

"Feel the heat. Don't analyze. Just do it." Rush's voice came to her like a dream.

She conjured the feelings he'd evoked and flames sprung to life in the sconces. She had but a moment to feel proud of herself before she busied herself with getting dressed, intuition taking her straight to the outdoor and weatherproof clothes. Leather pants, blouse, thick sweater, boots and a fur-lined cape. Rush's old strip of fabric went over her ears. He'd told her she might be able to disguise them with a glamor, but she hadn't gotten that far in her training. For now, she was going on a journey.

First, she needed help.

Clarke went to leave her room, but then noticed something on the table near the hearth. Two carved wooden figurines and her sundial, now with a leather cord attached. She put the sundial around her neck, and then picked up the wolf pup, turning it in her hands. She picked up the human female who had long hair, round ears and little dots over her nose. Freckles. It was unmistakably Clarke. So if that was her, then who was the wolf puppy? She picked it up again and stared hard, wishing she could get some kind of psychic imprint. But as usual, anything to do with Rush or her was empty.

But these carvings looked familiar. She went to the closet and rummaged in his rucksack until she found the wolf from the cabin. She placed it with the other two figurines. Her, Thorne, and a smaller pup. Her breath hitched and her hand went to her stomach.

When was the last time she'd had her period?

"Shit," she mumbled, and sat down. But the elixir should have stopped any chance of her getting pregnant. How long had she been awake in this world for? A month? How long prior to waking had it been since... "Double shit."

All the symptoms had been there. She'd been hungrier than normal. Tired. Occasionally nauseous. She looked at the little carving. Rush knew, and he said nothing. He knew and—wait. Why wasn't Rush a part of the carved figurine family?

She swallowed.

And then she was up, ransacking the room, looking for evidence that he was still around, but everywhere she turned, she only found more signs that he was gone. The coin in his rucksack, gone. A brand new Guardian jacket from the closet, gone. His sword, gone.

Why don the Guardian jacket now, when he'd purposefully avoided it before?

A well of emotion sprung in her body, mixing and swirling with horror. The way he'd kissed her last night, the way he'd made love... she *knew* it had felt different. She thought it was because he'd given up, but it was more than that. Tears burned her eyes. He'd left her alone. Alone in this new world.

Why?

He loved her. He may not have said it, but she felt it in her heart. A little voice whispered in her ear, *"If you loved someone, you wouldn't leave them."*

Years of self-doubt pressed on her chest. A mother was supposed to love her child, yet Clarke's had walked out of her life. All this time Clarke reasoned that her mother didn't love her, that she'd been disgusted with Clarke's abilities, or even afraid of them. Rush had accepted that part of her without question. She'd thought, yes, this is love. Unconditional. But maybe she'd had it all wrong. Maybe this was as good as it got, and she'd been too stubborn to accept it.

Forcing the tears away, she lifted the hem of her sweater and created a sling for the carvings to collect in.

The sun hadn't come up yet. Clenching her jaw, she left her quarters and gravitated toward a particular suite. She crossed the landing of the central grand staircase. Going up to the third door down the corridor, she raised her fist and knocked loudly. Within seconds, it opened.

A very naked Thorne glowered down at her from beneath a mess of white hair. *Did no one have decency here?* She could put up with the top half nudity, but the rest of it was just plain inconvenient. The past month had been a combination of her sorry hand-signs, and possessive growls and snaps from Rush every time she bumped into one of the half-nude buff residents, or worse, full-nude buff residents.

"What," Thorne grumbled.

"Rush is gone."

He lifted a brow, then tried to slam the door on her face. She stuck her boot in the gap. He made a frustrated sound and reopened it with a snap of his teeth.

It's okay, she thought. *He's not going to hurt me.* She forced the urge to run like prey. Sometimes she thought Thorne was closer to wolf than human. Sometimes he probably did too. His lip curled.

"Crescent Hollow has also been..." She couldn't even come up with a word for it. She looked at the ground as the vision of Anise almost dead in the cage swung into her mind. It wasn't only Anise, there were others feeling the wrath of Lord Thaddeus Nightstalk. Air rushed in and out of her lungs, gathering power along with her irritation. "I can't leave her like that. She was only nice to me."

"Crescent Hollow is none of my fucking business. Not anymore." He tried to close the door again, but she let the gathering storm of power go. She blasted the door open with a gush of air and threw a figurine at him. It glanced off his pec and toppled to the floor. He frowned down at it, then locked eyes with her, confused.

God, that felt good.

She threw another one, and then the last.

He snatched both out of the air with a superior look on his face. She couldn't stand it.

"You think you're so high and mighty with your sharp claws out all the time, but I got news for you. You're behaving the same way as Rush." She changed her tone to mocking. "Oh, we don't get involved in politics. We're all about protecting the Well. I'll give you a well. Well, fuck you all and your high horses. None of you are any better than the greedy assholes who lived in my time. Nothing has changed!"

His eyes glowed from the darkened recess of his room. His alpha fury licked across her skin and grew in power. He spoke through gritted teeth with a gravelly voice, no longer human. "You dare to come into my room, make demands, use offensive magic on me, and then you insult me. Damn straight I got sharp claws, and you're about to feel their wrath."

Claws sprung from the ends of his fingertips. Skin pulled tight over slabs of muscle and tendon. Every human instinct in Clarke was telling her to back the hell up, lay down and submit, but her newly honed instincts shouted for her to stay. Thorne was her only chance. He was the outlying ripple.

"Go on. Do your best," she taunted, and just when he stepped her way, she added, "I never pegged you for one to harm a pregnant woman."

He froze, face deadpanning. The claws retracted. "What?"

"Somehow Rush knew. And now he's left. So, in a way, you were right. Are you happy? He's gone."

Unable to accept the pity in Thorne's eyes, Clarke stared at the ground and waited while he put some pants on. She rubbed her forehead and forced herself to calm. It would do no one good right now if she caved to the panic growing in her body. It hurt to think of why Rush might have left. And then there were the other things.

"I had a premonition last night," she murmured. "Premonition, or vision... it was... I saw many wolves in cages. Some in fae form, some in wolf... I looked closer and recognized a female with a tail. Her name is Anise, and she worked in the bar at the Laughing Den. She's Caraway's friend. She was kind to me, and now Thaddeus is making her suffer for it." She paused, noticed Thorne had turned silent and watchful.

"Did Rush see the Prime before she left?"

She whirled to see Leaf standing in Thorne's doorway, hands dipped into the pockets of silk pajama pants. He lowered his brows, eyes laced with suspicion.

"Did he?" Leaf asked again.

"I don't know." She thought back. "He was different after that first night—the one she left."

"What do you think?" Leaf shared a look with Thorne. "Is he capable of hurting her?"

Thorne shrugged. "Whose sword other than his would leave such marks in her desk?"

"And on her windowsill."

"What's going on?" Clarke asked.

Thorne and Leaf shared a look over Clarke's shoulder. Damn it, these Guardians would never get involved in non-Order business. Not unless she forced them.

Her jaw lifted. "I know what happened to your missing Guardian."

She dropped the bomb and then pushed passed Leaf. Goddammit she was hungry all the time.

Thorne's footsteps came thudding after her. "Who?"

She hurried down the staircase. "You know very well who I'm talking about... but if you need me to prove I know too, then fine. His name is Jasper. He's the king's bastard."

Just as her feet hit the foyer floor, Thorne was there. He took hold of her wrist, stopping her before she entered the kitchen. "Rush told you that. It's nothing new. Don't lie to us, human. Don't play us."

Long, elegant fingers wrapped around Thorne's wrist. The air became thick, so stifling that it was hard to breathe, and then Thorne started gasping for air. From the concentration on Leaf's face, she knew he was behind the solidifying of air. Thorne's eyes watered, and he glared at Clarke as though he wanted to skewer her.

"Let the lady go," Leaf said through gritted teeth. "You of all people should understand her position."

Thorne's wild eyes darted to Clarke, down to her stomach, and then back to Leaf, who stood calmly through it all. Clarke's opinion of him went up a notch. She'd thought because of his sun-kissed looks and calm demeanor, he'd be a laid back pussy cat. But what she saw in the depths of that crystalline blue gaze was not calm. It was the tempest of an ocean. The waves that sucked you under. It was the reason he was the team leader, and no one else.

Thorne choked on the thickened air. His face went red. He shot Clarke one last look and then let go. He even hand-signed an apology. Oxygen came whooshing back, and he could breathe again.

She stalked to the kitchen and found it empty. The brownies hadn't been yet with new food, so she had to find some. She started by opening and closing every cupboard she could find, not caring if the loud bang of shutting doors woke the house.

The tension in the room shifted as others entered the room. Taking up residence beside the butcher block, Leaf flicked wrinkles from his pants. Thorne came in behind him.

"Now. Let's try this like civilized beings." Leaf gestured at Clarke. "What is it you know about Jasper?"

Her gaze darted between Thorne and him. He was right. She didn't know enough for them to go on, but they didn't know that. Every great con was steeped in truth.

"I know the Prime and the king had something to do with it," she said. "They conspired. That's all I'll tell you until you help me find Rush and rescue Anise."

With her hands locked on two different doorknobs, she bowed her head and took a deep breath. There. She'd said it. She wanted to find Rush. Even if the bastard had left her. She had to know why. She'd always thought that if it came to it, his curse would be the thing that took him away. Not his own... she swallowed the shameful words. Rush was *not* a coward. Not the Rush she knew. There must be something else going on.

Part of being a new person was not waiting for things to happen to her, she had to build the life she wanted. And she wanted Rush. There had to be a way. They might not have exchanged vows, but being mated was as good as being married in this time. They might not have said they loved each other, but Clarke knew she loved him. *This* was love. This aching longing squeezing every cell in her body. This *need* to chase him down until the ends of the earth just so she could wrap her arms around him one last time. Love was never giving up. Never quitting. Staying until the end.

Clarke opened another cupboard. Slammed it shut.

"What are you looking for?" Thorne asked.

"Food! I'm starving."

He came over, bent low and opened a base cupboard. Inside was a plate of bread, some sort of jam spread and the sweetest smell known to mankind. Coffee. Or something like it. While Thorne took out the bread and began slicing, Clarke opened the canister and sniffed. It was enough to make her relax and to feel like home. She didn't even need to drink it. But her father had. Those tears she'd held back leaked from her eyes. She missed him so much.

Thorne's eyes widened. "Don't cry."

"Shut up." She pointed the coffee canister at him. "It's hormones."

He held his palms up in defeat, but then cocked his head, listening to something near the door.

Was someone there?

Clarke narrowed her gaze through the other entrance of the kitchen where the dark hallway led to an entertaining area. A shadow moved. She almost choked when she noticed two others watching. The vampires. They blended so easily into the darkness that she'd not seen them. The moment she did, they knew, and came out of hiding.

The model, and the muscle, still dressed in their Guardian uniform.

Leather creaked as Shade folded his arms. He narrowed eyes in accusation at Leaf. "I *told* you."

Thorne pointed at Leaf in agreement. "Jasper's not on hiatus, or some secret mission. The king has him. Are we going to just let that slide?"

"We're Guardians," Leaf reminded them. "We don't get involved. Jasper knows this as much as anyone. The war we're fighting is very different to keeping everyday peace. If we don't draw the line, then our resources are expended."

"No," Clarke snapped. "Don't you dare hide behind your excuses. Staying isolated keeps your hearts hard. There's nothing wrong with getting involved to protect the ones you love. In fact, it separates us from the cold-hearted 'Untouched' humans you think are your enemy. Don't you see that?"

None of them argued with it. They knew it was true. They all used their position as Guardian to keep relationships at arm's length. But it was worth the pain. Being with someone you loved, even if it was fleeting, was the beautiful part of humanity she was fighting for.

"And what if the Prime is gone for good, too? What if staying out of politics got her killed?" Shade grumbled.

Clarke's hand went to her throat as she read between the lines. "You think Rush killed her."

"If it walks like the guilty and talks like a coward—"

Leaf silenced Thorne with his glare. "We don't know what happened. We don't know if she is dead. We don't know if the king has Jasper. We don't even know why Rush left. Let's be calm."

Hearing Leaf say it out loud made Clarke feel ashamed, for she was the first one who had lost faith in Rush. Her self-preservation reflex had been to revert to the defensive girl who'd run away from a man who'd used her. She owed it to Rush to give him the benefit of the doubt. She only wished he trusted her enough to tell her what was going on.

"There's something else you should know." Clarke swallowed. This would change all of their opinions. "The other half of the bargain your Prime made with the king was for him to keep the breeding law in place for another few years."

"What do you mean?" Thorne asked.

"I mean, the king was going to abolish it because Elphyne is flourishing. She made him keep it in place in return for handing him Jasper. Now why do you think she'd do that?"

Thorne stared at her long and hard while the pieces clicked together. Then he shoved the plate of bread and jam to the floor. Leaf raised a brow at him. Shade rolled his eyes. And Haze... the big vampire was the only one whose gaze landed on Thorne with concern because if what Clarke had seen in the vision was true, then the Prime had orchestrated the death of Thorne's mother. Why else would she have wanted that law to stay in effect? Because she wanted to control Rush. Because she wanted him to bring the chosen one to her.

Clarke just couldn't figure out why the Prime had to take this exact path.

"My point is," Clarke added quickly, "that your Prime can't be trusted. I think Rush figured it out, and that's why she hasn't been back. She's hiding... or scheming."

"Or she's dead," Shade said.

"We'd know if she was dead," Leaf defended. "And she has a realm to protect. It's not easy being the Prime."

"But at what expense?" Haze added. "She's made us all stay out of the affairs of the kingdom, but she's in the thick of it."

"It's *because* she's in the thick of it," Clarke pointed out. Silence compounded until all she could hear was the beating of her heart.

"Very well," Leaf said to Thorne through a clenched jaw. "You will go with Clarke and help these people at Crescent Hollow." He then met Clarke's eyes. "When you get back, you will help us find Jasper in return."

"Agreed."

"Or we can just make her tell us." Cloud walked in, cracking his knuckles. "Then we don't have to do anything but find Jasper."

"No," Thorne said with a sigh. "Clarke is right. Those are my people. I won't abandon them if they're in need. Jasper taught me better. I'm going."

"I don't answer to you," Cloud said.

"But you do to me." Leaf straightened.

"You lead the team, you don't make the rules."

"You don't have to join Clarke, but you won't force her to give up the information about Jasper until she's ready."

Cloud gave Leaf a derogatory stare and then left. When he was gone, Leaf turned to the rest of them. "Anyone going to Crescent Hollow, be ready and armed within the hour."

THIRTY-SIX

Life had never gone Rush's way.

From the moment he'd come out feet first, his unnatural wants had always ended in tragedy or suffering. But the alpha, Lord of Crescent Hollow, was never who he was supposed to be. If only it wasn't those closest to him who paid for his desires.

His father.

His lover.

His son.

His sister, mother.

And now... Rush's throat closed.

Damn that Prime and her always prepared answers. He'd gone to her all those nights ago, ready to annihilate, so sure that he was the one who'd known it all. But he wasn't.

"Did you ever consider that it wasn't fate doing these things to you? But yourself?" The Prime's smug voice was like honey clogging his throat.

Rush bared his teeth and planted Starcleaver's point in the female's desk. "You're the one who's doing these things, Prime. You. Not the divine Well. You've manipulated everything since... how long?"

She stared out the open window to the stars twinkling in the clear night sky. "Since before you were born."

"And after?"

"After too... but there is one thing I've never had a hand in—who the Well chooses." She glanced at Rush. "That has nothing to do with me. Not now, not ever. I just make the most of what I receive."

"Why?"

A laugh coughed out of her. "Why? You know why. So the Well doesn't dry up. So we have a bountiful land with plenty to grow. You may not remember the famine that plunged this planet into chaos, but I do. I was around when the last of our ancestors who'd fought tooth and nail to establish a stronghold on this land were still alive. And now because of the legacy they leave, it flourishes with beauty."

She was talking about the old ones. The ones who'd lived among Jackson Crimson's time, two thousand years ago. Was the Prime truly that old?

"You talk about legacy, but you have ripped mine from me."

She clicked her tongue, admonishing him. "That you have no legacy has nothing to do with me. All I did was put you in the right place at the right time. The rest was you."

The anger Rush had fostered over the time of his curse flourished anew. It seethed like a rolling ocean. How could she think she had nothing to do with his plight?

"Innocents have died because of your meddling," he ground out. "What about those?"

"No one is truly innocent. You know that."

Rush stared at his sword. He stared at her.

"I needed someone to bring her to us," the Prime conceded.

"Clarke?"

"Yes. We looked into many potential outcomes, and you were the only one who kept her from sinking to the inky depths of the Well. Has she told you what life she led in the old world? I'm not even sure if she told her friends at that time."

"If you're referring to her hand in the destruction of her world, then yes, I know. And I don't care."

"I'm not talking about that. I'm talking about the fact she used her gifts to steal from people. Cheat. Lie. Swindle. That was her motto."

He shrugged. Who was he to judge? "Perhaps. But the woman I know has honor."

She'd saved his life when she could have walked away.

"She has honor now," the Prime said. "Do you see?"

Rush turned away and clenched his jaw. She was saying Clarke would be a bad person if it wasn't for him. But he wasn't pure himself.

The Prime continued, "Because of your curse, you were the only one the Void could not See. And the only way to have you there, ready for her awakening, was to—"

"I get it," he snapped. Nothing she said mattered anyway. Even if it was the truth, it was her truth. She'd played with his family, his life, as though they were all expendable pieces of a game. His fingers wrapped around the Starcleaver's hilt. Felt the familiar heavy weight in his hands.

She licked her lips. "I may have made it so you were cursed, but I had faith you would return. I made sure your quarters remained untouched. As far as I was concerned, you were always part of the Twelve."

He'd had enough of her excuses.

"Trust me, Rush."

"I'm done with trust."

"Don't," she warned, eyes on the sword. "You'll get sick. It will push you over the edge."

His upper lip curled as he tugged the sword from the desk. The heavy metal lowered to scratch the floor. He sauntered, etching a line in the ground as he made his way to her by the window.

"You forgot one thing when you cursed me," he said, looking at her from beneath his lashes. "A loophole, if you will." He lifted Starcleaver and inspected the special glyphs etched into the blade. They were useless. Metal was magic free. It repelled magic. It was why the Guardians used metal swords to fight magical monsters. It rendered the magic of monsters impotent. "You left me Starcleaver. That was your mistake. It blocks magic. It blocks the curse from affecting me when I use it as an extension of my arm. As long as no other part of my body touches another, the sickness won't affect me. Who do you think has been culling wayward humans in our territory all these years? Or the errant monsters cavorting in Seelie territory? I know you know about them."

A small confident curve of her lips. "It wasn't a mistake. I left you Starcleaver on purpose."

He shook his head. "I don't think so. I think it was an oversight. I can scent the lie on you."

"Ah, Rush. Have you been so isolated from your kind that you've forgotten the fae cannot lie?"

"You know what I mean. You deal in half truths and misdirection."

Her big brown eyes widened a fraction, and then she pursed her lips. "History is repeating. Do you understand?"

Another step closer.

"Rush—" she put her hand up. "Killing me isn't the answer."

"Then what is?" He drew his arm back, braced, and readied to parry.

"She is. And the child growing in her womb."

Time stopped.

There was no sense, no rhyme or reason. A child? Growing in Clarke?

Rush's surprise was the break she needed. She burst into a ball of white light. Energy slammed into him. Wind ruffled his hair. He turned blindly, arcing his blade in an almighty swing. It cleaved through something, caught on the windowsill and embedded. When he could see again, a white feather beneath his blade was all that remained.

"If you want to save Clarke," she said, now suddenly behind him. "If you want to save your unborn child from suffering the same consequences as the first, then you have a choice to make."

He whirled to face her again. Drew back his sword. "You took my choice from me."

"This time, I'm giving it to you. A mouth for a mouth. Whose mouth will be the sacrifice for the new one coming into the world? Yours? Clarke's?"

There had been no question.

Rush checked his surroundings to make sure he'd landed through the portal in the correct place. The stench in the air was the first clue that he had.

Cornucopia was a sometimes shanty trading town, sometimes luxe getaway, for those who wanted debauchery, anonymity, and indulgence. Half the city was a mess of clay and stone houses. The other half, glass and precious gems glittering in the sun. The problem was, it all mixed together. Walk down any street and you'd get a shanty next to a mansion. The rough next to the sweet. The rich next to the poor.

It was why people loved it there.

He chewed on some sweet grass and stared at the city with the morning sun peeking over the horizon of jigsaw building tops. Already the bustling sounds filtered down to him. Cornucopia never slept.

The fact you have no legacy has nothing to do with me.

Fuck the Prime.

If you want to save your unborn child, then you will do exactly as I say.

Ditching the spent portal stone into the bush beside a dirt track, Rush adjusted Starcleaver on his back and set out toward Cornucopia.

Clarke would forgive him for this. She had to. It was for the good of Thorne and the good of the unborn. The Prime may be a manipulative pain in his ass, but he believed her. She'd said the only way to save Clarke and the child was to end Thaddeus. And then put another Nightstalk in his place as leader of Crescent Hollow. His sister. He didn't have to like that the Prime used him again, but he would not leave this world without a legacy. It was exactly what that scheming owl had counted on.

A mishmash of Seelie and Unseelie poured in and out of the front gate. It wasn't really a gate, per-say, but an opening in the wall twenty feet wide. There were no guards and no soldiers manning the entrance. Enter at your own peril, the sign said. The line bottle necked, and he slowed behind a group of shifters, careful not to bump into them. He could smell the fire-taint on them but could distinguish no breed. They weren't wolf, that was all he knew.

Beggars held out their hands for food or coin, but as he walked past, their eyes glazed over and they shifted their outstretched arms to the fae behind him. A buzzing overhead alerted him to a harem of pixies flying. Four males and their queen heading the formation with pride from the front.

Damned pixies and their wings, always skipping the line.

Now he was just plain grumpy. He ground his teeth. He hated being here on the Prime's insistence. Especially since he'd regretted being her puppet for so long. It was like she'd beat him to this conclusion. He'd never know if he would have come here on his own. But he knew it was the right choice.

Just as he got to the delta, his impatience wore thin. A commotion had stopped the progress of entry. He spat out the masticated mess of sweet grass and withdrew his sword. He used the length to prod and poke fae folk out of the way so he could get to the front with minimal contact. For the rest of them, his curse worked to move people and leave them forgetful in his wake. He got near the front and stopped to see a young female fae with her wrist caught by a meaty looking orc covered in dirt. The satchel bag that had been over the orc's shoulder had spilled to the floor. The smell of sour mud, sweat and shit made Rush want to gag, but the scent hadn't come from the bag. Inside was exotic red fruit the orc had probably come to sell.

The girl had red stained fingertips and lips. She'd also pissed her pants because the moment they had caught her, she'd signed her warrant to be sent to the Ring. Unless she paid for the fruit, that was, but from the looks of the scrawny thing, she had no coin.

"Not magic, not my problem," was the first thought to enter Rush's mind. Guardians were there to deal in magical disputes, magical monsters, and the preservation of the well.

But that was the Prime's legacy. Not his.

He tightened his grip on Starcleaver and sized up the orc. How to deal with this?

The orc just wanted to make a living.

The girl just wanted to eat.

Was one more right than the other? Should either die?

He grunted. Fuck this meddling shit. He sheathed the sword and dug into his pocket to find some coin. He tossed it between them. The instant the coin left his hands, it became visible and glinted in the sun. Every fae in the vicinity caught sight of the red flashing glass and pandemonium broke loose. Bodies dived for the money. Big. Small. Winged. Furred. Fists went flying. Jaws got punched. Weapons were drawn.

And that's when a gap opened, big enough for him to slide through untouched. He entered the bustling metropolis unaffected. On a whim, he glanced over his shoulder and caught sight of the red-stained-lip girl escaping under the legs of greedy fae.

With a smile, he turned toward the Ring. It was the last known location of his sister, and hopefully where he would find her working today. What the Prime counted on was that Rush had kept some kind of relationship with his sister. And she was right. There had been little Rush's curse let him do. He'd tried to write letters, but every time he put pen to paper, the curse knew his intentions. He couldn't finish the words. But he'd found loopholes. He had managed to drop coin for Kyra every time he visited. He had managed to use Starcleaver to prod the odd overzealous patron at the Ring, stopping them from causing Kyra mischief as she provided security. And then he'd managed to stay out of her life when it became clear she'd sensed his presence and not being able to communicate had caused her grief.

A clean break always healed the quickest.

And now he was back.

In the past weeks, the Prime had written letters explaining the new situation. If Kyra had received them, and believed the content, then she would have finished up work and now be waiting for him. A small part of him hoped she believed the letters. The rest was convinced she would take one look, laugh hysterically, and then incinerate them.

And stay safe.

Kyra's life had been ruined too.

Rush arrived outside the giant colosseum and searched along the outskirts. If this were night, the inside would roar with bloodlust. This morning it was eerily quiet and emptied. The last battle it served had finished hours ago. He could scent the water being hosed to wash away the blood and eviscerated body parts left on the Ring's floor.

As Kyra worked the security at the doors, she most likely had worked all night. While the battle inside the Ring was to settle scores, occasionally the bloodlust spilled into the crowd. Especially if the two fae settling the score were representatives of a larger group.

He walked around the perimeter until a familiar scent hit his nose. Kin. He crested a corner to see his sister standing tall, tough, and proud against the buttress of an alcove. Long silver hair caught in a segmented ponytail dangled over a shoulder, almost hitting her ass. Folded arms. Set jaw. And a scrunched up letter in her hand.

She'd aged.

He wondered if she'd say the same for him. Humans believed the fae to be immortal. But they only aged in different, more subtle ways. The light in her eyes, the hard set

210

to her shoulders, the way she favored one leg. It was all a sign of her times not within his orbit. He'd missed so much.

But she was there. Waiting.

Holding his breath, he stepped up to her and dropped his sword on the ground at her feet. The Prime had told him that all he needed to do to let her know he was there was to activate the portal stone, but he wanted to do more. He needed to show he was putting his faith in her, that he was there for her and that together they would take down their tyrannical uncle. The only way to do that was to lay down his prized weapon. A symbol of the organization that forbade him in the past from getting involved.

But this was his choice as much as the Prime's. It had been a long time coming.

Kyra blinked as Starcleaver came into being and then her eyes hardened. She threw the letters on the ground. It took her a long time before she gathered the compunction to speak. "I don't hear from you for years, and then I get these? What am I supposed to do with this?"

He couldn't answer. Even if he did, she wouldn't hear.

She put her hands on her hips and paced a few feet of the colosseum wall. "I thought you were dead. You're a stranger to me. Your son—who is a Guardian—is more known to me. And now you want me to go back to the Hollow to fight an evil son-of-a-bitch for a title I don't want? That I never had?" She threw her hands up in the air. "I mean. You didn't want it either. Right? You're the one who told me to stay away."

She paused, crouched and squeezed the bridge of her nose. Taking deep breaths, she finally said, "I thought I'd put this all behind me." She steeled herself and stood up. "There is nothing left for me there. Why go back?"

Rush did the only thing he could think of. He picked up Starcleaver and fought the curse to scratch a word into the stone path. REVENGE.

REVENGE

THIRTY-SEVEN

In the field outside the cadre houses, Leaf triggered a portal with his power, and sent the three winged Guardians through first. Then Thorne shifted into wolf as he went. Clarke was next.

Her stomach already churned at the thought of what would greet her on the other side. Bile hit the back of her throat and her hand flew to cover her mouth. She hadn't even traveled yet.

"You'll get used to it," Leaf said from beside her.

"When?"

He shoved her between the shoulder blades and pushed her through.

She landed in the field before Crescent Hollow and vomited. It took her a good few minutes before she could straighten, and when she did, there was no sign of life. No fee-lions flittering about. No soldiers manning the gate. Even the wind failed to blow.

Cages lined the walls as far as she could see. Each had a body inside. Each was dead silent. Including that of Anise, closest to the gate.

Fear gripped her heart and she started running. She got two feet before brawny hands slipped under her arms and lifted her clear off the ground. Kicking in a mad panic, she almost screamed as she lifted higher. Something had her.

"For a Seer, you're terrible at looking."

A shadow crossed her face as something blocked the sun, and the beat of wings gave her the final clue. Her gaze clashed with Shade's scowl. In angel form, his wings flapped from his back. He dipped and arced, turning them around in a deft maneuver, coasting to where Leaf closed the portal with some kind of hand signal and push of power. Rush had said the elves were better at using mana than any of them combined. She guessed that included creating natural portals without needing to imbue stones with a spell.

The moment her feet hit the ground, Clarke rounded on Shade. "Why did you stop me?"

"Are you mad? You never run into a hostile environment. Not without checking to see if it is safe."

She bit the inside of her cheek. He was right. Just because she could set books on fire and blast candle flames out, didn't mean she was a warrior. She had to calm down. Her strength lay in reading the future, and that was all about being calm enough to see the waves rocked by the boat. But... Anise. Still no movement in the cage.

"Are they dead?" she whispered.

Leaf's blue eyes narrowed with focus. "I don't think so, but Thorne's wolf ears will hear best." He looked at the big white wolf.

Thorne cocked his head, pricked his ears up and then dipped his head in what could be construed as a nod. Leaf turned to Cloud, Haze and Shade and pointed to the sky. He swirled his finger up.

All three took to the sky and spread out, flying in opposite directions. Two with the dark leathery wings of a bat, and the third with feathered wings as deep as the night sky. Soon, they disappeared against the backdrop of the azure and Clarke couldn't tell if it was because of their distance or if they'd used some kind of magical glamour to hide their appearance.

The sound of air ripped behind them. All three spun in time to see another portal burst into existence with blinding clarity.

Thorne's hackles raised. Leaf put his hand out, signaling for Thorne to stay. Clarke concentrated on her inner gift but felt no ill omens. Whoever was coming through wasn't the enemy.

A white-haired woman walked through holding a long curved bone scimitar in each hand. Tall, striking, and formidable, the female fae looked akin to a shield maiden stepping out of Viking lore. She was not someone Clarke wanted to get on the wrong side of. Her fur tipped ears flattened in a sign of aggression, but her eyes softened when they landed on Thorne. With that white hair, Clarke thought she must be a wolf, and perhaps related. Yes. Clarke knew who she was.

"You're Rush's sister," she said. "Kyra."

Kyra turned her way, narrowed her eyes, and then she said to Leaf, "Are you here to hinder us, or help us?"

Us?

Another figure came through the portal and paused, eyes wide and glued to her. *Rush*. Her stomach flipped. In the short time he'd left her, already her heart sang to see him again. Already she'd forgotten how terrible she'd felt when he simply disappeared. No goodbye. No explanation.

A yawning chasm of the unknown gaped between them. It could be closed with a simple few words, but the thoughts flitting behind his eyes were no sign he was ready to speak. No. He looked furious that she was there. Nostrils flared. Jaw clenched. Tendons at his neck taut.

His anger gave way to confusion as he caught sight of Thorne and Leaf. He closed the portal and then threw a mana-stone on the floor. It bounced and sizzled on the grass, spent.

"What are you doing here, Clarke?" He took a step her way with a growl of frustration. "You should be back at the Order, safe."

"And yet here you are."

"I'm a Guardian." Gold lightning flashed.

"Oh, cut the shit, Rush. I know a con when I see one. You're not here because of some duty to the Well. It's for Thaddeus and Crescent Hollow. Why won't you admit that?"

Why wasn't she good enough for the truth?

He stared at her.

She stared back. "What difference does it make if you tell me the truth? I'm here for the same reason. Why can't you speak plainly for once?"

"Clarke," he ground out. "Get Leaf to make a portal and send you home. Before it's too late."

"You know what?" she laughed. "Maybe if you had told me what you planned from the start, I'd still be there. Did you ever think that?"

To the rest of them, she must look like a crazy woman shouting at thin air, but they all knew who it was. She didn't need to make him visible. And she wasn't sure she was strong enough for them to hear her worst fears come into existence.

"It's not safe here," he said. "For you, or—"

"The baby?" She raised her brows. "Yes, I know. I also know that you conspired with the Prime to be here. But what I don't know is why you're doing it alone. I would have supported you in this. Why not tell me?"

And there it was on his face. The same look he'd given her in the library. The one that had said he'd given up. He didn't expect to come back.

Her face screwed up. Anger, denial, and pain lashed out. "No! You don't get to do this! I was working on a solution, Goddammit."

She was going to track down that forbidden part of the library. She'd sensed it there. Just a few more days was all she needed. It was the next step. She was good at stealing things. They would never know.

"There is no solution for unsanctioned breeding. This is the second time for me. Véda took the brunt of the punishment before. A mouth for a mouth. That's the law. If I don't die, then you will have to. Do you understand? I may as well do it protecting this village."

"A mouth for a mouth? Is that what the Prime said to get you to do her bidding? She's using you!" she hissed low. "Did she tell you it's her fault the breeding law is still active? The king was going to end it, but she convinced him to keep it. She gave him Jasper as an incentive."

From the way he took the hit of news without a flinch, he already knew. Or he didn't care. He knew his life had been one big manipulation, but he was here anyway. Because it was the right thing to do.

"What did she tell you to get you here?" Clarke pushed.

"She said only one outcome predicted you stayed alive after the birth. I have to make a stand with Kyra and fight for Crescent Hollow."

"Make a stand and fight with Kyra," she repeated the words for the sake of those listening. "And why did that mean keeping secrets?"

"Because... you know why."

"Because you'll die. That's why."

"Clarke," he said, voice flat. "It was always going to end this way."

"Says you!"

"Says everyone." Rush unstrapped the dagger from his belt and held it out to her. "Take it."

"No." She stepped back, throat clogging. "Stay away from me."

But he wouldn't stop coming. The bastard knew she'd asked for his dagger once, and he didn't trust her enough to arm her. Now he was freely giving her one. Coward.

She was the coward. She pointed at him. "You're going to leave me."

He stepped closer.

She stepped back. "Without even saying goodbye. Who will hold me at night? Who will keep the nightmares at bay?"

Kyra came up to Clarke. She had something in her hands. Some papers. Or letters. She held them out to Clarke. "These will explain everything."

While her face was full of compassion, her eyes were full of painful understanding. It was a look of shared heartache. She knew what Clarke was going through. What she would go through. Clarke's gaze darted to Leaf and the wolf standing further back... even they looked at her like she was some poor victim.

She was never the victim. But she'd never been alone. First her father, then her girl-friends Laurel and Ada. It was clear to her that she needed to be surrounded by good people. She couldn't stop anything on her own, let alone face an omnipotent black void she couldn't even identify. And now... her hand fluttered to her belly. She had another little life growing inside, one that needed her to be strong.

She didn't want to be like her mother. But what if that was her destiny? All the fight left her, and then her eyes locked onto Rush. "I can't do it without you. I'm not a good person."

"Of course you are."

"I'm not!" She turned to Leaf and Thorne, tears now making her vision blur. "I lied to them to get them here! This whole time it's been you keeping me on the straight and narrow. Not because you're better than me, but because you make me want to be a better person. The moment you're gone... I don't know what I'll do."

"Clarke," he said, all matter of fact. "Everything you've done while I've known you is good. It was you who guided me."

"But you didn't know me in my past life. What if this new me *is* the con? Lying to yourself is the greatest con of all." She wiped her eyes. "Did you know that?"

"I know you." He made it to her side just as Kyra held out the letters. She had no idea her brother was approaching at the same time.

"Read them," Kyra said. "They'll explain a lot. The Prime has been very forthright in her letters."

216

But there was no chance to read. There was no chance to blink. Another portal opened behind her, so fast and so bright that heat lanced along her spine. She only had enough time to register the wide, shocked looks on Kyra's and Rush's faces, and then she was pulled back into a vortex. A Void.

CHAPTER
THIRTY-EIGHT

Clarke tumbled to the ground, rolling across a hard and bumpy surface smelling like broken bracken and leaves. The wind knocked out of her. Half-blind from the portal flash, she couldn't see except to register the vague outline of trees, sky and shadows milling about. Ringing in her ears deafened her. The smell of ozone she associated with portals was rife in the air.

This wasn't Crescent Hollow.

She spat out dirt and breathed through the pain in her knees, hands, and side of her face. Nausea rolled in her stomach. She kept it down with a few gulps of air.

The ringing in her ears eased with every breath, but then shouts of battle in her periphery took over.

Horror locked her muscles. The cages at Crescent Hollow. It had been a trap. But who was the prey? Who was the bait? She blinked a few times, and figures came into focus. Kyra. She must have come through the portal too. She had two scimitars out, slicing, parrying, stabbing, locking and twisting. She plowed through two attackers with the skill and force of any Guardian. But then someone who made her skin crawl turned up.

Thaddeus. His scar puckered as he scowled at Kyra from behind. That unadulterated contempt in his eyes. Too busy fighting, Kyra was oblivious to the long sharp bone sword dangling from his hand.

Clarke opened her mouth to warn Kyra, but a croak came out. She coughed and spat out more dirt.

"Behind you!" she shouted, threw her palm out and pushed air with her power. A gust of wind blew at Thaddeus. It tripped him, knocking him into a tree, but wasn't enough to do lasting damage.

Kyra's fierce gaze caught on Clarke. She paused. And then she shifted. Her face elongated. White fur sprouted over her body. But she wasn't fast enough. A stag horned fae—the same one she'd seen at the Laughing Den—hit Kyra over the head with a club. She went down and her shift reversed.

Thaddeus kicked her swords out of the way. "Put her in the cage." His scarred face turned to Clarke. "And put her in too."

Rough arms picked her up from behind. She hadn't noticed anyone behind her. But now she was coming to her senses, she saw her location clearly. They were in the woods. Unless there was another forest full of spindly spooky trees, and dark shadowy light, it was the Whispering Woods.

Trees had been lopped around them to make a clearing. There were tents. Fireplaces. Chairs. It was a camp. This was Thaddeus's hunting party headquarters, and it appeared as though they'd been there for a while. Perhaps months.

But if he had control of Crescent Hollow, why would he need the subterfuge of a camp in the woods? The obvious answer was to keep secrets. But why would he need to do that?

"We're not allowed to play with the other humans we found, but you're not on the list. It means you're mine." That's what Thaddeus had said to her the first time they'd met. Coupled with how he'd reacted upon seeing her at the barracks, and how he'd been meeting with Bones... it could mean only one thing. They were working with the humans to hunt humans. Ones Thaddeus was prohibited to play with. Humans who could be useful, like Clarke, frozen from her time only to wake in this time with powers.

If the Prime had schemed and plotted for decades to ensure Clarke was delivered to her, then what would someone else do for another?

The fae dragged her across the soil. Swaying in the wind, one solitary metal cage hung suspended from a tree branch, five feet from the ground.

Metal.

Not wood.

Metal would block her powers and cut her from accessing the Well. The terror of it dawned on her. Even the cages along the walls at Crescent Hollow were wood. They just raised you high enough to cut your access. But Rush had said those would never work on Guardians. Maybe these metal bars were thicker. Stronger.

Was this why Thaddeus had met with the Dark Mage and Bones? They wanted cages strong enough to control the most powerful fae in Elphyne.

She suddenly wished she'd taken that knife from Rush.

"Get off me." She kicked out behind her, but a sharp pain gripped her hair, causing her to cry out. She gritted her teeth and pushed fire backward.

A curse and the stench of smoke meant she'd made her mark, but once again, her power and skill with the elements just wasn't strong enough.

Within seconds, she was at the cage and being pushed through. Her head slammed into the metal bars as they shoved her in. Pain spiked at her temple and white spots danced in her vision. Then it was quickly move to the side or be squashed by the dead weight of Kyra's unconscious body as they shoved her in. Sticky red stained the back of her white hair. Alarmed, Clarke pushed her fingers into Kyra's carotid, but relaxed when she felt a pulse beating strong. She checked Kyra's wound. The bleeding had already stopped. Thank God.

The cage door slammed with a clang.

And... a feeling switched off in her body. As though an organ had been removed, she felt like she'd had something, and now it was gone. But this displacement was nothing compared to how Kyra faired. She moaned and clutched her head. Sweat broke out on her forehead as she started panting. This was more than the injury.

For someone born with the power of the Well, being cut from it was far worse. Kyra trembled, shaking all over.

"Hey," Clarke whispered and squeezed the female's arm. "It will be okay."

"Now, isn't that better?" Thaddeus gloated as he locked the gate with a padlock. He put the key in the pocket of his regal embroidered jacket. Much fancier than what he wore last time. He appeared like a high lord, or a member of the royal court. He must expect a visit from someone important. Where her air blast had knocked him into a tree, a small sliver of blood wiped onto his thumb. His face hardened. "Oh, I'm going to have fun with you."

He walked away and motioned for the fae who'd shoved her in to follow him. Left alone with Kyra, Clarke tried to comfort her, but she was now out cold. It was probably a blessing. Rush had once said being cut from the Well was like the worst hangover you'd ever experience. The square footage of the space wasn't big enough for two people. She had to hold her knees to her chest.

Clarke rested her head between her knees. How did she get into this position? By diving head first without caution. Her mind was awash with all sorts of panicking nonsense. She took a deep, purposeful breath and exhaled. Then she looked up. Her eyes locked with Rush's.

He was there.

But lying prone on the ground, off to the side near a cluster of trees. Clarke pushed her forehead to the bars to see better.

At the time someone had pulled her through the portal, the rest of the Guardians were flying off scouting around Crescent Hollow, or had been standing too far away. But Rush had been right next to Kyra, and if she'd come through, then he must have done so by grabbing hold of her.

No, he wasn't injured. It was the contact sickness. His face glowed blue. She couldn't spot an inch of clean skin. Coming through the portal had cost him mana. Maybe all of it.

His eyes glittered with pain. Wincing, he reached over his back and unleashed Starcleaver. He held it in his hands as though it would ward off the agony.

"Hold on," he rasped. "Leaf knows... how to... trace portal."

And then he passed out.

THIRTY-NINE

She sensed him before she saw him. It was a shifting of the light composition in the woods. A shadow flitting over the sun. The temperature dropped along one side of her body. But he was neither God nor fae. He was a human in a tailored black business suit. Rose in the breast pocket. Standing by the trees, watching.

Gray at his temples sliced into the short black hair slicked from his forehead. Shrewd eyes looked out from an unremarkable middle-aged face.

Now that she'd seen him, and he knew, he moved toward her with a confident stride. Bones followed. No longer in a hooded robe, but wearing a SWAT like tactical outfit. Bulletproof vest. Black fatigues. Guns at his utility belt. Rifle in his hands. He looked like he did back in her time.

For a moment, Clarke needed to pinch herself. She had this surreal feeling that she'd stepped onto a movie set. They were so displaced. That maybe it was a dream. She rubbed her eyes. When she opened them, the Void stood before her cage, studying her. With the cage suspended, they were eye to eye.

"Clarke O'Leary," he said, voice like chills down her spine. "You've been a hard lady to find."

She said nothing and kept her eyes on him, not on Rush still recovering on the ground not far behind him.

"Well," he added with a wry smile. "To be fair, I didn't know I was looking for you until a few weeks ago. Somehow, you avoided the eyes of my Seer. I'm wondering if she didn't want the competition." He shrugged. "I killed her. So I suppose it doesn't matter now, does it? But now I have an opening for a new psychic."

She held her silence. He put his finger on Kyra's white hair and then cocked his head.

"Aren't they strange?" he murmured. "These animals? The more we learn about them, the more it seems to defy logic."

His tone suggested he spoke about a bug. Something he could squash beneath his feet or put under a microscope.

"You know," he said. "When I first awoke in this time and found this new evolution of homo sapiens, at first I was furious. I'd worked my entire life on a plan only to see it turn out differently. They weren't supposed to be here. It was meant to be the humans I'd prepared to live in a bunker, and I was supposed to be their king." He curled a strand of white hair around his finger. "These beasts were living on the land that should have been mine. They ate me out of house and home." He burst out laughing. Like a maniac. But when he came down, the humor had left his eyes. "I was their father. Their creator. If it weren't for me, none of this new evolution would exist. But just like children, there's always a use for the naughty ones."

He tugged on the hair and snapped it off Kyra's head. She cried out. Clarke reached out to soothe her.

And the Void watched it all with unbridled curiosity.

"You like these savages," he said. "You actually identify with them."

She lifted her chin. "From where I'm sitting, the savages are outside the cage."

Something flickered in his gaze, but then he stood back. "When I learned I had been gifted with some"—he looked at his hands—"abilities like these animals, I was pleasantly surprised. I was even happier to learn that this substance from their so-called magic Well of life kept me from aging. It also gave me incredible powers. On the outside, I looked the same, but inside was just as powerful as these immortal fae gods the new human settlement feared. It was so disappointing to see how regressed humans had become. Especially when I left such a detailed plan to keep them thriving." He sighed. "But, I'm a patient man. It was easy to spin a tale about being lost in the wilderness. It was even easier to convince them to install me as their leader and make them forget I didn't age, not like them. But the longer I stayed there, the more I learned of their fear for these beasts you so love. You know they'd tried to take Elphyne once and miserably failed." He shot Clarke a shark-like grin. "But they didn't have me. Or you."

"I'll never work for you."

He laughed. "Oh, we both know that's not true, don't we?"

He gestured to Bones, who left the campsite and came back with Thaddeus. He opened the cage and dragged Kyra out. And then Bones shut the gate, leaving Clarke still inside. She reached through the gaps in the bars.

The Void locked eyes with her. "You've always just needed the right motivation."

Tugging on the cuffs of his suit, he walked back a few steps to where Bones had retrieved him a chair. He sat down and waited.

For what?

Thaddeus pushed Kyra to her knees. She snarled and tried to shift. But the Void made a gesture in the air. Bones lifted his rifle, sighted, changed his mind and then pulled out a handgun from the holster on his hip. He pointed and then squeezed the trigger. A bullet ripped into Kyra's shoulder. She jerked, hit. Her shift halted mid-turn, leaving her face frozen in a state of flux. Half-wolf, half-fae. She was something between and howling in pain.

"You bastard!" Clarke shouted and rattled the cage. "Leave her alone."

"Oh, but it's so entertaining. Tell me what you see, Clarke." He gestured at Kyra. "Is that something you can identify with?"

"You're cruel. You're a cruel monster and you need to be exterminated."

"No. I'm a visionary." He tapped his temple. "They think they are ruled by some god of the earth, but we know better from our time, don't we? *We* are the gods. The fae existed once before in our time, but we got rid of them then. We can get rid of them now."

Kyra howled again, but Thaddeus pulled her head back by the segmented ponytail.

"How can you side with them?" Clarke shouted. "How can you do this to your own kind?"

Unguarded hatred and ego spilled out of Thaddeus's narrowed gaze. "My kind are stupid. They let the Order of the Well dictate how they live their life, but it's all been a lie. We need not follow their rules to be powerful. I make my own." He pushed his thumb on Kyra's wound. "No exit wound. The metal inside her prohibits the shift."

Clarke gasped. "That's why you're working with the humans. You want the weapons so you can take over Elphyne."

Thaddeus laughed, and the two humans smiled. The Void looked at Clarke. "Why bother with taking over Elphyne when you can let them destroy themselves?"

Attack themselves?

The White Woman. The drained Satyr. There were probably more.

"You're the one who's been making it look like Unseelie are attacking out of their territory."

Bones pulled a glass canister from his belt. It reminded Clarke of the one Rush had used to catch manabeeze. And when Bones walked toward Kyra, Clarke's heart stopped.

"No," she gasped. *Don't you dare.*

But he didn't slice her throat like a warada. He handed the canister to Thaddeus and pulled out a glass syringe, sloshing with metal in the tube. He depressed the needle, testing the pressure, and then jabbed Kyra in the neck.

Liquid metal injected into her veins and she screamed in agony.

"You see what's happening, Clarke?" the Void asked, fascinated. "With iron in her system, and the magic's aversion to the substance, the life force has to go somewhere. It's being forced out." He lifted his palms. "There's nothing special about it. Just science."

Little balls of light popped out of Kyra's chest. Thaddeus held the canister and trapped them as they escaped.

"Stop!" Clarke shouted. "I'll do whatever you want. Just let her go."

The Void nodded and Bones pulled the syringe out of Kyra's neck. The light stopped leaving her body, and Thaddeus screwed the cap on the glass canister. He handed it to the Void, who opened it and drank the contents. Light moved from inside his throat to his chest and then dispersed. Within moments, his pupils contracted. Every aspect of his body language projected bliss. It was like seeing a junkie take a hit. And then other changes happened. The color on his cheeks brightened, the lines on either side of his eyes lessened, and the gray in his hair disappeared altogether. He'd grown younger. He made a satisfied sound and patted his stomach. "Not purified, but I'm sure I'll manage a few memories of a measly female wolf."

"You will destroy the world," Clarke ground out. "I've seen it."

"No, Clarke. You must be mistaken. I will save it," he drawled.

She sat back in the cage and shook her head. He was deluded. Completely unaware that his actions would have devastating consequences. For him. The world. One day, there would be a painful reckoning for him. And she looked forward to being the one to show him the truth. The Prime's machinations made sense. She had told Clarke that truth could be a weapon and now Clarke was finally seeing the possibilities. One day it would come down to Clarke and the Void. Truth against delusion.

"Until then," the Void said, as though he'd read her mind. "I promised Thaddeus here that he could play with you." Then he turned to Thaddeus. "A psychic needs to keep use of her mouth, otherwise she can't speak the future. So just... you know, stay away from that area. Understood?"

Thaddeus nodded, evil eyes never leaving Clarke.

"Good. And when you're done, collect the last remaining mana from the she-wolf. She was tasty. There will be more people Clarke loves coming soon. More we can torture."

His sidekick helped him stumble away, wasted.

FORTY

Drowning in agony, Rush could do nothing but lie on the dirt and watch as a bullet tore into his sister, and then they injected liquid metal into her system. Some blend of iron he could scent. Then that filthy rotten scum stole and drank her mana.

It was a violation of the highest order and they wouldn't get away with it. None of them. He would hunt them down and rip their innards out first. His inner wolf battered at Rush's restraint, wanting out. It wanted revenge. And he would give it to him.

The pain crippled him, but it gave him time to formulate a plan. He saw in perfect clarity how he would pick up Starcleaver and run them through. They wouldn't even know he was coming. Many long minutes later, Rush pushed onto his trembling hands and knees to breathe through the last remnants of pain. As his senses cleared, he zeroed in on the conversation.

"Until then," the human said. "I promised Thaddeus here that he could play with you." A pause. "A psychic needs to keep use of her mouth, otherwise she can't speak the future. So just... you know, stay away from that area. Understood?

Rush's head snapped up, and he locked eyes on Clarke in the cage. That's why the scum wanted her. For her gift. Control the future, control the world. A world he created. Wide-eyed and full of defiance, she ground her teeth and stared at the man in the black suit as though she could kill him with a look.

But he was too far gone on the mana he'd ingested. He swayed and then said to Thaddeus, "Good. And when you're done, collect the last remaining mana from the she-wolf. She was tasty. There will be more people Clarke loves coming soon. More we can torture."

A snarl ripped from Rush's lips. But he wasn't ready to attack. Not recovered. He had to be error free as he ran his enemies through. Any wrong movement and they'd touch him. He looked down at the bright blue lights twinkling over his hands and reflecting off Starcleaver's blade as it lay between. The weight of understanding settled in his heart. This was it. His last battle. He would make it count.

He lifted his gaze, but the humans were gone, and Thaddeus whispered animosity to Clarke.

"No." Rush pushed to his feet, every muscle and bone aching with each breath. "Stay away from her."

The pain forced him to rest his palms on his knees and catch his breath. But despite his weary body, the wolf inside was ready to go. It howled with indignation. It scratched at its cage. It filled Rush with adrenaline.

Where were the Guardians?

Leaf had to find them soon. He had been right there when the portal was opened. Rush just needed to keep Thaddeus at bay for long enough until the Guardians tracked the portal remnants and arrived. But when Thaddeus gave a shrill whistle, and two others from his hunting party returned to the camp, Rush's hope squashed. Three of them. How could he stop three? Kyra still lay on the floor, half shifted, but not dead. If he could get that bullet out of her shoulder, then finishing the shift might be enough to purge the remaining iron from her blood. Hopefully.

"Clarke," he croaked. "The cage isn't strong enough to keep all your power at bay."

Clarke's eyes darted to him, but then shifted back to an indeterminate spot. She didn't want to give him away. But she heard him. "Remember I said the metal cage couldn't hold me? That's why they used a curse?"

She gave a minute nod.

"So reach for your power. All I need is for you to feel enough to get Kyra to see me. Just her. Can you do that?"

Another quick nod, and then her brows drew together in concentration. Rush checked Thaddeus's status. He barked orders at his hunters. They would turn on Clarke and Kyra any second.

Come on Clarke.

He couldn't wait any longer.

"Kyra," he croaked.

She moaned but didn't respond.

Gulping air, he tried again. "*Kyra.*"

Rolling to the side, her searching eyes landed on him. If she could get through this, he could too. "Get the bullet out," he said. "Dig into your wound with your claw and scoop it out. Do you understand?" He caught his breath. "It will allow you to shift and heal."

Shift and heal. The words stuck in his mind. If he shifted too, the last of the sickness would wash away... but it would also use the very last drop of his mana. Nothing would be left to hold the curse at bay. He'd age.

It might be enough.

"I think this will work better with you out of the cage," Thaddeus said to Clarke. "But we don't want you to cause any trouble."

"I will be nothing but trouble, asshole."

"Very well." Thaddeus paused with the key in the padlock and scanned the camp.

"We need something metal to stick into her. It will prevent her from using magic. Bring me something."

The bastards discussed her torture as though ordering something from the butcher at the markets. They disgusted him. Rush went to pick up his sword—

"Hey, Faddeus," the ram said, coming from the right. He picked up Starcleaver. "What's this?"

Shit.

Thaddeus glared at the ram, but when his eyes hit the sword, he froze. "That's my nephew's sword. He's here."

Like a switch being flipped, Rush burst into action. Willing strength into his legs, he launched at the ram. He covered the ram's hands on the hilt, twisted the sword tip to face the ram and then ran him through. To anyone else, it looked like the ram had stabbed himself. He went down to one knee, eyes wide in confusion, blood bubbling at his stomach. He wouldn't have known it was Rush.

"You idiot," Thaddeus snapped. "Find him!"

But the contact sickness doubled. Rush had touched the ram's hands. There had been no other way to control the sword. He collapsed on the ground while the other fae started looking around, stupid enough to check behind tents and chairs. Thaddeus went for the ram. He tugged the blade out of his stomach.

"I have to do everything myself." Thaddeus stood still and searched the clearing, but he didn't have to search far. His eyes landed on Rush and he laughed. "Oh, if you could see you now. All lit up like blue fireworks and crawling like a coward toward your mate."

He can see me?

But of course he could. Rush's mana was depleted. That last touch to the ram had tipped him over the edge. The curse was ending. Death waited for him on the other side of the veil. The wolf inside him howled—in fury, in pain, in longing. They could see Clarke. Just out of their reach but the weariness of time dragged him down, and he could barely breathe.

He was starting to age. But with the weakening curse, came access to the Well. He could feel the life of the planet in the ground beneath his touch. The connection wasn't as strong as a sacred place, but it was there. He just didn't have days to replenish his mana stores.

He had to get to Clarke. Whatever he gleaned from the source beneath his fingers, he'd give it to her. She'd broken through the metal cages restrictions enough to make him visible to Kyra. Maybe he could boost her somehow. At the very least, his mana would show her his memories, his feelings, his love. All the things he'd failed to say.

Clarke leaned back in the cage and kicked at the door, trying to get out. "Rush!"

"You're pathetic. Just like your father." Thaddeus stood between Clarke and Rush, a smile splitting his face as he watched Rush crawl to his mate. "You know he crawled too... at the end."

Rush choked and coughed. The blue glyphs moved on his skin as though they, too, heard the horrific confession. *Fuck him.* Rush wouldn't give Thaddeus his last moments. Pushing to his hands and knees, he tried once more to get to Clarke. The air moved in his raw lungs. His throat was sandpaper. His eyes were fire. He'd thought he could do this without her, to end Thaddeus and bring something right back to Crescent Hollow. To build a legacy. But now that he was here, in this moment, all he cared was that he couldn't leave this existence with things not right between them. She was everything.

His entire life had been one long winding path with her at the end.

"Clarke," he croaked. He was almost there.

Thaddeus booted him across the middle, sending him sprawling to the ground. He coughed into the dirt. He didn't have the energy to talk back.

"You didn't hear me." Thaddeus pointed the tip of the blade into Rush's arm and pushed.

White-hot agony lanced down his arm, and he roared in pain.

"I killed your father," Thaddeus clarified. "It wasn't you and your quest to join the Guardians. It was me and my men. I still can't believe how easy you were to fool."

Shock blanched Rush's face, draining the blood.

"Oh yes." Thaddeus grinned. The scar under his eye puckered. "Now you're listening. Well, let me tell you more secrets.... Your mother? I was in her ear every night, telling her to end it. Your lover? The mother of your child? Who do you think paid her to lie with you? Who do you think told her to keep the pregnancy a secret? And that magical monster that needed extermination on the exact day of her execution?" Thaddeus whispered into Rush's ear, "*Who do you think asked the Order for you to do your Guardian duty?*"

Fury burned and churned in Rush. He'd thought it was all the Prime... but Thaddeus had orchestrated the worst parts of his life. His uncle. Rush couldn't see straight from the vitriolic rage coursing through his veins. The wolf crashed to the surface. Rush could feel his teeth elongating. He growled through fangs, catching Thaddeus in his sight, and he forced his claws to drag his useless, semi-shifting body. Closer. Closer. He pushed Thaddeus back to the cage.

The struggle to keep the wolf in check pushed Rush's control to the limit.

The pleased look on his uncle's face said it all. He thought he'd gotten away with it.

And then Clarke's pale hands poked between the bars of the cage. She swung her favorite strip of torn cloth around Thaddeus's neck, caught it in the other hand, and then yanked hard. It pulled tight across his neck, choking. She put her feet against the bars for purchase and pulled with her weight to garrote.

Seeing her like this, fighting for his honor, for their lives, it gave him the strength to push to his feet.

Taking a life left a stain on one's heart. He wouldn't let Clarke tarnish herself for this. So he did the only thing he could think of. He let the wolf out.

CHAPTER
FORTY-ONE

The grip Clarke had around the garrote slipped. She cried out. No no no. She had to hold on. Even though the pain in her palms felt like she was slicing right through her hands. She would not go down without a fight. This fae was the reason for all the pain in Rush's life.

This evil fae.

White hair pushed through the cage and she bit down, capturing a chunk in her mouth and pulling to keep his head against the bars. It was dirty street tactics. It was disgusting. But she was desperate. It took so much effort to will Kyra to see Rush, and that had been a part of her power she was more confident with. The fire and wind, less so. Nothing was easy behind the metal bars.

And then an unearthly howl pierced her ears. A flash of blue light.

She spat out the hair and looked around Thaddeus's head. What she found wasn't possible. Rush. Not Rush. His wolf. Beautiful. White. Large. Its head came up to Thaddeus's armpits. The wolf's golden eyes met Clarke's. She didn't know how, but she sensed his intention. His plan. As though deep underwater, a calm settled over her. Her breath bloomed. And then she let go.

Thaddeus threw up his hands. He faced Clarke, as though she could somehow help him.

"Please..." he rasped.

Clarke looked him straight in the eyes and said, "Oh yes, you'll beg. You'll beg right up until the end. Cowards always do."

And then the wolf attacked. She shut her eyes so she didn't have to watch. She blocked her ears so she didn't have to hear. And when she thought it was safe, she looked again.

Thaddeus was hidden from view, somewhere beneath the cage. And Rush... he was still in wolf form, head on the ground, tongue hanging out of his bloody jaws, panting.

"Rush," she cried and wrapped her fingers around the bars.

Somewhere behind them, another fight was happening. Kyra had managed a full shift. She was in the corner eating something... or someone.

"Hold on, Rush." She spotted Thaddeus's key, still in the lock. "I'm coming. Just hold on."

Tears burned her eyes as she fumbled with the key. And when it dropped, the tears flowed over. She reached out, grasped air, but caught nothing. The key bounced on the dirt. Collapsing to the base of the cage, she dangled an arm through the bars, just like she remembered the pixie doing. The other hand, she placed over her womb.

"Rush..."

She squeezed her eyes shut. This couldn't be it. No. Please no.

"I love you," she whispered.

Now the tears were big, wracking sobs. Goddamn this world. Goddamn it for giving her everything and then taking it away. She wanted to scream. To hurl curses at the wind. But then a wet, warm pressure pushed into her palm. She looked down. It was the wolf's nose. He lifted his head, got to his paws, and touched her. One last time.

"I love you, you stupid fae." She cupped his muzzle. "You're so beautiful."

He whined.

A spark zipped from his body to hers. Power. Light. Life. Mana. It ripped into her body, wrapped around her heart, swirled around the life they'd created, and settled bone deep. Suddenly, she could feel him as though he were a part of her. She could sense his emotions. Knew he was there. A burning sensation itched along the part of her arm dangling out. It started small, like a tickle, and then built to an inferno in a way she'd never felt before. Blue light leaked from her pores in ripples of light. It enveloped the wolf. Sparked in his eyes. And then wrapped around both of them at once.

A bond snapped into place.

And through that bond, Clarke felt Rush's emptiness. He'd drained his mana stores, so she filled it up. She gave him energy. It wasn't much. The cage weakened her, but with her arm outside of the barrier and free, she sensed a sliver of the cosmic energy holding their planet together. The Well.

Rush had been right.

It wasn't something she could find. It had to find her. To find them. And it had been waiting.

Slowly Rush's wolf strengthened its touch at her hand. Tears spilling from Clarke's eyes turned joyful because the blue light that had leaked from her pores turned into a pattern along her forearm and hand. It reminded her of contour lines on a geographical map. The evidence was right there—the marking of a Well-blessed union.

The air around Rush shimmered, blistered, and then he shifted into his fae form. Naked as the day he was born, and with his own Well-blessed marking, he reached through the cage and pulled her lips to the gap. Mashed together between the bars, they kissed. Embarrassing sounds came out of Clarke as she cried and whimpered. He was okay. There were no curse marks on his body. He was young. Alive. This was it.

"I don't know if you heard me as a wolf, but I love you, Rush."

"I think I've loved you since the first time I carried you in my arms," he whispered, forehead on the bars.

"But that was so long ago."

"The heart wants what it wants."

She brushed his beard with her knuckles. "How? I mean, you said a Well-blessed union was instantaneous."

"I don't know. I think... I think because the curse cut me from the eternal Well, it couldn't approve of our union. It had to wait until the last of my mana was spent, and the end of the curse triggered. With nothing blocking that connection anymore, the last piece of the puzzle clicked into place when you said you loved me."

"The Prime. She knew. It's why she—"

Rush kissed her. "Doesn't matter. I used to think her manipulations mattered." His eyes softened, taking her in. "I don't need a blessed union to tell me I love you. I did that on my own."

"As did I."

He pulled away and picked up the fallen key. Two seconds later she was out and in his arms. They only had time for a small reunion, and then a portal ripped into being at the center of the camp. Bright light flashed, blinding them all. When it all came into perspective, the Guardians were there.

A white wolf. Three avenging winged fae. And a furious looking elf.

"You're late," Rush said.

CHAPTER
FORTY-TWO

From the moment Thorne stepped through the portal and found the bloody destruction waiting, he knew the battle wasn't over. The scent of fresh blood burned his sensitive wolf nose. Three bodies, two beyond comprehension. One still writhing from a sword wound in the shoulder. But the most arresting thing of all was seeing his father, curse free, and in a passionate embrace with his mate—no, *Well-blessed* mate.

It had been Clarke all along. A human.

The matching blue contours rippling up their arms proved it.

Seeing his father happy tied Thorne into all sorts of knots. A part of him saw how they loved each other, how the Well had approved, and something twisted inside. It wasn't hate. It wasn't jealousy. It was... an emptiness waiting to be named.

After arriving, the Guardians had spent the following hour canvasing the area, looking for further threats. Rush had mentioned there were humans who'd worked with Thaddeus. And the secrets he'd revealed were disturbing. Thorne had listened to it all from within the confines of his wolf form. Somehow, being on four paws made the truth easier to handle.

He couldn't see the Order staying out of it now. Not when the threat to the integrity of the Well was so glaringly obvious.

This was war.

And other secrets were revealed. About Thorne's mother. How she'd been paid by Thaddeus. It wasn't as though he'd thought his parents loved each other, but the truth had cast the situation into new light. How could he be angry at Rush for the part he played?

He couldn't.

But he *was* angry. That part hadn't changed. He just had no one to direct his rage at.

So he would filter it into finding Jasper. He would find the missing wolf, and then fight this war he'd never asked to be part of.

Pacing by the campfire someone had set up, even though it was midday, Thorne decided he'd waited long enough. Someone had found a blanket and cast it over Rush's shoulders. He pulled a corner to cover both he and his mate. They spoke in low, hushed voices to each other while Leaf and the remaining crew who hadn't gone back to the Hollow were doing last sweeps of the area.

Thorne shifted from wolf to fae form, and then went over. Rush stiffened. Clarke made a point to stare at his face and not the naked half of him most females enjoyed.

"Rush. Clarke." He nodded.

She broke free and before Thorne knew it, she hugged him. Going tense all over, he looked to Rush with wide eyes. "What...?"

Rush smirked. "Let her have it."

The redhead lifted her gaze, eyes glistening with tears. Thorne frowned.

"Thank you," Clarke said.

Both Rush's and Thorne's eyebrows winged up. She didn't. Oh, yeah. She did.

"And before either of you rub in the fact I said thank you. I don't care. I'll say it again."

"Why?" Thorne asked.

Clarke stepped back to see him better. "Because in the end it was you who said you wanted to come to Crescent Hollow to help Anise. Leaf told me you were the first to get her, and the rest of them, down from the cages."

A weird feeling rolled in Thorne's chest. "I was just doing my job."

"Ah," Clarke laughed. "But you see, it wasn't doing your job. Anise is alive and recovering because of you. So thank you. This is me telling you that when you need something in return from me, I'll be here."

"Within reason." Rush held out his finger.

All three of them stared at each other, no more words coming to mind.

Well, this is awkward.

He turned to leave.

Clarke took hold of his wrist. "Wait."

She opened her mouth to speak, but no words came out. Her irises turned white and seemed to go somewhere else as the Seeing vision took her in its grip. With a gasp, she let go of Thorne and her eyes returned to normal.

"I lied," she said. "When I told you I could help you find Jasper at the Order."

"I know," he growled. "I heard your confession at Crescent Hollow."

"Well. The thing is... after touching you, just now, I saw something new."

Thorne tensed. "What did you see?"

"I saw the person who will lead you to Jasper." She bit her lip and slid a look to Rush.

"Whatever it is, you can tell me," Thorne said. "I promise I won't bite your head off."

Right now. Maybe later. If she lied again.

"Okay," Clarke replied. "It's just that... the person who will lead you to him is a human from my time. A woman."

Thorne folded his arms, chewing over the scenario in his mind. Okay. It wasn't so bad. Clarke had turned out... semi-bearable. And she was loyal. Strong-willed. A good mate for his father. He supposed.

"That's fine," he said. "Where do I find her?"

"She won't thaw for some time, but... there's more."

He growled, "And?"

"And," she flinched, "Never mind."

He narrowed his eyes at her. She was clearly hiding something. And it festered already in his mind. These humans, even the ones imbued with power, were tricky creatures. They lied as easy as breathing. It was enough to make him sick.

Rush must have seen the fire in his eyes, because his alpha energy swelled, brushing down Thorne's front in warning.

"Enough," Rush said to him. "When it's time, she will tell you."

"Jasper might not have time."

"He does. It's all he has." Clarke cuddled into Rush, her expression turning melancholy.

Thorne opened his mouth—

"Thorne." Rush's deep voice cut through the night. "I know you don't want to hear this, but I've always tried to be there for you. Being a Guardian was forced on you. If you want to leave, I will support your decision. When it comes time to go on the hunt, I will be right there next to you. Until you're ready to accept that, I need to be with my mate."

Rush lifted Clarke in his arms and carried her to where Leaf stood with Shade, discussing the containment of the area.

"Where are you going?" Thorne asked.

The only reply was something mumbled about a cabin. And when Leaf activated a portal, the two of them went through on their own.

Just before the portal closed, Clarke shouted to him, "We'll talk soon."

And then they were gone.

FORTY-THREE

With the moon lighting the way, Clarke held Rush tightly as he carried her across the snowy shore of the lake near his cabin. Icy air nipped at her skin, but he shrugged the blanket from his shoulders and kept walking. Straight into the warm water. As the level hit his knees, he sank down. She gasped as they immersed in the heat. Steam curled between them. It was like a bath. A glorious bath. With deft, strong hands, he positioned her so she straddled his front, until it was just the two of them staring into each other's eyes.

She wiped silver hair from his furrowed brow. He was here. He was safe. He was alive. The emotion was too much for her fragile heart to contain and she felt it slide down their bond. She still marveled at how his injury healed when he shifted into a wolf. She'd seen Thaddeus stab him, but where the sword had entered his arm, only a pink scar remained. She lightly traced her finger around it, and then slid her hands over his shoulders to massage the hard knots on his back.

The long, guttural groan that came out of him rattled Clarke to the core, setting her pulse on fire.

"Feel better?" she purred.

Two eyes shuttered. His brows lifted in the middle as his body lost tension. Hands gripped her hips and pushed down, proving that not all parts of him had relaxed. He hardened beneath her and lifted his hips brazenly to prove it. A small moan slipped out of her.

"Yeah. Feels better," he muttered. "Mate. Mine."

She smiled. "Mate. I like that."

His eyes opened. Clashed. And he growled, "*Well-blessed* mate. The first in centuries. Us." Humor fled as his gaze turned smoldering. He lowered it to the luminescent blue markings twirling her arm. And then the mirror markings on his. Suddenly, Clarke couldn't breathe. His love fed down their bond, gushing like a tidal wave. Electricity rippled across the water. Wind buffeted their hair, tickling her skin. There was something in the air, in the water that... that was alive.

"Can you feel it?" she whispered, looking around in awe. Tree top shadows rustled against the gray sky. The wind whispered. The water swirled and eddied... and little sparks of bioluminescent blue swam about their bodies in a lazy dance. Her breath hitched. "What is it?"

"This lake is a source of power," he said, voice hoarse. "It's welcoming us. Here we can replenish our mana faster than from the land. But it's not only the lake feeding me, refilling me. I feel your power through our bond, seeping into my body, making me whole. I feel your love. I feel..." He snarled and cupped her face with his hand, forcing her gaze back to his. Dark pupils dilated... almost helpless. "I feel..."

And then she saw it. It wasn't the world around them she was feeling. It was Rush. His power. His spark. Everything his curse had blocked was now coming back. At the academy, he'd mentioned he could control the elements as well as shift into wolf. When she'd first met him, she likened him to a storm. And now a storm raged around them. Swirling wind. Sparks skipping over his shoulders. Electricity in the air. Thunder crashing. All from him. And here he was, tense and full of energy, eyes and skin barely containing the tempest crackling within.

"This is you," she whispered. "The real you."

"This is what you do to me. This is us."

His lips crashed against hers. Tongue pushed into her mouth. He deepened the kiss with a shuddering groan. So much feeling bursting in her chest. Falling. Falling. She was drowning in his scent, his emotion, his heat.

Frenzy came over them. She couldn't get close enough, and he couldn't touch her enough. Her clothes? What clothes. They were gone. Only the sundial on the leather cord remained. The rest had simply burned off. Disintegrated. It had been him. His magic. She knew from his wicked smile. His male satisfaction, and the possessive thrust of his cock into her now unimpeded entrance.

She gasped and fell back until her head landed on the water, eyes on the star filled sky. Reveling in the way he filled her completely, she yielded to his passion because it felt like her own. There was no way to tell where it ended or began. Strong hands braced her back and kept her afloat, while he slid into her from beneath. Hot lips trailed down her front. Fire skipped over her body, electrifying every nerve ending. He pulled her nipple into his mouth, growling around her flesh. "Mine, Clarke. You're mine."

She didn't need to speak, just feel, and he knew how much she loved him. The sensations hurtling through her body were almost too much. She felt his desire. He felt hers. They shared their very life-force. They were more than married. More than mates. They were one.

And they would be unstoppable.

⚖

Sometime later, Clarke cuddled Rush within his cabin. Lying on the bed, a fire crackling in the hearth, they couldn't let go of each other. The sprites were happy to see them, and danced in the flames.

But her stomach rumbled.

Rush pushed up onto his forearms. His laughing eyes landed on her stomach and then he pressed his ear to her womb.

"Is the little wolf hungry?" he asked.

She laughed and stroked his hair. "How do you know it will be a wolf? Maybe it will stay human."

He sat up, a serious look on his face. "Any babe this ravenous is surely a wolf."

"Yeah, okay. Whatever you say, Dad."

His expression turned somber, and he laid back to stare at the canopy of leaves branching across the cabin ceiling. She felt his guilt spear through their bond. With a gentle pat on his chest, she rolled to face him and rested on her elbow.

"Thorne will come around," she said.

He shrugged.

"He will," she insisted. "He has his own journey to go on first. Remember I mentioned my friend? The one who will lead him to Jasper? She's going to be his Well-blessed mate. I just didn't want to let him know. Somehow, I don't think he'll be receptive to a mating not of his choosing, and to be honest, she's not going to be happy either."

Rush turned to her, eyes hard. "There will be more unions like ours?"

She nodded. "I think many more. And for every one I find thawed from my time, there will be a Guardian as their mate. I think it's for a reason."

"Because you give me power. Power unlike any I've felt before." He rolled onto her, and crowded her with his strength. Muscles bulged. Tendons flexed. She had no doubt he would be lethal, dangerous, deadly. As if reading her mind, he gave her a smile that displayed sharp wolf-like fangs. "With your mana replenishing mine through our bond, I feel invincible."

She bit her lip. It was like she was Rush's battery. His personal source of power. "Our ability to transfer power will come in handy when the war finally hits."

"Then we will be ready when it is time." He arched a hesitant brow. "When will that be?"

"Hopefully, if we keep fighting, it will never be time. But if you're referring to when will I need to go and find the next person from my time? Not for a few years."

He loosed a breath. "Good. I want to be alone with you first. Time without the pressure of fate scratching at our door."

A scratching came at the cabin door. Their eyes widened. And then a wolf whined outside.

Rush returned her grin. "Gray must be hungry too."

FORTY-FOUR

TWO YEARS LATER

A lifetime of manipulation, machination, and sheer joy had brought Rush to this —sitting by his lake, watching a half nude woman wading in the shallows, hunting for pebbles. She was beautiful. Still. The same as the day he'd first laid eyes on her. And still, he leered like a horny teen.

He doubted he'd ever stop.

"What do you think," he mumbled to the cooing toddler wriggling on the blanket next to him. He tickled the child's stomach. "Does she look good enough to eat?"

She giggled and rolled on the blanket, trying to fight her way from Rush, but he caught her and dragged her back to him. Named aptly for the place of Rush's and Clarke's first kiss, Willow had redefined Rush's definition of life. Even though she was yet to shift into a wolf and prove her daddy proud, Willow had carved out new places in Rush's heart.

A yip came from Rush's right, and Gray came bursting out of the forest, followed by his own litter of new pups. Three little white and gray wolves chased him into the water, where they stayed, barking and yipping from the shore. Gray pranced around Clarke, splashing in the shallows. Rush hadn't thought the old wolf had it in him to rear another brood, but there he was, eyes lit up with new life.

In the past two years since Clarke had been in this time, the weather had warmed. The snow was gone from the mountains. For now. She said it would be back next year.

But Gray and his pack had stayed. The damned sprites had stayed. Even Thorne had begrudgingly visited a handful of times. Granted, each time had been to push for information on when they'd find Jasper, but he'd come. And each time the gap between them had closed just a little.

Kyra had established herself in Crescent Hollow as the new Lady Nightstalk. She was doing it on her own. No alpha mate to join her. But she had friends. Anise, Clarke's barmaid friend had also made a full recovery and supported Kyra's leadership, along with most of the town.

A trickle of unease traveled down their mating bond to Rush. Clarke patted Gray's old head. She pulled out the sundial on the cord around her neck, checked the time and then squinted his way. He knew that look.

Their blissful break was over. Things were about to change.

The End.

Thank you for reading Clarke's and Rush's story. I hope you liked their journey. Please consider leaving a review online to share the love. Thorne's and Laurel's story is next.
Lana
xx

THE SOLACE OF SHARP CLAWS

FAE GUARDIANS BOOK 2

BLURB

Sharp claws keep you safe.

That's the brutal lesson Thorne learned as a young wolf-shifter. Abandoned as a child, singled out by an evil uncle, and then forced to work for the ruthless Order of the Well, Thorne's anger was a weapon as much as his claws. Now a vicious Fae Guardian, he hunts monsters, the human enemy, and anything that gets in his way. On a mission to find his missing mentor, Thorne finds himself suddenly mated to Laurel, a beautiful, driven, but damaged human awoken from a time long since past.

A forced marriage is something neither of them want.
But everything they need.

Spending time with her teaches him that arm's length might not be a good thing. Learning to love will mean scratching the surface of both their souls, revealing truths more painful than any wound. If he can get past the hurt, the pain, and the pride, Thorne will find a new use for his claws... to bury deep and never let her go. But when a dark figure from Laurel's past catches up with her, it's not Thorne's claws in question. It's hers. If he can't stop her from exacting bitter revenge, she'll cost him the safety of his mentor and perhaps trigger a war. If he can learn to put his angry past behind him, open his heart and trust new friends, he just might be rewarded with more than an advantage in their ongoing war. He'll find love.

the SOLACE of SHARP CLAWS

CHAPTER
ONE

Thorne stepped through a portal into a field of long grass just outside the burning village of Mornington. Dressed for battle in his Guardian uniform, he unhooked Fury from his holster and held the silver-tipped battle-ax at his side. Decades of use molded the grip to fit his palm perfectly.

He dropped the spent portal stone and took in the scene. The overcast sky hid nothing from his sharp wolf-shifter senses. Screams and desperate cries floated across the field as the nearby village oozed flames and the acrid scent of fear. Caustic ozone from the recent portal mixed with undertones of blood, urine, disturbed dirt... and... Thorne inhaled, tasted notes on the air... A storm is brewing.

Prepare for battle.

Hushed murmurs reached him. He used Fury to cleave a path through the long grass. The voices stopped as his footsteps drew near.

"It's me," he said, voice low.

Aeron and River were huddled together, scratching a game plan in the dirt. The two Guardians were distinguishable not only from the similar leather battle uniform, but the twinkling blue teardrop tattoo under one eye. Aeron's long brown braid trailed down his back and over his baldric. The elf was adept at all forms of magery and was the cadre's most knowledgeable when it came to the monsters they hunted.

River's wings fanned out behind him, a reflection of his unique feathers when in crow form. They shimmered in shades of blue and black, just like his three-inch hair rustling in the wind.

Aeron scowled at Thorne. "I asked for Leaf. Or Forrest."

"Fuck you, too." Thorne kicked dirt on them.

"Harsh, bro," River snapped and then dusted himself off.

"Shh." Aeron waved them back down. "The djinn will hear us."

"A djinn." *Well-damn.* No wonder Aeron wanted another elf. Leaf, in particular, the team leader of their Cadre of Twelve, was adept in airborne elemental magic. Something Thorne could do in small doses but avoided in favor of shifting into a wolf and tearing through things with his fangs.

"What's the plan?" Thorne crouched low, leather breeches creaking.

"I say we trick the damned genie back into its bottle," River suggested. "Then we control it."

"What bottle?" Aeron scoffed. "Have you found it?"

River raised a snarky brow. "So what's your plan then, Preceptor Know-it-all?"

Aeron glared at River and then wiped the dirt until he had a flat surface again. He used his knife to draw a shape. "This is the djinn."

River snorted. "Looks more like a blob."

Aeron pointed at him, and River swallowed his retort.

Aeron then poked a hole in the middle of the shape. "This is the djinn's heart. It's the only solid part of the creature. Actually, the djinn *is* the heart. It just uses copious amounts of energy to create a storm-like smokescreen to hide its true self. We catch that"—he pointed at the heart—"and we live to see another day. The villagers live to see another day."

"How do we destroy it?" Thorne asked.

"We don't. We capture it," Aeron replied sternly and put his knife away.

"Why don't we just get rid of it?" Thorne's tongue swept over his lethal fangs. "It would save a lot of trouble. Djinns have a habit of escaping."

"Isn't a djinn's heart worth a lot of coin?" River asked, blue eyes twinkling.

Well-damned crows, always thinking of coin.

"Forget it. The Prime will want to question it," Aeron confirmed.

The Prime.

Thorne's ears flattened, and he bared his teeth. Her meddling talons had been shredding his fate since before he was born, but as the leader of the Order of the Well, she had a right to do so—as long as it was in the name of protecting the integrity of magic in Elphyne. The last thing any fae wanted was to revert to the barren world of the past where they aged and couldn't access the magic of the Well.

Screw the Prime.

There was one thing Thorne and Fury were good at—decimating. "Let's do this."

He stood and surveyed the field, but the moment his head cleared the long tips of tall grass, a malevolent force struck him in the face, sending him careening backward. He landed with a thud, heavy body crunching over sharp twigs and blades of grass. His breath knocked out of him. Fury skittered to the side. Groaning, Thorne blinked at the stormy sky until his senses became functional. And then he heard River snickering.

Bloody crow.

Thorne's anger, his old friend, swiftly rose to heat his face. He collected his ax and crawled back to the group with a throaty growl. "You could have warned me."

"Where would the fun be in that?" River wiped a tear from his eye.

"Why do you think we're staying hidden?" Aeron shot back. "The djinn is just waiting for your head to clear."

"Tell me how to capture it," he said. And then kill it.

"We need to use a deionizing spell to weaken its tempest and slow it down. But we have to be sure it will be a direct hit. The spell will use the vast majority of my stored mana. Once it's slowed, we cast the silver net over the bulk of its energy." Aeron tossed a fine silver mesh at River, who caught it and opened it. The elf continued, "River, you hover up high, get ready to cast the trap. Thorne and I will be on the ground to keep it contained. Sound good?"

Thorne's knuckles whitened on Fury. "I'm ready."

River beat his wings until wind gushed around them, and he launched vertically.

Aeron glanced at Thorne. "My hands will be occupied casting spells."

That he had to check made Thorne wonder if trust and camaraderie were ever going to run smooth between them.

"I've got your back," he replied.

Twelve in total, Thorne's unit had once been tight-knit, not only guarding each other's backs, but bonding in friendship. The sad truth was since Jasper, Thorne's wolf-shifter mentor, had disappeared over a decade ago, things had gone downhill. Although, if you asked Aeron, or any of the Guardians around before Thorne's time, they would have said the decline in morale had happened long before, when Rush, Thorne's father, had been exiled.

A curt nod from Aeron, and then they both stood cautiously. Heads above the horizon of grass, they surveyed the field making waves from the gentle, not gushing, wind. Where was it? Eerie silence greeted them. Somewhere above, River hovered, watching with sharp eyes, waiting for the right moment.

"You smell it?" Aeron muttered.

Thorne lifted his chin. Took a sharp breath. Caught it. Then started prowling east, back toward the village. It was stronger there. Perhaps it got tired of waiting for the Guardians to show their heads.

They stalked through the field, listening carefully. The hairs on Thorne's arms lifted, and an almighty crash snapped his head toward another direction—toward the other end of the village—a farm. A female's scream. It had someone.

"Fuck." He ran toward the helpless scream, every protective instinct in his body on high alert.

With his heart pounding, his breath heaving, he pumped his legs and sprinted.

"Wait," Aeron shouted as they cleared the field and came across the outbuilding of a farm.

A gray smokey tornado of destruction tore through the tiny settlement. Wood, debris, crops, it all went flying into the air as the djinn circled through. They were in the midst of a hurricane of roaring chaos.

A female faun crouched under a wagon with a child huddled in her arms. Thorne threw a blast of energy at the tempestuous djinn, but he only angered it more. The storm turned Thorne's way. Two smokey arms peeled from the tornado. Red eyes glowed in the midst.

"That's right, come here." He waved his hands over his head. "Fight someone your own size."

The djinn's elemental body turned back to the female and child.

"We have to lure it away." Aeron pulled up to Thorne's side, chest heaving. "I can't throw my spell at it when they're so close."

Thorne cupped his mouth and shouted. "Here!"

He gritted his teeth. He'd have to expend mana by using a spell—meaning he would have little left to shift into wolf. He hated taking that option off the table. But, Well-damn it, he had no choice.

Drawing on his power, he fashioned another blast of energy and threw it at the elemental. It would do nothing to it, maybe even feed it. But it got the djinn's attention. Red eyes locked on Thorne.

He backed away and pointed his ax at Aeron. "Stay there and attack from behind."

With every backward step into the grass field, Thorne threw more energy at the beast. The djinn followed. Its elemental arms lashed out, slashing at Thorne's face, cutting through his jacket, slicing his skin. Blood dripped from him. Dirt got in his eyes. With every stinging hit, Thorne's rile grew in intensity until he was ready to roar.

"I s-see you, wolf," the djinn hissed. "I s-see into your weak and angry heart."

Thorne faltered. The storm surrounded him, darkening the sky.

"I s-see you have hate. Wantsss revenge. You can use me. Make wisshes."

Flashes of Thorne's past hit him. Orphaned. Living with a cruel uncle. An aunt who tried to save him but failed to protect even herself. Being forced into the ceremonial lake, not knowing if he'd float and bloat, or come out alive. The taunts his childhood peers sent his way for being a child of greedy unsanctioned breeders. Then finding out it was all part of some bigger plan the Prime had cooked up. His pain was nothing but collateral damage. And now he worked for her.

"I'll tell you where my bottle is. S-seek revenge."

No. He wouldn't succumb. This was classic djinn behavior. It fed off the mana of others and used vengeance as a lure. Whoever ruled the djinn now would have little mana left in their body, and because it was leached out by a magical monster, that mana wouldn't be replenished. That fae would no longer be immortal.

Thorne roared his fury, dug deep, and drained his power to hurtle an energy wave at the djinn. Wind gusted from his fingertips, leaving him drained and tired. He stumbled.

"Now!" he yelled.

Nothing.

Crimson, what was Aeron waiting for?

And just as Thorne was out of magical means, Aeron threw his spell at the monster. Air crackled and fizzed. Thorne tasted metal on his tongue. The djinn-storm slowed, the smoke and wind of its tornado disintegrated, and then a sparkling net dropped from the sky.

With a whoosh, the storm was contained under the silver mesh. Thrashing about beneath was a dark, twisted blob of goo with red eyes. It squealed and bucked. And it spat vitriolic and unintelligible words at Thorne.

"Litter box trash," Thorne muttered and then lifted Fury, aimed, and chopped down.

He caught the djinn dead in the middle. It broke in two. A popping sound rent the air, and the remnants of the storm vanished. The clouds cleared, and the sun shone down.

"You idiot," Aeron snapped.

River landed with a windy thud, wings snapping in tight behind him. "Thorne?"

Thorne only grimaced at them, anger still firing in his system. He shrugged.

"Think you can call the shots?" Aeron shoved him. "You can collect the tax from the village, then."

Shock splintered through Thorne. Aeron rarely lost his temper.

"What?" He shook his head. "I'm here on your request. It's not my mission."

"Exactly." Aeron put the net and broken djinn body into Thorne's hands. "It was my mission, and you went against orders. I told you the Prime would want to question it."

Shit. Yes, he did.

"Time to go, River." Aeron threw his hand out and cast the spell to trigger a portal back to the Order.

Bastard. Clearly, Aeron had enough mana left to conjure a portal. He could have cast that deionizing spell earlier.

It seemed like Thorne was the last fae on earth willing to sacrifice his last mana drop for others these days.

River gave Thorne a one-shouldered shrug and then sauntered after Aeron through the portal. The bright shining light flashed and then disappeared as the portal closed, leaving Thorne in a resounding post-battle atmosphere. In one direction was the battle-torn village, in the other, a wild field leading to a forest that called to Thorne's inner wolf.

What he wouldn't give for the mind emptying freedom of running through the woods. The rushing wind. The myriad of scents. The burn of his muscles. All his worries and demons gone.

Simplicity. Bliss.

Sometimes he wondered which part of him came first. The wolf, or the fae. If he let his wolf take over permanently, would anyone miss the fae part of him? Why not just shift, let the beast out, and stay out? Stay animal.

Jasper's voice responded loud and clear from Thorne's memory. *Because the wolf is a part of you, not the other way around. Never forget that.*

CHAPTER
TWO

Looking worse for wear, Thorne returned to the Order through a portal. He ditched the spent stone into some bushes outside the gates and heard a clunk as it hit the others he'd thrown before. He needed to find a new dumping ground, or actually learn to create portals himself. But he didn't have the patience or the reserve mana to waste.

His wolf agreed with him. It liked having reign.

Approaching the gate, he gestured to the guard on the high stone wall and entered the Order grounds. As one of the Twelve, he lived in a house near the back. Having his own room was the only blessing in this place.

The folk at Mornington Village hadn't been pleased to hand over their only red coin, but monster hunting was expensive and resource heavy. They would have felt worse if the Guardians weren't around to stop the djinn. After he'd collected the fee, he'd seen the destruction up close and realized Aeron was right to be furious about the kill. Knowing why the djinn targeted Mornington would have been a good thing.

Damn it.

His pent-up rage and energy had nowhere to go. He felt like a demon pushed beneath his skin, wanting to burst out. It itched. It twitched. All he wanted was to head home, bathe, then go down to the Mess Hall and find a nice soft female to bury himself in. He would take her behind the academy library where the gardens provided plenty of cover, and then head back to his room, alone. Maybe he'd have a few drams of whiskey and—

"D'arn Thorne."

Every muscle in his body locked tight. He turned. "Prime."

In her angel form, the owl-shifter's long white wings brushed the ground. Curly white hair bounced on her bare, brown shoulders, and large knowing eyes took in everything. As usual, she wore the distinctive blue flowing gown that reminded Thorne of a goddess of old. It was probably why the Prime wore it, to attach any association to godliness to herself that she could.

She pursed her lips and held out her hand.

He dug into his pocket and retrieved the coin for her.

"As I understand," she said, "you're the reason there is no djinn to question."

"If you saw the destruction, it left—"

She held up her hand. "We both know excuses aren't what I'm looking for."

Thorne's fists clenched at his side in an attempt to remain stoic, despite the blood boiling in his veins. It would be so easy to let it out. To show her what he'd been thinking and feeling all these years. The rage and the turmoil over her leadership... among other things. Even the wolf inside him howled for a piece of her flesh. He flexed his fingers and exhaled. *I'm not like her.*

He had control of his beast.

Barely.

"What are you looking for then, Prime?"

The loaded question had a double meaning, and rightly so. He was sick and tired of her misdirections and machinations. He was tired of it all. She was the reason his mentor, Jasper, had been missing for over a decade. The only reason he'd learned Jasper was missing, and not on hiatus like the Prime had insisted, was that his father's mate, Clarke, had revealed the truth to Thorne. The psychic human had also said another like her would thaw from a two-thousand-year sleep and would lead him to Jasper. But she had said that two years ago. He started to wonder if it was all another misdirection. Or even an outright lie.

Humans could lie. Fae could not.

The Prime looked him over, long and hard. Then her gaze softened in a rare show of emotion. "It is not I who will be searching soon, D'arn Thorne. You will be going on a journey, and all I ask is that you remember one thing."

"What."

"The Well chose you to protect it. For whatever reason you hate me, believe I had no hand in that. It is real."

A growl slipped out. "You had no hand in shoving me into the ceremonial lake when I was twelve? Because I remember that a little differently. I remember all the tributes differently."

Less than thirty percent of Guardian applicants survived the initiation ceremony. When submerged in the lake, the cosmic Well of Life looked deep into their hearts and judged their worthiness of the extra power it imbued to successful initiates. But to be judged correctly, one was dragged to the bottom of the lake where the connection to the Well was the strongest. One had to truly believe they were dying and to face their moral demons. But if deemed worthy, the new power granted was instantaneous. You could rise a new fae. Stronger, but indentured to preserving the Well.

The six fae who'd entered before him had sunk. Then their bodies had bobbed to the top of the lake, dead, floated, and bloated with the shame of rejection. He knew he'd be the next to do so. He knew that a boy like him, the product of unsanctioned breeding, would never be chosen as a symbol of righteousness. He was the lowest of the low.

The shouts of acolytes and Guardians still rang in his ears when he remembered being pushed down the jetty that led into the sacred lake. He remembered his struggles, the warmth of urine as it ran down his legs on the cold day, and his bare heels burning as they collected splinters from the wood underfoot. He remembered the confusion as some of his captors had fallen into the lake themselves. Then he remembered the wolf inside him taking over, and the all-consuming terror as he looked down into the moving shadows of the deep water.

Something was in there.

Then he was pushed, he went airborne, and into the water's icy embrace.

"What would you have us do, D'arn Thorne?" the Prime asked, snapping him out of his past. "Wait until there are no more novitiates, no more Guardians, and no more protection for the Well? Elphyne will die."

"There has to be another way of getting fae to volunteer."

"There isn't."

He pinched the bridge of his nose. "I've had a long day. Are we done?"

The Prime turned her back, took a deep breath, and then walked away. But not before she tossed some last words over her shoulder. "Your day is only beginning."

He shook his head and continued toward the Twelve's house. The two-story behemoth sat tall and proud at the end of a lawn used as an informal training field. He'd only made it halfway across that field when a small, two-legged, white-haired toddler tottered down the porch steps. She lifted her nose, scented he was kin, and broke into a run toward him, chubby arms flailing in the air. He couldn't help the twitch on his lips at the sheer thrill on his half-sister's face and her high-pitched squeal of delight. It was the look of escape, of pure freedom, probably only linked to her state of undress, but infectious all the same.

He scooped up Willow's wriggling form.

"No no no." She kicked and struggled.

"I think you're a little young to be running across campus with half your clothes off." He cast a wary eye at the house next door where the only other cadre of Guardians lived. The Six were made up of Sluagh, Unseelie fae who'd led the Wild Hunt against the humans who invaded Elphyne centuries ago. They lived in the shadows and rarely came out in daytime, but stranger things had happened.

Some described them as fallen angels; others as demon monsters. Thorne couldn't say. He'd only caught glimpses of them over the decades he'd been at the Order. He'd heard the Sluagh still kidnapped humans. Since Willow was a halfling, he didn't like leaving her unattended on Order grounds. The Sluagh answered only to themselves and on occasion the Prime.

Curtains twitched at the dark windows of the house of the Six.

"Where are your parents?" he asked Willow.

"Mom-mom-mom." Willow pointed back at the house. "Dad-dad-dad."

A panicked woman came tearing out from the house, her long red hair sailing behind her. She saw Willow in Thorne's arms and sagged with relief.

When Thorne arrived, she thanked him—something she kept inexplicably doing, despite knowing that thanking fae would put her in their debt—and then took the wriggling toddler from his arms.

"You're a lifesaver, Thorne," she said, flustered. "Honestly, if Willow would just learn to shift, we'd have no fear with her running around on her own."

He raised a brow. "Still no luck?"

Exasperated, Clarke ushered him in so she could close the door and then released the struggling child into the house. "No, but your father thinks it will happen any day. She's got some long canines coming in. Rush has even tried shifting around her, which apparently is something shifter fathers do with their young to teach them..." Her voice trailed off and she slanted him a guilty look.

He ignored the tweak in his chest at the f-word. It was still odd to hear. He also chose to ignore the fact that Rush hadn't been there to teach Thorne to shift. It had been Rush's sister Kyra. And then later, Jasper.

Thorne cleared his throat. "Where is he?"

"Ah. Yes." Clarke's lips flattened. "That's why we're here."

Her pause gave him a flair of hope. Was this the time?

"Yes," she added, searching his face and reading his expression. "This is the time. Laurel will wake soon and we have to find her before someone else does. Rush is collecting supplies for the journey. It's going to be long and arduous." She flinched. "And unfortunately, Rush and I will have to continue on after you bring Laurel back here for training."

He folded his arms. Laurel. The human. A swarm of old hatred scored his blood. All his life he'd been trained to abhor humans. They stole from Elphyne, from the land and its people. They bled the very life from the soil. Over the past two years, the human raids had petered off and remained small enough to remain negligible to the leaders of Elphyne.

But the Order knew better. One human, a man Clarke had dubbed the Void, was stealing mana from magical creatures, utilizing it for his own means, and planning an invasion that every Seer in the history of Elphyne had warned would mean the end of existence. The problem was, every psychic vision showed a different series of events. The only true common element of victory was that Clarke was leading the way.

This Laurel that Clarke had mentioned was human. She deserved Thorne's suspicion and caution regardless of being a friend of Clarke's.

"This is the human who will lead me to Jasper?"

"Mm-hmm." Clarke scratched her head, seemed to avoid his gaze, and then looked for her daughter who had already vanished somewhere in the big house. "You best be changing, Thorne. We'll head out very soon. And dress warmly. She's in the Elation mountains, but I'm not sure exactly where. We'll have a search on our hands when we arrive."

TRAVELING through the cold Elation mountains hadn't been fun for Thorne. With his mana stores so low from the recent battle with the djinn, he'd been unable to change into wolf and the urgency of their mission prohibited him from stopping off at a natural source of power, like a sacred lake, to rapidly replenish. Instead, the magic slowly seeped back into his body during the journey. He wasn't comfortable knowing his power was so depleted. Especially when his father's was not.

Being Well-blessed meant Rush could borrow mana from Clarke any time he wanted. And Clarke was a rare thing indeed. Human, yet possessing the strongest capacity for holding mana the Order had ever seen. She could go for days at full strength without needing to replenish from the cosmic Well of Life. She could also filter that power to Rush as he did his duty as a Guardian.

Why her? What made this human so important?

A good hour into their journey, snow started to fall as they trekked up the rocky path. Evergreen trees made it difficult to see where they had come from. The snow made it harder. Rush had offered to cast an insulation spell around Thorne, as he had with Clarke, but he'd declined in favor of using his cape. He wasn't in the habit of accepting help from a father who'd never been there for him before.

He now regretted his choice.

They came to a grassed plateau edged by a rocky cliff. Clarke stopped and searched about the cliff before turning to Thorne and Rush.

"There's the cave," she said, pointing to a hidden entrance behind a fallen tree gathering a drift of snow.

They dropped their bags just inside the cave. Thorne also left his cape, as the temperature inside was strangely warmer. Thorne's and Rush's sharp wolf-shifter senses took them a few yards into the tunnel until they came to a three-way fork.

While Clarke and Rush discussed which way to go, Thorne put his hand on the tunnel walls. They were striated, as though the cavity had been drilled by someone... or something. Wyrms were known to inhabit these mountains.

A gasp sent his attention Clarke's way. Residual light shone from the cave entrance, enough to see her irises had turned Seer white. A pinch to her lips and paleness of skin revealed her vision wasn't good. When her blue eyes opened and searched for Rush, she swallowed. "We have to hurry."

"What is it?" Rush asked.

Her hand fluttered to her throat and she shook her head. "Something is wrong. I keep seeing fire."

"So where?" Thorne pointed into the dark recess of the cave system. "Which direction?"

"Unfortunately, my visions haven't shown me where to find Laurel, only that she's hidden somewhere in here."

"So we split up."

"Yes."

Rush frowned at Clarke. "I go with you."

She scowled back. "If the three of us separate, we'll cover more ground."

"You said something is wrong. I can feel you're hiding something from me." Rush folded his arms and stared her down. Like cartography contours, or a fingerprint, their matching bioluminescent Well-blessed markings curved around a hand and arm on each body. It told the world they belonged to each other, and their souls were bound. They could share mana and emotions. Humans could lie, but with that soul-connection, she couldn't lie to him.

Danger sizzled in the air. Urgency. Thorne's heart beat faster and he reached over his shoulder to release Fury.

"Fine," Clarke said. "Rush with me. Thorne, you go on your own. Meet back here in an hour. If the other party isn't back by then..." She looked at Rush. "How do we communicate? Seriously, someone at the academy needs to invent a magical cell phone."

"Because Thorne and I are kin, we can communicate through water with the right link-spell, but that's not always reliable, especially if there is no water around." Rush went to his rucksack and pulled out two glowing glass canisters. He handed one to Thorne who lifted his for inspection. Inside was an air sprite. Made from sparks of light, it shed luminosity wherever it went, leaving a trail. The inside of the canister was already smeared with by-product.

"Sprites," Rush explained. "Already bargained with. They'll also provide light for you to help see."

Thorne raised his brow. Bargained with? That meant the sprite wouldn't just float away on her own agenda, she'd follow Thorne around until she was released from her bargain.

Thorne unscrewed his canister and the tiny winged female zoomed out, circling him with a high-pitched buzz of annoyance.

"Don't listen to her," Rush grumbled. "She got a good deal. A blue coin and all you can eat prickleberries for the rest of the year."

Thorne looked down the three tunnels and sighed. "I'll start with the right."

"We'll take the left."

Thorne was about to head off when he caught Clarke's hesitation. More danger?

"What?" he prompted.

Her eyes widened. "It's just that Laurel has been through a lot. She might not respond well to an unfamiliar face, and you're very... imposing."

"Then hope you find her first."

Crimson, he could handle a female, regardless of the fact she woke from another time. Frustrated, he went down the narrowest tunnel, ducking to avoid the rocky bulk overhead. The tunnel shrank the further he went, until he was half crouched as he walked. Continuing for long minutes, his patience wore thin. Clarke had been frozen for thousands of years and she'd awoken, thawed in a lake. But this human? She had to be hidden in tunnels created by Crimson-knew what. The ridges and striations on the walls solidified his theory that the tunnels were bored by a creature.

Better find the human fast.

Thorne had no clue what kind of human he'd find. Clarke had been difficult to process when she'd first arrived. She spoke strange. She had too much energy. And—

Thorne ducked when the sprite flew across his face, leaving a cold splash on his cheek. No doubt there would be a luminescent track left. He smudged it away, but when he pulled his hand back, an unfamiliar scent halted him. It came from the dark hollow ahead. Sulfur... and—he sneezed—something burned and bitter. The hairs on the back of his neck stood to attention. The sprite flittered about the cavern, knocking into walls erratically. Something was definitely off.

"What is it?" he muttered. Was the borer of the tunnels here?

His grip tightened on Fury's handle.

Smoke oozed from the hollow ahead. The sprite refused to move forward and squeaked with panic.

Shit.

Thorne broke into a jog, pushed through the hollow and into a larger cavern. Fire flickered beyond the smoke. His eyes stung and watered but... there was something in there. He could sense it. It was a tug to his chest. A twist to his heart. A need. An urgency. It went beyond logic. Proceeding could mean imminent death, but he would do it anyway. This incessant need inside urged him forward.

Coughing, he swatted the smoke away and approached with caution. The mana he'd replenished over the journey from the Order might be enough to conjure a spell. He reached deep within to grab the power the Well granted him. He drew on his energy, converted it to water, and sent it toward the epicenter of the inferno. Water shot from his hands and doused the flames. Sizzling smoke hissed. Firelight extinguished, casting the cavern into darkness. He squinted through burning eyes, coughed, and then unbuttoned his jacket. With access to his sweater, he pulled the collar to cover his nose and mouth, filtering the air.

"Get help," he rasped to the sprite then ushered it out of the cavern. It flew out, taking the light, and a little smoke, with it.

Thorne turned back to the darkness, eyes narrowing toward the corner. His wolf-sight kicked in and picked up a figure laying on the ground. Blood thudded in his ears. It was her. The human. He felt it as surely as if someone had carved her name across her heart. Laurel.

His instinct urged him forward. "All right, wolf. Let's see what this is all about."

He took a step. Then another. The dark shape didn't move. His ears pricked up and strained for a heartbeat. It was there, faint. And fading.

She was unwell.

It was no wonder with this smoke-filled cavern. If he'd been a minute longer, purged the smoke later, she'd have suffocated. Crouching down by her side, he took in her face.

His breath hitched.

His mind stalled.

He blinked, a little befuddled and unsure of what he'd expected. He hadn't really prepared himself. Consumed with the second part of this meeting, the part where this woman would lead him to his lost mentor... he'd failed to think about the woman herself.

She was beautiful. Painstakingly so. Sensual lips like a dream, yet her face held an unyielding harshness even in her repose. Dark short hair cut directly below her sharp jaw. Glorious body swathed in tight black clothes that pronounced every sexy curve. Muscular. Taut. Trim. She looked at peace. Her hands pressed under her face as though she'd fallen asleep.

Somehow Thorne had the sense she wouldn't be caught vulnerable like this often. The arousing thought sparked a kernel of curiosity in his long since dark soul.

And then he saw her ruined and twisted nails. Some of them were thick and stubby.

Laurel has been through a lot, Clarke's voice floated from his memory.

His lip curled in a snarl. He knew why nails grew like that. Someone had done that to her—ripped her nails clean from her fingers.

There was more to her that didn't add up. Scorch marks radiated from her body along the cavern floor. Her clothes were left smoldering, but her skin was blemish free.

Clarke had power. This human—Laurel—probably had it too. Maybe even an inferno's worth. But despite the strange recent fire, her lips held a blue tint. He touched her cheek and hissed. Ice cold. The fire hadn't been enough to thaw her from the ice. The cosmic Well had brought her this far, but she wouldn't survive if he failed to warm her up. He needed to get her blood pumping.

Reaching within himself, he scraped the last remnant of his power and cast a warming spell. But it fizzled and sputtered. His mana was spent. Damn. He glanced at the entrance to the cavern but heard no incoming footsteps. Rush and Clarke could be an hour away or more. Only one thing to do.

He peeled off his jacket, rolled it, and tucked it beneath her head. Water from his dousing spell sloshed along the rocky floor as he moved. It had already turned cold, like the frozen cavern around him.

Laurel made no move. No sound. The wolf inside him paced and whined in a restless cycle.

"You will survive this," he decreed. *I won't let you die.*

Next was his sweater and undershirt until he was top naked. Shifters were fire-fae. Their body temperature ran high, but since his lack of mana meant he couldn't shift, he'd have to warm her a different way. Lying down next to her, he ripped her shirt open until her chest was bare except for a small dark covering over her breasts. He peeled her wet and torn shirt away and threw it to the side, then gathered her close. He used his sweater to cover her bare back and trapped their body heat.

He cupped the back of her head in one hand, and with the other, he rubbed her back to create friction. He tried not to think of the icy bloom of his breath. She would wake. She had to. She was his key to... everything.

And she was limp, her heart sluggish, her face pale.

Come on. At least shiver.

He placed his palm over the center of her chest. A spark of mana. It was all he had left to give. Heat zinged down his arm, hit his palm and melted into her chest. Warmth spread from his touch. Blue light bloomed on her skin until it pulsed along her veins, striating outward like a star. It should have melted and joined her life-force, but the light didn't leave. It shone brighter. It burned hotter. It spread to her extremities until it wrapped around her arm and his at the same time. He shut his eyes against the shine. When the heat lessened against his face, he opened his eyes and gasped.

Up his arm and hers was the contoured blue bioluminescent markings of a Well-blessed union.

This human was his mate.

QUEEN
FITNESS

CHAPTER
THREE

Laurel's smart watch buzzed, telling her it was time for her next appointment. She packed up her desk, straightened her papers, locked her computer and gave the picture of her family one last look. It was of her parents and Laurel next to her twin brother, Lionel, in his hospital bed before he died. Taken fifteen years earlier, Laurel and Lionel were freshmen in high school. He never finished.

Her watch buzzed again.

Right. Brunch with the girls.

She strode through the office floor of her business empire. Under the Queen Fitness umbrella, she sold equipment, a fashion line, as well as dominated the franchise gymnasium real estate in Las Vegas. She wanted to be in every hotel by the end of the year. Impossible was not a word in her vocabulary.

A young blond in yoga attire rushed up to Laurel and held out a smoothie. "Your wheatgrass protein shake is ready, Miss Baker."

"Thank you, Dee." She flicked her gaze down to the woman's feet and frowned. "What's that?"

Dee stopped. Laurel stopped, arched her brows, and then decided it was best they walk and talk, so gestured toward the exit. "Follow."

Laurel had too many things on her agenda to be policing employee fashion. Goddamn, she missed her old assistant, Belinda. That girl had been a walking machine. This one... well... she pursed her lips as Dee scurried to catch up. She was a work in progress.

But Laurel would whip her into shape. Just like she did with everything.

"I'm waiting," Laurel said, walking.

"Um..." Dee scurried. "Sorry, what was the question?"

"What's on your feet?"

"Sneakers?"

"Incorrect. They're the wrong sneakers. The competitor's. Everyone on this floor must wear the Nike-Queen Fitness branded shoes. We didn't spend thousands to secure that partnership for nothing. Do you understand? Good. Grab a pair from the marketing department on your way out today. Next?"

"Sorry, next?"

Good God. "Yes, what's next on my agenda?"

She already knew she had brunch with the girls, then a meeting with the CEO of Luxor, and a quick twenty-minute sojourn down to the shooting range with her father. He'd much rather her take time off to go fishing in the real wilderness, but she'd stopped doing that when she had opened her business. Now she didn't know the meaning of vacation. The shooting range would have to do.

"Okay, first up you have... um... I'm sorry I forgot to bring your planner."

Laurel stopped. She glared. "Well? Chop-chop. Off you go."

Dee scurried away. Laurel tapped her custom Nike covered foot. She took a slow sip of her smoothie and thrummed her glossy blue nails on the cup. Her eyes narrowed with predatory focus on a worker's cell screen—at the brightly colored little gems being locked in a row. Fury tightened her posture. She ground her teeth and strode over. She didn't get to these dizzying heights of success by playing games on her cell, and she expected nothing less from her staff.

She arrived behind the man in question. With a clearing of her throat, the noises in the office died off. There was no other sound except the tapping of her foot. Slowly, the employee rotated in his chair and lifted his gaze to her face. He paled.

She held out her palm. He regretfully placed his cell in it. Then she tossed it into the trash on her way out. What did they think life was? A ride? A game? No. You had to earn your place in it. You, more than any other person, had been given a gift. She certainly didn't squander hers.

A flash of her twin's face hit her hard. Her throat clogged. But she shook it off before she stepped into the foyer and heard Dee's voice echoing behind her.

"Laurel."

"Laurel."

Dee sounded underwater. Deep. *That's odd.* In fact, everything seemed out of place. The bright lights were blurry. The lobby moved. It smelled like someone had set the trash on fire. Maybe the cell phone had exploded.

She shook her head. *Have to get to brunch with the girls.* No time to dawdle. *Clarke and Ada are waiting.*

Laurel took a step. Felt sluggish.

"Laurel."

Dee's voice had deepened. Suddenly, it wasn't Dee chasing her, but another. A man from her nightmares. His long face warped into something hideously overlong. His expression was a mask of bland depravity—the only emotion she'd ever seen in his dark, soulless eyes.

Pain ripped through her fingertip. She looked down and saw why. He'd pulled her fingernail clean off with a set of pliers.

"No." She thrashed her head. She refused to give this man any satisfaction. "Don't give him the numbers, Clarke!"

"Laurel, wake up."

A spark of heat at her chest punched her out of her dream. Her eyes snapped open to a blue glow in a dim room.

The urge to vomit rose within her like a tidal wave and she puked something disgusting. It dribbled down her chin and landed on her chest. It wasn't smoothie. It was dark, viscous muck. Her heavy eyelids wanted to close again. Every muscle in her body ached. Cold air nipped her face and legs, but inexplicable heat surrounded her torso.

Blue light flashed. Nausea rolled again. She groaned. What the hell was happening? Forcing her gaze open, she tried to take in her surroundings. In the glow, a face. A... man.

Fierce. Handsome. Shockingly blue eyes glowing as much as the surrounding light.

Naked, brawny chest. Powerful arms locked around her.

He caged her in.

She screamed.

He blinked. He let go, and she shuffled back. Rock scrapped against her bare back. Hissing in pain, she looked down at her puke-stained bra and yoga pants. Someone had painted glow-in-the-dark blue lines over her right hand and arm. What was this, a rave? Had she ended up in some nightclub? He had the same on his arm. The markings felt hot... alive... as though something lived beneath her skin. Something powerful.

What the hell?

A quick look around the room showed her it wasn't a room at all, but the inside of a cave. Panic flooded her, threatening to drown out all common sense.

"Laurel." His voice was deep. Calming. He held his hand out like one would to a wounded bear. "You are safe."

Safe? Then why was her heart beating a hundred miles a minute? Where was her t-shirt? Why did the stench of burned things and smoke fill her nose? Where the goddamned hell was she? How did he know her name?

He moved toward her, but she shuffled back and winced when her bare back hit the rocky wall again. "Stay away."

Oh God. What if this was the next step in Bones' torture? What if he hadn't let Clarke and Laurel go? No. She shook her head as more memories came to her.

Bones *had* let them go. He'd pulled out every last one of Laurel's fingernails and was about to move onto her teeth when Clarke caved. She'd given him the numbers. *Bishop, that bastard!* Clarke's ex-boyfriend was the one who'd sold them out to Bones. He'd told the mercenary about Clarke's psychic powers. Laurel's throat choked up. Clarke's eyes had been red and raw from crying. Tears had run in tracks down her face. Until that point, she'd held her tongue. She'd done what Laurel had ordered her to do. Because anyone willing to resort to torture to get some numbers had to be evil. Those numbers had to be bad.

More memories surfaced.

Watching the news reports on TV. Bombs going off around the world. Those numbers had been nuclear codes. Like dominos, civilization collapsed. Then the fallout. The sky. The nuclear winter. The sudden catastrophic ice.

"Did he send you?" she croaked. Maybe Bones wasn't done. Maybe the end of the world wasn't enough for him. "Clarke won't tell you anything now. You can torture me all you like."

Laurel had a stern word to Clarke after Bones had let them go. She'd told her friend that if they were captured again, to never give anything up. Laurel could take it.

A darkness washed over the strange man's eyes. His jaw set. And then he answered, slowly and calmly. "I'm... ah... friends with Clarke. She sent me to find you."

Laurel pointed her finger at him and accused, "You hesitated."

She caught sight of her damaged fingernail and snatched her hand back.

"I hesitated because she's human," the man muttered. "I'm fae. I'm still getting used to our alliance."

"Fae?"

He gestured at his ears. With a start, Laurel realized they were pointed at the top. Pointed with a light dusting of fur. The sides of his head were buzzed. The pale, silver hair on the top was scraped back from his forehead and pulled into a Viking-like twisted braid that dropped down his brawny back.

His ears twitched. His head cocked, and he slanted a look to the dark hole serving as the cavern exit, and then he tensed. That behavior was decidedly not human, but closer to animal and otherworldly. Laurel sensed danger from him, as though he were a wild, vicious beast calmly watching its prey, getting ready to pounce.

"Something is coming," he muttered.

He scrounged about the floor for something. When his fingers latched onto a dark shape, he tossed it her way. Another scream bubbled in her throat, but when the thing hit her, she realized it was cloth. No. Not cloth. Leather. A jacket. She relaxed.

"Put it on," he grumbled and collected something else, a belt. With a goddamned holster of some sort attached. And in that holster was a big, scary ax glinting with the blue light cast from their matching markings.

When he turned to strap his weapon over his naked torso, Laurel noticed a large tattoo between his shoulder blades. A howling wolf. Back muscles rippled as he lifted the leather straps over his head. The wolf shuddered menacingly. Laurel knew what kind of work it took to carve out a body like that. She'd built her life's business around it.

She also knew how much strength was within his body. His big fists were twice the size of hers. If he wanted to hurt her, she stood no chance. He looked over his shoulder and locked eyes with her, perhaps waiting for something. He didn't find it and frowned.

"You must dress. We have to get out. Danger is coming. Do you understand me?" He spoke as if he expected her to speak another language.

Her cheeks heated. "Of course I understand you. It's the only thing I do understand. What the hell is going on? Where am I?"

"I'm sure Clarke will have plenty to say to you. My name is Thorne."

Clarke.

Her mind got stuck on the familiar name and suddenly there wasn't a place she wanted to be more than near her dear friend. Clarke had been a crafty and sometimes morally ambiguous woman, but she always knew what to say, and she had a knack for knowing what to do. Underneath it all, she had a good heart, and Laurel loved her.

Right. So now Laurel had a plan. Find Clarke. Talk to Clarke. *Work out what the hell is going on.* With this new point to focus on, she slipped her hands within the arms of the fae's oversized and heavy leather jacket. It looked like a badass biker jacket, and it smelled like man. She cast a quick glance at Thorne. He looked like a badass biker. With an ax. And pointed ears.

She shook her head. Again. And couldn't move the feeling of displacement.

Find Clarke. Feel centered. She could do that.

"Where's my top?" she asked.

Thorne bent and picked up something soggy. He squeezed water out of it and offered it to her like some kind of cat with a dead mouse. *Are you fricking kidding me?* Her shirt was torn, in pieces, and half disintegrated. That was a custom Lululemon yoga shirt.

He frowned down at it. Sniffed it. And then remarked, "This has forbidden plastics in it. It will have to be destroyed. But we can do it later."

Forbidden plastics?

Laurel begrudgingly took the top from him but didn't put it on. She wiped her front where her vomit had dribbled, then dumped the top and did up the buttons on the jacket. She gestured to the big guy. "After you."

They'd gone two feet down the exit tunnel when a bright white firefly buzzed and squeaked near Thorne's face. He stopped and inexplicably seemed to listen to the hovering fly. Laurel almost bumped into him. Then he swore. Two-seconds later, his fist clenched around the ax handle.

He craned his neck to look over his shoulder at her. "Can you conjure fire again?"

"What?" she spluttered.

"Fuck."

Panic started to creep up her body. "What's going on?"

But he didn't answer. He started to undress, fingers unbuckling his baldric.

She blinked. What was he doing?

He shoved his baldric at her—battle-ax and all. Then he undid the button at his breeches placket, shoved it all down, and toed off his boots at the same time. "Bring my things. And stay back."

The air around him shimmered. Her blue arm markings burned, and she felt as though something was sucked from her—like the sensation of having blood drawn, but all over—and then he *changed.*

One minute, he was fae, the next a large, white wolf. Two blue eyes locked with hers, looked down at Thorne's clothing in reminder, and then bounded toward the exit.

"Shit." Laurel gaped. "Shit shit shit."

What the hell?

What the goddamned hell?

Was this real? Was she in actual hell? Her mind whirled, spiraling out of control with all the possibilities. She rubbed her eyes. Light from the buzzing white firefly kept her surroundings visible, but it was dark in the direction the wolf had gone.

A growl, an echo, and the sound of something tearing. Snarling.

Laurel's heart stopped beating.

The firefly landed on her finger and bit.

"Ow!" she cried and shook her hand out.

The creature bit her again. This time, Laurel looked closer. It wasn't a bug. It had two arms, two legs, a human face... and wings.

"I'm on drugs," Laurel reasoned. "Must be some kind of psychotropic torture."

Bones was back. There was no other logical explanation.

The little thing jumped off her hand and landed on Thorne's fallen breeches and boots. It squeaked at her with urgency. Laurel jolted with understanding. It wanted her to pick up the things and go.

The tunnel shuddered and groaned. Little rocks and sand fell from above. An almighty roar trembled her bones. That was not... that was not from the wolf. That sounded like a beast. Big. Dinosaur big. In here. In these tunnels.

Danger.

The glowing white firefly tugged on her collar.

"Right. We need to go. Got it."

Urgency skittered up Laurel's spine as she collected Thorne's items and took off after the glowing thing, all the while chanting to herself, "You're not insane. You're *not* insane. Speaking to a firefly is perfectly normal."

She followed until they got to an intersection about ten feet across and stopped. Which way? There were at least three other passages. Chest heaving, she calmed and focused on where the soft natural light came from. *There.* Glowing streaks were on the same walls, similar in color to the little winged creature. Most of the streaks led down that tunnel. It must be the way out. She took a step, but then jumped back the way she'd come as something big came at her. Snapping piranha teeth and a wet, eyeless face on the body of a giant wyrm. She shrieked, hugged her package and retreated further into the tunnel, hoping to hell the thing would just keep going down another tunnel. And prayed.

The walls rumbled. The giant slug-thing slithered past.

A flash of white followed it, nipping at its tail. The wolf. *Thorne?*

In Laurel's heart she sensed it was him, just like after he'd made the change.

Once again, the feeling of displacement was so big that her mind emptied. She shook her head and thought of Clarke. *Get to Clarke.*

"Can you take me to Clarke?" Laurel asked the lady-fly. She squeaked in return. Then buzzed away, turned back, and hovered. Waiting. "Okay. Let's do this."

CHAPTER

FOUR

Laurel burst from the dark tunnel system into the light of day. She squinted to protect the ache in her eyes. Fresh air gusted into her face. Snow everywhere. Trees. She blinked as her eyes adjusted and hugged herself.

Goddamn. This wasn't Vegas.

"Laurel?"

She turned. Cried. Her good friend Clarke was sitting on a rocky outcrop beneath a fir tree and next to a fledgling campfire. Laurel dropped her package and ran. The two collided and hugged. God, it was good to feel something familiar in her arms. The same red hair she'd known for years. The same freckle-faced bastion of fun who'd always made it her business to keep Laurel from working too hard.

Sobs wracked her body.

Laurel *never* cried.

Not when her twin had been diagnosed with his auto immune disease. Not when he died. Not when her fingernails were ripped from her fingers. And not when the sky had rained ash. Tears weren't useful unless they were the tears of your enemies. Well, that's what her father used to say. The military general had been a driving force in her life.

A new kind of choking took hold of Laurel when she realized she had no clue what had happened to her family. Were they safe? Maybe her father had her mother holed up in some government bunker somewhere. Surely a general had access to something like that.

Swallowing, she drew back and hastily wiped her eyes. She took in Clarke's worried face. The same, but different. Something shrewd existed in her blue-eyed stare that hadn't been there before. Clarke looked... grown up.

And what the hell was she wearing?

Laurel gingerly fingered the fur-lined cape, the carved wooden sundial on a leather cord around her neck, and the scrap of fabric around her hair. Clarke captured Laurel's roving hand.

"There's a lot to tell you," Clarke said. "Come and sit down. The boys will be finished playing soon."

"Boys?"

Clarke bit her lip, eyes assessing. "I'm taking it you've met Thorne?"

Yeah, she'd met that dangerous fae... or wolf. The one who'd been half-naked and hugging her when she'd woken. Intense. That was the only word she had to describe the man. Instead of answering, she looked around at the snow-capped trees. "Where *are* we?"

"I think the better word is when. *When* are we."

"Come again?"

"We're two thousand years into the future—give or take a few years."

Laurel's head swam. "What?"

Clarke sighed. "You really should sit down. And look"—she opened her rucksack to pull out some clothes—"I brought clean clothes for you to change into. Something I wish someone had done for me." She mumbled something about a stubborn wolf and then tossed the clothes to Laurel with a fresh smile. "You'll feel better. Trust me. The praxis wool is warmer too."

"Praxis?"

"A new kind of goat thing. The animals have mutated in this time. Some are the same, but, never-mind. You'll find out one day."

Goat thing? Mutated?

The ground moved beneath Laurel's feet. The horizon shifted. Her head lolled, and she landed hard on her butt. Clarke ran over to her, but she pushed her away. "I'm fine."

Laurel tried to stand. Her eyes rolled. Okay, maybe she wasn't fine. She sat and rested her head between her knees, ignoring the cold snow seeping into her already sodden pants.

"Take it easy, Laurel," Clarke cooed. "Deep breaths."

The cold air was exactly what she needed on her hot and prickly skin. A wave of nausea rolled through her and she retched until more black goo came out. Clarke went to her rucksack and pulled out a waterskin. A *waterskin!*

"Oh, God," Laurel mumbled. "What the hell?"

"Don't worry. I vomited that stuff too. It will pass."

Fight for control. Laurel forced the breath in and out of her lungs. She focused hard on a single twig poking out of the snow. She used the resolve her father taught her. *Tough situations build strong people.* She'd used the same mantra in all her gym centers. Queens don't whine. They work. And then they are *fine.*

Laurel unbuttoned the jacket and peeled it off. She went to add the woolen sweater, but Clarke stopped her. "Bra too. Anything with plastic and metal in it has to go, which, to be honest, is all the clothing you're wearing. Probably why it lasted so many years without completely deteriorating. My clothes practically fell from my body when I woke. Oh. And you'll have to give me your shoes. And your watch."

Laurel gingerly covered her watch. Without it, how would she know what day it was, or when her next appointment was, or how many steps she'd done? She needed it. "Why?"

Clarke's grave expression gave Laurel chills. "Because those bombs that went off destroyed the world. What grew out of the ashes isn't the same. Magic is a part of this world now, but it only flows where no metals or plastics are present. So..." She gestured at Laurel's bra. "The sooner you get it all off, the sooner you can access your full powers."

That took a moment to settle in. Powers. Magic.

Wolf shifter.

Flying fairy thing.

Hungry, giant slug-thing.

Great. Just great. Laurel looked around again as if she could orientate by sight. The sky was blue, not the dusky haze she remembered from... yesterday? Last week? Thousands of years ago? Good lord. *Thousands of years ago!*

She shivered and rubbed her arms. It certainly looked like a new world. What other explanation could there be?

"What happened exactly?" she asked Clarke. "I don't remember how I came to be in that cave."

"We were all at my place. Do you remember that?"

Laurel frowned, squinting to try to recollect, but shook her head.

Clarke continued, "We were in the living room watching the news. Vegas had pretty much shut down at that point. Then it started snowing, and we all went outside to look. Then... I guess the temperature dropped so fast that we froze." She clicked her fingers. "Snap-frozen. Just like that. Rush said the land has shifted since our time. Some ruins remain, but nothing looks the same." Clarke took a breath. "My working theory is that the cosmic Well chose us to survive and somehow worked to keep us frozen and preserved all these years."

"Cosmic Well?"

"Yeah, it's like the life-force that all magic draws from. These fae worship it like a deity. Only, it's not a real person. It's just... life. All powerful. All consuming. All nourishing."

There were so many more questions Laurel wanted to ask but settled on one. "Who's Rush?"

"My husband. I suppose you could call him that." Her lips stretched into a wide-mouthed grin. "He's so awesome. Hot. Sexy. The best. God, I love him. And our daughter, Willow. I can't wait until you meet her."

Daughter? Laurel's brow lifted. Clarke had zero sign of a baby belly. "Goddamn. How—?"

"I thawed about three years ago and had Willow two years ago." Her expression darkened. "There's more I need to tell you, but... Come on. Get dressed and warm first."

Laurel unhooked her bra and quickly slipped the sweater on. Her smartwatch joined the pile. It was dead, anyway. She replaced her yoga pants and sneakers with tight leather pants that fit her like a second skin, and then she tugged on the waterproofed fur-lined boots. The glow from her arm markings glanced off her surroundings every time she moved.

"What is this?" She held her palm out. "You have them too."

"Thorne didn't tell you?" Clarke frowned and then muttered under her breath. "Of course he didn't."

Clarke shook out the cape and wrapped it around Laurel's shoulders. The warmth immediately settled her nerves. Laurel hugged it tightly while Clarke avoided her gaze.

I know that look.

It was the look of secrets.

"Clarke, what are the markings? And why did he ask me if I could conjure fire? And, come to think of it... I saw him turn into a wolf. Right before my eyes. And then there was the glowing little firefly that—"

"It's fine. Don't panic. Remember I said some animals had mutated? Thorne is fae—evolved from both human and animal and with the capacity for using magic—mana—which you now have too. Apparently, fae existed once before, like in the fairytales of old, but as humans industrialized the world, covering it with metal and plastic, magic disappeared." Clarke paused. "And your markings are that of a Well-blessed mating. It means"—she winced—"that... um... your souls are bound. I guess to put it in a way you might understand, you're married to Thorne."

Laurel's heart gave palpitations.

"Uh-uh. No." Nope. Nopety, nope. She shook her head. Married. Never. She was not the marrying type. Let alone to that big, over-muscled warrior that turned into a mother-fricking-wolf? "No fucking way! In no version of life will I ever be married to a feral animal! What the hell, Clarke? You better start bringing out the prank cameras or something, because I'm starting to lose my patience. You know I'm not the marrying type."

Clarke's eyes flashed and caught something over Laurel's shoulder. Laurel stiffened. She turned. Two giant white wolves stood before the cave, holding the tail of the large wyrm between them like a rope, red blood dripping down their maws. One wolf was golden-eyed. The other blue-eyed—Thorne.

FIVE

Thorne spat out the wyrm's tail. His side of the catch thumped wetly to the ground. Laurel's words twisted through him.

Feral animal?

This feral animal just protected her from the wyrm. This feral animal just caught her next meal. This feral animal was her Well-blessed *mate*. Anger swirled and churned. Who did she think she was? A human. That's what. A filthy, lying human who hadn't earned her right to hold mana within. She never went through the harrowing initiation he did as a child.

She'd sacrilegiously worn metals and plastics her entire life. No training. Whatsoever. Born in a bed of red coin. That was the kind of female she was. Thorne didn't need to learn any more to see that. Entitled. Sour-faced. Whining woman.

His lip curled, wanting to snarl, but he wouldn't give her the satisfaction. Instead, he drew her mana through their bond and used it to fuel his shift to fae form, reveling when she shivered as the magic left her body to replenish his, smug in the knowledge that she'd have no idea what that feeling meant, or that he'd taken her magic without permission.

It's what she deserved.

Laurel watched him with thinly veiled precaution as he stalked toward her. He stopped inches away. Tension vibrated in the air, but she held her ground while Thorne studied her with open hostility. In the full light of day, she was even more striking. It was a shame she was human and had a soul like murky ink. Good looking. Sharp jaw, small nose, big brown eyes, wide lips, dusky skin. Dark, straight hair cut to her chin. From what he could see of her beneath the cape, and what he remembered from within the cave, she was also fit. Healthy. The kind of body a male drooled over and begged to be under.

Not him.

She did her best to keep her eyes locked on his, but he could tell she wanted to look down. Not to cower to his alpha presence, but to inspect him as much as he had her. Despite her strong outward countenance, her inner turmoil exuded curiosity as much as fear... and a little something beneath it all. Attraction.

Good. Let her pine.

"Jeeze, Thorne." Clarke rolled her eyes. "Put some clothes on."

He stared at Laurel, a silent challenge in his eyes, daring her to turn away, to snarl or squeak at the blood still coating his jaw, to faint or swoon at his nakedness. She stared back, right into his eyes, never losing gumption. It made his heart pound harder, but for which emotion, he was at a loss. Then his rile rose like a flooding river.

Through their bond, he sensed her fear quake. And that made him smile, a baring of teeth. Good. She should fear him. At least then he knew where he stood.

He dipped to the ground, picked up a handful of snow and used it to wash the blood from his mouth, and then ran another handful over his chest to clear the remnants, eyes never leaving hers.

She backed away to the other side of the campfire.

That's right. Move away, human. That's where you belong. Humans on one side, fae on the other. Somewhere behind him, he heard Rush's feet crunching as he came back from wherever he'd transformed, but Thorne kept his gaze stolidly on Laurel.

"Lost my clothes," Rush grumbled. "Somewhere in the cave-system."

"I knew you'd lose them. So I brought extra," she replied.

"What would I do without you?" A kissing sound.

"Probably starve."

A snort.

Finally, Laurel broke eye contact. Her gaze shifted to Rush.

While Rush was Thorne's father, the fae stopped aging once they achieved maturity at about twenty-one. To a human, he and his father would look like brothers.

Thorne found his clothes and stalked into the dense trees to dress. Not for any sense of propriety, he just didn't want to stare at the human any longer. After he'd slipped his battle uniform on, he worked on his hair. The leather cord binding it had gotten lost in the shift. He fiddled with tying it into some sort of knot to keep it from getting in his face and stared out into the forest, contemplating what to do.

Clarke came up quietly behind him.

"I knew you'd lose it. And I know what it means to you to keep your hair long. Here." She smiled gently at him and held out a new cord.

Damned Seers. A little of his anger released and he touched his fingers to his lips, then pushed his hand out in the fae hand-sign for gratitude. Voicing his explicit gratitude would mean he owed her a boon, and he wasn't ready for that. Even if she treated him like kin and apologized and thanked him all the time. Family would do anything for each other anyway. Debts didn't matter.

"Don't mention it." She returned to where the others sat, leaving him to his peace.

Thorne preferred to shave the sides of his head to keep his ears exposed, and he used to keep the top shorter for ease of care after a shift, but he'd promised himself he wouldn't cut it until he found Jasper. He'd started growing it two years earlier when he'd learned the Prime had sold Jasper to King Mithras in return for keeping the unsanctioned breeding law active. The same law which saw Thorne's birth mother executed, and Rush exiled. There was nothing good about Mithras, not anymore. Once he was an adventurous king, but now, a cruel coward sitting in his glass palace. No doubt he wanted Jasper because he was a direct descendant. A bastard, but a potential threat to his throne all the same.

Thorne hated Mithras.

He'd ruined Thorne's life. His parents' lives. And now Jasper's. As Mithras's illegitimate son, Jasper had escaped the culling of royal offspring by joining the Order—an organization above the law of the royal courts. For a century or three, Jasper had been safe.

The question was, how much of Jasper, if any, would be left when they found him?

Thorne ran his finger down the long length of his hair. Too long.

Rush approached and cleared his throat.

Thorne should feel some sort of kinship with the fae, but there was a part of him that knew they weren't there yet. He regretted not knowing the kind of fae Rush was, not the way he knew Jasper or the other Guardians. Haze. Shade. Leaf. Even Cloud. They occupied an ever-present space in his mind, like family. But it had been two years since Thorne had learned of Rush's existence, and most of that time Rush had been isolated in his cabin, living his life with his mate and new child, Willow.

But they'd earned the solitude. Even Thorne couldn't fault them for wanting that.

Thorne fitted his ax-baldric over his Guardian jacket, grateful to have Fury at his back once again.

"Congratulations," Rush said.

"Don't you mean commiserations?" Thorne angled his blue marked arm before his face and sneered.

Silence. Then an awkward sound. "Look, you may not see it now, but she *will* be a blessing to you. And soon, you won't be able to live without her. The Well is never wrong."

Thorne scoffed.

Admittedly, when he'd heard about the rare Well-blessed matings and seen how loved-up Rush and Clarke were, he'd expected more of a visceral reaction when the mating triggered in his own body. But nothing beyond the trickle of her emotions, and the power of her mana pushing at his own, twisting and entwining as though they were one. That part had been good. He actually hadn't meant to take that first amount from her, but when she'd not noticed, he took more. And then the wolf wanted out when he found the wyrm.

The wolf wanted lots of things these days.

When his wolf wanted to mate physically, the fae part of Thorne would have a hard time resisting. Clarke still wore the bite scar on her neck from when Rush had taken her. Thankfully, beyond a general appreciation for her attractiveness, Thorne had felt no such compunction with Laurel.

He supposed the mating response was different with everyone.

"Just because that's your story, doesn't mean it will be mine," he replied to Rush.

Rush folded his arms, brows lowering.

Oh, here we go. The parental talk. The one Rush had no right to give. Being Thorne's sperm donor didn't make him his father. Tension rode Thorne's system as he waited for the lecture.

It didn't come.

"You're right," Rush admitted. "In fact, I hope it's nothing like mine. I want better for you, Thorne. You deserve to be happy."

Thorne ground his teeth. A bird twittered in a nearby tree, hopped from branch to branch, and displaced a clump of snow that landed on Thorne's boot.

"But," Rush continued, "I know as well as anyone how much it hurts to hold that wall up. Just keep an open mind. Take her to the Order. Train her. Put in some effort and she'll lead you to Jasper when the time is right. You never know, you might find you both have more in common than you think. Clarke and I need to head out to find the another frozen human. When we get back, we can hunt for Jasper together. He was a friend."

"Why can't Laurel lead us now?" It grated there was no timeframe, no date, just vague ideas from Clarke about when or how they would find Jasper.

"You know why. A Seer doesn't see all. Just guides. I don't even know if Laurel knows she's meant to go on this quest."

Thorne was sick of waiting.

Rush clapped him on the back. "Come on. Clarke needs to tell you both something before we leave."

When they returned to the camp, Clarke had bolstered the fire and roasted the wyrm tail on long skewers, much to Laurel's clear distaste. She sat on a stone, hugging her cape, frowning at the fire. Thorne grinned wickedly. He had a feeling he'd enjoy eliciting more discomfort within the woman. He'd make her truly see how animalistic and feral he could be.

There were two kinds of mating. One of the soul and one of the body. His wolf knew that this woman was his soul-match and was curious. It wanted to sniff her. To find out if she was good enough to bite. To feast on. The wolf urged Thorne to go to her, to sit with her, and rub his scent on her... but he didn't. Never. Just because the Well announced them as mates, didn't mean he had to accept it. Did he?

Clarke's head lifted as he neared. She slid out her wooden sundial pendant and left the shadow of the trees to check the time. Concern ghosted her features.

"We have to get going, Rush."

Laurel jumped up. "Great. I'm ready to leave. Where are we going?"

"Oh. Um." Clarke looked at Rush and relaxed, simply by laying eyes on her mate. Thorne wasn't too stubborn to admit a small part of him was jealous. Clarke also had that look when her gaze landed on her daughter. And every time Thorne saw it, an emptiness in his chest hollowed further. It was a look he'd never shared with anyone. Maybe his aunt Kyra in his youth, but that was decades ago.

"You're going to the Order," Clarke continued. "I'll be going somewhere else."

"You're leaving me?" Laurel said in a small voice.

"But not alone. Thorne will be with you."

The look Laurel cut Thorne would hurt if he didn't feel the same way about her.

"Don't worry," he said. "I don't bite." Much.

"But..." Laurel started, then stopped.

"I know it's not ideal," Clarke added. "But we have to search for Ada."

"Ada? Of course I'll come with you. Is she sleeping? Where is she?"

Clarke sighed. "I'm sorry, Laurel. You can't come. You need to train the powers growing inside of you before you have an accident, and Ada will be fine. She's asleep, frozen in ice, just like you were. We'll go to her and bring her to the Order where you can see her. She'll be excited to see a friendly face."

"I'm fine. You know me. I'll work anywhere, anytime. I want to see Ada."

"She's not fine," Thorne added with a sardonic glance at Laurel. "When I found her, she was surrounded in fire, almost dead from smoke inhalation. It was lucky I was able to douse the flames without having time to replenish my stores since my last mission."

Rush's brow rose. "How did you?"

Thorne showed Rush his blue marked arm by way of explanation. "Point is, she needs training."

"*She* is the cat's mother. I have a name and it's none of your business what I can or can't do."

Thorne deadpanned.

"Anyway," Clarke said. "You can't come with us, I'm very sorry."

"Where are you going?"

"I can't tell you that either. We learned that the Void is here, and he had Seers working for him. You know, the more I think about it, he may have woken a long time ago. He's worked out how to harvest mana and ingest it to keep himself young. He could be more knowledgeable about this world than we realize. The more people I tell about Ada, the easier it is for him to find out, and the last thing we want is for him to send Bones, or some other henchman to get to Ada before us."

"Bones?" Laurel's face paled.

"Oh shit. I should have warmed up to that part."

Laurel grabbed Clarke by the arm and pulled her to the side where she spoke in a rushed and hushed tone. Thorne fought another grin. Laurel had no idea he could still hear with his keen wolf ears. But his amusement dropped when he caught the word "torture." The woman was so feisty and full of life, he'd forgotten about her past. He supposed it wasn't like people carried a sign around their neck that told the world about their past.

Rush cleared his throat and stood before Thorne, blocking his view of the women. Rush scratched his beard.

"What?" Thorne snapped.

"It's just that I wanted to ask if you could keep an eye on Willow while we're gone."

"As in... babysit?"

"Not babysit. I know that's asking too much. But just to check in on her. You smell like kin. Like it or not, you *are* kin. She'll feel better with you around. I know the house brownies are excellent sitters, but the rest of the cadre won't look out for her as a brother would."

Half-brother. He clenched his jaw but nodded. Even if he wasn't related, young fae were treasures to any fae race. There was a time any birth was celebrated and lauded, as each child was a sign their species would thrive in the harsh post-apocalypse landscape it used to be.

Rush exhaled and hand-signed his thanks.

"If you're worried about the Sluagh, she'll be fine," Thorne said.

"Why do you say that?"

"I have a theory that they only hunt humans because they lack mana. Clarke was never attacked on campus. I don't think Willow will be either."

"I'm not so sure," Rush added. "The Sluagh eat the souls of fae, too."

Thorne shrugged, but then his ears pricked up at the sound of his name, and he listened in on the conversation the two women were having.

"It's much safer for you to be with Thorne," Clarke insisted.

"That means nothing to me. I don't know him."

"He'll protect you with his life."

"I can't trust that. You said we were married! What if he wants... things I don't?"

"You can trust the Well-blessed markings. They connect you both on a metaphysical level. There is no way he'll harm you. It would be like harming himself. And trust me. I've *Seen* things. I know it will all work out fine."

What did that mean?

But Thorne had no chance to ask. Clarke cut the conversation, went back to the campfire, and resumed eating. Fifteen minutes later, everyone had eaten their fill. Laurel chose to wait until they arrived at the Order to eat.

Clarke handed a portal stone to him. "This is imbued with the essence of the Order. It will take you there. We'll leave after you. The less you know about where we're headed, the better."

Thorne activated the stone and a rift in the air opened. Glowing light exploded and buzzed with energy. He stepped through to the other side and waited for Laurel in the field just before the gates of the Order. When she hadn't come after five minutes, he was about to leave without her, but a flash of light and power sparked and then her shape finally appeared.

He closed off the portal. The stone sizzled in his hands.

Alone at last.

He ditched the stone on the floor and bared his teeth. "Let's get this straight. I only want you for one thing—to find my mentor, Jasper. Clarke said you would lead me to him. That's the only reason I'm here."

"What about the... marriage?"

"Marriage. This is what you humans call mating?"

She nodded.

He stared at her long and hard. The Well had matched them up. Apparently, the Well was never wrong. But he couldn't see it.

"You're the last person I'd choose to be married to."

Turning his back, he strode toward the gates.

CHAPTER
SIX

Laurel fumed.

She followed the rude wolf-shifter beyond the walls of some medieval type compound—high stone perimeter, oversized gates, and guards questioning anyone who dared approach. Once inside the lush grounds, Laurel could still see the red-leafed forest outside, towering over the perimeter walls. Those trees were huge. She was trapped. A prisoner.

Any hope that she'd find something familiar from her time was dashed, and she both wished for her friend to come back and silently cursed her. Why did Clarke have to leave her so soon?

The sound of trickling water followed Laurel everywhere. There were little gullies of water beside the paths, water fountains, and water dripping from rooftops of buildings as though it had rained recently. But it hadn't.

If she weren't feeling so displaced, she'd appreciate the verdant landscaping mixed with Byzantine type architecture, simple stone and wooden dwellings.

Fine. Maybe it was like a paradise, or a spa retreat... but she still felt trapped. Lost. Alone.

A wave of irritation washed over her, and strangely, she felt as though it wasn't hers. Like the emotion was a foreign body in her own. Brushing it off, and trying to look inconspicuous, Laurel kept her head down and strode swiftly as she followed Thorne along a path and into the depths of the campus. Large impressive buildings with arched and mosaic windows were to her left, and to the right, behind the barrier of a box hedge, was a grassed training ground for soldiers. Shouts of acknowledgment from the field drew Laurel's attention. Three men, or fae as they were called, were on the outskirts of the field gesturing for Thorne's attention. But he kept walking, staunch and determined, so Laurel followed.

What else could she do?

Clarke had left her. And she got it, she really did. If Laurel had awoken to find herself alone, she might not have survived. Madness or panic would have overwhelmed her if the fire hadn't. That was hard enough to grasp as it was. Fire. From her. Goodness.

If Ada was the next one to wake from their time, she shouldn't have to go through it alone. Ada may be a woman who could look after herself, but even her survivalist training wouldn't cut it at this time.

This training was how Laurel and Ada had met. Laurel had been looking for new ways to bring some spark into her fitness clubs, and survival weekends in the Nevada desert were just the thing. They had trekked a few trails, headed into the canyons, and learned a few empowering skills.

Since arriving through the portal, she'd seen no snow. The air was still nippy, and the vegetation was foreign. Blood-red leafed forests? She shuddered to think what the wildlife was like, and she wasn't keen on exploring. Not until she understood what the hell was going on with her.

Clarke had said Laurel had magic now. It wasn't entirely impossible to believe. She'd seen the evidence in the cave and, on some level, she felt magic living inside of her. It was an energy that reacted to things around her as though it had a life of its own, and it was mainly concentrated on the blue marks on her arm. It almost seemed she could feel someone else's emotions, which was stupid.

Shaking her head, she continued her journey. They made it to a large two-story house toward the back of the campus. Sitting on the porch were two women. One was tiny, about waist high and with small pointy-ears, leathery skin, tufts of hair peeking from random places, and a yellow ribbon in her hair. The other woman had white feathered wings.

She had *wings*.

Laurel's eyes widened as she took in the sight. Glorious white feathers, glossy and catching the sun, swept down from this woman's back to dust the floor. For a moment, Laurel thought perhaps they were a prosthetic, but then the feathers fluffed out, like she'd seen a bird do when cold. Laurel's breath hitched.

Thorne swore under his breath upon seeing the winged-lady. A surge of foreign anger rose within Laurel. Once again, it wasn't her emotion. She had no reason to be angry at the winged woman she hadn't met before.

Could the emotion be coming from the only person scowling in her vicinity? The one with matching twin markings on his arm?

Thorne stomped up the steps and attempted to head straight into the house, but the winged woman cut him off.

"D'arn Thorne." The tone in her voice was hard, sharp, and imperious.

He tensed, knuckles white on the doorknob, then released and met the woman's wide-eyed stare. "What."

"Are you going to introduce us?"

Thorne waved at Laurel. "Laurel, meet the Prime. And the brownie there is Jocinda."

He tried to enter the house again, but the Prime's hand lifted and clenched. Power tingled Laurel's tongue, air whooshed, and the door slammed shut.

"Thin ice, D'arn Thorne."

A low growl rumbled from his throat and he faced her once again. This time, he said nothing and stared.

Laurel rubbed her forearm. The overwhelming urge for anger definitely seemed to come from the markings. She narrowed her eyes at Thorne. It had to be his emotion. There was no other explanation. She concentrated. Something else laced the anger. Hate. Bitterness steeped in regret.

He had a history with this winged-woman. Twisted and painful. The Prime straightened her spine and gave Laurel the once over. Laurel narrowed her eyes suspiciously back.

"It's a pleasure to meet you, Laurel. I'm Prime Aleksandra. You can call me Prime. I am in charge around here. Welcome." She inclined her head regally. "Waking thousands of years after an apocalypse must be harrowing. I'm sure you have many questions and must be tired and hungry. Jocinda has graciously prepared your rooms. There are clothes, bathing water, and refreshments."

Laurel's suspicion eased. Thank God a woman was in charge around here. Laurel held out her hand and said, "Thank you."

Sound stopped. Every hair on Laurel's arms stood on end. Thorne grunted. The Prime glanced down at Laurel's extended hand. Her white brow lifted at the blue glowing marks etched on her skin.

"I will collect on that debt one day in the future. For now, I will leave you to gather your bearings with your new mate. Being Well-blessed so early in your relationship is a boon and a sign that the Well looks favorably on your coupling. I'm sure you will make a formidable team. Tomorrow morning a Guardian will escort you to the temple for testing. Then you will resume your training at the academy."

A team? She and Thorne. Ha! With difficulty, she forced her laughter down, and when Thorne shot her an inquisitive stare, she realized he must sense her emotions too. He was curious about her sardonicism. She felt that echo back at her.

So it was true. The emotions she'd been feeling over the journey were his.

The Prime ignored Thorne's and Laurel's interaction. She hiked her blue floor-length dress to clear her bare feet, nodded to the brownie and then padded down the porch steps and strode away across the lawn, her wings sweeping regally behind her like a glorious white mantle.

The brownie became a bulldozer of action. "Right. Follow me and I will take you to your room." She barged past Thorne and entered the house, stomping right up the grand staircase that led from the foyer to where Laurel presumed were the living quarters.

Without waiting for Thorne, Laurel pushed past him and followed Jocinda. Having her own room was appealing. A bath, some food, and a rest to gather her bearings, even better.

Outside the house had been limestone, arched windows, and terracotta tiles. Inside, the house reminded her of an old medieval castle. Rugs. Glass windows. Tapestries. Leather and wooden furniture. The smell of citrus and cedar. Candles in candlestick holders. Candelabras hanging from the ceiling, but not made from metal. Something else. Glossy pottery perhaps? Opaque glass?

While Laurel ogled at the decor, Thorne took two maroon-carpeted steps at a time to overtake Laurel and catch Jocinda as she scurried to the next floor.

"Where are you going?" he asked the brownie.

"Taking Laurel to her room," Jocinda replied. She took a right on the landing, and stopped at a particular door down the hall.

"But that's my room," he noted.

"You're mated, are you not?"

"Yes, but—"

"Are you arguing with me, D'arn Thorne?"

"No, I'm just... we're not mated like that. Well-blessed mating is different from one of the bodies."

She blinked, flabbergasted at Thorne's tone. "I think not, D'arn Thorne. Would you prefer to arrange these sorts of things yourself?"

Thorne immediately backtracked and showed his palms in surrender. Laurel even sensed a dash of fear down the bond. Fear over a few chores?

"Jocinda, you're completely right," he returned. "We are mated. This is our room." Then he touched his lips and motioned his hand outward and down toward the brownie.

Odd kind of hand signal. Laurel wondered what it meant. She'd seen it a few times already. Another thing to catalog for later.

The brownie opened the door and ushered Laurel inside, brusquely rattling off instructions on how to draw the bath, where more clothes were, and about the food choice selected on the table. Breakfast was served in the kitchen an hour after sunup, lunch at midday, and dinner was an hour after sundown in the main dining room. They'd *foretold* that she was coming, so did their best to find food that Laurel liked, but since the world was vastly changed from Laurel's time, she wasn't so sure.

Again, there were a few things the brownie had said that Laurel didn't understand and hoped she remembered to ask later when she wasn't so brain-fried.

After the whirlwind was gone, it was just Laurel and Thorne together in the chambers.

A window overlooked the large lawn at the front of the house. A decorative temple rose in the distance, tall, regal, and with water running from the roof to cascade over the eaves. Two armchairs faced each other before the window. A table with food was between.

One king-sized bed.

Through an archway, in another chamber, was a steaming bath, and more doors she assumed went to dressing rooms or closets. Hopefully a toilet too.

Good God. What if these people didn't have toilets? It didn't seem like there was electricity. You needed copper wiring for that, right?

Laurel's hands pierced her hair, and she pulled. This was all a bit much. She went to the window and stared while her heart thudded in her chest. She took in air slowly through her nose and exhaled through her mouth, wishing her nerves would calm.

Behind her, Thorne toed off his boots and strode into the bathing room, where he promptly unbuckled his weapons and shed his battle uniform. She had a few seconds to glimpse a taut, shapely rear-end, and then he sank into the bath. The muscles in his back rippled as he supported his weight. The howling wolf tattoo danced.

A long, husky deep sigh escaped him as he immersed, and Laurel felt it vibrate down to her core. For a moment, the anger she sensed from him switched to emptiness and she almost forgot about his caustic attitude. He was just a sexy man in a bath.

With pointed ears.

He rested a muscled arm over the rim of the bath and reclined his head, his long warrior's tail dangling outside the tub.

But he *was* an asshole. Given the chance, most men were. She didn't expect them to be any different in this time than in hers. They'd tried to beat her down when she rose to the top of her fitness game; they'd betrayed her, and one had even tortured her. The only man Laurel had trusted was her father. And he was dead. Gone.

Her throat closed up. Her eyes watered.

They were all gone.

Except for one.

Bones. Apparently he still lived. She shivered, felt the ghost of pain in her fingers, and rubbed them on her thighs. Catching herself in a nervous habit, she tugged her cape around her body until it squeezed tight.

She would *not* cry.

But she missed her father's rigid outlook on life. Her mother's way of softening it. Every creature comfort in her home. Green protein smoothies. Her Nikes. Being CEO of her own company, she owned a penthouse apartment in one of the big chain hotels on the strip. She didn't have to do anything but workout and be a boss. That was her life. She had been a queen. A queen who was living twice as hard because her twin hadn't.

Now what was she?

She shuffled over to the window and sat on an armchair, tucking her feet beneath her bottom. It wasn't so different out there. Blue sky. Green grass. Grumpy people.

Winged people.

Bossy people.

Fae. Not people.

She groaned and grabbed her head. This was going to take some getting used to. She picked through the food on the table, looking for something familiar. Strange fruit. Odd smelling bread. Meat and gravy, which she wasn't a huge fan of. Usually, she stuck to fish or vegetables. Then her gaze landed on one item in particular. Potato croquettes. Her father was part Flemish and would make them at every family gathering. How did they know this about her?

Magic.

Laurel took a bite of the croquette and almost cried. Melt in her mouth. It tasted so good. So like how Papa used to make. She could almost see him standing over a frying pan, testing the sizzling rolls with a spoon. The smell of butter. The friendly ribbing her mother gave her father because he was an overachiever. And then the loving looks her parents shot each other, even though they were well into their third decade of marriage.

What would her father think of this situation?

"He who fails to plan is planning to fail," he used to say. She'd hung the quote on the wall of her office in her first gym. It originally came from Winston Churchill who also said, "There is nothing wrong with change if it's in the right direction."

She'd left the world a destroyed husk. A big, empty, gaping hole stretched in her chest. No rock concerts. Famous artwork. All that history. No airplanes to another continent. People, families, children. Gone.

A small sob escaped Laurel, and she covered her mouth, holding it in as she faced the window. It was stupid to try to hide it. Thorne could sense everything. And that made her feel even worse. Not even her thoughts were private.

Outside, she saw the sun setting. The pink and orange hues mixed with turquoise and navy. Beautiful. A group of fae casually strolled across a path at the end of the lawn. They looked to be dressed in long blue robes. And they were laughing.

Laurel's hand touched the glass window pane.

They were happy.

Her world was gone, but now a new one was alive. Alive and seemingly thriving with magic, new life, and hope. If Clarke believed Laurel had a job to do in this world, then she should do it. She was never one to shy away from responsibility, and Laurel would be damned if she let those same evil humans try to take the laughter away from this new world. Not this time.

Tomorrow, Laurel would make her five-step plan. She'd get her body back into shape, work on this magic growing inside her, and then she would find Thorne's missing friend and shove her success in his face.

Because that's the way to deal with naysayers. Prove them wrong.

She knew it was petty, but it was her only defense mechanism at this point. It was something to hold on to.

The sound of water sloshing alerted Laurel to the wolfish fae getting out. With only her instincts thinking, and the need to be somewhere she wouldn't have to interact, she pulled back the covers on the bed, intending to claim it for herself and pretend to be asleep. He got the tub first, fine, but then she would get the bed. He could sleep elsewhere. That was the intention, anyway.

She took off her boots and shed the cape. But the rest she kept on. A bone-deep weariness sank in and she found herself not caring if she dirtied the sheets. She just wanted to sleep and to wake tomorrow clear-headed, like she usually was.

The moment she rested her head on the soft pillow, her body sank into the mattress, and her eyelids grew heavy. An unavoidable sigh fell from her lips. She tucked her hand beside her face and let her lashes slowly drift closed. Tomorrow she would start her plan. Tonight, she would take it easy on herself. Tonight she would mourn the family and friends she'd lost from her time. She would dream about her mother tickling her face when she fell asleep as a child, or even how she brushed Laurel's hair from her face when Laurel was a sad adult. She would pretend she was still only a phone call away.

The padding of feet got closer, and she schooled her emotions to deadpan, and her breath to calm. She feigned sleep. He'd have to physically force her out if he didn't like her taking his spot.

He was quiet so long she thought maybe he'd gone. And she almost fooled herself into sleeping. Oblivion edged in.

Steps drew close, and she didn't have it in her to tense. Maybe it was because there was no hostility coming from him. No. It was an emotion she'd not expected... relief trickled through the markings in her arm. Thorne's calloused fingers traced over hers, lingering around the scars of her nail beds, and then over the fresher scars on her knuckles from when she'd taken up self-defense lessons after Bones' torture. A touch of sadness leaked through the bond. Then... compassion.

The heat of his body—fresh from the bath—blasted her face as he leaned close. Now she tensed, ready to fight, knowing this alerted him to her wakefulness. If he dared touch her... but he took hold of the blanket she'd neglected and drew it over her shoulders. Then he shifted the hair from her face and tucked it behind her ear.

Thorne left the room.

Laurel stayed tense, muscles locked and heart-pounding for long minutes. He'd tucked her hair. He'd covered her with a blanket. The next thing she knew, her eyes flew open and everything was dark.

She'd fallen asleep.

SEVEN

Lying in the bed, stretching languidly, Laurel realized it must be close to dawn because she felt rested. She was also an early-to-bed, early-to-rise kind of girl. Perhaps it was something being an army brat gave her. Everywhere they'd moved when she was younger was at some army base. There was always activity in her house during the early hours.

She sat up and rubbed her eyes. The first thing she noticed was an ambient blue glow. Oh. That's right. She had a weird, shimmering tattoo. She poked at the blue lines, testing. On the outside, her skin felt the same. But on the inside, there was a restless energy swimming beneath her skin. Like she'd just taken a pump class, downed a wheatgrass shot, and perhaps even had a coffee.

Coffee. Wheatgrass. Pump class. Her face crumpled at the memory of favorite things she may never see again. But the ache in her heart over losing her family and the rest of the world wasn't so raw after sleep. It was still there, but the deep shock had faded. With that mind numbing emotion gone, she had the clarity to approach her situation with a level head, just like her father had always taught her. *Control your controllables.*

Laurel smiled. She wasn't sure if controllable was even a real word, but her father always made up vocabulary to suit his purpose. His sentiment was right. She couldn't control the fact she was in this time, or that she was in some kind of arranged marriage with this wolf-shifter, but she could control her attitude toward it. The divine source of power they worshipped had chosen Laurel and Thorne as mates, as partners. The Well had imbued her with power. It had faith in her. Laurel should respect that, even if she didn't understand it.

Changing her frame of mind was harder than it sounded. She had to steel herself against her natural objections and ignore her skeptical instincts. It wouldn't happen overnight, but perhaps with time, she'd grow to love this place... maybe even... her mind shifted to Thorne, but she wouldn't finish that train of thought. Not yet.

She had a plan to make. A course of action. But what?

A few things stood out. Clarke believed Laurel was the key to finding this person lost to Thorne. Laurel had to learn to control her powers. And this Prime lady assumed Laurel was going to fall in line, get tested, and go to her academy. There were too many questions, and it was unlikely Laurel would receive answers from Thorne. He also needed an attitude adjustment.

One thing she knew for sure was that she'd solve nothing sitting there thinking about it.

The best thing to do when feeling displaced was to go back to routine, to find something familiar and ground herself. Her favorite old routine was her morning run. It made her feel like she had her shit sorted. She didn't. But it made her *feel* as though she did.

She patted her cheeks. *Wake up beauty, it's time to beast.*

She looked around the moonlit room. No light switch or lamps. But she did find another person in the bed with her. Her jaw dropped. Thorne had slept next to her all night. The steady sound of his breathing ensured her of his slumber. Between the blue glow of their markings and the moonlight, she could see the fae clearly with a blanket draped over his brawny, muscular body. Arms behind his head, his biceps bulged. In rest, he looked attractive. Hot. Mouthwateringly so.

She blinked at the direction of her thoughts, but once started, she couldn't stop. Didn't want to. Her gaze magnetized on his body, starting with a face that almost looked boyish in sleep and in no way as intimidating as in wakefulness. *Puppy* was her first reaction, but then her eyes trailed down, grazed over his scruff covered jaw, thick neck, and sculptured shoulders. Every feminine instinct tingled in appreciation. Down the V of his torso, to the eight-pack stomach where a bolt of desire hit as her gaze snagged on the tantalizing dark hair just below his navel but above the sheet line. She patted her hot cheeks. Must be something wrong with her.

Although... she glanced back at his face... a one-night stand had never bothered her much in the past. Maybe that's what this partnership could be. Physical.

Relationships for her existed only between the sheets, even before Bones ruined her trust in men. Men were intimidated by her drive, they never stuck around, and she ended up finding a use-them-and-lose-them tactic was easier for everyone. Her body reacted. Her skin flushed, her nipples pebbled, and she clenched her thighs together at the thought of how she would use his body to work out her own sensual kinks. She imagined he was the kind of partner who would take all she demanded and then ask for more.

Her hungry eyes shifted to the bulge between his legs. Yes. He could take her demands, and she'd happily give them.

Work to do.

Clearing her throat, she eased softly off the bed, and then quietly explored the anteroom where the bathtub was. More arched windows let in enough light to see. Behind a curtain, she found a closet. Hanging from rails on one side were multiple copies of the blue and black leather battle gear Thorne had worn. On the left side, she found a range of feminine clothes. Thumbing through the collection, she was disappointed to find no yoga pants, no workout clothes, and no sneakers. But Clarke had mentioned plastics being prohibited, and a key proponent of Lycra was synthetic. Still, there were knit fabrics she might be able to source. In the meantime, Laurel would have to be resourceful and come up with alternative active attire.

First, she needed something to bind her breasts. She needed a sports crop top. Tapping her lip, she thought of alternatives. She supposed she could tear a sheet into strips and bind it around her chest. Then her eyes landed on a long, dangling piece of fabric hanging from the rail. Shifting clothing items out of the way, she realized the strip was exactly what she had in mind... as though they'd known about her needs. Clarke had either told them, or they were all truly psychic.

After three attempts, she fashioned the strip around her chest and one shoulder in a way that looked good and felt comfortable. Then she cut off the wool leggings at the thigh with one of Thorne's daggers, and slipped them on, satisfied at how the pants clung to her hips. They wouldn't give her trouble as she ran. Lastly, shoes were a problem. It was either wear solid leather boots or go barefoot. Perhaps they just didn't make the kind of shoes she needed yet. Maybe that was a business opportunity for her.

She decided to keep her feet bare, and tiptoed through the house, intending to be quiet to avoid waking anyone, but soon discovered that was pointless. Three fae were sitting in the open living room near the front, playing cards, carousing loudly. She considered stopping to say hello, but could already see the sky lighten outside. Her favorite time to run was dawn. The rising sun promised a fresh start. Missing it ruined her day.

She slid by and let herself out of the house, closing the door softly behind her. Standing on the porch, she deeply inhaled the fresh air and took a moment to appreciate the smell. She had to force her brain not to take shallow breaths to avoid the air pollution from the nuclear fallout. In her time, the air quality had been abysmal toward the end. But here, early birds were calling, a purple hue ghosted the sky, and the pleasant sound of water trickled. She briefly allowed the memory of helplessness to enter her system, then forced it aside. The time for feeling sorry for herself was over. Another few deep, concerted breaths and she was calm. Strong. Queen.

She was here.

Alive.

She would make the most of it.

Setting off, she jogged down the steps and onto the lawn. Soft grass greeted her feet, and she almost wept at the profound sense of rightness. This was Laurel Baker. Running. In control. Always moving.

On the first lap of the lawn, the pleasant familiar burn in her lungs warmed her and she relaxed. She was able to take in the houses and structures nearby. The house she'd come from dwarfed the house next to it, which was dark and steeped in shadows. It gave her the creeps every time she looked at it, so she passed quickly. After the third lap, all her irrational fears ebbed away. She sank into the fall of her feet, the beat of her heart, and the drag of her breath—at first shallow, and then deep and freeing. Her mind became numb to everything but the next step, the next breath, and her rhythmic heartbeat.

This. Right here.

It felt good. So good she couldn't help smiling.

That was why when the hairs lifted on the back of her neck, she paid no attention. But when hot air, like breath, puffed behind her ear, she stopped suddenly, heart-skipping, and whipped her gaze around. Swallowing nervously, she surveyed the empty lawn. Predawn light glinted through a murky mist and painted the buildings and plants in gold and pink. Like a magnet, her eyes drew toward the smaller house, still somehow creepy and dark, as though even the sun was afraid to touch it. Black curtains were devoid of light. Crow statues sat on the steepled roof, frozen in their regard of her. Cobwebs dusted the porch eaves. And standing in the shadows of the open doorway was a man.

Tall, lithe, hauntingly handsome. He had the kind of beauty that stole her breath. Eyes like gray smoke. Silken medium length black hair. A dark business suit fitted his graceful body like a second skin. A gothic cape hung from his shoulders and kissed the ground beneath him. Long pale delicate fingers tapped his thigh, as though he were deep in thought as he watched her. Laurel's stuttering steps drew her closer until she stopped before his house. It was as though his gaze pulled her there. She couldn't tear her eyes away, nor step in another direction. She was locked in his curious, smoky sights.

Eyes burning with intrigue trailed down her body. Another hot puff of air blew across the back of her neck. A lover's breath. As if he stood behind her, not before her.

She glanced over her shoulder. *Nothing.*

Snapping her gaze back, she almost yelped to see him a few steps down on his porch. *Closer.* One foot was on a higher step. Those long fingers grasped a rail, but his simmering, intense gaze still locked and devoured. Despite his perfect appearance, every instinct screamed for her to run. But there were other instincts. Baser ones that felt... hot. Heavy. Swollen. Aroused.

What the fuck was going on?

The puff of hot air on her neck shifted. It trailed down behind her ear, tickling her skin, and then it explored her body... wrapping around the blue markings on her arm, and then back up to her torso. It was as though he touched her. Intimately. Brazenly. The whisper of wind entered her clothes, somehow slipped beneath the tight straps she'd wound against her body. Sensation caressed her breasts, nipples, and then navel. She gasped as goosebumps erupted, and the phantom touch went lower.

Terror warred with desire. This was... she couldn't move. Could barely breathe while the beautiful man drank her in, head cocked to the side as though she were a curiosity in a museum. He seemed to look beyond her skin and flesh, to the inside of her very soul. Her body wanted him, would do *anything* if only he came closer and touched her for real.

But while her body engaged in sex, and velvet, and sinful desires, her mind screamed in terror. She opened her mouth... nothing came out.

EIGHT

Thorne woke with a jolt. Something was wrong.

Terror surged down his bond, hard and sharp. He checked the bed next to him. Empty.

Laurel.

Her scent was fresh. She must have left recently. He shot off the bed, and ran through the house, past the three vampires playing cards in the living room, and out the front door. Two steps later he launched off the porch and had shifted into wolf by the time his paws hit the ground.

Scenting her, he found her standing stiff before the house of the Six. Uncharacteristically, one of the Sluagh was on his porch, staring at Laurel as though she were his next meal. Dumbfounded, Thorne had never seen one of them in the light of dawn before. Only at night. But from the acrid scent of magic in the air, the Sluagh wasn't just staring. He was breaching Laurel's will, the way only a soul-eater could.

Thorne *ran*, prepared to strike. He skidded to a halt between Laurel and the house. Hackles raised, ears down, claws out, he snarled.

Fuck off, Sluagh. She's mine.

The Sluagh's dark eyes slid Thorne's way. He cocked an indignant brow and then darted his gaze to the rising sun as if that were his only concern. For a fleeting moment, the cape draping from his shoulders fluttered with menace. Not a cape. Wings. Big, featherless ones like the vampires... but with draconic talons. Then the Sluagh's gaze snapped down to the blue markings glowing through the fur of Thorne's right paw. The Sluagh's brows lifted in surprise.

A velvety smooth voice entered Thorne's mind. *Truth.*

And then the Sluagh gave a respectful bow and stepped back. Energy blasted from behind Thorne. Wind ruffled his fur. Not energy. The Sluagh's soul. It rejoined its host body and a ghostly outline of the Sluagh's skull crackled and flashed like lightning beneath his skin.

Death. Fallen angels. Soul-stealers.

The Sluagh had many names that fae and humans alike whispered to their children in tales of warning and woe. Never leave a west window open when a loved one was near death because the Sluagh would steal their soul away. But for humans, they cared little if you were near death. They'd steal you alive, kidnap you and keep you in their dark dens, supping on your soul until there was nothing left—if you were lucky. If you weren't, you'd eternally belong to them, a part of the Wild Hunt that flew through the skies during battle, full of locked and moaning souls desperate for release but condemned to live all eternity, serving as the Sluagh's spectral soldiers, only called out of hibernation to hunt down the enemy or serve as sustenance.

Sluaghs answered to no one, could exist on the spectral plane, and were impossible to control. Unseelie to the core, they were borne of chaos and Queen Maebh's need for protection during the first great war against the humans. It was the Sluagh who'd turned the tide of the battle and pushed the humans back behind their high crystal walls. The humans' war machines could not decimate the spectral offensive of the Wild Hunt.

It baffled Thorne that there were six of them, *here*, ordained by the Well—lauded and accepted by the very nature of life.

These six Sluagh were Guardians who fought magic-warped monsters and upheld the laws of the Well. They were monstrous protectors of fae but were virtually monsters themselves.

But then again, it was the way of the fae. Without darkness, there could be no light. Without the sun, there would be no moon. And... Thorne had been chosen too. One look into his own dark heart confounded most people.

Shifting back to fae form, Thorne rounded on a still shaken Laurel. Her chest rose and fell, fists flexing at her sides, eyes like two big saucers.

"What are you doing out here by yourself?" Thorne ground out before she had a chance to speak. But then frowned when he took in her strange attire, pink cheeks, and sweat-glossed skin. Was she... training? "You should never be out alone, especially at night."

"It was dawn."

"Close enough."

She blinked, and then met his stare. "I was... going for a run. That's all."

"Stupid human. Did you ever stop to think that it wasn't safe?"

All timidness dissolved. Hard fury flashed in her eyes and then she punched him.

In the nose.

Pain and yellow light exploded. A scalding sensation licked his face. His eyes watered and he doubled over, groaning. That hurt more than usual. It also smelled burned. *Fire?* He wiped the blood from the tender flesh of his nose and forced his eyes open. Fire engulfed her fist—the one that punched him. She had no idea.

"No, Thorne," she said. "This *stupid human* did not think that going for a simple run would be dangerous. No one has told me jack about this place. Whatever that *thing* was, it didn't exist in my time except in nightmares or the movies."

He pinned her with murder in his gaze. "So he's a *thing* and I'm a *feral* animal. And yet you're the violent one. You're the one using your mana against me." He gave her fist a scornful look. "And you wonder why no one has volunteered to help you."

She gaped, saw her fist, and the fire guttered out. "I... oh my God. You're right. How the hell did I do that?" She blinked rapidly, eyes shooting all over the place before finally lowering. A pink tinge hit her cheeks. "I'm so sorry."

Thorne stepped back, shocked by her admission because, to be honest, he *was* being a dick. He'd deserved that punch. There was no need to put herself in debt by apologizing. But then again, she hardly knew about that fae law. Could he fault her for his shortcomings in teaching her?

Her eyes immediately tracked down his naked body. The pink tinge on her cheeks reddened further as she saw what hung between his legs. *Damn.* He should cover up. But then again, that would mean he gave a shit.

She was still looking.

"You want to touch it too?" he drawled. "Maybe paint a picture. It will last longer. Honestly, I don't mind."

Now, where had that come from?

"Um," she stuttered, eyes darting back up to his. "S-sorry. It's hard not to look when it's so—"

Crimson, this was getting messed up. He wasn't... flirting, was he?

No.

Stop it.

He growled, "Don't go anywhere on your own. Understood?"

"Why?" She lifted her chin.

He pointed at the house of the Six. "That's why. The Sluagh steal souls, and they like the taste of humans best. If they don't eat yours, they conscript your soul to fight in their battalion of ghosts for eternity. There are six of them living in that house and their loyalty lies nowhere except to the Well."

For a moment she appeared shocked. But then her eyes turned thoughtful, and she frowned. "Um... I don't think it was stealing my soul."

"What do you mean?"

"I mean." She lowered her voice in a conspiring way. "It kinda felt me up."

Her words blanked every thought in his head. His inner wolf snarled, wanting to take over, to seek reparations from the Sluagh at this infringement to her person. His next words came out slowly and through a clenched jaw. "It *touched* you. Inappropriately?"

She nodded cautiously, clearly sensing his anger down their bond, perhaps even thinking it was directed at her. And that made him madder. He'd seen her warped fingernails. Knew exactly what had happened. She'd been tortured.

It took Thorne a moment to understand, and then all the frustration he'd been holding exploded. The Sluagh had felt her up. Without permission. Caustic rage surged within him. His wolf snarled, frenzied to get out of the confines of his body. It wanted to tear the Sluagh to pieces.

"Not with his actual hands," she continued, "but with... you know. His energy, soul... or wind, or something. You look pissed. Maybe I shouldn't have told you."

The confident woman dissolved.

Well-damn that Sluagh and its unwelcome and perverted energy. Thorne's fangs sprouted. He stormed back to the Sluagh's house, stomped up the steps and pounded on the door, not caring if he roused all Six and signed the death warrant for his eternal soul. No one touched what belonged to him. His fist kept pounding until eventually, he realized what he was thinking.

She was his.

He'd thought it so adamantly.

But he didn't want it. Did he?

So why was he knocking?

Stupid.

Conflicted, he felt torn apart in many places. On one hand, it offended Thorne on so many levels to see a female taken advantage of like that, on another hand... there was a primal part of him that wanted to be the one she let go there. And that confused him. It was all wrong. This must be the mating marks speaking. Another low growl later and he went back down the steps, glaring at Laurel. "Go back to our house until you're called by the council for your testing."

He strode past her.

"Thorne."

He halted. Turned.

"I think we got off on the wrong foot. I'm... sorry I punched you. I don't like feeling helpless... and... I guess"—her bottom lip quivered—"I'm thousands of years from my world, my family, and my home. Everything here is different. Running makes me feel like I'm in control. I promise I'll ask before I head out again. Please, let's start again." She held her hand out. "My name is Laurel Baker. I know you don't like me, and to be frank, I'm not sure if I like you. But I won't shy away from responsibility. I'll help you find your friend."

His gaze dipped to her outstretched hand. "What do I do with that?"

"Shake it. In greeting."

"Like a bargain."

"I suppose it can also be used as a sign of closing a business deal. Or one of respect."

He straightened. "Then what bargain do you wish of me in return?"

"Nothing."

Shock and hurt flittered down their bond, as though he'd offended her. Thorne narrowed his eyes. She couldn't truly be offering her services for free. "Every fae wants something in return."

It was the way of life in Elphyne.

"In case you missed it, I'm not fae."

He scoffed. Didn't he know it?

She continued, "Well, I suppose if there has to be something, then I would like you to teach me the ways of this new time, including how to use my power." She hugged herself. "You said I made that fire in the cave, yet when that Sluagh had me in his control, I could do nothing to protect myself. I don't even know how I made the fire after I hit you. Again, sorry about that. I don't want to be helpless like that again."

Curious. She not only held her own against his sharp tongue, but it was dipped in honey. In a few sentences, she'd managed to steer the conversation and push further. And potentially put herself in his debt multiple times. He needn't bargain with her to get what he wanted. The laws of Elphyne said he could just take it from her as part of that debt.

But, again, she had no idea what she'd unwittingly done.

"The academy here will teach you to control your mana. Why not just wait for them to do so?"

"I want you."

Those three words struck a chord inside him. "Why?"

"I suppose," she bit her lip, clearly thinking hard. "I suppose it's a few things I'm slowly coming to terms with. Not only did you come to my rescue, but Clarke trusts you. Your Well chose us to be together, and I should try to honor that. Don't you agree?"

Regretfully, a part of him did. Since the dawn of Elphyne, and Jackson Crimson's discovery of mana and its link to the Well, fae learned that the more they followed the lead the Well set, the longer they stayed alive. That's why metal and plastic were outlawed. It halted the natural flow of mana in nature and in your body. As long as he listened to those laws, he could shift into wolf. He stayed young. He didn't like that a human mate was chosen for him, but he respected the Well.

Laurel mistook his silence for hesitance. She added, "I also want you to teach me because with this bond between us, you can't lie to me."

"Fae can't lie, anyway."

Confusion flittered over her expression, but then shrewd insight shone through. "I'm sure there are ways around that. Remind me to tell you about lawyers one day. But for now, you need something from me. I need something from you. If you don't want to work with this partnership idea, then perhaps consider it a classic business arrangement."

He was probably going to regret this, but he prowled toward her and clasped her hand. "Done. I will help you learn to utilize your mana. You will lead me to Jasper. And then we will go our separate ways."

"Agreed."

He sent mana into his hand. It wrapped around her palm, circling and tattooing the bargain on her soul.

Hours later, Thorne stood in the shadows of the armory, watching a sparring match on the training field while Laurel was being tested for her affinity to different elements at the temple. A winged fae—possibly an eagle shifter—battled a young wolf he'd not met before. Most wolf shifters knew each other, if not by sight, by scent. He must be new.

"You going to show the young pup how it's done?" A deep voice came from over Thorne's shoulder.

He turned and found Caraway, a muskox-shifter who towered at over a foot taller than most others. Two horns curled from the shaggy mop of hair on the top of his head and curved down and out at his scruff covered jaw. His brown doe eyes watched Thorne with amusement. Caraway was big, jolly, and always ready for a laugh, but a surprisingly deadly addition to the Order.

"He seems to have it under control." Thorne nodded at the sparring match. The wolf had the winged fae's neck in his jaw.

Caraway's eyes darted down to the blue markings on Thorne's arms. "Much has happened since we last saw each other."

Much was an understatement. They hadn't spoken for the past two years, not since Caraway's good friend Anise had been held hostage and Thorne was the one who rescued her, not Caraway. It mattered not to Thorne, but clearly there were some underlying issues between Caraway and Anise. Thorne preferred not to get involved, and the hunt for Jasper had kept him busy.

"How have you been?" Caraway ventured.

"Good. You?"

"Good."

They stood in silence for a few beats, and then Caraway folded his arms. "You haven't seen Anise, have you?"

Thorne frowned. "I thought you were friends. It's been two years."

"At first she wouldn't see me, then she disappeared. I just want to check in with her and make sure she's okay after what happened."

Being in a cage for two weeks, cut from the Well, would have been torture for Anise. Having no access to the lifeblood of nature was akin to a harrowing hangover. The very thought sent a shudder through Thorne. He couldn't grasp how the humans lived without that access permanently.

"You sure you're not keeping her whereabouts from me?"

"Why would I do that?"

Caraway's forlorn flicker made Thorne think the big ox had feelings for the feisty female fae. Thorne's brows knitted together.

"You know Guardians are discouraged from having a relationship for good reason, Caraway."

Caraway laughed, big bellied and loud. "You can talk, wolf. You and your father are lighting the way for all us loners."

"But we didn't have a say in it."

"I don't see Rush complaining. And from the looks of your human, I dare say you won't be either. Stop it. Don't scowl at me. You know I'm right. If I got to wake up next to that every day for eternity, I'd die happy."

A possessive growl rumbled from the base of Thorne's throat and Caraway laughed harder.

"Don't worry, old friend. It's a good thing my type has furry ears. I won't go near your mate."

"You shouldn't go near a female, period. Guardians shouldn't be in long-term relationships. We die sooner than others. It's too complicated."

"Screw the Prime's relationship rule. After what you two have been through, I'd say you deserve a little happiness. It's better to be happy for what little time we have, than none at all. My friendship with Anise has been the best years of my life. Now she won't talk to me... I hate it. I think being cut off from the Well would be worse."

That wasn't true. Rush had been cut from the Well during his fifty-year long exile. He'd almost died from lack of connection. The Prime had cursed Rush as punishment for siring Thorne when the law still stated all new births had to be sanctioned. Rush had suffered because Thorne was born.

Everything inside Thorne clenched tight. Anger surged, and he wondered if he'd ever be free of that weight, of the suffocating self-loathing that encircled him every time he remembered how he'd blamed himself simply for being born unwanted, a thorn in someone's paw.

Irritated, Thorne turned back to the training field. The battle was done. He supposed he had some time to kill before Laurel was done with the testing. He raised his brow at Caraway and then nodded at the field. "You want to go? For old time's sake?"

Caraway shrugged. "All right, but no shifting."

Thorne scoffed.

A change in atmosphere signaled Cloud's arrival. Irrefutable, electrified tension permeated the air. The scent of the night sky and spice hit Thorne's nose as the Prime's assassin landed in a flutter of black feathered wings.

The crow shifter was covered in neck-to-toe power-enhancing tattoos. Like an oil slick, they reflected incandescent, prismatic light and some said the inky depths of the Well—where necromancers and dark mages drew from, where anarchy reigned. Thorne preferred not to dabble with the unknown side of their power. It was a dance with disorder that could only end in sorrow. But then again, Cloud was Unseelie, and they were creatures of chaos. Perhaps the enhancing tattoos didn't affect them as it did the Seelie fae.

Blue lightning crackled in Cloud's amused blue gaze.

"Heard about your little mishap this morning," he drawled.

Thorne's eyes narrowed. "Wasn't my mishap."

"But it was your human's, ergo..."

"She's not mine." *Yes, she fucking was.*

Fuck.

As if hearing Thorne's silent turmoil, Cloud grinned knowingly, but the smile didn't reach his eyes. It wasn't genuine humor. It was the cruel, mocking kind. Cloud had been kept captive by the humans in their Crystal City decades ago. It was something he never spoke about, but from the way he spewed vitriol about them, and the way he'd declared to cut every single one of their heads off, the experience hadn't been good.

Thorne gave Cloud and his austere demeanor the once over. Did he need to warn Cloud away from Laurel?

"If the Sluagh wanted a taste of her soul, she must be as desolate as the rest of them," Cloud teased.

Claws sprung from Thorne's fingertips. "Careful."

"Or what?" Cloud stepped closer.

"Or next time I rip into your wings with my teeth, I won't let go."

Blue lightning flashed in Cloud's eyes. Electricity skipped over his skin.

Before he could respond, Thorne continued, "It wasn't Laurel's soul the Sluagh wanted."

Thorne lifted his blue marked hand, meaning, in other words, the Sluagh had wanted Laurel's power. Whether that was true didn't matter. It made Cloud believe Thorne had bested him. Despite Cloud's myriad of enhancing tattoos, the Well-blessed union with Laurel had given Thorne access to more power than Cloud could ever hope for, unless he ended up with his own union. And considering his disdain for humans, or anyone else, that was unlikely. Thorne honestly believed the fae would keel over and vomit if he had to share his sacred mana, let alone his emotions.

If he had any emotions left.

Cloud narrowed his eyes at the markings, then sneered and left.

Caraway scratched his beard. "Well, he's a ray of sunshine."

Thorne raised a brow.

Caraway boomed a laugh and clapped Thorne on the shoulder. "You're not as bad as that. Trust me."

"Fuck you."

This made Caraway double over in a fit. The raucous laughter drew Leaf's attention. The tall blond elf was the team leader of the Twelve, a council member, and an all-out overachiever. He must have come straight from the temple which meant Laurel would be done.

Thorne looked around for an escape route. He didn't particularly feel like being bossed around, but he was too late. Leaf and his Well-damned aristocratic nose arrived.

"D'arn Thorne. D'arn Caraway."

Always with the official titles. Thorne's lip curled. "Leaf."

Leaf glanced at Caraway, who took the hint, mock-saluted Thorne, and strode off.

"As expected, Laurel has tested in abundance with mana. Her capacity for holding it within herself is enough to carry her for days at full power without needing to refill. But I suspect you knew that already."

Thorne gave a tight nod. He didn't need to reveal that he'd already been borrowing from Laurel on occasion.

"Right, well, I'm sure she'll let you know, but her affinity is strongly skewed toward fire. With a little in chaos and spirit, she's basically a ticking time bomb if she can't control it. Her training will resume tomorrow and most likely take weeks. In the meantime, we have a job that requires the nose of a wolf."

Thorne folded his arms. "Give it to someone else. I'll be commencing my hunt for Jasper any day."

A sigh of exasperation left Leaf. This was the same argument they'd had for years. Thorne would want to leave his duties as a Guardian behind and scour Elphyne for signs of Jasper. Leaf would always remind Thorne that his destiny was with the Order, and that Jasper didn't want to be found.

Thorne didn't believe it.

Jasper was not the understated kind. He couldn't hide if he tried. Thorne once remembered Jasper drunkenly declaring to all of Cornucopia that he was the Seelie High King Mithras's bastard son, and that the king wanted him dead, but being a Guardian, Mithras could do nothing to hurt Jasper without aggravating the Order, so who wanted to fuck the king's son.

Jasper had hordes of female fae lining up to bed him. He laughed in the face of danger and taunted destiny. Thorne used to look up to him, but now Jasper was missing, Thorne couldn't help but worry that it was his untouchable, reckless attitude that had put him in danger.

"I'm not asking," Leaf said. "You'll leave first thing tomorrow. Be ready."

Anger surged. "How can you forget one of your own so easily?"

Storm clouds gathered in Leaf's eyes. "While you've been worried about your own little world, Elphyne is on the brink of war. Or have you truly been so blind as to the fresh slate of attacks on Seelie soil?"

"As the Prime always says, if it's not magic, it's not our problem."

"Unseelie unleashing mana-warped monsters *is* magic. It *is* our problem. Two years ago, we learned that humans from Clarke's past have been manipulating fae into doing their bidding. Those humans have been quiet, but we know they want our resources. We have news of a Seelie attack, this time in the Unseelie territory, on Queen Maebh's soil. She's requested an outside opinion of the crime scene before she makes up her own mind as to whether the threat is authentic. It could very well be part of the plot the humans are hatching. Whilst we try to stay out of fae politics, any kind of war will be detrimental to the integrity of the Well, don't you think?"

"This goes against everything the Prime has peddled about getting involved."

"Times are changing. The threat to Elphyne is more complicated. If we war amongst ourselves to the death, the humans will have free reign to come in and take what they want from our soil. They will mine it for metals, and spread their toxins all over the earth, killing it once and for all. Your duty is to the Well, D'arn Thorne. Not to Jasper."

"You're as heartless as the Prime."

"I'm doing my job." Leaf's eyes flashed. "Be ready at sunrise. I'll ensure your mate is kept safe while you're gone."

Like hell, he would.

LEAF

CHAPTER
TEN

Laurel eased her aching body into the tub and submerged in hot steaming water. The so-called testing had taken all day. At the temple, she'd had to stand in various ponds of water and watch a little obelisk light up or not light up. It was the strangest thing. Each pond was apparently keyed to a particular type of element and revealed where her powers were strongest. She was strongest in fire.

She'd always been a practical woman, and the idea of making fire with her mind baffled her, but with each pond she'd stepped in, she'd felt an echo of *something* move deep within her soul and burn down her marked arm.

She sighed and dipped her head back to rest on the lip of the tub, staring at the simple wooden ceiling.

So this was her life now.

No electric lights. No vents from a cooling system. Her gaze trailed around the bathing chamber and tried to make sense of what she saw, how technology was different. No electricity, no computers, no gorgeous rubber-soled shoes. Much of the decor was remarkably familiar. Rugs on the floor. Linen drapes on the window. A closet stacked with clothes—no heeled pumps, dresses or makeup, mind you—but still something so common and mundane that it felt comforting. Pants. Blouses. Jackets.

Soft incense burned with the scent of ocean and forest. Of Thorne, she realized with a start.

The wolf-shifter's grouchy face sprung to mind. Always frowning, that one. Except when she'd seen him sleep and the pressure of his worries had melted away. Had he always been so distant, or had something happened to him to make him so? She held her scarred fingers before her eyes, watched them tremble and then submerged them.

It was none of her business.

But aren't you married to him?

Wasn't that what Clarke had said? Laurel had a sudden stab of longing for her friend. What she wouldn't give for a hug from her mother right now, or a chat. Her mother always knew what to say. She'd tamed her own alpha male, after all. Tears stung Laurel's eyes and she dashed them away. *Crying over the matter won't help. Feeling sorry for herself won't help.*

This time, it was her father's voice drilling her, just like he had when she was younger during one of their "training" sessions. General Baker had always wanted her to join the army. Lionel had been a sickly boy, and preferred the couch and his video games to the outdoors, but Laurel had always liked to run track, and so her father focused his army-trained energy on riding her ass until she made Nationals. At the time, she had hated him. Distance endurance was hard. But when she had won gold, she couldn't argue with his drive. Lionel had also been so proud. Laurel owed much of her success to the discipline her father had taught her.

Laurel cleared her throat and forced herself to rally. She'd been given a second chance at life, none of her family had, so she had to make this worth it. First, she needed to learn how to use these powers building inside her. She hadn't seen Thorne all morning and was already concerned he'd backed out of their bargain. It seemed like none of the fae here at the Order knew he was the one teaching her.

The door burst open and Thorne rushed in, closing it behind.

She craned her neck to see him. Looking fierce, he promptly unbuttoned his leather battle jacket and hung it on a hook behind the door. His white undershirt clung to his form and accentuated every hard muscle as it bunched and rolled with his movements. It took her mind a moment to recover from the impact of the raw male strength he exuded, and then he stormed over, blue fire in his eyes. Spell broken.

Forcing her fingers to remain relaxed on the lip of the tub, she watched him circle the room, pull out a knapsack and fill it with various items—small stones, coin, weapons.

It was on the tip of her tongue to make a retort about privacy, but she knew it would just glance off him. If he had no qualms walking around campus in the nude, then why would he care about her state of undress?

After a few minutes, he still hadn't acknowledged her. She wondered if he'd noticed her. A sense of unrest trickled through their bond and, for once, it wasn't aimed at her. She cleared her throat.

His gaze flicked over to her. He frowned, and then returned to his packing. Finally he collected a small stone bowl, came over and dipped it into the bath water, then went to a vanity with a black shiny mirror. He perched on a stool, lathered a soapy mixture and applied it to the sides of his head. He unclipped a bone knife from his belt and shaved from ear to the strip of silver hair on top.

Two scrapes in, his deep voice rumbled, "We're leaving tonight. Prepare for travel. Dress warm."

Their eyes met in the mirror. Held. Then he resumed shaving. The knife tinkled against the bowl every time he washed it clean of soap.

"They said my training at the academy would commence tomorrow morning and would last for weeks."

He paused. "We agreed I would train you."

Relief washed through her. "Good. I was just checking nothing had changed."

"We made a bargain." He shot her a quizzical look, as if bargains were never broken, and she should know better. "We leave tonight."

Thorne scraped his knife from his neck to his high hairline. He got to the part at the back of his neck and struggled, trying to find a good angle in the mirror.

Laurel wasn't sure why she did what she did next. Maybe it was because, despite being mated, married, or whatever they were, he was as distant about it as she was. It was the complete opposite to how Rush and Clarke had behaved. They were so loved up, it wasn't funny. Laurel hadn't thought she'd wanted a connection like that, but the emptiness of missing her family was starting to make her feel like maybe she did. Maybe this was a moment of weakness.

She stood up. Water sluiced down her body. Steam curled from the tub.

Thorne froze. He locked eyes with her in the mirror. The air seemed to thicken.

Despite his frozen countenance, and his failure to drop his gaze to her nudity, a bolt of lust seared through the bond and he fumbled with the knife, almost dropping it.

Her body had always been fabulous, shaped from a lifetime in the gym. She never had an issue with showing it off. But this was a bad idea. She lost her nerve, changed her mind, and gathered the towel around her body. What was she thinking?

Hugging the towel, she padded over to him and took the knife from his hand. She smirked. "In case you drop it again, maybe I should finish shaving you."

Without complaint, he acquiesced. She held the blade to his skin and hesitated. If he was her enemy, this would be the perfect opportunity to hurt him. But she met his eyes again, felt the mix of lust and longing he tried to hide, and couldn't move. Couldn't breathe. It was unlike anything she'd experienced before. A tempest whirled in her soul. Outwardly, he looked like he always did, but inside...

He wasn't her enemy. She swallowed and concentrated on the blade scraping roughly along his head.

"Why are we leaving?" she asked, voice huskier than intended.

"Because you won't lead me to Jasper here." His voice sounded dry too.

"Okay," she said. "Fair enough."

He released a breath of relief. Perhaps he'd expected her to argue.

"Tell me about him," she prompted.

"Jasper? He's a wolf-shifter. Of the Mithras line."

"Mithras?"

"The Seelie High King." Thorne grimaced at her confused face. "Elphyne is split into two territories, Seelie—fae of order and light, and Unseelie—fae of chaos and night. Within the Seelie territory, the High King Mithras rules over the Summer and Spring Courts. High Queen Maebh rules over the Unseelie territories, the Winter and Autumn Courts. Mithras is Jasper's biological father."

"Tell me more about Jasper."

"Jasper is the king's illegitimate son, and as such was a target for assassination. Mithras wants no one taking over his throne, and in Elphyne, thrones can be won by blood, whether by war, or by kin. Jasper always knew if the king found out about his existence he would be in danger, and so he volunteered to take the initiation ceremony.

He survived and fell under protection of the Order of the Well. Even High Kings have no jurisdiction over the Order. Jasper was safe for years. But now we know Mithras has him, and we don't know where. I've searched everywhere. And still I come up with nothing."

Laurel paused in her shaving. "You don't think Bones or the Void have him?"

"I never thought to look in Crystal City. It's one of the places fae can't enter. It's a city in the wasteland and is full of so much metal that no mana flows there. It's completely cut off. It could be why it's been hard to scry for him." Thorne's gaze turned thoughtful. "But Rush spent time in the human city a few years ago. If Jasper was there, it's likely he'd have heard about it. A fae like Jasper would be big news."

He didn't look too convinced. Neither was she, but she didn't push it. She continued shaving and pretended like that wasn't the most she'd ever heard him speak. "And the Order won't search for him?"

"It was the Prime who sold Jasper to the king for a promise. I highly doubt she has the same motivation to find him as I do."

Jesus. Now she knew why Thorne hated the Prime.

"Then what the fuck are we doing in this place? Why on earth would Clarke align herself with an organization that betrays its own employees?"

Thorne's eyes locked with Laurel's in the mirror. Approval flickered over his expression, and then his brows snapped down. "The Prime isn't the Well. She's one person with a god complex. Ultimately, none of us here have sworn our service to her specifically. We're sworn to the Well. Clarke knows this. She walks to her own tune. The Prime allows it because Clarke is currently working to the same ends—protecting Elphyne."

Thank fuck for Clarke's common sense. And if Clarke didn't trust the Prime, then neither would Laurel. "So where will we start the search?"

"I think we sweep Elphyne before heading into the wasteland. Cornucopia is a neutral trade city between Seelie and Unseelie territory. Jasper used to have an apartment in Cornucopia. May as well start there."

Finished shaving, Laurel took a hand towel and patted the last of the soap from Thorne's head. With a palm pressed on one of his rock-hard shoulders, she took the tail of his hair and let it run through her fingers. It bumped every time she hit a ridge of leather cord. His hair was very long. Down to the middle of his back.

"Does the length mean something?" she asked.

He paused. Then nodded. "I pledged to only cut it when I found Jasper."

"He's been missing that long?"

"Over a decade."

Sadness spread as her fingers trailed back up the hair, slipped over the newly shorn scalp and found the lightly furred tip of his pointed ear. It twitched. Her breath hitched. It *moved*. Like an actual wolf's ear. Unable to help herself, curiosity led her finger down over the fur and stroked.

That lust she'd felt earlier barreled toward her down the bond, kindling her own in response.

A growl came a moment before his strong, vice-like grip took her wrist. Suddenly he was up and facing her. Fire, passion and fury warred over his expression and simultaneously down their bond. He wrenched her offending arm behind her back and pressed her to him. Each time his chest lifted with ragged breath, the towel rubbed her sensitized skin. Confusion danced in his eyes.

"What game are you playing at, human?" he snarled in her face.

"I don't know what you mean, *wolf*," she replied. "I'm still learning. Teach me."

His eyes narrowed, assessing. For all their talk about an alliance, they were still treating each other like enemies. But she didn't shrink back. She held her ground, waiting for whatever sharp words were sitting on the tip of his tongue. They didn't come. Instead, he let go of her hand and said, voice rough, "Don't touch a fae's ears without permission."

She stepped back. "Why?"

"Because they are erogenous."

Oh. Well, that would do it.

A high-pitched squeal at the door came before a little ball of two-legged energy burst through. Pink cheeked and with damp silver hair, the little girl wore simple night-clothes—pale blue linen pants and a t-shirt. Looking severely flustered, the brownie Laurel had met yesterday followed the girl.

"Willow," the brownie admonished. "Leave your brother alone."

Brother?

This must be Clarke's daughter. Laurel's gaze snapped to the girl who had now found her way to Thorne and was attempting to crawl up his legs to tug on his hair. He tried to scoop her up but she deftly evaded him and became a white blur until she climbed on the bed and bounced.

"This is unfortunate, D'arn," Jocinda said. "It's time for her to sleep but she can smell kin in the house."

Laurel expected Thorne to grouse or shout, but he waved Jocinda down and said, "It's fine. I'll get her."

He strode to the bed, but Willow saw him coming. She crouched, fangs sprang from her teeth, her ears elongated until they were severely arched, and claws springing from her fingertips. Transformed before Laurel's eyes, Willow snarled at Thorne.

He paused. "That's new."

"No-no-no sleep." Willow pounced. Thorne caught her midair and tried to take her to Jocinda, but Willow screamed and wiggled and bit Thorne. "No," she whined, tears brimming. "Sleep with you. Here!"

Jocinda gave Thorne a questioning look.

Willow did too.

He sighed heavily. "Fine. I'll put her in her own bed later."

With a nod of approval, Jocinda left.

Laurel followed the two to the bed and was given a possessive warning growl from the little girl. Then she sniffed the air, looked at Laurel's blue marks on her arms, and promptly relaxed.

"She knows you're kin, too," Thorne murmured, seemingly surprised.

A little piece of Laurel's heart melted. Her throat thickened, and she had to force the tears away. She and Lionel used to always jump into their parents' bed, despite her father grumbling. Her mother would always make room.

Clarke was her family. She might not be here, but her daughter was. Soon they would all be together.

"Hi," Laurel whispered, her throat dry. "I'm Laurel, your momma's best friend. Has she spoken about me?"

Willow nodded shyly, then gave a little growl and jumped on Thorne, nipping his face and doing her best to be vicious. Irritation swam over his features. "Willow. It's time for sleep."

But she thought it was fight time. Not sleep time.

Laurel smiled. The girl had moxie, just like her mother. Laurel hugged her body towel and laid down on the bed. She patted the pillow next to her. "Come on. Time to sleep. I'll stay with you."

Reluctantly, Willow peeled off Thorne and came over. She used her claws to pluck the blanket and crawled in circles before finally finding a comfortable position to settle. Her big eyes watched Laurel curiously.

Laurel gently rubbed her finger down the bridge of Willow's nose. With every stroke, the little girl's eyes grew heavier until eventually, they stayed closed. Through it all, Laurel could feel the weight of Thorne's attention and when Willow finally fell asleep, he whispered, "How did you do that... magic?"

She almost laughed. "No. My mother used to do it to me when I was little. Children just need touch. If she thinks we're family, then she misses hers. I know what that's like."

CHAPTER

ELEVEN

After seeing Willow to her room, Thorne returned to his chambers and was surprised to find Laurel dressed in travel attire as he'd requested. He'd expected a bit of push back, but the woman continued to defy his expectations.

Since he'd seen her with Willow, he'd been in a constant state of unrest. His skin felt tight. His pulse elevated. The wolf in him heartily approved of Laurel's maternal behavior. It also cautiously liked how Willow had treated Laurel like kin.

It was getting harder to keep Laurel at arm's length. And part of him didn't want to. Part of him liked the idea of family. Of her. His father, Clarke, and Willow as a unit. But the other part remembered how cruel the world was. It remembered his mission and that she would lead him to someone who might not smell like kin to Thorne, but *was* family. A fae who had saved Thorne's life in more ways than one.

"Okay," Laurel stated, "I've got warm leggings on, a sweater, and this furred cape on the bed. Was that the kind of warm you're talking about? And what about food? Do we need any?"

The woman rattled off more questions, but harrowing memories forced a burn in his throat. Twelve-year-old Thorne had just arrived at the Order, and Jasper had been chosen to settle him in his room at the barracks.

"Breeches, shirt, sweater, jacket, cape," Jasper said and pointed at the uniform hanging in the closet.

Thorne stood in the doorway to the shared dormitory, hating the single bed in the corner, hating the matching bunk on the other side. It looked like a prison and Jasper was the tattooed prison guard behind him, blocking the exit. Thorne wanted to transform into wolf and run out of there, into the poisonous forest surrounding the Order grounds. Maybe he should. He'd traveled through worse places. Then again, maybe he should eat the toxic red leaves. Never come back.

The idea was so appealing that it consumed his thoughts. Nobody would miss him. They'd just sigh and say, "Oh well, there goes another Guardian."

"You get three sets," D'arn Jasper continued. "You're in charge of laundering them."

Thorne set his simmering gaze on the tall fae, loathing his pretty face. What did Thorne care what he asked him to do? Thorne didn't choose to be shoved into the ceremonial lake. He would have preferred to die—to float—to never worry about where his next beating was going to come from. Never fear the snide looks from people casting him as unwanted. Trash.

"Go away," snapped Thorne.

It only made the d'arn laugh heartily.

"Go float yourself," he snarled again, fury welling to overtake his despair.

"Been there, done that. Didn't stick. Just like you."

"So what, you think we're the same?"

Jasper's dark brow rose. "We're more alike than you think. One day, you'll get that. Until then, launder your uniform, or don't. I don't really care. Here." He removed a small package from his pocket and held it out. "It's a bit of mana-weed. Just don't smoke it before training. Preceptor in charge won't be happy if you turn up wasted."

Thorne took the package and a little thrill skipped up his spine. His aunt Kyra had always said he was too young for this and prohibited any sort of inebriation. At the time, he'd thought she was just being a stick in the mud... but after his Uncle Thaddeus and cohorts had beaten Thorne to a pulp, he knew his aunt was only looking out for him. Better to keep your senses so you could protect yourself, even if that meant lifting your hands to cover your face.

Jasper must have seen the question in Thorne's eyes as he reverently accepted the package. "Yeah, I know you're a bit young, kid, but the training will harden you. Smoke it with some friends. We work hard here, but we play hard too." Jasper's eyes twinkled with humor. Thorne almost missed the angst haunting his expression. Almost. "You're among family now, Nightstalk. Get some rest."

Laurel's hand waved before Thorne's face. "Thorne. Are you listening? I asked about food."

"Food?"

She smirked. "Yeah, I was hoping you'd have smoothie supplies around. But I guess not." She bit her lip at his blank face. "Never heard of the drink?"

"Aren't all drinks smooth?"

Laurel's eyes widened. She blinked. Then she burst out laughing, doubling over and clutching her middle. Her melodious sound pierced his hard shell. Humor shot down their bond and warmth spread throughout his body like whiskey. It was like nothing he'd felt before. No humor, no laugh, no joke had brought this kind of rebellious freedom to his heart. His lip twitched.

He didn't know what to do. She was so... alluring. That smile was transformative. Eyes so bright. Skin flushed.

He took a step closer. And another.

Want to touch her.

Big round eyes watched him approach, and she stopped laughing.

"Do that again," he demanded.

"What... laugh?"

Still mesmerized, he nodded.

"Have you not"—she swallowed—"seen someone laugh before?"

He took her neck gently in his hand and lowered his nose to breathe her in, letting her scent take hold of him further. Something sweet, yet musky. Black raspberries laced with female. No mission, no hate, no Well. Just her. And him.

She stilled, letting him have his moment, and it was bliss. An ache in his fangs. Alpha instincts. *Mark her.*

"Thorne?"

"I have seen it," he murmured against her skin. "I've just not *felt* it."

"Oh."

Such a tiny sound from her. Breathy, soft, feminine. But something in her tone gave him pause, and when he sensed her emotions change down the bond, he stepped back, lip curled. "I don't want your pity, Laurel."

Her eyes turned sad and that made it worse. She'd been tortured, lost her whole world, and yet she felt sorry for him. She didn't even know him.

Fuck this. He finished getting ready, strapping his battle-ax baldric over his jacket and fit weapons to his belt. Then he slung the knapsack over his shoulder and went to the window to peek outside. Darkness swathed the grounds, but it was still early enough that walking to the stables wouldn't appear out of the ordinary. Seelie and Unseelie fae resided in equal amounts on the campus, so the nightlife was as active as the day. Thorne's best bet to avoid Leaf would be to go now, when the elves and other cadre members would often go down to the Mess Hall and take advantage of the Mage Brew and social atmosphere.

"Let's go," he said.

Laurel joined him at the door.

"Are you telling me what the plan is, or am I to follow you around like a lost puppy?"

He frowned. "There is no plan."

"Surely there's something."

"Get to the stables, take a kuturi, and fly to Cornucopia."

"Okay." She thought about it. "Wait... what's a kuturi? Why aren't we using a portal?"

"Because Leaf can trace portals. I don't want anyone knowing where we're going. And you'll find out what a kuturi is when you see one."

"Oh. Sure. That makes sense in no way possible." She searched his face. "Are we going to get in trouble?"

He shrugged, opened the door to his room, and ushered her out. If there was a chance she'd changed her mind, this would be it. But she returned his shrug and followed him.

Just as he'd hoped, the residents of the house were either out, or in their rooms. Thorne led Laurel outside and through the grounds, taking the long winding paths shadowed by trees wherever he could. They bypassed the horse stables and went straight to the kuturi stables without missing a step. Thorne stopped outside the gate and searched around for the only fae who might be here—Forrest.

The auburn-haired elf, also in the Twelve, was almost a permanent fixture at the stables. He had an affinity with animals and art. But like Leaf and Aeron, he should be at the Mess Hall eating and drinking. Scanning the area, Thorne couldn't see him. Good.

He turned his attention to finding a bag of sugared treats. They would keep the kuturi happy and incentivized.

Clawing, squawking, and rustling came from the stalls. The animals knew they were there.

While he scrounged through a supply sack, Laurel shifted uncomfortably.

"What is it?" he asked.

Her gaze darted nervously to a stall. "I'm guessing a kuturi is some kind of giant bird?"

He frowned. "Giant birds were not around in your time?"

She blanched. "I'm right, aren't I? Oh, Jesus. We're going on a bird. Shit."

"How did you fly from one place to another?"

"We made machines that carried us. Planes. Helicopters. We were safe and inside. Not on some bird." She patted her face as though trying to cool it.

So she had no clue. His lip curved slightly as he remembered the warmth of her earlier humor, and in that moment, there was nothing he wanted more than to feel her laughter again. Eagerness twitched through him. With a watchful eye on her reaction, he opened the oversized gate.

"Holy fuck," she gasped.

Inside was a kuturi. With the head of an eagle and the body of a fox, the white-feathered and furred breed was mostly docile, and happy to fly long distances. Useless during a battle, but as long as sugar treats were involved, a perfect alternative for traveling long distances.

The winged beast was big enough to carry two adults on its back comfortably. It squawked at Thorne and pranced on its paws, long tail swishing in excitement. Black patterns marred the white coat in an artistic way Forrest would probably wax poetic about.

"This is a kuturi," he said.

Laurel gasped and then shoved Thorne. "Get out."

Um. What?

He glanced over his shoulder at her. "Why?"

"No, it's... um. Oh, God, it's a figure of speech. I'm just... wow. It's so beautiful. Can I pat it?"

He nodded. "It won't bite unless it's mistreated, and we spoil them here."

She couldn't stop grinning, and that happiness he'd felt earlier bloomed again. Laurel cooed and fawned over the animal with lively expressions. The kuturi ate up her attention like it was a sugar treat. Rushing warmth flowed down their bond when Laurel hugged the animal and nuzzled its neck. The way her hand stroked rhythmically and tickled under the kuturi's chin made Thorne's chest ache in envy.

He shook his head and cleared his throat.

"Move. I have to put the saddle on."

"Oh, sorry." Laurel jumped back. "I'm in the way."

Her smile didn't leave her face until he'd fitted a double saddle and reins, and when he led the creature out of the stalls to the lawn outside, her skin took on a sickly hue.

He should say something to calm her nerves.

He opened his mouth, but was cut off by a crow cawing in a nearby tree.

Fuck.

Thorne closed his eyes and counted to five. Don't kill it. Don't. He continued counting until he got to ten, then opened his eyes and sought the crow out. Up on a branch, lurking in shadows, was the glossy black crow, watching him with knowing eyes.

"Just let us go, Cloud."

Laurel did a double take as she caught the power struggle but remained silent.

The crow cawed.

"What do you care if we leave?" Thorne asked. "I'm taking the human with me."

The bird's beady eyes flicked to Laurel. Stared. Then left in a flutter of black wings. Whether that meant Cloud was giving Thorne a head start, or simply had flown to tattle on him, Thorne couldn't tell. Best be quick about it or Leaf would be back to haul his ass on that mission.

He gave Laurel a boost onto the kuturi and then climbed on behind her. Laurel fit snuggly between his legs, her body slotting in next to his perfectly. He retrieved a treat from the knapsack at his back, made a clicking sound with his tongue, and reached around Laurel to give the kuturi a treat. It was the promise of more to come at the end of their arduous journey. When he returned to his correct position, Laurel pressed back into him, and a feeling of rightness bloomed further.

Laurel still tickled the kuturi around the head. He couldn't see her smile, but he could feel it.

On a whim, he decided a small detour would be warranted. Holding the reins in his hands on either side of Laurel, he guided the bird to the lawn runway behind the stables.

"*Hiya.*" He kicked the bird with his heels.

Wings snapped out, taloned paws trotted, and within moments, equilibrium shifted as the animal picked up speed, beat its wings in a frenzy, and lifted. Laurel squeaked in excitement, knuckles white on the grip of the saddle before her. Her short hair billowed and tickled Thorne's face, eliciting a smile from his lips.

Lift off.

CHAPTER

TWELVE

Laurel was flying. *Can't believe it.* Actually flying atop a bird-animal-thing. Wind buffeted her face. The fresh, clean, and restorative air reminded her of home before the fallout. It was the kind of air that energized her on a hike in the Yosemite National Park with Ada. Tears burned in her eyes, her throat tightened, and she had to force her mind back into the present. She gripped the saddle, kept her knees locked and pressed against the wall of muscle behind her. Not only did she feel safer inside the cage of Thorne's confident arms, but he provided much-needed warmth at this altitude.

It was better to focus on that, on the adventure, than to sink into melancholy over her lost life. Her lost world. She couldn't turn back time, only move forward. Or fly.

Night made the journey extra thrilling. Sometimes she could see lights below on the ground, other times nothing, but the clear air made the stars and moon so bright. It painted the earth below in surprising clarity. She saw blobs of trees and tiny thatch-roofed villages that looked like she'd stepped back in time, not forward. In some places, the stars were beneath them as they flew over water.

Thorne steered the kuturi by the reins and knees, clenching his powerful thighs next to Laurel's. There were so many questions whirling around her mind, but with the wind rushing in her ears, the beat of wings, and her blood quickening, she kept her mouth shut, afraid she would miss the wonder if her attention lapsed.

After an hour or so, Thorne tapped Laurel on the thigh. His lips hit her ear, and he pointed to her right. "Look down."

A shiver ran through her at the sound of his voice, smooth and deep. She tried to angle to the side and peer down, but she wobbled and squeaked. Her arms ached from holding the saddle so tight, for so long, and she didn't trust herself. She shook her head. It was a long way down.

Thorne shifted the reins to one hand and then slid his other tightly around her middle. Steady. "I've got you. Go on. Take a look."

Instinct shifted inside her like a clock ticking or cogs turning. Her eyes landed on the blue glowing marks on her arm, and the twin ones on his forearm circling her stomach. The blue was brighter at night. It painted her front and the kuturi's head. The connection between them pulsed, stronger than before. It felt... it felt... like *trust*. She trusted the fae behind her. It was more than knowing he needed her for a task. It was the kind of person he was, the one he tried to hide. He had stood between her and a Sluagh. He had let his young sister climb into his bed and disrupt his travel plans. He had never felt the joy of laughter, but wanted to. That unguarded moment they'd shared in his chambers had done more to give her insight into her partner than any words. The feel of his fingers curling around her neck. The way his nose dipped to her skin and breathed in deep. The open wonder in his eyes when he'd demanded she laugh again.

I don't want your pity, Laurel.

Somehow that made her trust him more. It meant his small confession had come from an honest place. Inhaling deeply, she nodded, and tilted to the side, confident he would keep her from falling. Lashes lifting from the wind, hair blasting back, she scanned the ground below. She didn't have to look far. Something truly magnificent and full of awe was about one hundred feet below her.

Glowing patterns in all shapes and colors drew a gasp from her lips. What was it? So big and vast. Was it some kind of light show? A circus? She frowned as Thorne guided the kuturi lower. It was nature.

Bioluminescent, ethereal nature.

All of it glowed in shades of blue, pink, purple, yellow, and green. A rainbow of life. Flowers bloomed at night. Leaves, trees, a body of water so large it seemed like a glossy mirror of the night. Lower still brought them perilously close to the lake so vast she couldn't see the end. Their slipstream disturbed the water behind them. When Laurel craned to look behind, she saw they'd rocked the surface of the lake. Swimming stars churned and eddied as though alive and were as excited to meet Laurel as she was for them.

"Where are we?" she asked, trying to meet Thorne's serious stare.

"The ceremonial lake," he replied. "It's the original source of power. Some say it is access to the Well itself."

The Well.

The cradle of life. Of everything the Order dedicated their service to. During her testing, she'd heard plenty about it. Now she truly saw it. It was more than immortality. More than mana. It was the very core of existence. Stardust itself.

Suddenly she felt so small and irrelevant in the grand scheme of things. But she wasn't irrelevant, she was chosen. Maybe not so insignificant after all.

"I need to see it," she declared. "To touch it."

"Now?"

She nodded.

Anguish filtered down their bond and, for a moment, Laurel thought Thorne would shut down, but he didn't. He gripped her middle tight, and the side of his lip curled in a seductive half-smile. "Ready?"

She lost control of her mind. *Dimples.*

"What?" she said.

"Hold tight."

He urged the kuturi faster and Laurel had to turn back to the front. Her cheeks tightened at the speed. She could do nothing but hold on and enjoy the thrill of magic-laden air, of anticipation and awe as they zoomed. Every time the kuturi lifted and dipped, her stomach gave way, and her body filled with sensation. An incomprehensible squeal escaped her lips. She felt like Bastian upon Falkor from the Neverending Story. Thorne must have liked it, too, because he urged the kuturi up higher, despite Laurel's proclamation to go down. His arm became iron around her middle, and then his deep voice whispered near her ear, "Do you trust me?"

"Yes," she replied. No hesitation.

"Then when I say to let go, let go."

She nodded. Okay. Weird. But Okay. Maybe they had to dismount in the lake. She'd sky-dived out of a plane before. She could handle this. Sure.

Then he barked words she didn't understand, clicked his tongue, and the kuturi barrel-rolled. Her stomach lifted into her throat. Her eyes blurred. And the luminescent horizon shifted as they rotated until they were upside down. Her whirling mind only had enough time to grasp they flew upside down and then the gap between them and the water suddenly closed. A scream caught in her throat. Would they crash? On their heads? At this speed, impact on the water would be like hitting concrete.

A second later, the kuturi's wings snapped out, and they glided. The roar of wind whipped past and she could *smell* the salty water as they zoomed.

"Now!" he barked.

She let go of the saddle. Gravity took her hands and flung them toward the lake beneath. Her fingers hit the icy surface. Contact was a hammer to her hand, but the stars in the water, the glowing balls of energy... they were an interstellar galaxy just waiting to zoom up her skin as though iron to a magnet and then the world shifted again and they were upright, flying along as though nothing had changed.

Except everything had.

The contents of her stomach wanted out, an incandescent rainbow patina coated her hands, and... she'd never had more fun in her life. Gasping, heart-pounding so hard it wanted out of her chest, and so full of feeling she would burst, she twisted to see Thorne. But did it too fast, too hard, and they all wobbled.

He steadied them, chuckled, and a puff of hot breath brushed her neck, eliciting shivers that she felt down to her toes. His humor slid into her like a blanket wrapping around her heart.

"Sorry," she gasped. "I just... oh my God, that was fun."

"It's called whiffling," he explained. "It can only be done quickly and for a few beats."

"It was incredible." She shouted another *woohoo* to which he responded with another silent chuckle she felt along her spine. His humor morphed to joy and she almost wept.

I have seen it. I've just not felt it.

He'd lived twice her years, but in all that time he'd not felt true mirth until from her, and now it echoed back at her down their bond.

Her grin stretched until her cheeks hurt.

Thorne directed a descent that took them down to land on a long wooden jetty covered in glowing barnacles. Like the rainbow patina on her arms, it oozed over the underwood and cast rays of prismatic light through the gaps in the planks. As their ride trotted to a halt, coming off the jetty and onto the sandy shore, Laurel felt a shift in Thorne's demeanor. Joy fled.

Hate. Loathing. Disgust.

It mixed with... duty? An ache?

The trees surrounding the shore provided a tall canopy that seemed to expand into a forest. Not all of it glowed. That glory belonged mainly to vines and creepers growing from the ground, winding into the forest, making it look like a part of the trees.

Crickets chirped. The mating sound of aquatic life called. Something skittered in the foliage. Little balls of lazy lights broke away, as though disturbed. Laurel could have sworn she heard giggling and narrowed her eyes. What had Thorne called the flying firefly thing in the cave, a sprite?

Along the shore, human sized stone huts were scattered among the vegetation. No light came from the windows. Perhaps they were empty.

"Do people live here?" she asked as Thorne helped her from the saddle.

He didn't answer, only fed the kuturi some sugar snacks, and tied its lead to the trunk of a tree. "Wait here," he told it, and then joined Laurel.

Every line of his body was tense.

"What's wrong?" she asked.

Icy fire sparked in his eyes as he glared at the lake. How could he be so irritated in such a wondrous place?

"Thorne?" she prompted.

He scowled, picked up a pebble, and then threw it against the water, making it skip until something in the deep leaped out and sucked it in. "I hate this place."

She gaped at the dark thing in the water, then shook her head and refocused on Thorne. How could he hate this place?

"Why?"

A beat. A breath. An anguished look. "Because they forced me in. No one asked me. I didn't want it... still don't. And do you know what the worst thing was? The Prime herself pushed me in, knowing full well the odds were stacked against my survival."

"That sounds harsh."

"Guardians are a dying breed. No one has volunteered in decades, yet the realm must be protected from the greed of humans and the corruption of fae, so she forces everyone to offer tributes. Even royalty. Even paupers. Farmers. Females. The starting age is twelve."

The greed of humans. Corruption of fae? Wait... "You were twelve?"

His clipped nod was her answer.

"I'm so sorry."

His gaze hardened. "Once again, I don't want your pity."

"Then why tell me?"

"I don't know." He started walking back toward the kuturi. "Let's go."

"Wait." She grasped his hand, tugging him back. At their connection, their bond markings flared brightly. She felt a zing journey down her arm and warmth between their palms. It was as though their souls talked to each other.

As they both considered their blue markings, silence passed. His eyes caught on her gnarled fingernails. To her horror, he shifted them into the light of the moon and inspected them. She snatched her hand away.

"Why do you keep hiding them?" he asked.

A sharp, sad laugh shot out of her. "You know why. They're broken."

His gaze held her captive. It was clear he wanted to say something, but she was a coward. She wouldn't let him. Where he'd just laid out a secret from his past, she ran from it. So she changed the subject. "You said you would teach me, Obi-Wan. I want to be a Jedi like you."

His lip twitched. Something like stifled confusion, awe, and curiosity warred through him. She knew how she must look to him. A strange visitor from another time. Someone who looked like his enemy but acted like something else. Everything inside him wanted to know more about her—she could sense it. He held it all back behind his stiff posture and near implacable expression, but the emotions he tried to corral in his body soared through their bond. She was confounding him. And she liked it. She'd raised the bar her entire life. She was that woman no one expected to succeed, but did.

Your only limit is you.

Yet another quote she rattled off to her clients. They would groan and moan as she put them through their sweaty paces in pump class, but she was living proof. The nails had been ripped out, and when they grew back gnarled, she took up MMA lessons. Then she installed the same training into every Queen Fitness gym. More than self-defense, it was an offense class. Designed to help a woman take the first step in protecting herself. To help her become a powerhouse.

It was something Laurel desperately wanted to believe about herself.

Sometimes she wondered if the motivational quotes she spouted were all a ruse. Just a show. An act. Think yourself strong, and you will be. Maybe. But like a clown who was sad inside but projected jokes, she felt like a fraud sometimes.

"So," she said, "Are there drills? Training exercises? How do I make fire come out of my hand again?"

"We don't have time. It's getting late."

"Give me thirty minutes. You promised you would."

He turned his back on her. She thought maybe he'd declined, but he took two steps, unbuckled the menacing ax from the baldric around his shoulders, and then unbuttoned his leather jacket. He dumped it on the sandy beach and then faced her, now dressed only in a fitted white shirt and breeches.

"Take your cape off," he ordered.

For a single, panic-filled moment, her instinct shouted at her. *Look at his muscles.* That strength. He could rip her in two and not break a sweat. Pulled out nails could be a blessing compared to having a wolf's claws shred her heart.

Cautiously, she studied him and sensed no animosity.

Okay. Let's see where this is going.

A little thrill tripped in her stomach. Good. This was good. She could do this. She unlaced the cape and dropped it to the ground. Her knitted sweater gave her plenty of freedom to move, so she left it on. How would this training go?

What's his plan?

Anticipation thrummed against her skin. She darted a glance at the lake, then to him.

"We're not going for a swim," he noted her direction.

"Then what?"

He lifted his fists, boxer style. "You have a good right hook. Show me more."

A grin split her face. Her MMA training had only lasted a few months before bombs were set loose on the world, but it had been enough to give her the confidence to fight back, or at the very least, the urge to. If Bones came at her again, she wouldn't stop fighting. No matter what.

But he's so much bigger than Bones, a little voice in the back of her head warned. An undercurrent of doubt and fear began to tickle her skin. She shook it off. Surely by now, after everything she'd been through since that terrible day, she could defend herself. Strike first, ask questions later.

He gave her much smaller body a scornful once over and then arched an indignant brow. Was that meant to intimidate?

"You might regret this," she warned, feigning courage.

"Famous last words."

THIRTEEN

Laurel's voracity took Thorne by surprise. She didn't stop coming until she'd landed a few hits. Impressive. There was something else driving her actions, and for once, Thorne didn't think it was something he'd done.

He blocked easily, but it didn't stop her from trying. She came at him. He stepped to the side and elbowed her, causing her to stumble. Did she give up? No. She twirled like a dancer and came back, this time learning his patterns.

Clever.

She didn't stumble from the same move again.

Maybe it was the lake's mystic energy filtering into his cracked soul, or the air of anticipation from the sprites watching from both the forest and the water, but he found himself sinking into the sparring match with full-body composure. No anger fired in his veins. No fury. Just... latent fun.

After twenty minutes of rigorous sparring, she paused, chest heaving with effort.

Disappointment flooded him. Was she going to stop?

No. She only removed her sweater, shot him a dazzling grin, and then came at him again—this time making sharp shouts with each strike. *Hya. Hya. Hya.* And he got distracted. Jacket off, there was more of her skin to admire. More fire in her eyes. In her body. She looked alive. Not only did he feel her effervescence whittle his composure, but he saw it on every inch of her face.

Desire speared through him. The woman was a marvel. Sweat cast a pearlescent sheen across her skin, highlighting every feminine curve—the dip of her collar bone, the grace of her neck, the smooth skin on her arms.

Her natural scent invaded his nose, hitting some button in his primitive nature and it took everything he had to stop from jumping her, forcing her down and making her submit. And that would make her run screaming in the other direction. She didn't want a man to dominate her. She wanted an equal.

The bargain they'd made urged him to keep within the boundaries of decency. Onward.

Didn't make it easier.

He slapped her away as she came for his face. "You can't beat me with your fists."

"Watch me." She tried again.

But his patience wore thin. Her musk drove him to distraction. The wolf in him was done with sparring. It wanted between her legs. He shouldn't be here, doing this. They should be flying toward Cornucopia. For Jasper. He swiftly took her wrist, twisted, and secured her arm behind her back in a punishing maneuver. She cried out in pain, but he held.

"Don't like it?" he taunted. "So get out."

"Not funny." She whimpered. Struggled. "Thorne, I mean it. That hurts. Let me go."

Her scent changed. *Fear.* Every predatory instinct in him perked up. *Laced with sweet feminine musk. Black raspberries.* A growl slipped out. His teeth elongated into fangs. Claws slid from his fingertips, pricking into her. Sensation zipped down his spine and heated at his groin. He was so aroused. Painfully so. Surely she felt the press of his erection against her back. Her hot, sweaty body—trying to be strong—but not enough. When he spoke next, his voice had become gravelly, beastly. "Make me."

He expected her to fight back as she had after the Sluagh. She'd punched fire in his face out of instinct. She should have fought. That's what he would have done. It's what he'd done his entire life. But she didn't. Her terror crashed into him like an ocean storm. He choked on her fear, doubt, and panic. This wasn't her. This wasn't the woman he'd come to know.

"Make me," he said again. He tightened his grip. Hoping the strong woman would resurface, to strike him in the face. The thought sent another wave of arousal over him. He liked his love-making a little rough, passionate. He liked his lovers feisty.

"I can't," she whimpered, squeezing her eyes shut.

"You can. You have the power of a thousand suns at your disposal. Your emotion is your trigger. Use it. The depth of your inner well is deep. And when that's dry, you can access mine. Take it. Your nails might be broken, Laurel, but you aren't."

She gasped, perhaps offended. For long, hard moments, silence compounded. Crickets chirped. And then something must have clicked within her. Fire exploded at his hand, searing his skin. He let go, grinned wolfishly, and bounded back. She whirled on him. Rage transformed her beautiful features, screwing them into a face full of determination. Then she attacked.

The fiery being that came at him was a divine thing. *This is what I want.* Elemental. Goddess. Skin illuminated as though her very blood had incinerated. *Yes.* Flames licked her skin. In her eyes. In her mouth. And still, she advanced.

He stood stock-still, ready to take the hurricane. *Hit me. Make me feel alive.* She kept coming. She wasn't going to stop. He braced.

Volcanic vengeance. A harpy's scream. She dove at him. Catching her, he stumbled back, pain burst along his flesh as it burned. He thought he wanted this. Nope. No, he didn't. He slammed up an insulated wall of protection with his mana, but too late. Searing pain coated him.

Water. Get to water.

It only took seconds, and then they were submerged in the shallows of the lake. Smoke sizzled and hissed. Thorne felt burned in patches over his skin. Laurel spluttered and gasped as he took her under. *Cool off, woman.* But she hit him. Struck him again.

They emerged, gasping.

"Hey." He took her wrists. "Settle."

The survival instinct in her eyes wouldn't fade. *"Don't* tell me to settle."

"Laurel. You got me. You won."

She raged and hit again, but it glanced off his solid chest.

She pushed off and stood back, eyes like wildfire. Water lapped at their waists. The slick rainbow residue from the lake dripped down both their bodies. Her shirt was virtually gone. It hung off her torso in strips of charred mess. His was less ruined, thanks to his last-minute wall of mana, but the skin she'd burned blistered on his arms. Hastily, he splashed water over them. The healing waters soothed the skin. It wasn't bad. He'd survive.

Two steps and he was back in her space, gathering her trembling form gently. She was traumatized.

Guilt flooded him. Shit. Damn. He was a Well-damned cocksucker. A floater. Litter-box trash.

"Are you okay?" he mumbled. *I'm sorry.*

Chest heaving, she wiped the water from her face in irritation. "I'm fine."

"No. You're not." He raised his brows at her shredded top. Perky, perfect nipples glistened in the gaps of her shredded shirt. The arousal he felt earlier bloomed again, hardening between his legs, wanting back into his system.

He swallowed. Couldn't lift his eyes from her chest. He shouldn't be looking.

She glanced down, gasped, and covered herself with an infuriated pout. "How come your shirt is still there?"

"I used my mana as insulation," he rasped, still looking at the same spot, only her arms were covering the pert breasts.

Damn. He scrubbed his face and tore his gaze away.

"You did this on purpose." She pointed at him.

"I didn't. But—" he shrugged. Honestly, if he knew she was going to lose her shirt, maybe he would have.

"I don't mean the top. I mean the goading. You wanted me to hit you."

A growl dragged out of his throat.

It was then he realized their emotions were abnormally heightened. It was the lake. The power.

The wind picked up. Ripples in the water lapped at their skin. But it wasn't cold. It was warm, like between a woman's thighs. Like the dangerous lure of a honey trap, it reacted to Thorne's and Laurel's presence. Energy zinged into him. Into her, too. He could tell by the goosebumps erupting over her flesh. The black of her pupils dilated. Her full lips parted.

Their Well-blessed markings flared, casting blue refractions over the rippling water.

The lake, the source of primordial power around them, urged them together. It *wanted* them together. Wet. Streaked in luminescent color. Sexy. Laurel looked up at him, all lashes, and fizzled fury. Just how he liked it. His warrior's gaze turned heated and she inched closer. She traced a finger down his front and his abs sucked in.

He couldn't breathe. Her lashes lifted to assess his reaction, then she gripped his shirt as though to throw him down.

He tensed. Pushed his jagged lust at her. Let her read it in his eyes. *Do it. Throw me down.*

She raised a dark brow. *You'd like that, wouldn't you?*

I would.

Her grip loosened. His heartbeat raced as her touch turned explorative. Over his pec. Down to his abs. Around. Slippery. Wet. Friction. Everywhere she went, fire ignited like a sharp claw scratching his skin. Fuck, he was so hard. Bursting. Painful. He wanted more. *Scratch me. Make me bleed.*

The wind picked up around them, lifting their hair. He should mind the changing weather. The turbulence. He should warn her about the seductive call of the lake. Its infallible wants. But it was *this* between them. An attraction stronger than any he'd ever known. And it was because it had already been there, simmering beneath his skin from the moment he'd laid eyes on her.

All the more reason to warn her.

To stop this.

"I feel... weird," she admitted.

"It's the power from the lake," he muttered, eyes drinking her moonlit skin in.

Soft lips. Obstinate jaw. And her body... *Crimson.* Glistening. Perfectly toned and begging for touch. His cock twitched. The wolf inside him panted. Want.

Want to kiss her. Taste her. Bite her.

A strangled groan escaped him. He didn't care about anything else and let his hands roam over the slick surface of her skin. His thumbs brushed her nipples. Her lids fell to half-mast and moan of appreciation shuddered through her.

He couldn't stop this. Whatever was happening.

Stop.

"Laurel." Her name on his tongue. That's all it took. She grabbed at the thick source of his braid and pulled him to her, slamming his lips onto hers. Instant, heady euphoria. He groaned into her mouth and tugged her closer. Her tongue thrust past his fangs, making demands. They licked, sucked, nipped. Incomprehensible pleas chirped out of both of them. More. Deeper. Harder.

This was how he liked it. Fiery. Urgent. Passionate. And she'd instigated the kiss. She was perfect for him.

Mate.

Mark her.

Bite her.

Keep her. His wolf was in a frenzy, but... something was wrong. He could feel it in the water, rippling. Something slick and heavy swirled around his legs. *Alarm. Panic.*

They're here.

He spared no thought for her decency, hefted her over his shoulder and raced out of the water. Three sloshing strides and he was on the shore, settling her back to her feet. Her skin had gone pale. She'd felt it too. Their eyes clashed. She realized she still clutched him, let go and then stepped back.

"What was that?" she asked, hugging herself.

He frowned at the shore, searching for signs. "That was"—everything he hated—"Inkeels."

"What?" she gaped.

"The Well isn't all glowing things and magical powers. There is an inky side. A greedy side." He flinched at the memory of his initiation ceremony. Of the suffocating and horrifying constriction of his body as the *things* slithered around him, dragging him into the deep and further below.

His chest constricted. He flinched, trying to suck in a breath of air. *You're not drowning. Not now.*

He jolted at her touch on his arm. When he looked, he found only concern in her eyes. The fire was gone. And it was this gentler side he had no idea how to handle.

"They're why you hate it here, aren't they?"

She saw right through him. He felt flayed open. Raw. Cowardly. Like a child to be horrified of such things. Was he a warrior, a wolf, or worse? Thorne flexed his fists, as though the action could shift the slimy memory from his skin.

Fuck it. They should never have stopped here. He turned toward the kuturi as it sharpened its beak against a tree trunk.

"Thorne. What about the inky side?" she asked, scurrying to collect her cape and sweater. "Tell me."

He stopped at the kuturi, took a moment to gather his composure, and slid her a dark look. He had to answer her, it was part of her education. He already felt the magical compulsion build from their bargain. Didn't mean he enjoyed it.

"It's the stuff of nightmares. Where beings like the Sluagh come from. Where there is no love, no family, no right. Only wrong. Chaos. A dark chasm of despair. Do you understand, or do I have to draw you a diagram?"

"No need to get snippy. Jeeze." A deep line appeared between her brows. "And this is the Well you all worship?"

He snapped around. "We don't worship it. We respect it. And this"—he pointed at the water—"is a place where the connection is strongest. The Well is..." He struggled to come up with the right words. "Life. Cosmic. All-powerful. In our blood. Us."

Slipping her sweater over her shredded shirt, she added, "And the things in the water?"

"Inkeels. They drag you down during the initiation ceremony. They take you to the darkest depths, look into your soul, and strip you of everything you identify with until you feel violated in the most heinous way possible. You would do anything to get out of there. You want to know more? How they invaded me? You want me to take you there? Show you for yourself?" He leaned in close and bared his teeth. "You want those things in you too?"

His harsh words seemed to bounce off her, but then her eyes glistened with tears.

Still, she didn't back down. She lifted her chin. "But you didn't, did you? Get out of there, I mean. You took the harrowing experience and... it shaped what you are. A Guardian. Someone the Well chose to keep this world flourishing."

She wouldn't stop staring. Looking into his soul. Awe filled her eyes. "You're—"

"Stop," he snarled.

"You don't know what I was going to say!"

"I'm not a good person."

She scoffed. "Keep telling yourself that. Maybe someday it will stick."

He glared at her, hoping to somehow burn her words away with his sight. "That kiss was a mistake, Laurel. We should leave. The lake has a way of calling you back in. Well-blessed markings don't mean we're exempt. It might decide to test us again."

FOURTEEN

The adrenaline from training and the argument energized Laurel, but after a few hours of flying, not even the buzz of thrill-seeking could sustain her energy levels. Or the awe that she was a frickin' powerful woman.

That fire.

An inferno of power.

It had come from her.

Emotion is your trigger, Thorne had said.

He'd also lost all sense of personality since their kiss, and all she felt down their bond was a coldness that worried her. *That kiss was a mistake.* Try as she might, she couldn't stop thinking about the words he'd hurled at her. Slimy things pulling you down, drowning you... violating you?

No wonder no one wanted to become a Guardian anymore.

And Thorne? He had some issues. That was clear as day. To switch so mercurially in mood when she brought up his morality. He'd done a complete nosedive. It horrified him to think that he might be a good person. But he was. She was sure of it.

Was she? Now, that was another story. Given the power, she had reacted with flames. When he'd taunted her, a switch had flipped inside her. Something dark drove her to attack him, to take no quarter, to burn him alive and make him pay for his words and patronizing grin. It was like he didn't think she could take him.

She'd had to.

A sigh escaped her. Maybe they were a good match. Maybe the Well knew what it was doing when pairing them up. Her body certainly wanted him.

Exhaustion crept in, and she was about to suggest setting down for a rest when something on the horizon piqued her fancy—a yellow stream beaming into the night sky like a spotlight. An ethereal orange glow was near the ground. *More bioluminescence?*

No. It was stronger than that. She squinted. More dark shapes, silhouettes of all shapes and sizes before the light. With a start, she realized it was a city of sorts.

Her interest flared.

The closer they flew, the more she saw. No skyscrapers, but a mixture of squat buildings and tall architectural wonders spread out from the orange glow that served as a center beacon. Some buildings were shiny and luxurious, others looked as though they'd been scraped from a forest and brought in. The surrounding citadel wall was almost for show. Its substance, a mixture of solid brick or dilapidated stone next to open and wonky planks of wood. The orange column of light came from a stadium atop a hill, alight with some sort of entertainment currently in progress. Across the currents of the wind she heard roars and shouts. Cheers. Curiosity filled her. Maybe a sports game?

The smell in the air changed. It became a little pungent, a little dirty, and a little like food. Definitely a city.

This must be Cornucopia.

Thorne glided the kuturi down and landed just outside the city limits, alongside a wide river where jetties and docks were punctuated by various warehouses and buildings. It seemed like a common flight path, because they weren't the only ones landing on the dirt airstrip. Other winged creatures, some with passengers on their backs, others with wings sprouting from their own backs, milled about. Many carried cargo in nets. Sometimes the cargo wiggled. It took restraint to stop curiosity and wonder from dominating her expression.

It must be close to midnight, but it was as busy as a midday rush. Not only were there commuters coming in, but soldiers on the ground. It seemed like there were two kinds. Those dressed in coats of red and yellow embroidery, and those in dark tunics. They seemed to stick to their own color groups and looked warily at the others.

With protesting muscles, Laurel dragged herself off the kuturi. Thorne cast a cautious eye at the soldiers milling about and then fished in his pocket for a treat. He retrieved something like sugared jerky and handed it to her.

Upon sniffing the new treat, the kuturi pranced excitedly.

"Give it this," he said. "I'll be back in five."

Laurel's eyes were glued to the griffin-like creature, so she paid little attention to where Thorne disappeared to. Somewhere behind her. Probably to pay for boarding for the kuturi. She didn't care. The kuturi had the only attention her energy allowed. Its lungs heaved as it caught breath, and it nudged her arm with its beak.

"Easy, does it." She fed the animal small pieces of jerky and patted its neck affectionately. She couldn't believe she'd just flown on its back. It was almost like a dinosaur, or a dragon, or... nothing like in her time, that was for sure.

Thorne returned with a tall, mustached, and bald man who had deeply discolored and disfigured features. He had a severe under-bite on his lower jaw. Two fangs protruded up and over his top lip—like a cartoon dog. Arched ears, as was the norm with the fae (so she'd been told), clearly showed his heritage. He narrowed shrewd eyes at her, assessing.

Alarm prickled her skin, and she wanted to check that her hair was covering her ears, but held her fists calmly at her sides. If there was any need to panic, Thorne would let her know. After a moment, Laurel realized the new fae's resentment wasn't aimed solely at her, but at the big warrior at her side. Why?

The attendant's eyes kept darting between the teardrop tattoo beneath Thorne's eye, to his battle-ax strung over his back, and to the jacket—beaten and hardened from countless battles—and the logo of scales over the breast pocket.

Ah. She got it now. He disliked Guardians.

With a final scowl at the attendant, Thorne gathered his knapsack and gave the kuturi a ruffle under the chin. "We'll be back for you in a few days."

Then he gestured for Laurel to head down a long dirt path toward the city. After a few hundred feet, she commented, "He didn't like that you were a Guardian, did he?"

"None of them do."

"Them?"

Thorne glanced at Laurel as though she were crazy. "Everyone."

"Why?" After the sacrifice Guardians had made in the ceremonial lake, after the life of servitude to keep the realm safe and plentiful with magic, it seemed ridiculous. They should be revered. At least lauded.

He shrugged. "Maybe because we can use metals and still access our mana. Maybe it's because we can't fund the Order without taxing them for monster kills. Maybe they resent us prohibiting the use of metals or plastics. Maybe it's jealousy. Who knows? Why don't you ask them?"

More sharp words.

As they entered the city through the unmanned ragtag gates, many passersby looked at Thorne's Guardian uniform and balked. If Laurel wasn't sufficiently overwhelmed with the visual delights of the new mini metropolis, she might have been concerned, or at least angry on his behalf. As it was, her attention was almost completely and irrevocably taken with the atmosphere of Cornucopia.

The streets were a mix of cobblestone and dirt. Shanty type buildings sat next to tall, luxurious and decadent visual delights like the three-spire, mini castle that seemed to be an eating and housing establishment. A hotel! It was that last structure that made her chest swell with nostalgia.

"This is almost like Vegas!" she exclaimed, turning in circles, eyes wide. "My hometown."

Hawkers peddled their wares on street sides, their carts overflowing with an assortment of food, drink, or merchandise. The mouthwatering smell of something salty yet fruity coated the air with a layer of desire. Scantily clad women of all shapes and sizes were next in line as Thorne and Laurel walked past. They stood before a loud raucous establishment with fae leaning out from balconies, laughing and shouting in merriment. Rhythmic drums, lights, and conversation came from inside buildings. The nightlife here was magnificent. Laurel, Clarke, and Ada used to burn up the dance floor on many occasions, in many clubs, and always in sexy dresses. What she wouldn't give to go back to those carefree times.

"Hurry up," Thorne said, already two steps ahead of her. "You can gawk tomorrow."

She caught up with him. "Where are we going—*oof!*"

A body bumped into Laurel at the hip. She almost fell backward.

"Watch where you're going, elf." A grumpy, squat dwarf with a big nose glowered at her.

"Sor—" Thorne slapped his big palm over her mouth, cutting her off.

"Fuck off, dwarf," he barked.

The dwarf took one look at the blue Well-blessed marking on Thorne's hand, widened his eyes, and then stepped back. He seemed to gather himself, he spat at Thorne's feet, and then scurried off.

What was that about?

Suddenly, every sensation in the lane amplified. The shouts and conversation from the balcony above became deafening roars. The sizzle of a food vendor's makeshift stove sparked and spat. A woman with green skin and big, under-bite teeth shouted and waved a fist. She looked like the She-Hulk. A small, furred rat-like creature scampered by Laurel's feet and she jumped to the side.

Thorne let go of her mouth and growled, "Don't get lost. Don't apologize. And don't say thank you."

"Because I'm huma—rfh?"

He did it again! Palm to her mouth. He lowered his face until it was inches from hers. "And *don't* say that."

She glared at him over his hand. After a decidedly dark stare, he released her mouth. Slowly. "Just keep your mouth shut."

Argh! She flattened her mouth and thought of a million nasty things she wanted to say to him, but realized she didn't need to. She could send it all surging into him from their bond. And that was exactly what she did—speared her fury straight to him.

His breath hitched. Nostrils flared, infuriated. He sent his scolding emotions right back. "Well-damn it, Laurel. Don't push me."

"Or what?" *Go on. Kiss me again.*

"Or I'll—" he bit off his words, glared daggers, and then scanned the lane. "Off you go, then. Take the lead. Clarke said you'll lead me to Jasper, so go."

He folded his arms smugly.

"Yeah. Well. To be honest, I just want to sleep. Is that too much to ask?" They could work out the plan tomorrow.

He smirked, as if he'd won the argument they weren't even having, and then made a flourish with his hand toward the direction he was originally going. "After you, m'lady."

"Cordiality isn't becoming on you." This time, she hurried to stay at his side. "Where are we going?"

He sighed. The tension in his shoulders eased, and he said, "Jasper has a place. We'll start there, rest, and then resume our hunt tomorrow."

Jasper's place turned out to be an apartment in one of the more luxe buildings in the center of the city, not far from the nightlife. Nowhere luxe in comparison to her apartment in Vegas—still no electricity—but not as simple as some places she'd passed. It was a top floor penthouse of a three-story building. Thorne entered via an unlocking spell of some sort that involved a drop of his blood. Inside, the decor was simple bachelor style. Dusty bed in one corner. A couch, table and chairs for entertaining in another. Cool ceramic tiles. No kitchen. But an open fire pit that seemed more appropriate in a backyard if it weren't for its designer decor vibe.

The condo hadn't been visited for a long time, yet the indoor potted plants thrived. When Laurel looked closer, she realized the plants weren't potted, but part of some chain of nature that linked each apartment through gaps in the floor.

"Where is the bathroom?" she asked. The journey had been long, and she was dying to use the toilet.

Lost in thought as he trailed a finger through dust on the tabletop, Thorne indicated toward a door at the back. Laurel's lip curled as she tiptoed through the quiet place. She wasn't sure why she was being quiet. Maybe it was because it felt like walking through a dead person's home. Weird.

Thankfully, the bathroom was in working order. A flushing toilet, small bathtub, and basin under a black glossy mirror. There was a candle on the countertop. She blanched when she realized she'd either have to work out how to light it herself, or call Thorne, and with his mood, she wasn't willing to broach the subject.

So that meant she had to try.

The last time she'd used her fire power, she'd been filled with fury, hatred, and survival instinct. But none of that mattered now. She picked up the candle and stared at it. She tried to remember how it felt to have the shifting power living inside her. Of how it jumped to her call when she was upset. The burn in her cheeks. The roaring of her pulse. She connected all that with the candle and urged it to light, to spark.

The candle spluttered.

It flared brightly, so brightly that she almost dropped it. But she'd had practise at tapering off her power already, so she shut it down.

When she checked the candle, a little flame flickered gently.

She grinned. And look at that, her sweater stayed intact.

Once done in the bathroom, she returned to the main room. Thorne had thrown open the large bifold glass doors and was on the balcony watching over the city. Laurel placed the candle on the table and joined him.

"You seem disappointed," she said.

"No shit."

He was hurting. He probably had hoped Jasper would be there. Laurel bit her lip and looked inside at the decor again. It was simple, but not completely something she'd expect in a Guardian's home.

"I didn't realize the Guardian game was so lucrative. I thought you said you couldn't keep the Order running without taxing monster kills."

"We get a wage. And we live a long time. Most of us have collected holdings and wealth. Jasper liked to frequent Cornucopia during his time off. So he bought this place. I have the family Nightstalk home in Crescent Hollow."

"Crescent Hollow. That sounds cool. I'd like to go there some day."

He frowned at her. "You're here to help me find Jasper. Not go on vacation."

"Ah," she replied, with a twinkle in her eye. "But I'm the one who will lead you to him. Who's to say it's not while I'm on vacation?"

Nostrils flared.

She laughed. "You hate this, don't you?"

Another glare.

"Relax, Growly." She shuffled back inside. "Tonight, I just want a hot bath, a change of clothes, some food, and sleep."

Thorne followed her, shutting the doors behind him. The sounds of the street muffled. The air inside had lost its staleness. Much better.

"You humans don't want much, do you?" Thorne commented sarcastically.

"What does that mean?"

He watched her rifle through his knapsack. "Rush calls Clarke his princess because she's full of demands."

Laurel snorted. "I'm sure that's a gross exaggeration. And they're not demands. We just know what we want, and we aren't afraid to ask for it. But, for the record, I prefer queen, not princess."

Thorne barked a laugh. "Right. Of course."

"Hey." She pouted at him. "Not for the reasons you think. I used to run a very successful chain of fitness establishments for women. I called my business Queen Fitness. It's a state of mind, not just a title. You think like a queen, you become one. It's very empowering."

"A fitness institution for multiple queens. Sounds horrifying."

"We're not really queens. It's a state of mind. It's just a place women go to work out."

"Like a training yard?"

"Sure. Go with that." She'd pulled out half his knapsack by now, and still, no spare clothes for her. "I can't find another top. Tell me you didn't plan on us being here for a few days and not pack a spare change of clothes."

He gave her a shrug, then headed to the door. "We can go shopping tomorrow. For now, I'll get some food. Don't open the door. Don't open the windows. Just... don't do anything until I get back."

FIFTEEN

By the fourth day in Cornucopia, Thorne had followed Laurel as she'd wandered the entire market square and questioned residents. They'd come up with no intelligible signs that Jasper had been there recently, or even in the past few years. Now they were stuck at a fresh produce vendor Thorne had once saved from the Ring, and who subsequently owed him. He ducked under a brightly covered awning to shield himself from the late afternoon sun and watched Laurel turn a piece of gilly-fruit over in her hands as she haggled with the merchant like a local.

"One clear coin," Laurel said. "That's my final offer."

The merchant laughed. "That's not enough for five gilly-fruit." She raised her brow at Thorne. "Tell her she's joking."

Laurel sighed and put the fruit down. "Very well, then. We'll find another vendor for our needs."

"No, wait!" The merchant said. "I'll take two coin for five gilly-fruit. That's still robbing me blind."

"Deal." Laurel made the gimme-sign to Thorne.

He sighed and fished out two clear glass coins from his pocket and handed them to her. With a wide, triumphant grin, Laurel collected her prize, and they moved to the next stall. The counter was littered with tiny glass animals, baubles and rings. Why on earth Laurel would want to stop there was beyond him.

Thorne leaned against a wooden pole while she sampled the rings. Her attention stayed on a particular blue, clear and gold item. She even held it to the light to catch the rays of sunset.

Frowning, he turned back to the market streets, folded his arms, and kept a wary eye on passers-by. As usual, the population of Cornucopia was as random as its architecture. Seelie and Unseelie together in a mish-mash.

A posh elf in the Seelie gentry walked next to a vampire from the Unseelie gentry. Both dressed disgustingly in wealth. Embroidered jackets, frilled shirts, pompous hair, and a touch of rouge on their cheeks. By rights, the two should have been at each other's throats like the guards loitering in the space they had no jurisdiction in. But in Cornucopia, the companionship between the vampire and the elf was on a level playing field.

Neutral territory.

Neither the Seelie nor the Unseelie could claim it without inciting a war.

It was why Jasper had loved it there. No one cared about his parentage. No one cared about his pretty face. And if he removed his Guardian uniform, he usually found someone who cared naught about his job. Fae came to Cornucopia for one reason. To have a good time. Whether it was to watch the blood sports at the Ring, to visit the elven-elixir dens, or to dance and fuck a stranger at one of the nightspots. For a few years, even Thorne had fallen prey to the city's allure. That was until Jasper went missing, and he realized the same city that granted anonymity also couldn't care less about each other.

"Hurry up," he declared.

Laurel ignored him and then shifted to the next lot of jewelry.

He wondered how she kept her spirits alive after four days of training, searching, and coming up short. She was still alight, bright with passion and excitement. She was in an element she didn't know she had, or maybe this was Laurel all the time. Confident. Strong. He'd done his best to let her lead the daily expeditions, hoping that if he did, then Clarke's prophecy would come true. But not one fae knew who Jasper was. It had been too long since he'd gone missing. The carousing, charismatic three-hundred-year-old Guardian had disappeared from the collective memory of the city that had cradled him his entire life.

They hadn't hit the nightspots yet.

This will take forever.

Not only did Thorne have to train Laurel in self-defense, but he also had to educate her about their world, and how to use her mana. Some of it came naturally to her, but trying to explain the theory behind the mystical art of accessing one's personal Well was harder than he'd initially thought. She'd blustered her way through lighting a candle, but there were other elements she had an affinity with that he was failing in teaching her about. He could see the benefit of returning to the Order and letting the Mages take over her education.

Laurel wasn't swayed. She woke every morning with a bounce in her step, eager to commence the day. It didn't matter if Thorne wasn't in the mood for a jog around the block, she insisted on going anyway, and he was left scrambling to catch up to avoid a repeat of her incident with the Sluagh. Cornucopia was a strange place. Some said lawless, others said the opposite. One offense declared and you were sent to the Ring— the gladiator pit where differences were settled by blood.

The first morning, he'd had to chase her down the street at dawn, still only in his breeches and casting a glamor on her ears as he went to make them look pointed. While her short hair had covered her ears when they'd disembarked the kuturi, he'd made it a habit to glamor her ears from the first day they'd left Jasper's apartment. There were too many ways this could go wrong and letting Laurel forge her own path was beginning to wear.

Since that first morning, it felt like all Thorne was doing was playing catch up to the woman. Catch up to her as she relentlessly shopped for new clothing in the fabric district. Catch up as she quickly learned the nuances of society and wended and wove through the streets. Catch up as she *made friends* with residents and *redecorated* Jasper's apartment. It was enough to make him snap.

"Time to go," he barked at Laurel.

Her lips pursed, she held her finger up for the merchant to wait and turned to Thorne. "I'm almost done, Growly."

He frowned. Another thing he'd gained over the past few days was that infernal nickname.

"Laurel. I'm done."

She sighed and met Thorne's gaze.

"All right. I'm done too. Let's go home, eat, and then maybe head out and try the only places we've not been to."

She meant the elixir-dens and nightclubs. A surly wash of—something—hit him. He didn't like the idea of Laurel in one of those places, filled with inebriated and horny fae, half-naked Rosebuds, and trigger tempers.

"Not a good idea."

"Unfortunately, it's not your idea. It's mine. And I won't feel like we've exhausted all avenues unless we go there."

He stopped walking and stared at her. "Are you giving me an order?"

She tapped her lip. "Why, yes. Yes, I am. Is that a problem, Growly?"

Everything in him wanted to say yes, it was a fucking problem, but he knew in his gut he had to let her guide the activities. *Crimson*, save him.

"Good," she added, "Chop-chop. Let's go. I want to be bathed, fed, and dressed by the time the Birdcage opens."

He inwardly groaned. The Birdcage was the worst of the elven-elixir dens. He would regret this, but he gestured down the street, tinted in sunset. "After you, my queen."

As Thorne stood behind Laurel in the short line for the Birdcage, every instinct inside him screamed to turn the other way. A giant orc in front of him already pawed the behind of a scantily clad elf wearing the mark of a Rosebud courtesan on her upper arm—a rose with no thorns. It was a symbol of beauty, without the pain. The Rosebuds were skilled in their sensuous craft and also physically incapable of getting with child. For the females, their wombs had been removed. For the males, their ability to produce active seed had been cut, ensuring there would be zero repercussions for any regarding the unsanctioned breeding laws.

Clarke had revealed to him the law should have been abolished before Thorne's birth, but King Mithras was not a man of his word. If this same charlatan held Jasper, the sooner they found him, the better. Jasper's move to work at the Order should have pulled him out of the king's crosshairs, but if that was the case, then why had the Prime handed him over to the king?

Like falling dominos, the Prime's machinations all fell into place. The unsanctioned breeding law meant Rush was cursed after Thorne was born. Rush's curse meant he was exiled and invisible to scrying eyes. Because Rush was invisible, when he'd discovered Clarke, and triggered her Well-blessed union, she became irrevocably linked to the Prime's team and would some day turn the tide of the coming war in the favor of the fae.

Infuriatingly, this meant Clarke received many concessions from the Prime the rest of the Order did not. And Jasper had been the victim because of it, nothing but collateral damage. Just like Thorne's mother. Just like Thorne.

Maybe that was why he had left the Order without permission. Part of him resented the woman who'd birthed his half-sister. If it weren't for her arrival in this time, much of Thorne's life would have been different. He'd have two parents alive. Not one. His mentor would be here, and he'd never have been forced into the servitude of the Well. Was that so selfish of him to want?

Rhythmic drumbeats from inside the establishment vibrated the dirt floor and traveled up Thorne's body to itch his ears. They twitched uncontrollably. As did his nose. They weren't even indoors, and yet he could already scent the sex, drugs, and sweat. He hated this place. And he hated that Laurel was pushing him to the edge of red. He'd tried to explain what she would find inside, but all she'd focused on was dancing. It seemed his human companion was a fan.

The dress she wore was no better than a Rosebud courtesan's. Diaphanous silk wrapped her perfectly toned body, giving everyone a clear view of her seductive shape. If it weren't for a strip of opaque linen over her breasts and waist, he'd have an eye of everything. No tattoos, no Well-blessed markings in sight. She'd insisted on extending her glamor from giving the round shell of her ears a pointed look, to hiding their bond. His teardrop marking refused to be glamored, so she painted him with something dark, like a tattoo. He felt ridiculous. She also glamored away his arm markings and insisted he dressed in civilian clothing—buckskin breeches and a form-fitting black shirt rolled up to his elbows.

The worst part was no weapons allowed. He had to leave Fury on the bench at Jasper's apartment. But he never went without a backup. He'd carved a transference rune into Fury's wooden handle. If there came such a time that he needed his old friend, he could summon it. Because he was a Guardian, the metal would come too.

When he questioned Laurel's reasons for hiding their Well-blessed union, she blinked at him innocently and said, "What does it matter to you? You keep insisting we aren't mated in *that* way. That kiss was a mistake. Your words, not mine."

True. Those words had come out of his mouth. Four days ago. He shifted uncomfortably and tugged on his sleeves.

"Besides," she added, "hiding your Guardian status will make you more approachable."

His heart leaped into his throat. Was she trying to make them appear uninvolved? As though they were free to explore others? He narrowed his eyes, studying her intensely. He couldn't flat out ask her. She would think he cared.

A low growl of frustration rumbled in his throat. This was a bad idea.

SIXTEEN

Laurel hopped from foot to foot as she stood in the queue for the elixir den Thorne had studiously avoided the entire time they had been in Cornucopia. But she was ready to let loose. She was dressed in a sexy outfit, had kohl makeup around her eyes, and her hair was slicked and clean. She'd also found a shimmering substance to rub over her skin from a really nice female fae who looked more like a sheep than a human, and she was so friendly. The shimmer had always been part of Laurel's routine before she headed out clubbing back in her time. Laurel used to have money, and she enjoyed spending it. She was a self-made queen and didn't deserve the gruff treatment Thorne threw her way. Especially since she *knew* of his undeniable feelings for her. He couldn't lie. Constant lust and attraction simmered down their bond, and yet he stifled it and changed the subject any time she commented.

She might have enjoyed their short moment at the ceremonial lake but wasn't one to wallow or pine. She *was* one to take control of her life and steer it in the right direction. To be honest, spending the past four days doing whatever the hell she'd wanted was invigorating. Finally, she felt like she had control back in her life. Control, strength, and purpose.

What more could she want?

Silently, she glanced over at Thorne's brooding face. He looked uncomfortable in the clothes she'd picked for him. But he looked hot. Sexy. There was no denying it. If he were on her arm at one of the Vegas clubs, they'd have jumped the queue because of all that presence he threw. She could virtually feel his energy in the air. Her dad would have respected him. Her mother would have loved him. The last phone call Laurel had with her parents was about Laurel's need for a big protector in the changing world. That's when they thought the nuclear fallout was the worst thing they had to face.

An image of her family swam into her mind, but she pushed them aside. As much as she missed them, they weren't coming back. So she would live for them. She would flourish for them. And she would do it with the fire she'd been graced with.

Butterflies fluttered in Laurel's stomach. The hard, handsome man on her arm only made tonight better, regardless of his sour expression. The moment he'd seen her dress, he'd paled. As far as she was concerned, when men look like they're going to faint at the sight of your body, it was a compliment. She was ready to party, and perhaps ready for something more from their relationship.

The multilevel Birdcage was the perfect place to explore those feelings. It could have existed in the pages of a magazine. Artisan facades made from a mixture of polished tree limbs and some sort of smooth substance for cage bars. Obviously not metal, but from her vantage point, she couldn't tell the difference. On a balcony above their head, two male fae stood sipping from a glass, eyes languidly drooping from whatever toxin they'd ingested. One had long lustrous brown hair. Very humanlike except the ears. Embroidered jacket, pearlescent buttons, wealth dripping from his pores. His companion was someone of similar social stature, you could tell by the detail in his velvet coat and the stiff spine.

The line moved forward. Thorne guided Laurel closer and she dragged her gaze away from the suave couple.

"Last chance," Thorne murmured. "We can turn around and leave right now."

"Don't be a stick in the mud. You said Jasper frequented here. It's the last place we haven't visited." Well, not *the* last place. The Ring was that. But Thorne didn't think anyone there would know about Jasper. Apparently, his aunt used to work as security and said she'd never seen Jasper there before.

"This isn't a place for someone like you," Thorne mumbled.

"What's that supposed to mean?"

"Nothing."

Nervous tension emanated from him. Looking up at his brooding profile, she appreciated the hard lines, straight nose, and square jaw. She'd urged him to trim his scruff for the night. That dimple in his cheek had been revealed. One thing was for certain, she was no longer simply attracted to him, she was in lust for him. Hard. Every cell in her body sang when they touched, and it was starting to hurt when she restrained her desires.

She wanted the touch of his sweet lips on hers again.

"Well, I say we go in. If anything, it will be good to let off some steam. I can have a drink and a dance, maybe get lucky while I'm at it." She paused, waited for a reaction— down their bond, or otherwise.

Icy thunder snapped her way. "What does get lucky mean?"

She arched a brow salaciously. "I think you know what it means."

A low growl rumbled in his throat. "And what exactly will I be doing while you *get lucky*?"

Trying to hide a teasing smirk, she thwacked him on the chest. "Oh, I don't know. I'm sure you'll think of something. Scope out the joint. Find a lady. Ask questions. Up to you."

"Find a lady?" His eyes widened. "You're serious. But we're—"

"What... mated?" She leveled her stare at him. "You said it wasn't like that. You said there was another kind of mating that Rush and Clarke shared, and we don't have it. So... I guess, call this an open marriage."

Angry eyes turned away and glared at some indeterminate spot in the distance. Part of her churned, but she kept her doubts down and out of their bond. If she didn't force him to think about what he wanted, he would continue to keep her at arm's length, and she couldn't live her life like that. Being in Cornucopia had helped Laurel take back control. It was time Thorne learned that his actions had consequences.

"You know," she continued, "the fae really aren't that bad. After talking to them at the markets, I'm starting to feel like I'm fitting in."

"Don't get complacent. Some might look normal, but they could be using a glamor to hide their true form. They could also turn on you the moment they find out who you really are."

"I'm sure I'll be fine. Ooh goodie. Look. Our turn." The queue had brought them right up to the front entrance, where a pink-haired pixie collected a door fee. She was flanked on either side by two male pixies in charge of security. They also had pink hair, but where the female was small and dainty, the males were Laurel's height and packed plenty of muscle.

The female pixie narrowed her eyes at Thorne, but then shifted to Laurel with a broad smile. "Welcome to the Birdcage. We ask all patrons to leave their weapons at the door and to keep their wings latent." She received Laurel's cape and continued rattling off information. "Happy hour is at nine, and we have a special on contraceptive elixirs tonight. Two for one."

"There you go," Thorne grumbled. "Perfect night for you."

She ignored his snippy remark, despite the hurt simmering beneath her skin. This was the reaction she wanted from him. Jealousy never reared a pretty head, and he had to know that if he was jealous, then there was a reason for it. Namely that he liked her too. Her brow puckered, and she did her best to get on with it.

"What do you mean by keeping wings latent?" Laurel asked the pixie.

"Some of us can't shift, but if we're caught spreading our wings, it's immediate eviction. Despite being called the Birdcage, we respectfully ask that all patrons keep their wings dormant."

Thorne dug into his pants and handed some coin to the pixie.

The pixie handed Laurel a cloakroom token and ushered them inside. Two-seconds later and they were walking through a dark tunnel, following the tribal beat of drums. Nearing the end of the tunnel, the air thickened. When they emerged, it was into an aviary-like interior. A large open column reached up high—no roof, just twinkling stars, and open sky. On all sides, up various split levels, cages jutted out, acting like open rooms. Moss and vines spilled from each cage floor, both dangling and entwining up bars. The foliage provided a semblance of privacy for the fae inside the cages, but not entirely. She glimpsed writhing naked bodies betwixt the greenery. Wow. It really was one of those places. Glass spheres suspended from cages contained glowing balls of light that cast a soft—or shady—ambiance. It was dim, but bright enough to see.

"The cages are filled with natural and live foliage to negate the feeling of being disconnected from the Well. Air fae can also be higher than most others before suffering that disconnection."

"Right."

That made little sense to her, but she had to give him points for trying to educate her.

All manner of fae existed here. It was better than the marketplace. Some were humanlike, some were humanoid. Many were more animal than fae. Orcs. Pixies. Scaly skin. Fae with their wings tucked tight. Skimpy clothing on both males and females. Three haughty looking elves holding a faun by a lead and collar around her neck. They walked to the thriving dance floor that existed around a platform at the center that housed a magnificent archaic cage. It looked more like the bones of a ribcage.

Inside was the band.

Laurel gasped. *They're human.*

No pointed ears. No animal characteristics. Must be.

One violinist. One flutist. One person on the drums. And one woman who sang haunting opera notes. Not one was manacled, or in a state of physical disarray, but she couldn't shake the sense they were prisoners. Each artisan smiled wistfully as they played their instruments, but their eyes screamed in horror. It was surreal, especially compared to the happy, carefree vibe of the patrons dancing around the stage.

Could they be forced? Somehow magically induced to stay there? Was that look in their eyes real?

Laurel scanned the dancing fae to see if anyone noticed, or cared, but they didn't.

"They're human," she whispered to Thorne as he led her toward the curved bar at the back of the establishment. They skirted the dance floor and the surrounding booths.

"Still want to *get lucky?*" he mocked.

"Should we do something?"

He shot her a look as if she was stupid. "Causing trouble here will only have one outcome, being sent to the Ring. And if you want to get out of Cornucopia alive, I highly suggest you don't. Those humans will be spoils of war. I kill their kind."

In other words, they were not worth their time. Anger flashed in her eyes. *She* was their kind. She dropped hold of his arm and strode to the bar. She needed a drink. Things weren't going according to plan. It was supposed to be a fun night where they'd tick one last place off their search list. Just when she thought she was getting used to this place, it surprised her.

She scowled at the barmaid, a cute female fae with wolfish ears, black kohl-rimmed eyes, and with a swishing tail at her rear. She had a similar hairstyle to Laurel, short and dark. Polishing a small glass with a towel, the barmaid noted Laurel's arrival and tipped her chin.

"What will it be?" Husky words.

"Your best elixir." Then she lifted two fingers. Thorne needed to loosen up too.

Two short glasses slammed on the counter, and then the barmaid almost did a double-take at Thorne. Maybe they knew each other?

Huh. Maybe this getting lucky thing wasn't such a good idea after all.

The barmaid was about to pour something blue and glowing into the glasses, but Thorne blocked with his palm. The barmaid raised a brow at Thorne.

He scowled at her. "Not *that* good."

Laurel sent him a questioning look.

"Trust me," he returned. And then darted a glance up at the cages with the writhing, naked bodies. "Unless you were serious about joining them."

When she still looked baffled, he leaned in close and lowered his tone. "It was an aphrodisiac."

Ah. The two-for-one contraceptive offer was starting to make sense. Her brows lifted. "That might not be so bad."

He choked on his drink. "Not in a place like this."

The dim light cast the sharp angles of Thorne's face into soft relief, and she quite enjoyed seeing his face without the stubble. He pretended to be unaffected by the topic of conversation, but his telltale nervous emotions gave him away.

"You've tried it," she accused.

A half shrug was her answer.

She was so right. The thought of Thorne, hot and sweaty, engaged in endless hours of sex made Laurel's heart thump loudly in her chest. She picked up her waiting glass. "You know, for the record, we didn't have places like this back home." She took a sip. Minty. Apple fresh. Delicious. It warmed her throat and sent a pleasant sensation of ease into her muscles. She would pay the barmaid a compliment when she ordered the next drink. "Well, I mean, we did have places where people went to have sex, but they weren't advertised so publicly."

Once again, he coughed. "And. Um. Did you, ah, frequent these places?"

A smile touched the corner of her lips. "Wouldn't you like to know?"

For an electrified few seconds, they stared into each other's eyes. There went his simmering lust again, straight down their bond like liquid fire.

"Right," she said and cracked a crick in her neck. She downed the last of the drink and surveyed the room. Her mood darkened when she landed on the band. Before the night was done, she'd have to do something about that. She couldn't leave knowing people were being held captive against their will, whether human or fae. She needed to get closer first. "I'm going to dance. Will you come with me?"

He blinked, perhaps a little panicked, then his familiar mask of discontent slammed down and he sneered at her revealing dress. "If you're going to act like a courtesan, then don't forget to take your pink elixir. Unless, of course, you want to be executed for unsanctioned breeding."

Her jaw dropped. He just called her a whore. Her heart shattered into a million pieces. This jealousy thing wasn't quite working out. But then again, if he was shooting this low with his comments, then she was getting under his skin.

"Suit yourself." She stole his remaining drink, gulped it down, and then wiped her mouth with the back of her hand. She was ready to let loose, dance, and work out some kinks. A giant Thorne-sized kink. Time to feel alive again. Time to feel human. Appreciated.

Just don't look at the musicians in the cage and you'll feel like you're back in a club at home.

SEVENTEEN

This was *not* going according to plan.

Thorne stewed in his dark thoughts on the sidelines of the Birdcage main floor. He regretted every harsh word that sent Laurel to the dance floor. Her hurt had pierced him down their bond, wrapped its barbed wire arms around his chest and squeezed until he hurt too, proving that he had a heart, after all.

Damn. Damn him for saying those nasty things to her, but he was right. She couldn't just let anyone stick their cock in her, fill her with child, and send her to her death. The damned king's stupid law was still in effect and he would not stand by idly and let her fuck her way to her grave.

Shit.

He flinched. He was doing it again. Letting his anger dictate his thoughts. She had done nothing yet. She just wanted to dance. Guilt speared him. Even if she wanted to— he swallowed a lump—do something with another male fae, then shouldn't that be her choice? She was right, he'd been clear to her that he didn't believe their mating was the same as one of the body. But this Well-blessed thing was so new and he was fast surrendering to the idea that it was not only the same as a mating of the body, but more.

Fuck. He scrubbed his face.

He had no other option but to wait with his arms folded and watch over Laurel while she danced. And watch he did. She was hypnotizing. Mesmerizing. The way she closed her eyes, felt the music, swayed, and undulated to the beat was almost like she really had the expert training of a Rosebud courtesan. Seduction pulsed in her veins. It frightened him how she affected him. Every tug of her body, every swerve, roll, dip, twitch of her lip was a direct line to his cock. It sprung to attention the second she went down there. Every now and then, she'd lift her lashes, home in on him, and clash eyes. *Like a hit of divilxir.* A fluttering in his chest. His stomach. The sense of falling. And then the searing hard lust crushing his soul.

Bad. Idea.

Mouth dry, he swallowed. Once again she gave him a beckoning look and then went back to her solo performance. But she wasn't solo for long. He wasn't the only fae watching her. From the dark recess of a booth, a dark shadow had his head riveted in Laurel's direction. Always. Flanking the shadowed figure were two burly orcs who looked more suitable as guards in the Unseelie army. Perhaps they were part of the private security here.

An object on the booth table caught Thorne's eye and a curse slipped from his tongue. It was a djinn bottle. Ceramic, inscribed with runes and uncorked. Meaning it was empty. Used. Was this the fae who'd sent the djinn after the people in Mornington?

He looked closer at one of the orcs and noticed he had saggy skin. Aged. As though he'd used a precious part of his soul to operate the djinn.

Instinctively, Thorne reached for Fury but remembered it was back at the apartment. Twitching, he drew his hand back to his side and made a mental note to pass on this new piece of information to Aeron when he returned to the Order.

Thorne shifted his gaze back to the dance floor and the more pressing concern. Two male pixies, shirts off, wings plastered to their sweaty backs—bumping and grinding around Laurel—potentially looking for a new queen for their harem. *Damned pixies.*

He would kill them. Gut them, pull their entrails out, and stuff them back in their mouths. Maybe he'd use their wings for decoration. Jasper's apartment decor was still a little sparse.

"Another drink," he barked at the bartender. "Ale. Strong."

When the glass slid across the hardwood counter, he caught it and turned his back on the dance floor. Watching Laurel was torture.

Stick to the goal. Interview the patrons. Staff. Anyone.

At least she was enjoying herself. He couldn't fault her for wanting a good time. Crimson knew he'd drowned himself in this place more than once in his younger years. *Just... don't leave with anyone,* he thought. Silently begging.

Thorne pulled out a coin from his pocket and paid.

"Before you go," he said to the barmaid, "Take a look at this."

He cast a spell over his drink and pushed the image of Jasper from his mind into the reflection. A shimmering image of his old mentor appeared in the ale. Not perfect, but good enough. "Have you seen this fae before?"

Thorne waited for the usual clamming up of the tongue—standard response to a Guardian. But the barmaid just stood back with an unimpressed look on her face. And then he recognized her.

"Anise!" he exclaimed.

She raised a vexed brow. "You save my life and you forget my face?"

"No, it's just that I didn't expect to see you here." He frowned. She lived in Crescent Hollow and worked at the Laughing Den. Or had Caraway said he'd not seen her in a while? "Why *are* you here?"

"Not that it's any of your business, but I couldn't live there anymore."

"But isn't Kyra a better alpha than Thaddeus?" He thought the place would be a sanctuary now.

Anise's eyes lost their fire and she picked up a cloth and started polishing a glass. "She is. It's not that."

He nodded solemnly. "It's the memories."

"I can't turn a corner without thinking they're there waiting for me. I can't walk outside the front gate without seeing the cage I was kept in." She shrugged. "It was time to leave. People here don't seem to care about my appearance as much. I should have left long ago."

She said the words, but it didn't look like she believed them. Thorne knew how cruel people could be. They were the same whether in Cornucopia, the Seelie Kingdom, or the dark, chaotic Unseelie. Anise was born to two wolf-shifters, but she couldn't shift. Her tail was permanent. Her nose had a dark tint at the tip. Wait.

"Does Caraway know?"

She scowled at him. "Why would I care? That floater knew the red-coats were in town. He knew Thaddeus and they were up to something, and yet he did nothing. If he'd acted when I told him, maybe a few lives would have been saved. Maybe I wouldn't have nightmares."

"You know Guardians are prohibited to get involved with politics."

"It hasn't stopped you."

He toyed with the rim of the glass. "But I'm an outcast, even with the outcasts."

"No, you're not. You just think you are. And, anyway, I'd rather that than be someone with no backbone." Anise finished polishing her glass and started vigorously cleaning the counter. "Why are you here, anyway?"

He thumbed the dance floor. "I'm with her."

Anise narrowed her eyes at Laurel. "Oh, yeah. She's cute."

"Clarke's friend."

"No shit. Same... like... from before?"

He nodded. Anise scrutinized him for a long time and then pointed at his face. "You know the black shit you put over your Guardian mark is rubbing off."

He scrubbed it. "Stupid idea anyway."

Anise looked back at the image of Jasper in the drink. "So... who's this? He looks familiar"

"An old friend. He's been missing for a long time. He used to frequent this place."

"I've only been here a year. I haven't seen him, but I can ask around."

A little thrill flipped in Thorne's stomach. He cleared his throat and tried not to look excited. "That would be appreciated."

"Stay here a minute." She took the glass and walked over to a security guard, showed him, and moved on. Thorne tracked her as she asked a few more before she came back.

"Apparently he was a regular." Anise blew air from her mouth, raised her eyes to the ceiling, and searched her memory. "I think Fern said the last time they saw Jasper was at least a decade ago."

Bogey's Balls. Thorne knew it was too good to be true.

"Can you tell me more about that last time?"

"Not really. All I know is that he spent a lot of coin. Fucked a lot of Rosebuds. Drank a lot of divilixir."

Same old Jasper-shit. An exasperated sigh slipped out. Thorne hand-signed his thanks and took a swig of his drink. He swilled the fruity taste around his mouth.

Anise paused and frowned. Her eyes darted over to the dark booth in the corner. "Although," she said. "Mind you. Things have changed a bit since then in here."

Thorne nodded slowly.

"If you need more info, ask Patches."

"He the new boss?"

"As good as. Been around for a couple of years. Right about when the entertainment started coming from captive humans. Honestly, it's the first time I've heard about this kind of captivity outside of King Mithras's Court."

"You don't mind it?" Thorne asked. He didn't think Anise was this kind of person.

"Between you and me, I won't be around for long." She glanced behind Thorne. "That's Patches."

"Right." Thorne followed her gaze to the booth in the corner with the empty djinn bottle. The same booth with the shadowed resident watching Laurel. The one where the resident wasn't sitting in the dark anymore, but standing at the edge of the dance floor, watching Laurel.

The scent of Patches' breed wafted over to Thorne and he tensed. Wolf. Probably Seelie since most wolves were. Fucker wore nothing but leather pants, meaning he was ready to shift at a moment's notice. Yellow eyes. Power-enhancing tattoos slicked over his scarred body. Pumped and threaded muscles. Furred, pointed ears twitching. Patch over one scarred eye.

During Thorne's teenage years, Jasper had taken Thorne to a place just like this and hired him a Rosebud to "break him in." Some people might think Jasper was a delinquent sexual fiend, but Thorne knew better. It was a cover. Sure, he'd enjoyed the perks of the role, but that first visit hadn't just been about hedonism. It was battle practice. Thorne still remembered walking in behind Jasper and being lectured quietly.

"Scope the joint on entry. Check the exits. Check for threats. Who do you think is the one you need to worry about most?"

"The big one with the tatts."

Jasper whacked Thorne over the head. "No, grasshopper. The biggest threat is the calmest person in the room. Look again."

Tonight, that person was Patches.

A disturbance at the entrance interrupted Thorne's attention. Air shifted and electrified with warning. Sound warped. His ears pricked at the gasps of patrons as they begrudgingly made way for a new arrival. Anise cursed under her breath. The bewitched musicians stumbled, the beat skipped, and then the magic riding their captivity kicked in again and the music flowed as if it hadn't stopped.

Once upon a time, Thorne looked at the latest artisan captives with pity and compassion, but that time had long since past. Being a Guardian had whittled away any part of him that cared for the fate of anyone that failed to fall under the scope of a

Guardian's protection. Did it make him jaded? Probably. But no worse than the two Guardians currently walking in a direct line toward Thorne.

Cloud and Shade. Crow and Vampire.

Both resplendently fearsome in their Guardian battle gear, hard eyes, and contempt for those around them. The crowd parted to make way. Cloud's feathered wings draped with menace, and Shade's leathery wings twitched with barely veiled tension. They cared little about the Birdcage's rule to keep their wings tucked tight. Guardians cared little about the opinions of others in general.

Thorne tried to move so they wouldn't see him, but it was no use. They were here *for* him. *Well-damn it.* Probably here on Leaf's orders to drag him back to the Order and face repercussions for leaving when he'd been given a mission. Screw the Order. He was sick of them.

He slammed down the last of the fruity ale just as Cloud strode up to him.

"The fuck you done to your face?" he asked dryly, either meaning Thorne's black smudge over the teardrop tattoo, or the missing beard.

Thorne ignored him and smiled apologetically at Anise. She smirked and went to prepare a drink for the new arrivals.

Shade picked up Thorne's empty glass and inspected it.

"If you're here to haul me back to the Order," Thorne said, "save yourselves some time and turn around now. I'm not coming back. Not until I find Jasper."

"Good," Shade drawled as he put the empty glass back down.

Surprise lifted Thorne's brows. "Then why are you here?"

"Hungry." Shade's predatory gaze scanned the patrons, now over their initial disturbance and back in revelry.

Liar. Shade was hungry, clearly, but they weren't here for the food. A good-looking vampire, as experienced as Shade, had willing donors falling at his feet. To prove Thorne's point, Shade pushed off the counter and crooked his finger at a pretty faun with curved horns flowing out of her curly red hair. She broke away from her group, cloven feet tick-ticking on the marble floor, and the two of them disappeared into the shadows.

That's all it took for Shade. A crook of the finger and females wet themselves. If only Thorne had that much control over the opposite sex, maybe he could get Laurel to follow his instructions more. No. It was Laurel who only needed to crook her finger at him, and his insides turned to lava.

She would be the death of him.

"Why are you here, Cloud?" Thorne ground out. He needed to see if it was the djinn bottle, or something else. "The Prime send you? Leaf?"

Cloud accepted his drink, tossed the ridiculous garnish, and sniffed it. "Nope."

"Then why?" Still didn't trust them.

"Maybe we care about Jasper too. You ever think that?"

Thorne scoffed, "You don't care about anyone."

"Harsh."

"True."

Cloud stared intently at the drink. "Maybe my wings have been clipped, and that's why I haven't helped in the hunt for Jasper."

Clipped? As in the Prime had something over him? "Fuck the Prime."

"Not today. Not any day."

Thorne slid eyes at Cloud. The fae returned his solid stare. Well-damn. Color him inky. Cloud was serious. Of all the fae to throw in their lot with Thorne, he'd never expected it to be the human-hating, Prime-loving, crow. He was wrong about the Prime-loving part. Which begged the question, who was Cloud loyal to?

"Just so you know," Cloud added. "The young wolf who filled your mission is dead."

Thorne's stomach dropped. "The fuck?"

"Yep. He's monster meat." Cloud leveled his gaze at Thorne. "This is the fallout from neglecting your duty."

Shit. Fuck. Shit. Heaviness closed Thorne's lids. The same weight settled on his shoulders. He braced the counter and breathed deeply. Poor kid. The wolf inside Thorne howled in grief. Another wolf down. Thorne's fault. There was no denying it.

"What happened to your markings?" Cloud asked, eying Thorne's arm.

"Glamored."

A cold, derogatory laugh burst out of Cloud and he slung his gaze at the dance floor. "Trouble in paradise already. Can't say I'm surprised. Didn't expect anything less from a filthy human."

Thorne bared his teeth. "Watch it."

"Then again, she's dancing between an orc and a pixie. Maybe she's about to redeem herself," Cloud added sarcastically.

Thorne tensed. Couldn't look. The wolf in him, already worked up, was now frantic. Part of him wanted to throttle Cloud for his disrespect, the other part wanted to throttle the fae no doubt with their hands all over Laurel. Nothing but fun and elation trickled down their bond. Damn. He needed to figure out a way to block their shared emotions... or accept it. Neither would be easy.

Cloud continued, "And with that dress on—wait. Isn't she your mate?"

The counter creaked under Thorne's punishing grip. "Why?"

"Then why is she—oh, yeah, that's not good. Time for us to get what we came for." Cloud made a shrill whistle, calling Shade back.

Thorne snapped around, heart pounding in his chest. There, in the center of the dance floor, Laurel was stuck between a growing group of male fae and trying to stop a brawl. One of the orc guards, a few pixies, and some elves. Motherfuckers.

This ends now.

Pushing off the counter, he strode into the fray, only vaguely aware of Cloud and Shade heading toward the table where the djinn bottle was. Of course those fuckers would be all about work.

Without thinking, he palmed two males beside Laurel—an orc and a pixie—both staggered back. The pixie's wings flared and vibrated on instinct, knocking a glass from the fae next to them, which in turn spilled on another. The orc bellowed in fury. The sound echoed off the high aviary column and disappeared into the night sky above.

"I had it sorted, Thorne," Laurel snapped.

"The fuck you did. Come on. Let's go." He tried to take Laurel by the arm, but she shrugged out of his hold.

"Don't," she warned.

"Lady said no," the orc grunted and stepped up. He shoved Thorne back.

Despite the big fae's height and brawn, Thorne barely flinched. He looked down at the beefy hand, still pressed to his pec. Red leaked into Thorne's vision and he rubbed the remainder of paint from his eye tattoo. He snarled and shattered the glamor holding his true appearance at bay. The Well-blessed markings on his arm and hand flickered into life, and the fire in his eyes doubled.

The orc's eyes widened. "Guardian?"

"Remove your hand, orc."

"The fucking Seelie-priss started it." The orc snatched his hand back, but recollected his composure and glared at the pixie, still glowering behind Laurel's back.

The pixie's fangs bared and he hissed. "Unseelie trash. You think you can just take what you want. She was with me first."

The orc took a swing. The pixie went down. And then chaos let loose.

The brawl moved over the dance floor like a tumultuous ocean. Lurkers in the shadows made themselves known. Orc bouncers. Shifters. Other reprobates with sharp bone weapons brandished. Blood would be spilled if this wasn't stopped.

Before Thorne could shift into a wolf, a thunderous crack rent the air. Lightning flashed. Everyone ducked, protecting their head from the elemental fury that was Cloud as he gathered electricity into his body. Next to him, Shade had materialized from whatever nook he'd been supping in, a drop of blood at the corner of his mouth, lethal prowess in his dark eyes. Shade commanded the shadows, and they crept toward him ominously, ready to swallow up anyone who got in his way.

Patrons screamed and shuffled out of the way, hiding wherever they could. A stampede almost crushed Thorne, but he shouldered free and watched the spectacle the Guardians put on.

Casually, as if Cloud had all the time in the world, he strolled over to where Patches stood and collected the djinn bottle from the table.

"This yours, wolf?" Cloud asked him.

"What's it to you, freak?"

Cloud laughed and looked at Shade. "You hear that? He called me a freak."

Shade looked impressed. "Yeah, I did. Must have balls. Because it also means I'm a freak. And, ah—" he looked over to Thorne. "Mean's he called our buddy over there a freak too."

Fuck. *Don't involve me.* Thorne clenched his jaw.

Patches calculated the odds, didn't like them, and then pointed at the orc who'd tried it on with Laurel. The same one with a slightly aged look to his face. "He's the one who brought the bottle in here. Ask him."

Cloud raised a brow at the orc. "That right?"

The orc paled. Nodded.

"Guess that's us done, then." Cloud secured the bottle to his belt loop and then gestured at Shade.

Shade looked Thorne squarely in the eyes. "You're welcome."

The two of them took one meaty orc arm each, flapped their wings, and then took off vertically, carrying their prisoner kicking and screaming between them until their bodies were nothing but shadows in the dark sky.

Patches hadn't offered the whole truth. That orc may have been the one who brought the bottle in, but somehow Thorne didn't think the orc was the one who'd orchestrated the attack on Mornington. Cloud and Shade weren't stupid. They'd be back for Patches.

"Time to go," Thorne said and looked for Laurel.

But she wasn't there.

Confused, he searched for her. Only then did he notice the music had stopped. The musicians weren't in their cage. The knowledge of what Laurel had done hit him with the force of a hurricane. She'd freed them during the disturbance. The moment he'd noticed, so did Patches. In the space of seconds, more guards appeared from the darkness of the club and dropped from the cages hanging above. This time, it was only one Guardian against many.

Thorne still liked those odds.

Until they dragged Laurel from the bathrooms, kicking and struggling, bleeding from her lip.

"The lady has caused this establishment offense," Patches boomed.

"Take your hands off her," Thorne warned. "Or this won't end pretty."

"Stay out of this, Guardian," Patches replied. "This doesn't concern you."

"Oh yes, it does."

Thorne's fangs and claws elongated, ready to let the wolf out, but Laurel shook her head. He paused. What? Why the fuck not? Forcing himself to calm and assess the situation, he realized there was no fear hurtling down the bond from her, not like it had done with the Sluagh. He arched his brow at her. Her lips quirked. *Trust me.*

Crimson, save him.

"What is the offense?" Thorne asked.

"She released our humans. She can't pay in coin, so she must pay in the Ring."

Shocked, Thorne couldn't stop the snarl that slipped out. But yet again, Laurel didn't flinch. Her smile widened. Which meant only one thing. She'd planned this.

He leveled his stare at Patches. "If you're taking her, then I invoke the rights of a Well-blessed union."

He lifted his marked hand. A chorus of gasps floated around the room.

"But you can't enter the Ring," someone said. "You're a Guardian."

"I'm also her mate. You either take both of us or none."

Patches looked at Laurel, at her still bare arm. "I don't see the same marking on her. And I don't see a wolf's bite on her neck. You don't smell mated, and you don't act it." He slid his narrowed eyes back to Thorne. "I don't want the Order breathing down my neck if we send you in. She goes alone."

EIGHTEEN

"She goes alone."

Patches' words echoed in the room. Laurel tensed, waiting for Thorne to protest. She supposed she could let the glamor on her Well-blessed markings drop. That would solve the argument. But she liked watching Thorne squirm.

That unsanctioned breeding comment Thorne had made cut her deep, but it was a festering wound for him. His pain was worse, and he'd lashed out to keep it hidden. So, when she'd danced, and the orc had danced with her, she couldn't help asking questions about Jasper.

To her surprise, each of the male fae that had danced around her had been more than forthcoming, each eager to please her more with tid-bits of information. Before he'd been taken by Cloud and Shade, the older-looking orc had confessed that he'd been working for Patches for a long time. And he'd been around when another orc had boasted about taking the bastard son of the king to the Ring. Of course, this other orc—Gunther, his name was—was also a prisoner at the Ring and resided under the hill.

From what she'd gathered, "under the hill" was the colloquial term Cornucopians called the place where prisoners were kept before they had to battle in the Ring. Some prisoners never left this jail. They would do battle, and then would be returned under the hill until the next time they were needed. Some battles negotiated were until death, others were first blood, and then if you were lucky, you could walk away.

The only way of gleaning more information from Gunther would be to get herself arrested.

The moment the two visiting Guardians had caused a commotion, Laurel knew that she could help the human prisoners escape and get herself caught in the process.

The guards holding her made to take her away, but Thorne shouted, "*Stop.*"

"You want us to act mated?" he snapped at Patches. "Fine."

Thorne strode to Laurel, fierce intensity in his blue-ice stare. He gripped the back of her neck, pulled her toward him so fast her mind sloshed, and then crushed his lips to hers. Maybe she should have been confused, or surprised, or angry, but all those feelings she'd told to wait, didn't want to wait. They rushed to the surface at the taste of him, and when he gripped her rear with his free hand, she forgot to breathe. She forgot to think.

There was nothing but his tongue, his taste, and his heat. She was so lost in him, she almost missed his whispered words. "If you don't drop the glamor, they'll drop it for you. All of it."

Panic petrified her.

Her ears. She'd forgotten. With her mind whirling with the potential consequences, she let him gently nibble her bottom lip as her mind caught up. Being a human in front of all these human-hating fae wouldn't mean being sent to the Ring. It could mean immediate execution, or entrapment like the artisans. Thorne was right. She dropped the glamor on her arm and when he eased off, she held her arm up for all to see.

Patches' dark eyebrow lifted over his eye-patch. He looked at Thorne. "Your funeral."

THERE WASN'T a moment of privacy the entire walk from the Birdcage to the Ring, and Laurel had been warned by Thorne not to give away any secrets with so many sharp ears listening. She couldn't tell him about her plan. It would have to wait until they were securely under the hill.

Their guards pushed them up the dirt path toward the colosseum at the top of a hill of rock. There was a fight on tonight, and the bright beam of orange light shot up from the colosseum into the sky. But it was beneath the colosseum that held Laurel's attention. No access points to the hill anywhere she could see, meaning they had to walk up to the top.

Inwardly, she groaned. It looked about four or five floors high. Her heels weren't going to cut it.

Thorne prowled at her side. Not a peep out of him the entire journey through town. She had no idea if he understood why or how she'd done this. He was big and strong enough to take down the four guards flanking them. He didn't.

He knew.

Must.

Or he could be doing what he'd done the entire time they'd been in Cornucopia—letting her lead.

Finally at the top, and with sore feet and heaving breaths, Laurel and her companions came to the large stadium. Fae milled about the many arched entries. Some looked excited about the show, others were nervous or in tears—probably friends or family of some prisoners. Seeing that side of it, Laurel's own nerves hit. Was she stupid to think she could handle this? Even win a battle? Or escape?

Don't lose faith now.

"Here we go," a guard said as they arrived at a small, nondescript hatch in the floor. "Your new home."

That's it? A hatch?

"And we wait down there until when?" Thorne demanded.

"Until you're called upon."

"Which is...?"

The orc smirked. "Whenever we say. You had your chance, Guardian. You gave it up. Now the bargain has been set. You can't leave until you win."

Why did Laurel suddenly have a bad feeling about that? "Who do we have to beat?"

The orc pulled out a strange tool that reminded Laurel of a branding iron, but it wasn't metal. It was made of smooth ceramic.

"What is that?" Thorne growled.

"For your binding." The orc's lips stretched to reveal his fangs. "We can't very well have prisoners portal out of here whenever they want."

"Is that all it's for?"

"Once you're released, it will disappear."

Thorne's brows slammed down. "That's not what I asked. I said, is that all it's for?"

Irritation swam over the orc's features. "It also prohibits your magic leaving the stadium."

Laurel supposed that made sense. Thorne, on the other hand, was infuriated for some reason. Perhaps he'd had another plan up his proverbial sleeve. But neither of them had time for more questions. The orc stamped their cheeks, burning their flesh. Laurel screamed. White hot agony lanced the side of her face. She wanted to touch it but couldn't manage more than a trembling hand hovering over the area.

Thorne took it much better. Not even a wince. When his was done, she was surprised to see no glaring red branding wound, but a blue rune, glowing and glittering with the power of the Well, just like her hand markings and his teardrop tattoo.

"Oh. And it's embedded with a transference spell, meaning when it's time for you to fight, you can't hide. You'll be transported into the arena."

Then the orc pushed Laurel down the hatch. Briefly, she became airborne in the dark. A scream froze in her throat. *Weightless.* And then... her ass hit slippery dirt and she flew down a slide, hands flailing, desperate to grasp something to slow herself down. Down, down, down she swirled like Alice down the rabbit hole. Until finally, light burst, hurting her eyes. She squinted, became airborne again, and then landed on soft green grass, tumbling until she came to a halt.

When she gathered her bearings, she gasped.

Trees. Grass. Sun? Light came from somewhere. The trickle of water. A sparkling river. Little huts made from sticks and bark. People—fae—of all kinds everywhere. At first glance, at least fifty. Maybe a hundred. She thought perhaps she'd knocked her head. It sure seemed like a Wonderland. But then she looked closer. The fae were rough, brutal, and the type that looked like they would stab you in the back the moment you weren't looking. But there was also fae who looked like they'd lived down here for years. As though they'd been forgotten.

Thorne landed gracefully next to her. He rolled and found his feet swiftly. Immediately, he took up a position of wariness—crouched in a fighting stance, eyes scanning the new Wonderland as though it were about to eat him whole. After he assessed, he relaxed and helped Laurel up.

"You good?" he asked, eyes never leaving those fae residents, now staring at the newcomers with hungry eyes.

She nodded. "Just peachy."

Her ass and thighs stung from the ride down the slippery dirt tunnel. If she looked, she'd bet she'd find scratches under the layer of mud. Her shoes were missing and her beautiful new dress was torn to shreds. If she thought it was revealing before, that was nothing compared to now.

"Shit," she muttered and pawed at the torn shreds.

Thorne reached over his shoulder, grabbed his shirt by the neck, and pulled it off. "Put this on."

With the weight of a thousand eyes on her, she had no trouble doing as she was told. She ripped off any straggling gauze and used a long strip to tie Thorne's shirt around her waist so it looked like a dress. When she was done, she tilted her nose to the shirt. It smelled like him. Now it was on her. She liked that. Their scents mixing.

He gave her a quizzical look. She blushed and quickly looked away.

"So," she said. "What now?"

"You tell me."

Their eyes met. Held. Yeah, he knew.

Laurel glanced around to see if anyone was within hearing range. They were halfway down a soft grass hill that led to a valley below where the people gathered.

"Is it safe to talk?" Even though he seemed to trust her, it was time to explain.

His ears twitched. "Probably not. But also probably the most privacy we'll get in this place."

"While I was dancing, I questioned the orc guard about Jasper. He said another guard many years ago had boasted about sending Jasper to the Ring. That guard is here himself and has been for years. His name is Gunther."

"So you got arrested on purpose. And you didn't think it pertinent to include me in on your plan?"

"Well excuse me for thinking you had no faith in me, especially considering you had just called me a whore."

His eyes widened. "I called you a Rosebud courtesan. There's a big difference."

"What's the difference?"

He didn't answer.

Jesus Christ. With that, Laurel started her trek down the hill.

His footsteps pounded behind her, as heavy as the god of thunder himself.

"Laurel," he said. "I..."

She stopped at the base of the hill. "You're what?"

You're sorry?

He opened his mouth. Shut it. Then scowled at something behind Laurel.

"We're looking for a fae named Gunther," Thorne bellowed.

A line of hard-looking fae stepped up. Each of different breeds, each with a home-fashioned weapon in their hand. Some were made of bone, others of wood. Maces. Clubs. Axes. Swords. Sharp things. Dangerous things.

Next to her, Thorne sucked in his abs and started plucking buttons on his breeches.

"What are you doing?" she hissed.

"I don't want my only pants to be ruined in the shift," he replied casually, put his thumbs in the loops of his belt and got ready to drop.

She held out her palm in a placating way. "No need to get your panties twisted, Growly. Let's just take a breath before we wolf out." To the line of hardened criminals edging their way, she waved hello. "We just want to talk to Gunther. No one needs to get hurt."

One stepped forward. No teeth, crooked nose, bald, and a stink she whiffed from ten feet away. Pointed ears. Probably elf. For a species that didn't show age, he looked ancient with crow's feet around his eyes and a gnarled and bent figure. But the muscles in his shoulders were corded. He'd be a tough nut to crack. His snarl was full of contempt.

"What do you want with Gunther? What will you give?" He eyed her bare legs salaciously. Perhaps they didn't get too many females down here.

Already in the process of letting his wolf out, Thorne's eyes took on a feral glint, his claws distended, his canines elongated. It was a breathtaking sight.

"Name your price," she said, turning back to the elf. Hopefully he would ask for coin, food, or protection.

But what the fae came back with, she could never have been prepared.

"Your underwear," he said.

He had to be kidding. But he wasn't. A sharp laugh burst out of her. Thorne turned to stone.

Another fae next to the crooked nosed elf stepped forward. "I'll take you there for only half your underwear."

"I'll do it for a quarter," said a third.

"I'll do it for free," piped up a small voice.

"Yes." Laurel pointed to where the sound came from and landed on a scrappy looking boy of about thirteen. "You. You're the winner. Let's go."

Laurel hurried the rest of the way to meet the boy. As she drew near, she found a timid satyr. Wide and low pointed ears twitched and flicked as though a fly landed on them. Curly brown hair. Big doe eyes. But a hardness in them that saddened her. His clothes were hole-ridden and smelled. He looked half starved. She hated to think what had happened to have him thrown in there.

"I'm Laurel." She stuck out her hand. He eyed it as though she had a disease, so she took it back. Right—handshaking wasn't a thing. "This is Thorne."

"I'm Sparrow."

"He's my Sparrow. That's what he is." The crooked nosed elf stood between Sparrow and Laurel. "You want him, you pay for him."

Laurel lifted a brow. "And I suppose you want my underwear."

"Mention her underwear again, and it will be the last thing you utter." Thorne loomed over the elf, jaw clenched, part wolf. "I will cut your tongue out, elf. Don't mistake my words."

The elf looked warily at Thorne, caught the teardrop tattoo, lowered his gaze and stepped back. "What's a Guardian doing here? You lot ain't allowed in here."

"They made an exception."

"I own him." The elf pointed at Sparrow.

"Now I do," Thorne returned.

"You ain't paid me."

Thorne leaned forward an inch. "The fact I leave your tongue in is your payment."

The elf nodded emphatically and stepped back. He shooed the rest of them, and the bystanders eased away. Was Thorne truly that frightening? Or had the reputation of a Guardian preceded him? Laurel was yet to see Thorne in battle.

She'd seen the disgust toward Guardians, but not so much the fear. Come to think of it, even Patches had been hesitant.

When Sparrow led them away, Laurel asked him. "Why do they fear Guardians so much?"

It felt like a silly question, considering he was a warrior, but she also felt there was more to it and wanted to learn more about their culture. Thorne slid her an indecipherable glance, considered, and then shrugged. "Perhaps it's because we're stronger, magically and physically. Or that us using metal can stop them using magic altogether."

"What do you mean?"

"If we use metal to pierce, cut, or wound a fae, or mana-warped monster, with our weapons, it can dampen their magic. Leaving metal in a fae's body will completely stop a shift, halt a spell, and..." His focus turned inward, sad. "Push your mana from your body in an excruciating way."

"You sound like you're speaking from experience."

"Rush and Clarke witnessed my aunt, Kyra, have a liquid metal injected into her veins. They saw her mana pop out of her body. Then that bastard drank it."

Laurel shivered, knowing exactly who Thorne spoke about. "It was the Void. And Bones."

He nodded grimly. "They harvest mana like it's a delicacy."

Once Bones popped into her head, she couldn't get him out. The fury. The hate. The need for revenge. She was lucky to have gotten away with only her fingernails ripped out. They'd grown back. Twisted and warped, admittedly, but still they grew back. If she ever met Bones again, she wouldn't flinch. She would end him and his sick, black heart. The same went for the Void.

"Laurel," Thorne paused. "You good?"

She cleared her throat. Must have let her emotions slip. She nodded. "Let's go."

Sparrow took them through the strange underground world that was its own microcosm of the world above. They left the grassy knoll behind and ventured into a forest of elm trees where water dripped from the sky in a never-ending sprinkle of rain. Insects chirped. The smell of damp earth and wet leaves restored her mood.

Sparrow ducked and weaved through brush, skipped over fallen logs and damp blackberry bushes. After a five-minute walk, they emerged in a clearing where the sun shone brightly and a lone, wooden shanty sat in the middle.

On the porch, rocking in a chair, was a toothless, haggard, and ancient-looking orc. White hair tufted on the sides of his head. Wrinkles sagged his face.

Laurel stopped. Thorne raised a brow at her.

"He's old," she whispered. "How?"

"My guess?" Thorne rubbed his chin, stubble now forming. "He's paid for his possessions with his mana. Could be the only currency down here. And since mana is what keeps us fae immortal, he's almost out."

"But I thought you could replenish it."

"You can. But there's a way of giving your mana that takes a piece of your soul, of your capacity to ever hold it or sense the magic of the Well again. Think of it like filling up the bottom of a well with sand, reducing its ability to hold water. When that well is full of sand, it doesn't take long before you can't sense the magic of the Well at all. You become human. Or in his case, mortal."

"So he's no danger to us."

"I wouldn't go that far. He's kept these possessions down here with no contest. He's got something."

Laurel took a deep breath and let it out slow. She caught Thorne's eyes. "You ready?"

He darted a glance at Gunther, where all his questions might be answered. "Feels like I've been waiting my whole life for this."

NINETEEN

Thorne strode toward Gunther's hut with single-minded tenacity. He was *this* close to getting answers, and his patience wore thin.

"Stop!" Sparrow chirped.

Thorne halted. His hand whipped out to catch Laurel on the sternum and halted her too.

He turned to the boy. "This better be good."

The boy licked his lips. "You were about to walk into a trap."

Thorne's brows winged up. Yep. That would do it.

He looked down at his feet, didn't see anything suspicious, but when he shifted his gaze to Gunther, the old orc threw his head back and laughed heartily, eyes crinkling, open mouth a black hole.

"What's the trap?" Thorne asked, cringing at the sound of the orc's wheezing laugh.

"It's, um." The boy seemed to shrink away from Thorne. "I, um."

"Spit it out."

"Thorne," Laurel admonished. "Give him a second."

The boy's shy eyes shifted to her in gratitude.

"If it helps," Laurel continued. "You can talk to me, and not Thorne. He scares me too sometimes."

Sparrow picked up a rock and threw it at the orc. A few feet away, the rock hit an invisible force-field and disintegrated in a spark of electricity.

"Wards," Thorne grumbled.

"What does that mean?" Laurel asked.

"It means," Gunther said as he stood up, creaking in his old age, "that you can't get in unless I let you in."

If Thorne had Fury, he could get in. The metal ax would obliterate the magic. He frowned, brooding in his bitterness.

"We don't need to get in. We just need to ask you a few questions," Laurel replied.

"Answer is no," Gunther shouted.

"You don't even know what I was going to ask."

"Come on, Laurel." Thorne touched Laurel on the shoulder. "Let's go. He's probably a waste of time, anyway."

"Now, I didn't say that." Gunther hunched and shuffled closer. "Tell you what, you ask your question, and I'll tell you if I know the answer."

"Well, that doesn't help us," Laurel replied.

"It will if you do something for me as payment for the actual answer."

"What do you want?" Thorne asked.

"Food."

Thorne turned to Sparrow. "What's the deal with meals down here?"

"They drop food down the chute every day, but you have to fight to get it."

"Don't want no chute-food," Gunther said. "Want fish."

"Are there fish here?" Thorne asked Sparrow, who replied with a dubious look.

"Yeah, but... they're ika fish. Too fast to catch by hand. Big, and they have teeth."

"What if we scorch them?" Thorne suggested.

"Won't work. Too fast."

There were a myriad of other spells he could try, but he had no idea if his mana stores would replenish down here in time for the impending battle, and without Fury, he would probably have to borrow from Laurel as it was.

"What about using a fishing line, bait and hook?" Laurel asked. "Make the fish come to us."

"What would we use for line?" Thorne turned his shrewd gaze to Gunther, then to Sparrow. Both gave no indication that they could help. To be sure, he raised his brows at both of them.

"If I could hunt my own ika," Gunther crowed, "do you think I'd ask for help?"

Thorne supposed not. He had no clue as to how to get the fish if they were too quick for magic and too fast for hands to grab. He wouldn't have much better luck if that was the case.

Laurel glanced at his long hair. "You know... we could cut your hair, as weird as that sounds. It's very long. It could be fashioned into a line."

Thorne's hand went to the tail of his hair and ran down the length. Cut it off? But he hadn't found Jasper yet. He shot Laurel a wary glance.

She smiled gently. "It's long and strong. We can split the strands and braid them together to make a long fishing line. Put a hook at one end, and a rod at the other, and we've got our tool."

Thorne's fist clenched over his hair. Seeing his turmoil, Laurel placed a cool palm on his bare chest and pushed him to the side, under a tree canopy, where they had a little more privacy. She kept her palm there and looked up at him.

Moments ticked by until the burn of her touch far outgrew the sensation where his palm met his hair. The blue of her Well-blessed markings seemed to get brighter with their proximity.

The hair was a constant reminder to never give up.

Laurel's palm slid up his chest, curved around the back of his neck, and held.

"Please let it go, Thorne," she said, eyes somber.

"You don't understand."

"I do."

"How?" The word was a whisper, a ghost.

"Because there was a time once when I held onto someone I loved too."

A lover?

Tightness constricted around his chest.

She let go of Thorne, eyes downcast. "I had a twin. His name was Lionel. And he was everything I wasn't. Funny. Smart. But he was always getting sick. Somehow he was the twin that got the weak genes. He died, and I lived. For years I blamed myself for being the one who survived. What made me so special? Why me and not him?" Her eyes teared up when she met his again. "And then my father said 'You can't base your future on the what ifs and dreams of the past. You can only work on the dreams of today'." She rubbed her eyes. "Anyway. He was always spouting shit like that. I decided to put my energy into something I can control, into having a business where I could help others stay strong, and do you know what? I actually did help people. Lives were changed. The point is. Right here, right now, we put our energy toward something we can control."

Thorne's stark gaze landed on Gunther. "I need information."

"Right. So let's get it."

She made to move, but he let go of his hair and stopped her, bringing her back to face him.

"Is this why you work so hard?" he asked. "Every day you're up and running as though you have a kuturi squawking at your heels."

She gave him a sad smile and trailed her fingers down his braid. "I respect why you did this. In a way, it gives you the same drive that running gives me. And because of this, I feel I can say this: You're not alone anymore. I'm here with you. I'll be your drive. We won't rest until Jasper is safe. Trust me."

Something cracked inside of him. It hurt.

To avoid looking at Laurel, and making the hurt worse, he turned to Sparrow and walked over. "Do you have a knife?"

Sparrow darted a guilty glance to the orc who still stood a few feet within the boundary of his wards. He reached behind him and pulled a small bone carving knife from his waistband.

The orc shouted, "That's mine."

"Well you shouldn't have left your hut a few weeks ago when the wards were down," Sparrow replied and handed it to Thorne.

Thorne swallowed. He took his braid in hand, held the blade to the scalp, but couldn't do it.

Laurel put her hand over the knife. The look in her eye said that she had his back. She would do it.

Trust me.

Gravity failed and he floated, head dizzy, before suddenly crashing to his knees. His skin prickled hotly. Couldn't breathe.

Laurel's cool touch was an oasis. Fingers were on his shoulders, then pressing the sides of his head, fluttering around as she got herself in position. She lifted the tail of the braid. The knife pushed at the scalp.

No no no.

He squeezed his eyes shut.

And then... snip.

A freeing of weight. A sensation of floating. And Laurel.

Laurel behind him, pressing up against his bare back. Laurel's hands on his head as she used the knife to tidy the rest of his hacked hair. Wisps of white hair floated around and tickled his nose. And Laurel's emotions down the bond... compassion, melancholy... love?

His eyes snapped open. He craned his neck to look at her. Up. Up into her eyes where a fondness gazed back at him. No. It was too soon for that. She cupped his jaw and said with a raw voice, "I'll start on the line. Perhaps you can take the knife and find some wood to fashion into a rod."

When Thorne returned to Laurel with two thick, long sticks he'd removed from a tree, he found her tying off a long, thin and braided line made from his hair. He'd only been gone half an hour, yet the woman had not only created the line, but managed to convince Gunther to grind and shape a fishing hook out of stone. He watched from the tree line and marveled at the tenacity of the woman.

Not long ago, she woke from another time, and yet she'd accomplished so much. Faced with a changed world, Laurel had swiftly moved from someone who believed fae were things and feral beasts, to dancing with them in a club, and protecting a wee one in a prison. She'd somehow cajoled the grumpy orc to help secure her end of the bargain and convinced a timid fae boy to guard her back while she worked.

"How did you manage that?" Thorne asked, pointing to the hook.

"Oh, it wasn't hard." She smirked. "I only needed to remind dear old Gunther that the sooner he helps us, the sooner he eats. I know you fae have to do this exchange thing, but it really would be great to have someone doing something nice and not expect anything in return."

Like you? He wanted to say. Because it was true. He hadn't believed it at first, but Laurel was a quick study. If Thorne hadn't bonded to her, she would have learned about her powers all on her own. She didn't need him. This bargain she'd entered to help him find Jasper hadn't been about her needs at all.

Another unsettled feeling snapped between his ribs. This was not a feeling he was used to, and he was hesitant to put words to it, but the undeniable trust blooming in his heart grew with each act of her kindness.

Thorne took the knife and shaved off any lumps and bumps from the wooden length they were to use as a rod. He notched the end, and they tied the long line to it.

When it was done, Laurel stood with a proud look on her face. She grinned and gave Sparrow an affectionate pat on the shoulder.

"We did it, buddy."

Sparrow looked up at Laurel as though she were the sun. She didn't know the kid from an inkeel, but she hooked her arm around his shoulders and tugged him to her side.

A rush of primal desire flooded Thorne's system. The wolf in him woke. Its gaze leveled on Laurel. Intensified. She would make a good mate. She could protect cubs while the hunter was away. She was caring, kind, strong. A perfect mate.

"All right," Laurel said. "All we need now is bait. And I have just the right people to ask."

"Dare I ask?" Thorne replied, wondering if she had removed her underwear after all.

She looked pleased with herself and shrugged evasively. "Let's ask the natives and see."

Five minutes later, they had secured scraps of food from some other prisoners. Mostly it was worms, bugs, and other insects foraged from under logs and dirt. As it turned out, it wasn't the underwear she used as currency, but the promise to leave the fishing rod to them after they left. Once again, she'd surprised him.

By the time they settled into position by the stream, Thorne was completely and utterly at a loss for words.

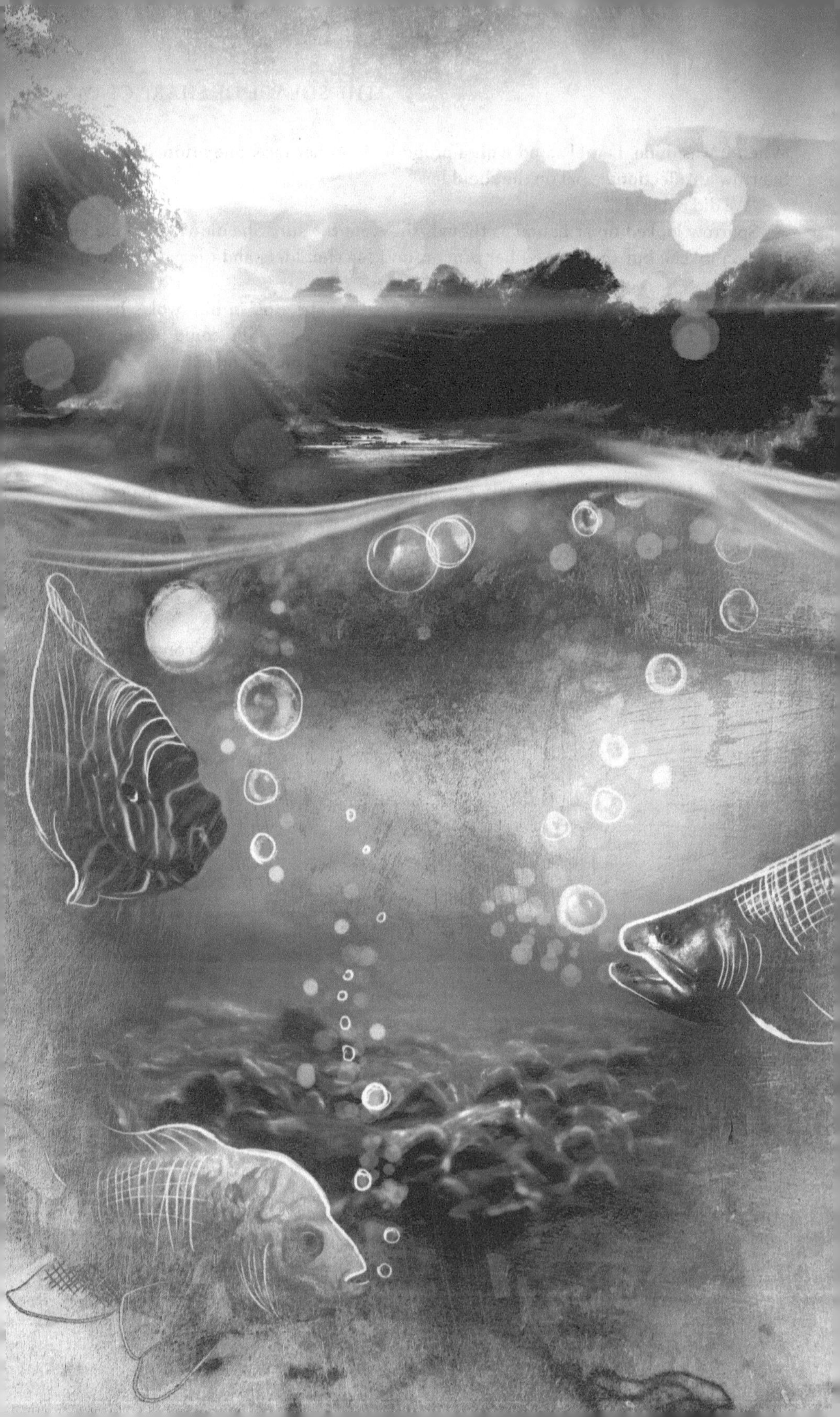

CHAPTER

TWENTY

After Lionel's funeral, it had taken six months for Laurel's father to go fishing again. His declaration had come as such a shock. Lionel and her father had always done this together. The exclusive boys fishing trip was an easy task and suited Lionel's poor health, plus it was a cheeky way to get away from the "nagging" women in the family. While they would go, Laurel and her mother would spend the time pampering and doing mani-pedis at home. It had worked for everyone.

But that first day.

When her father had quietly dressed in his gear and packed the tackle box, Laurel and her mother had watched with heavy hearts. Today there would be no Lionel. There never would.

Laurel used to take the fishing trips for granted, and only saw them as a way she got to spend time with her mother, but her father needed her too. It had been too heartbreaking to ignore. She went with him. At first it was to spend as much time as she could with her father, of replacing the hole Lionel had left. Then it became about living for Lionel. It became about being someone worthy of taking his spot in life. She was the first twin. The bigger one who took more sustenance in the womb. It could have easily been the other way. It could have been her who got sick, or both of them. Or even her parents. But from that day forward, Laurel knew that she would never waste her time on earth again.

It was a pity it took the monotony of waiting for an ika fish to bite to remember those quiet moments of solitude fishing with her father. Just being present with each other. Her business had sucked too much of her time, and she'd stopped those important trips with her dad. Shamefully, she'd been so wrapped up that she hadn't even made Christmas the year before the nuclear bombs went off.

Sniffing, she wiped her nose and continued braiding a second line with the last of Thorne's hair. They might have enough for another one. Sparrow was trying to stab a fast swimming fish a few feet down the meandering river while Thorne manned the fishing rod from the shallows.

He needed some work on patience. He cursed and scoffed every time he gathered in his line and found the bait had been eaten, or worse, that the bait was there and not a nibble had been taken. Once or twice, whole pieces of the line went missing and they'd had to make repairs.

Smiling inwardly, Laurel appreciated the simple sight of the large, well-muscled fae doing something so familiar from her time. Gone was his long warrior's tail. A part of her mourned that. She knew what it meant to him, what it had taken for him to make the sacrifice, and what it meant about his faith in her.

In his rolled-up pants, smooth skin and sharp haircut, he was almost a perfect match to the type of men she dated back in her time. A slow bloom of heat unfurled in her lower stomach. In another life, she could almost imagine the two of them spending time together, relaxing by a river, fishing, camping, swimming—playing. Maybe she would splash him. He'd scowl, grouse for a bit, and then when she thought he had moved on from the joke, he would dive under the water and take her down with him. Water would envelope them. Embrace them. Then maybe while they were down there, he'd kiss her. Breathe air into her lungs. Keep her alive.

Her smile came out to dance on her lips and she had to bite down to contain her growing emotions. She glanced at Thorne.

Icy blue rimmed with electric blue already aimed her way. With breathless awareness, she realized he'd intimately felt the journey of her daydream.

Slowly, never breaking eye contact, she got up from her spot on the lawn. When she joined him, she stood at his side and watched the water meander past in the small river. If she forgot about it being a prison, it was peaceful there. The strange light warming their faces, insects chirping, rain pitter-pattering in the forest. Laurel closed her eyes and immersed herself in the moment.

"Why are you so driven?" Thorne's rough voice entered her reverie. "I mean, I know it was about your twin, but I want to understand more."

She opened her eyes and smiled sadly at him. "Lionel was the sick twin. I felt guilty at first because I was the one who grew strong in the womb. But then this turned into staying strong. To avoid getting the same sickness he did. When Lionel died, I needed to prove I was the right choice."

Silence ticked by.

"And how do you know if you are?"

"See... that's the thing. I used to think the more successful I was, and the fitter I was, the better I was, but now I look back at how I lived my life, I realize how many important things I missed while I was striving to be the best. I missed spending time with my family, the single most important people in my life, and I screwed it all up for green smoothies and spin class."

"I don't know what they are, but I can assure you, your family loved you."

"How could you possibly know that?"

The look he shot her, so open, raw and honest, dug deep into her heart. "Because you're not hard to love."

She stared hard at the ground. "And what about you?"

"Naturally, I'm easy to love too. Just ask Cloud."

Laughter burst out of her so hard and fast that she had to cover her mouth.

A smile stretched his lips. A dimple flashed in his cheek. And somewhere, fireworks went off.

Thorne's gaze turned serious. He took her fingers from her mouth and reveled in her smile. She'd never had someone who looked at her like this. Like she was the source of his joy, the battery that sparked his heart.

"Why are you so driven?" she asked him.

A dark cloud took his smile away and his intense gaze shifted to the river. Laurel wasn't sure he would speak, but he did. And it stole her breath.

"Jasper was the only person I had in my corner."

It stole her heart because that was never the impression she had. "Are you sure?"

His burning gaze slid her way. "What do you mean?"

"It's just that... um... well. And this might be none of my business, but—" She took a deep, steadying breath. "Before I came through the portal with you that first day, Clarke told me a few things. She told me Rush has been trying to be there for you and you're cutting him out."

Thorne huffed. "Of course I'm not receptive. I've been on my own for decades."

"But is that really true?"

"What are you getting at?"

"Rush was cursed. You may not have been able to see him, but he was there for you. Clarke said he used to follow you around as a child. He used to leave you little carved animals. He would—"

"Fuck. How much have you talked about me behind my back?"

"Only a little. She wanted to give me some background since we're married."

A sharp retort was on the tip of his tongue, but he swallowed it down. "I'm not talking about this anymore."

Thorne shifted to get up, but Laurel stopped him.

"Don't, Thorne. Don't stuff this down in a dark place and let it fester."

He bared his teeth. "What do you know about it?"

Her eyes widened. She gasped. "Are you seriously asking me that? Everyone I've ever loved is dead. My whole world is gone, wiped out by some dickhead because I wasn't brave enough to withstand his torture." Her bottom lip trembled because it was the truth she never wanted to admit. If she had been tough enough to withstand Bones, or even strong enough to fight back, maybe none of this would have happened. She'd been helpless. "But if you let all this hurt and pain block your happiness, you will be lonely for the rest of your life. And it won't be circumstance that put you there, but *you*."

The truth echoed in the air, hanging between them. Hostility burned in his eyes. Laurel watched him fumble with the line for a few seconds before helping him.

"You're doing it wrong. Fishing is a study in patience."

She put her hand over his, but he wouldn't give up the rod. His knuckles whitened. The muscles in his torso were threaded and sinewy with agitation. Veins popped. There was a sense of a caged bear about him. One more poke and he'd snap, ripping her to shreds with claws and teeth. Exhaling deeply, she took her hand away and went to leave, but he spoke.

"I don't know how to be any different." The words were raw, deep, and rough.

The courage it took to say those words was evident in every rigid line of his body.

"Start with this."

She kept her hand on his and then ducked under his arms until she was between them. He stiffened. She adjusted their grip so his big hands engulfed hers on the rod. Body heat seared down her back. Breath ghosted her ear. Her pulse quickened.

Biting her lip, she murmured, "First we make sure the line will fly when released. No tangles. Then we pull back"—she lifted the rod—"take a step forward and then let go of the line when the rod is pointed straight ahead. You ready?"

She felt it more than saw it—his readiness. A hitch of breath, a thud of his heart against her spine, his slow and steady exhale tickling her ear.

"Let it go," she rasped.

Together, they cast the line. It zinged from their hands and landed in the deeper part of the river.

"Now put your finger here so you can feel the tension."

"I feel it."

She swallowed.

"Good. Now we wait."

"How long?"

Her eyes fluttered. "However long it takes."

She went to move, but he tensed, locking her in. No words. Just his solid stance, the weight of his stare—on her, not the water—and the prickle of awareness down the hot side of her face that told her he was shifting closer. Closer. Until he did the strangest thing.

He nuzzled into her neck, inhaled deeply, and then rested his teeth gently on the flesh between her neck and shoulder. That's all he did as long seconds ticked past. For a moment, she thought he might bite her, but then he unlocked his jaw and shifted his chin to the top of her head with a heavy sigh.

"We wait," he repeated.

She nodded dumbly.

And wait they did. Minutes passed. Five. Ten. Fifteen. They did nothing but brace against each other and feel the tension in the line as they watched Sparrow play downstream, giggling softly every time he stabbed a fish and came up short.

The weight of Laurel's lids grew heavy, and she hazily realized they'd been thrown down the chute during the night. Light still sparkled on the water.

"Why is it always daytime down here?" she asked with a yawn.

Behind her, Thorne took a breath and answered. "It's the manabeeze."

She craned to look up at him with questioning eyes. "What?"

"Remember I told you how stolen mana can be used for artificial purposes."

"Well, you didn't quite elaborate. You said the orc may have sold his in some bargains and that once gone, you can't replenish it."

"Right. So manabeeze are little balls of sacred energy. Some say our very soul. They release naturally from your body when you die. They buzz about until eventually they rejoin the cosmic Well. If you look closely at the ceiling, it shimmers. My guess is a vast amount have died down here over the past few centuries. The manabeeze are somehow trapped. Enough has amounted that it creates an artificial light."

"Ghosts," Laurel murmured.

"Pardon?"

"Just like the stars in a night sky, only brighter. I don't know if you're aware of this, or if time has erased the knowledge, but stars are suns from solar systems far away in space. But the sad thing is, by the time the light travels millions of light-years to us, the actual star would be dead in real time. So when we're looking at the stars in the night sky, we're looking at ghosts. It's a bit like this." She sighed. "I suppose it could be romantic."

"Why?"

"If two people who loved each other were trapped up there, they'd be together for eternity."

She glanced over at Sparrow. The boy was too young to lose his life down here. For stealing food?

Thorne let go of the rod briefly. His touch came to the side of her face where the binding rune itched. Tracing around it, she felt his frown in every place his body connected with hers. His stomach tensed, drawing tight across her spine. His arms bracketing her locked.

"I hate that they've done this to you, marred your face."

"It's temporary." Right?

She sensed he was about to say more, but then the line under their fingers *pinged*.

Years of honed fishing instincts launched into action. She locked the line around a notch they'd created and yanked.

"Help me," she gasped.

The line vibrated with tension and promise. She yanked, gathered the line. Yanked. Gathered. Each time the fish came closer.

"We caught one!" Thorne exclaimed.

"Not if you stop reeling it in."

"Right." He joined her again, keeping the line from unraveling and drawing the fish in.

With each tug, a shadow popped under the water, coming closer and closer until finally it broke the surface, flip-flopping about. It was heavy. Thorne took over and hauled the three-foot beast onto land where he clubbed it and then held it up with an incorrigible grin.

"Dinner."

CHAPTER
TWENTY-ONE

Thorne kept watch while Laurel slept. After they'd reeled the fish in, she was dead on her feet. He'd gutted the fish, cooked it on a campfire, and the three of them ate in companionable conversation while the nasty orc watched from his side of the ward. Gunther would give them information, but not until after Thorne was clear about who was running the show.

Thorne didn't think they would be called into battle immediately. Having their first ever Guardian would be a draw card. They'd want to advertise the battle and find an opponent worthy enough of bringing in a crowd. Someone who would likely have beef with the Order.

That's what he'd do, anyway. It would make for the better show.

He threw around options in his head as he continued to fish while Laurel and Sparrow slept. Standing in the river shallows, waiting for another bite, strangely settled him. It didn't take long before his tension ebbed away and a calming peace washed over him.

Enjoying the moment, he kept fishing. Even when he caught another, he threw in a line for a third.

He felt the unseen eyes of other prisoners all around him, always watching, waiting for him to slip up. It wouldn't happen. Hours later, he'd caught a total of three large fish and kept them in clear view of Gunther by laying them on the lawn between their camp and the wards. It was probably courting danger, knowing many other eyes were wanting, but he couldn't help himself. The orc had the balls to bargain with a Guardian, then he'd suffer the consequences. *A study in patience*, Laurel had said. He was beginning to see the benefits in that. They would get their information, whether now or later didn't matter. And they would get it on their terms.

With the fish caught, and not much else to do, Thorne found himself staring at his reflection in the river water, pondering over Laurel's words earlier about not having someone in his corner. Rush's curse had made him invisible and untouchable. It wasn't the first time he'd heard Rush had been around Thorne as a child, and the more he thought about it, the more he saw old memories in a new light.

The time when he'd been a tribute to the Order, and pushed into the waters of the ceremonial lake, there had been Guardians who'd strangely fallen in the water. Thorne's young mind had reasoned that it was his own kicking and screaming that had somehow pushed those Guardians in, but now he knew the strength it took to move someone as solid as him. If those Guardians fell because someone had pushed them, someone like Rush, then it was true—he'd been around. And the act of touching those Guardians would have made Rush violently ill from the curse.

That notion sank in. His father had made himself *ill* trying to protect him.

There were other times Thorne had noticed Rush's presence.

Once a group of young wolf shifters had teased Thorne about his lack of parents. They'd been playing by the Whispering Woods near Crescent Hollow, and Thorne distinctly remembered more than one of them accidentally hitting themselves with the sticks they'd been playing with. They'd thought the spirits of the woods had come to tease them.

Thorne rubbed the back of his neck, contemplating. Perhaps he should reach out to Rush and Clarke. Let them know where they were and to check on Laurel's other friend who would wake soon. Laurel would want to know.

A communication spell through water might work. He had a blood link to Rush. The Well would connect them. Thorne used Sparrow's knife to cut his finger and drip blood into the river. Then he allowed a tiny drop of his mana to drive the spell. The water shimmered a bright blue, and then Thorne mentally sought out Rush. Because the Well connected everything in Elphyne, if Rush was also around water, he'd be alerted by a glow.

It took a few goes, a few drops of blood and a few of mana, but eventually an image formed in the reflection. It was dark and shadowed, but Thorne made out branches and night sky. Then a tense face loomed over. White hair. Golden eyes. Rush.

"Thorne?" Rush said, voice hollow through the connection.

Because it was never just Rush, a shock of red flashed over Rush's shoulder. Clarke poked her head into view. "What is that?" she asked curiously.

"Communication spell," Rush explained. "Works best between blood relatives."

"Cool." But then Clarke narrowed her eyes. "Hi Thorne. What's wrong. Why are you calling?"

"You mean you don't know?" Thorne joked knowing she hated that she couldn't control her visions.

"Har-har," Clarke replied. "Very funny. When did you get a sense of humor?"

Rush pushed her out of the way so his face filled the view. "Is something wrong?"

"Not exactly." Thorne scrubbed his newly shorn hair. "Have you returned to the Order?"

Rush shook his head. "We've only just arrived at the site where Clarke thinks she'll find her friend. But"—Rush's gaze hardened—"you wouldn't be asking that if you were at the Order."

"Willow is fine," he assured Rush. "It's just that I left with Laurel. We've got a lead on Jasper."

"You were supposed to wait for me."

"I didn't."

Silence.

"Okay. So what's the plan?"

"We're under the hill."

Rush's eyebrows lifted. "You mean, under the Ring?"

Thorne nodded. "Laurel's plan. Trust me, if I knew about it, I wouldn't be here."

Thorne could almost feel Rush's exasperation through the connection. "These human females are hard to deny."

"I heard that!" Clarke called from the distance.

"I'm calling because I think you should know where we are. Just in case."

"Do you need help?"

"Not at the moment."

"Understood."

Thorne darted a glance to Laurel's sleeping form, then back to Rush. "Laurel is sleeping, but she would want me to ask about her friend."

"Not much we can tell you at this stage, but now that we know this connection spell works, I'll try to contact you when we know more."

"Until next time." Thorne dipped his chin.

Rush nodded and the connection ended.

Thorne collected the fishing rod and went back to where Laurel and Sparrow slept huddled together. He settled down, with his back to Gunther, and kept his eye on the forest where he sensed their voyeurs. The fish were behind him, and there was nothing between the fish and the wards. But if anyone else tried to steal the fish, Gunther would see. Knowing how long it had taken to catch the fish, Thorne was sure Gunther would sound an alarm.

Thorne stayed like this until hours later, Laurel began moving in her sleep. She twitched, frowned and whimpered. Must be a nightmare.

Leaning over, he trailed his knuckles down her rune-free cheek and sent calming emotions down their bond. Within moments, she settled and then didn't wake until he supposed it was morning. There was no way to tell with the artificial light.

She sat up, rubbing her eyes. "How long was I out?"

He shrugged.

"Right. No way of knowing, I suppose." Stretching, she met his eyes. His were still locked on the way her lithe body moved. His inner wolf paced restlessly. Since he'd almost marked her when they'd been fishing, it had set off a chain reaction of primal instincts. He'd teased the wolf with completion, now it wanted to finish what he'd started.

It wanted to bite the sexy human.

It wanted to mate with her.

It wanted to keep mating with her until she was tired, spent, and satisfied, but still hungry for his cock. Until she looked much like she did now, after sleep. Puffy eyes. Rosy cheeks. Plump lips. Messy hair.

She smiled hesitantly at him. "Your turn. I'll keep watch."

His brow lifted with indignation, to which she returned with a roll of the eyes.

"You need your rest for this coming battle," she insisted. "Even big strong warrior types like you need rest."

"Not going to happen. Let's speak to Gunther first." He pointed to his stash of fish. "We have plenty to pay him with."

"Oh great. Well done, Thorne. I can't believe you caught more!"

He had the sudden urge to go to her, to bask in her praise. He wanted it.

Laurel's mood sank when her eyes hit Sparrow, still fast asleep. "He's so innocent like this."

Thorne shrugged. "Not too innocent to get put in here."

She shot him a glare. "Do you even know what he did?"

"Doesn't really matter. He's in."

She clicked her tongue. "That kind of attitude sucks. What are you fighting for, Thorne, if not for a world where injustice doesn't rule? I think we have a duty to this kid. The system here has failed him."

He opened his mouth to retort. Then shut it. She was right. And Thorne knew better than anyone about collateral damage from a broken system. He'd failed in his duty recently. A young Guardian wolf shifter had died. Cloud had berated him for it.

"We'll work something out for him."

"Really?" Her eyes lit up, and it was everything Thorne wanted to live for.

That hope.

Trust.

Validation.

He cleared his throat and bent over Sparrow to wake him gently.

"Nap time is over," Thorne said.

Groggily, the boy woke up, but he didn't complain. Tough kid. Thorne handed Sparrow's knife back to him and kneeled until they were at eye level. At first, Sparrow blanched, but then Thorne spoke, and Sparrow's eyes widened to big saucers.

"Thank you for the loan of the knife," Thorne said.

"Y-y-you said thank you," Sparrow stuttered. "Y-y-you owe me."

"Well, look at that. So I did," Thorne agreed, a twitch to his lip. "Guess that means you can now make me do anything you want."

"Keep me safe," Sparrow blurted.

"Already doing that. Pick something else."

A small frown between those tiny brows. "Keep me... fed?"

"Try again."

"Help me escape?"

"That'll do. Agreed." Thorne clasped the boy's hand and sent mana into the agreement, marking it as binding between them. "We will get you out. Alive."

He leaned down closer and whispered, "Don't forget to be specific. If we didn't specify the alive part, escaping could also mean in death."

"Oh. Got it."

When Thorne straightened, he found Laurel smiling at him. And for the first time in a long time, he didn't revolt. He smiled back.

Together, they strode toward the barrier line for Gunther's warding. He held up the catch of three fish by the tails. "I think you've waited enough."

Gunther, who'd seen them coming, had come off his porch chair to meet them with a sour look.

"Tell us what you know," Laurel demanded, chin up.

A rush of affection surged in Thorne. It was enough for Laurel to dart a questioning glance at him. And what do you know, he Well-damned smiled again. When he turned that smile toward the orc, it turned wicked. He let his fangs elongate.

"If we're satisfied with your information," Thorne said. "You can have the fish."

"The king's guard paid me to bring Jasper in."

"Which king? Mithras?"

"Yes."

Thorne narrowed his eyes. "How long ago?"

The orc shrugged.

Laurel, the brazen female that she was, arched her brow and took the fish from Thorne's hands. Or tried to. It was heavy. In the end, she decided to let him keep hold and put her hand beneath the catch. Fire sparked on her fingertips.

"I don't have any problem cooking an early breakfast," she said. "I'm sure we have plenty of others watching in the wings who will want what we're too full to eat."

Gunther raised his palm, crinkled eyes widening. "He's the champion," he blurted. "Or he was the last time I fought."

Shock reverberated through Thorne. Jasper was the champion? Pushing his reaction way down, he continued. Now they were getting somewhere. "Is Jasper still the champion?"

"I don't know. The champion gets his own quarters, separate from down here. I ain't seen it, but heard it's real luxury."

"And you have no idea if he's still fighting?" Laurel asked.

"No. Now can I have the fish?"

"I don't know." Thorne rubbed the stubble on his chin. "Doesn't sound feasible that they would be able to hide a Guardian in plain sight, fighting in the Ring all these years."

"They put a mask on him," Gunther added. "It's metal. Hides his face."

A snarl ripped out of Thorne. His voice came out animalistic. "Metal? How is it the Order hasn't discovered this?"

"They painted it to look like bone. Maybe done some other things. But..." Gunther hesitated.

Laurel's flames sparked brighter.

"The mask stays on because it's bolted to his flesh. Even a Guardian can't resist the magic halting effects of metal piercing flesh. They force him to start the shift, then put the mask on. When he fights, he's frozen mid-shift."

Cold fury settled in Thorne's stomach. He'd heard of an undefeated beastly warrior of the Ring, but never had he imagined it would be a wolf shifter. Rush and Clarke's enemies had used that tactic on Kyra to halt her shift. They'd put a bullet in her and left it in. Until the bullet was clawed out, Kyra had been stuck mid-shift, a grotesque half-beast, half-fae. A permanent mask would also hide Jasper's distinguishing Guardian tattoo, eliminating any chance of discovery by the public.

The metal being a part of him could have been what was stopping Thorne's scrying attempts at finding him too.

But what about his other tattoos? Jasper had a myriad of them over his body. He'd sullied his skin as much as he could, gotten tattoos, and brawled and reveled regularly as a way to counteract his pretty face. He hated that his appearance took after the ethereal beauty of his father, the king.

Jasper had been here all along.

Sparrow let out a pained shout. When Thorne looked over, the binding rune on Sparrow's cheek glowed. He was being called to the Ring.

No. Not now. Thorne wasn't finished questioning Gunther. But as the rune glowed brighter, burned hotter, he knew they were out of time.

Thorne threw the fish at Gunther's wards. He leaped at Laurel, took her hand, and then grabbed Sparrow just before the transference spell finished activating. And when it did, all three of them teleported.

A whooshing displacement shot his equilibrium, but he dared not release his hold on Laurel or Sparrow. If he did, Laurel and he could end up in pieces. When the transference was over, and the dust settled, they found themselves standing in the middle of a large oval dirt stage. A multi-tiered crowd roared around them. And twenty feet away were two other prisoners, just coming out of their transference, getting ready to fight.

They were in the Ring.

CHAPTER
TWENTY-TWO

The roar of a crowd surrounded Laurel.

It took her a moment to gather her bearings. Sparrow had been called, and Thorne had latched onto Sparrow and her, so they all came. They were in the Ring.

About two-hundred feet long, and one-fifty wide, the fighting arena smelled like dirt, blood and urine. Sky and sun above. A twelve-foot-high wall surrounded the fighting floor. Three closed gates led somewhere and were possibly the only way of escape. Laurel shielded her eyes and looked higher. Three levels of bleachers housed patrons cheering from their seats—what looked like fae gentry and the echelon of Elphyne were on the ground level, then the general public were on the next two. It was like a football game. Only, there was no game. No. From the spilled blood in the sand beneath her feet, it was a fight for survival.

For the first time since she'd hatched her plan to find Jasper, she had doubts.

Worse. Could she keep Sparrow safe? The small boy was trembling with fear and as pale as the bone sword in their opponent's hand. Thorne looked ready to decimate as he scanned the arena for threats and presumably exits. Skin pulled taut over the slabs of hard muscle on his body. Fists flexed at his side.

"Stay behind us," Laurel said to Sparrow, eyeing the only other inhabitants of the Ring—two prisoners from under the hill.

Sparrow had been called up here on his own, which meant the people who ran this farce would make him fight those two much older, more capable, fae. Two adults against one boy? It sickened her.

To the side of the arena, behind a barrier of thick glass, she saw a cluster of guards or soldiers manically discussing the run sheet they had in their hands, most likely wondering how two other people had appeared with Sparrow.

So they were the ones to speak with.

Knowing Thorne would keep Sparrow safe, Laurel lifted her chin and strode straight for them. In all her experience rising to the top of her business, she learned the best way to succeed was to go in guns blazing from the start. The last thing she wanted was to be sent back under the hill. She must do this now.

"Laurel," Thorne growled, halting her.

"I'll be back," she replied with a look over her shoulder. "Look after him."

Laurel continued her brisk pace until guards manning the boundary started to approach. Most of them were the big burly orc type, but a few were her size. She could take them on if necessary. She could burn them all.

But she'd only get one chance, and then they might use a spell to protect themselves much the same way Thorne had during training.

She just needed to talk to the organizers.

She dared a quick glance back over her shoulder. Thorne, Sparrow, and their opponents weren't engaging. Everyone knew something wasn't quite right. Good. The longer they avoided fighting, the better.

"I'd like to talk to the person in charge, please," Laurel said to the orcs blocking her way.

"How about we send you back downstairs instead?" one replied with a smirk at his comrade.

"How about I set *you* on fire?" she returned. Flames sparked at her fingertips.

They scoffed, unperturbed. They wouldn't be so complacent if she sent the full force of her power at them.

"You either get your boss, or I'll get him myself." She eyed the fae who'd turned from the run sheet with sharp interest. His nose had been recently broken. Long brown hair was fashioned into braids at the front of his face. A thorny headdress perched on his head like a crown. No. It wasn't a crown. It was a part of him. Antlers. He must be the boss with his entitled posture.

"Try," said the guard.

Back at the ceremonial lake, Thorne had said emotion was her trigger. So she let the anger already building in her body have free rein. She thought about them bringing Sparrow up here to fight two adult fae. A growl slipped out. Then she thought about the fact the boy had been thrown under the hill in the first place. Then it was the humans she'd released from the cages. Whether they were even alive. She thought about the unfairness of feeling guilty about how her world ended. At feeling partly responsible, just like Clarke had. It wasn't their fault. They were the victims. *It was Bones's fault. The Void's fault.*

Flame grew from her hands, licked up her arms and became an inferno of mana pouring out of her hands. The heat was a pleasant companion to her rage and she let it all shine on her face, oblivious to the sound of the crowd shouting their excitement.

She wasn't doing this for them. Sick, sick bastards.

She was doing this for all the victims of this cruel world, all the women who'd had men pulling their metaphoric nails out. Rage turned her vision red.

"I'm only going to offer this once," she shouted to the organizers, still safely ensconced behind the boundary wall. But they were engaged. "Let the boy go, unharmed, and we will voluntarily fight your champion."

The antlered fae broke away from the pack, a self-satisfied smile on his twisted face.

He sneered at Laurel. "You're in no position to *volunteer*. We can send you back under the hill until we're ready for you."

The audacity in his eyes made her fingers twitch, and she ached to raze the smug dismissal from his face. She leveled her stare on the stag fae and welcomed the power brimming in her soul. She opened the floodgates. Let it out.

The flames from her arms cast a glow of orange and yellow and white, but also emanated from her body, her skin. She felt nuclear, like she was going to explode. As power rose through her body, a gust of wind tousled her hair. At once, all glamor on her body melted away. The rune on her cheek crumbled to dust, and the glamor on her ears dissolved.

A half smile curved her lips. "Clearly, your binding rune isn't as powerful as me."

The breath of the collective crowd held. The organizers gaped. The guards paled.

"What are you?" The stag-fae stuttered.

"Unstoppable. And human."

Shocked silence deafened her.

She hurtled onward. "This will be your first and only chance to have a powered human with her Well-blessed and mated Guardian do battle. You can either accept that, or we leave. What do you say to my offer?"

The stag nodded, but then stopped when his colleague tapped him on the shoulder and whispered something. Returning to her with an indecipherable expression, the boss said, "Be the last ones standing in a fight with the champion, and then you become the champion." He held up three fingers. "We get you for three battles. If you win all, then you are free to go after the third. Consider your sentence over."

Remembering Thorne's warning to Sparrow about being specific, she added, "Two battles, and you let the boy leave unharmed and unhindered after the first battle."

The organizers conferred, then nodded in agreement.

Laurel snuffed her flames out. She cast a glance over her shoulder and flinched at Thorne's furious face.

Surely he knew this was the only way to get what he wanted. She waited for his approval. He gave a surly nod and she released a breath. Good.

"We have a bargain," she said to the organizers and turned away. With any luck, they wouldn't realize they hadn't shaken on it, or made the binding, or whatev—

"Not so fast," one of them called.

Dang it.

Biting her lip, she turned back slowly. Sure enough, the boss had stepped onto the floor and approached, flanked by two guards. "We need to make it official."

To his credit, he repeated the bargain terms word for word. When it was done, he asked for Sparrow.

From the simmering anger down their bond, it was clear Thorne would have words with Laurel later, but for now, he squeezed Sparrow on the shoulder. "We will win. Don't worry."

Sparrow's eyes watered. "Than—"

"Don't!" Laurel interrupted. "We're not doing this for a favor. Thorne is a Guardian. It's his duty to protect Elphyne, and you're the best part of that." She turned to Thorne. "Where will he go after he's released?"

Thorne crouched low so he was at eye level with Sparrow. "There is a female fox-shifter who is the merchant of the vegetable cart in the south end of the markets. She is looking for someone to help her with her stall. If you permit, I will leave an endorsement on you to take to her."

"What is that?"

Thorne took Sparrow's thin arm and pointed at the inside of his wrist. "It is my mark spelled with a message. She only needs to touch it, and she will see. It may hurt a little."

Bravely, Sparrow nodded. Thorne's claw sprung from his fingertip and he scratched a shape onto the boy's soft skin. But Sparrow didn't cry. He nodded grimly once it was done and left the floor, joining the organizers on the sidelines.

Now it was just Thorne, Laurel, and the two prisoners. The murmurs and occasional shouts from the crowd meant they were getting restless. They'd expected a bloodthirsty fight to have started minutes ago. When Laurel glanced up, Thorne's mask of hate and anger was back. He stared at their opponents, but the irritation simmering down their bond was for her.

"Do you not agree with what I did?" she asked.

Still, he stared forward. "I don't agree with you thinking you speak for all of us."

Thought so. Damn. She felt a little bad about that. It ended okay, but like he said, it wasn't her place to decide. Thorne was more knowledgeable. He may have had an alternative solution that didn't mean they had to fight two battles.

"And you revealed your true identity," he growled. "You put yourself in jeopardy. Even if we get out of this, even if the champion is Jasper, they could be gathering armies beyond the walls, waiting for it all to be over." Now he glared at her. "Did you even think about the consequences of that? Word will get around about a powered human. Word might get to our enemies. It's bad enough the Void knows about the humans waking from your time, but if Queen Maebh or King Mithras get wind of it, don't you think they would exploit powered humans too? Maybe they'll want payback for all the fae humans have harvested mana from. Maybe they'll come for you!"

He growled again and looked away.

Shit. She really did mess up. "Sorry?" she tried.

But not even the tempt of a debt placated him. All she could do was face the two prisoners, wait for the champion and hope she wouldn't die.

TWENTY-THREE

Thorne sized up his opponents. Both hardened criminals had horns, were brawny, and scarred. But the most despicable part of this scenario was the bone weapons. One held a sword. The other, an ax. And they had been prepared to use them on Sparrow.

Something about that situation hit too close to home. Instead of Sparrow, Thorne saw himself as a child. He saw his uncle, Thaddeus, hand him over to the Order. Saw the Order pushing him toward the ceremonial lake—the inkeels.

Thorne bared his teeth.

It was time to bring Fury back. The binding rune on his cheek blocked his magic from leaving the arena, but Laurel had broken her rune. And with the bargain she'd made with the organizers, he didn't think there would be repercussions if he did the same to his own rune. Who cared if there was? He could take them. He would have Fury. The battle would be as good as won.

The crowned stag took the podium at the end of the arena and lifted his arms like a showman. His voice echoed across the bleachers as he riled up the impatient crowd with shallow words and inflammatory taunts. The crowd would get their money's worth.

Thorne used the opportunity to talk quietly to Laurel.

"When you used your power, how much did you spend?"

"What do you mean?"

"Do you have a sense of how empty your personal well is?" He frowned at her confusion, so clarified. "The abundance of magic within you."

"It feels the same. Why?"

Crimson. She'd expended that much and felt the same? Truly she had a bottomless well, but it gave him an opportunity.

"How did you remove the binding rune?" He tapped his cheek.

"I just got angry and let myself fill with power. Like, really angry. I think you were right, and emotion is my trigger."

It could be a confluence reaction. He'd stopped her from getting too mad at the ceremonial lake, but hadn't now, meaning that without boundaries, she excelled. The problem with uncontrolled magic was that combined with unchecked emotion, it could have combustible consequences. Not only could the power pulled from the Well be stronger, but it could be more chaotic. There was no certainty that if Thorne did the same, he would have the same outcome, but he had to try. If for some reason he was cut from his ability to shift, he would need his metal ax. It would kill any magical creature they threw at them.

He had to try.

A stab of guilt pricked him at the thought of taking her mana again without her permission, but she had spared no thought to his opinion when she'd strode over to the organizers and demanded her terms. Nor had she consulted him at the Birdcage.

Slowly, he focused on their bond. Her mana leaped to him as though waiting for his call, such was the connection of a Well-blessed mating. Such was the harmony of their unique soul bond.

As he drew on her mana, he burned his own, sending it into every fiber and cell of his body, letting himself welcome his old friends: wrath, fury and rage and hate. More. More, he drew, until Laurel shivered and didn't know why. Until his cheek started to burn. And yet more he took and tried not to let the disbelief get into his system and taint the confluence. *So much power. And there was still more to take.*

If anyone found out about this, anyone like the human leeches from Crystal City, then Laurel would be in danger of having her mana harvested.

"... And they think *they* can dictate how the game is played in the Ring," the announcer continued. Thorne pushed his voice out of his head, ignored the consequent roar of the crowd, and concentrated.

With a crack like thunder, the binding rune crumbled on his cheek, littering dust to the floor. Crouching, he distended a claw and scraped a rune into his right palm, the same rune as on Fury's handle back at Jasper's apartment. Now all he had to do was wait. Wait for the spell to find his ax, and wait for it to arrive in his palm. But when Laurel landed on her knees beside him, he wasn't sure they had enough time.

Her pallid skin held a sheen of sweat. Her head looked too heavy for her neck. Short dark hair was plastered to her cheeks. She looked at him with glassy eyes.

"Are you not well?" he asked.

No words. Perhaps no energy. She shook her head.

He took her hand, tested her pulse at her wrist and found it sluggish. Was this his doing? Had he taken too much of her mana, too fast? Well-blessed matings were rare and untested. Apart from Clarke and Rush, the last pairing was centuries ago. He should have searched the archives at the Order academy library before they'd left, and then perhaps he'd be armed with knowledge before attempting a drawing of this magnitude.

She will gain it back.

Simply by having her feet on the earth, she would start to replenish from the cosmic Well and rebuild her stores. Finding a source of power would be better, faster.

Thorne zoned back in on the announcer's speech. Something about making Thorne and Laurel pay for their disobedience. The hairs on the back of his neck raised in warning.

"What do we say to that?" the announcer shouted.

A roar of defiance merged with an undercurrent of collective boos and disgruntled comments. The spectators wanted blood, and Thorne and Laurel had taken that away from them. They wanted compensation.

The announcer waved down the horde. "Never fear, my friends, I may have bargained for only two battles for their freedom, but I never specified how long those battles would be." A roar of excitement. "Or how many opponents they shall have." Even more excitement. "Or what species they will be fighting!"

Deafening.

The crowd was inconsolable. Thirsty. They wanted blood? Thorne would give them blood.

"Laurel, you may have used too much of your mana at once. Take it easy. Let me handle this." Thorne stood before the crowd and let his claws loose. He met Laurel's curious stare with steadfast certainty. "You may change your opinion of me after this."

Too tired to respond, she simply met his gaze.

The cacophony from the crowd grew to a stadium-trembling roar of white noise and sparks exploded between Thorne and the prisoners. Must be the signal to start.

Begin.

The prisoners rushed toward Thorne, their eyes full of fury and desperation. Unfortunately for them, there was another Fury, the one that arrived via transference spell into Thorne's hand. He clenched tight around the handle and almost sighed at the relief of having his sworn weapon back where it belonged.

A slow, wicked grin stretched his lips.

Upon seeing the ax, the prisoners balked, but only for a stutter-step, and then they kept coming.

Thorne widened his feet. Braced. He rotated the ax in his hand. Once. Twice.

His opponents split, intending to go around him. He snarled, held Fury to the side, and clotheslined a prisoner at the neck with Fury's handle. With the first opponent down, he kept swinging the ax around and embedded Fury's bit into the other fleeing prisoner's back. The prisoner bowed, screamed in pain, and then collapsed to the ground.

Thorne ground his teeth and yanked Fury out, but the prisoner's body lifted with the ax. He used his boot to separate body from blade and then slid a warning glance to the first prisoner on the floor. He wasn't moving. *Probably broke his windpipe.* Possibly neck.

Briefly, Thorne considered chopping those antlers off to use as a makeshift weapon, but the binding runes on both prisoners' cheeks flared blue, and they sank into the ground, heading back under the hill. Surprised, Thorne lifted his brows. He expected the transference spell to react differently. Perhaps there was more they'd neglected to tell Thorne about the binding rune. *Doesn't matter now.* No doubt they would continue to travel through the dirt until they landed somewhere under the hill, and if they died, manabeeze would escape their body and join the rest of the ghosts in the false sky.

He tapped the ground with his foot. Maybe the earth was spelled, and that's why no manabeeze could escape from under the hill. But that was a question for another day. He lifted his face to the crowd, held his ax high and roared, "That all you got?"

The crowd cheered. He cast his gaze around at the tiered seating and tried to commit to memory the brutes and heathens who believed this sport was righteous. He caught sight of a cluster of black-coats, Unseelie royal guards with their eyes locked in the distance, somewhere on the opposite side of the arena. Thorne followed their gaze and found a group of red-coats, Seelie royal guards staring right back at them.

Thorne sneered. Perhaps he should shift to wolf. Perhaps he would break the boundary of the Ring and meet some of them in the stands. They might be tasty.

"Thorne?" Laurel asked, now holding Sparrow's puny knife as she stared at something over Thorne's shoulder.

He whirled and caught one of the arena gates opening, cranking heavily upward. Something pawed at the gap beneath. Dust clouds bloomed. Muzzles sniffed, jaws snapped in haste to get out. With each increment the gate lifted, more of the beasts became visible. One. Two. Three. Four waradas. Small and hoglike, their insectoid armor made it extremely difficult to pierce and maim. Unless you knew where to hit. But the pincers on the sides of their jaws were sharp. If just one of them got Laurel...

"Holy shit," she gasped.

"If you are cornered, strike beneath the jaw where it is tender," he barked at her.

Waradas may be small, but they were quick. Once again, he considered shifting to wolf, but the ax would have better luck cutting through the wararda armor than his fangs. The little beasts broke free of their containment and charged.

With his left hand, Thorne threw a blast of hard air, and then propelled himself forward in the slipstream. The waradas scattered from his spell, but Thorne caught two of them in the head, splitting their skulls before they knew what had happened. The other two had rolled and recovered, then charged him. One. Two. He chopped. They were down. Dead. He twirled like a dancer, swung his ax, and caught the final warada under the chin as it charged. It flew back, airborne, and then crashed. When the dust settled, nothing moved.

It was all over in a matter of seconds, but he'd got them all. Laurel was unharmed.

He thought.

He turned back to Laurel and his stomach dropped.

She stood at the center of the arena, unharmed, but it was what he saw behind her that worried him. Another gate had fully opened. Bright light shone from the tunnel, and the dark silhouette standing in the hollow was tall, bulky and humanoid. But it wasn't human. Nor animal. It was something between.

Tribal drums started beating. The crowed whipped into a frenzy.

The thing in the tunnel was head to toe black fur. Sharp claws protruded from gnarled fingers. It had a thick neck, broad shoulders, and a bushy tail. Was this a wolf shifter caught between shapes? Jasper? While his face was covered by a bone mask that only showed yellow eyes through two holes, shaggy brown hair and pointed ears aimed skyward. Thorne sniffed, catching the metallic tang on the air. Not bone. *Iron.*

A growl ripped out of him. Gunther had been right.

Fur covered any power-enhancing tattoos. The mask hid the Guardian teardrop tattoo. But it was Jasper. Thorne knew it by the champion's scent.

Gripping Fury until his knuckles hurt, Thorne stalked warily toward his old mentor, one eye looking out for more danger.

The tick-tick-ticking of the gates opening.

The thump-thump-thumping of the drums.

And then a gurgling, hissing sound Thorne would never forget in his life. Well-hounds. Without turning, he knew there would be one, maybe two or three waist high beasts behind him. Canine cousins of wolves, but warped by mana so much that it bled from their eyes in a stream of blue iridescent acid. But he dared not turn, for the most dangerous beast was to his front, on the other side of Laurel.

TWENTY-FOUR

Yeah. This wasn't good.

Laurel didn't know which was worse, the strange Doberman like dogs stalking closer behind Thorne, or the thing she knew was behind her, but was too afraid to look at. Thorne's hard eyes locked over her shoulder, and he took slow and wary steps toward her, almost as if he didn't want to startle what was behind her.

She squeezed her eyes shut, imagining the worst. Something from Stephen King's IT maybe, or a fricking T-Rex. Who knew with this world? Who knew what fricking monsters were going to attack next?

Something had happened to her earlier and she felt wretched. Like she needed to sleep for days. Her arms were weighted. The breath dragged into her lungs. And her lids drooped heavily. But after seeing the dogs with dripping eyes, adrenaline hit her system and she started to wake up.

Taking a deep breath, she reached for her magic and held it ready. Plenty was still there, so it made no sense why she'd felt so woozy. The moment one of those dogs came at her, she was letting loose.

Thorne got to her side. Blue eyes crystalized with alarm.

"What is it?" she asked. "Behind me... no. Don't tell me. I don't want to know."

"It's Jasper," he grunted.

"Oh." Maybe that wasn't so bad.

And then a howl ripped through the arena. She slowly looked over her shoulder. Froze. That was *not* Jasper. That was a fucking werewolf.

"Holy mother of all."

"I'll take care of him," Thorne said. "You fire at the Well-hounds. Once they're burning, try to get the blade into them." He gritted his teeth. "No. Actually, you can't. I'll have to do it."

"Why?"

"Because the little dagger you have will be eaten by their acidic blood. The only reason my ax won't is that the Well-hound is a magical creature. Its blood is only acidic because of magic. My ax will nullify that. I'm not even sure if your fire will work on the Well-hounds. Their coats can deflect magic."

"So, I have to..." She turned fully to face Jasper realizing that her only other option was to fight him. She gulped.

"Just keep him busy. Throw fire at him, but don't... don't hurt him too much. Make a smokescreen. The metal mask will not only stop him from accessing his magic, but impede his sense of smell."

"Got it."

And then it was on.

The hounds leaped and Thorne whirled to fight, ax brandished high, and then cleaved down, taking his first hound. A devil come to life, his muscles bulged with deadly intent, and his eyes were lit by the blue fires of hell.

Laurel turned back to Jasper who ambled, slow but steadily toward her. Big wolf ears pricked forward over his mask. Shaggy brown and black hair, a matted mess behind his head. It was a small mercy his teeth were hidden. But not those claws. She licked her lips. "You can do this, Laurel."

Find your fire. Your only weakness is you.

Goddamn it. Those sayings worked better in picture frames on her gymnasium wall. The crowd roared louder. The drums beat faster. And Jasper threw his head back and howled from beneath his mask. The sound wrapped around her bones and rattled.

Good God. This was Thorne's mentor? He was *enormous.*

Flexing her fists, she waited for him to come. She intended to let him get closer before she released her flames, but in a blink of an eye, he launched, faster than her eye could see. She let the flames go on instinct but had no idea if they burned.

She was hit. Full body. By a big, furry, shaggy human-shaped monster.

She screamed and felt hands around her shoulders, claws digging into her skin. *Don't hurt him.* This was the person Thorne had been searching for. But the pain stabbing into her flesh, it was frightening. She didn't want to die.

She used fear to gather power. It gushed like a geyser and exploded from her in a blast that rattled the arena. Not fire. Just a tornado of air. How she'd managed that, or if Jasper had been disabled from the gust, she had no idea. Without waiting for the dust to settle, she got to her feet. An enormous cloud of arena dirt bloomed, masking everything. She tested her shoulder wound. It was shallow. She was fine.

For now.

The werewolf had caught her in its claws. It could have killed her, but it had gripped her more... out of curiosity?

She looked for Thorne in the screen of dust.

The crowd booed and her pulse sped up. Why were they booing?

Was it because they couldn't see through the dust cloud? Or was it...

A dog whined. Shrieked. Snarled.

"Thorne!" she shouted urgently.

She put her hand to shield her eyes as if that could help with visibility. Another whine cut off mid sound. Another snarl. The kind that sounded like a beast had something in its mouth and rattled from side to side. Twirling, she squinted, trying to see.

"Thorne!"

No answer. She coughed. The dust was thinning.

A shadow. Ahead. Was that the direction Thorne had gone? Or was she disoriented? Was it the werewolf—Jasper?

"Laurel!"

Her heart leaped. It was Thorne. Where? Where? She waved her hands before her face, trying to clear more dust-smoke. Thorne strode out of the bloom, more bloody than before. His ax dripped with a blue substance that hissed upon meeting the ground. Bright eyes scanned wildly, landed on her, and then burned with a light that squeezed her heart. He rushed to her, gripped the back of her neck and forced her to look into his eyes.

"You good?" he asked.

She nodded. "Just a few scratches."

"Jasper?"

"He's... I don't know. I was scared. I blasted. I... I don't know." *I'm sorry.*

Thorne gave a short, grave nod, and then pushed her behind him.

With nose lifted and scenting, he strode forward into dust. At least they could see the blue sky now. His hand moved from her hip, down to her hand, and forced it to a belt loop on his pants.

"Hold on until we get to a clear spot."

She nodded. Took hold. When she'd been body hit, she'd lost the bone knife. It was somewhere on the ground, buried beneath the dust. Thorne stepped forward cautiously, scenting the air, letting his nose guide them. Every so often, he would sneeze, clear his olfactory, and start again.

Suddenly, the boos stopped. The drums stopped.

Eerie silence.

The crowd cheered. Crazed. Dread coated Laurel's bones. What the...?

A thud. Another thud.

Footsteps?

Something drew close.

Out of the dust, a face from a horror movie. Yellow frenzied eyes peering from a full-faced mask. Gnarly claws. Brown fur.

Thorne ran to meet Jasper, but Laurel was still holding onto him. Her arm almost ripped from its socket as she was dragged along. She unhooked from his belt loop just in time. Thorne clashed with Jasper. He used the ax butt to push against Jasper's chest, forcing him backward. They wrestled. Went to the ground. More dust and sand exploded.

"Jasper!" Thorne roared. "It's me."

Laurel felt like a dumbass just standing there, but what could she do?

Nothing Thorne did changed Jasper's single-mindedness. The feral glint in his yellow eyes raged as he attacked.

"Have to get the mask off," Thorne muttered, grunted, and tried to rip it from Jasper's face.

Jasper howled in pain and lashed out.

"Fuck!" Thorne cursed.

Blood ran from Jasper's neck, where the mask was attached.

"What if I melt it off?" Laurel suggested. "Can we insulate his skin at the same time, as you did at the lake?"

Thorne pushed the long ax handle across Jasper's throat, choking and incapacitating him.

"Do it," he bit out. "I'll insulate him. Do it now."

Thank God. Fire was the only spell Laurel knew how to do well. She summoned her magic, let the flames build until sparks ignited at her fingertips.

"Move!" she shouted.

Thorne jumped back. She thrust her hands at Jasper and sent napalm his way, hoping to dear God that Thorne's insulation spell kept the heat, as well as the fire, from Jasper's skin because if it didn't... she didn't want to know.

"More!" Thorne yelled through the inferno. "Hot. Like at the lake."

She did as was told.

More fire. More flames. More heat. Until she felt giddy with it.

"Enough!" he roared.

Laurel snapped her hands closed, shutting the valve to her power. When it cut off, she felt like it rebounded in her body. Waves of dizziness came over her. The same lethargy she'd experienced before hit. But this time, she rolled to the side and vomited as she vaguely heard Thorne's voice.

"Jasper. It's me. Fuck, what have they done to you?"

Laurel gagged again. God, she felt awful.

A male moan. A groan. "Rush?" A gasp. "Rush." A whimper. "You came. You... I don't deserve it. I don't deserve to be rescued. Not when I left you... not when—"

"Hush, Jasper. It's Thorne. Not Rush."

"No. no. No. I shouldn't have let her die. Véda. She was pregnant. Not her fault. I should have said something."

"Jasper!"

"I looked after your son, just like you asked. I kept an eye on him for you." Another moan. A whimper. "Please don't hate me."

The air was clearing. The dust was settling. Laurel heaved in a breath to steady her nausea. The shadowed silhouettes that were Thorne and Jasper became clear. The plan had worked. The mask was now a molten puddle beside the fae with shaggy brown and black hair, pointed ears, and deeply tanned skin. Blue glowing marks circled his neck like a collar. He was naked. Distraught. Tortured. Manic.

Jasper's untamed eyes fixated on Thorne but failed to see him.

The look of anguish in Thorne's expression said it all. Jasper wasn't quite right in the head.

Drip. Hiss.

Drip. Hiss.

Laurel frowned. What was that?

Drip.

Hiss.

She turned her head, glimpsed black animal, blue leaking eyes, and then fangs snapped at her. She lifted her arm to shield herself. Teeth clamped down.

Pain exploded. Her scream curdled. Something snapped. Bone. Oh God, it was her bone. Crushed. The hound dragged her backward by her arm. Kicking and whimpering, she tried to keep up so the arm wouldn't tear from her body. That was her fear.

A roar of fury rattled from somewhere and she couldn't tell where. Tears ran in streams from her face. She managed to look down her body, to where she'd last seen Thorne.

Time stopped.

Pain stopped.

It was as though they'd split the fabric of the world and there was a space between breaths as her eyes met Thorne's across the distance.

His eyes were *torn*. Just like his emotions hurtling down their bond. Desperation. Indecision. He had Jasper in his grasp. Finally...

And Laurel?

What was she to him?

Nothing.

She exhaled. Tears brimmed. And she hurtled all her fury and rage and pain back at the beast still locked around her arm. She had no other weapon but her magic. Drawing on it as best she could, she sent fire at the beast, but it fizzled and sputtered as it hit the hound. Flames died out... doused as though drowned in water.

Helplessness swamped her. Magic didn't work against the beast.

This is it. I'm dying. Maybe this was why I was given a second chance. To help Thorne rescue Jasper. Now it's done.

Her eyes shut. Blackness. Then opened heavily. Tired. Tormented.

An anguished roar created an earthquake. She heard thudding. And then the beast latching onto her arm was gone. Or maybe her arm was gone. She couldn't tell. It hurt so much. Acidic fire burned in her veins.

"Laurel." Thorne's sweet, rough voice. "Hold on."

Pressure on her arm... or what was left of it.

He kept his hand clamped on her wound, a deep furrow to his brow. "You'll be fine. They have healers here. I can triage a little. Here. Bite down."

He put something between her teeth. Hard. Dirty. Salty. The ax handle. It barely fit between her teeth, but it did the job.

Searing white-hot agony engulfed her arm. She screamed around the wooden bit, eyes streaming with tears. Blinking, she craned her neck and saw a bright light bleeding from Thorne's hands. He was doing something. Healing her somehow... the pain ebbed like cold water had been thrown on it.

She spat out the handle.

"Jasper?" she croaked.

Thorne's brows lifted in the middle. He looked beyond Laurel's body. She followed his glance and found Jasper, safe, and sound. One knee up, elbow resting on it, looking at them with a strange curiosity, as though he should know them.

Those blue glyphs around his collar winked in the sun. Like Thorne, Jasper was well built. But where Thorne was hewn from rough rock, Jasper was smooth marble. Stunning face, perfectly carved, almost pretty in his masculinity. The rest of him was solid, strong and infallible, but for his mind and confused golden gaze.

"He's cursed," Thorne explained quietly. "Doesn't quite remember me. But I don't think it's the curse that's done that to him. I think his mind is protecting itself. He's been tortured. Maybe it's both."

A hush swept over the crowd.

And Laurel's heart stopped. This was the moment of reckoning. Would the organizers send more opponents out? Was this enough to beat Jasper?

As if reading her thoughts, Thorne grit out, "I won't kill him. I'll kill everyone in the crowd if they try to make me."

Turned out, they didn't.

Jasper's blue glyphs flared brightly. He howled in pain, clutching his head.

"No!" Thorne shouted. He darted a panicked glance to Laurel's arm then back to Jasper. "I can't." He choked. "I can't get to you, Jasper. *I'm sorry.*"

Then, like the transference spell that had taken the first prisoners, Jasper started to melt into the ground. All around them, the animals did too.

"I'll come for you," Thorne shouted, and then one by one the hounds and Jasper all disappeared until nothing but blood and acid stains were left.

"Ladies and gentlemen," shouted the announcer with a note of disdain. "We have our new champions!"

TWENTY-FIVE

Thorne glared at Laurel. Bitterness leaked from his eyes like the acid from the hounds, and it was all directed at her.

She was to blame. She was wounded. She couldn't protect herself. She led them here.

Here—where he'd found Jasper and lost him. Thorne's entire life had boiled down to that moment when he couldn't save the male who had saved him.

He'd chosen her instead.

Pain squeezed his heart at the image of Laurel being dragged by one of the hounds he'd failed to dispatch. The sight burned into his retinas. The blood. The caustic acid. Her blood-curdling scream. His hand trying to stem the bleeding. Her pale face and blue lips and blood pooling on the ground beneath them.

He sucked in a deep breath, let air fill his lungs, and then *roared*.

It frightened Laurel. She balked from his touch. His fingers slipped from her blood-wet arm. But it didn't matter, the bleeding had stopped. It wasn't as bad as he'd originally thought, just messy. The healers would take care of the rest.

He roared again.

And the crowd thought it was in victory.

Not again.

He rubbed his aching chest. *Not again.*

"Thorne," Laurel tried. She reached for him, but he shook her off.

Storming to his feet, he picked up Fury, and then scooped Laurel into his arms. She was his now.

CHAPTER
TWENTY-SIX

Thorne carried Laurel with confident strides toward the gate leaving the arena. She felt safe cocooned in his arms, protected by his body, despite the turmoil coming from him. So much pain, confusion, and just... feelings. It suffocated Laurel. Full body trembles wracked her body. Her arm stung, itched, and she was afraid to look at it. But it was functional. Her fingers moved. She could bend at the elbow. Thorne had saved it.

He'd saved her.

The enormity of what had happened sank in.

He could have let her die. There was a moment she wasn't sure what he would do. But he'd chosen her. Over Jasper.

The words kept repeating in her head—he chose me—along with disbelief. Everything after that happened in a blur.

They stopped at the exit in the shadow of the tunnel that led from the arena. The smarmy announcer waited for them.

"You think you've won?" he sneered. "Maybe this time. But you'll be back for another battle, and we'll be ready for you."

Thorne's return stare said he wanted to rip the announcers crown of antlers from his head and then gut him.

"What did you do with the champion?" Thorne pulled Laurel in tighter.

"He's not the champion anymore. You two are. At least for tonight. Enjoy it while it lasts."

The ground rumbled. The walls shook. Thorne leveled his glare at the announcer. "Don't make me repeat myself."

"Relax. He's gone under the hill. He'll be back for a rematch. We can't let the crowd miss out on that opportunity." Sweat over the announcer's brow betrayed his nerves.

"When?"

"Whenever we decide."

With that, Thorne turned and called for a healer like he owned the place.

Laurel patted Thorne's chest. "Sparrow?"

His eyes softened on her and then hardened as he turned to the announcer, still watching from the wings. "Where is the boy?"

"We let him go."

"You're not holding him?"

"We don't need another mouth to feed. He's gone with the crowd."

Laurel breathed a sigh of relief. With any luck, Sparrow would be just about at the market stall with Thorne's acquaintance. Still, she couldn't help but worry.

"Where is the healer?" Thorne barked.

"You'll get one in your room," the announcer replied. He gave them one last scornful look and then shouted some directions to the guards and left. Five guards weren't enough to hold Thorne back. One look at his battle-ax told them that. But they did their job anyway. Because if Thorne got through them, there were probably more somewhere. Thorne was strong, but not invincible. They escorted Thorne and Laurel through a labyrinth of dark tunnels until they came to a stone staircase and went up.

At the top of the stairs, they walked down a corridor to a single bolted door at the end. Waiting was a slim, female elf who pushed through the soldiers to get to them. Voluminous pantaloons gave Laurel pirate vibes. Various bottles and tinctures dangling from her belt tinkled as she moved.

Thorne gently put Laurel on her feet.

"Are you hurt anywhere else?" The healer reached for her arm.

Thorne caught the healer's wrist and growled in warning.

The healer didn't balk. She glared back at Thorne. Laurel liked her already.

"What are your qualifications, healer?" Thorne demanded.

"I studied with the Royal Apothecary in the Autumn Court for fifty years under Rubrum rule."

Thorne let go of her wrist and gave a disgruntled nod.

The healer quickly took Laurel's arm, assessed no immediate threat to her life, and then ushered them inside the room.

The guards left them at the door.

Inside was a vast suite with polished marble floors. Furthest at the back, enormous ceiling-to-floor windows overlooked the arena. Before the window was a giant bed, bigger than king-sized, and with fabric overhangs draping from the roof. Closer was a series of lounges with velvet embroidered cushions. And before the lounges, inset in the ground and surrounded by brightly colored and glittering tiles, was a long Roman-style bath fit for at least ten people. Steam lifted from the vanilla-scented water.

"Sit," the healer ordered and pointed to two facing wooden benches before the bath.

Thorne helped Laurel to one bench, and then sat on the opposite with his fists on his thighs, glaring at them, silently daring the healer to make a wrong move.

The healer took Laurel's arm, tested it, and asked a few questions about pain and mobility. She cleaned it, found Laurel's skin was healed over, and then was in the middle of applying a salve that tingled and burned when a group of beautiful female fae came in. Dressed scantily, each carried different supplies. Food. Clothes. Drink. Perhaps wine. A large bowl of hot water, soap, perfume, and towels.

The healer massaged Laurel's arm, and she felt her entire body relax. Her lazy gaze wandered back to the new arrivals.

Three females. Two elves. One a brunette, the other with long black hair and a plump-lipped smile. The third was a pretty faun with cloven feet, small bumps on her head for horns, and voluptuous curves at her hips and breasts. All were stunning. Each wore similar pants to the healer, but where the healer wore a modest jacket, these wore revealing bustiers that showed ample midriff and cleavage. A rosebud tattoo graced their upper arms.

Rosebud.

After putting down their trays, two walked over and demurely offered each Thorne, and Laurel an elixir.

"For your energy restoration." The black-haired fae curtseyed.

Laurel accepted her elixir with a smile and drank it. She licked her lips. It tasted like ginger.

Laurel's curiosity turned to irritation when all three Rosebuds went to Thorne and began washing him, doing their best to lather him with extra attention. He stiffly watched Laurel, blue eyes blazing, hardly paying attention to the female attendants, even when their small hands slipped and caressed his body, inching lower over his abs, closer to his belt with each pass.

Could he not see what they were doing?

Laurel squirmed with irritation.

"Sit still," ordered the healer. "They'll relieve you next."

Relieve me!

As in... she snapped her gaze back to Thorne, then down to the very big bulge in his pants. He was hard. Was that there before or after the Rosebuds had touched him?

Sensing her unease, the healer clarified. "A warrior's body is flush with excitement post battle. It is customary for the champion to have his needs met. In this case, we have two champions. You'll have to wait until I'm done before your turn."

Oh, hell no.

The Rosebud attendants made cooing sounds and little feminine moans of appreciation as they washed Thorne. As if they were getting off from cleaning Laurel's man. And he *was* her man. She knew that now. He may pretend otherwise, but deep inside, he knew it too.

They'd gone through too much.

The black-haired elf with the killer lips bent to Thorne's ear and whispered something. When he didn't answer, or even flinch, the elf nodded to her companions. The faun began to unplug the buttons on his breeches. He did nothing. The brunette's hand slipped down his stomach, bumped over his abs, and dipped inside his pants, gasping in delight at what she found.

He did nothing.

Enough.

Laurel shot to her feet, yanked out of the healer's grasp, and slapped the Rosebud's hand away.

"Out," she ordered, pointing at the door. *"Out!"*

They blinked in surprise at Laurel, so she screamed it again. And again. Until everyone in that room scurried in fear. Even the healer picked up her things.

Laurel chased them all out, not satisfied until the last pair of bouncing breasts left the room. She slammed the door behind them, only vaguely registering the five guards still outside before they closed and bolted the door. She whirled back to Thorne.

He had just sat there while they fondled him. While they put their hands on places that even she hadn't touched yet.

She stormed back and stood before him, hands on her hips. His gaze still looked ahead, his fists were still clenched on his thighs. Was he... in shock?

No. He had a fricking boner. It strained against his pants. He'd let them touch him. The image of that slut's hand moving down his pants infuriated her. How dare he let her do that. Laurel wanted to shake him. Wanted to shout in his face and slap him.

"What's wrong with you?" she accused and shoved him squarely in the chest.

He barely moved backward.

Slowly, his eyes lifted to hers and her stomach bottomed out. Something dark flickered in the depths of his blue ocean. Dark, dangerous, furious.

"Me?" He tensed. Sinews and tendons became visible. Veins popped. Red-colored his face. "What's wrong with *me?*"

He stood so fast, Laurel stepped back. And then he advanced, crowding her space. Hot, demonic eyes glared at her. Another step back and she fell onto the bench, staring up at him.

"You're the one who got me into this mess," he growled, looking down at her. "From the very beginning, you've been a thorn in my side."

She gasped. A thorn in his side? Flabbergasted, she wanted to rail at him. She thought they were beyond this! After everything they'd been through.

Then it hit her.

Maybe he needed to work through it all verbally. Maybe they needed clarity.

She scowled at him. "You're the one who's so Goddamned angry and mean. You called me a whore!"

"You danced and dressed like one," he shot back.

"You're an ass!"

"You do whatever you want, no thought for the consequences."

"That was the point! You wanted me to. I did that for you!" Because she was so eager for his approval, she realized suddenly. All the fight left her. The next words came out a vehement whimper. A bitter accusation. "All you've wanted to do was to save him. But you saved me."

He blinked. Deadpanned.

"Why did you pick me?" Tears stung her eyes. Her throat clogged up and in that one question, the weight of the world suffocated her.

Why her?

Why did she get to live when others died? Why not her family, her parents, her neighbor? Why not someone who was a saint in her time, a soldier or a philanthropist? Why the woman who worked herself to the bone, and the woman who was afraid she was broken inside. Why. The. Fuck. Her?

Thorne growled, grasped the back of her neck, and roughly lifted her to her feet. Gasping, her eyes flared. Her heart hammered painfully against her ribcage. He squeezed the column of her neck, tight and almost painful. He studied her, seemingly at a loss for words. All she could feel down their bond was a raging torrent of emotion. Nothing she could decipher.

"Why?" she whispered bravely. "Why choose me?"

Confusion warred with hate on his face. "Because... because..."

"Let it go, Thorne. I can take it."

His gaze hardened. But still, nothing.

"Say something!" She shoved him, caught the sight of her twisted nails, turned her fingers into fists and hit him again.

And again.

Each time she lost energy until she slid her palms up his smooth chest and stilled, over the thudding beat of his heart.

The rough pad of his thumb swiped up the delicate front of her neck and circled against the hollow of her throat, her airway. Was he going to strangle her? Snap her neck? She held him with her stare, the question in her eyes.

"Because I can't breathe when you're around," he rasped. "And I detest it. I can't think. I can't move. I've survived a decade without him, but the thought of a single day without you... I hate it. I hate that I chose you. Hate that I want you so bad I can't sleep at night. Hate that it took me so long to realize you want me too."

He crushed his lips to hers and flattened her to his body. Thank God. *This*. This is what she'd been waiting for. A sign that he wanted her. That he needed her as much as she needed him. A strangled groan escaped him as his tongue demanded entrance to her mouth. She opened to him, and surrendered as he sank into the kiss with wild, hungry strokes of his tongue.

I hate that I chose you.

She shoved him away. "Fuck you, Thorne."

Heaving in ragged breaths, they both stared daggers at the other, but he refused to let her go. His fingers flexed against her shoulders.

No. Fuck him because she wouldn't be that person to him, the reason for his hatred, an excuse for his behavior. It wasn't fair. This wasn't her fault. She never chose to be mated to him. She never asked to be brought back to life. She didn't deserve it. Lip trembling, she broke the hold he had on her and turned her back on him, intending to go anywhere she could.

He grabbed her wrist, yanked her back, and slammed her body against his where he held it.

"No," he growled, eyes on fire... desperate. "You don't walk away from me."

"I do whatever the fuck I want. You hate me."

His eyes widened. Then his brows slammed down again, infuriated. "I hate me, Laurel. Not you. *Me*."

Oh, God. No.

No, Thorne.

Her anger melted away. She cupped his stubbled jaw and he flinched. She brought his gaze back to hers. What stared back at her wasn't a fearsome Guardian, but a lost little boy. Someone hurting for so long, the pain had become the poisoned air he breathed.

"I don't hate you," she murmured.

"You should."

"But I don't."

His breath turned ragged, rough, big. He gulped in air, pressed her to his chest. Harder. As though he really were afraid she would leave him. His heart pounded as though it would break through his flesh and leap into hers.

"Laurel." Panic tightened his deep voice. "I don't... I don't..."

"Know how to be different? I know," she said gently. "Let me show you."

More panic down their bond. More ragged breaths.

"Thorne," she whispered, lifted on her toes and drew close to his lips. "Let me show you how to be loved."

She kissed him. At first, he tensed, so she pressed her lips to his jaw. Then to the corner of his mouth. To the other side. To the bottom of his ear where she licked and suckled his lobe lovingly. Slowly, he relaxed.

"Let it go," she muttered. "All that armor you wear over your heart, let it go."

A long guttural moan rattled his body. His legs buckled. He spun them until he landed on the bench and she straddled him, still cupping his face. He buried his face in the crook of her neck, nuzzled into her hair and inhaled deeply. He held her tight. So tight.

"Don't..." he whispered against her neck. "Don't ever walk away from me."

It was more of a plea than a demand. And that's why she shook her head and replied, "I won't."

Another long shuddering breath left him. His teeth grazed over the skin running from her neck to her shoulder, kindling her desire. Beneath her, he hardened again until she felt it between her legs.

"Be mine, Laurel," he murmured against her flesh as he licked and suckled her sensitive spots.

"I already am."

His teeth sank in. She gasped, arching into him. Pain and desire held court in her body. The sting of his teeth versus the pleasure between her legs, at her breasts pushing against him, at his mouth as he suckled her skin, licking and paying homage to it. Part of her wanted him so badly, she rocked wantonly. The other part was aghast. He'd bitten her! Aghast, but delighted at his passion. His need for her was so strong, he played rough. She needed that too. Needed to know how much he wanted her.

She wanted all the fire. Even if it burned.

He came off her, pupils dilated, drugged, fangs elongated and bloody. Her blood.

And he was happy.

Her hand clamped over her neck. "Is it bad?"

The propriety glint in his eye sent shivers down her spine, right to where it pooled with heat in her groin. She squirmed. He steadied her on his lap.

"I marked you," he replied, voice thick and deep. "Now everyone can see that you're mine."

Laurel touched her tender skin, cupping her palm over the bite mark. Her badge of honor, the markings of love. She grinned.

"Maybe next time, just buy me a ring?"

"I'll do that too. Whatever you want. And this is the one and only time my teeth will sink into your flesh. Mating is for life."

His lazy, heated gaze raked down her body, what he could see of it anyway. Deciding her shirt was a hindrance, he pushed it up her thighs and then growled with barely restrained longing as her underwear came into sight. He thrust his hips and watched where their intimate parts joined through the fabric. He did it again. She moaned as sparks of bliss shot from their connection.

Thorne pinned her with his icy-blue stare. Something wholly inhuman stared back at her. It was the wolf. Hungry. Demanding. Primal. "I'll have my mate now."

Claws distended from his fingers and ripped her shirt clear down the middle. She gasped in delight. Bolstered by her response, he did the same to her underwear, flinging bits of torn fabric until there was nothing left on her body. He drank in her nakedness, loved what he saw, and licked his lips.

"Let's get you cleaned up."

"I don't mind if you don't mind," she said cheekily. Dirty sex. She was down for that. Down for it dirty. Down for it clean. Down for it all.

He shot her a hard stare. "Laurel. I'm going to lick every inch of your body. I mind."

Oh.

Plumping the pillows of her bottom, he gave a self satisfied grunt and then slapped her. The sting hit her ass and rocked her most sensitive part. She moaned in earnest. Then he carried her to the bath, where he lowered her feet first into the hot water. She slithered down his body and immersed alone, bereft.

The water was thigh high, but she sank until completely under. Heat infused her tired muscles. Laurel held herself underwater for a moment to collect herself. She was about to do this. With Thorne. He'd marked her. She was his.

I'll have my mate now.

A yearning so strong and pure surged through her. He'd finally let go of his hatred and put his passion to good use. And he was invigorating. She surfaced and found him staring at her, eyes at half-mast and full of greedy need. He idly played with the button on his pants, erection straining so hard it looked painful. He caught the direction of her gaze and a slow, indecent smile curved his lips.

There went those dimples, stopping her heart. *Damn, boy.*

Pretending she had control of her hormones, she paddled backward until her back hit the tiles and she rested her arms along the bath length. Her top half emerged from the water, and he clearly enjoyed the sight.

"Strip," she demanded.

With a cocky lift of his brow, he did. Slowly. He hooked thumbs in the belt loops and lowered his pants to the ground. No underwear. A body made from every woman's fantasy. Defined musculature, broad shoulders tapering to a narrow waist of perfection. The light fuzz of dark silver hair. And she knew she'd seen it before, but never like this. His cock was thick, proud, and long. Rock hard and waiting for her. He took it and squeezed.

"I like the way you look at me," he murmured hoarsely.

"Don't make me wait too long," she teased.

He slid into the bath and swam to her where he crowded her with his big body. All that power under the skin. Strong enough to cleave through those vicious arena beasts all on his own.

God, he was hot. Sexy. Heady. Vanilla steam everywhere. Coming right off his skin. His gaze dipped to the mark on her neck and flared with possessive pride. He kissed the wound gently, licked around it, and rumbled appreciatively. It drove Laurel wild. Then he came up until his lips hovered over hers, teasing with his breath. The look on his face showed he struggled to believe this was real too. That it wasn't some dream gone in the morning.

A drop of water trickled down Laurel's cheek and ran to her lip. His pink tongue darted out, licked, lapped, and then ran along her bottom lip until he sucked it completely into his mouth, biting between his teeth. The same teeth that had pierced flesh but were now so gentle.

That was it. The button on her restraint.

She pawed at him, touching everywhere, scratching, needing, dying... until she found his shaft, wrapped her fingers around it, and pumped. His breath came in ragged bursts as he thrust into her. But he didn't forget his promise. He licked and kissed over her entire face, shoulders, ears. He nibbled, nipped, and drove into her hand. And then he drew back, eyes glassy and full of dark promises.

"You're incredible," he said.

Stupefied.

A breath later and he lifted her onto the edge of the bath. She gasped at the cold tiles beneath. He tasted her lips, her stomach, breasts, nipples. She threw her head back. "Yes, Thorne. Everywhere."

"Everywhere," he grunted and spread her thighs. Upon seeing her intimately, his eyes lit up. They flared blue. She was sure the color changed... became vibrant. Luminescent.

"Fuck." He gave a throaty groan as he stared between her legs. And then he buried his face there, feasting. He kept going. Licking and laving and thrusting with his tongue. He inserted a finger and stroked, plunged, and thrust deep into her core. Like a relentless machine, he worked her until her nerves coiled tight. Until she felt it coming but was helpless against it. Screaming, she broke apart, thighs quivering around his head with her release, fingers clawing into his hair as she struggled to hold on.

When the last of her throes died, he dragged her from the tiles, turned her, and bent her over the bath edge, face first.

"I'm going to have you like this," he growled softly into her ear. "And then I'll take you again with you on top. But for the first... like this."

She nodded and grinned. "For the first."

He slapped her rear. She jolted, felt the echo of her orgasm between her legs, and then went liquid against the tiles. Couldn't speak. *Do it again.*

"And I'm going to spill my seed on your back."

She nodded. Whatever he wanted. God, that was sexy. Even the way he spoke about it. Men were so crude in her time. This fae was...

"So I don't get you with child."

Her heart clenched. She held her breath and turned slightly to lock eyes and then nodded. *My poor baby.* The damned unsanctioned breeding law had done a number on him. She placed her palms on the hard, wet tiles and lifted her rear in invitation. His big hand landed on her head, almost completely covering it as he pushed gently until her cheek pressed against the tiles where he pinned her.

For a moment, she froze, confused. Fear wanted to rear its ugly head, but... *Trust.* She trusted him. Completely. This was more about his fear.

For the first... like this.

Once the realization hit, and she'd surrendered to that trust, every feminine muscle clenched in anticipation. She was excited. Intoxicated by his masculine smell. The heat of him against her spine. The steady press of his hand against her head. Firm, but not unforgiving. Pleading. He needed her to stay still.

A finger, maybe a claw, traced lightly down her spine, eliciting a gasp from her lips. He traced a circle on each cheek of her bottom. She squirmed and tried to look, but he pushed her head back down. This time, he curled fingers into her hair and gripped tight, perhaps readying himself. *Please ready yourself.* The sensation of her hair being strained at the roots did something inside. It was tight, but not painful. Passionate, but gentle. Loving, but rough. A rush of pleasure surged at her swollen apex. She would come again, without even being filled.

The anticipation was killing her.

A desperate moan released from her lungs. "Hurry," she pleaded.

But he didn't. With his free hand, he continued to explore her rear, smacking her playfully, tickling her right where the blood rushed and still pulsated from her recent release. He swiped his fingers through her wet entrance, dipped inside, pressed against her nub. She bit into her palm, whimpering.

I'm so ready.

Blunt pressure at her entrance came in a gentle, almost hesitant manner. She wiggled to let him know she was good, and he slid his length along her wet folds, through the gap between her thighs. A strangled groan later, and he murmured, "I could come just like this. Your ass and thighs are so firm."

Gasping, she pushed back into him. "Don't you dare. I want you inside me."

A hoarse chuckle. "Yes, my queen."

And then he thrust in. All. The. Way. In. She cried out, palms slapping the tiles. Water splashed. Sensation exploded inside her. He filled her completely. Stretched her. But he didn't move. He held her prisoner.

He cursed repetitively, coming to terms himself.

God, she needed to see him. She could imagine his incredible physique straining too. Muscles that were corded and sinewy. Neck tendons and veins distended. His sexy face contorted in determination.

The weight at her head disappeared only to reappear at her waist. He gripped steadily, fingers flexed, and then he pulled out... only to slam back in with a force that sent her sliding along the tiles. He dragged her back into position and held tighter.

"You will take me," he declared. Thrust. "Always."

Her eyes rolled in pleasure.

"Always." He thrust again. "Just me." And again. He kept going, mad, driven, hard, fast. Skin slapped. Pounded. "No fucking dancing pixies."

And again.

"No fucking dancing orcs."

She grinned.

He picked up the pace. Heat gathered at the base of Laurel's spine again. She bit her finger and let herself come apart, whimpering in breathless gasps as he grunted, pulled out, and released on her back, using the gap between her bottom to wring the last of his desire. When he was done, he yanked her back to him in a punishing embrace.

Boneless, they sank into the water and almost submerged until he swam backward to settle on a step. He positioned her between his legs. They floated in a way that felt like heaven, but as her gaze slowly lifted to the ceiling, she knew they weren't.

They were prisoners.

TWENTY-SEVEN

Hours later, Thorne had taken Laurel in the bed, on the couches, and against the glass windows facing the empty arena under the moonlight. They couldn't get enough of each other. With her beneath him, she was accommodating, encouraging, and always eager for what he wanted. Patient for what he needed. And she was sure to tell him what she desired too. With her on top, she was a minx with never-ending stamina.

And if he panicked about releasing inside her, she handed him control. Without question.

After their last time, they'd ended on the big bed and were now tangled in silk sheets. She was quite honestly his perfect match, meeting him pound for pound of flesh until they'd both dropped exhausted and slipped into sleep.

Thorne didn't sleep long. He woke near dawn and stared at the overhang of fabric above them, gently stroking her arm as she curled into his side, drifting in and out of sleep. There were no words to describe how it felt to have her in his arms, knowing that she would be there every night from now on. He couldn't stop thinking about what his future would hold. They would get out of here, there was no doubt in his mind. And there was no going back. He'd marked her. Completely and irrevocably, she was his mate. Forever. Both in soul and in body. The idea both scintillated and worried him. He was uncertain if she understood the gravity of this commitment.

She'd thought the bite mark was cute. She'd grinned when he told her she would never dance with another male fae. But there was more to this than cute or a grin. Every male fae would be able to smell Thorne on her. If they were decent, they would treat her respectfully. He would also react viscerally when seeing other males too close to her. He would get possessive and irrational if they overstepped their bounds. The wolf in him would react differently too, now that he'd sunk his teeth and claws into her.

It wouldn't let go, no matter what. Even if she came to hate him for it. Even if she tried to walk away.

You know I'm not the marrying type.

Those had been her words on the day he'd met her. Was marriage the same as mating, or was it different? At that time, he'd not been keen about it either. But now he found he hoped for things he dared not dream before.

The blue Well-blessed markings sparkled on both their arms, shining brighter than before. Perhaps the Well had been right to pair them up. He would give it that. And he would not give her up. Even for Jasper.

A rush of guilt swamped him. His touch tightened on her arm. She stirred and opened her eyes.

"What is it, Growly?" she murmured, running her fingers over his stomach.

She caught sight of her warped nails in the dawn light and snatched her hand back.

"Don't do that," he rumbled.

"What?"

"Don't hide yourself around me, Laurel. We're beyond that now."

"I know." She exhaled and rolled to her back. She said nothing for a long time before speaking again. "It's just... no matter what I do, how boss-lady I feel, it's still there in the back of my head."

"What is?"

"Bones is here. In this time." Her eyes flared with emotion. "And I hate him. I want him gone. I've never said that about anyone before."

He kissed the top of her head. "Then I will make it my life's mission to remove him."

"Just like that?"

He nodded. Whatever she wanted, he would give it to her.

She frowned and looked away again. "I hear you say that, and I believe you—I mean, jeeze, you're a one-man army—but then I wonder if it will be enough. Is it even right? I don't want this need for revenge to define me. Do you know what I mean?"

Sometimes pain occupied a permanent place in your soul. It was an unwelcome tenant, festering until it came back to haunt you when you least expected. Jasper's iron mask came to mind and Thorne knew that his mentor would have his own tenants to worry about when they found a way to get him out. But looking at Laurel, flushed and spent in his arms, he knew that his pain was smaller. His tenant grew quieter, more obedient.

She touched him again. "You're thinking about him."

"Are you sure your arm is healed?"

"Bit late to ask now," she joked. She gave him a look that said she knew he'd avoided the topic but nodded. "It's been fine since we got back from the Ring. I don't know what you did, but it's like new."

This brought a frown to his face. His spell wasn't supposed to completely heal her. He didn't have the skills. His healing magic was triage at best. But he did heal her. And the only explanation he could come up with was that their union was Well-blessed. Perhaps this knowing of each other's emotions had helped. There was much to learn about their special, intimate union.

"There's something else." She sat up and brushed loose strands of hair from her eyes. "I can feel it. You're the one who said we're beyond hiding things now, so spill."

He didn't want to burden her with this, so he pushed aside the silken sheets and got to his feet. He went to the window. The first rays of dawn peeked over the horizon of the arena. They were on the uppermost level, above the highest tier of bleachers. Around the stadium, he saw their room wasn't the only one above the stands. But he couldn't see into any windows and suspected the glass was manufactured to allow users to see out, but not in. All the better to manage secret prisoners.

Jasper could have stared out at the arena, just like this.

He could have done it for years locked in here, wondering if any of his friends were down there, or if they'd come to view a match and recognize him... to save him. Thorne wondered if Jasper had worn the iron mask permanently, or if it had been removed while he was in this private space. If any attendants came again, he'd ask, but he was afraid he knew the answer. The mask had nails that pierced Jasper's skin at the sides of his face and neck. He'd seen red welts festering around them. The blood when he'd tried to remove it.

A Guardian was resistant to the mana-damaging effects of holding metal, yet they couldn't resist it invading their bodies. The iron had halted Jasper's shift mid-way. What was the point of suffering the inkeels in the ceremonial lake if this advantage over metal didn't extend inward?

Laurel's cool palm on his back startled him. Her hands wrapping around his waist made him soften.

"Please tell me what's on your mind," she whispered against his back.

He turned, slung his arm around her, and brought her to his side where she joined him watching the dawn of a new day.

"I was thinking about how much I never wanted to be a Guardian."

"And now?"

"I don't know," he admitted. He couldn't remember a time he'd wanted it. But he wouldn't give up the advantage it gave him over his opponents. Not when it meant keeping her safe. "Now you make me want things I've never wanted before."

"Such as?"

"Such as this. Us." He swallowed, thought of Rush and Clarke... and little Willow. "Family."

The confession sent his pulse sky rocketing.

She tensed beneath his arm, and for a moment, Thorne thought he'd scared her silent. But then she spoke quietly. "You make me want things too."

His lip quirked. "Such as?"

"I've never been a relationship type of person," she admitted. "I was too busy running my business and being a queen. But here's the thing. Queens are lonely. Spending time with you, fishing of all things, made me remember how much joy there is to be present in a moment. And after everything I loved was taken from me, I realized how little time I spent on what mattered. I don't want to make the same mistakes I made before."

He looked down at her. "Are you saying I matter to you?"

She smirked. "You could say I'm warming to you."

He feigned shock and smacked her gently on the rear. "We're mated. You have no choice."

"So we're mated. And that's that? No wedding ceremony? No party? Do fae not have them?" she pouted.

"We have them. Usually if one wants to mate with another, they must go on a quest the other has set for them."

Her eyes lit up. "What, like, to prove your undying love you must go behind enemy lines and steal their most precious jewel then bring it back. That sort of quest?"

His eyes danced at her interpretation. "Behind enemy lines. That's a high task indeed. Usually it's not so dramatic and something well within each betrothed's means. Like picking special flowers for the garland crowns, or something."

"Oh." She laughed. "Okay. Go on."

"On the day of the mating, each betrothed will present the result of their quest to the other at the ceremony."

"Where the male bites her before everyone?" she exclaimed.

This time, it was his turn to laugh. "Every fae breed has a different ritual. The pixies have a queen and she has a harem. She mates with multiple males. If they all bit her, she'd be covered in scars."

"So what do they do?"

He waggled his brows. "You'll have to ask a pix. Anyway, the celebration goes for seven days. Three before. One on the day of the commitment. And three after."

"Sounds like fun." She tweaked his nose. "I especially like the quest part. I'd be down for that. Sounds like an adventure. We just didn't do that sort of thing back in my time. It was all about the clothes, the looks, the money..."

He stared into her eyes until he got lost in them. "Do you want one, a celebration?"

"I don't know, I just... I guess so. I mean, isn't that what you want?"

"I've never thought about it. Guardians don't mate." Lowering his lips, he touched hers gently. "More things that are changing."

Thorne was mid-blink, trying to decipher her body language when a knock came at the door. Laurel rushed to cover herself with a blanket. He strode to the door in his current state—nude.

He was about three feet from the door when it opened. The black-haired and plump-lipped Rosebud from yesterday came in holding a tray of food. Behind her was the healer. The Rosebud winked at him and then went to place her tray on a table. The healer eyed him warily.

She stepped inside and a guard shut the door behind her, bolting it.

"Are you well?" the healer asked.

He nodded. "Clearly."

"And your mate?"

Laurel arrived at his side, now dressed in similar pantaloons to the healer and with a wrap top. It looked good on her. Laurel didn't seem to have the same appreciation for his state of undress. She shoved a package into his arms.

"Dress," she ordered.

His lips curved at how she glared at the Rosebud, even though the courtesan was busying herself with unloading the tray. He liked Laurel possessive. His wolf liked it too. But there was no need to poke the bear. He slipped on his pants, grimacing at the pantaloon style. Breeches were much better for battle. Less voluminous fabric to get caught in claws or weapons. He left the disgusting vest.

"I would like a word with you, healer."

She ignored him and went to Laurel. "How is your arm?"

Laurel tested her movement. "Perfect."

"Amazing." The healer traced Laurel's Well-blessed markings, perhaps having the same thoughts as he about why Laurel had healed so well. "And your energy?"

Laurel's gaze turned inward. "Excellent, actually. I should be tired, but that restorative elixir worked a treat. I'm as chirpy as a cricket."

"Healer," Thorne repeated. "I would like a word with you."

She met his stare. "Unless it's about your injuries, I am bound not to talk to you. Neither is the Rosebud... unless it is about your pleasure, or your wellbeing, that is."

Laurel stepped closer to Thorne.

"You have a geas on you?" he asked.

The healer nodded.

"Of course you do," he replied bitterly. A magical geas was like a curse, but less harmful to one's soul—for the fae casting it. Where a curse was rigid and difficult to break, a geas was bendable. There was always a workaround or a loophole to a geas. He just needed the right words to say.

"I have an injury, healer," he said.

She narrowed her eyes at him, understanding where he was going with this.

As the fae do not lie, the healer had to take his word for it. She glanced at Laurel, then at the Rosebud, just finishing up. Thorne understood. She was wary of listeners, of someone who would reveal her betrayal to her boss.

"Rosebud," Thorne shouted. She looked over. "That will be all. I will speak more about my injuries with the healer. In private."

The Rosebud nodded, and then made her exit.

"Go on," the healer said. "Tell me about your injury."

"It is one of the heart. Someone dear to me was kept prisoner in this room for decades. It has caused me many years of pain. In order to heal, I need to know more about him."

"Are you saying this act of imprisonment was what caused your injury?"

"Yes."

"What can you tell me about the previous champion?"

The healer lifted her brows and then went to the setting of food where she bit down on some fruit. "This is going to take a while, so I suggest you get comfortable."

For the next hour, the healer told Thorne and Laurel how Jasper was brought in forcibly almost a decade ago. His power-enhancing tattoos were stripped from his body, but they couldn't remove the distinctive teardrop tattoo of a Guardian no matter how hard they tried, so used the iron mask to cover it.

The person who'd ordered Jasper's imprisonment was someone well off. This person had paid for a Dark Mage to paint the curse runes around Jasper's neck. When Thorne questioned the iron mask, she told them of a human companion to the Dark Mage. A man wearing all black, who had the look of a hawk, and held metal weapons for his own defense. Two years ago, this same human returned, this time wearing the colors of Seelie High King Mithras, a red velvet coat with flames embroidered along the hem. The human no longer had round ears but pointed.

But it was the same human. She'd been sure of it.

Upon hearing this last bit, Laurel went quiet.

"Is the old champion under the hill?" Thorne asked. "This still relates to my injury."

"He was last night."

"And now?"

"I don't know."

Thorne scratched his chin. "One last question," he said. "The champion. Was the iron mask always on his face?"

The healer nodded gravely. "But occasionally it was removed to allow him to shift back to fae form."

Banshee's balls. This meant Jasper had been stuck between a wolf and fae form for most of a decade. The iron might have poisoned his brain. There was no telling how dark Jasper's state of mind would be when they rescued him.

And they would rescue him.

Thorne hand-signed his thanks to the healer. "Your time has been invaluable. So I will give you something of value in return. This establishment has committed a grave offense against the Well."

"The iron mask," she said.

He nodded. "There will be a raid. The Guardians will come. You should be very far from here when that happens."

The healer signed her gratitude and then left.

Laurel picked at the last of the bread. Her eyes were unfocused, and anxiety trickled down their bond. She'd been like this since the healer had talked about the human turned fae. It was this Bones person. Must be. The one Thorne was going to hunt down and kill for her.

While it twisted his gut to see her so upset, he knew it would have to wait. First, he would see to the raid.

He collected the bowl the Rosebuds had used the previous night and refilled it will bath water. He went back to the table, pierced his finger, and instigated a communication spell. While he waited for it to connect with Rush, he thought it was regrettable that Jasper's only blood relative had been the king, the very man who had imprisoned him. Jasper was unable to get word out, as those communication spells only worked for blooded kin. It might not have mattered anyway if the iron mask had kept Jasper in a state of flux the entire time. His mind might not have been lucid enough to cast spells.

"Thorne?" Rush's deep voice came from the bowl.

"Rush," Thorne greeted, relieved to see his father's visage in the water. "Have I caught you at a bad time?"

Clouds of air puffed from Rush's mouth. He must be somewhere cold.

"You could say that," Rush replied in a grave voice. "But I'm afraid, there won't be a good time for a while."

"What's happened?"

"It's Ada," Rush replied. "We found her, but she won't wake up."

Laurel's hand covered her mouth. Thorne reached over and squeezed her on the shoulder.

"But she is safe?" he asked.

"Yes. We are about to leave for the Order where the healers can see to her. Her blood is pumping. But she will not wake. You didn't contact me for that, though, did you?"

Thorne's fingers clenched on the bowl, and he couldn't make the next words come out. He must have taken too long, perhaps frowned too much, because Rush noticed.

"I know that look," Rush remarked.

"How?"

"When you were young and Thaddeus asked you to collect water from the lake as punishment, you would wear that face and stand on the shore for hours until you knew someone would come and hasten you. And only when the time you'd been allotted for the task was drawing close, would you complete the task. So, I know that face. You are procrastinating. You need help."

Yes, Thorne had made that face at the lake. The realization swam from his deepest memories. He'd been afraid of the lake because, even though the one where he'd been tasked to collect water wasn't the ceremonial lake, it still reminded his young mind of the place he'd been told had taken his grandfather, the original alpha of Crescent Hollow.

Thorne stared at Rush, at the male he'd accused of never being there for him, somehow only now understanding that Rush had *always* been there. Just not seen. Thorne scrubbed his face. He swallowed.

"Yes. I need help."

"Anything."

A warm feeling flooded Thorne and the next words spilled out of him. He told Rush about what they'd discovered, about the iron mask, the need for a raid, and then Jasper's words to him in the arena.

Before Jasper was Thorne's mentor, he was Rush's friend, possibly his mentor as well. Rush had asked Jasper to look after his son. It should dampen Thorne's feelings about Jasper's involvement in his life, but it didn't. He could see how both had only wanted the best for Thorne.

Someone spoke out of view from Rush. Rush turned, listened, and then met Thorne's eyes again.

"I will arrange the raid and be at the Ring by the time the sun sets, if not before. The rest of the Twelve will be with me."

"What about the Prime? She's not my biggest fan."

Rush's vicious growl of discontent came through the connection, rippling the water. "You leave her to me."

"Good."

"Thorne?"

"Yes?"

"I'm proud of you." And then the connection cut. Rush's visage disappeared and the water turned opaque.

"What do we do now?" Laurel asked.

"Now we wait."

TWENTY-EIGHT

Later that day, Laurel sat on the floor of the champion's room, her head pressed to the glass window, watching the fight happening all the way down at ground level. She hadn't expected Rush to pull together something so quickly, but when a flock of shadows passed across the sun, and a squadron of winged fae dropped to the arena roof, she knew it could only mean one thing. The raid had begun.

"Thorne!" she shouted, hopping to her feet. "It's happening."

He rushed to her side from where he'd been listening at the door with his keen wolf ears, hoping to garner some nugget of information from the guards. She pointed at the opposite roof where two Guardians had taken position. He squinted.

"That's Indigo and Shade," he said, then cast his eyes around, noting more fae he recognized. "Haze. Cloud. Ash, and River." He turned to her, eyes wide. "That's all the winged fae in the Twelve—the crows and the vamps."

"Why are you surprised?"

"I just didn't think they'd all come."

She squeezed his arm and smiled. "You asked for help, and they came."

His nostrils flared, and he nodded. "There's always a ground fleet during a raid. With this many on top, Rush probably has the rest of the Twelve down below. Plus more." He shook his head. "I still can't believe it."

"Get used to it, Thorne," she said. "Your friends support you. And Jasper."

"I don't know how Rush convinced the Prime to let them come." He narrowed his eyes. "Unless she's only approved the bit about the iron-mask, and not taking Jasper."

"We'll find him."

He nodded, collected his ax, and ushered her to the front door. "Let's go. Stay behind me. We might have to fight our way out."

"Wait." She stopped him. "What about the bargain I made with the organizer to have two battles?"

Thorne shot her a wolfish grin. "Fighting these guards outside our door consists of a battle, does it not?"

She returned his smile. "Yes. Yes, it does."

"Perfect." He shooed her back a step. "Don't want to hurt my queen."

"Of course."

When she was a safe distance back, he cleaved his battle-ax at the door, splitting the wood straight down the middle. Shouts ensued on the other side. Guards rushed and called for backup, but within another two strokes, Thorne had burst through the bolted door and kicked it wide open.

Laurel's fierce warrior cast a glance over his shoulder and said, "A blast of your fire will suffice."

Bouncing on her toes with excitement, she let flames consume her fingers and sent an inferno through the door, pulling the power at the last moment when she heard a pitiful scream. When the smoke and flames died down, there was no one in the hall. For a moment, she thought she might have burned them all to a crisp, but then one by one, the guards came back up from the stairwell and charged. Thorne threw a spell of dense air at them, knocking them back like a tidal wave, and then dispatched each guard by clocking them with the flat edge of his ax. When it was done, his ears pricked up alert, checking for more danger. Satisfied there was none, he waved Laurel onward and went down the stairs.

They reached ground level and found the gate to the arena wide open. Sun shone from the bright entrance. Thorne slowed his approach, wary and steady with his ax at the ready. When a shadow blocked the light, he lifted his ax, ready to inflict pain, but then dropped it to his side.

It was Rush.

Standing as tall and broad as Thorne, Rush looked fearsome in his Guardian uniform, great sword gripped in his hand, silver hair tied back and ready for battle. Golden eyes landed on Thorne, then flicked to Laurel.

"Vacation is over," Rush joked and gestured for them to exit the tunnel.

"Har-har," Thorne replied. He took Laurel's hand and walked out with her. When they emerged, they found the arena virtually empty. Only a few Guardians combed the bleachers.

"Jasper?" Thorne asked Rush.

"He wasn't down there."

Thorne let loose a string of curses.

Two Guardians came over. One was the tall gilt-haired elf, Leaf, and the other was the serious brunette elf who at first glance somehow looked more suave than the rest, even though he wore the same badass battle uniform.

Leaf opened his mouth to speak, but Thorne cut him off. "If you're going to reprimand me about skipping out on my mission, don't."

Both Leaf and the other elf narrowed their eyes at Thorne. Rush also cast him a wary look but said nothing.

"I wasn't," Leaf replied. "A new tribute will have to replace him. Your guilt is reprimand enough."

Thorne's face reddened, and true to Leaf's word, guilt surged down their bond to plunge into Laurel's heart. This was the first she'd heard of this. Someone had died because Thorne had left?

Thorne frowned and rubbed between his eyes. He turned away and took a few steps where he stopped and stayed with his back to them.

Two vampires landed in a whirl of leathery wings and dust. One was the sinfully good-looking vampire she'd glimpsed at the Birdcage, the other was one she'd never met. He was tall, athletic, and had light brown wavy hair—longish on top, buzzed on the sides. Somehow, there was a carefree vibe to him, despite his blood-streaked leathers. She could almost see him partying on a yacht in the Caribbean or part of the Brazilian soccer team. Maybe both.

And then she looked closer. He wore spiked metal rings on his knuckles. They were covered in fresh blood.

He caught her looking, gave her a curious once-over, and his lips curved on one side, flashing fang. His pointed tongue darted out to lick the blood off his knuckle-duster.

"Fangs to yourself, Indigo," Thorne growled at the vampire. He rested a proprietary arm over Laurel's shoulder.

Indigo kissed the air in Thorne's direction, then turned to Leaf.

"D'arn Shade. D'arn Indigo," Leaf acknowledged. "Status report?"

"Clearly no one is accepting blame for the iron mask," Shade drawled. "But we found evidence of it in the dirt on the arena floor. What was left of it, anyway. Completely melted."

Laurel gingerly lifted her hand. "That was me."

A stare from six extremely tall and lethal Guardians, all dressed in black battle gear spattered with blood, was the most intimidating thing Laurel had ever experienced.

She lifted her chin. "It was necessary to remove the mask from Jasper's face."

"And you did this with your power?" Leaf confirmed.

She nodded. "Thorne put an insulation spell on him for protection."

It was the brunette elf who responded. "Interesting. I would like to know more about the spell you both used when you get a chance."

She didn't exactly use a spell. It was more like instinct. She nodded. Thorne's grip tightened on her shoulder.

"Right," Shade continued. "As I was saying, no one is owning up to it. But Cloud isn't finished interrogating them."

"And Jasper is missing," Thorne added. "Is there news on where he was taken?"

"Unfortunately," Shade continued, "the most we have is that he went under the hill, but not for long before a portal opened and he was taken away by someone wearing the colors of the Seelie High King."

"How long are we going to let him get away with this?" Thorne growled. "Let's just infiltrate Helianthus City, find Jasper, and take him back."

"Sign me up." Indigo's eyes flashed. "That sounds like fun."

Rush shook his head. "He might not be in the city. Even if he was, there's no evidence. We can't just break in without just cause. Not with the power of the Order behind us."

"What if we do it without?"

Leaf's blue eyes blazed. "I've told you once, and I'll say it again. We have a duty to the Well. We can't spend years chasing Jasper down. There simply aren't enough resources."

"More like you're the Prime's little lackey," Thorne shot back.

"Actually," Rush interjected. "The Prime has given us permission to run an extraction for Jasper. He is one of our own. She regrets the outcome of her bargain with the king. It just needs to be above board."

"You mean the bargain where she gave him Jasper in return for keeping the unsanctioned law active. So she could ensure you were cursed, unseeable to the scrying eyes of the enemy, and in the right place and time to find your mate," Thorne shot back.

The air thickened with tension. Thorne became solid rock next to Laurel.

Rush's brows lowered at Thorne. "You want to do this here? Now?"

Laurel looked up at her mate. *Let it go*, she tried to tell him through their bond. He had to let it go. This poisonous hold on his past was eating him. As if hearing her plea, Thorne looked down. His eyes softened, and he released a breath. He looked at Rush, his father, and hand-signed an apology.

"It's not your fault. I shouldn't have spoken out," Thorne said.

Shade made a choking sound. Indigo coughed and raised a brow at Thorne. "Did you just apologize?"

A few of them chuckled. Rush just gave a short nod, then changed the conversation. "I suggest we gather some intel before we make a decision."

"Yes," Leaf added. "When Cloud is done with his interrogation, we might know more about the link between Patches and the Birdcage, this place, and the Seelie High King."

"He's only going to confirm what I've been saying for the past two years," Rush growled. "The humans are setting up the Unseelie. They're trying to instigate a war. They know that with the Sluagh, they can't kill us, so they're trying to make us kill each other."

Leaf scrubbed his jaw. "It's certainly the kind of crafty we've come to expect from them, but all we have to go on is hearsay and circumstantial evidence. No one has caught the humans in the act."

Thorne opened his mouth to say that they had—when the humans had kidnapped Kyra and Clarke two years prior, but Leaf lifted a finger to silence him.

"No," Leaf added. "That wasn't catching them in the act. Only Rush laid eyes on the humans. Not a single one of us did. And the only evidence we found showed that the humans were feeding Thaddeus metal, not the king. Thaddeus is now dead."

"So we're back to playing the same cat-and-mouse game we've been playing for years," Thorne replied, throwing his hands in the air. "Why can't we tell Queen Maebh or King Mithras that it's all a setup?"

"That might have worked a few years ago," Rush said. "But we've learned today that

Mithras is working with a human. How else would he get his hands on enough iron to make a mask?"

"Yes. He is working with a human," Thorne confirmed with a grave look at Laurel. "His name is Bones."

Rush's golden gaze narrowed. "He is the right-hand man of the one Clarke calls the Void. The human leader. And you know this for sure?"

Thorne nodded. "The healer here was under a geas not to talk about anything except our injuries, but I found a loophole. She confessed she had witnessed a person matching Bones' description was here two years ago as a human, then more recently dressed in Mithras colors and with elven ears."

"Once again, this is hearsay," Leaf pointed out.

"Well, we won't have hard evidence unless we go on the offensive," Thorne said.

For some reason, Thorne's words threw the group into silence... almost as if *offensive* was a dirty word. Laurel supposed it might be. From what she'd gathered, their roles were to preserve the integrity of the Well. Up until recently, this duty had revolved around hunting mana-warped monsters, policing metals and plastics, and keeping the current day humans from entering Elphyne. But their duty was becoming convoluted as time wore on. Clarke foretold another war, one where the man who'd originally defiled the world did it again, ending life once and for all this time.

"Has Clarke *seen* anything?" Laurel asked.

Rush winced. "Not about this. And to be fair, her mind is occupied with the health of her friend."

Laurel's heart clenched. Ada was in a coma. How could she have forgotten that?

They continued talking, but Laurel tuned out. All she could think was that she couldn't handle this for another decade. Jasper had already been missing for that long. She didn't know how to help. She was a fish out of water.

"More discussion is required," Leaf declared. "We will return to the Order until we exhaust all avenues and come up with a plan of attack."

As each Guardian took off through a portal, Laurel caught the bitter look on Thorne's face, and if she guessed correctly, she knew why. It seemed the Prime had indoctrinated the Guardians to her way of thinking. They couldn't make decisions without consulting her. They weren't living in a democracy. It was a dictatorship.

CHAPTER
TWENTY-NINE

As they crossed the threshold to the house of the Twelve, Thorne watched his mate draw Clarke into a fierce embrace. From that moment, Thorne was not much but an afterthought in Laurel's eyes. Seeing the twinkle in them, and the way she invigorated around her friend, he couldn't help feeling a little envious at the friendship. And then there was the rush of love he sensed from Laurel. They must be close friends, indeed. But when Clarke's expression turned grave, and she gestured for Laurel to follow her, the twinkle in Laurel's eyes disappeared. She cast a concerned glance to Thorne, and he gestured that he would be right behind.

"Is she still asleep?" Laurel asked Clarke as they took the staircase.

Clarke nodded. "Hasn't moved an inch. The healing Mages don't know what is wrong. They're trying to use magic to keep her sustained, but if she doesn't wake soon, I'm afraid she'll slip away."

Laurel's nose turned pink and her eyes watered. "Where is she?"

"We put her in Jasper's old room." Clarke sent a nervous glance to Thorne. "It was the only room free, and we need her close."

He gave a short nod. There wasn't much he could say to that. Jasper wasn't here. And if this newly awoken woman, Ada, was as close to these two as they were to each other, then she must be like family.

Thorne followed the women down the hall and stopped at the open doorway to Jasper's old room. He leaned against the frame with a shoulder. Lying on Jasper's bed was a petite female with long, wavy golden hair spread around her like a mermaid. Her eyes were closed, her body still, her mouth pinched as though she were in pain. She'd been cleaned and dressed in fresh clothing.

Laurel sat next to Ada on the bed.

Thorne watched his mate brush her friend gently down the arm and was reminded of the time she did that to Willow. Laurel would make a good mother one day. It wasn't the first time he'd thought that, but it was the first time he'd done so knowing what it meant to him directly.

He should give them some space. Rubbing his chest, he turned and headed to the kitchen, hungry and ready for food. Or a drink. When he got there, he found Rush scrounging around too. Both still in the attire they'd been in during the raid, and both led by their stomachs. Their eyes met briefly, and then Thorne joined him in the search. It was too early for dinner, but food was required before he cleaned up. Silently, they found a collection of nuts and dried berries, and a jug of ale before heading outside and into the back garden where Willow played while under the watchful eye of Jocinda as she tended to a patch of herbs.

They sat on a wooden bench before a long table used for communal meals. The weather had been unseasonably warm. A few years ago, it snowed at this time of year, but now the sun shone brightly and the flowers bloomed. A long strip of lawn stretched from the back of the house to the tall stone wall that separated the Order campus from the poisonous forest surrounding them. Before the wall was a thick grove of Willow and Cherry trees, blocking much of the wall from sight and catching most errant poisonous leaves from the external forest. They still had to watch Willow in case she found a leaf and ingested it.

"You are comfortable with her outside now?" Thorne asked with a nod in the direction of the house of the Six.

Rush poured ale into two steins and exhaled deeply. "I've accepted she's not going to shift into wolf, it would have happened by now, but she has shifted from human into a fae form, or rather something closer to an elf. I don't think the Sluagh will bother her."

Thorne frowned as he recalled her change in appearance that night she'd wanted to sleep in his bed. "I remember fangs coming out, and her ears elongating."

"Claws too," Rush added, "but that is all."

"Should be enough to mark her as different from the humans."

"Agreed. Plus, her mana-holding capacity is strong for her age. We will still keep her indoors when the sun goes down, though."

Thorne settled back on the wooden bench, the stein in his hand, and joined Rush as he watched the little silver-haired child chase down a butterfly—or a possible sprite —with single-minded tenacity.

"She is fearless," Thorne remarked.

"She is," Rush agreed.

Willow landed, caught something, carefully opened her hands, and then pouted. Not there. She resumed her hunt.

"Leaf has called a meeting with the Council first thing in the morning," Rush said. "We will discuss a plan of action."

Weariness coated Thorne's bones. "I don't know what more we can do being shackled as we are by the rules the Prime has put in place. We have exhausted our options."

"There are always more options," Rush replied. "Ada has been found. Now I am free to go on the hunt with you. If we can't use the Order to get to him, then we do it on our own. We won't stop until we bring Jasper home."

Thorne let those words settle, and something tight around his heart loosened. He was learning Rush was a fae true to his word, a male who didn't mince words or skirt around manipulation and misdirection. He'd promised to go on this hunt when he could, and now he would.

"There is something you should know," Thorne said.

"I'm listening."

"When Jasper was freed from the mask, he confused me with you."

Rush's brows snapped together.

Thorne scrubbed his hand through his newly shorn hair. "He babbled about looking after me like you'd asked, but not deserving to be rescued." Thorne paused. "He apologized."

Rush went still.

Even though Jasper was fae, and his words should have been the truth, Thorne had to ask. "Was your request why he mentored me?"

"Jasper and I were longtime friends and would often partner on missions into the wolf territories. When your mother was executed, and they took me into custody, I threw some regrettable words at him." A dark shadow passed over Rush's expression. "Jasper had refused to help Véda, and I found it unforgivable. It didn't make sense. Now I understand that perhaps the Prime had something to do with it." Rush's gaze fogged as he stared into his stein. "While I'm eternally grateful he looked out for you, I had no idea he took those harsh words to heart."

"He failed to remember me," Thorne muttered into his stein, took a breath with his lips on the rim, and then sipped.

When he lowered the cup, he felt Rush's shrewd gaze on him. "This is most likely because of the curse marks that were on his body. Or his state of mind. Not because of you."

"I never said it was," he groused.

"But you were thinking it."

Thorne kept his mouth shut. Had he been thinking it? Perhaps it was there, simmering beneath his conscious thoughts. Perhaps his face showed his inner turmoil more than he liked to admit.

"I know," Rush added. "Because—"

"You know me," Thorne finished.

Willow leaped over Jocinda's feet as she kneeled and dug into a herb patch. She took two wobbly steps and then launched with her whole body onto something on the grass. She looked over to Rush with excitement—*look at me!*—opened her fingers, squealed in excitement, but then her catch flittered off.

"Dad!" she shouted. "See?"

"Yes, squirt. I saw." Rush turned to Thorne. "I see your mate has been marked. These mana-filled humans are hard to resist, no?"

Thorne barked out a laugh. "That is one way of putting it."

Rush smiled over his stein. "They are also very bossy."

Thorne laughed some more. When his humor died down, he confessed, "I think I needed that."

"Me too."

They shared a small smile, and it was... nice. But Thorne wasn't settled. He wouldn't be for a while. Not with Jasper in the wind, and Laurel worried over her friend. And when Laurel worried, he worried. It was more than their shared bond.

Rush noticed Thorne checking the door to the house and raised his brows in question.

"Laurel is unsettled," Thorne explained. "About this new friend."

"So is Clarke," Rush agreed and scowled into his cup. "I don't know what to do. Usually, Clarke is the one who knows such things."

"And they are strange things, are they not?" Thorne replied. "From their time, I mean."

"Yes. This is true."

They both turned their scowls to their steins. A few minutes of awkward silence, then Thorne offered, "Laurel used to own a business where females would pay coin for her to show them how to make their bodies physically fit."

Rush frowned. "Like the training we do on the fields?"

"I guess so."

"And these females would pay Laurel. Not the other way around?"

Thorne shrugged. "Something like that."

"The training. Did that make her a general of her own army?"

"She said she was a queen. But not like our queens. I don't believe she had subjects. Or a castle."

"Odd."

"Indeed."

"Clarke was a thief," Rush blurted.

Thorne sprayed out his mouthful of ale and laughed.

Rush's lips quirked. "Don't tell her I told you."

The sun warmed Thorne's face and he tried to experience this moment for what it was. Laurel had mentioned this sort of simple awareness was something she'd regretted. He could see the wisdom in that. It was the first time he'd come together with his father on level ground. They had something in common. Both had Well-blessed mates —the first fae in centuries to do so—and both were mated to women of the days past. Humans with power. Another first. They were the only people in this time to share such a bond. And they were kin. Thorne knew that Rush and he would stand together, united, if anyone came for their humans. It was because of this notion of connection that he was prompted to speak his next words.

"I would like to do something for Laurel," he said. He felt a little silly, but continued. "She talks about something called a smoo-thie."

Rush lifted his gaze to Thorne's. "Smoo-thie?"

"Yes. She wishes for one in the morning, usually when she is hungry, yet she talks about it as though she drinks it. I don't know what it is, but I would like to give her one."

Rush's gaze turned foggy, and he looked inward, as though trying to remember. He tapped his lip. "Smoo-thie."

"I believe it is green. Perhaps it involves fruit."

"I suppose if it is a meal, we could enquire with the house brownies. I could also ask Clarke when Laurel is not within hearing distance, if you permit."

Thorne studied Rush for a moment and decided he liked this new thing between them. He sensed Rush did too. "I would like that."

"Consider it done." Rush chugged back the last of his ale, thumped his chest, belching softly.

"Da-*ad*." The sound of a little voice trying to entice attention drifted over. "Where's Willow?"

Both Thorne and Rush looked to the garden.

Thorne barked a laugh. There, behind a sparse bush was Willow. He could see her clearly, but a single leaf covered her lower face. She clearly thought it was enough to hide her entire form. Earnest eyes twinkled at her father.

Thorne raised his brow at Rush, who chuckled back and then shouted, "Oh dear, I've lost Willow. Wherever can she be?"

Giggles.

And then Rush stood, clapped Thorne on the shoulder and walked past to collect a squealing and giggling Willow before zooming her around and lifting her onto his shoulders. Then he returned and headed for the house.

"I'll be back," Rush said and mimed having a drink.

The smoo-thie?

"You're going to ask now?" Thorne asked.

"No time like the present." Rush shrugged. "I'll no longer put off for tomorrow what I can do today. You never know when time is taken from you."

AFTER DINNER, Thorne took a plate of food up to Jasper's room where Laurel still sat a vigil at Ada's beside by candlelight. Night had long since fallen, and he'd already bathed and dressed. Clarke was asleep next to Ada. She must be weary after keeping vigil herself for so long.

Laurel was still in the clothes she'd taken from the Ring. Her feet were tucked under her bottom and she rested in the high-back chair by the window-side. Her melancholy reflected down their bond. It reminded him of her first night awake in this time, where she'd sat on a chair just like that in his room, brooding out the window while he'd taken his bath.

She didn't think he'd paid attention, but he did. She'd been homesick, and he'd felt every last minute of it while he'd taken a bath. He'd lifted the blanket to cover her and tucked her hair as she'd drifted to sleep. It was then that he'd first thought maybe she was worth getting to know more thoroughly. He was glad he now had.

He rapped his knuckles gently on the door.

Laurel looked over.

"I have food," he said.

She smiled. "Perfect."

He took the plate to her. She raised her brows, impressed at the selection. A selection of roast vegetables and savory pastries filled with fish and cream. She made short work of eating the selection.

"Will you be retiring soon?" The thought of having his mate in his bed awoke every instinct in his body. Since he'd marked her, it was all he'd thought about, but he wouldn't push the subject. As he'd mentioned to her, a mating ceremony lasted days. But what he hadn't mentioned, was that the last three days were spent in privacy, enjoying each other's bodies while the rest of the family continued the party without them. This may not be practical given their current situation.

He would, however, push the subject of her needing rest.

She glanced at Ada. "Clarke and I are taking shifts watching her. When she wakes, I'll come."

A sound at the door drew their attention, and a little white head poked around from the shadow of the doorframe. Willow came stumbling in, hair wet from a recent bath, and dressed in sleepwear. The scent of fresh powder wafted in. She looked over at them hesitantly, then dragged a small blanket into the room.

"Sleeping Pretty is cold," she mumbled and looked at the bed.

Thorne thought perhaps Willow meant her mother, but she crawled onto the bed and tried to cover Ada. Seeing her difficulty, Thorne helped her spread the blanket. When Willow was done, she curled between her mother and Ada.

Laurel came to stand next to Thorne. "That's weird."

"Not really. The temperature is dropping."

"No, I mean..." Laurel shook her head. "It doesn't matter."

Thorne pulled her into his arms. "It does, else you wouldn't have mentioned it."

"It's just that we used to call Ada 'Pretty Kitty' because she used to rehabilitate big wild cats, and clearly, she's very pretty. Eventually, we shortened it to just Pretty." She bit her lip. "Maybe Clarke said something."

"Most likely." Thorne lifted Laurel's face and kissed her deeply, making sure to let her know what would be waiting when she made it to his bed. *Their* bed.

"Don't be too long," he said, patted her gently on the rear, and went back to his room.

CHAPTER

THIRTY

After Thorne had left, Laurel sat on the bedside chair, occasionally testing the temperature on Ada's forehead with the back of her hand. She was afraid that Ada would suddenly stop breathing if she stopped checking. Laurel didn't want to lose her, not when she'd lost so much already.

Ada had a dry, sarcastic sense of humor that not everyone understood, but Laurel and Clarke did. They were often in fits of laughter over something Ada refused to believe was funny, only the truth. Of course, that made it funnier.

Seeing Clarke and her new family gave Laurel a taste of what a future could be like here and sharing that with Ada would be even better. Laurel dug into the pocket in her pantaloons and pulled out a small vial of pink elixir. After learning Laurel's relationship with Thorne had gone to the next level, Clarke had given it to Laurel the moment they were alone. Take a drop a day and it would stop Laurel from becoming pregnant.

Laurel had taken her first dose hours ago. She would tell Thorne about it as soon as she could. It would relieve his concerns and allay his fears about the unsanctioned breeding law.

She put the vial back and went back to staring at her friend, watching the air draw in and out of her lips as she slept. Since Willow had brought the extra blanket, Ada's cheeks had taken more color. Maybe she had been cold, after all. Perhaps Willow had a little of her mother's psychic powers.

Either way, if Ada had been cold, and now she wasn't, it could only be a good sign.

Hours passed, and Laurel's eyes grew heavy, but she didn't want to wake Clarke. The poor thing had a small child. She'd be exhausted. Laurel looked over at her redheaded friend and noticed a deep frown between her brows. Laurel picked up the candlestick holder at the table and brought the flame closer to Clarke. She was definitely whimpering with shallow breath.

Dreaming?

Laurel put the candle on the bedside table and took hold of her friend's shoulder. "Clarke," she whispered.

"No." Clarke spoke vehemently through her teeth. "You stay away from her."

Clarke's eyes pinged open and seemed to look beyond Laurel's shoulders. The hairs on the back of Laurel's neck lifted, and she checked, half expecting to see Bones, or perhaps the Sluagh, but there was nothing. Clarke kept talking. No. It was more like pleading with someone not there. Glistening tracks of tears ran down her cheeks.

"Wake up," Laurel said and shook Clarke's shoulders.

With a gasp, Clarke's eyes focused. "Laurel?"

"Yeah, it's me. You were dreaming."

Clarke jackknifed up, and drew Laurel into a hug, whimpering, "Oh, thank God. I thought he had you again."

"Shh." Laurel stroked her friend's sobbing back. "I'm fine. I'm fine. It wasn't a—" Laurel swallowed the lump in her throat. "Vision, was it?"

"I don't know. It felt more like a regular nightmare. Did you see my eyes? Where they white?"

"They looked normal."

Clarke exhaled heavily. "Nightmare then."

Willow stirred on the bed. Clarke wiped her nose and then checked on her daughter. Once satisfied she was asleep, Clarke picked up the candleholder and took Laurel's hand. She dragged Laurel into the adjoining bathing chamber—as far as they could get from little fae ears.

"What's wrong?" Laurel asked.

Flickering candlelight revealed the panic in Clarke's eyes.

"I keep dreaming about *him*."

"The Void?"

Clarke nodded. Her lip curled. "It's worse than before, and it's also not only him but..."

"Bones."

Another nod. Then Clarke burst into tears. "I'm sorry."

"Hey. Hey, don't cry." Laurel squeezed Clarke's arm. "Whatever it is, we'll work it out. We've got badass warriors for husbands."

"Mates."

"Same thing."

"Better. But here's the thing," Clarke continued. "Every version of the future I dream, it's not our fae warriors who beat the Void. Well, it's not them alone."

Laurel stiffened. "You mean it's us?"

"They're trained to avoid fae politics. It's ingrained in them. But the Void uses fae politics to infiltrate Elphyne. Don't you see?"

No. She didn't see. Clarke wasn't making much sense. Laurel frowned at her friend while her brain whirled. The healer at the Ring had mentioned the human who'd been described as looking similar to Bones coming back disguised as a fae in the king's colors. Was that what Clarke meant by politics? The Order might have the power, but they were ill-equipped to battle on the same frequency as someone so manipulative and deceptive as Bones.

This man who had destroyed their world could be sitting by King Mithras's side, right now, plotting the end of another world, but this time, he'd have the power of a fae king behind him. Not just any king, the High Seelie King. Ruler of half the land.

Clarke's eyes met Laurel's. "Before you woke up in this time, I had a vision of you walking ahead with Thorne, Jasper, all of us behind you. You lead us to a table where we enjoyed a meal together. I know it's you, Laurel. You'll somehow lead us to Jasper. Some decision you make is going to make us all very happy. For a time, anyway."

Silently watching through the doorway to the two sleeping on the bed, the profound realization of their situation hit home. This was their life now. They were alive. The world was flourishing. Laurel had *hope*. She had dreams. She wanted her own family some day.

A ghost of pain in her fingertips caused a tremble in her hands. She rubbed her nails on her thighs.

Clarke had a *child*. She had a family now. That was too much to lose.

"We need to kill Bones," Clarke said grimly. Perhaps she'd been thinking the same things.

"I agree. But I need to kill him. You need to stay here."

The words hung in the air.

Laurel? Kill. Had she really said that?

Yes. She was strong, now. More powerful. The Bones she knew didn't have magic. Not like her. He was here, in Elphyne. In their realm, on their terms. Now was the time.

"I want to help more," Clarke whispered. "I hate that you're the one who has to do this when it was my fault we're all in this mess."

Laurel turned to her friend. "Clarke, it was never your fault," she said vehemently. "It was none of our faults. It was theirs. Bishop. Bones. The Void. *Theirs*. You want to help? Tell me what you know. Then Thorne and I can be ready."

Clarke nodded. Her eyes watered.

"Rush would help too, but... there are too many variables in that chain of events."

"What? Have you seen something?"

"I know that Bones is directly linked to the end of the world. I know that the Order want to help, but they need us to finish it. I know that sometimes, they have the right intentions, but they don't get the job done." Clarke glanced to where Ada was sleeping in the other room. "We're the only ones who know what Bones and the Void are really like. We've seen the old world. We know what was lost. I'm afraid... I'm afraid that if they get their hands on Bones, they'll keep him alive to question him."

"He's a cancer. It's better to cut it out and be done with it." Dark bitterness coated Laurel's vision, and she was surprised at how right those words sounded. *Cut it out. Be done with it.*

"Exactly. We don't need to interrogate him. We can find out the Void's plan some other way."

None of them wanted to voice their fears. Could they really do this? Take this ruthless and cold step? Could Laurel become a killer?

Were they acting irrationally *because* of their fears?

Laurel rubbed her aching nails again.

"We need to keep this between you and me," Clarke said, meeting Laurel's eyes. "I'm talking about our end game. If we tell Rush or Thorne, or even the Prime about how serious we are about this, they might try to stop us."

"But Thorne said he would kill Bones for me. He wants the same thing."

"He might not have the choice. He might have to choose between you or Bones, or Jasper and Bones. I just..."

"I know what you're getting at." Laurel inhaled deeply and exhaled. If it came to Laurel's life, or Bones', Thorne would pick her. Without a doubt. But Laurel wouldn't stop until she cut out the cancer. She had to. "We keep the killing part between us then."

"At least until the deed is done."

"Agreed."

"In the meantime, I'll work on the Prime. The Guardians might not be trained for manipulations and politics, but she is. She's a master of it. If I can find a reason to convince her to help us, perhaps we can get you into the Summer Court, and then half the job is done."

Laurel nodded grimly. Already, she was preparing her mind, making herself harder, colder. She could do this.

Just think about how it would feel to finally know Bones wasn't in the world anymore. That he was never coming back.

LAUREL RETURNED to Thorne's room not long after midnight. After their decision to kill Bones, she and Clarke had gone over as many variations of a plan as they could, but there came a point where they couldn't continue without going around in circles, so Laurel left. Now, she pushed it all out of her mind, telling herself that for the rest of the night, she would pretend things were as normal as they could be.

That she didn't have to turn herself into a cold, ruthless killer just yet.

Closing the door softly, she padded quietly into the room and to where Thorne was fast asleep on the bed, naked and twisted in his sheets. The soft warm glow of her candlelight clashed with the blue of his Well-blessed markings. It was breathtaking. She didn't think she'd ever get used to these magical moments. Of course, ogling his perfect physique could also be another reason she was out of breath. The sharp lines of his body, the slabs of muscle, the smooth skin, and the peaceful expression on his face as he slept. It all made her insides ache with want. She put her candle on the bedside table and then undressed.

She would get in and curl up beside him.

But she wasn't tired anymore. Her mind was buzzed from what she'd discussed with Clarke.

Crawling onto the bed, she straddled him gently and began kissing down his front —starting with the hard column of his neck, and trailing down his torso. When her lips tickled the hair at his groin, he stirred with a low, pleasure-filled moan and she was pleased to see a hard rod take shape beneath the sheets. Big hands landed on her head. Fingers threaded into her hair and massaged meanderingly.

"Laurel," he murmured, voice deep and husky. "What is the meaning of this?"

"Are you complaining?"

She hooked her finger in the sheet that covered his hips, drew it down to reveal he was indeed hard and ready. She lowered her lips and licked the long, responsive length, taking special care as she hit the crown.

Another masculine groan, an instinctive gentle thrust of his hips, and his cock entered her mouth. She hummed appreciatively and sucked deep.

Thorne cursed and bolted upright. She jerked back, grinning and licking her lips. Now completely awake, his eyes landed on her state of undress, settling on his favorite parts of her with smoldering intensity. He reached for her.

She straddled his hips, fitted him beneath her, and sank down on his length, shuddering at the sensation of being filled completely. He steadied her waist and looked softly into her eyes.

"You should be resting," he insisted.

She undulated her hips, reveling in the way stubbornness eased out of his expression. Loving how he soon forgot about his protests and started kissing down her neck, licking around the mark he'd put there, and moving with her.

Hard pants. Ragged breaths.

"My queen," he murmured, half to himself.

Laurel took her pleasure in her warrior fae and enjoyed the night for what it was— possibly the last time he'd look at her without hurt or betrayal again.

Secrets never ended well.

But sometimes, they were necessary.

WHEN MORNING CAME, Laurel woke to find Thorne already gone. But next to the bed on the side table was a pottery cup with condensation running down the side. She shuffled over and looked inside. Frothy green foam. Next to the cup was a small piece of parchment with the words "Drink me" written in a chicken scratch scrawl she could only guess was Thorne's handwriting.

She sniffed it. Fruity, yet... herby.

Her eyes lit up and she braved a sip. Her taste buds rejoiced. Full of dense flavor and exactly what she'd been craving. A smoothie. Not exactly like the wheatgrass one she had every morning, not as smooth, but similar. A taste of home.

Tears sprung to her eyes, and she gulped it all down, trying not to think about how this made her task even more difficult. She had to lie to Thorne.

And that made her feel sick.

She didn't want to do it.

But if anything, sleep had solidified the notion that Bones had to die. And Thorne would always pick her if it came to it. She couldn't just send the Guardians on an assassination mission. Clarke was right not to trust them to complete the deed. They might keep Bones. And then he might escape. He might do something worse.

No. It had to be this way.

Laurel bathed and dressed into something she could jog in. She needed to feel that burn in her lungs today more than any day. She needed to chase her demons away. Once ready, she headed out.

The house was abuzz with activity and large, half-naked male fae. Some she recognized and gave a shy wave to, others she stayed clear of. The dark crow-shifter, for one. The way he looked at her gave her the heebie-jeebies—as though he wanted to knock her out, gift wrap her and deliver her next door to the thing that ate souls.

No. Not *thing*, she reminded herself. That's how she used to think. She was different now. She was a part of this new world. Every creature in this time was owed respect, even if it lived off the souls of others. She was sure there was no other way for it to gain sustenance. Like vampires.

The door to Ada's room was closed, and Laurel suspected Clarke was in there with a sleeping Willow, so avoided going in. Clarke would have told Laurel if Ada's condition had changed.

She went out the front door in search of Thorne and found him and a group of three other fae in hand-to-hand combat on the front lawn. Rush, Aeron, and a big, bodybuilder type vampire she thought was named Haze. Behind them, about a hundred feet away, and across the grass field, were the Guardian barracks where those who weren't in the special cadres resided. A few Guardians she'd never met sat out the front, watching the informal sparring match while they ate breakfast.

Thorne must have sensed her arrival. He turned, got knocked in the head by a meaty fist, scowled at his attacker—Haze—and then jogged toward Laurel. When he arrived, all sweaty and in leather breeches, he drew her to his frame and gave her an open-mouthed kiss.

"Mm," he said, licking his lips and looking very pleased with himself. "You found my gift."

Laurel didn't know what to say. She was all warm and gooey inside. He'd not only made the most public display of affection, but he'd given her the taste of home, and he was... smiling. Dimples and all.

She wasn't the only one lost for words. All three fae on the lawn stood agape. But Thorne didn't care. He put his lips near her ear. "For the record, any time you want to wake me as you did last night, is fine with me."

Clearly, fae had good hearing, because one of them let out a taunting wolf whistle. Laurel's cheeks heated.

"Don't be shy," Thorne chuckled. "They probably heard last night too."

"What!" she gasped.

He shrugged. "You took me by surprise last night, but I'll spell the room tonight to give us some privacy." Then his gaze turned wicked. "Unless you want me to spell it now. I think we have a few minutes before the council meeting."

Apparently, they didn't. Across the lawn, Leaf strode toward them, his golden hair gilded by the morning sun. He wore a grave expression on his face.

"Something is wrong," Thorne murmured, eyes on Leaf.

When Leaf arrived, he gestured for them all to go indoors.

"What is it?" Thorne asked.

"I'll tell you when everyone is together."

"Just tell us now."

Leaf put his hands on his hips, shot a glance to the other concerned Guardians, and exhaled. "We received an invitation from High King Mithras last night."

Thorne tensed beside Laurel.

Leaf continued, "It's for a ball in honor of his announcement to recognize his first and only heir."

"Fuck off, he is," Haze spat.

A growl ripped out of both Thorne's and Rush's throats. The rest of them held a glower on their face that could cut stone, but Laurel wasn't quite understanding.

"Why is this not a good thing?" she asked.

"The king assassinated his offspring years ago—both legitimate and illegitimate," Leaf explained. "Unless he's secretly produced an heir none of us know about, his only living heir is Jasper."

"Who is the invitation for?" Thorne asked.

"The Prime, plus one."

"I'll go with her," Thorne decreed.

Leaf raised a brow. "I think not."

Thorne raised his palm. "This has always been *my* hunt."

"At the expense of your duty to the Well," Leaf reminded.

"I understand that. And I will make amends, but this is—"

Leaf shook his head, cutting Thorne off. "It is not up to me to decide. The Prime will bring someone with her."

"Then we find a way to get in ourselves," Rush added.

"This is impossible," Aeron, the brown-haired elf, said. "This ball will be by invitation only. Unless we find due cause to enter the citadel, we won't be able to get in. We can't even disguise ourselves." He pointed at his teardrop tattoo. "Glamor won't cover this."

"Is it a masquerade?" Thorne asked, eyes hopeful.

Leaf shook his head. "It matters not what we discuss now. The Prime has requested we all meet in the council chambers as soon as possible. You lot head there, and Aeron and I will gather the rest."

Leaf strode into the house with Aeron. The remaining Guardians got into a heated discussion about how, and who, would be the best person to go with the Prime. Laurel stood back, letting them talk, because her mind was already whirling.

The opportunity was too fortuitous. An invitation. She just had to make sure her name was on it.

THIRTY-ONE

Thorne led Laurel up the temple steps and into the room adjoining it where the Council usually met. An open pantheon, the temple overlooked the entire Order grounds. They'd passed acolytes and novitiates seeing to the upkeep of the floral arrangements, and water integrity as it flowed in a stream from the fountains to culverts to staircases, all leading down to ground level.

He'd not been up there often. The sacred pools, with the elemental obelisks sticking out of the center, always grated on him. One of his earliest memories of entering this place was moving from pool to pool after his initiation ceremony, and having his elemental affinity tested before being sent to his rooms at the barracks the first time. When Laurel tensed next to him, he realized she would have her own memories of this place now. She, too, had been tested upon arriving in this place.

The council chamber was crowded with Guardians from the Twelve. Three blue robed Mages, council members, were also there. Barrow was a preceptor at the academy. He'd had an accident with his mana a few decades ago that left him a little aged and with long white hair. Colt, the pixie, was also a preceptor, and Dawn was the head Seer.

The Prime stood at the front of the room, at the edge of the pantheon, and with her back to the view of grounds below. White feathered wings draped like a mantle over brown shoulders and blue gown. White coiled ringlets bounced when she turned her head Thorne's way. Her large owl-shifter eyes tracked him as he made his way into the room with his hand gripped tightly around Laurel's.

This should be fun, he thought bitterly.

As Thorne was the last to arrive, Barrow cast a privacy ward around the room, ensuring not one word of their conversation would be heard beyond their immediate proximity. Thorne took Laurel to where Rush and Clarke stood near a pillar. He faced the front and drew Laurel to his chest, firmly clasping his arms around her front.

"I have asked you to come here today as there is some news pertinent to us all and we must come to a decision together," the Prime said.

Thorne scoffed. Since when did she consult them all?

The Prime cocked her head Thorne's way. "Do you have something to say, D'arn Thorne?"

"Why bother asking us?" he replied. "You'll make up your own mind, anyway."

She stared at him long and hard. So long, that Thorne believed she would either erupt with offense or ignore him. But her face suddenly lost its defense. She sighed.

"This is the way it has been in the past. True. But..." She glanced at Clarke, of all people. "I am learning that change is a good thing, and I must embrace it if we are to overcome this new threat."

New threat. Did she mean the humans from Crystal City or King Mithras? Perhaps it was both?

"It is no secret I am responsible for the loss of D'arn Jasper from our ranks."

"You mean you sold him," Thorne shot out again. "Don't mince your words, Prime."

Her jaw clenched, but to her credit, she didn't back down. "This is one way of naming what I did. Another way is to say I have secured us your mate."

She gestured at Laurel, who tensed in his arms. He tightened his grip. "Clarke is the one who led us to Laurel."

"And who led Rush to Clarke?" the Prime raised a brow.

Dammit. She was right. He knew it. He knew it a long time ago, yet he still couldn't let it go.

The Prime lowered her brows at Thorne. "You cannot believe that the events that led to Clarke's discovery were easy for me to decide. The fae who have died as a result will be a burden I, and I alone, carry. It will weigh me down when I finally rejoin the cosmic Well."

A hollow ache filled Thorne's chest. He'd not yet met these humans they were so fearful of, the ones who'd destroyed the planet the first time around, but he'd seen the evidence of their destruction, not only in the icy wastelands that covered most of the planet today, but in the aftermath of Clarke's kidnapping two years ago. They'd preyed on Thaddeus Nightstalk's vulnerable inky side and used him to carry out their wishes, harvesting mana from the souls of fae to feed the humans and their false immortality. Thorne still remembered the cages lining the Crescent Hollow village boundary walls. He still remembered Anise's weak body as he drew her out of the cage suspended from the ground. And if these humans were the same ones somehow behind Jasper's capture at the Ring... a low growl rumbled in his throat.

"I may not have shown it," he said to the Prime, "but I understand this threat. I am here, Prime, because I stand on the same side as you."

She gave him a slight nod and turned to the rest of the congregation. "High King Mithras has invited me, and a guest of my choosing, to a ball in honor of naming his new heir. It is in a week's time. Considering Jasper's recent sighting, we're all assuming he is the one the king is naming as his heir."

A murmur of discontent and discussion arose, but the Prime raised her hand.

"I'm not finished. As anyone who is over the age of three hundred is aware, when the thaw began, and King Mithras broke away from the Unseelie Kingdom to create the Seelie Kingdom, he subsequently and systematically assassinated every fae he'd sired. The only offspring he was unable to touch was Jasper, and that was because Jasper sought refuge with the Order and his identity was stripped from him, thus removing any claim to the throne."

"He's also a bastard," Barrow said, his white busy eyebrows drawn down. "What makes you so sure he's the one the king is naming as heir?"

Cloud stepped forward, dark smudges under his eyes. "Because Ash, River, and I have spent the night confirming this is true."

Thorne straightened. All three crows in the Twelve had gone on a reconnaissance mission. To Helianthus? "You've seen him?"

A solemn nod. "We flew over the citadel, gathered gossip, and then watched in the palace grounds. Not only did the serving staff talk freely of the new prince, but we saw him being fitted for his party attire."

Rage surged in Thorne.

"How is it Dawn hasn't *Seen* this?" Leaf gestured toward the Seer.

But Thorne knew it was the same way that Rush was able to go *unseen* during his curse. It was the reason he was cursed in the first place.

"Jasper has curse marks around his collar," Thorne said. "Both Mithras and Bones have been linked to this act."

The Prime's wings flared dramatically with an irritated snap. "They're working together, and they've used our own technique against us," she noted. "They're fast learners."

A rumble of dissent rippled across the room. Cloud muttered general insults at the human race. Thorne glared at him.

"So Mithras is working with them?" Colt asked.

"It seems so," the Prime answered.

Colt frowned. "Then we need to stop the spread of their blasphemy before the rest of Elphyne believe they are more important than the Well. If we don't make a move against these dissenters, they will soon have the upper hand. Clearly it's time to bring the kings and queens in on this threat. We must warn the other rulers."

The Prime looked to Clarke for answers, who cowered a little under the intense gaze. Laurel gave Clarke a slight nod, an act which seemed to bolster Clarke's confidence.

Clarke lifted her chin and leveled her gaze at the Prime. "You know who you must bring with you."

Good. Finally some sense. Thorne let go of his mate and stepped forward. But the Prime's gaze settled on Laurel. The walls closed in, and, in a rush of paranoia, Thorne suddenly felt as though he was the last to come to this conclusion because everyone in the room nodded as though it made perfect sense. Even Laurel. Why her? Because of her fire power?

"No," he barked, pre-empting the Prime's response. "She is not going with you. Take a Guardian. It doesn't have to be me, but you need a warrior beside you."

Laurel's eyes flared in irritation. "I fought with you in the Ring. I'm not that incompetent."

"You would have died if I didn't save you," he shot back.

"I know the humans, I've seen what they look like, I can point them out. I know how they think. I can help the Prime get the information we need to bring Jasper home."

Maybe that was true, but it still wasn't good enough for Thorne. Blinding panic heated his face. "Are you mad? You're not ready. You've been awake in this time for but a week!"

"You've trained me well enough."

"Don't be daft, Laurel. You can't even sense when I'm siphoning your mana without your permission."

She gasped and the silence in the room became deafening.

Shit. He shouldn't have said that. Not here. Not in front of everyone. He'd planned to explain how it all worked properly when they had the time. He needed to ease her into what he'd done. What he'd already promised himself he wouldn't do again.

"You've been doing what?" Laurel ground out through her teeth.

He looked to the ceiling and tried to calm the rising sense of helplessness. May as well let her know all. Then she'd understand what a fool's errand this was. He was sure everyone would agree. "During the battle, when I broke the binding rune they put on me, I used your mana to do it. It is why you almost collapsed in the midst of the battle."

"You put your mate in danger?" Rush growled. "Without even asking her permission?"

"I needed to use a transference spell to bring Fury to me," he shot back. Could none of them see that had been the only decision to make, whether he'd asked permission or not. "Having Fury was the only reason I defeated the Well-hounds." He rounded on the Prime. "So you see, I can do whatever you need her for. She doesn't need to be in the thick of it. Just nearby in case I need to replenish my mana."

"If I had known that's all I meant to you, Thorne, I wouldn't have..." Laurel choked. Hurt, betrayal, and pain surged into Thorne through their bond. She was taking this all the wrong way. How could she not see that he only wanted to protect her? Couldn't she *feel* that from him? Wasn't that enough?

And then she did something that cleaved his heart in two, more than any stroke of a blade. She straightened her spine, walked over to him, took his hand, and looked him squarely in the eye. "We have located Jasper. You have taught me the ways of this land to my satisfaction. Consider our bargain ended."

"No," he said. "You can't walk away from me. We're bonded."

She shrugged. "That's your rule, not mine."

"It's the Well's rule. You're stuck with me, Laurel, whether you like it or not."

She glared at him. "Being *stuck* with you isn't exactly how I imagined this going. If you can't trust me to be on my own, without you, and with the Prime, then what are we doing? As far as I can see, the Well-blessed mating works well when we're together, but there are no adverse affects when we're apart, except the strength of our shared mana and emotions is weakened. So, technically, I can walk away."

"That's not what I meant. You're getting this all wrong." His heart thudded. His skin went hot and prickly. She promised she wouldn't.

"Well, let me say it in a way you understand. In the binding words of our original bargain, we must walk away from each other."

A spark of heat zapped between their palms as their agreement ended with a snap.

Laurel turned and walked out of the temple.

She Well-damned *walked away* from him.

"We need her, Thorne," the Prime said gently. "Not only can her Well-blessed markings be hidden by appropriate attire, but I believe your mate has the power within her to keep a cloaking spell active for an extended period. She can get into places in the castle none of us can. We just need to train her."

All he heard was waffle because the blood in his ears was roaring. The wolf in him snarled with fury. Claws sprung from his fingertips. Fangs elongated in his mouth. He glared at her and spoke with a voice no longer human.

"You," he spat. "What more will you take from me?"

The Prime blinked, surprised.

And it infuriated him all the more. But then she filled with her power, letting the electric currents of the Well crackle along her skin, sparking and lighting with raw energy.

"Now you, D'arn Thorne, must walk away before you go somewhere dark you may not return from."

Every pair of eyes in the room watched him warily, readying their own power in case he released his. But they weren't worth it. None of them were. If his own mate couldn't understand him, then why was he trying? Thorne turned to the only one who'd given him comfort over his years... his wolf. He shifted, burst out of his clothes, and trotted out of there.

CHAPTER

THIRTY-TWO

Laurel stood at the window in Ada's room and looked at the front lawn as the sun came up. A fire crackled on the hearth, keeping the brisk cold air outside, but condensation had gathered on the window, casting much of the view into warped bubble patterns.

It had been three days since Thorne had shifted into wolf and ran out of the Order compound.

Three days and she'd not heard a peep.

The markings on her arm told her next to nothing. Just a distant presence meaning he was alive, somewhere out there in the wild, poisonous forest surrounding the Order campus walls. And that was the icing on her pain-filled cake. Thorne preferred to live in a poisonous forest, possibly as a wolf, rather than coming home and working through their argument.

He'd hurt her immensely.

She would have given her mana freely if he'd asked at the Ring.

If he'd asked.

But this was about keeping the truth from her. The fae couldn't lie, but they could certainly keep the truth to themselves and, in doing so, he'd unwittingly committed the most heinous crime to her person. He'd taken away her ability to protect herself.

He *knew* how Bones had made her feel.

He *knew*, and yet he'd said nothing about what he'd done.

She felt like she didn't know him at all. What kind of man would do that to someone he supposedly loved?

But did he? Did he love her?

She'd felt warm emotions from him, but who was to say that was love? Their mating wasn't one of their choosing. They didn't even have a wedding ceremony. When he'd described one to her, it had made her pine for one. She felt like they'd missed a whole part of a normal relationship. The part she never used to want, until him.

Thinking back on the time they'd spent together, it had always been Laurel making the sacrifices.

It ate her up inside.

But she wouldn't chase him. No. She was done with telling him to let his anger go. Done with being the one to sacrifice. It was his turn. The ball was in his court.

Maybe this was a good thing. A blessing in disguise. Everyone else believed the Prime and Laurel were going to gather intel, and to rescue Jasper, but Laurel knew. Clarke knew. Laurel wouldn't come back without seeing Bones' dead body with her own eyes. After Thorne's behavior, it was clear there was no way he'd let her go through with this secret mission.

Rush had tried to apologize for Thorne. He'd said a male wolf shifter was highly possessive after mating, but this didn't excuse Thorne's behavior prior to their mating. The stealing of her mana. That was inexcusable.

"I wish I could come with you," Clarke said from behind Laurel. "But someone needs to stay with Ada."

Laurel turned to her friend sitting next to Ada on the bed. "Pretty is lucky to have you as a friend, Clarke. I am too."

"I hope that is true."

"After I go to Helianthus City, you'll see it is. I won't let you down."

Laurel turned back to the window and ran her finger down the condensation on the window. Water trickled to land in a pool at the bottom windowsill.

"Thorne will be back," Clarke declared.

Laurel couldn't find it in herself to feel. "Is this something you've *Seen*?"

"No. It's something I know because he's mated to you. I know how he would be feeling right now."

Like his heart is being ripped out? She hoped so. Because hers was.

"I don't think it's the same for us, Clarke. Thorne and I are different from you and Rush."

"The only difference is that Thorne is extra stubborn." Clarke took a breath. "And he was extra hurt. He never had a loving family like you."

"I know that," she snapped.

"I don't think you do. And don't take this the wrong way, but the scars of a broken and lonely childhood stay with you forever."

Laurel wanted to snap her anger at Clarke again, but her friend was right. Losing Lionel hurt. Deeply. But she'd had two loving parents to fill the gap. She'd had *people*. Some had no one. Some were empty for a long time.

Clarke had grown up with a mother who hated and vilified her. Her father had died young. She was alone until a bad man seduced her vulnerable state and manipulated her. If it weren't for Laurel and Ada befriending Clarke, she might still be with that bad man, but the world as they knew it would still be gone.

Including the loving family Laurel left behind.

A surge of defiance ran through Laurel. Clarke was wrong. Laurel deserved to feel anguish over missing her family. What made Thorne's pain more worthy than hers? It was all relative. Everyone had a right to hurt in the way that mattered to them. It didn't mean they could take it out on those they supposedly cared for. What allowed him to get away with his behavior? He'd had Jasper. He'd had his aunt. And now, he had Rush, Clarke, and Laurel. Yet it still wasn't enough for Thorne.

No. She frowned at the window. She was a queen. A boss. She wouldn't be treated this way. By anyone.

"Are you prepared?" Clarke asked.

"The dress is made. I've practiced the cloaking spell until I've gone cross-eyed."

"That's not what I meant."

Laurel turned and met her friend's grave eyes. She glanced at her ruined nails, but this time, she resisted the urge to rub them on her thighs in an attempt to erase that feeling. No. She curled her fingers into a fist and used that sensation to drive her resolve.

"I won't hesitate when I see him, don't worry. I don't care if it's in a crowded room." Dark, bitter anger filled Laurel. "If I see Bones, I'll burn him to ash."

THIRTY-THREE

In his wolf form, and from the shadows of the trees surrounding the Order walls, Thorne watched the procession bound for Helianthus City leave the grounds. It was unusual that the Prime had chosen to travel by horse and carriage. A portal would have been faster, unless she wanted to travel the long way on purpose.

He hated not knowing why.

A curtain in the carriage window twitched, and Thorne caught sight of his mate's sweet face as she stared out the window, perhaps looking for him. He'd never know because she turned her face back into the dark recess of the cabin where a shock of white ringlets bounced before the curtain was dropped.

Bitterness seethed anew.

And then with each passing moment, the carriage drew away, his battered emotions ebbed, draining away with the distance.

The sense of Laurel's presence lessened in his soul until she became naught but a ghost of a feeling down his bond, and he was once again as lonely as he'd always been. An ache in his chest grew.

He let loose a howl that shook the trees. When the last notes died, his ears pricked up at the sound of footsteps. His hackles rose as he concentrated on the sound: crunching fallen leaves and twigs. And then he scented kin. A white wolf padded out of the shelter of trees and turned to him, golden eyes piercing.

Rush.

A shimmering light haloed the wolf's body, and then Rush shifted into fae form. The deep scowl on his face softened inexplicably. He opened his mouth to speak, but Thorne, still in wolf form, growled at him.

He didn't need a lecture. He knew exactly what a floater he'd been, but he didn't know how to handle the feelings that had been choking him in that council room. He'd only meant to come out here until he could breathe better... and somehow he couldn't work up the courage to find his way back. He couldn't face Laurel with his tail between his legs. Shame had never been in his emotional canon.

Until her.

"I don't know how to help you mend this wound between you and your mate," Rush said. "That's not why I'm here."

Thorne stilled. He sat on his hind legs and looked up at Rush.

"Laurel will need your help where she is going." Rush scrubbed his beard, anguish on his face.

Alarm prickled Thorne all over. Laurel needed his help? He shifted back to fae form.

"What is it?" His throat felt raw from under-use.

"I overheard them speak." Rush met Thorne's eyes, then looked away with a frown. "Shit. If Clarke finds out I'm here, she'll have my balls in a vice."

"Rush," Thorne growled, now filling with apprehension.

"But just because we're mated, doesn't mean we always agree. I'm the only one who knows how you feel right now, Thorne. I understand these overwhelming feelings you must have. The urge to protect is so strong after mating. It drove me to do something that almost ended in Clarke's death. If you don't travel to Helianthus City, you won't be able to stop Laurel from making the worst mistake of her life. She's going to kill the one who tortured her."

"Good," Thorne spat. "He will deserve to have his life cut short."

Laurel deserved a little reparation.

"Yes, he does. But does Laurel deserve the burden of such an act?"

Thorne's blood slowly drained from his face.

Rush continued, "Perhaps she's not told you enough about her time and where she was from. Before the very end, they lived peacefully. The only death they knew was from disease or old age. Murder was reserved for the lowliest of them, and few and far between suffered the consequences. Not like now."

The gravity of what Rush said settled in Thorne like a falling stone. If Laurel took on this mantle, it would ruin her. Such an act would eat at her soul. He thought back to all the ways she'd used her power. None of the times had ended in the death of the enemy. She'd been strong, powerful, and at times ruthless. But she wasn't a killer.

He was.

It had been Thorne who'd ended their opponents without a second thought in the Ring. If her time had truly been more peaceful, then having to become this person that killed, so soon after waking from her time, it would irrevocably change her.

"There's more," Rush added. "Cloud and Shade went back to interrogate Patches about the djinn bottle. With what they gathered from his guard too, they've pieced together more mercenary acts of terror paid for by Mithras coin."

"Meaning?"

"Someone close to the king has been paying Patches to make it look like Unseelie are attacking the Seelie."

"So it is true. Someone is inciting a civil war between fae-kind."

"Yes."

"You think it's the humans?"

Rush nodded. "Clarke and I suspected it's been happening for some time, but after we were rid of Thaddeus, there wasn't much activity. When I'd visited the human city while I was cursed, I saw nothing of this magnitude. That coupled with the fact Clarke's recent visions were mainly about finding Laurel and Ada, we thought we had time to deal with the Void. Now we know the humans were using this time to get a stronghold within the Summer Court."

A new flood of irritation swam through Thorne. "Knowing all this, then how can you be happy with the Prime's plan to take Laurel with her? There is more we can do on behalf of the Well. The Order has a right to raid the palace."

Rush scoffed. "No, we don't. We need more evidence. But if you'd stuck around long enough, you'd have learned the Guardians pushed for our own extraction plan for Jasper. And the Prime has approved it."

"She has?"

"It is why she left by carriage and not portal. She is creating a distraction, making the journey to the Summer Court in Helianthus a spectacle. And we have time to prepare." Rush's gaze turned inward. "Do you know I almost killed the Prime for what she did to us? I went to her office, drew Starcleaver, and swung it at her head. I caught naught but a tail-feather as she flew out of the window. And now I am glad that I missed." He leveled his stare on Thorne. "Killing anyone because of perceived injustice is no way to honor the Well. It makes us no better than the ones who came before us."

"Perceived injustice?" Thorne growled. "How can you say that? It was real."

"I only meant the Prime has been different since the news about Jasper came out. I believe she is regretful. I now understand the toll it takes to keep Elphyne flourishing. She had to make an untenable decision. Any way she chose, someone was going to get hurt. She picked the fate that ended with Clarke alive. And with Clarke alive, Laurel is alive. More will live because of this choice. Possibly the rest of the world will be born anew. I will never forgive the Prime for what she's done, but I believe she deserves a chance to make amends for her mistake with Jasper."

His words hit Thorne hard.

It *had* been an untenable decision. Less death vs more death. Could Thorne say he'd be able to take that burden on?

No.

Which meant Thorne had been a fool. A giant floating piece of useless, Well-rejected trash. Not only to Laurel, but to the Order. He'd let his anger get in the way, and because of his inability to see past it, they'd have learned about the link with the djinn's owner before he'd even met Laurel. They'd know the humans had infiltrated the Summer Court long before Jasper was removed from the Ring. But it took Laurel to teach him to let go of that anger. So, in a way, Clarke had been right. Laurel had led him to finding Jasper in more ways than one.

All they knew about the Void now was that he wanted Elphyne for himself, and he believed he could use magic without having to follow the rules the Well had given them. He wanted to bring metals and plastics back. He wanted to dominate the new world. The fae knew that this would have catastrophic consequences. For centuries, the world struggled to gain its life back. Survival in the harsh, frozen landscape was nothing more than that... survival. There were those among the fae—the Prime, namely—who still remembered that world. She made sure to remind them of it often. They weren't living back then. They were surviving. It wasn't until Jackson Crimson discovered the link to the Well, and the rules about metals and plastics, that life flourished anew.

Life came back to the planet. New species were made in both animal and plant life. Some species thought extinct had thawed and were brought back to the living. And it was only through the grace of the Well that this happened. Letting the Void go back to the old, greedy ways would spell the end, and if they got rid of Bones, the Void would only find another to fill his place.

"We should capture this Bones person. He is the Void's right-hand man. We should capture him and not kill him because it could set off a chain reaction of revenge with the Void. For all we know, they are lovers. They've traveled through time to be here. I might not be anywhere near the truth, but if there's one thing I've learned this year, it's that I don't know everything," Thorne said. "We should capture him, and then give him to Cloud to interrogate."

"Agreed."

Thorne's gaze snapped to his father's, a mirror image of his own except for the color. Thorne inherited that from his mother. It may have taken Thorne some time to come to terms with Rush's presence, but now Thorne could see he was a fae of honor, and he was doing his best to put the painful past behind them—something they couldn't change—and look to the future. Something they *could* change.

There was much Thorne could learn from his father.

"If Laurel is allowed to end this human," Rush continued. "It could cause catastrophic consequences. I don't know why or how Clarke has not *seen* this. I think sometimes we rely on her knowing too much from her visions, we fail to see that she is just as fallible as the rest of us. Her emotions get in the way too. She is afraid. I sense it every day. We all make mistakes. How we deal with them is our true test of character."

"How are you so wise?" Thorne joked.

"I've spent a long time watching the behavior of others."

This made a sadness well inside Thorne. "You were there when I grew up," he acknowledged.

"Yes. Until you got to the Order I shared in your pain. And then... seeing you with Jasper." Rush looked away. "It was then I realized you were moving on without me. It hurt too much to watch, so I moved away. I trusted Jasper to look after you."

It took a long moment before Thorne had the courage to say, "I understand this now. And... I am sorry no one was there to share your pain."

Rush's eyes watered. His jaw clenched. And he nodded.

For it was known that only family apologized so freely to one another. Only family didn't expect a boon in return.

Emotion clogged Thorne. And then, for the first time in his decades-long life, he hugged his father.

THIRTY-FOUR

The journey south from the Order of the Well to the Helianthus City took three days.

It was only three days.

She could wait three days to hear Bones scream as he melted in her fire. To smell his scorched flesh. To feel an echo of the pain he'd inflicted on her. It was all she cared about now, and somehow, she'd equated the end of Bones with the release of the bitterness left from Thorne's betrayal.

How could he?

He'd used her.

Left her vulnerable.

He'd left.

And didn't come back.

She knew he was hurting. She knew she'd walked away from him first. But she was hurting too. She'd had her whole world ripped from her, and she was tired of trying to stay positive about it.

The long journey to Helianthus City meant they had to stop at many villages along the way. At each stop, the Prime would get out and wave regally and bestow blessings on the townspeople. Laurel would stay in the carriage or regale herself to any room or lodgings volunteered by the grace of townspeople loyal to the Well.

Without Clarke, or the distraction of keeping Ada hydrated and alive, Laurel slipped into a dark, resentful state of mind.

No guards traveled with them, only two Mages. One was the Prime's assistant, Maryweather, who was another owl shifter. Maryweather looked very similar to the Prime, minus the curly hair. Maryweather's was straight. She sat up on the driver's box seat with Thistle, the coachman—a male fox-eared fae with red hair. Occasionally,

Laurel caught shadows flittering over the carriage, and she looked outside, expecting to see clouds, but only caught a white owl coasting. Occasionally a crow or two.

But after the first day, she'd stopped checking to see who followed them and her thoughts became consumed with how she would find Bones and assassinate him. He might not be in the palace. He might not be in Elphyne. But if he was, she would find him.

She also had to go along with the Prime's plan to rescue Jasper.

Thistle was extremely zealous in his newly self-appointed role as the tour guide and narrated stories about the towns they passed. Annoyingly, he kept interrupting her dark thoughts with his chirpy rundowns of the towns they stopped in. Like a proper gentleman, he would help Laurel and the Prime down from the carriage when necessary. He confessed to Laurel that they wouldn't be able to do this sort of fanfare in the Unseelie Kingdom. Residents there would shut their doors and stay inside, and it wouldn't be a personal insult, it was just how the Unseelie were. They didn't like outsiders, even those who dedicated their lives to serving the Well.

Maybe that was where Laurel needed to go. She might need to escape the Seelie kingdom after what she planned to do. Surely there would be someone willing to help her relocate. And if not, she had a handy cloaking spell in her canon of skills now. She would find a way. Living in the Unseelie kingdom, undisturbed by outsiders... it was definitely appealing.

As they neared Helianthus City, Laurel decided she wouldn't get another chance to discuss something that had been playing on her mind. The Prime wasn't particularly talkative during the journey, and she was a little frightening. Men trying to mansplain things to Laurel, she could take. But a strong woman, possibly as powerful as Laurel, *that* she found intimidating.

But there was one thing that had been playing on her mind. If she didn't speak up now, she might never have a chance to ask the Prime again.

"Is it really necessary to force tributes to obtain more Guardians?" she asked. "Can they not be sourced another way?"

The Prime, who had been staring out the window on her side of the carriage, a stack of papers in her hand, turned to Laurel with a knowing smirk. "I see D'arn Thorne has been in your ear about the subject."

"He has," she agreed. "But I would also like to hear your version of the truth."

The Prime looked at Laurel with a mix of suspicion and something Laurel believed was respect, then she turned back to the window.

"Our numbers are dwindling," the Prime admitted. "Elphyne is growing, flourishing, yet there are empty beds in the barracks. Guardians perish too often. Mana-twisted monsters are springing up from the depths of the Well. The threat from humans is also expanding." She sighed heavily. "Once, there was nothing more important than dedicating your life to the service of the Well. The fae knew that if we made sacrifices, the Well would reward us with a treasured world beyond our imaginations. Now we live in our imagination and our dreams have become reality. It is hard to see beyond into a future where we don't dominate. I fear the fae will have to see nightmares again before they realize how good they have it."

Laurel agreed, in a way. "Humans suffered the same affliction. We are too smart for our own good. We built the bombs, we destroyed the land, and we suffered for it. It is a pity I don't have a lesson learned you can use to teach the people of this time. We were always aware of the sinking ship but could never stop it."

The Prime leveled her stare at Laurel. It lasted so long that Laurel squirmed. "Has anyone told you the tale of the first fae who discovered the link between the Well, the magic within us, and that of the planet?"

"Jackson Crimson?" she suggested. She'd heard snippets about their first leader during her training at the academy for the cloaking spell.

"Did they tell you what happened to him?"

Laurel shook her head.

"No," the Prime said. "I suppose no one has told you. It's nowhere near as glamorous as the start of his story."

"What happened to him?"

"He dedicated his life to building the Order. He built everything you see that we have today. And then he went to the ceremonial lake, offered himself, and never came out." A sadness came over the Prime, as though she had been there, as though she'd known him. "The scriptures say he'd reached enlightenment. The Well took him into its depths and he became one with it, all-powerful, all-seeing. But... I know the truth. He was tired. Tired of fighting for Elphyne, when it didn't seem like the fae were learning from the mistakes the first humans made."

"Are you talking about metals and plastics?"

The Prime nodded. "And more. The magic. Dipping into the dark arts, thinking of themselves as gods. Cruelty. Greed. You will understand more when you meet King Mithras. I fear it is as you said. A sinking ship."

With that, the Prime turned back to her papers, effectively dismissing Laurel. But she wasn't done with the Prime.

"The fae don't need nightmares," Laurel said. "People are defensive when they believe no one is on their side. Your trouble with recruits is a classic branding problem." The Prime arched her brow at Laurel, so she continued. "In my time, we had businesses and corporations that had thousands of staff. My own company employed twelve-hundred people. To make my workplace attractive to work at, I offered free fitness clothes, free equipment, and free gym memberships. It not only made them feel of value, but it encouraged them to look after their health, which in turn made them more productive. I marketed Queen Fitness as, not only a place to work, but a way of life. Work healthy, live longer."

The Prime snorted. "We can't make that promise. Living longer isn't necessarily something we can offer. You're more likely to live longer if you *aren't* a Guardian."

"You're taking me too literally. There are plenty of things you can offer."

"Such as?"

"Such as a place to live. A warm home and a roof over their heads. Belonging. Clothes. Food. Education. Power. Glory. The knowledge that you are doing something good for the world."

"Altruism has never been a core value of the fae, despite Crimson's best efforts."

Laurel shrugged. "Perhaps. But it's a start. I saw how much the fae liked watching the ruthless battles at the Ring. Maybe you could host something like the Guardian Games, where you pit each Guardian against each other and they battle for glory—not to the death, obviously—but maybe something more sporty. Children could collect cards or place bets on their favorites. If you make these games a regular thing, soon others will want to join. It doesn't have to be a sport, but it's a popularity contest. We need to make ourselves look better than the Crown."

The Prime tapped her lip. "I think sometime later, I would like to hear more about your time and how your businesses handled these situations."

"I also would like that," Laurel replied. She hoped that one day the Order could do away with tributes. With a pang in her chest, she realized Thorne would have liked that too.

Thistle shouted down from his position outside the carriage.

"Helianthus City coming up on the right."

Laurel pulled the curtain from the window and peeked outside. Her breath sucked in hard at the beauty and found her mind inexplicably shift to Thorne. She would have liked to share this experience with him.

He'd hurt her, and she'd hurt him back. It was petty, childish, and not the way she'd normally behave.

She'd waited for days in their room for him to come back so they could talk about it, but he didn't. And with each passing day he stayed away, her heart broke a little more, and the scars between the broken parts had hardened. It was easier to turn her attention toward Bones and let him be the focus of her wrath. But now, as the city came into view, all that hatred ebbed away, and all she could think was that she wanted to share it with Thorne.

Those little small moments of joy they'd been collecting were missed.

Pushing aside her sadness, she focused on the magnificent city they approached. Helianthus City was unlike anything she'd seen before. No such cities existed in her time. This one sparkled in the sun as though it were made from diamonds.

While the carriage traveled over the uneven road, Thistle explained the impenetrable citadel walls were made from mana-fortified glass that looked like someone had frozen a wave of water as it reached breaking point. Laurel honestly couldn't tell if there was actual water inside the glass walls, or if it was sparkling manabeeze like the false sky under the hill. Would this wall glow at night, or was it the sun's rays reflecting in it now?

The weather had turned warmer. Seagulls squawked. It still wasn't the summer as she remembered it, but she supposed to these people, who had lived centuries in winter, this would indeed be very warm.

The carriage crossed a long, arched bridge to get to the city walls. As they traveled over it, a sparkling river ran from the city harbor and into a vast turquoise sea. This was the first time Laurel had seen the seaside since arriving in this time, and it was incredibly clear and pristine. Laurel gasped as they drove by a rocky beach with white sand where she could have sworn humanoid creatures basked on a warm slab of stone. Each had a fish tail. And a human head.

She whipped around to the Prime. "Were they mermaids?"

The Prime, who'd not been paying attention due to her flicking through some documents, shrugged. "Possibly. There are such fae named mermaids, but there are also fae emerging from the oceans who've lived there unnoticed for millennia until recently. With the habitable stretch of land increasing every year, we're still discovering new breeds of fae."

Holy mother-of-pearl. Laurel turned back to the window as they arrived at the citadel gates and were stopped by the soldiers guarding the entrance. All were distinguished in coats of shocking red, clean-cut appearances, shiny bone weapons or bows, and arrows. After the guards checked in to see the Prime, they were allowed through the gates. Within moments, they were moving again and driving into the citadel itself.

Laurel didn't think she could be filled with more wonder, but once inside the citadel, she saw there were not only streets, but canals that led from the estuary and wound through the packed houses, like those she'd once seen in Venice. Most townhouses weren't made from glass, like the wall, but they had glass features, enough to make it all twinkle brightly, making Laurel wish for a pair of sunglasses. Fae of all kinds came out of their dwellings to see the Prime's carriage. Some of them opened the hatches of their windows, smiled and waved. Others frowned.

Most frowned.

Definitely a branding issue.

As they took the main road, Laurel noticed fae putting up decorations in the streets. Some were already celebrating roadside with food and drink. She supposed the festivities tonight in the palace would spill out into the streets, making the king's announcement something the entire city could be a part of. Laurel's mood darkened when, as they drew closer to the palace, she noted more food, more drink, and more wastage.

What had happened to having too many mouths to feed that they resorted to killing fae for having children?

An animal roasted on a spit, but the people carousing next to it had completely forgotten. It had burned black, and they didn't care because they'd already had their fill with other food. Empty plates and cups were scattered everywhere. Seagulls scavenged and gorged. Rotten food had flies buzzing around. Had they been celebrating for days?

It certainly didn't look like the people here in the city wanted for necessities so much that they needed an unsanctioned breeding law to ensure enough resources went around. It looked like they had too much.

A tomato, or similar fruit, smashed against the carriage window and she drew back suddenly.

The Prime sighed. "Here we go."

"Why are they throwing fruit?"

"They see the Order of the Well emblem on the carriage."

"You know," Laurel commented dryly, "You should be taxing the king and this city for your monster-hunting services, not the people you save."

The thud of more fruit hit the carriage, the occasional derogatory shout from a passerby, and the responding curse from Thistle.

Laurel faced the Prime, who watched her with unguarded curiosity. Laurel thought perhaps she'd spoken out of turn, but the Prime nodded.

"You first humans are constantly astounding me. You and Clarke, I mean. The ones who live today, they're descended from your kind, but I believe they're different. Before you and Clarke arrived, I never would have thought working with the humans would be a possibility. But you keep proving me wrong, and for that, I am grateful. Not only because all the sacrifices I've made are founded, but because it gives me hope for our combined futures. Crimson always wanted us all to live in harmony. Until then..." The Prime tapped her lip. "I believe taxing the king just might be a solution we can entertain." She pointed at Laurel. "Remind me when we return to the Order."

Pride swelled in Laurel as she turned back to gazing out of the window. Yes. Perhaps she was going to find her feet in this world, after all. Whether it was with Thorne, the Prime, or otherwise. She wouldn't let Bones take this away from her. Not this time.

THIRTY-FIVE

Standing before a black-glass mirror, Laurel watched her reflection as Maryweather fussed about, tying Laurel's turquoise blue shoulder straps and securing a small beaded headdress. The dress was too much, but the Prime had insisted Laurel look eye catching enough to gain the king's attention.

Eye-catching meant a neckline that dipped to her navel and showed ample cleavage. The same cut existed at the back, showing skin all the way down to the curve of her very awesome rear-end. So low that she couldn't wear underwear. The dress hugged her hips and then flared near the floor, fishtail style, ending in patterns of red, yellow, and orange.

Sky on fire.

That's what her dress reminded her of.

Scattered along the base hem of the dress, sparkling beads glowed sporadically as though powered by electricity. Her favorite pearlescent crushed powder highlighted her smooth skin. When she walked, she shimmered, as though she truly were on fire.

With strong black eye makeup, pale glossy lips, and long dangling earrings, she felt like she was going to the Met Gala. She'd been once with a Cross-fit champion on her arm. It had all been for publicity, but it was fun. Maybe this could be too. The fae certainly knew how to dress. She was truly extravagant, and she wasn't ashamed to admit it. The only part she didn't like was the way her pinned back hair showed her very round ears.

They'd discussed at length whether Laurel would go in disguise. In the end, they decided that the king was already liaising with humans. Laurel had already declared to Cornucopia she was human, so why not use her humanity to their benefit? This was essentially Laurel's debutante introduction into the fae society as a powered human. It not only signaled that she was here, but that she was accepted by the Order, and that they would stand behind her if anyone tried to hurt her. Still...

"It's too much," she said. "The cloaking spell works better if I'm already inconspicuous."

The Prime barely looked up from the letter she penned with quill and ink at a desk. Her simple white dress draped down her legs to pool at the floor.

"We've been through this," she said, eyes still on her work. "The cloaking spell is a backup. First, we want you to attract attention. The king has been refusing to grant me an audience for the past two years. The only way to speak privately with him is for you to catch his eye. He likes new things. He likes beautiful things. He likes collecting human artisans and holding them captive. Word about the human with fire power who fought in the Ring will have reached him by now. And since you have Well-blessed markings on your body, he will be very curious. He and I have a history. We compete. He won't like that I have you and he doesn't. He will endeavor to steal you for himself. Even seduce you."

"Even knowing I'm mated?"

"Nobody can erase that mating, but he won't want to do that. He'll want to conquer you and use you. Then he will throw you away."

"You make this sound so appealing," she muttered under her breath. And then louder, "Why can't you demand he hand Jasper back to you? You're the Prime of the Order of the Well. I thought you were above Elphyne law."

The Prime lifted her head, smiled, and arched a brow. "Now, if that was the case, we wouldn't be here, would we?" She went back to her letter. "No. The sorry fact is that the courts are starting to shun the Order, and powerful as we are, we are small. On our way in, I noticed emissaries from the Autumn and Spring Courts. This does not bode well."

"Why not?"

"Because the Autumn Court is part of the Unseelie kingdom. If Mithras is attempting to sway them, he's trying to amass power. He wants them to defect and to join him with his attack on Queen Maebh. Our job at this ball is not only to retrieve Jasper as one of our own but to put in a show of force. To say that we know what is happening, and we are as strong as they are."

"Force?" Laurel asked. "But it's just you and me."

The Prime blinked. "Whatever gave you that idea?"

"Oh. I just assumed because you never told me otherwise."

"Why would I tell you my plans? You've yet to pledge loyalty to the Well. You haven't even discussed tenure at the Order. The only reason I trust you this far is that my Seer, Dawn, has foretold that for us to have a beneficial outcome from this ball, you are necessary."

Laurel turned back to the mirror and tried to keep her beating heart to a minimum. What else had the Prime planned? Was any of it going to interfere with Laurel's intentions to assassinate Bones? Should she tell the Prime? Unease swam through Laurel's stomach and she pressed her palm there. Maybe going out half-cocked and just killing some random person in the royal court might not be a good idea, even if he was one of the worst humans in history.

She felt sick with doubt and ached for Thorne's steady presence. A hard lump formed in her throat. She missed him. More than she'd ever imagined. Would he miss her too, if all this went south?

Laurel cast one last glance at herself in the mirror. It was a beautiful dress. Sky on fire. She flared her fingers at her stomach. Maryweather had offered to glamor her nails, but Laurel declined, as she always did. They were her battle scars, a reminder of everything Bones had taken. A reminder for her to stay the course. She rubbed her nails against her thighs.

⚖

HUES of the setting sun glimmered into the palace through the crystal clear ceiling. Laurel waited patiently with the Prime in an anteroom beside the ballroom, catching glimpses of the ballroom every time a guest entered through the long red, velvet drapes. From what she could see inside, more curtains lined the walls, covering masonry so that it looked like a room made from velvet and glass, opulent to its core.

From the loud conversation, the string quartet, and the jingling of bells—something the Prime explained probably belonged to a jester—it seemed like festivities were well underway. Laurel had yet to glimpse Jasper, or Bones, or the king. But she saw plenty of glamorously dressed fae, just like her. She didn't feel so out of place.

The Prime stood next to Laurel, and fumed. They'd been waiting for at least thirty minutes to be admitted to the ballroom and announced. Her great white owl wings were packed away—shifted into her body, so she looked virtually human, if it weren't for the aura of otherness to her.

Finally, a fae with large curling ram horns and a waistcoat called them through the drapes. Once inside the ballroom, he made them stop. He pinched his lips. Looked down at them, and then raised his trumpet, taking the attention of the ballroom. He read from a sheet where they'd written their names down.

"May I present Aleksandra, Her Illustrious Prime of the Order of the Well, and, er... Miss Laurel Baker, Fitness Queen of Las Vegas."

Laurel grinned at her title. None of them knew where Vegas was, but like the Prime had said, they needed to use her humanity to an advantage. It would intrigue the king, and it would flush Bones out. If he was here.

She strode into the room with her chin held high, her spine straight, and her eyes wary.

But she couldn't see past the crowds of curious gentry, the lords and ladies of Elphyne. Perhaps even a queen or a king. And she couldn't see past her own disgust. Not only were the fae here grossly overdressed, but the food was extravagant, as was the drink. Hanging from the glass ceiling were large chandeliers with half-naked fae dangling, performing acrobatics and swinging from thick, green vines. As they walked around the perimeter of the room, Laurel heard dallying laughter, and the occasional sound of couples clearly enjoying themselves. There must be hidden alcoves behind the curtains.

At round tables, fae behaved badly, throwing food into each other's mouths, shooting back drinks from the bosoms of ladies, dipping under the tables to play with pet animals on leashes. Some of them weren't even animals. Some were fae. Or perhaps... human.

And then they walked into the center of the room, right before the dais leading up to the king's throne, flanked by Jasper on one side, and Bones on the other. Laurel's heart threatened to pound out of her chest, but she forced herself to ignore both of them and keep her eyes on the king. As they stopped before the dais, Laurel's eyes lifted and landed on the golden-haired, svelte fae with eyes like honey. His wolfish ears stuck out from the weight of a delicate blown-glass crown. His long golden locks looked more like a lion's mane than that of a wolf.

But it was clear he was a wolf. She could see it in the wild shadows of his eyes. They were the same as Jasper's. But where the king was golden, Jasper was dark. Laurel bet that he would shift into a black wolf with that brown and black-tipped hair. He looked better than he had at the arena—face cleaned, no wounds in sight. His high, frill-neck shirt covered his curse marks, and a velvet orange coat hugged his physique. On his head sat a smaller, blown-glass crown. Clearly, he was the heir, but he wasn't even allowed to sit.

A statue with empty eyes.

Was he drugged?

Sadness bloomed in Laurel, and then she shifted her gaze to the other side of the throne where a face she'd never forget stared back at her. Bones. In a red embroidered coat. He was part of the king's royal guard.

Heat prickled Laurel's face and under her arms. Without helping herself, her fingers rubbed and flexed against her thighs. There he was. And with pointed elf-ears. He watched her with a black, evil gaze. He caught the movement of her fingers and then smiled.

He fed off fear. She wouldn't give it to him. She stopped rubbing her nails. Cold, hard fury seethed in her blood. That's all he would receive from her now. That was the last time she'd let her panic take over.

The king looked at Laurel, then down to the Prime. His finger tapped on the arm of his throne as he stared at her in contemplation. But then Bones whispered something in the king's ear, and his gaze snapped back to Laurel.

The king stood up.

He stepped down the dais and came toward Laurel, like a lion stalking its prey. Mithras pushed past the Prime and stopped mere inches from Laurel's feet. This slight was exactly what the Prime had hoped, but she acted affronted, all the same.

The crowd cleared around them, giving ample room for the king to inspect Laurel. The Prime made a very loud, obvious huff, and then retreated to another table where she struck a conversation with two bronze-skinned and auburn-haired fae.

"Human," the king drawled, drawing her attention back to him. He gave her the once over, like she was a prized mare on auction. His golden gaze, a brand down her body. "You are simply breathtaking."

Laurel met his gaze and nodded. "I am."

The king blinked, shocked by her admission, and then paused as though recollecting his strategy.

In Laurel's experience, men didn't like it when an empowered female accepted their compliment. They wanted to be the one with the power, lauding their attention as though it were a gift from a god—them. So the easiest way to establish a power balance was to meet him halfway. Laurel knew she was beautiful. She knew she had a trim body that men drooled over. She'd worked damned hard for it. She'd earned her confidence.

She held out her hand. The one with her Well-blessed markings glowing brightly on her skin. The king's gaze flared with some hidden emotion, and then he took her hand and lowered his lips to it, ensuring he smelled her with his keen wolf senses.

Laurel didn't miss his gaze catching on her nails and watched curiously to see what he would do. He rubbed his thumb over her hand and straightened but didn't let go.

"You are a most curious human."

"My name is Laurel."

"Laurel," he tested. "A name as beautiful as the person it belongs to. Tell me, Laurel, do you have any special artistic gifts?" He gestured to the string quartet currently playing in the corner. Like the musicians she'd seen at the Birdcage, these played with bleeding fingers. "I most like the human artisans from Crystal City. They're unlike anything we experience here in Elphyne."

She smiled at him. Name dropping the impenetrable human city was a veiled display of his influence and reach. Perhaps he assumed that Laurel thought because he could take these humans whenever he wanted, he could take her too. They were chattel to him.

Laurel darted a glance to Bones. He'd traded in metal cages and weapons to Thaddeus, and now he was using his own kind to get in the king's good graces.

"I'm not from Crystal City."

His brows winged up. "No?"

He still held her hand, idly rubbing his thumb over her skin, making sure to touch her blue mating marks. He also looked occasionally to the one at her neck and it seemed to titillate him further, as though he planned to take what belonged to someone else. She had the sudden urge to vomit, or to take a long hot bath and wash his taint away. But she settled for letting her power build until it heated her hand. He gasped and let go, looking at her shocked. Her grin stretched.

"No," she repeated. "I'm not from Crystal City. But I suspect you knew that, even before I had it announced at my arrival."

His playfulness disappeared and something wild flashed in the shadows of his eyes. His wolfish ears twitched, dislodging golden hair and nudging his crown. Laurel imagined the wolf he shifted to was dark, ruthless, and a little mad. And then the king's countenance snapped back to one of joviality.

"Come," he said, holding out his hand, proving he wasn't afraid of her fire. "Dance with me."

A murmur of surprise, shock, and awe rippled around the room. The king dancing, let alone with a human, probably didn't happen often. And she also got the sense that one didn't refuse an invitation to do so. She smiled thinly and put her hand back in his while holding the bile down in her throat.

He tugged her to his frame. Beneath the embroidered suit was a hard body she had no doubt was lethal and strong. She forced a smile on her lips. "I'm afraid I'm not versed in the dances of your world. I may step on your feet."

"Oh"—he smiled darkly—"It's not hard to follow my lead."

One hand clasped hers and lifted to the side, the other grasped her rear. No. Grasp was the wrong word. Groped was better.

A surge of fury gushed down Laurel's bond. It wasn't hers.

Thorne?

Hope flared in her chest. She cast her gaze around the room but couldn't see him. The king must have sensed her distraction. He lowered his nose to her neck, right over the bite scar, and inhaled deeply.

When he came back to face her, she saw his eyes had turned slumberous.

"You smell divine, even with the taint of your mate on there."

She frowned at him. He could smell that? "I haven't seen him for days," she mumbled.

The king gave her a rakish grin. "I wouldn't care if you did."

In other words, he might be the only male in Elphyne who couldn't care less about the rules of mating. She was told that no other male would want to be with her after she'd been sworn to Thorne—a fact he'd neglected to tell her before he'd bitten her.

Her chest constricted. *Better get this over with.*

"Why did you assume I was from Crystal City?" she asked demurely.

The king's grip on her rear tightened so much, it impeded her movement. He shifted and danced them around in a circle. "Where else would you be from?"

"The same place Bones is from."

He didn't stutter. He didn't flinch. "Bones," he said. "Such a barbaric name, don't you think?"

"So you don't deny it. You know him."

"And you lie. There is only one human city."

Two realizations hit Laurel. If the king believed there was only one human city, then Bones hadn't revealed he was from the past. The second thing was that the king clearly knew Bones was human, so the glamor on Bones' ears wasn't for the king's benefit, but for the people of Elphyne. The king knowingly colluded with Bones and didn't want them to know about it. This was all the Prime needed to know to take the matter further.

"Can Bones use mana as I can?" she pressed.

"Why so many questions about my advisor?"

"Your advisor?" she laughed. "I'm just curious if he woke from my time with the same unending power, or if he was shunned by the Well, as I've heard."

Mithras narrowed his eyes. "What do you mean, 'he woke from your time.' And no one has unending power."

"Well, perhaps not unending. But close. It's true. The Order hasn't seen the likes of this much power in one person since they started recording it. Ask the Prime if you don't believe me." She waggled her arm with the blue markings. "And I can share my power with my mate, making him all the stronger too. Did you hear about our little situation at the Ring?" She leaned closer. "My mate drew enough power from me to shatter binding runes, and I'd done the same to myself only moments before."

The king stopped dancing. She could virtually see his thoughts ticking over, wondering about the prize he had in his hands, and why Bones hadn't revealed he had this kind of power, or if Bones had it at all. Whatever he was thinking, Laurel knew she'd cast doubt into his mind.

"I want to make you an offer," she said, as a sudden thought came to her. "Release Jasper, and you can have me for as long as you want."

"Why would I want you over my kin?"

That riled. She glared back. "Because I know you like to collect things. I know you like to look better than Queen Maebh, but the sad fact is you simply aren't as powerful. Correct me if I'm wrong, but she commands the Sluagh, right? Didn't she create them?" She blinked innocently. "Tell me, King Mithras. What have you created? I'm fascinated to know."

Cold, hard menace flickered in his dark eyes.

And there it was. She'd found his core trigger. He'd broken away from the Unseelie Kingdom years ago to create the Seelie Kingdom, but Queen Maebh was one of the original fae. She was far more powerful than him, and he knew it. He feared it.

He swung her roughly around in a pirouette.

She leaned in close to him and lowered her voice seductively. "I can burn your palace of glass down in one sitting and still have power left over. Isn't that worth having in the war you're about to incite?"

"Killing you won't have the same rallying effect, I'm afraid. Even with your power, you're not worth as much as the fae upon that dais."

They were going to kill Jasper? Laurel gasped. Of course. Why else would a selfish king announce an heir when he'd assassinated all other offspring? He was greedy. He wanted to rule Elphyne. But he only had half of it, and he was no match for the Unseelie queen.

But if he made it look like she killed his only heir, then he had a symbol to rally fae armies behind. They would seek revenge, not just for the fake attacks around the realm, but for the murder of his only son.

"This was Bones' idea, wasn't it?" she accused.

The king smirked and then shrugged. "So what if it was?"

"You realize that whatever he's told you about his origins is false. Humans can lie, or have you forgotten that? He is one of the people who destroyed the first world. And the reason they did that was so the new world was smaller, more manageable, easier for them to take over." She studied the king's face. "You seem to be proving them right."

Outrage shattered the king's superior countenance. "If that were so, then why are they stuck behind their Crystal City walls, deep into the barren ice wastelands?"

"But they're not stuck, are they?" she replied. "I can see at least five in this room. The musicians you assume are your prisoners. And Bones. How many more has he smuggled into Elphyne under the guise of captives?"

The king blinked, shocked. Obviously, it had never occurred to him that this could be occurring. Laurel had no idea if it was, but at least the idea cast doubt in his mind.

458

She pressed on. "If the humans get the fae to kill each other, then they won't be stuck in the wastelands, will they?"

Indignation colored the king's cheeks. He glared at her and stepped away. "Enjoy the rest of the ball, Laurel. And tell that bitch owl that her plan failed to work. Jasper is my kin. I decide what to do with him."

And then the king walked away, back to take the steps of his dais to take a seat on his throne. Laurel noticed with great triumph that he gripped the glass arms until his knuckles were white. And his crown was crooked. Through it all, Jasper didn't even flinch. But on the other side, Bones stared at her with glimmering eyes full of dark thoughts, hatred, and a promise of pain.

Had he heard her interaction with the king? Were those glamored ears also spelled to hear better? She hoped so, because if they were, then he'd know she wasn't the demure, frightened woman she was the last time he met her. *Bring it on, ass-wipe.*

A hit of emotion hurtled into Laurel from her mating bond. Hurt, anger, and eye-watering, skin-prickling fury wracked Laurel's body. She almost choked on it and had to push her way through the crowd toward the sides. She needed a breathing space. Somewhere quiet. The volume of noise started to suffocate her. The chandelier lights were blinding. Too many things sparkled.

That king was infernally stupid, greedy, and cruel. He deserved to be burned to ash, too. Her fingertips heated as she got to the curtained wall. Combustible red velvet drapes hung from the ceiling on all sides. This would be a good place to start the fire.

She glared at the king until the crowd started to swirl around her, partially blocking her view as they returned to dance and shenanigans. It was time to move to Plan B.

Her breathing calmed. She was ready. She would burn both those suckers right there on the dais. So strong was her focus, that she failed to register the sense of Thorne's emotions getting stronger, and when she took a step toward the dais, but was stopped by an arm, she almost screamed. A hand covered her mouth, and then she was dragged through the billowing drapes, between a gap, and right into a dark, hidden alcove only big enough for her... and Thorne.

THIRTY-SIX

Thorne pushed Laurel up against the dark alcove wall and pinned her with his hips. He held her shoulders and glared at her, despite every cell in his body rejoicing to hold her again.

"I know what you're planning to do," he growled.

He could still smell traces of Mithras on her skin. His wolf howled with indignation, with outrage. It also wanted to make Laurel submit, to pay for flirting with someone *not* him. That's what she'd done, flirted and allowed the king to paw at her in places only Thorne had the right to touch.

She struggled beneath his hold. "It's none of your business, Thorne."

"Yes, it is," he said, digging his claws into her. He wanted to let his fury out, to stoke the fire, but he didn't want to go back to being that person he was before he met her. That person was angry all the time. That person was bitter. That person missed out because of his pride. Thorne exhaled and let her go. "I made a mistake, Laurel. I should have told you about the sharing of our mana."

She blinked. Her lips parted.

He continued. "But I'm not sorry I took what I needed to in order to save your life. I will never be sorry for keeping you alive. I am, however, very sorry that I let you walk away from me without fighting for you."

Her hands lifted to rest on his stomach, and damn, he wished he wasn't wearing his Guardian uniform. He wanted to feel that touch on his bare skin. Like he had once before.

"Laurel," he pleaded. "Don't do it. Please."

"Do what?"

"You know what I'm talking about. Don't kill Bones."

Darkness entered her eyes again.

"He's the man who tortured me. You should understand that. He's the one feeding lies to the king. And guess what? He's the one who's convinced the king to name Jasper as his heir... so they can murder him."

Thorne's breath froze in his lungs. "Murder Jasper?"

"The plan is to set Jasper up as the treasured heir to the Summer Court, then to kill him and make it look like Queen Maebh ordered it. This is the spark that will set all of Elphyne ablaze. Bones has to be stopped. The king didn't even know Bones was from my time."

"This is what you were discussing with the king?"

She nodded, eyes still alight with emotion. "He thinks he's invincible. Unaccountable. He didn't care that I knew he colluded with a human. I tried to offer myself in exchange for Jasper. I figured it would get me closer to Bones *and* set Jasper free, but he saw through it. He doesn't even care that I have the kind of power I do, or that I'm human. There must be something else they're offering the king to make him betray his own kind like this."

Thorne's mind whirled.

The air in the small confined space grew thick.

She'd offered herself as an exchange.

She would take Jasper's place.

Sacrifice herself for one of them.

Fuck. He'd made a big mistake in letting her go. Big mistake.

"Let me out, Thorne," she demanded. "He's right there. Right through that curtain. All I need to do is get within a few feet and hurl fire at him until I'm drained. He won't survive."

"No," he ground out. "I'm not letting you go."

"What?" she gasped. "You can't stop me."

Sharp claws sprung from his fingers and he bared his teeth. "I won't let you make the same mistakes as me, Laurel. Only a week ago I destroyed something in anger, where if I'd approached it with a level head, we would have known about the king's plans earlier. Don't you see? You taught me to let that anger go. Now I need to do the same for you."

She scowled. "I'll burn you if you don't release me."

"Then we both burn."

"*Thorne,*" she pleaded. "I have to do this."

He shook his head. "The Guardians are about to raid. They have this in hand. Let them capture Bones and take him back for questioning. Let us figure out what he's offering Mithras that's more powerful, or more enticing than you. It must be something dangerous to give him an edge over a war with Queen Maebh. Or at least he *thinks* it is. You know this is the best course of action."

"He'll get away."

"No. He's human. And I don't believe Well-blessed like you. He steals his mana. You were gifted with it. If you think any other way, that's your fear talking. Rush believes it was Clarke's fear talking too. You need to let it go."

Laurel's fury surged through their bond. Panic engulfed him. She was going to leave. What he'd said hadn't been enough to sway her.

"Laurel." He took her face gently between his palms. "I'm sorry. What more do you need from me? An oath to the Well? Because I will gladly make that oath, just tell me what to say."

"What is that?"

"It's a mana-infused bargain you make with the Well, not another fae. It's an all-encompassing vow. But be careful. If you want me to say I won't take your mana without permission, the oath will be enforced forever. It's unbreakable. Even if you're dying and you need me to take your mana in order to protect you, I won't be able to do it. Even if I need it to save my own life, or the life of our future children, I won't be able to. But if that is what you need for me to prove that I love you and that I never wanted to hurt you, then I'll do it."

She tensed beneath his touch. Her fury dissipated. Something else flickered down their bond, like a tiny candle coming alight, something he dared not hope for in his wildest dreams.

"You love me?" she asked, eyes glimmering.

His face screwed up with the flood of emotion engulfing his heart. He loved her so much it hurt. So much he couldn't speak. So he nodded. "I would die for you. I would die with you."

Her lips parted. Air puffed out as though she'd been holding it tight. Her face crumpled too, and he knew from their shared emotions that she was trying not to cry.

"You love me?" she asked again, hand moving to his heart.

"Yes," he managed. "I've been so caught up with worrying about being left behind, that I failed to realize I should be holding onto you. And Laurel"—his voice deepened —"I'll hold on to you until we become ghosts in the sky."

She slid her hands around his neck, locked them fiercely, and then pulled his lips to hers, whispering, "I love you too."

He claimed her mouth in a searing kiss. There was no restraint holding him back, no care for the ball guests beyond the curtain, no want or responsibility. Just her lips. Her heart.

She was his.

He felt it.

Knew it.

He'd been stupid to doubt it. Stupid to not fight for it.

He kissed her with all his passion until his balance slipped. His palms slapped on the wall beside her head, and he deepened the kiss, making sure to press against her with his body. She plucked at the studs holding his battle jacket closed. He let her. *Crimson*, he wanted to touch her as she was touching him. To put his fingers where the king's had been, to claim his rights back. Undeniable primal instinct urged him onward.

But he pushed apart and heaved in a ragged breath. "Laurel," he whispered.

Her hands had finished with his jacket, and were now at his belt, already working at the bindings, trying to get to his achingly hard erection. He threw his head back, hissed at the sharp pleasure of her touch as she found her mark.

"We can't," he growled at the ceiling. "There's work to do."

Her touch left him.

When he looked back down, he found her lust-filled eyes suddenly focused. She wiped her mouth. "You're right. Bones. I have to kill him. I promised."

Panic flared in his heart again, and he dipped to take her mouth in another hot and demanding kiss. She groaned as his tongue pushed in. He knew she loved it. He felt it. She dueled back.

Maybe this was what he needed to do. Keep her distracted. It just had to be long enough to let the Guardians' plan kick into action and stop her from making a mistake.

Yesterday, Cloud had finished interrogating Patches. As it turned out, Patches was ready to make an oath to the Well, one that confessed the king was the one who paid him to use the djinn bottle. The king directly. They had him.

The Guardians were poised to raid the ball. Ready to blackmail the king into releasing Jasper. Ready to take Bones into custody. And then they would get their answers about the Void's plans, and then Thorne would end Bones once and for all. But they had to do this the right way. All Thorne needed to do was keep Laurel busy.

He grinned into her mouth. "I'm going to take you, Laurel, hard against this wall. Shall I put up a privacy ward, or can you stay quiet, little queen, so as not to rouse attention?"

"I can stay quiet," she breathed and dipped her hands deep into his pants. She took hold of his length and squeezed. "Can you?"

Pleasure sparked at his groin. Thorne's vision lost focus.

"Fuck," he grunted and thrust involuntarily into her hand. He buried his face into her neck, kissed her skin, licked his mark, bit down gently. But...

He pulled back so their eyes could meet. He wouldn't start this relationship the second time around with deception. It might be their ruin, the nail in their coffin. He had to be truthful.

"I'm distracting you," he confessed, studying her face.

"I think you got it the wrong way around." She smiled and pumped his length.

His eyes rolled at the bliss.

"I don't think you understand," he ground out.

"Mm." She licked along his bottom lip, nipped him, and then every primal instinct in his body surged.

"Laurel," he warned. "I'm distracting you so you don't make the biggest mistake of your life. Because I don't want you to regret the dark stain on your heart from taking a life. I'm doing this because I love you. Do you understand?"

She paused. Silent. Eyes glistening under the blue glow of their mating marks. His words were finally sinking in. Hitting home.

"You're keeping me from Bones," she accused.

"You have to trust me," he said. "There is a plan to take him into custody. It's a good one. He will receive his justice. This is the best way to honor the people of your time, and the family you lost. We will get the Void's plans from Bones. We will *use* him before we *eliminate* him. Do you understand?"

"Distract me," she demanded. "So I'm not thinking about it. So I don't go out there and..." She swallowed.

His lips curved.

Then he gathered her dress and hiked it up her smooth legs. The raucous cheers and shouts from the party-goers blended with the music. Anytime now, the Guardians would have the place surrounded.

Thorne slid his fingers between Laurel's thighs, found her naked and wet. It should have turned him on, but he saw red. All he could think was that the king had his hands on her, so close to this... this that was his. *Mine*, his wolf growled. All he could see behind his eyelids was the imprint of it happening. He imagined the king's scent still on her. Every possessive instinct flared to life. The wolf snarled. He would kill the king.

"He touched you," he growled. "No one will touch you like that again. No one but me."

"If they try, they'll lose their hand," she agreed with a smirk. "I'll burn it off."

"I'm serious, Laurel." He plunged a finger into her tight, moist sheath.

Her lips parted with a gasp. "Again."

"Laurel," he ground his teeth. "Do you understand? You and me for life. However long it is. The wolf in me won't have it any other way."

"Tell your wolf not to run away next time."

He smiled. "I think that can be arranged."

"Yes," she breathed. "Let's get married."

He took her mouth, plunged his tongue, and worked her harder with his fingers. Then just as she started to make little sounds signaling she was close to her release, he changed their position. He hooked her legs around his waist, leaned her against the wall, took hold of his shaft and entered her, watching as she moaned with the feel of him stretching her. Every time, this part held him captive. His eyes fluttered with the sensation of her surrounding him.

She'd been wrong.

She couldn't keep quiet.

THIRTY-SEVEN

Laurel was still coming down from her high, hugging Thorne, so grateful that they were now past their troubles when a loud crashing sound came from the ballroom and she jolted.

"What was that?" she asked.

Screams.

Shouts.

Men barking orders.

"Sounds like they're here," Thorne grumbled against her neck. "Is it so terrible that I don't want to leave this spot?"

He drew back, and they straightened each other up. Somehow, Laurel's beaded headdress was gone. Thorne's ax-baldric had ridden up his neck. His hair was adorably skewiff. And he had a look about him that seemed very pleased. She gave his jaw a fond caress.

This moment right here was one that she would remember with joy, despite the chaos brewing in the ballroom.

Another loud crash—this one like breaking glass. All straightened, Thorne's expression grew hard. He held Laurel back and peeled open the curtain so they could peek outside.

It was pandemonium.

Red-coated royal guards were running about. Fancy dressed fae panicked and screamed as they ran from the room. A draft came from somewhere. As the people cleared, the throne dais came into view.

King Mithras sat with a furious scowl on his face, watching as Guardians dropped from the broken glass ceiling. The king's guards had taken up formation between the king and the ballroom floor where more Guardians approached, including Rush, Leaf and the ground fleet.

Mithras's eyes located and locked on the Prime, who was still sitting at a table, calmly sipping from a teacup.

Rush snarled at the king and released his sword, Starcleaver. Not even a king would get in the way of a Guardian's metal weapon. Laurel's heart gave a little flip as Rush climbed up the dais and took hold of Jasper's hand.

After Jasper had confused Thorne with Rush at the arena, Laurel would have thought he'd recognize his old partner, but all Jasper did was stumble vacantly as Rush pulled him down the dais to where the Prime sat.

Movement on the other side of the dais caught Laurel's attention.

"Look," she said and tapped Thorne. "Bones is getting away."

While the king was refusing to budge, Bones slinked off to the side and disappeared down a back exit.

"There are too many red-coats between us and there," Thorne said. "We'll not make it through without joining the fight."

"Bones will escape then."

Panic welled inside Laurel. She couldn't let that happen. Not after coming so close. For a minute, regret surged through her, as did guilt over ignoring her original mission. Thorne caught her change and cupped her face. "Don't," he started. "Don't go there. We will find him. And we will work together."

"I can cloak us."

"Good idea. I can track his scent."

Within seconds, Laurel had completed the cloaking spell, exactly like she remembered from training. It involved using light and shadows against each other. She nodded to Thorne, and he opened the curtain, taking them into the fray.

Both invisible, they kept their hands locked and kept to the outskirts of the room, hurrying as fast as they could between the gaps of frightened fae and scattering staff. The guards were amassing to protect the king.

Laurel glimpsed the severe gazes of Guardians as they formed a circle around the Prime and Jasper. Things were about to get heavy.

"Should we help them?" Laurel asked.

She wanted to find Bones, but not at a cost to their allies.

Thorne glanced over his shoulder as they hurried. "No," he replied. "Rush is there. They'll have it under control."

Laurel and Thorne jumped up on the dais and then darted out the door Bones had run through. It was a service corridor.

"Keep the cloaking spell up," Thorne said and pulled her behind him as he tracked Bones by scent.

Laurel gave herself over to Thorne, trusting his instincts. She concentrated on keeping the spell up. This was what their partnership should be—working together.

A shout ahead and then a clash of utensils had Thorne increasing their speed. The smell of food grew stronger. They reached the kitchens, and Thorne caught her eyes, put his finger to his lips, and released Fury.

They entered the large kitchen together. It was at least fifty feet long. Aisles of counters lined the kitchen. Stoves were against the walls. Cooks and servants everywhere tried to straighten the mess someone had just made by running through. Herbs and food had scattered over benches. And down the center aisle, at the other end of the kitchen where the only other exit was, a furious chef bared his fangs and blocked Bones from leaving.

They'd found him.

Laurel's heart leaped into her throat.

Thorne let go of her hand, releasing himself from the cloaking spell. He quietly motioned for Laurel to go around the counter and head down to the back of the kitchen until she was behind the cook. He would block this exit to stop Bones from retracing his steps.

Sheathed in her cloaking spell, she skipped and darted through the staff in the other aisle as they cursed and shouted at the intruder to get out. Coming around to the chef's rear, Laurel searched for a weapon she could use before dropping her cloaking spell, just something else in case the fire wasn't practical.

She picked up a ceramic knife, brandished it, and then dropped her cloaking spell. Standing behind the enormous cook, she couldn't even see Bones, but she was ready. She tapped the cook on the shoulder.

He glanced over his shoulder, confused.

She smiled sweetly. "I got it, big guy."

But the cook didn't believe she had what it took to stop Bones. He frowned and turned back, but not before Bones pilfered a knife from the bench and drove it into the cook's belly.

Well, that's what he intended to do. Thorne grabbed Bones by the throat and wrenched him backward. Bones was smaller than Thorne, but an experienced mercenary. He flipped the knife in his hands, aimed backward, and stabbed in the gap under his arm. The blade sank into Thorne's stomach.

Thorne grunted. But didn't stall. Bones must have missed. His face contorted into blind rage and he threw Bones across the counter as though he weighed less than a sack of flour. Bones slid across the surface, crashing into bowls of salad, knocking cucumbers and potatoes, skittering glass to the floor with a tremendous crash.

"Let me past!" Laurel shouted at the cook and tried to shove him.

"No, little lady. You stay back. Stay safe."

Rage filled her. She let her hands burn. The cook's eyes widened at the flames and he quickly moved to the side.

Laurel squeezed past him, intending to go to Thorne, but he'd moved around the counter to drag Bones to his feet. Thorne's huge fist crunched the wiry wrist, slamming it onto the counter. In Thorne's other hand, Fury rose behind his head. Laurel's comprehension lagged behind her mate's actions. It wasn't until Bones' skinny fingers were convulsing on the floor, reaching for the wrist still in Thorne's grip, that she understood.

"Cauterize it," he said.

She nodded and sent fire to Bones' arm. His screaming intensified, but she didn't burn him for long. When it was done, Bones cradled his arm. Sweat poured down his face. His eyes rolled, but he locked them onto Laurel with pure, obsidian hatred.

"You'll pay for that."

Thorne took Bones by the neck and squeezed painfully. "Shut up. Or I take your other hand, and she won't cauterize it."

Bones spat into Thorne's face. Thorne dodged, and that infuriated Bones even more. "Doesn't matter what you do to me. You won't make me talk."

"But I will," drawled Cloud as he prowled into the room, eyes full of something wicked and frightening as he locked onto Bones. "I'll make you sing like a little bird."

Bones' eyes widened in what looked like recognition. *"You."*

What was going on here?

Laurel's gaze darted between Bones and Cloud. Did they know each other? How was that possible?

Cloud and his fellow crow shifter, River, collected Bones from Thorne and dragged his sorry ass out of there. Just before they got to the exit, Laurel shouted, "Wait!"

Cloud tensed and looked over his shoulder. With Bones dangling between him and River, they turned to face Laurel. She clenched her jaw and strode over. She leaned down so she was eye to eye with Bones. "Pity your Seer didn't see this coming."

She punched him in the face.

Both Thorne and River looked at Laurel with amusement. Cloud held something else in his electric blue gaze. Respect? Understanding?

And then the crows took him away. His feet dragged on the floor and his obsidian gaze was still locked on Laurel.

She shivered. She knew it was more important to keep him alive, yet she couldn't shake the feeling they should kill him while they had the chance. Fear.

That's what it was, nothing more.

Thorne came up to her and held out Bones' dismembered hand.

"I know it's not his nails, but hopefully this is retribution enough," he said. "For now."

She stared at the disgusting hand, then back at Thorne's eager face. And then she burst out laughing.

Tears watered her eyes. This was so surreal. She felt as though she were in a dream. She didn't think she'd ever shake the feeling. Wiping her eyes, she looked at her mate with warmth and touched his cheek tenderly.

"Thank you, my love," she said. "But I don't know what to do with that."

Thorne frowned and turned the hand over. He fiddled with the king's signet ring on the little finger. "Interesting. Perhaps we should rejoin the main party and take this with us."

Laurel linked arms with Thorne. "Okay. But you're carrying it."

The first thing Laurel noticed was the king no longer sat calmly on his throne. He stood on the ballroom floor surrounded by his guard, shouting at the Prime about her audacity to accuse him of treason to the Well.

470

The rest of the ballroom had been cleared of guests, and all that remained were a few Guardians manning the exits. Haze and Shade were at the front entrance, and to the back of the stage, Aeron stood next to a new auburn-haired elf she'd not met. Deeply tanned and with brown eyes, he looked as though he spent a lot of time outdoors. He might be Forrest.

Up high on the glass ceiling, to the backdrop of a starry night sky, was Indigo dangling his feet. The vampire had seen Laurel enter and winked when she looked up. A hand shot from the darkness to thwack him on the chest. Laurel vaguely saw the shadowed outline of another fae with wings. She did a quick calculation in her head of all the winged Guardians and realized it must be the third crow-shifter she'd also not met, Ash.

Eyes back to the floor, Leaf and Rush stood guard next to a docile Jasper. The Prime was in the middle of laying out the offenses the king was charged with. Letters she'd appropriated from her handbag were being unfolded on the table. So that's what she'd been working on during the journey, an official record of the treason.

Rush noted their arrival and caught Thorne's eyes. Thorne nodded and held up the severed hand. Rush nodded back. Laurel almost smiled. They were getting along so nicely. Clarke would be proud.

Oh, no. *Clarke.*

She would be furious that Laurel couldn't go through with it. She bit her lip, worried. No, it would be okay. Cloud looked like he would take care of Bones. He'd get the information they needed.

This was the right thing to do. She would help Clarke understand that.

Thorne strode right up to the base of the king's dais and dropped Bones' hand.

Mithras looked down, sneered, and then scolded Thorne. "You dare?"

"Does the ring look familiar?" Thorne asked.

"I don't answer to you," he clipped.

"Well, you should," Thorne replied. "How else are you going to explain why one of your advisors is wearing a metal ring with your signet on it. It matches the wax seal on the letters instructing a certain shifter from Cornucopia to commit acts of terror against the Seelie, your own people." Thorne gave a smug smile. "I hope you weren't planning on activating that transference rune beneath it. You know, the one the metal ring hid from our scans. Possibly the one that would return Bones to you if he was ever taken captive."

The king glared at Thorne like he wanted to chew his heart out. "All that proves is that a man wearing that ring wrote those letters. Not me. I accept no responsibility for the acts you're accusing me of."

The Prime stepped forward. "We don't need you to accept responsibility. We have a witness who will swear an oath to the Well. We have your human. We can try you for treason right now."

"What you have is circumstantial evidence at best."

"You put curse marks on Jasper," Rush accused.

"They were there when we rescued him from the Ring. And for the record, he belongs to me. You can't take him."

"Oh, we'll take him," the Prime said. "And you'll let us because if you don't, we'll go straight to Queen Maebh with proof of your machinations to incite a war. Whether you admit it or not, she will invade your territory and find out for herself. Or perhaps she'll send the Wild Hunt to collect you and bring you back to her."

"You don't get involved in fae politics," he spat back.

"For this, I will make an allowance."

King Mithras stared down at the Prime. "You've turned into a cold-hearted bitch, Aleksandra."

"And you, a spineless coward."

"Fine. Take him." Mithras gestured at Jasper. "He is broken, anyway."

Assuming he was free to go, the king turned to leave, but the Prime had one last demand.

"You will end the unsanctioned breeding law," she said. "As you promised the first time."

"A promise is not a bargain," the king said over his shoulder.

"No. It's worth more. It's between friends," the Prime shot back. "Clearly, I was wrong to trust you. You promised that if I handed Jasper over to you, you would treat him as your treasured son. I was stupid to think you would treasure your children a different way. I won't make the mistake again. Fail to follow through with your word, and not only will I try you for treason, but I will visit Queen Maebh."

King Mithras's eyes glowed molten gold. He ground his teeth and then eventually said, "By the morrow I will send out a decree that the unsanctioned breeding law be abolished in Seelie territory, and then I trust this insane idea of my treason will be forgotten and you will focus your attention on where it needs to be—toward the humans invading our land."

He glared at Laurel. Thorne growled low in his throat. The king looked back to the Prime.

She nodded brusquely. "If you do not make this decree, and stick to your word, I will personally portal into the Obsidian Palace and go directly to Queen Maebh. You have until noon tomorrow, and then I expect to see fae all over Seelie territory fornicating in celebration."

Mithras gestured to the guards. "See them out. I want no Order representatives left by the time the moon is high."

Thorne's lip curled at the king's retreating back. "We were leaving, anyway."

THIRTY-EIGHT

JASPER – THE HOUSE OF THE TWELVE, IN THE LIVING ROOM.

There were things he remembered—things he didn't.

He knew he shifted into a wolf. He knew he'd lived here before. The smells were the same. He knew he should recognize these people who'd taken him from the king's palace and into their home filled with leather-clad warriors, fussing brownies, and citrus and cedar cleaning solution.

He should know how to play the game of cards the three vampires engaged in at the table in the adjoining room. He should know why they sat him in the worn, comfortable chair by the empty fireplace, or why they handed him a rolled-up stick of mana-weed to smoke. But it sat dwindling on a tray, unused.

Fae would come before him, speak to him, and welcome him home.

But he didn't know them.

He didn't know anything.

Days passed.

Eventually, they stopped trying to get him to talk. They left him alone, watching from his chair, frowning at the empty fireplace. He wasn't sure how long he stared.

Something touched his arm. He looked down. A small, pale and chubby hand rested on his forearm. His gaze followed the arm and found a cherub face with silver-white hair. She bared little sharp fangs and growled viciously. Did he know her?

He bared his teeth back.

She relaxed, cocked her head, and inspected him. Then she pouted and tugged on his hand. "Sleeping Pretty needs you."

He looked over to where the people who'd brought him talked at a table. They looked happy. Comfortable. Friendly. He didn't belong there.

Quietly, unnoticed, he stood and followed the little girl up the staircase and down the hall to a wooden door. He'd been here before. Many times. Long, long ago. The little one pushed open the door and told him to hush. Then she creeped inside and pointed at the bed in the dim room.

Lying on it was a golden-haired female. Asleep.

The little girl tugged him closer. He stumbled until his knees hit the bed.

"Sleeping Pretty needs a kiss to wake."

He looked down at the child and frowned. He looked back at the sleeping female. His frown deepened.

An undeniable urge to go to her swam through him. It was as though something pushed him.

He didn't know how, he didn't know anything, but he knew her.

So he went to her. Her mana called to his like a siren at sea, and like a wave rising to meet the shore, his mana called back. He touched her arm. A spark of heat zipped up his arm. Blue flames engulfed them both, and then he heard a scream.

Behind him.

A redheaded woman.

"Leave her alone!"

Footsteps thudded up the stairs. Down the hall. The people he should know came barging into the room, scowling at him as though he'd done wrong. They frowned at his golden-haired female on the bed. The one inexplicably linked to him. They wanted to take her away from him.

She was his. *Mine.*

Something wild and feral within him growled. His fangs elongated, and a snarl ripped out of his lungs. He picked up Sleeping Pretty, carried her in his arms, and he wished himself gone.

THIRTY-NINE

"Any news?" Laurel asked as she fitted a floral wreath to her head.

Clarke turned to her friend with a placating smile. "Laurel, you've asked me that every day for the past three weeks and the answer is always the same." Clarke shrugged. "I can't *see* anything about Jasper. Since he took Ada, his curse marks block him from my visions. They must still be together because I can't see her either."

"Yeah, but that's a good thing, right?" Laurel asked.

"I think so." Clarke gave Laurel's floral headdress one last tweak. Her eyes glittered with worry. "I was so afraid when I first saw him with her, but she'll be fine. Jasper is her mate. I saw the blue markings with my own eyes before he took her away. They have to be fine."

Laurel took her friend's hands and squeezed. "They will be. I just wondered if there was news. It would be nice to share this day with her, that's all."

"I know," Clarke said with a sigh. "I also know that I was wrong to ask you to kill Bones. You can't know how sorry I am."

"I wanted to. Don't think it was only you."

"I'm glad our big, overbearing mates stopped us."

"Me too."

Clarke checked her appearance in the mirror. She straightened her bridesmaid floral garland on her head. "Maybe we'll keep them."

Laurel chuckled. She gathered herself and stood back for one last look. Yeah. She looked like a boss. Like a queen. She'd even painted her nails and displayed them proudly.

Clarke came up behind her and hugged her. "Your parents would be proud. I'm proud."

Laurel's eyes teared up. "You'll make me cry and ruin my makeup."

"Then let me focus on how amazing you look." Clarke quickly gave a low whistle of appreciation. "Thorne is going to carry you off and have his way with you before you even finish walking down the aisle."

Laurel's cheeks hurt as she smiled. She dashed away her burgeoning tears and picked up her bouquet of jasmine. "But that's what the last three days of the celebration are for, right?"

They laughed and left the bedroom together. It was sad that Ada wasn't there, but none of them could dispute the coincidence that Jasper had triggered a Well-blessed mating with Ada. They had to have faith that the Well had chosen their union for a reason. It's what their partners kept insisting, and none of them were worried. They couldn't keep putting their lives on hold while they waited for them both to turn up.

Clarke led Laurel down the staircase to the kitchen where they walked through to the back door. Outside in the sun, set up on the back lawn, was a seating arrangement reminiscent of a classic wedding ceremony. All the Guardians, some Mages, and even a friend or two were present. Rush sat to one side with Willow on his lap, both of them grinning at the fun "first human tradition" they shared in. Thorne stood at the end of a floral carpeted aisle, waiting nervously. The Prime stood behind him, ready to officiate.

Thorne had promised Laurel a mating celebration, and she'd realized she wanted a wedding. Old school. Something to remember her time. So he wore a suit, and she wore a white dress.

Laurel stood at the start of the aisle, not a tremble in her fingers, not a doubt in her mind.

This war with the Void may only be beginning, and King Mithras was up to something. She also hadn't forgotten that she owed the Prime a debt for thanking her, as was the fae custom, but she was starting to trust her too. She might collect one day, she might not. Things were changing in Elphyne, and Laurel was proud to be a part of it.

For now, she would enjoy this small moment for what it was—perfection.

When the flute started playing, Clarke turned to Laurel and smiled. "You ready?"

She nodded. When they arrived together at the front, Laurel handed her bouquet to Clarke. Thorne took her hands, and without waiting for the Prime's instructions, he slipped a glass ring on her finger.

"Is this right?" he murmured, voice hoarse.

"You're supposed to wait for the celebrant to tell you when."

He made an awkward face. "I couldn't wait to show you."

Laurel looked down at the ring he'd put on her finger and gasped. It was as beautiful as the day she'd first admired it at the Cornucopia markets. A clear glass ring that sparkled with trapped light. He'd gone back for it.

"I may have not told the whole truth when I said I wouldn't take your mana again without permission," he confessed. "I took a single drop and infused it in the ring. I also added one from mine. Now a part of us will always be together. For eternity."

"Like ghosts of the past. The stars in the sky."

He nodded. "You're never alone, Laurel."

Tears burned her eyes as she blubbered, "Neither are you, my love."

She looked around at all the people who had gathered to share in this momentous occasion. And from the sheer joy radiating down their bond, she believed him.

She only wished this moment would last forever.

The End.

That's not the last of the Fae Guardians... Keep reading for some exclusive awesomeness.

OF KISSES AND WISHES

BONUS FAE GUARDIANS NOVELLA

BLURB

Wolfish Anise has always been teased for being a lesser fae of Elphyne. She wishes for two things: the kisses of a long-time friend who never dates outside his breed and to find the elusive Ice-Witch, who promises to give Anise magic and the ability to shift.

Caraway left his pacifist family to join the Guardians and became a ruthless protector of Elphyne. He wants to prove his oxen-shifter breed can be more than docile prey, but two years ago, he failed at protecting the most important fae in his life—his best friend Anise.

When a new mission forces them together on a quest, secret desires are revealed—but have they been revealed too late? Even if Caraway can stop Anise from making the worst mistake of her life, no one walks away from the Ice-Witch with their soul intact.

ONE

Glass coin tinkled as it landed in Anise's hand. She counted, and then checked down the length of the bar to see if her coworkers watched. Once sure she was free, she pocketed the amount instead of adding it to the Birdcage's nightly takings. She reached beneath the bar and pulled out a small vial of red glowing liquid. Forcing a smile on her face, she handed it to the awaiting female wolf-shifter with wide, earnest eyes.

"You get caught with this outside of Cornucopia, you didn't get it from me. Understood?" Anise warned.

The female smiled tightly, looked down at the tail swishing behind Anise, and struggled to hide her disgust. "I know the deal."

Anise scowled back, immediately on the defense. Any fae who stared at her tail like it was monstrous, classed themselves superior to those *lesser fae*, those like Anise who appeared different to humans, but held no mana from the Well, and thus couldn't shift or use magic. Lesser fae were considered only one step away from animals.

The shouts of cruel children surfaced from Anise's memories.

"Without your tail and ears, you're basically human!"

"Take that back!"

"You can't shift. You can't hunt. You can't even protect your own kind."

"Shut up!"

Sing-song taunts. *"Human. Dirty, dirty human!"*

"If you don't stop, I'll tell on you."

"Who will save you? You have no friends."

"Are you going to give me what I paid for, or what?"

Anise's gaze returned to the white-haired female shifter. Like all wolf-shifters, her fur-tipped pointed ears gave her away. She also had an unremarkable body squeezed into a straight dress that hugged her skinny frame. And she smelled like wolf beneath all that perfume. There was nothing special about her, yet she clearly thought so. Probably the daughter or a distant cousin of some high fae Summer Court lord.

"What are you dumb as well as less?" The female snatched the vial from Anise's hand, unstoppered the cork, and downed the contents in one hit.

"Easy there." Anise flinched. "You didn't even wait for the right dose."

"I didn't come to Cornucopia for the right dose. Just like you didn't come here to feel like the second-rate citizen you are. I've taken Scarlixir before. I have plenty of elves as friends. I know exactly what I'm doing."

Anise had to bite her lip to avoid scoffing. Elves may have been the original fae who'd concocted the elixir, but they had no idea how the magical and inebriating *mana*-infused mixture had been cut and diluted with other chemicals to save coin in production. Anise didn't even know. She had to go by what the dealer had told her. They didn't call it Scarlixir for the scarlet color. No. It was because if you overdosed on the euphoric inducing drug, it made you want to claw your skin until it bled. Hence, the scars.

"Suit yourself." Anise smirked and watched the wolf sashay away to the dance floor. "Ooh, you're going to be paying for that later, too."

She glanced up. The three-story verdant nightclub overflowed with greenery. The central column reached all the way to the ceiling where a hole revealed the night sky. The crescent moon had crossed to the other side of the observatory. If she'd looked five minutes later, she'd have missed it, and the signal that her shift was over.

Elation lifted her soul. Finally. She'd been waiting for this moment for five years. Time to go on vacation. She patted the coin in her pocket. There was enough for where she needed to go, but that last sale was the icing on the cake.

Bidding adieu to her co-workers, Anise collected her jacket from the staffroom and checked her bone dagger was safely strapped to her belt before heading home. Not only was the dagger reinforced with mana to make it stronger, but she'd paid extra to spell it to always hit its mark. It cost a fortune, but after she was attacked two years ago and held hostage, she liked to feel secure.

The walk home to her modest apartment was not a safe one, but there were no safe parts of town. Cornucopia was not ruled by any fae kingdom, neither Seelie nor Unseelie. It existed as a neutral territory where all fae-kind could come together. No rules applied. Well, not many. Those rules were enforced by the Order of the Well, who were more like the magic police in terms of offenses to the integrity of the Well. If you were like Anise and held no mana with which to pervert, or held no forbidden metals or plastics, you weren't even a fly in their swamp. The only other law was that of The Ring, a gladiator-style pit where you solved your differences.

Lucky for Anise, she'd kept to herself during her stay. She'd only left her home town of Crescent Hollow because it was no longer safe there either. As the closest fae settlement to the humans in the wasteland, she'd met the unfortunate fate of being kidnapped and tortured two years earlier. The ringleader of this torture was the Alpha of Crescent Hollow at the time, Lord Thaddeus Nightstalk. He'd been secretly working with humans to bargain for metal cages and weapons so he could control Guardians—the mana-enhanced warriors who worked for the Order of the Well. As part of the deal,

Thaddeus had also tortured many of the lesser fae residents of Crescent Hollow, Anise included.

It was pure cowardice. Not only had Thaddeus picked those fae who were more vulnerable, but he also sucked dry what little mana they had so he could give it to the humans for their own nefarious purposes. It was Anise's only blessing to have no mana to give.

Shivering with reasons nothing to do with the cold, Anise kept her hand poised over her dagger and her eyes wary. Every shadow and insect scuttle made her jolt. By the time she made it to her place, she was a bag of raw nerves. Once inside the one-room apartment, she double bolted the door and lit a candle. Not only did she check every dark crevice of the room, but also beneath the bed. Once satisfied, she crossed to the window, tweaked the drapes, and peeped outside into the dark alley street. Her room was on the second floor, and there was no other way to get into the room other than the front door.

After she washed her face, she pulled the pillows from her bed and stuffed them under the covers so it looked like someone slept there. Then she unsheathed her dagger, got to her knees, and crawled beneath the bed. There she had set up her own little den. A woolen blanket, another pillow, and a collection of her most precious items. A box with her saved coins, a dried flower her friend Caraway had once given her, and a secret invitation addressed to Anise from the Ice-Witch. Her salvation.

Clutching her dagger, she settled and tried not to let the darkness bring the wails and screams from her nightmares. The memories of being trapped in a cage, elevated from the ground, starved, and emaciated.

Two weeks.

She'd been held hostage for two weeks. Little food. Little water. And no one came to save her. Not even the one friend she thought she had.

"Who will save you? You have no friends."

Anise sniffed and wiped her nose with the back of her hand. Cradling it to her chest, she clutched the Ice-Witch's invitation until she fell asleep.

CHAPTER
TWO

Caraway always fancied himself a big fae. As a muskox shifter, he towered above most others at an inch over seven-feet tall. Taller than even the legendary Guardians in the Cadre of Twelve. Caraway's big bones and large frame were stacked with slabs of hard muscle honed from decades of heavy training under the tutelage of the Order's ruthless preceptors.

All manner of fae shrunk when he arrived in his black leather Guardian uniform. And most looked in fear at his sharp, curved horns as they flowed from the top of his head, then down and out at his cheeks. But it was truly the giant metal broadsword strapped to his back that incited the most knee-knocking terror. One cleave of his mighty blade, Reckoning, and any creature in Elphyne would be cut in half. Metal had the ability to not only halt magic in its tracks but pierce almost any manner of surface. Apart from the Guardians, who'd earned their endorsement through a painstaking ceremony, no other fae was sanctioned to carry metal. Touching the forbidden substance would cut their magic supply from the Well and cause a painful headache.

But not Caraway. Not the Guardians. They could decimate the enemy *and* use the full force of the gifts the Well had given them. This dual power made them nigh unstoppable in Elphyne.

So he should feel tall. He should feel big. Invincible. But standing where he was, on the Guardian training field at the Order, with the sun blinding him, and facing one of the Twelve, he felt like a four-foot-tall dwarf.

Facing him from about ten feet away was Rush, a wolf-shifter who'd recently mated with Clarke, a human who inexplicably had, and could use, mana. She'd been exposed to the Well over a two-thousand-year sleep, frozen in ice. She thawed a few years ago and brought with her news of an evil human who'd caused the destruction of the old world and had awoken in this time with the intent to reclaim Elphyne's resources for himself.

Clarke was Rush's, Well-blessed mate.

That meant the silver-haired shifter in front of Caraway, was not only lethal because he could rip Caraway to shreds with sharp teeth, or slice Caraway with his sword, but also blast him with endless offensive magic without running out of power. If his stores of mana were low, all he needed to do was siphon some from his powerful mate. Rush was indestructible.

How was Caraway going to fight that?

"You're a disgrace to the herd," Caraway's mother's voice filtered from his memories. "Us muskox don't fight. We don't spill blood. We live in harmony with the Well."

And when a human raiding party had invaded his family's territory, their pacifist ways could do nothing to protect their kind. Half their herd had been wiped out. But did losing so many lives make Caraway's mother change her mind? No. She still looked on in disgust as he left on his way to submit to the Guardian initiation.

"Are you going to stand there all day staring into space, or spar with me?" Rush laughed, scratching his gray beard.

The Guardian hadn't yet released his sword. The handle poked over his shoulder, taunting Caraway.

Caraway's grip tightened on his own sword, Reckoning. He narrowed his eyes and then charged. Heavy feet thudded across the grass.

Rush pushed his palm out, the blue Well-blessed markings on his hand glowed brightly, and a gust of sharp, cold wind came at Caraway. Like a wall, the element hit and knocked him backward. He landed hard on his rear, jarring the senses out of him.

"Use your sword," Rush shouted back. "It's broad enough the metal will displace the mana I send your way."

Gritting his teeth, Caraway planted Reckoning's tip into the grass and used it to lever himself up. Well-damn it. This was embarrassing. Get him in hand-to-hand combat and he would come out on top. But he needed this. The extra training.

The human enemies emerging didn't play by the rules, and he needed to be ready. He'd failed too many times already.

Anise's smirking face came to mind and he almost lost his footing. Cute wolfish ears twitching in irritation, dark stain on her nose, big golden eyes with long sweeping lashes. Something squeezed hard in his chest. His old friend had moved away and hadn't told him where, which meant she didn't want to be found. He couldn't blame her. He'd fucked up.

"Stop!" A male shout came from the sidelines.

Caraway squinted into the sun, shielded his eyes. The team leader of the Twelve, Leaf, a golden-haired elf with a superiority complex, waved him over. Leaf was also a council member. This could mean only one thing.

Caraway had a mission.

Wiping the dirt off Reckoning, Caraway sheathed the great sword at the baldric on his back and then strode over. Leaf, Rush, and his son Thorne almost converged to meet. Fae stopped aging at about the age of twenty years, so both father and son looked almost identical except for their eyes and hair. Rush's eyes were golden, and Thorne's were icy blue. Rush's hair was long and silver, Thorne's was buzzed at the sides and short on top. All three looked at Caraway ominously.

Why were they looking at him like that? As though he wasn't about to like what they said next.

"What is it?" he asked.

Leaf folded his arms, his black leathers creaking. "Cloud has finished interrogating the human who worked with High King Mithras."

"Oh?" Caraway raised his brow and did his best to hide his blatant disgust for both the Seelie High King and the human he'd conspired with. The same human who'd manipulated and worked with the fae who'd tortured Anise for two weeks. "Does that mean we can kill him now?"

Thorne shot Caraway dark eyes. A feral glint shone back at Caraway, and the pacifist in his blood wanted to shrink back. Oxen and Wolves were enemies in the animal world, but Caraway had found this one to be his greatest ally.

Thorne bared his fangs. "The prisoner is mine."

Caraway folded his arms. "That human tortured Anise."

"He tortured my mate first. If there's anything left of him after I've had him, he's all yours."

Caraway bit back a retort, because Thorne was well within his rights to take revenge on the human. Laurel was Thorne's Well-blessed mate. They shared not only mana but emotions. Thorne would have relived Laurel's pain as though it were his own. Anise wasn't Caraway's mate. She might not even be his friend.

Not after she blamed him for failing to notice she'd been locked in a cage for two weeks. That tightness in his chest constricted again.

"I hate to burst your bubbles," Leaf drawled. "But neither of you will get your hands on him yet. Cloud has failed to draw worthy information from the human. His mind is locked tight like a vise. Cloud is finished with his interrogation, but we have other methods we will try next. There is one lead we need you to investigate, Caraway."

Caraway looked at the other three, more capable Guardians. All of them were part of the Twelve, the most feared and revered warriors of the Order of the Well. Each of them vicious and uniquely powerful in their own way, it was every Guardian's dream to one day earn their place in the tight-knit cadre of brothers-in-arms. Not only were they powerful, but two of them had already attained a status all Guardians secretly wanted but denied they did—they had found love in this impossible world.

Up until now, it was assumed the life of a Guardian was lonely and empty when it came to mating. Long term relationships weren't encouraged. Not only was a Guardian's duty demanding, but dangerous. Lives were often cut short. Short dalliances were encouraged.

Until recently.

Thorne had worked on abolishing the unsanctioned breeding law. Rush had a two-year-old daughter that ran around the Order campus. Times were certainly changing.

"Why me?" Caraway asked. "Clearly I'm not the most experienced in this group."

"But you have the best connection to the person who has the information."

"Who?"

"Anise."

Caraway's heart stuttered. His mouth dried. *They'd found her?* "You want me to interrogate her?"

"No," Leaf replied. "None of that. But we want you to infiltrate her journey. Go where she is going and conduct your own investigation."

"I'm not following."

"She's been invited to see the Ice-Witch."

As though the hag was standing next to him, Caraway's bones froze. The Ice-Witch was a powerful sorceress who, not only made the most heinous magical bargains with fae, but did so without scruples or discrimination. Every Guardian knew you didn't bargain with the witch unless you were prepared to offer your soul and submit to eons of torture. If you came out of her ice cave with anything less, then you were having a good day.

But did Anise know this?

"The witch is a powerful adversary," Caraway said. "Any of the cadre would do a better job."

"It's Anise," Thorne replied with a soulful gaze. "It was me who pulled her from that cage, Caraway. But it was you she called for. If she's heading to the Ice-Witch, then... she's going to need a friend."

Caraway swallowed the lump in his throat and he stared hard at the ground, trying not to let the burn behind his eyelids overflow into tears. Anise had asked for him, even after he'd failed to realize she was in trouble. He'd left Crescent Hollow before she'd been taken because Anise and he had argued. She was fed up with the red-coated royal Seelie guards causing havoc every time they came to town. She was fed up with the town's Lord and Alpha, Thaddeus, ruling the village so cruelly. And she was frustrated that no one took her seriously as a lesser fae. As usual, Caraway had stayed out of the unrest. Guardians were forbidden to get involved with general fae politics. If it didn't involve mana, then it wasn't their problem.

Guardians were a dying breed and the war against warped magic and keeping the integrity of the Well alive was growing every day. They simply didn't have enough resources to be the police of everything. A line had to be drawn, and fae politics was on the other side.

"How did you find her?" Caraway asked, throat dry.

"You know how Laurel and I got sent to the Ring by causing a disturbance at the Birdcage?" Thorne asked. "We ran into Anise there."

Caraway nodded. The Birdcage was an elixir den in Cornucopia. Fae from all over Elphyne went there to unwind with dance, drink, or to screw, and to satisfy their deviant urges. Being in Cornucopia, the establishment got away without adhering to any laws that restricted revelry in the Seelie or Unseelie Kingdoms. Usually, this freedom leaned toward the hedonistic side, but Caraway had seen darker rooms and cages with strange sadistic goings-on.

That was where Anise had been working?

"We need you to drill the Ice-Witch for information," Leaf continued. "All our prisoner gave us was her name. But it's more than we've received after days of interrogation." Leaf plucked a feather from his shoulder and flicked it to the ground. Then he met Caraway's eyes. "You're authorized to use force if necessary, but if you discover the witch is the source of the perversion of magic the humans have been using, then don't do anything. Bring the information back and we will assess. At the very least, get a location for us."

Granting wishes to make someone taller or more beautiful was one thing, but lately, mana-warped monsters had been emerging all over Elphyne. If the witch was responsible for those, then she would be dealt with by the Order. If she was also the one feeding the humans secrets on how to use mana, then she would rue the day she betrayed her own kind.

Something else occurred to Caraway. "What would Anise want with the Ice Witch?"

"What does anyone want?" Leaf replied.

Anise's cute tail swished into Caraway's mind and his heart stopped. It was the one thing she'd always been self-conscious about, and he'd bet his sword that she was going to bargain away her soul so she could look like a normal fae.

The two of them had become friends over a mutual bond—they'd both been branded as outcasts. He, for his Guardian status and his family's disdain for violence. She, because she couldn't make the full shift into a wolf. She couldn't shift at all. It had never bothered Caraway, but he knew she stewed about it.

This was not good. He couldn't let her make this mistake. Anise was perfect, just the way she was born. Becoming a shifter was not worth the damnation of her eternal soul. That was priceless.

"I'll go," Caraway said. "Just tell me where and when."

CHAPTER

THREE

Anise woke to the sound of knocking at her door. A peek from beneath the bed showed sun rays had escaped the confines of the curtains to lighten the room. She rubbed her eyes. She should already be awake and on her way by now. Damn it.

Sleeping under the bed felt safer, but it was also darker and she'd missed her dawn wake-up call.

Knock-knock-knock.

Frowning, Anise found her dagger and shimmied out from beneath the bed. Cracking her back, then neck, she eyed the door with suspicion. She'd been living here for over a year but hadn't told anyone. There was no reason she'd have a visitor. She gripped her dagger hard and darted a glance to the window, suddenly cursing the lack of opening for an escape. She supposed she could break the glass.

"Anise?" came the muffled deep voice. "It's me."

Anise stared at the door.

It's me.

Oh, how she'd dreamed of hearing those two little words over and over whilst captured and tortured in that cage. How she'd hoped and longed for them, held onto them as though they were a lifeline.

A lifeline that never came.

The tension in her body shifted until it crumpled her face. She opened the door and scowled despite her heart galloping and her stomach fluttering. *Damn it.*

Caraway loomed in the hallway, his big bulk taking up most of the room. His head and curved horns almost brushed the ceiling. Segmented pauldrons on the Guardian uniform hit the walls on either side—he was that broad. Bone stud buttons ran down the front of his flat torso. Blue piping accentuated the shape of his body—bulging

493

where his biceps stretched the leather jacket almost indecently. A broadsword was holstered over his back.

And the most dangerous part of all—his big, brown, long-lashed doe eyes staring right into her, reaching inside and tugging on her atoms, sending them into a frenzy.

His presence stole Anise's breath away. Nothing had changed in the way her body reacted to him. Only her mind.

She looked closer and took in his face, surprised to note his usual jolly, flushed coloring was gone. Messy shaggy hair fell over his curved horns. Scruff over his square jaw. Dark, bruised circles beneath those long lashes.

His usual nonchalant vibe had been replaced with hard lines. A pinched look to his face, a flattened press of his lips, and tendons in his temples pulsed from a clenched jaw.

It didn't suit him.

The old Anise wanted to ask what had happened to suck the jolly out of him. The sound of his big-bellied laugh had warmed her on many cold nights during their friendship. But the new Anise, the one he'd left in that cage to rot, didn't give a shit.

"Go away," she said and tried to close the door.

Caraway shoved his giant boot in the gap, stopping it from closing. He put his big meaty hand on the door and pressed. It seemed effortless, and the marked difference in their body strength drove her nuts. This was why she was going to see the Ice-Witch. *This.*

Helplessness swam over her and she stood back. Caraway ducked to get under the doorframe, came in, and closed the door behind him. He surveyed the room with trepidation.

"This is where you've been staying?"

His gaze landed on the pillow decoy in the bed, tilted to see the blanket and sleeping arrangement beneath, and then caught the dagger still in her hand. When his shrewd gaze lifted to meet hers, it softened.

"I don't want your pity, Caraway," she said, pointing the dagger at him, and then the door. "And I told you to go away. So you should respect a lady's wishes and do just that."

But he didn't go. He started poking around the room as though he owned it. He went to the window, opened the curtain, looked outside, and then tested it to see if it opened. Turning, his eyes tracked around the room until they landed on her knapsack, filled and ready for her journey. His brows lifted.

"Where are you going?"

"None of your business." Anise folded her arms. "Why are you here, Caraway?"

Those brows lowered darkly. "I've been looking for you for a long time, Anise. Why are you running away from me? I thought we were friends."

Her eyes narrowed. "Friends don't leave friends to the mercy of evil, twisted people."

"I didn't know about that until it was too late."

"I told you things were getting dire in that town. I *told* you." The accusation was a spear of vitriol. The moment the words were out of her mouth, Caraway flinched as though hit.

He sat heavily on the bed. It creaked from his weight and the great sword at his back twisted to accommodate the new position. He put his head in his hands.

"I know," he said softly. "But I'm not allowed to get involved with—"

Anise held up her hand. "Oh spare me the same rigmarole. I've heard the Order's mantra before. 'Not mana, not my problem,' right? You and I both know it goes deeper than that."

She'd meant deeper in the sense that the world wasn't painted in shades of gray, but when Caraway shot her hurt, accusatory eyes, she knew he thought she'd meant something else. She stuttered and sighed. The tension in her body melted. "You know I didn't mean it that way."

"I think you did," he shot back. "You of all people know what my family thinks of me."

She worried her lip with her teeth. A band of guilt wrapped around her chest. When they'd been close friends, Caraway had confessed his darkest shame one night while they were both inebriated. His family was peace-loving. He wanted to save the world and had embraced violence. At least if it was in the name of the Well, he had a higher, holy purpose no one could argue with. If he resorted to helping Anise out and doling out his own version of justice to the humans and other fae reprobates who'd kidnapped her, then the lines were blurred and perhaps he really was this lower-than-low person his family accused him of being. He'd be a monster no different to the mana-twisted beasts he hunted.

The real, open regret on his face plucked at Anise's heart and for the first time, she realized that perhaps those hard lines he'd grown were from her, just another person in his life who'd asked him to make an impossible decision.

She sat down next to him with a heavy sigh and hand-signed an apology. She put a fist to her chest and made a circle motion. Fae don't voice their thanks or say sorry, for it left them in another's debt. Only family freely spoke these because it was known that true family would do anything for each other, regardless of debt.

Caraway hand-signed his apology too. "I should have been there to protect you, no matter what. You're right. Ignoring the plight of others because it isn't my job isn't a way to live."

"I get it," she soothed. "The Prime doesn't want you to get involved."

He gritted his teeth. "But that's not stopping the Cadre of Twelve. Rush and Thorne have both broken the rules recently. And the Prime's not reprimanded them." He scrubbed his face. "What difference does it make if I'm fighting to preserve the integrity of the Well if the world it goes to is turning to shit?"

Her heart reached out to him. It might have only taken him a few decades, and almost losing her, but he was finally getting it.

"It was also unfair of me to throw the burden of my capture at you," she said. "I know you would have been there if you knew."

He turned to her, eyes brimming with hope. "Can we go back to being friends?"

Her heart lurched. Her hand slid under the cover on the bed and grasped the paper invitation that had consumed her life for the past year and more. Indecision rocked her. What would he think of her choice?

"What's that?" he asked, eyes toward where her hand moved.

Alarmed, she looked down. The white letter poked out from beneath the blanket. There was no way he'd let her go without an explanation, so she took a deep breath, and let it out.

"It's an invitation to see the Ice-Witch."

Silence.

She closed her eyes and waited for the reprimand she knew was coming. Caraway had always been a come as you are kind of male, but while he'd spoken the words, his actions were louder. He'd only dated high fae. She never saw him with a lesser fae. None like her.

Warm, rough fingers touched her cheek. Her eyes flew open and met his. In them, she saw pity. She knocked his hand away and stood up.

"Don't judge me, Caraway."

"I wasn't."

She looked sideways at him. "You weren't?"

"No. But visiting the Ice-Witch for any reason won't have a happy ending. You know this."

Bitter pain and failure swirled in her gut. He had no idea what it was like to be sub-par. To be teased your whole life, first by cruel kids, then by even meaner adults. That last customer at the Birdcage hadn't been a one-off. Fae like her treated Anise differently all the time. It was the tail.

She'd considered cutting it off once, just to be rid of it. But then there was the discoloration on her face. The darker nose. The black-rimmed eyes. The bigger than normal wolfish ears.

"You know the reason I'm visiting her," she said to him. "And you know the hurt I feel is bone-deep. I'll do anything to be rid of it."

"What are you asking the witch for?" he asked softly.

"I want the ability to shift. To protect myself."

"I'll protect you."

"You can't be there all the time. It's not your job."

He growled, eyes flashing possessively. "It should be. I should never have let you be taken."

"I should be able to protect myself as all the other wolves can."

"There are other ways to keep yourself safe."

"Don't." She held up her hand. "Don't try to dissuade me. I've made up my mind."

A heavy sigh. Then, "If you want to see the Ice-Witch, then I won't stop you."

"You won't?"

"No." He stood, his big body crowding the room. His eyes turned hard. "But I will go with you."

Her lashes flew wide. "But... but you can't. The Prime won't allow it."

"Fuck the Prime," he replied. "I won't leave you unprotected. Not anymore. Do you understand?"

Slowly, she nodded, hardly believing her ears.

"Good. When do we leave?"
She collected her bag and fur-lined cape. "Now."

FOUR

Caraway followed Anise through the Meandering Woods. A smidge of gray sky could be seen through the tall, still wet trees from recent rain. Sticks and twigs crunched and squelched underfoot as they trekked. They'd been walking for two hours, and yet the fallen log marker was nowhere in sight.

The moment Caraway read the letter's instructions, he'd become wary. *Meet a troll at a fallen log, and then be told of the true location of the Ice-Witch?* It seemed preposterous. Trolls were notorious for misdirection. Fae couldn't lie, but they could send you on a wild wolpertinger chase just to mess with your head and then claim it was to reveal your heart's desire. Trolls were also carnivores, and didn't discriminate between their meat. Animal, monster, human, or fae, it was all the same to them. That Anise had planned to go there alone did not sit well with Caraway.

Doubt crept into his mind. He'd been instructed to keep the mission as reconnaissance only, but he would prepare himself for action if necessary.

"How far do we have to go?" Caraway asked.

Anise shot him a sardonic look. "Are you tired, big guy?"

He snorted. "No. I just don't want you to be taken for a fool."

She waved the folded letter. "This prevents that. The gully should be just up ahead."

They cleared bracken and stepped into a ditch, boots landing in soggy leaves. A burst of woodland sprites exploded, fluttering and zipping about, cursing in their high-squeaky voices for him to watch his step. Then, as if hearing something he couldn't, the sprites scattered to the winds.

The hairs on Caraway's arms lifted. He checked around and looked for something... anything. Being so close to Unseelie territory, where the fae of chaos ruled, there were many dangers, not to mention mana-warped monsters.

The ditch he'd stepped into was, in fact, the gully they'd been searching for. It widened ahead and extended into the distance. More lush greenery littered the bottom.

The birds stopped chirping. The insects silenced.

Anise, not picking up the tension in the air, made a jubilant sound and pointed to a moss-covered fallen log.

"That must be it!"

A shadow emerged from behind the log. The troll, a five-foot gnarly beast, walked on two legs. Its overlong arms extended to the ground where clawed fingers scraped the dirt. His brown fuzzy hair extended from the top of his head and down to his bare back. Pointed ears twitched as his beady eyes watched them approach. Tense posture said he was not to be trifled with, and the scars over his almost naked body proved it. This troll was a survivor.

No weapons, as far as Caraway could see. The troll wore nothing but a torn, dirty loincloth and a necklace made from some sort of leathery dehydrated chunks.

When the troll darted a nervous glance to where Caraway's hand gripped the hilt of his broadsword, Caraway's lip curled but he released and lowered his hand to his side. No good would come of starting this with an altercation. Best to act like there was nothing to be worried about.

Caraway put his boot on a small rock and leaned casually on his knee.

Anise held up her folded letter and raised her voice. "I have an invitation to see the Ice-Witch. It says to come here and you will show me the rest of the way."

The troll squinted at her, then at Caraway. "We don't want no Guardians around here. We eat Guardians."

For a moment, Caraway thought the troll was simply trying to sound threatening, but then he took a closer look at the troll's necklace. Those leather chunks were familiar. *Pointed ears.* Some big, some small, and some child-sized.

Caraway's stomach bottomed out. This troll had eaten children, and it was proud of it. Ice washed through his veins, tensing every muscle.

"Who him?" Anise laughed, pointing at Caraway. "He's not here to cause trouble. He's just my bodyguard for the trip. You won't hear a peep out of him. Right, Car?"

Anise's eyes pleaded with him, and he knew he couldn't jeopardize this mission, not without getting instructions first. He bared his teeth in what he supposed could be called a smile, and then raised his palms to the troll in surrender.

The troll glared at Caraway's glistening blue teardrop tattoo under his right eye—his Guardian mark—then at the sharp horns curling from the top of his head where his gaze lingered. The troll backed away. For a moment, Caraway thought he'd retreated, but then the troll tossed a glance over his shoulder and snarled to Anise, "You coming?"

A grin split her face. Elation brightened her skin. She trotted after the troll, her long dark tail swishing at her rear. It had been a while since Caraway had seen a swish in his friend's tail, and he liked it.

He followed, but unclipped the fastening strap securing Reckoning to his baldric. Now if he needed to draw his magic-cutting weapon, there would be nothing hindering the release.

The troll took them to a cave entrance where bones and body parts hung on strings, curing over a smokey fire. They looked fresh. Two, three, maybe four legs which equaled *two fae* that had been killed and trussed up. A quick glance around the cave showed no signs of contraband, which made these deaths not Caraway's problem.

Strange items and knick-knacks stacked in high, precarious piles were hoarded around the place, both inside and outside the cave. They were remnants of the old-time before a nuclear winter had swallowed the land and spat out a destitute, icy planet. Glancing deeper into the cave, he caught sight of a straw bed covered with a soft woolen blanket. It looked strange in a rough troll cave.

Something moved in the darkness, and his senses lit up.

Another troll?

He sniffed the air, but his senses weren't as attuned as a wolf's. He glanced at Anise and caught a crease between her brows. She'd smelled something she didn't like, but shook her head and dismissed it.

The troll rifled around in a wicker basket by the cave entrance until he found a portal stone. He grunted at his find and then gestured with urgency for Anise to show him the invitation. Instead of reading it, he sniffed it.

"Yep. Smells like witch," he muttered and then handed Anise the stone. "This will take you to her."

Anise received the stone but slumped. "I can't activate portal stones. Could you do it?"

The troll shook his head. "Not part of the deal. You go now. We hungry."

"I can do it," Caraway offered.

"Good," the troll picked up a long, jagged bone machete that had been resting against the cave. He jabbed it toward Caraway and Anise. "You go."

Caraway frowned at the troll's haste and moved between the sharp bone weapon and Anise.

"Come on," he said. "Let's go do this elsewhere."

He walked Anise out of the gully but, try as he might, he couldn't shake the sensation something was very wrong back at the camp. That blanket. Those curing body parts... He paused just as they climbed out of the gully and into a clearing. Anise handed him the stone, but instead of activating it, he turned back to survey the direction they'd come from.

Smoke curled from the troll's campfire, winding it's way up through the treetops and into the overcast sky.

It had been too easy.

Trolls were evil bastards when they wanted to be. Trying to get one of them to do something for you was a hard task. They were deceptive, too.

And then the cutting sound of a baby's cry pierced through the trees. Caraway's heart leaped into his throat. His eyes locked with Anise's. She'd heard too. But it was the diminishing hope turned resignation in her eyes that broke his heart. And when her ears flattened and she turned her gaze away, he understood that her faith in him was gone.

No words were needed. She'd thought because he was a Guardian, he'd ignore the plight of a baby, just like he'd failed to pay attention to the signs leading up to her capture two years ago.

He unsheathed Reckoning and growled as he shoved the portal stone at her. "Stay here and wait for me," he ordered, and then headed back toward the cave.

FIVE

Anise stood dumbly as she watched Caraway's big, leather-clad body disappear down into the gully.

The baby cried again, and it sliced right through her heart. She hadn't expected Caraway to return to the troll. The shock of it still atrophied her muscles.

Caraway—getting involved in the plight of others, even when it seemingly had nothing to do with his job. This went against everything he stood for, or rather, everything the Order of the Well stood for.

Maybe the Order *was* changing. Maybe the world was.

The frozen, harsh landscape that had taught the fae to be so brutal and ruthless was decreasing. The world was getting bigger once more.

Anise blinked and looked down at the portal stone. It was her ticket to seeing the Ice-Witch, to garner the ability to shift and hold mana, but it had been left in the safe-keeping of a child-eating Unseelie troll who wore trophies of his kills around his neck. She wanted to hurl the stone into the sky and forget about her journey, but a small part of her reasoned away this knowledge.

Maybe the Ice-Witch didn't know the troll was like this. Maybe she did.

Did it matter?

If Anise acquired the ability to shift, then did it matter who helped her get it?

Anise knew the witch was Unseelie. She knew the morally obtuse woman would have different methods, and that was precisely why Anise was going to see her. No fae in Seelie territory offered the ability to grant changes to her physical makeup. Dark magic was the only way to inject chaos into creation, and the Unseelie had no compunction when it came to dealing with the inky side of the Well.

The baby's cry pricked her ears forward and goosebumps erupted over her skin. Whatever Anise thought of the witch, there were more important things to do right now. She pocketed the stone, unsheathed her dagger, and jogged after Caraway.

When she arrived at the cave, her heart leaped into her throat. The troll's head was on the floor—separate from his body—and Caraway stood with his broadsword to his side, its tip bloody and scraping the ground as he stalked closer to something beyond the campfire at the mouth of the cave. She'd never seen that kind of fury in his expression. He was formidable.

Caraway stopped. The campfire blocked him from his quarry.

Anise could tell he was calculating how to approach the situation. The tension in his shoulders pulled tight. The tips of his horns quivered. And an unearthly breeze gusted his hair, as though the mana he held ripe within his body, ready for hostile release, was quivering to get out. It just needed a target.

Anise crept up behind him and almost lost the contents of her stomach when she saw what was in the cave beyond the fire. Another troll, this one bigger and fatter. The orange firelight cast sinister shadows along its craggy body. It cradled the wailing baby in its arms and held it to the side as if it were protecting the baby, but Anise knew it was the opposite. The troll inched toward the campfire near the cave mouth and snarled, the evidence of its last meal dangled between its teeth.

She palmed the hilt of her dagger. If either her or Caraway struck the troll, the baby would fall. Whatever they decided, they must act fast before the baby ended up in the fire.

Caraway frowned at Anise. "I told you to stay put."

"When do I ever do what I'm told?" She edged up to his side and whispered, "What do we do?"

"I can't strike and cast a spell at the same time. I'm not that good."

"But I can strike," she replied. "Be ready to catch the baby."

"Anise," Caraway warned, but she'd already taken a step closer.

She threw her dagger at the troll's face and wished it to land true. Its blade whistled past the flames and sunk into the troll's eye. It let loose an almighty roar and released the baby so it could pull the dagger free.

Panic choked Anise at the sight of the falling baby. She was already halfway around the fire as the troll stumbled backward, but Caraway beat her. He hadn't taken a step, yet the baby hovered in mid-air. He'd cast some kind of air-hardening spell around it to keep it safe.

She'd never been more relieved to have a Guardian as a friend, and even more so that he'd insisted on coming on this journey. If he'd not, she'd never have been able to rescue this baby on her own. It would have ended another trophy around the trolls' necks. She found a fluffy blanket on the straw mattress and swaddled the baby before gathering it into her arms. Then she quickly got as far into the gully as she could to avoid the smoke.

"It's all right, little one," she crooned. "We've got you."

Anise washed the baby's red face and gave it something to drink from a waterskin she'd had in her bag.

Caraway came back, blood dripping from his sword in one hand, and her soiled dagger in his other.

"Is it okay?" His deep voice cracked with concern.

She nodded. "For now, but we need to get it—" she took a peek inside the blanket. "Him. It's a boy." She gulped a deep breath. "No fur on his ears. No wings. How will we know which fae race he belongs to, or where to take him?"

"We take him to the Order."

Anise winced. "But you went against Order rules." Her watering eyes locked with her friend's. "Why?"

Why, when he'd always avoided getting involved in the past?

He held her stare.

"Maybe what happened to you has taught me some things. Maybe right or wrong doesn't have defined borders." He shrugged. "You were right, Anise. If I've got the ability to do something, I should."

The smile she sent him stretched so wide it hurt her cheeks. "Good to see something is getting through that woolly head of yours."

Their moment didn't last long before she saw something flicker in his eyes. Consequence. He may be finally understanding that saving all lives matters, but nothing happened in a vacuum. Caraway's actions could have dire consequences, and if his convictions weren't strong enough, then he'd ultimately blame her for any punishment he received as a result of saving this baby.

The Guardians took following orders seriously, and if you failed, you weren't much use to the Order.

Her smile faded. "I hope you didn't do this just to make me happy."

"I thought this is what you wanted? Me getting involved."

Turmoil swirled in her stomach. "I want you to get involved with things like this because it's the right thing to do, not because you think it would make me happy."

The baby started crying again, and Anise tucked it close.

"We can finish this conversation later," he said and pulled out a portal stone from his pocket. "For now, we'd better get the infant to safety. This is the only stone I have keyed to the Order, but I can get another while we're there. Unless you had an alternative route back from the Ice-Witch."

She shrugged. She had planned to shift into a wolf form and use her more weatherproof animal body to trot home. Wolves could travel miles through the snow in one day. Failure hadn't been an option. But now... now she understood things could go wrong.

Caraway's boss, the Prime, might let him off with a wrist slap for what he'd done, but if Anise let him follow her to the Ice-Witch, and he got into more trouble, she wouldn't forgive herself. This rebellion thing of his was new to him, despite herself harping on about it for years. He needed time to process his actions and motivations. Anise refused to be the one who ruined the life he'd built for himself, not when he'd struggled after leaving his pacifist family behind for the violent life at the Order.

When they arrived at the Order, she would find someone to activate the portal stone to the Ice-Witch, and she would leave Caraway behind. It was the right choice.

⚖

WHEN THEY ARRIVED in the field outside the Order of the Well compound, Anise handed the baby to Caraway.

"I'll wait for you here," she said.

He frowned. "Are you sure? Clarke is probably inside."

As tempting as it was to see her friend, Anise already felt her resolve weakening, and visiting the Ice-Witch had been her sole purpose for half a decade. She couldn't chicken out now.

"I'm good," she said.

He raised a brow, but turned and left. When the big compound gates closed after he'd walked through, she turned and pulled out the troll's portal stone from her pocket. The smooth, warm surface fit in the palm of her hand. She assumed there would be a magical reaction when she touched it—if she held mana within her body. She wondered what it would feel like to be connected viscerally to all the magic in the world, to have her own internal Well that fed from the grand Cosmic Well.

But she didn't.

And it was because she didn't that Caraway had already gotten into trouble. The Prime wouldn't be happy about his meddling, let alone bringing home a stray baby. And if he kept assisting in Anise's journey to the witch, then she would feel the same as she always did—useless.

The stone could be another test. The Ice-Witch knew why Anise sought her out. She'd have known that Anise couldn't activate a portal stone on her own, that she'd need help.

If Caraway hadn't been there, she'd probably have had to barter with the troll to get him to activate it, or to travel to a village and find a high fae to help her.

With a sigh, she faced the guard on top of the wall surrounding the Order compound. He wore a helmet made from hardened leather and a black leather Guardian uniform. A longbow was in his hands, and a quiver of arrows strapped to his back.

"Excuse me," she said, waving up to him.

He looked down.

"I'm running late for my appointment. Would you mind terribly if you activated my portal stone for me? I'm afraid I'm not as strong as you and lack your power."

When in doubt, she always found a well-timed ego-stroking compliment worked. He blinked, glanced over his shoulder to the other side of the wall, and then nodded.

"Toss it up."

Trying not to hide her smile, she threw it. He caught it deftly and pointed to where he was going to activate the portal. Within moments, a bright light tore a slice through the fabric of space. The light grew in size until it became a giant circle, her destination showing through the middle in a brightly blurred scene of snow and ice.

This was it.

Her heart pounded. She experienced a flicker of doubt at leaving her friend, but knew it was for the best. If she couldn't even see the Ice-Witch on her own, then what was the point of going on this quest?

She tossed a grateful smile at the guard, and then walked through the portal.

CHAPTER
SIX

After leaving the child with a Mage, Caraway returned to the gate with an incorrigible smile on his face. Even the Prime's tongue-lashing about working outside the scope of his station hadn't ruffled his fur. He'd done something that felt good.

Because of him, this child would have the chance to grow up.

This was why he'd left his family in the first place—to save those who couldn't save themselves. It was why he became a Guardian. He couldn't believe he'd forgotten that, despite Anise's urging to do so. Some part of him must have still been locked into an old way of thinking, one where he could only do his job if he colored inside the lines. But life wasn't ordered. It was chaotic.

"Violence begets violence," his mother had once said.

"Violence protects. It teaches your enemy to be afraid of you."

"Well, congratulations, son. We are now afraid of you."

He shoved the memories down and focused on the one shining light in his life. Anise. He couldn't wait to tell her what he'd said when the Prime had tried to block him from leaving. He'd told her that if she wanted to keep him as a Guardian, then she'd better get used to him stepping in to help those unfortunate, whether it was Well-related or not. He'd said the Order needed this kind of image boost after the Prime's totalitarian ways, and then he didn't stop to wait for the Prime's response.

Coming up to the gate, he gestured for the guard on top to open it and let him out. When he emerged into the field outside the Order compound, he couldn't find Anise. At first, he thought perhaps she'd gone inside after all, but he'd barely spent time at the Academy where he'd flagged down a healing Mage. The Prime had accosted him on the way back out. If Anise had entered the compound, she'd have walked straight past him.

He lifted his gaze to the sentry's post and squinted into the sun.

"Where did the female go?" he asked.

The guard shrugged. "Somewhere snowy, I guess."

Caraway's heart clenched. "What do you mean?"

"She asked me to activate her portal stone. Said she couldn't do it."

No.

Caraway shook his head, refusing to believe it. She wouldn't leave without him, would she? He'd felt like they were finally connecting again. But she had left. Not only had she entered dangerous territory on her own, but she was still planning on going through with her quest for the ability to shift. No bargain made with the Ice-Witch would be safe. And then there was the mission part of his reason for following her. Caraway might not agree with the Prime's way of leading sometimes, but he stood behind the Order's mission to keep magic alive in Elphyne. They needed to know whether the Ice-Witch was responsible for supplying the human enemy with mana-warped monsters.

Mild panic swarmed his skin like prickling ant bites. He had to get Leaf. Without preamble, he headed back into the Order to find the Cadre of Twelve's team leader, and resident expert at tracing portals.

CARAWAY STOOD behind Leaf and Aeron as they assessed the space in the air where Anise's portal had been activated. Leaf glared at the space with glowing blue eyes. It seemed as if he saw through the air to another dimension. His compatriot, Aeron, also looked at something Caraway couldn't see.

They were tracing the portal—tracking where it had sent Anise.

Both elves were adept at casting spells with their inherent mana. As far as Caraway knew, there was no one more skilled than Leaf. He shuddered to think how powerful Leaf would become if he gained a Well-blessed mate like his cadre members, Rush and Thorne.

Aeron's braided brown hair swung down his spine every time he nodded to Leaf with another increment of portal remnant he assessed.

Caraway could see none of it.

This skill took decades, possibly centuries, to hone. It was why these two were part of the cadre, the Order's most elite warriors, and not Caraway.

"I've almost got it," Leaf murmured. Small droplets of perspiration dotted the skin over his smooth top lip.

"She's far north-west," Aeron added. "In the cold."

Leaf made a swiping motion with his hand, and a tearing sound ripped through the air. He reopened the portal and turned to Caraway, "I hope she brought a woolen cape."

Caraway gave a curt nod. He didn't need one. Being a muskox-shifter, and one of the fire-fae, his temperature ran hot.

Aeron put something smooth into Caraway's palm. When Caraway looked down, he found another portal stone. But he'd already taken one from the Mage Academy. He raised a brow at Aeron.

"It's from Clarke. It's keyed to Rush's cabin."

"Why?" Caraway asked. Clarke was psychic. Had she seen some reason that he'd be needing to take a detour home?

Aeron shrugged. "Who knows with Clarke? I'm guessing she'll want to meet you there before you come here."

Caraway nodded his gratitude, braced, and then headed through the portal.

Leaf reminded Caraway as he left, "Just reconnaissance."

⚖

THE ICE-FOREST WAS APTLY NAMED for the trees of frozen water. Clear crystalline trunks four hand-spans wide stretched high into the blue sky. Icicle leaves swayed and tinkled with the arctic breeze as Caraway navigated the only path available. The portal had taken him to the brink of the forest. It was either head backward over a vast icy tundra, or deep into the forest. It made sense the Ice-Witch would live in a frozen forest—he hoped—and not the barren tundra.

But the further he trekked, the more doubt crept into his mind. Every few hundred feet, he picked up a new worrying sign that things weren't going according to Anise's plan.

Specks of blood were stark against the ice. At first, the drops looked like they'd come from a scratch, or a shallow wound, but then he came to a place in the path where ice had chipped away from trunks, the ground was littered with fallen icicle leaves, and the tiny red droplets arced in a line as though someone had been cut and blood had spurted. With each passing minute, he stared at the blood spatter, his chest constricted painfully until it felt like his ribcage squashed his heart.

Anise *had* to be okay.

He wouldn't accept another outcome.

A screech shook the leaves and a shower of ice rained down on Caraway's head. He released Reckoning and crouched into a battle stance, ears straining, and eyes searching the sky. A light shadow blocked the sun. Then another, and another. Screeching grew in timbre. More powdered ice dropped from the trees.

What's up there?

Air trembled.

Crushed shards of leaves fell to the ground, hitting his shoulders.

Glamor was a common tool in the fae arsenal, and whatever hunted him could be using it to hide from sight. Then again, it could also be a camouflage system of the beasts. Caraway closed his eyes and focused on senses other than sight. He let the air enter his lungs, held, and then exhaled slowly. Through it all, his ears strained and he sent out a blanket of magic to surround him. Whether it was his pacifist roots or something the Well had gifted him during his initiation ceremony, Caraway had learned that as a Guardian, he excelled in protective spells, including casting forcefields around his body—or the baby he'd saved.

Any being entering his immediate surroundings would trigger his alarm system, and he'd know where to strike.

All he had to do was wait.

So he breathed, and he listened, and he sensed. Like trying to catch a fish, he waited for a thrumming ping down the line he'd cast.

Ping.

He spun and thrust Reckoning into a solid ice wall. An ear-piercing shriek rattled his bones, and a crashing sound like breaking glass followed. When he opened his eyes, he paused from the sheer shock of what he saw. A broken sculpture of a gargoyle made from ice, not stone. But he could've sworn it had been moving through the air, rattling the leaves of the trees enough to shatter them.

Caraway nudged the large broken chunks of solid ice with his sword. No blood, just a clear crystalline body through and through. If he'd needed any evidence the witch was creating mana-warped monsters, this could be it. Except... the ice would melt soon, and there would be nothing left. He needed more.

The ice also meant the blood he'd seen on the way had indeed belonged to Anise.

He was still lost in thought when he heard another screech, only then remembering that he'd heard more than one creature calling earlier. A thud behind him had him tensing. He gripped the hilt of his sword painfully. A bloom of white breath ghosted over his shoulder. He whirled, ready to strike, and came face to face with another angry ice-gargoyle. It opened its jaws, screeched again. Its white breath turned putrid and green.

Was it... poison?

Dark spots swam before his eyes. He tried to swing at the beast, knowing the magic-nulling properties of his sword would help, but staggered like a drunk to the floor where everything went dark.

Too late.

His last thought was of Anise's sassy smile.

SEVEN

Their prison was a domed room made of solid snow. Light came from the only exit, guarded by two winged beasts carved from ice. There was no water, no food, and no toilet.

Anise gently patted Caraway's cheek but he didn't stir.

Crimson, when those frozen beasts had dragged his lifeless body in, she'd felt sick. It still hadn't returned to normal. He had to wake soon. *He had to!*

She patted his cheek again. No reaction. But at least he was warm and breathed evenly.

In an attempt to calm herself, Anise shifted her position so she could sit against the solid snow wall and lifted Caraway's big head into her lap. It felt better to hold him.

He moaned. She let her knuckles graze his cheek and then rasp over the scruff on his jaw. She'd always fantasized about touching him... his face, his jaw, his horns. But the horns weren't there this time. He was a shifter, so perhaps he'd morphed them away. She'd just never seen him do that in all the years she'd known him.

It wouldn't surprise her if he'd chosen to keep his horns visible when he didn't have to. Usually, a shifters' natural fae-form was close to human, with only arched ears as a sign they were *other*, touched by the magic of the Well, but never Caraway. He'd always had his curved lethal horns proudly jutting from his head. He'd probably left them there to look as far from human as he could.

Humans were manaless, untouched, greedy leeches that constantly tried to invade Elphyne and reap the benefits of the Well, yet refused to follow the rules that provided Well's magic in the first place.

No metal. No plastic. Two simple rules.

But the humans had run out of metals in their city. They'd come raiding in Elphyne to look for places to mine for resources.

Caraway's peace-loving family were victims of one such raid. As nomads, they'd lived amongst the western snowy tundra. A human-led raiding party had massacred half his tribe. His family's answer was to migrate further inland. Caraway's answer was to join the Guardians where he gained enhanced powers to help him hunt humans and return the favor.

Anise's home town, Crescent Hollow, was the closest fae settlement to the human city. Because of this proximity, Caraway was always there, sitting in the tavern where Anise had worked. Sometimes before a hunt, sometimes after, but every time he spoke of the race that murdered his kinsfolk, his cheeks would redden with fury.

"That's what I like about you folk here in Crescent Hollow," he'd once said. *"You're so far from human even though you're so close. You never forget what it means to be fae."*

Crescent Hollow was a wolf-shifter town. But Anise couldn't shift.

"Without your tail and ears, you're basically human!"

The cruel taunts of her childhood still haunted her. She couldn't be the thing that Caraway hated. She had to stand on her own two feet and hold her own the way mana-filled fae could.

Caraway stirred again.

Long lashes lifted slowly, warily. Warm brown eyes focused on her and then widened.

"You're okay," he said, incredulously. "But I saw blood."

She smiled gently and showed her healing forearm. "I cut myself on one of those ice beasts, but I had some elven healing cream in my bag. I've stopped bleeding now."

He blinked, seemingly processing her words. Then he sat up sharply and enveloped her smaller body within his. The force of his strong arms locked around her. She stiffened on reflex until his hold tightened, and then she melted into him.

For long, silent minutes, they held each other and the world was right.

It was just the two of them, warm bodies fused together in an icy world. Why couldn't life be this simple?

Caraway pulled back just enough that he could look down into her eyes.

"Anise," he said, voice deep and rough. "I thought I'd lost you."

"I'm here," she replied.

Charged awareness bounced between them. They were close. So Well-damned close that she could stick out her tongue and lick his lips. *Crimson,* she wanted to. They'd never been in an embrace like this, and they both knew it.

How would he react? Would he pull away and act as many others did?

What are you dumb as well as less? The voice of her last customer rang through her mind. Her heart sank. She lowered her eyes, but Caraway used his finger to tilt her chin up. This time, there was an intensity in his gaze that rocked her to her core. Heat and desire stirred in her lower belly. Confused, she frowned at him.

His intensity held until she squirmed. Then he licked his lips, looked down at hers, and leaned in until there was no doubt in her mind what he was about to do. She froze with anticipation. Her nerves thrummed with energy.

The tips of their noses touched and his lashes shuttered as though he was in pain. Their breaths came in stilted gasps... and then he moved his lips an iota. *Closer.*

They didn't kiss. Not yet. Maybe he was thinking the same things as she—that this kiss would change everything. That this was the one thing she'd always wanted, but feared would never happen. That he would turn away and change his mind. That she was less, and not good enough.

But he nudged his lips toward hers. He closed the gap. He lifted her chin. *Almost.*

And then... soft lips landed on hers, capturing her mouth, leaving her breathless. She went liquid with a moan.

Caraway growled with approval, splayed a big hand at her back, and tugged her closer as though she weighed nothing to him. Damn, he was strong. It sent a thrill tripping through her stomach. Her soft front slammed against his hard chest and he deepened their kiss.

Yes. He wanted this too.

Knowing it flipped a switch inside her. She speared fingers into his hair, tightened her grip, kissed harder, and drank him up. Her tongue dueled with his and plundered his mouth for more. His taste was like a drug, and he must have felt the same way because he held her so tight she could barely move. When they finally broke for air, they still couldn't let go of each other.

He felt hot, hard, a little sweaty, and she wanted more.

"Anise," he rasped deeply, eyes searching hers. Something flickered in them, and her doubt came hurtling back.

He's going to say this is a mistake.

Before he could speak, she blurted the first thing that came to mind. "Your horns are gone. I've never seen you without them."

He blinked. His jaw clicked shut. And he frowned. "What?"

She gestured to his head.

Caraway's looming body pulled back. His warmth went with him.

"So stupid. I forgot," he admonished himself.

The air shimmered around his head, and then two sharp horns grew from above his temples until they curved down and outward from his cheekbones.

The shame in his posture surprised Anise. His eyes turned downcast.

"It's because you think you look human without the horns, don't you?" she asked, and then elaborated. "You keep the horns so you look different to those who killed your family."

He jerked back. "Why would you think that?"

"I don't know. I guess you're always talking about how much you hate them, and how much you love the shifters at Crescent Hollow looking so different to them."

His brows lowered. His gaze darkened. "Anise, I don't love the shifters at the Hollow because they *look* different from humans. They *are* different from humans. Especially you—you're kind, selfless, and brave." He shuffled closer and lifted her chin to look hard into her eyes. "I keep my horns because you're self-conscious of your tail. I do it so you think we're the same outside and in—" He tapped her sternum. "From the moment I met you, Anise, you've accepted me for who I am. Unlike my family, who disowned me for wanting to protect them, you've always taken me as I came. I keep my horns to show you I accept you as you are."

Anise's mind whirled with his confession.

He kept his horns so she didn't feel left out. So she felt less alone. He thought she was kind, selfless, and brave.

Her fingers wrapped around the smooth length of his horns and tugged until his lips came back to hers. This time, there was no hesitation. The two of them kissed as though their hearts pulled their puppet strings, directing them with passion, desire, and need. They were so lost in each other, they failed to notice their companion until she spoke.

"This is so sweet I'm getting cavities."

They broke apart. Caraway shoved Anise behind him and bared his teeth at the intruder.

The Ice-Witch was here, and she wasn't anything like the hag Anise had expected.

A tall, willowy female fae leaned with her shoulder against the doorway. White ringlets bounced around a pale, heart-shaped face. She had a dusky nose, flushed cheeks, and white rabbit ears that poked through an orange top hat and pointed straight up. Her outfit was a mix of black, white, and orange lace and wool. A corset squeezed abundant breasts out the top, and slick black woolen pants revealed a twitching bunny rabbit tail at the rear. When she smiled, two large front teeth touched her bottom lip.

She shifted red eyes to Anise. "I'm ready to see you now."

When Anise moved, Caraway held her back.

The witch clicked her tongue. "Now, now, Guardian. Is that any way to behave?"

"Don't make the deal, Anise," he said over his shoulder. "You don't need to change. You're perfect the way you are."

All humor in the witch's face flatlined. She glared at Caraway. "You don't get a say in her choice when you haven't been honest about your true reason for being here."

Anise stiffened and locked on Caraway. "What's she talking about?"

Guilt flashed over his features.

"Caraway?" she prompted.

"I'm here on a mission," he admitted. "For the Order."

She stepped away from him, shocked. So... he wasn't here to support her? It had been a ruse?

"Anise," he reached for her, but she stepped further back and he flinched. "It doesn't change the fact I don't want you to make a bargain with this female. Please don't. I'm begging you."

"All this time," she said, "I thought maybe you actually missed me. That's why you came to see me after two years, but it wasn't. You're only using me to get to the Ice-Witch, aren't you?"

His lack of an answer was all she needed to know.

CHAPTER
EIGHT

Caraway roared his anger at the ice-gargoyles from his prison, but the two beasts blocked him solidly. There was no way through.

The witch had taken Anise away before he could explain, *before he could say sorry*.

He punched the snowy wall until shards of stalactite ice dropped from the ceiling. One was so sharp, it cut the back of his hand as it came down. He landed heavily on the ground and dipped his head into his hands.

Damn him.

He should have been honest with Anise from the start. She would have understood, surely. Now he was stuck in an icy prison while his love was about to make the biggest mistake of her life.

He needed his sword, and he needed it now.

The gargoyles were magical creatures. They wouldn't have touched Reckoning for fear of it affecting themselves. It was probably rusting on the path where he'd been poisoned.

Caraway's head lifted.

A slow smile formed as a plan came to mind. Recently, Thorne had shown him a handy little trick. As one of the Cadre of Twelve, and Well-blessed to boot, Thorne was more adept at spell casting than Caraway could ever hope to be. The wolf-shifter had been recently imprisoned in the Ring—a gladiator type pit where differences were decided through a battle to the death. He'd been thrown in without his weapon, but years earlier he'd carved a transference rune onto his battle-ax's handle. When he was in the Ring, all he'd needed to do was scratch that same rune onto his palm, and the spell would hunt down the weapon and bring it to him. Thorne had single-handedly won a battle against multiple mana-warped creatures because he'd had the might of his magic-cutting ax.

514

After hearing the story, Caraway had immediately carved a transference rune into Reckoning's handle. Collecting a broken shard of stalactite, Caraway carved the rune into his palm and activated the spell, then he positioned himself behind the gargoyles and waited. A whooshing sound came, the air twisted and heated, and then Caraway felt a solid familiar weight land in the palm of his right hand.

Reckoning.

He grinned.

ANISE FOLLOWED the witch through a long hallway carved from clear ice. While the witch didn't seem to feel the cold, Anise felt it through to her bones. She hugged her cape around her shoulders and forced her teeth to stop chattering.

It wasn't only her skin that was numb, but her heart and mind. She couldn't comprehend Caraway had only followed her on this quest to use her. Did she know him at all? It hurt to think it was all a manipulation.

Her heart didn't want to believe it. His kiss had been real. He couldn't fake that.

I keep my horns to show you I accept you as you are.

Anise's chest constricted. Her eyes watered.

"Here we go," the witch's sickly sweet voice echoed.

Anise looked up and found they'd emerged into a large hall. Like the rest of this part of the world, it was all made from ice. Cobwebs hung from the ceiling like a sick sort of decoration. Prismatic light filtered through the ceiling from outside, making Anise realize it must still be day. As she followed the witch, Anise noticed strange shadows encased in the ice walls. The closer she got, the more she wanted to vomit.

The shadows were people, frozen with terror on their faces. Were they others like Anise, who'd come looking for answers, or were they fae who'd done the witch wrong?

Anise hugged her cape tighter.

The witch took steps up to a podium where an ice-throne sat. She sprawled into the seat and crooked her finger at Anise.

"Come closer, dear."

Anise shuffled forward but stopped at the foot of the dais. "Where's my bone dagger?" she asked.

"You'll get it when you leave." The witch slipped out the dagger from her boot and stabbed it into the arm of her throne. The hilt wobbled as it took purchase. "I couldn't very well leave intruders in my home with weapons, could I?"

"Intruder?" Anise gasped. "I was invited."

"The Guardian was not."

"Nor was he excluded."

The witch's gaze narrowed on Anise. "He killed my troll."

Anise tried not to let her panic show on her face. She had also killed a troll, and no matter what Caraway had done to get into this place, she didn't want him to die for it. And she would never regret saving that baby's life.

"What are you going to do with Caraway?" she asked.

"Well, now. That depends on you."

Anise took a step back. "What do you mean?"

"Well, my dear. How are you planning to pay for the ability to shift?"

"I have coin. Lots of it. That's how I plan to pay."

The witch laughed. It was a high-pitched melodious tinkle. "What makes you think I need coin?"

"Then what do you want?"

"Two hundred years," she stated and then gestured to the poor souls trapped in the ice. "After two hundred years, you pay me with a soul."

Anise bit her lip. "But I get the power of a shifter for two hundred years?"

She could live as one of the wolves in Crescent Hollow for two centuries before she needed to lose her soul. And in that time, she could shift into a wolf, run through the forest, and feel the joy and freedom other shifters always waxed poetic about when they'd come into the tavern. For two centuries, she would hold mana within her body and cast spells without needing to resort to potions or elixirs. Wasn't that all she'd wanted? To belong?

"You don't need to change. You're perfect the way you are."

Part of her wanted to believe Caraway's words, and part of her wanted to not need to. She hated that she yearned for his approval, the same as everyone else's. She hated that she wanted to fit in, but the constant anxiety was a noose over her head. She'd never be rid of it if she didn't try this.

The witch squinted at her. "I can see you have doubts, and I know it's because of the male who followed you. Let me give you a piece of free advice." She leaned forward in her throne until her orange top hat tilted on her head. If it weren't for her rabbit ears poking through cutout holes, the hat may have fallen right off. "Males, of any species, are not to be trusted. They take what they want, but they'll never give you what you need. It's in their nature. They're the hunters, not the nurturers. The sooner you come to terms with that, the better."

That's when Anise realized every frozen body in the ice was male.

The witch stood and stepped down the dais. With wistful eyes, she trailed her fingers along the icy walls of her macabre museum.

"I wasn't always like this." She gestured to her ears. "I used to shift into a rabbit. And like you, I came looking for a way to become more than less. But then I found him." She stopped at a particular shadowed figure trapped in the ice. A tall fae, handsome and ominous in his expression, even as he was petrified. "He seduced me, and he stole my mana. He harvested it for his own use. But you see, he made a mistake. He believed that those lesser fae were beneath him." She snarled at the shadow. "He should have killed me when he had the chance."

"Caraway's stolen nothing from me," Anise said. Her experience wasn't the same as this female's.

The witch's eyes snapped toward Anise. "All males are the same."

Anise shook her head. Perhaps the witch's story was meant to convince her to give up on Caraway, but it only made her realize he wasn't Anise's enemy. He'd never believed she was beneath him. No, she loved him. She wouldn't involve him in this.

"I just want the ability to shift."

The witch held out her hand. "So we have a deal?"

Anise paused, but two hundred years of fulfillment was a long time. She could be happy.

She nodded and shook the witch's hand. "Yes, we have a deal."

Thunder cracked through the hall. The walls shook. Tiny icicles showered from the ceiling. Anise thought, perhaps, that it was because of the bargain they'd just struck, but the witch's facial expression was as surprised as Anise's.

They disengaged and Anise repeated. "You give me the ability to shift into a wolf for two hundred years, and I give you my soul after that."

"Oh, little wolf. It's too late to add specifics." The witch's peach lips curved into a wicked grin. "Now, I didn't say *whose* soul was payment."

Then she laughed a big cackling sound that shriveled Anise's resolve. What could she mean? Not Anise's soul? Then whose—

Caraway burst into the room, his face contorted in fury, his fist around his long broadsword. Long legs strode into the center of the hall.

"What did you do?" he demanded to the witch.

He stormed toward where she had retreated to her throne. He raised his sword high above his head, but before he could arc his swing downward, the witch flicked her wrist and ice shot out of the ground beneath his feet. Water sprung like a geyser to surround Caraway's body. It only took seconds, and his sword was knocked from his hands. It clattered loudly to the ground.

"No!" Anise shouted. "Leave him alone."

But the witch just laughed as the water slithered up Caraway's body and turned to ice. His doe-eyed gaze flicked to Anise, and then to his fallen sword with a forlorn finality before he became completely encased   frozen.

Anise hissed at the witch. "No! I don't agree to give him. Let him go."

The witch clicked her tongue and then pouted. "Yes, you did agree."

"He's not mine to give," Anise insisted.

"His heart is yours, therefore it is yours to give."

Anise snarled and ran toward the throne, aiming for her dagger. The witch flicked her hand, and Anise went flying backward. She landed hard and skidded across the icy floor, groaning in pain. But if she couldn't get close to the witch, how could she defeat her?

Gaining the ability to shift wasn't worth Caraway's life. It wasn't worth his soul. She couldn't do this to him. Groaning, Anise clutched her side where the ice had bruised. She rolled and faced the ground then tried to crawl away from the witch, but only managed to get to the base of Caraway's icy tomb. She used the column to drag herself into a sitting position, then scowled at the witch.

"You tricked me," she accused. "You never said it had to be another's soul."

"I said *a* soul, dearie, not *your* soul. You clearly weren't listening hard enough. How do you think you'll gain the ability to shift? It has to come from somewhere."

"Still, why his? Why not someone else's?"

"Because he's the only one who belongs to you. He's the only one you have a right to give." The witch's brows rose. "Don't you see? My ability was stolen from me, but I took it back, plus more! You can finally be powerful. You can have them all whimpering at your feet. You can take what you want, just like they do."

Anise squeezed her eyes and shook her head. When she opened them, her gaze landed on Caraway's sword. Her mind blanked.

His sword.

Caraway had glanced at it before he'd frozen. Thinking back, it had been a purposeful glance. *A message?*

Take the weapon and use it.

But the sword was metal. Metal was forbidden because it halted the flow of mana through the earth, air, water, and through bodies of any fae. The sword would cut through any magic the witch threw Anise's way. It would cut through the witch. But just as the thoughts formed in her head, Anise felt disappointment crush her breath. Guardians were the only fae alive who could use metal weapons, and not disrupt their own flow of mana. Anyone else would experience extreme pain when using it.

But... she wasn't just anyone else.

She already had no mana. She couldn't shift. There was nothing in her body for the sword's metal to disrupt.

Caraway had known that. The look he'd given the sword *was* a message.

Hope flared. Anise licked her lips and glanced at the witch. There was no way Anise could reach for the sword without the witch noticing. She would blast her with magic before Anise's fingers closed around the hilt. She had to trick her. She had to take a hit and fall within the range. The sword wasn't far, only a few feet to her right.

She steeled her resolve, hardened her gut, and growled before climbing to her feet, charging ahead but veering right. The witch threw out another hand of hard power. It knocked Anise senseless, and true to expectations, her body went flying backward again. The solid floor connected with Anise's shoulder. She cried out in pain, but went sliding backward, right within reach of the sword.

"When will you learn, little she-wolf?" the witch snarled.

Anise clutched her middle and feigned crawling away. Her body almost shielded her from view. As she reached for the giant sword, she had a moment of clarity. Caraway had been right. She didn't need the ability to shift. She was perfect the way she was. The very thing she'd cursed as lacking in her body was now the thing saving her life. It was all about perspective. No mana meant that when her fingers curled around the hilt of the magic-killing sword, she felt nothing but the overwhelming urge to protect what was hers.

She came to her feet, snarling and baring her teeth. Moving the sword to hold in two hands, she charged the dais using the sword as a shield. The witch tried to throw magic at Anise, but the sword cut it in half. The witch tried to send ice through the ground, like she had Caraway, but he'd been taken by surprise. Anise didn't make the same mistake. She sliced and cut her way until she made it to the dais and launched up, taking the steps in two giant leaps. She aimed the tip of the sword straight forward and kept running as though carrying a lance. It pierced the witch through the heart, pinning her to her ice throne. Blood welled from the witch's mouth and she tried to scream. Only a gurgle came out.

"I'll learn when you're dead," Anise said and twisted the blade deep.

The witch's last gaze was at the fae she'd first encased in the ice, and it was a look of longing and regret. The pain froze in her expression as the light left her eyes, and Anise knew she'd made the right decision. If she'd accepted the bargain, Anise would have lived a life as lonely as the witch's. What were two hundred years if it was spent alone?

Sniffing, she wiped her nose on her sleeve, then yanked the sword out of the witch. The witch's body slumped down the throne and tumbled to the ground. Then Anise set to chipping away Caraway's tomb, praying to the Well that he would survive. It took long, drawn-out minutes, but she chipped enough for Caraway to break through. His big, powerful body exploded through the ice and he staggered to his knees with big, ragged breaths.

"Car," she said and fell to the ground with him.

He lifted his frost-covered chin and met her eyes. "You did it," he rasped. "I knew you would."

She sniffed and tried not to smile, but the pure adoration in his eyes warmed her heart.

She joked, "I guess having no mana counts for something right?"

The grin that split his blue lips was contagious. He cupped her jaw and brushed a trembling thumb along her skin. "Anise, you have something, or else you'd have aged at a human rate."

She blinked. "But I felt nothing when I touched the sword."

"The Well works in mysterious ways, and I can't explain it, but it's true. You have enough of the Well inside that you are fae. We can live here in Elphyne where the land flourishes. You don't have to manipulate the magic to appreciate it. As long as we're together, isn't that enough?"

She looked deep into his eyes. "Are we together?"

Worry flared in his gaze. "I hope so. I mean, I want to... don't you? That kiss... um."

His ears reddened and his cheeks reddened in a blush.

Well-damn, it was the most adorable thing she'd ever seen, and it gave her the courage to say, "I want to be more than together. I want to be mated with you."

CHAPTER
NINE

The sweetest words had come out of Anise's mouth, but Caraway couldn't give her the answer she needed. Not only was the cold in his system taking over, but he didn't know if mating was in his future as a Guardian.

He shivered uncontrollably. Concern replaced the light in Anise's eyes.

"We have to get you somewhere warm," she said.

He nodded. "P-Portal stone in my p-pocket-t."

She dug into his pants pocket and drew out a smooth stone that she placed in his cold, shaking fingers. He gave the frozen museum a scathing once-over—there had been no evidence that the witch had been working with the humans, but Caraway hadn't really had time to conduct a thorough investigation and those gargoyles definitely weren't natural.

Now he'd been here, he could create his own portal stone back. All he needed was something native to the place.

"I need to c-collect some s-snow," he said. "F-for a portal stone."

Anise nodded and rifled around her bag for her waterskin. She emptied it and scooped some snow in. It would do.

He activated the portal, right there inside the hall. The transference of energy ripped a hole in space and time. He held out a hand to Anise. Before she took it, she collected her dagger from the throne and gave the dead witch one last look. Caraway thought he saw pity in her eyes and wondered what had transpired while he'd been frozen.

Then Anise took his hand and together they walked through the portal. They arrived not at the Order, as he'd thought, but on the snow-dusted sandy banks of a sacred lake near Rush's cabin. Rush and Clarke had lived here for two years while they raised their newborn away from society.

The sun dipped beyond the horizon, and darkness loomed.

Caraway searched in his pockets for the other portal stone, the one that would take them back to the Order, but Anise stopped him.

"Look," she said and pointed to the wooden cabin set near some trees.

Smoke curled from the chimney.

"It's Rush's c-cabin," he explained, still stuttering from the cold. "Before I left the Order, Clarke s-sent me a portal stone that came here."

Anise grinned. "Gotta love that psychic human. Wish all of them were like her. It's getting dark and the cabin looks warm. Let's make camp for the night."

He gave her a quizzical look.

Anise elaborated. "Where there's smoke, there's fire. Come on. Let's get you warmed up."

She took his cold hand and pulled him toward the cabin. On the porch, they kicked the snow from their boots and then entered the one-room cabin. Inside was a bed, a kitchen counter, and a crackling fireplace with two small fire sprites dancing on a log to keep it smoldering. One male, one female. They paused upon Caraway's and Anise's entry and squeaked at the intrusion.

Caraway showed them the spent portal stone. "C-Clarke invited us."

The sprites—glowing red and orange figures made of flames—stared and then resumed their dancing, ignoring Anise and Caraway.

But the heat... it was divine.

Caraway shuffled closer to the fireplace and crouched low. He held his palms out and let the warmth suffuse his body, vaguely aware of Anise's bustling behind him in the kitchen. When she brought a ceramic pot filled with soup over to the fire, he realized she'd been cooking and a few minutes had gone by.

"There were root vegetables under the counter," she explained and placed the pot so it would cook.

The sprites grew curious and looked over the pot at the contents.

Once satisfied the sprites weren't going to cause mischief, Anise turned to Caraway with a determined look on her face.

"Time to get you out of the wet clothes."

His lips twitched. The fire was doing its job superbly at warming and drying him. He didn't need to, but he *wanted* to, so he let her systematically set about helping him out of his Guardian uniform. First, she removed his baldric and sword, then his boots. When she got to his jacket, he was already warmed up and getting hotter by the second. Her touch took the chill away more than any fire could.

This female, his friend who'd shared so much with him, was taking care of him. No one had done so since his youth—since before his mother and father had branded him as a violent anarchist.

This female, with whom he was irrevocably in love with, had saved his life.

He watched with reverence as she unpicked the bone-stud buttons down the center of his jacket.

Flickering firelight cast a glow on her face, softening her features. He found himself becoming breathless from her beauty. She felt her dark-rimmed eyes were too wolf-like, but he found them stunning. She hated the black smudge of color at the tip of her nose, but he wanted to lick it. She tried to hide her extra arched ears by wearing a leather cord around her head, but he smiled where the ears stubbornly poked through the fall of black hair.

It was all Anise. It made her unique. It made her *more*, and it made her the one he loved.

She frowned as she peeled his jacket from his arms and shook it out. "It's so heavy and soggy," she murmured and then searched for a place to hang it. She found a hook on the back of the front door.

When she returned, she caught the heated look in Caraway's stare and blanched.

"What?" she asked. "Why are you staring?"

His lips curved on one side. "Because you're beautiful."

She ignored him and pointed at the rest of his wet clothes, his white shirt, and pants. "You should probably take it all off."

His grin widened and his laugh boomed out from deep in his belly. "You know, if you wanted to get my clothes off, there were easier ways of going about it than to get a witch to steal my soul."

It was meant to be a joke, but the pain in her eyes was real.

"Oh no," he murmured and reached for her hand. "I didn't mean it like that. It was a joke. Stupid."

Her lips flattened and she looked away. "I almost got you killed."

"I'm fine, Anise," he whispered. "And I'm not blameless here. I should have told you the truth about why I was with you. The Order may have given me the mission to follow you to the Ice-Witch, but it was because a prisoner had mentioned her name during interrogation. I was too much of a coward to come and find you myself and, for that, I'll never be sorry enough. But let me be clear, I'm not sorry the mission brought me back to you."

After his words were done, silence hung in the air. Then she slowly lifted her gaze to his.

"You said 'sorry'," she said.

He nodded. A spoken apology, or thank you, from one fae to another was an acknowledgment of debt. It gave a legally binding reason to forge a bargain to repay the debt. Caraway was essentially putting his life in Anise's hands. It was also known that debts were not acted on between family because they would do anything for their loved ones anyway.

How she responded would determine their future with each other.

"I'm sorry too," she said. "I should never have placed the blame on you for my capture two years ago, but you were the closest friend I had. You were the safest avenue. And if I didn't blame you, then I had to blame myself."

She flared her lashes in a way that made Caraway think she was trying not to cry, and when a tear spilled free anyway, it broke his heart.

He trailed a thumb across her cheek to wipe the moisture away. "Anise, what happened to you could have happened to anyone."

"But none of the shifters were caught." A sob wracked her body. "If I had the power, I could have protected myself."

"But you *can* protect yourself." He shook her gently. "You lived on your own in Cornucopia for years. You killed a troll and saved a baby. You bloody-well killed the Ice-Witch!" His eyes widened with the realization. "You're incredible, Anise. And you can't shift. You can't use mana to cast spells. So Well-damned what? You're *more* amazing for it."

He ran his hands down her arms and circled to her back where he let his touch glide down over the tail poking from her pants. She startled and looked up at him.

He grinned. "You can touch my horns."

It was meant to be a joke, to show that they were the same inside and out, but his voice came out low and rough, and once it emitted, he couldn't stop the train of his thoughts. Yes, he wanted her to touch him. Everywhere.

She licked his lips and then raked her heated gaze down his front. "That's not where I want to touch you."

His cock hardened instantly.

"Anise," he croaked, begged.

Her fingers curled beneath the hem of his shirt and lifted slowly. He sucked in a breath, abs curling inward, as her fingers brushed his stomach. She kept lifting. He raised his arms so she could remove his shirt, and then she started working on the drawstrings of his pants.

"Anise," he murmured.

"Shh," she scolded. "I'm enjoying this."

He was too, but desire raged inside him like an inferno. He was hard, tense, and coiled tight. When she slid his pants down his thighs, her hair brushed his skin. He threw his head back and cursed loudly. Every time she touched him, his senses sparked like fireworks. She lifted each of his feet to slide his pants free, and when she was done, he scooped his hands under her arms and lifted her clear off the ground.

With a molten, golden gaze, she wrapped her legs around his waist and cupped his face to snarl against his lips. "Last chance, Car. Once I start this with you, I won't stop. I'll mark you as mine."

The wolf-shifters marked their mates to prove to the world they were together. The thought of her teeth on his neck ripped a growl of approval from his throat and he slammed his lips on hers, only pulling back to say, "I've always been yours. I'm ready."

CHAPTER
TEN

Anise sank her fangs into the thick column of Caraway's neck. Her hormones went haywire and a mating-musk scent seeped from her pores, coating Caraway. Usually, two shifters marked each other. Caraway wasn't a wolf, but he *was* fae, and mating in any fae race was classed as a serious union of commitment. He was ready. So was she.

She clutched him tightly as she bit down.

He moaned, his eyes rolled back, and he staggered toward the bed where he landed heavily with her on top of him. She laved at the wound she'd created with loving care and relished the evidence of their commitment. He didn't wait long before he started peeling her clothes from her body. First, her cape. Then her shirt, and then his thick fingers were digging into her pants, fumbling at the buttons.

Somehow, they managed to both end up completely naked, sweaty, and in each other's arms. She thought she would be ashamed of being like this with him, but when he looked at her body... especially her breasts... his eyes heated with desire. A hungry growl rumbled from his throat and he latched onto her nipple, sucking greedily and sending showers of bliss coursing through her body.

They kissed and touched and played with each other, savoring this new level of intimacy. There was no doubt. He'd let her mark him, and from the way he fervently touched her and kissed her, it turned him on as much as it did her.

He rolled so he was on top and fit his hips between her legs. He took his erection in hand and entered her in one slick motion. She gasped, back bowing, as she adjusted to the sensation of him filling her. Moans and groans filled the room as they adjusted to the new onslaught of sensations, then he gave a self-satisfied masculine grunt and kissed her lips. Meeting her eyes, he braced his hands on either side of her head.

"You ready?" he asked, voice gravelly.

She lifted her hips. "Yes."

"I'm claiming you tonight, too. Are you ready?" he repeated, intense brown eyes pinned her so hard she lost her breath.

All she could do was nod and hold on as he pulled out and thrust back in until there was no doubt in her mind that he claimed her more thoroughly than any bite mark. Theirs was a claiming of hearts, bodies, and minds. Of futures and of pasts. Of wolves, fae, shifters, and ox. It didn't matter what they looked like, only what they *felt*. Their love was forged from ice and fire, from kisses and wishes. And it was real.

⚖

ANISE WOKE ENTWINED with Caraway's muscular, naked body. She was so happy, she didn't want to leave, but one look at the black leather Guardian jacket hanging on the door hook reminded her of reality. They might have claimed each other, but it didn't mean the world would let them be together.

A Guardian warrior, and a lesser fae.

The world was full of cruel boundaries.

She sighed and rested her head on his shoulder. Her exhale ruffled the hair on his chest. His rumble of appreciation brought a smile to her lips so she ran her fingers through the coarse hair, wanting to elicit more sounds from her sleeping giant. His hand snapped up and swallowed hers whole, and then he directed it downward with a cheeky smirk, keeping his eyes closed the entire time.

"So demanding, already." She laughed.

He chuckled. It came from deep in his belly and sent Anise's hormones crazy. She'd always loved his laugh. It was so genuine, so real, and she never wanted to lose it again.

He must have sensed the change in her mood because when he looked down at her, a solemn shadow flittered in his eyes. He rolled to face her and gently traced fingers down her arm.

"We'll figure it out, Anise," he promised.

"You can't quit being a Guardian." She touched the glowing blue teardrop tattoo beneath his right eye. "It's a part of you."

His brows joined in the middle. "So are you."

"How will we make this work, then?"

He shrugged. "Live with me at the Order."

"That's not possible."

"It is for Rush and Clarke, and Thorne and Laurel."

"But they're Well-blessed. Their union is honored above all else, especially by an organization that worships the Well."

"We don't worship it. We respect it and work to keeping it flourishing. There's a difference." Darkness formed in his eyes. "And I don't care if our union is blessed by the Well. I'm not leaving you again. They can all go and fu—"

"Shhh." She put a finger on his lips and sat up. Her ears twitched as she picked up voices. "Someone is outside."

She'd never seen Caraway move so fast, but within seconds, he was out of the bed. He threw a blanket over her and collected Reckoning. Heedless of his nudity, he went to the window and peered through. All the tension left his shoulders as his eyes latched onto their visitors, and then he turned back to her with confusion.

"It's Rush and Thorne."

She sat up with a squeak. "Don't let them inside until I'm dressed."

He went back to the window. "Clarke and Laurel are also here. And Willow."

"What?" Willow was Rush's and Clarke's small daughter.

Caraway nodded and slipped on his pants. "Maybe Clarke saw something in a vision. Could be why she sent me the portal stone. I'll go and greet them. You get dressed."

He put on his shirt and rested his sword by the door then went outside. While he was gone, Anise made quick work of clothing herself, and then straightened the cabin as much as she could. It wouldn't do to have the owner arrive and see it in such disarray. Thankfully the sprites had redirected the flames from burning the pot overnight. Only half of the wood smoldered. The soup was cold but not inedible. When she was done straightening the room, she put on her boots and ventured outside.

Fresh morning air greeted her. At least it wasn't snowing. Down on the shore of the lake, Caraway spoke with the two Guardians, while Laurel and Clarke collected stones with Willow by the waterside. Clarke's red hair was unmissable, and Laurel's dark bob just the same.

Anise didn't realize how tense she was until she saw the women were a distance away from her new mate. Her body viscerally relaxed, but the underlying protective mode was still there. It was a wolf instinct. She was sure it happened to the males of the species more, but she still had to make an effort to calm herself down. When she had, a new kind of anxiety entered her system. She didn't know which group of visitors to go to first. She'd not truly met Laurel, but had served her at the Birdcage elixir den in Cornucopia.

Anise was saved from making her decision when Willow spotted she was out of the cabin, squealed, and ran toward her with unrestrained delight. Anise had not formally met the little girl either but had heard about her stark white hair from Thorne. She was a halfling—half wolf-shifter, half-human—but one-hundred percent tenacious.

Willow's little legs brought her closer to Anise with every squeal. As she neared, Anise recognized the squeals were words.

"Gray is coming. Gray is coming!" Willow barreled past Anise and up to the cabin porch where she grinned and whirled around, hiding behind a wooden pole, intently watching the horizon of the nearby woods where an old wolf emerged, sniffed the air, and then spotted Rush. He trotted over, sniffed him too, and then yipped before heading up to the cabin to meet Willow.

"He's getting old," Clarke noted as she arrived and gave the wolf a pointed look. "He was Rush's long time companion when he was cursed, and he protected our cabin while Willow was a baby. This might be the last time she will get to see her old protector."

"Oh, that's sad," Anise replied.

Clarke gave Anise a gentle smile. "It is, but it's the natural order of life for those animals, and humans for that matter. Any creature without mana in them ages so fast.

I'm still getting used to the idea that I'm not one of them anymore. Anyway, it's good to see you, Anise."

Caraway had said something similar to Anise back at the witch's lair. If Anise was truly without mana, she'd have aged a long time ago. Somehow, knowing that made Anise feel warm inside. She smiled at Clarke. "It's good to see you too."

Clarke gestured to Laurel. "I think you might have met Laurel."

"Sort of."

Laurel bit her lip. "Yeah, that's my fault. I was a bit preoccupied the last time we met." She made the fae hand-sign for an apology—a fist in circles over her chest. "It was rude of me."

Anise laughed it off. "You weren't rude. I was the barmaid. I served you a drink. That's all."

"Yes, well, if it's all the same to you, if I hadn't been so angry at Thorne, I would have taken the time to give you a proper hello."

Clarke waggled her brows at Anise. "I see my little gift went to good use?"

"Gift?" Anise frowned.

Clarke tapped a bite mark scar on her own neck. Laurel laughed and tapped her own. Then they both made eyes at Caraway's fresh mating mark.

"Oh!" Anise blushed. "You saw us getting together in a vision? Is that why you gave him the portal stone for here? How embarrassing."

"Not at all!" Clarke replied. "Actually, we're here for another reason."

Anise cocked a brow.

"What reason?" Caraway asked as the Guardians arrived.

Laurel took Thorne's hand, and Anise couldn't help noticing the matching blue markings entwining both their arms. Rush and Clarke had similar identical markings on their hands. They were magnificent. Like water reflections living on their skin.

"I wanted to thank you for helping me out when I first arrived. Waking up two thousand years after my time wasn't so easy to deal with. And this lout didn't make it easier at the start," Clarke said, pointing to Rush who grunted irritably. She laughed. "Anise, you and Caraway were so kind to me that night in the tavern. So—" She shared a conspiring look with Laurel. "We've come up with a solution that keeps you two together."

Thorne frowned. "I told them they were meddling."

Rush also clenched his jaw. "But it's a good idea."

"What?" Anise asked. "Don't keep us in suspense."

Laurel grinned. "I've been working with the Prime to raise the public profile of the Order. Too many fae-folk don't look favorably on the organization and it's been a real problem lately. High King Mithras is gaining power, and it's not good. So I've convinced the Prime to station trusted Guardians in cities and towns around Elphyne so the Order always has a point of contact for anyone with questions. No more mystery. I think if we make each Guardian seem more approachable, like an ambassador as well as a protector, then more fae will want to volunteer to be initiated. The Order won't need to seek tributes from children anymore."

Thorne squeezed her shoulder and a look of sheer pride crossed his face.

"What does that mean for us?" Caraway asked.

"It means," Rush elaborated. "The two of you can live together in a city of your choice. Caraway won't need to live at the Order grounds, and instead of heading out into the wild on missions, he can work at improving the Order's image in the city he's stationed at."

"Couldn't think of a better Guardian for the job." Thorne clapped Caraway on the back.

"We can be together?" Anise could hardly believe it. Caraway could stay a Guardian, and they could stay together.

Their eyes met, held, and then Caraway rushed to pick her up in a bone-crushing hug. Her mind whirled. Could it be that simple?

He put her down, eyes searching hers. "Where do you want to live?"

Immediately, her heart took her home, to Crescent Hollow. But the familiar pang and panic of her attack left her mouth dry at the thought of returning there.

No, she told herself. This time it was different. *She* was different. She had to stop letting her fears take hold of her. Sure, she'd had bad memories there, but there had also been good memories. And fae lived a long time... possibly forever. Hopefully, she and Caraway would share a long life together. She smiled up at him and for the first time in a long time, wanted to go home.

"Let's go to Crescent Hollow."

He grinned back at her. "I was hoping you would say that."

Rush cleared his throat. "Let's go inside and you can tell us about the Ice-Witch while Willow plays with Gray. Thorne and I will take your intel and the sample of snow back to the Prime. Your mission is done, Caraway."

Clarke stopped her mate with a hand to the shoulder. "Let's just get the snow sample. I think the newly mated couple might want to spend some alone time together."

Rush's eyes widened when he caught the fresh mark on Caraway's neck. A blush hit his cheeks. Both he and Thorne quickly made excuses to leave. Both were so rushed, she knew they were contrived, but was grateful all the same.

Anise smiled when she looked at her new friends and realized just how far she'd come. No longer did those taunts from her memories haunt her because Anise *did* have friends. She had a lover. A mate. And she had a future. It didn't matter what she looked like on the outside. It only mattered how she lived her life and the love she invited in. That jaded Ice-Witch had it all wrong.

Anise looked up into Caraway's eyes, she knew her life would be the opposite of lonely. It would be filled with love, kisses, and wishes come true.

The End.

THE DREAMS OF BROKEN KINGS

FAE GUARDIANS BOOK 3

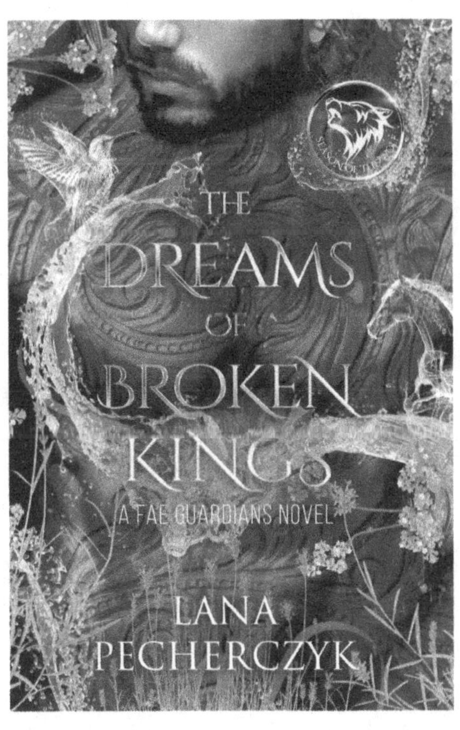

BLURB

After being abandoned as a child, Ada has learned to choose her friends and lovers wisely. And then a nuclear winter froze the world, taking everything she fought so hard to keep. When she inexplicably wakes years later in a new world full of magic, and where humans are the enemy, all she wants is to find her two best friends... if they're even alive.

Jasper knows he is someone damaged and dangerous, the scars on his body prove it. But his memories have been taken from him. He knows not why, or how, he came to be in the locked room with the pretty, vulnerable human, but he knows three things: the King wants him dead, Ada is his mate, and he'll do anything to claim her.

Trusting each other is their first step to uncovering the truth and avoiding certain death. But how can Ada feel safe with a strange fae who keeps dark secrets one minute, and then stokes the flames of her desire the next? How can she forgive the broken fae for hiding the most precious secret of all – his heart.

THE DREAMS OF BROKEN KINGS

PROLOGUE

The boy watched with wondrous eyes as his mother coaxed water sprites from the fountain. A ripple of energy tingled his tongue as her invisible *mana*—her *magic*—left her body, entered the garden fountain, and formed shapes with the water. First, a seahorse bounced on the fountain's flow. Then, an explosion of fireworks churned the water. She added horses, hummingbirds, and flying kuturi. The small water sprites squeaked in joy and clapped their hands, spraying a fine mist everywhere.

The boy's mother turned to him with the same crooked smile many fae had pledged their life to see. They'd kneeled before her when she'd flicked her long, lustrous black and brown locks. They'd tried to kiss her red lips, but she'd always turned her cheek and walked away. She would return to him, her son.

His mother shifted her magic. The watery show skipped from the fountain and danced along the leaves of nearby plants. Her waterhorse galloped and neighed. Sprites followed the procession through their extensive garden, leaving behind their watery mist and coating every surface with droplets that glistened in the sun like jewels.

"Your turn, my love," she said. "Send your mana into the water and make a shape. But make it fun. Everyone works better when there is joy to be had."

He gathered control of his mana and steeled himself against the surge of energy in case it flitted about like water from a hose. Mana flowed eagerly from the stores of his internal Well, rising to meet his summons like the tide during a full moon. Always sitting beneath the surface of his consciousness, his inner wolf came alive. It liked his thoughts of the moon. It wanted to shift from two to four-legged and run through the forest, roll around in the dirt, maybe even snap his teeth at the sprites along the way. They looked extra delicious as they danced and sparkled.

And he was hungry.

When his mother spoke, he realized a wolfish snarl had trembled from his teeth.

"Love," his mother crooned a warning as she ran a hand through his shaggy hair. "Kindness before killing."

"But, Mama," he said. "I want to play too."

Her crooked smile widened and warmed him more than any sun. "I know, and you will, but you must learn to control your animal urges. You *must* remember that the wolf is a part of you, and not the other way around. You are more than the sum of your ancestors. This is very important. Do you understand?"

He nodded sullenly. She always lectured him about controlling his wolf. He didn't see the problem. His wolf liked to play. His mother always talked about having fun. Why couldn't she see they were the same thing?

She took him by the shoulders and looked deeply into his eyes. Her smile dropped and her expression grew still.

"What is fun for some, isn't fun for others. Look at the sprites, darling, what are they doing?"

He threw his hands up, exasperated. "Playing."

She turned his jaw toward a plant where they jumped and pranced, showering the fronds with glistening rivulets.

"Look closer, my love."

Water dripped onto the soft peat beneath, showering it with sustenance.

"They're watering our garden!" he exclaimed.

She grinned. "And what would they have done if we simply used our strength to demand their obedience?"

"They'd have hidden in the fountain until we were gone." He knew. He'd waited once in wolf form, snarling and snapping at the water. He'd waited all night and day and, still, they hadn't come out.

A wolf's long, drawn out howl ripped through the air, and his mother's smile died. He didn't think a howl was unusual. They lived nearby a wolf-shifter village, after all. But she turned to him, eyes wide and black with panic.

"Hide. Where we practiced."

"Mama?"

She bustled him out of the garden and toward the small cottage. "Hurry. Faster."

Tears stinging his eyes, he stumbled. "You're hurting me, Mama."

No reply.

She took him into their living room, shifted a rug, and lifted the hatch in the wooden planks, then urged him to get into the dark crawlspace filled with musty smells and dirt.

Thundering hooves grew louder as horses crested the laneway outside their home. Howls lifted every hair on the back of his neck. His instincts knew the call. It was the call of a hunt. For blood.

"Hurry."

"Who is it, Mama?"

She bundled him down and then kneeled, a sad resignation in her eyes as she brushed his jaw with the back of her knuckles. The heart-shaped pendant dangling from her neck scraped along the floor, leaving a claw-like scratch.

"Remember how we practiced?"

He nodded. "No sounds. Don't come out until my wolf scents no intruders."

"You are kind," she said emphatically, and then cast a spell that felt like cotton wool wrapping his body. "You are brave. And you are worth it. Do you understand?"

"Mama?" his throat constricted. "I'm afraid."

"No movements, my love, or the spell will break and he will scent you."

"*Who?*"

A cold bleakness entered her eyes. "Your father."

She shut the hatch, swaddling him in the cold finality of muffled darkness.

He barely registered the rustling of the rug being pushed back into place and the bursting of the front door, but when the screams started, they pierced the dampening spell. He forced the thundering of his heart to calm and listened.

"You can't hide from me." A loud, booming male voice. "I am King of all the Seelie now."

"You may color your hair gold, wear gaudy clothes, and live in a castle of glass, but you can't hide the stench of rot underneath. I will *always* remember."

The silence raised the boy's hackles.

Crack. Like flesh hitting flesh. *Thud.* Something landed on the floorboards. His mother.

She made no sound, no cry of pain despite the trembling of her breath.

The boy lifted his face to where a shaft of light filtered through at the edge. Mama must have failed to flatten the rug properly. Too fearful to move further, he stared through the gap and tried to halt the breath in his lungs. Surely the intruder would hear the pounding of his heart.

Blurred shapes and shadows moved as boots and paws trampled across the wooden floor, shaking dust and sand through the cracks with every step. Louder and louder until they came to a standstill above the boy's head. A whimper caught in his throat.

"Where is the boy?" the King asked, voice flat and cold.

His mother was silent.

Something shifted above. Wolves snarled. Claws scratched against the wooden floor.

"This is the last time I ask you, where is the boy?"

"He is ten times the fae you are, ten times the soul, and he will be ten times the king."

"Search the place. Leave no stone unturned," the King boomed. Then his voice got closer, quieter. "And you will still be ten times the whore."

The choking sound that followed broke the boy's heart. But he'd practiced this moment, stayed beneath these floorboards, remained still and silent no matter what. No matter the sounds of teeth tearing through flesh. No matter the feel of warm liquid dripping onto his face. He squeezed his eyes shut and imagined the feel of fresh rain. The wet bracken beneath his paws. The smell of the forest. The call of the wild.

Tumbling with his cousins. Nipping at dragonflies. Today, he added the sprites playing. Their joy in the water. How it called to him too.

It wasn't until the last footfall died, the scent of wolf lessened, and the sound of dripping grew louder, that his mother's final words expelled on the hiss of her dying breath. *"... kind... brave... worth it."*

CHAPTER

ONE

Amber eyes shrouded in thick lashes stared at Ada from across the cold, grimy bedroom. It shouldn't be possible for a man to look like both angel and devil at the same time, but there he was, caught in limbo somewhere between sin and a miracle. *Such striking features.* Tall and muscular with statuesque bone structure, yet soft, sensuous lips. Even his brown hair was extraordinary. Each tip of the medium length appeared to be dipped in black ink, like an artist's paintbrush. On the outside, he was a masterpiece. He should have been perfect. But the closer Ada looked, the more she noticed cracks in his canvas. All was not well with him.

It started with his unblinking eyes.

Work long enough with wounded, wild animals and the familiar signs of mistreatment were easy to recognize. The old pain. The soul crushing emptiness of surrender. The fresh scars upon old scars at his neck. This man had suffered. He had been tortured. He had given up hope.

Whether his mind was still intact was another story.

He hadn't said a word, nor moved an inch, yet Ada sensed he was once as wild and carefree as the animals she'd rehabilitated. Now, he was at the end of his rope. She hoped she wasn't in the way when he snapped.

His blistering intent stayed locked solely on her, as it had done so for the past five minutes since her groggy awakening that ended with the vomit of something dark and viscous on the floor next to the old bed.

He didn't get up to help her. He never murmured a note of sympathy. He just kept staring.

He's cuckoo. Surely.

His linen clothing was as strange as hers which looked more suited to a cult that worshipped natural materials than her usual khakis and worn T-shirt. Someone must have dressed her because she hadn't been wearing the simple outfit when she'd... her

541

brow puckered. What had she been doing before coming here? She couldn't remember a thing beyond going outside Clarke's apartment and lifting her awestruck face to the snow falling in Vegas.

The small miracle, or curse, depending on how you looked at it, had taken their minds off the bombs that had dropped around the world, devastating humankind. The cities that survived, like Vegas, were scrambling to find normalcy in the fallout, when the nuclear winter fell like a freezing blanket with a speed that baffled the TV weatherman. The drop in temperature had been so fast that the Bellagio fountains froze midflight. And then it had snowed... and then...

Ada struggled to grasp what had come next.

Had she been drugged? Panic sparked, tightening her chest, quickening her breath. Was that why she'd been sick? Where were her friends, Clarke and Laurel? They had been with her in the yard, looking at the snow.

The silent man stared at her as though she had a list of algebra equations written on her face.

"Are you going to stare at me all day, or will you tell me how we got here?" she asked.

Dark lashes blinked, and then he resumed staring as though he could see into her mind. She shivered.

Christ. This was insane.

She cringed, disgusted that her head had rested on the decayed bed. Thank goodness she'd moved and now sat in the corner, hands wrapped around her knees, bare feet on the dusty floor.

While she had been asleep, someone had tattooed glow-in-the-dark ink in a strange glowing blue pattern around her right arm—his too. She rubbed her marks for the tenth time. Definitely tattooed on there. Definitely twinkling, as though the undercurrent of the summer sea ran beneath it. If only it gave her the summer heat. A shiver wracked her body as cold air seeped into her bones.

"Right." She stood and rubbed herself briskly. "If you're not going to help, then I'll find my own way out of here."

Just like she always did. No use waiting for a hero to turn up. A familiar pang in her chest reminded her of the first time she'd learned this truth—the first time her mother failed to come home with food—but forced the memory aside before it took root. She had no time for that.

The instant she stood, he echoed by unfolding his long body, and straightening to a height that crowded her and sucked the air from the room.

Creepy.

She looked for a weapon, but... she cocked her head and studied him. She didn't *feel* animosity coming from him, strange as that sounded. Her instincts had never taken a wrong turn, and they were the only thing that had kept her alive on more than one occasion. Whether it was hiking in the wilderness, hunting for food, or navigating unfamiliar terrain, she'd learned to trust her intuition. And right now, it was telling her this man wasn't a threat.

But he also wasn't helping.

"I'm Ada," she ventured.

His brow furrowed, but he said nothing.

"Can you speak?"

A slow nod.

"What's your name?"

Amber eyes darted around the room. He flinched and scratched blue arcane markings around the thick column of his neck. Red welts meant he'd been itching for a while. Whatever those blue markings were, they didn't agree with him. Not like the ones down their arms.

"Your name?" she prompted again.

"I don't know."

His voice was deep and smooth like honey. It matched his gorgeous face and perfect body. If he ever lost this creepy hesitancy, she imagined no woman would be safe from his charms.

"How can you not know?"

"Because I don't," he snapped, a faint snarl deepening his tone.

Ada startled.

Injured animal. Proceed with caution.

She held up her palms. "Was just asking."

He looked away. Not that there was much to look at in this room. Just a high, small window too tiny to climb through. She could break through the thin, stained ceiling, though. Debris littered the ground, but nothing she could use. Broken bits of wood, a few branches and some feathers as though a bird had nested inside. Damp puddles collected from leaking rain.

"Maybe this is one of those locked room scenarios," she murmured to herself. "I've seen *Saw*. Some Mad Max sicko has put us in here, drugged me, taken your memories, and painted weird cultist shit on us." She shot him a side-eye. "If you try to saw off my leg, I will kill you. Fair warning."

Perhaps the tall man was drugged too, because he just stared at her in confusion. Part of her didn't believe herself either. A locked room? No way. And she didn't feel drugged. But then again, she didn't believe the nuclear holocaust would actually happen. She didn't believe her precious wilderness would either be destroyed or covered in snow.

Maybe Vegas was gone too, and this dingy room was all that was left.

Maybe they were the last two people on earth and this was some rare pocket that had survived the fallout.

A new sense of urgency skated up her spine. This room was too small. She had to get out. She made an awkward face when he didn't move, so sidestepped and went to the door where she rattled the porcelain lock. It didn't budge. She peeked through the old keyhole. The lock probably worked from both sides. Light shone through, but all she could see was a wall.

"We need to get out of here," she mumbled. "I'm starving. And thirsty. And..."

And forget about sawing her leg off. The man in the room with her might try to eat her from the way he kept staring.

He moved. She flinched. A tiny twitch lifted one side of his lips, and she could have sworn she caught amusement dancing in his eyes before he shouldered her to the side and took hold of the doorknob. One wrench and it came off in his powerful grip. Ada's lips parted.

He uncurled his fingers, and the knob teetered in the dip of his palm. She reached for it, but he snapped his fingers around the knob and evaded her. Frowning, she looked up, expecting anger, but amusement flickered in his eyes again.

"You think this is a game?" she said.

Her irritation only made his lips purse as though he tried to hide a smile and then picked out the rest of the half-crumbled knob from the hole in the door. In moments, the entire contraption was gone. He jammed his fingers into the gap and yanked.

"Are you telling me you could have done that five minutes ago?"

Big shoulders bunched and lowered.

Joking one minute, brooding the next. Maybe he wasn't all there in the head—a few bricks short of a load. Maybe that tragedy in his eyes had taken more of a toll than she realized. Nobody deserved to lose their mind. She stepped into the hallway, but a big hand landed on her shoulder and tugged her back.

"I go first," he grunted and placed her behind his large frame.

"Oh-kay."

His bulk refused argument.

The corridor was as decrepit as the bedroom. Water trickled down the stone walls, peeling wallpaper and creating mold deposits in the hardwood floor that gifted her nostrils with tingling pungency. Ivy trailed down the wall, invading from holes in the terracotta tiled roof. Glimpses of cloudy sky flashed as she walked by. Small cameo oil paintings lined the wall, but the decay had eroded much of the canvas. Glimpses of faces watched Ada and her companion as they walked cautiously through the hallway. He snuffled, as though trying to get the scent out of his nose.

The next room was more jungle than living room. Plants and flowers climbed over old wooden furniture padded with patchy blue velvet. Arched windows let in light, but a flourish of thorny brambles blocked escape through the window.

The blue markings on their arms glowed and glanced off their surroundings as they passed. A flash drew her eye to a table toppled with a collection of junk. She strolled over and inspected the goods. They looked like something you'd see at a junkyard, or a hoarder's house. Perhaps the state of Vegas was more dire than it had been when she'd... she frowned again, frustrated that she couldn't remember how she got here.

Maybe she had amnesia too.

Rusted copper pennies lined the bottom of a shallow bowl overflowing with rain water still dripping from the ceiling in sporadic plops. Ada flicked a box-like rectangle that may have once been a cell phone. She touched a round smooth surface that was probably a squash ball and then flicked a thin garland that might have been Christmas tinsel in another life. She picked up a jar of rusty ball-point pens and jiggled them.

"Stop." A hand knocked the jar from her fingers. It clattered loudly to the floor.

"Why did you do that?"

He scowled. "Metals and plastics are forbidden by the Well."

She raised her brows and muttered under her breath, "Definitely a few screws loose."

I'm done with this. Shaking her head, she left the weird shrine and searched for an exit. She just wanted to find her friends. They had been with her in Vegas. Chances were, they'd be around somewhere. She hoped.

Dripping water echoed as it landed in puddles. Leaves rustled and a whisper of sound flittered behind her, but when she looked, she found nothing except the plant life.

Searching beneath vines on the wall, she asked, "How do you know metal is banned, but you don't know your name?"

When he gave no answer, she sent him a sidelong look. He seemed as perplexed as she was.

A beam of light filtered through a crack in the ceiling and landed on some ivy with a dark door shape behind it. *Bingo.*

"Help me get this off." She hauled great curtains of vines and tried to pull it off.

No help came. Ada turned and found the man staring at his feet, a deep crease between his brow as he studied a tattered, patterned rug.

"What is it?" she asked.

"I know this." He crouched and ran a finger over the pattern. His trail left a wake in the sodden rug. "I've been here before."

Here, as in this cottage, or here as in the city woven into the tapestry of the rug? Either way, he was more familiar than she was.

"You have? Well, that's great. You should know how to get out of here."

He shook his head. "I don't..."

The man was troubled. A stab of sympathy pushed Ada to meet him on the floor. Amber eyes clashed with hers. They were almost luminous in the dark. Coupled with his thick, dark lashes, she could get lost in his eyes. And that wasn't a sentiment she was familiar with. It unnerved her more than the small blue teardrop tattoo twinkling beneath his right eye. She hadn't noticed it before.

Fear stabbed through her. Was this her future? Would some nut job come and paint her and then take her memories too?

"We'll figure it out," she murmured, eyes darting to his sparkling blue tattoo collar. Welts scored his skin from all the scratching he'd been doing. Unable to help herself, she touched one of the blue lines on his neck. He hissed. A wave of *hurt* washed through her, as though she'd felt the pain herself. She lowered her hand. "Hurts, huh?"

He looked affronted, and a little defensive, but nodded.

"We'll figure that out too," she announced.

Drop Ada in the desert, and she'd survive. In high school, they voted her most likely to succeed in a zombie apocalypse. None of them knew she'd only attended school for the first time from her junior year. They were cruel enough without knowing she'd spent most of her childhood surviving on her own in the woods... well, there was Harold, the old-timer she would visit in exchange for hunting and reading lessons. But the point was, she would get through this.

Dusting off her hands, she straightened and went to the door. She lifted the last of the ivy, turned the doorknob, and used her foot to push the wooden length. It shifted an inch. Elation lifted her spirits. She turned to share her excitement, but almost bowled into a broad chest.

"Personal space, dude," she mumbled.

He'd better not be the type to imprint on her after a few moments of compassion. The last thing she needed was a sad puppy following her around. After she'd assimilated into society and graduated high school, Ada had taken a job rehabilitating animals. There had been a rescued cougar kitten that refused to return to the wild. She'd almost considered moving to live in the forest with it, or bringing it home, but by that stage, she'd made friends in the city and knew she would miss them too much. The city and her friends had tethered Ada to reality. Without them, she would have returned to the lonely life of a hermit like Harold.

Once again, he shifted Ada to the side and used brute force to open the door. It might have taken all her energy to move it a simple inch, but he'd barely twitched a muscle to shift the entire frame.

"What do you bench?" she asked. "Seriously, like, two hundred pounds?"

No answer, so she followed him outside and into a courtyard overrun by nature, much as the inside had been. But out here...

"I can't believe it," she murmured, eyes lifting to the sky. "Blue."

She'd assumed the gray through the gaps in the ceiling was the dull nuclear blanket of their scorched sky, but... *blue* interspersed with regular storm clouds. Could this be a surviving pocket, unaffected by the fallout? But the scorched sky had covered the entire globe.

Twittering birds leaped in the sunshine, hopping from branches to a three-tiered stagnant fountain, washing their beaks, and then dancing back. She turned in a three-sixty-degree rotation. Lush vegetation filled the garden courtyard. Vine-covered limestone walls surrounded them, along with the occasional shrubs and small fruit tree.

Ada rushed to the trees and searched for fruit. Who knew when she'd eat again? She riffled through the leaves, but disappointment dropped in her stomach like a stone. Nothing.

Wrong time of year, perhaps.

"This is incredible," she breathed, and scrambled on top of a long stone table that may have been for outdoor entertaining. In her haste, her foot slipped on the slippery moss and she tumbled. Strong hands caught her around the waist. For a few moments, she held her rescuer's gaze as he lowered her gently to the ground.

He looked at her as though *she* were the marvel.

She gave an awkward laugh. "I slipped."

"You did." A small smile tugged his lips. The light glinting in his eyes had only been fleeting, but a rush of reward hit right in her chest. She wanted to chase that high... to get him to smile again. He held out his hand and, when she reached for it, he snatched it back with an eyebrow waggle. She giggled like a damned school girl. Perhaps he enjoyed seeing her smile too, because he played the same game until eventually she stopped smiling. He got the picture, and he helped her onto the table like a proper gentleman. Heat warmed her cheeks.

He might be a little mute, or dumb, or whatever, but the dude had understated magnetism. Everything about him disarmed her. The random games. His heart-stopping smile. His weird chivalry. Clearing her mind, she forced her attention to the cottage surroundings and gasped.

The land beyond was a punch in the chest.

"It's back," she croaked. "It's all back!"

The nuclear fallout had stolen the biodiversity of her adored wilderness. Everything had been dying. But now... now there were rolling green hills damp with recent rain and luscious trees bursting with life. Some sort of farm animal grazed in a distant field. She couldn't see it clearly, but it had horns. Further afield, smoke curled from a cottage chimney. *People.*

Her temporary elation washed back with a wave of dread. Rotating, she surveyed the rest of the land surrounding the cottage. Land and forest stretched for miles... everywhere. While the abundance of natural life called to her carefree, nomadic spirit, the obvious and foreboding truth was too hard to ignore. No city scrapers. No lights. No hustle, bustle, and burnished party limos. They were nowhere near Vegas. Nowhere near home.

"Where are we?"

CHAPTER
TWO

The shock of displacement felled Ada. Her knees thunked onto the stone table. Big hands encircled her tiny waist, dragged her to the floor, and held her while she trembled at the knees. She brushed him off to stand by herself.

At best, she'd thought perhaps she was in a small pocket of untouched land that had survived the holocaust. Or maybe some crazy apocalyptic bunker. Visions of Mad Max types playing a locked room game with them had been her *logical* assumption. Ha!

Logic wasn't a factor in this reality.

They'd said the scorched sky would take decades, perhaps centuries, to clear. They'd said the land would suffer immeasurably. They'd said flora and fauna would become extinct, and it was inevitable. Farming had turned from green pastures to hydroponic warehouses. Forests turned from luscious to barren. Their best hope had been to ride it out and weather the storm of their own doing. This couldn't be Ada's world. It just couldn't.

"You look lost."

Ada pressed her lips together. "I don't know where I am."

"At least you have a name." His brow puckered. "And memories."

She sent him a merciful glance.

"Are we in a dream?" Were her friends alive? Was she? She pinched her arm. "Ouch."

"Why did you do that?"

"For fun," she snarked. He failed to pick up her sarcasm, so she added, "I wasn't sure if this is reality."

For a few heartbeats, he shared her silence, and then a blue glow at the stagnant fountain drew his attention. He cocked his head, as though listening to something. Ada heard naught but the aria of birds and the scampering of some tiny animal within the weeds. Every line of his body tensed, from his broad shoulders to his balled fists, and then, like a predator catching a scent, he stepped closer to the fountain. Long legs prowled silently. Ada was reminded of a wolf in a field of grass, stalking its prey. So sleek. So quiet. So unnoticed. Until its lethal claws ripped through the flesh of its next meal.

All she saw was the old three-tiered fountain, its pools filled with recent rain water. Slugs crawled along the base and deadnettle weeds spilled into the basin, leaving purple debris that had turned rancid. But the water glittered blue, much like their arm markings, as though a foreign force existed in the shallows.

That light had to come from somewhere.

She bent and checked for power cords, or perhaps a spotlight plugged in. Nothing. Strange. But maybe she needed to get closer. Wiring could be hidden within the base.

"What is it?" she asked.

"Shh." He held a finger out, halting her approach.

Her jaw clicked shut. The hairs on her arms pricked up. She searched the courtyard for a weapon, and found a long, wooden pole that may have once been a broomstick.

His boots hit the fountain base and then he stared into the water for so long she thought it had bewitched him, if such a thing were possible.

Clutching her broomstick, she inched close enough to see inside the basin where a moving picture flickered beneath the water, much like a video on a screen. An ageless man with smooth tan skin, long golden hair, and pointed, fur-tipped ears tapped his finger on his lips. The glass coronet balanced on his head wobbled with every tap. A Scandinavian king, perhaps? Also weird, considering half of Europe had been bombed.

His shrewd eyes locked onto the man next to Ada, as though he could see him, which was ridiculous. Television screens weren't two-way, unless there was a camera somewhere.

She glanced around the garden, but found nothing technological. She supposed if the comment about metal and plastic being forbidden was to be trusted, then there would be none.

And this wasn't a television screen.

"It's time for you to return, Jasper." The Golden King's decree warbled and echoed as though he truly were underwater.

Jasper. That was his name.

Jasper frowned at the water. "Who are you?"

The Golden King stilled. Thoughts calculated behind shrewd eyes. First, he appeared startled, then he looked pensive, and then his expression darkened with excitement. He spoke to someone off screen—or puddle, or whatever this was.

The King's expression lifted in surprise and he raised his brows at his companion, not seeming to care that Jasper could overhear his next words. *"Seems like it's holding. How long will it last?"* A pause. *"Good. The last thing we need is for him to realize who he is before we can get to him."* The man nodded, then returned to Jasper. *"Tell me where you are, and I will send someone after you."*

Send someone *after* Jasper? Not for, or to help, but after him.

"He seems like a real delight," Ada drawled, trying to lighten the mood.

Jasper's scowl clashed with hers, but his lips twitched in an almost smile.

"*Who's that with you?*" the King snapped, trying to see to Jasper's side. Ada felt the need to step out of view, just to piss the bastard off, but it was unnecessary—Jasper dashed his hand through the water, dispelling the picture, effectively cutting communication as one would switch off a device.

All that remained in the fountain pool were pebbles, broken glass, and purple petals covered with furry mold. And the slugs she might have to eat if she couldn't find food soon.

"So what was that all about?" she asked.

Jasper's growl started as a low rumble that built into a snarl of hostility. Ada could virtually *feel* his emotion vibrate through her as though it were her own. His lip-curling attention locked onto the fountain as the blue light flashed again. Something small and slick launched out of the pond with a splash. She glimpsed tiny piranha teeth, a monstrous face, and slimy knobby limbs. Claws pierced Jasper's front. He caught it moments before vicious teeth collected his nose. One clench of his fist, and the creature's spine snapped, wilting its body. He threw it to the side and rubbed the spots on his chest, now oozing a slow release of blood through the black fabric.

Ada nudged the slimy, small carcass with the end of her pole. Its skin had a layer of jelly over it, as though it lived underwater. Whiskers on its nose reminded her of a catfish. The stain of Jasper's blood still coated its sharp claws.

And then something strange happened—by far the weirdest since she'd woken. Tiny balls of glowing light lifted from the creature's body and floated like fireflies into the sky before disappearing altogether.

She jolted and pointed at the sky. "What the hell was that?"

Jasper didn't answer. His pained gaze was locked on the water in the fountain where the King had returned, this time with a dark hooded figure loitering behind him. Both had the black gazes of a serial killer as they watched and waited.

What were they waiting for?

Jasper grunted. His hand went to his wounds, fingers flexing against his shirt as though he had a heart attack. He dropped to a knee. Ada's heart leaped into her throat. Her instinct was to run to him, but the men in the water would see her. Panicked, she stayed, her heart warring with her mind.

"*That should do it,*" a snaky voice said from within the water. "*He won't survive a ponaturi bite.*"

"*He is strong,*" the King reminded him. "*He has survived worse. Much worse.*"

"*Not even a Guardian can survive the ponaturi.*"

A grunt of agreement, and then the communication cut off.

Goddamn. This was an assassination attempt.

Ada kneeled next to Jasper and put a palm to his clammy, scruff covered cheek. She lifted his shirt to inspect the wounds. They weren't deep but, if the shadowed figure in the water was to be believed, Jasper had been poisoned.

"Don't stress," she murmured, forcing herself to remain calm. "I know what to do."

She didn't. She did. Oh, God... did she?

"Take your shirt off," she said.

Jasper tried to lift his arms but winced in pain. He jolted forward and gagged. Oh shit. *He's going to vomit.* The wounds near his collar bone rapidly turned an angry purple. The toxin could already be working into his blood. She was probably too late.

Regardless, she had to do something, so she lifted the shirt, placed her lips on a wound and sucked. Bitter blood laced with something acrid filled her mouth. She spat it out and then repeated, trying to ignore the way Jasper's heavy body drooped as he used her for support.

"I got you." *I won't let you die.*

Because then she would have no one.

She moved to each of his four claw wounds and repeated. Suck, spit. Suck, spit. Each time she silently willed the poison to come out, to leave Jasper's body, and to end up on the floor. She envisioned it as black slime in clear water. Each suck removed the slime, leaving nothing but purity. On the final wound, Jasper's hold on his posture gave way. He collapsed onto Ada. They flopped to the floor. She maneuvered them sideways so she wouldn't be crushed, but jarred her shoulder painfully against the stone floor.

Frantically, she checked his wounds, thinking she might have to open the flesh to gain more access to the poison, but there was no festering around the site. It looked healthy and strangely, smaller. As though it were healing. Maybe she'd imagined it being worse. The King's dark companion had said something about no one surviving the bite of a ponaturi, but these were claw punctures.

"Hey, Jasper." She patted his cheek. "Wake up."

Long lashes fluttered, a deep groan rattled his ribs, but his lids stayed glued shut. Ada hovered her ear over his mouth and felt the warm push of even breath. Good. She pressed her ear to his bare chest, right over the blue glowing marks that gave him welts. Now that she'd pushed up his shirt, she could see the welts clearly. More marks and scars extended south over his torso.

She listened. Steady heartbeat. Good.

He was okay. At least for now. She needed to clean his wounds properly, but there was no clean water. Grimacing, she used the fountain water to rinse her mouth out. She wasn't sure she wanted to risk using the dirty water on his open wounds. Maybe she'd just given herself a disease, but it was that or the poison residue on her tongue. An overwhelming sense of helplessness filled her, and a burst of traitorous fear caused a small whimper to escape. She wiped her face with the back of her hand.

"Just stop it, Ada," she said. "This isn't like you. You can manage on your own, no problems. You've faced worse shit than this. You're the female version of MacGyver." But her pep talk did little to assuage her fear. She squeezed her eyes shut, felt the burn of tears, and squeezed tighter. Where were her friends? Where were Clarke and Laurel? The rest of her city? "I need help, damn it."

Even in the darkest days in Vegas, the city's first responders hadn't buckled under the nuclear crisis. They'd continued to take each drama as it unfolded with awe-inspiring, unwavering confidence. They just kept going.

So keep going.

Ada opened her eyes. Poking its head from beneath the purple flowers of a dead-nettle weed was a tiny, winged person. Green and brown all over, it was no bigger than her thumb. Ada rubbed her eyes and checked again.

Nope. Still there.

"You're a fucking fairy," she gaped. The little thing tittered angrily at her. She held her palms up. "I'm sorry, so... not a fairy?"

Or was it because she'd cursed?

It shook its head, but its eyes lit up. It pointed at her, and then at the ponaturi carcass, and then at itself, squeaking in a language too tiny for her to understand. She had the weird feeling that she'd offended it, and she owed it something.

"You want the body?"

It nodded.

"Fine. Take it."

It might have been edible, but Ada had eaten her fair share of poisonous plants, bugs, and animals. She'd made herself sick from them, too.

The little winged not-fairy jumped out, latched onto a leg of the tiny carcass, and then dragged it back into the weeds surrounding the fountain. The ponaturi's translucent skin wobbled and bobbed as it went over cobblestones.

Jasper started thrashing, twitching, and dreaming. He was afraid. And full of hate.

Why would she know that?

She lifted her blue tattooed arm and darted a look between her hand and his. Their marks were identical. Could it be they connected the two of them somehow?

"Hey," she whispered and placed a steady palm on his chest.

He released a slow breath and stilled almost immediately. She took her hand off and he frowned so quickly that she placed it back down.

"You like that, huh?" she murmured. She supposed if she couldn't find clean water, then comforting him was the next best thing.

Comfort and prayer to the higher entity she knew existed somewhere. In all her times lost in the woods, recovering from a snake bite, or hoping the berries she'd eaten wouldn't kill her, she'd prayed to this nameless being. She didn't believe in the Judea-Catholic God, or any other, for that matter, but she'd always believed in *something*.

Because each time she'd been close to death, fearful that no one would save her, she'd prayed and survived. She'd lived another day. Perhaps it was a guardian angel, except this benevolent presence had no wings. It was in every part of nature. It was the very lifeblood of the world. And it was thankful for the time she put into preserving its little furred residents.

She knew her romantic notion was dumb, but it was all she had for company on the many lonely nights growing up by herself. And it felt right.

Keeping her palm on Jasper's front, she let her thumb slowly graze the T-shirt fabric, bumping across the scars she'd glimpsed beneath. They'd looked like battle wounds. Maybe he was some kind of soldier.

He was hot, but not feverish. The shirt bunched at his abdomen, revealing tiny veins delineating the muscles and dipping into his pants along with a trail of dark hair.

Her heart beat faster. In repose, he was more stunning than awake. He smelled like unadulterated male but edged with something sweet like blackcurrant. Before she knew it, she'd shifted closer to inhale that intoxicating scent deep into her lungs.

"Don't be stupid," she mumbled to herself, then shifted back. "Pick something else to think about."

So she focused on the blue arcane marks peeking out from his shirt's collar. They were different than the pattern on their arms. Those marks were almost natural and flowed in a linear pattern that moved in harmony with the shape of their limb. It was almost like a fingerprint, or the contour lines of a map. She liked that idea. This man had a history as intriguing as a map. His body revealed untold stories. From the scars, to the slabs of honed muscle, to the callouses on his fingers, to the glowing tattoos.

He'd lived. He'd seen a lot. And that resonated with her. She had scars too, except hers were mainly on the inside.

The marks around his neck seemed cruel. Straight, angry slashes mixed with jagged curves. They didn't belong on his body. She swept her touch over them, and he murmured in protest, but soon fell back into the dream he seemed to be having. She hoped that was a good sign. He had no fever, no sweat on his upper lip or brow, and no discoloring of his wounds. They continued to close over cleanly.

"Remarkable," she murmured, and looked closer.

She tugged down the shirt collar and touched around a wound near where a claw puncture had hit the blue markings around his collarbone. The blue lifted under her thumbnail as she scraped, separating from skin, revealing a dark oil slick beneath. Gross. She wiped the dark residue away and glanced at the sleeping patient to see if it bothered him, but he made no move, so she kept peeling. She couldn't explain it, but it seemed like the right thing to do. Surely if they were creating angry welts, they should be gone. Another pick, another peel. And she kept talking to herself. The habit probably stemmed from a lonely childhood, or the years spent rehabilitating wounded animals, but she found her voice soothed both her and the animals she worked with.

"You should wake up soon, Jasper," she said, picking at more of his collar tattoo. "We've only just met, but so far, you're okay. I mean, you're kinda the *only* person I've met here, so I suppose that's not saying much. Unless you count the King and his buddy, but I think anyone would look okay next to them, if you know what I mean." She snorted, but then took a breath to force her usual sarcasm to disappear and started again. "I don't really know where *here* is, but it's definitely not home. There are weird things. Little fairy things that squeak at me for calling them a fairy. There are fountains that let you speak to someone through the water. There are fanged, slimy creatures that conjure out of said water when they hadn't been there before. And there are men with pointy, fur-tipped ears—" She cut herself off and glanced warily to Jasper's ears, partly hidden behind his tousled hair. Her heart stopped, and she resisted the urge to check beneath the dark locks. What if his ears were pointed too? *Only one way to find out.* She reached over, brushed some hair aside, and then snatched her hand back with a startled gasp. "You're one of them."

Whatever *they* were. Not human, that was for sure.

His ears were the same as the King's. Pointed with a furred tip that matched the color of his hair. Ada drew her studious gaze back to her patient's face.

"You're one of them, but the King wasn't your friend. He sent that *thing* to hurt you. Which means he knows you, and he's afraid of you."

Thoughtful, she went back to picking at the blue mark.

"To be honest, if you hadn't helped me, I'd probably be afraid of you too. You're pretty imposing. You belong in this place, unlike me. If you get better, maybe you can help me find my friends. Maybe we can help each other. But you need to wake up, Jasper."

A piece an inch wide, and two inches long came clean off, bringing with it another few inches of tattoo. She wiped the black oozing oil residue clean. Its darkness resonated with a sinister echo. She shivered and flicked it to the side.

Jasper catapulted upright with a roar so deep and loud, it rattled the air.

CHAPTER

THREE

Jasper dreamed he swam in the warm waters of the ceremonial lake, painfully aware of Well Worms circling beneath. Still to outgrow the weak trappings of his youth, his limbs burned from keeping his head above water. Time was running out.

Snowflakes drifted onto his face. Despite the arctic winter, the lake was always warm, lit from beneath by some primal furnace. His gaze locked onto the luminescent aquatic life beneath him and the same vibrant color along the trees surrounding the shore, winding up the trunks like festive decorations. The glowing life signaled a source of mana from the Well—the very cosmic energy that birthed life for all Elphynians. If he were to die tonight, at least it was pretty.

Wolves howled in the distance, breaking the silent night. His heart beat a little faster. His keen shifter ears picked up plants and underbrush, rustling as paws padded closer through the woods. Birds cawed and took to the sky as marauding sycophants and the King's fae invaded their peaceful home.

They're coming.

He tried not to sink too low and prayed he had the courage to survive what would happen next. The Well Worms would take him under. It was that or face a bastard's death by the King's hand.

He would rather face the worms.

He would rather let the Well judge his twelve-year-old heart.

His mother had bid him to be kind... to be brave. So he'd come to the place where the bravest go. The legendary Guardians came here as plain fae. They left as heroes. If deemed worthy, the Well blessed them with the gift of using magic-destroying metal weapons without having their own mana blocked. Fae had a limited supply of mana within their body from which to draw for magic casting, and no matter how many times they replenished from a power source, like this lake, there was a limit. But after completing the initiation, a Guardian's capacity to hold mana expanded. They could last longer in battle than even the Highest Fae, those like the King.

But this power came at a cost. Guardians dedicated their long lives to upholding the integrity of the Well. They slayed mana-warped monsters; they policed possession of forbidden metals and plastics—because these blocked the flow of mana—and they protected fae-kind from the human enemy which sought to return the world to its old, greedy and barren ways.

Two-thirds who entered the lake were deemed unworthy and failed to emerge alive. Instead of sinking and being imbued with the essence of the Well of life itself, their bloated carcasses floated to the surface, their shame for all to see and a warning against those who dared contemplate taking power when it was not deserved.

Could a cowardly boy be worthy?

His sins came back to taunt him. When he should have screamed, he had stayed quiet. When he should have fought, he'd hid. He should have done something instead of tremble in fear as his mother's warm blood dripped onto his face as he lay in the dugout beneath the floorboards.

The last thing he saw before dipping beneath the lake surface was his father's cruel smile from the shore, his hunting wolves snarling at his side. He didn't believe Jasper was worthy either. He assumed Jasper would float.

Slimy, thick worms wrapped around Jasper's ankles, and he plummeted.

Down, down, down into the murky cold inky water, to the fathoms no one dared venture. Only the bravest sank. Only the worthiest survived. Around his body, long worms coiled, tightening and constricting until his arms pinned to his sides. His lungs burned. His heart hammered.

Fear turned his blood to ice. The worms slid across his closed lips, begging for him to open and let them in.

No movements, my love, or the spell will break, and he will scent you.

If he survived this, he would become a Guardian. He could save the fae his father murdered in the name of secrets and power. He could protect them. All of them.

He had to be brave so the next time his father tried to silence a female, a mother, or a daughter, he would be there.

He stopped struggling. He submitted. The worms slid around his neck and invaded his mouth. They swam down his throat and judged him from the inside. They swallowed his screams.

The dream twisted. This time, the experience was unique. Initially, he had been judged on a mere twelve years of life. This time, he was no longer a child. His years numbered in the hundreds. Somewhere in the back of his mind, he knew he shouldn't be back here. That it must be a dream. No one submitted twice to the judgment of the Well. No one wanted to. But here he was. The worms choked. They invaded. They wreathed. They feasted on the ink in his soul. They surrounded his heart and squeezed.

Had he done what he'd promised? Had he protected the innocents—made sure those like his mother had been helped?

Tearing into flesh of the enemy for the applause of a fickle crowd.

Wasting his mind on hallucinogens.

Spending his coin on Rosebud Courtesans and welcoming the empty pleasures they offered.

Fae spitting at his feet as he walked through their villages to collect the tax the Order of the Well demanded, or their tributes of initiates—children.

Watching his best friend's female executed after giving birth... by decree of the King.

He could have done something. He could have protected her.

"You are brave," Mama's memory sneered at him. *"You are kind."*

The worms choked. They stole his breath. Darkness closed in.

Another voice warbled from a distance, a life raft for his heavy soul.

Her tone was gentle and carried a dry, husky sweetness that warmed him like spiced wine.

"We've only just met, but so far, you're okay..."

He tethered himself to her voice as she drifted in and out of earshot.

"You belong in this place, unlike me. If you get better, maybe you can help me find my friends. Maybe we can help each other. But you need to wake up, Jasper."

Pain sliced through him and he roared awake, heaving in great lungfuls of air.

A blond woman blinked at him, startled. Pain at his chest. *Her fault!*

Catapulting himself off the ground, he lurched at her, taking her down and pinning her by the shoulders. His inner wolf battered against the confines of Jasper's body. It wanted out. It wanted vengeance.

"You hurt me!" He snapped his teeth an inch from her face.

She flinched, shut her eyes and stilled.

She's not fighting.

She's breathing quietly. She's not afraid.

She was... concerned. He felt the emotion come to him through the blue marks on his right arm. She had the same on hers. He should know what they mean, but... his neck itched. It burned.

He eased a fraction and studied her. Blond long hair twisted into a messy braid splayed on the cobblestones. Pretty flushed face. Pink lips. Freckles. Fragile woman. His eyes tracked to the side. He snarled at her round ears.

"Human."

His wolf was so close to taking over. His eyes stung from the power of it. It wanted to do the protecting, the investigating, the surviving. But there was something about the human... *Different.*

He sniffed her. She reeked of mana, of power. His nose buried into her hair, then down the vein in her neck to her front. Lower. He took in the sweet-spicy scent of her womanhood, and a low rumble caught in his throat. A surge of carnal want slammed into him.

Need. Mine. Take.

The wolf demanded Jasper take his due. It took every ounce of restraint to hold his primal instincts at bay. He shut his eyes and breathed through his emotions.

"The wolf is a part of me, not the other way around," he mumbled to himself. Then repeated it, again and again, until the demanding urge to shift abated.

When he opened his eyes, she avoided his gaze. Prying his fingers from her shoulders, he eased back. Her alluring scent affected him in a way his logic couldn't comprehend. He needed her as though she was his mate—his one true match—the female he would spend the rest of his immortal life with. Yet she was human.

Enemy.

He clutched his head and pulled his hair. His mind was a fog.

"What did you do to me?" he rasped.

His hand went to the pain still radiating from his chest.

Finally, she met his gaze. He found caution, intelligence, and something he recognized every time he met his reflection's gaze—the will to survive. Well... he used to have it.

She wouldn't go down without a fight, this one. It sent another thrilling spark of the hunt jogging through his senses. So why had she submitted to him?

"I pulled this from your neck." A blue, gelatinous strip dangled from her fingers.

He looked down at his chest. From what he could see, more blue marks covered his upper torso. He poked his finger through a hole in his shirt and saw more blue beneath. When he touched his neck, he felt it slightly raised and irritated. The markings at his arm were different. Smooth, shaped in curved lines like the contour lines on a map, they felt like they belonged.

He rubbed his neck. Those marks were responsible for his foggy mind. They had to be.

"Take more off," he demanded and pointed to his neck.

"Um." She bit her lip and slowly lifted herself to a sitting position. "Okay. A please would be nice."

"Please."

She raised her hand, hesitated, then met his eyes. "It might hurt."

"I was unprepared last time. This time, I am ready."

He balled his hands into fists and sat back on his haunches. He nodded.

She stroked the skin of his collarbone. A shiver prickled through him at her touch. He shifted to get comfortable and then noticed four small healing puncture wounds on his torso. He touched them but had no memory of the injury.

"You know," she said. "I also sucked the poison out of your wounds. You're welcome."

"You're welcome," he murmured.

She laughed. His gaze clashed with hers and for a moment, he was lost in the flecks of gold dancing in their rich brown depths. Then something she said connected with primal satisfaction. A smile curved his lips.

"Your mouth was on me?" he asked slowly. "Sucking?"

"Yeah, well, I had to. I wasn't exactly going to let you die, now, was I?"

She'd protected him?

The profound notion tugged at his heart. On the outside, he stilled. On the inside, he became a raging torrent of sensation, desire, and possessive instinct.

Her brow puckered as she tried to pick a neck mark, but couldn't grasp it. "It's not working this time."

He barely listened. His mind was still on the hunger burning in his veins, urging him to draw her closer. Just an inch. Maybe more. It became an incomprehensible maelstrom of sensation. His eyes watered. If he didn't taste her soon, he would…

"I would advise you to step away, human."

"Why?"

He growled low, voice rattling with gravel. "Because my wolf wants me to claim you."

She startled and shuffled back.

Desire simmered in a volatile cocktail within his body.

Take her, claim her.

He would never take a female against her will, even a human. The act was despicable. So he stood, turned, and swiped at the first thing he could reach—a vase sitting on a stone table. It flew, then crashed against the stone wall, shattering into tiny pieces and crumbling to the ground. Next, he flipped the stone table itself. An almighty howl of defiance released.

Heaving great breaths through a clenched jaw, he lifted his chin and howled at the sky. When the last note died, he found himself on all fours and caged inside the body of a wolf. *No!* Without his consent, it had drawn on his mana and shifted. It had broken through.

The wolf was everything he wasn't. It was brave. It was ruthless. It was vicious.

It did what it needed to survive.

And it was hungry.

Nose tipped, it caught a scent. Female. *Mine. Mate.*

He stalked her, found her crouched by a fountain. She avoided his gaze and lowered herself further, as though she sensed not to provoke him.

But she wasn't a wolf, she wasn't even fae. How could she be his mate? Curiously, he paced before her. And then she started talking.

"I'm not your enemy," she mumbled, still not engaging in eye contact. "I'm Ada. You're Jasper. At least I think you are. You seem to have forgotten yourself. To be honest, it didn't really seem like you remembered much. But whatever we call ourselves, the same thing remains. We are in this together. We arrived at this place, neither of us with any clue to how we got here. I'm from somewhere called Las Vegas. It's in the United States…"

She continued to talk softly and in calming tones. It was the same voice that called him out of his dream. He cocked his head and sat back on his haunches and then listened to her story about how they both came to be in this place. It resonated. It felt right.

Slowly, with every word out of her mouth, his anger and fire washed away until eventually she stopped speaking. He whined softly.

She faced him and met his eyes. "Jasper?"

Jasper wrested control of his mana from the wolf. He changed back into fae form, panting from the strain. Lifting his sullen gaze to hers, he used his fist to trace a circular motion around his heart. Shame washed through him and he hung his head.

"I don't know what that means," she said. "The hand sign."

Crimson.

He scanned the moss-covered ground until he found his breeches and then shook them out to inspect. Still in one piece, thank the Well. He must have stepped out of them, however, his shirt hadn't survived the sudden shift. It lay in tatters. Clenching his jaw, he gave her his back and stepped into his pants, only facing her as he buttoned them.

"It means I have apologized," he explained.

"Why don't you just say sorry?"

"Because then I would owe you a boon. You would be well within your rights to use your mana to enforce a bargain with me." He raised his brow, feeling a little more like himself—whoever that was. "I'm not that sorry."

"Mana?" Her hands fretted.

The human probably had no idea what mana was. She'd saved his life, so he felt he owed her an explanation at least. So he explained the laws of the Well to her—that it refused to flow through metal and plastic, that it was the life force of the earth itself—and then pointed at her arm.

"Somehow, by some miracle, you've been blessed by the Well. I can smell it on you."

She raised a brow. "I can shift into a wolf, too?"

He regarded her round ears shrewdly. "Unlikely. But what you can do is a mystery to me. Perhaps it is linked to how you remove the markings on my neck."

She shook her head. "But this time I couldn't get it."

"Learning to harness your mana takes time and training." He frowned. "I'm not the right person to help you. I don't..." His neck flared again, halting his train of thought. He gave a frustrated growl and flexed his fists.

"So... what happened? Before?" she asked.

"You tell me."

"One minute you were staring into the water of that fountain, talking to that golden-haired man, and then this thing jumps out and claws you. It was poisoned. I leeched some poison out, but you passed out." She shrugged. "While you were out, you seemed in pain, but when I put my hand on you... I don't know. It's dumb." She raised her eyes to the sky. "This whole situation is insane."

"Tell me anyway," he urged.

"You calmed when I put my hand on you."

Mate, his wolf snarled. *Mine.*

He gave her an assessing once over. From blond top to dainty bared feet, she was attractive. Very. And she had the same blue markings on her arm. He frowned as an explanation tried to come to him, but a sudden burn and itch at his neck pilfered it away.

He scratched.

"Stop," she admonished.

"I can't help it."

"Whatever that is on your neck, it's not the same as what's on our arms. And I think it's connected to your lack of memory."

He had the same inkling. He couldn't escape the feeling that he should be somewhere else, that he had responsibilities. His memories were blocked, and she'd cracked them open… just a little, just enough to clear some fog.

"Do you remember who you are?" she asked with a quick glance at the fountain.

"No," he replied. The name Jasper sounded foreign.

"How did we get here?"

"I don't know."

"Do you even know that you turned into a big black wolf?"

His brow arched.

"Right. Stupid question, okay, so, what *do* you know?"

That question stupefied him more than anything else. His mind hurt to reach far back. His neck burned. He only knew what had come to pass since he'd awoken with vague feelings he should be somewhere.

"I know that you did something that seemed to help. I know that I should be somewhere else… that I have responsibilities. I know that my wolf wants me to claim you, that these arm markings connect us in a way I should respect." He looked down at his hand, mumbling, "Blessed by the Well."

It was inconceivable. She was human. It went beyond everything he felt to be right. "I know you're mine, human. But I don't have to like it."

She folded her arms and cocked a hip. "Yeah, and I'm just over here having the time of my life." Her brows slammed down. "And, hang on a minute, I am most certainly not yours. I belong to no one, thank you very much… whatever you are."

"Fae," he replied.

"Bless you."

His lip twitched. "What?"

"You sneezed."

"No, I said I'm fae. That's what I am. You're human, and I'm fire-fae, to be precise. I shift forms, unlike other fae races."

"Fae? As in the Fair-Folk from ancient fairy tales?" She looked at the sky. "What's next, flying pigs?"

He shrugged. "It's possible they existed in the old world."

"Old world?" Her brow puckered. "Oh, you're serious."

Another shrug.

"Right. You can't remember." She sighed. "We need to find someone who can help us. Neither of us is capable of much at the moment, and I really need to eat." She glanced toward the gate leading to the fields outside. "I've seen a few things around the place I can use to fashion a trap. I'm starving, and we need to get moving before the sun goes down or make camp here for the night. I'm guessing it gets cold in this place."

Jasper wasn't afraid of the cold. He could walk in the snow for miles and feel fine. His neck itched as though a memory tried to surface, and he grunted with annoyance. The human was right. Food first, and then they could find help. But he would be the one to provide.

"Stay here," he said, and walked to the gate.

"Where are you going?"

"To hunt."

Ada chased after him as they emerged outside. A forest lay to their left, and hills of grass to their right. Somewhere down in the valley, smoke curled from a cottage chimney. He sniffed but caught a whiff of enemy.

Ada pointed at the cottage. "Look."

He shook his head. "Don't go there."

"But they could help us."

His hackles raised. "Trust me. It's best we stay away, and you stay here."

"Why?"

"Whatever is down there will be no friend to us. Elphyne is a dangerous place, human. Dangerous things come in pretty packages."

And he was one of them. He slid his pants off and shifted to wolf form before trotting to the tree line without a backward glance.

CHAPTER

FOUR

The moment the fae shifted to wolf form and disappeared into the thick of the forest, Ada set about collecting items from within the junkyard cottage to build herself a snare trap. While he'd been assessing her, and perhaps arrogantly accepting her—for now—she'd been silently screaming in her mind.

This was insane.

He'd changed into a wolf before her eyes.

His ears were pointed. He'd said he was part of a mythical, magical race.

And the asshole seemed to think she belonged to him.

She *did not* belong to anyone.

They might be stuck together until they could find help, but she certainly would not let him think he could boss her around. She could take care of herself.

I know you're mine, human. But I don't have to like it.

Her nose scrunched up. *Whatever, jerk.* She didn't have to like it either.

She forced her mind to the task of setting traps. If she didn't set something soon, then she'd have to forage in the forest at night, or worse, eat the slugs.

First, she went to the hearth and picked out some old charcoal to rub against her hands. That way when she touched the trap items, her scent wouldn't transfer. Then she rummaged about the cottage, searching for things she could use. The best she came up with was an old curtain cord, a basket, and pens she could use as lever sticks for the snare. The stinky slugs were bait. Not as good as peanut butter or sardines. Hopefully she wouldn't need any of it if Jasper came back with food.

Feeling proud of herself, she gathered sticks from trees, and then set up stick-snares near the forest's edge, and the basket one closer to the field leading to the farm in the distance. If only Jasper let her go down and investigate the animal she'd seen grazing. It could be a cow.

Her environment looked innocent enough, but then again, she knew nothing about this Elphyne place. A goblin-like creature had jumped out of the fountain and almost killed Jasper—a man who seemed pretty hard to kill.

And that brought her mind to the most boggling thing of all. Magic was real, and he believed she had it. She shook her head, unable to let the overwhelming truth in. For now, she needed to focus on survival. Tomorrow, she would ponder the wonder of her displacement.

Once the traps were set, she ventured back into the cottage and found a bowl to collect rainwater. Thunder still rumbled occasionally, and the dark rain clouds hadn't left. Hopefully that meant a fresh supply of water.

Keeping warm was the next item on her list. The low overnight temperature could kill them quicker than any lack of food or hydration. While waiting for the traps to spring, she collected kindling for the fireplace, but without a flint or matches, she wasn't looking forward to setting it alight.

Finally, she settled against the outside garden wall, picked up the long cord length ending on the basket trap and waited for a poor unsuspecting animal to venture beneath it. With each passing moment, the golden sun set over the green rolling hills. She tried to stay positive. Snare traps were a numbers game. The more she had, the better chance of catching food, but she would be lucky to catch something tonight. Slugs might be crap bait.

For now, it was nice to take a moment to appreciate the sight of nature restored. Always a visceral reaction, tension unwound in her body, but the moment it went, a heavy sadness sliced through her. She dashed burgeoning tears away from her eyes, hating that the fae might come back and see her weakness.

Every thought she'd held at bay since waking crashed to the surface.

Her joy at seeing the world born again.

Her sadness at missing her friends.

Her warring fear and attraction with her new companion.

Her confusion at this world's rules.

Every emotion washed about inside until her throat closed and she coughed to clear the tension, shaking herself out of her melancholy. Falling into despair would only get herself killed. A shuffling sound snapped her head up.

A small fluffy animal hopped about beneath the cane basket cage. She yanked on the cord. The basket fell, trap sprung. Elation fizzed through her and she wanted to shout her triumph. Rabbit for dinner. Her mouth watered. Getting to her feet, she cast a worried glance to the forest. It had been hours and Jasper hadn't returned. Just as well she'd decided not to wait for him. He might never return.

Dangerous things come in pretty packages.

She snorted.

Jasper certainly was pretty. And she believed he *was* dangerous. That first time he attacked her by the fountain, she'd almost peed her pants, and she'd faced down a black bear once. Well, faced a bear and escaped by playing dead. Same thing. An ache in her marked arm flared, and she tried not to think about getting attached to him already. She was a loner. Always had been, always would be. With the exception of her two friends.

She was not the kind of girl to be owned or claimed by a man, let alone a damaged, wolf-man who just happened to have an incredible body. And face. And smile. Those lips...

Stop it.

As she drew close to the trap, the small animal came into clear view. It wasn't a rabbit like she'd first thought, but rabbit-like. It had the same body and face, but chicken wings sprouted from its back, and tiny antlers protruded from its forehead. Big eyes glistened as she approached. Her heart tugged. It was cute.

And another sign that this world was not as she'd left it, but perhaps had grown out of the ashes of hers. Jasper had said something about the old world, so maybe she'd somehow—*nah.* Time travel was impossible.

As impossible as no sign of an extinction level nuclear holocaust?

Wherever she was, there were similarities and differences. Maybe she could learn to live here. She could learn to love it... if she could get over missing her friends.

But she wouldn't be getting over anything if she didn't eat. She was so hungry.

"I'm so sorry, buddy, but a girl's gotta eat."

Readying the glass shard she'd taken from within the house, she crouched low and put her hand on the basket, ready to lift. She bit her lip, took a deep breath and then—

Air shimmered around the animal. A slice of recognition warned her moments before the creature exploded into a larger form with a roar. Hurtling backward, Ada landed hard. Her vision blurred. She bit her tongue and tasted blood. *What the hell?*

The tiny, winged bunny had become something else. No longer on all fours, the creature—*monster*—stood on two furred and clawed feet. Its grotesquely shaped body was humanoid, yet covered in patches of matted fur. Only the pectorals were bare pink skin. Long wings draped from his broad shoulders. His nose was part bunny. His mouth had buck teeth. His eyes were red, and long sharp antlers angled from his forehead— no longer tiny and cute. A long pink tongue whipped out to lick a strand of dangling drool from his leering mouth. She gulped as her eyes traveled south to where a very large and laden erection jutted out from the white fuzz of his groin.

Ada was never the kind of woman to scream. Perhaps it was her long-instilled survivalist instinct. Fear would only signal she was prey. Yet, as the monster leered and stroked himself with a very human hand, she screamed.

It grinned salaciously.

"You *owe* me, human," it declared. "You apologized, now you owe me."

She had?

Idiot, Ada. You just did what you weren't supposed to do. Regret pulsed through her. Damn it. She should have waited for Jasper. She forced her heart to slow, her breath to steady, and to assess the situation with a level head.

Jaws snapped at her.

Can't.

She shut her eyes and averted her face. Hot, putrid breath tickled her face, signaling he'd come closer. Vomit rose. She forced it down. Flaring her nostrils, she steeled herself and gripped the glass shard tighter, barely mindful of it stinging her own skin.

Come on. Do this. Toughen up. Destroy it before it destroys you.

It was the voice of Harold, the old crotchety hunter she'd met when wandering the woods as a child. Instead of calling the authorities and putting her in foster care, he'd grumpily taught her how to survive. She opened her eyes and glared.

Survive.

"Get away from me," she demanded. "Or I'll slice your dick clean off."

The rabbit-eared monster cocked its head and studied her with curiosity. A moment, that's all it gave her, but it was enough for her to go on the offensive. She lurched forward and embedded her shard somewhere into its front. Hot sticky blood spilled over her hand.

Strike the belly. Rip up, gut it. Hesitation means suffering for both sides.

She pulled her hand out and stabbed again. Its furious roar cut mid cry when a dark blur hit side-on. Ada's arm yanked, still stuck in the creature's gut. She let go of her weapon just in time to escape two snarling bodies as they grappled and rolled away down the hill. It was Jasper.

Dark hair, tanned and muscled body flashed against pink, furry and feathered. They moved too fast.

Who's winning?

Alarmed, she searched for another weapon, but found none. Didn't matter. The fight was swiftly over. Little balls of light floated out of the monster. Jasper levered off the body, blood coating his naked chest, hands, and dripping from his chin. Amber eyes glowed with adrenaline as he locked onto her with feral intensity.

Heart leaping into her throat, Ada backed up at the sight of an angry, virile, and naked fae stalking toward her as though he wanted to spank her. Worse… eat her.

"I told you to stay inside," he growled.

Her eyes dipped down to what hung from the nestle of dark hair at *his* groin. It wasn't erect, but long. Big. Thick. She resisted patting her too-hot cheeks.

"I was hungry," she murmured.

"I was handling it."

"Um. Do you want me to get your clothes?"

He grunted in frustration, searched the area and found where he'd left his pants. He shoved them on, then returned to her, still fuming.

"Happy?" he asked.

"Over the moon," she replied, a snipe to her tone. "I've already had one unwelcome dick wagging in my face tonight. I don't need another."

He jerked back and his expression turned thoughtful. "What?"

"That thing had a goddamn erection. And it was… you know. Pumping the ol' pipe. Spanking the monkey. Going to town with his hand."

His brows lifted in recognition. Amusement crinkled his eyes. "A wolpertinger has no females of its own kind to mate with, so it tricks females from other fae races into bargains. They lure you in with their cuteness and then kidnap and mate with you. You're lucky I sensed your fear and dropped the berries to come running. A mana-infused bargain is hard to break." He rubbed his stubbled jaw. "You know, if there are more around, my scent on you will deter them."

"You want to rub yourself on me?"

"No, pretty human. I want to mate with you. I want to mark you."

Her jaw dropped. She wasn't sure which part to comprehend first. The fact the beast had wanted to impregnate her, or that Jasper had found berries and dropped them, or that he'd basically just asked to have sex in a casual "It will save your life" sort of way.

"This is absurd," she murmured with a blush. "I'm not *mating* with you. And I will not end up as some horny bunny's sex slave. I need to wash this blood off."

Three things she never thought she'd say.

"I won't hurt you," he promised, and that made her gape even more.

"You don't even like me." Heat flared in her cheeks at the blistering attention. She swallowed and stepped back. "What's in the water here?"

"Fine," he said with a pout. "I will skin the wolpertinger. At least your stupidity has gifted us with a hearty meal."

She spun on her heel, furious at her body's reaction to the rich sound of his laughter following her.

Two hours later, they'd cleaned up as best they could. Jasper had returned with his berries, and skinned a fleshy portion of the beast, and then lit the fire with his mana. Like magic, the flames sprung to life on the hearth and they cooked their stew over the fire in a cracked ceramic pot.

It made her stomach curdle to eat the stew, but she'd had worse. And it tasted like chicken, so she just closed her eyes and pretended it was exactly that. As long as she replenished her energy, she could try to make it to some sort of city or town. Surely there must be a village nearby. She hadn't given up on the idea of finding her friends, although it was sounding less likely that they were also alive. She made a mental note to ask Jasper more about how much time had passed since her time.

With the food gone and their stomachs full, they settled on the floor by the fire. Jasper reclined against an old torn armchair and watched her with an intensity that made her shift and squirm. She hadn't forgotten his offhanded proposal, or his earlier comment about her belonging to him. The way he looked at her was proprietary and almost Machiavellian, as though he hatched devious plans to get what he wanted, and he was prepared to wait.

He chewed on a piece of straw Ada had scattered before the fireplace. If she didn't still sense a strange bond of trust between them, she would have run by now. As it stood, he'd said some things, but his actions were respectful.

He'd helped her down from the table earlier and then let go. He'd tried to keep her from harm, whether that had been by going through a door first, or by trying to keep her here while he went out to hunt.

"All right, fun time is over," she said, a little sleepy from the heat of the flames. "Time for you to explain some shit."

His lips quirked. "Fun time is just beginning."

He pulled out a handful of berries from his pocket. They were different than the ones they'd added to flavor the stew. He handed her one. "Try it."

She arched her brow. "Why do I have the feeling you're not telling me something?"

He shrugged. "You may feel a little relaxed from eating them, that's all."

"Those are relaxing berries, like a drug? Are you kidding me right now?"

He frowned. "They're no big deal. Just something to loosen up with."

He made a face she'd expect on a teenage boy when his mother confiscated his first beer.

"We're both lost, Jasper. You have no memories. We might not survive the night because it's going to be pretty cold. For all you know, I'm a serial killer. And you want to take some sort of drug?"

He dared her with his eyes, popped a berry into his mouth, and chewed.

She huffed. "Fine. Be an ass."

"We're not lost," he said, voice already turning a little slurred. The berries must work quick. "I used to live here. There's a village nearby. We can go there tomorrow."

"Have you remembered things?"

"Nope."

"Then how do you know?"

"Gut feeling. Just like the feeling that said not to go near that cottage. And look what happened. A wolpertinger lived there." He grinned smugly.

Damn him. It was cute. Puffy-eyed, grinning frat boy, cute.

"How can you be so nonchalant about this?"

But no answer came. He'd already started snoring softly.

Ada didn't get it.

He was important enough for a king to assassinate and for someone to block his memories. He was strong enough to kill a monster with his bare hands. He had scars all over him. He seemed like someone who should act a little more responsible.

"You've definitely changed," she murmured. Since taking the blue mark from his neck, more of a playful personality had shone through. If she could get more of the blue off, surely he'd recall some of their situation. If his gut feelings were right, then actual knowledge would be better.

Perhaps he had to be asleep for her to peel the marks off.

Shuffling closer, she checked to see if he noticed her. Once satisfied he was well and truly under, she went to work at the neck marks, picking at the edges with her fingernails. This time, she tried to channel some of this internal mana he had talked about but had no idea what she was doing. Perhaps she felt a tingle down her arm, perhaps not. In the end, she settled into a routine of how she'd approached it before—visualizing the bad stuff gone.

Maybe it was the lack of performance anxiety without his watchful eyes on her, or how she hummed quietly, but her nail caught on some blue. She picked and peeled until a strip came free.

His fingers wrapped around her wrist and held her immobile.

His eyes defocused, his brow puckered, and he tugged them to the ground.

"Tomorrow," he whined. "Sleep now."

She tried to remove her arm so she could shift back to her side, but he held tight.

"I'll keep you warm," he muttered.

"I'm not comfortable with that," she shot back.

He grunted. "I'll shift."

The air shimmered, and fur sprouted from his skin. Within moments, a stunning black wolf crawled out of a pair of pants and then curled around her lazily. He was big enough to shelter her. His fur was thick and, as she looked closer, she found it was like his hair—brown with black tips. He would be warm to sleep up against. The wolf cast a reproachful glance her way and then huffed in annoyance at her reticence.

"Fine," she muttered and curled into his side.

While she wasn't ready to sleep with a pointed-ear fae, she was completely at home next to an animal.

Unable to help herself, she reached out and scratched him under the chin. "You're gorgeous," she muttered.

The moment her head hit the floor, her eyelids grew heavy. She sighed. The wolf sighed. And it was... nice. It took her some time to let her tension go, but she didn't want to live her life destroying everything before it destroyed her. That may have been the way she had survived growing up, but it wasn't how she ended up living. Meeting Harold had taught her how to hunt and read, but after knowing he died alone in his cabin, she knew she never wanted that for herself.

The fire crackled, and Ada drifted, remembering the faces of her friends. Clarke's red, unruly hair. The way she drank soda like it was going out of fashion. Laurel's inevitable rebuke about Clarke looking after her health and how much sugar was in said soda.

Ada drifted to sleep, smiling at imagined conversations in her head.

CHAPTER

FIVE

J asper continued to chew mana-weed berries for the duration of their walk from the cottage to the nearby village. Fenrysfield, he thought it was called. Maybe. It took them half a day of walking through rain-soaked mud. He hated every minute, and it had nothing to do with the water falling from the sky, but with the manner with which he'd awoken.

He may have fallen asleep in wolf form, but during the night, his wolf had conceded control of his body. It knew the woman was theirs, that she was human, that she was Jasper's to claim. When he woke, his fae form was wrapped around her alluring body, hugging her within the shelter of his arms, his arousal hard and stiff between the nestle of her bottom. The situation had confounded him, and he couldn't place why.

Had he never awoken with a female in his arms?

Had he not embraced?

Surely he'd been with a female before. Plenty. He may not remember, but he knew it with a solid certainty. Why else would his blood sing at the thought of taking her, of licking her all over, and burying his face between her legs? He enjoyed sex. That was not why he'd been out of sorts when he'd awoken.

Perhaps it was because she was human. Although, he found he cared less upon waking because she was unlike any human he knew... he thought. Perhaps. She certainly held mana within her body. That in itself was highly unusual for one of the forsaken Untouched. The very name fae called humans—Untouched—meant the Well had failed to touch them.

She'd also helped him on more than one occasion and claimed to know nothing about the humans of Crystal City. She claimed to be from a place called Las Vegas. How could he place her in the same category?

All he knew for sure was that her feminine scent drove him to distraction. His skin had buzzed every time she'd moved in sleep, or her hair tickled his skin, or she made a little whimper-sigh that hardened him to the point of pain. He couldn't think, couldn't move, couldn't breathe because he feared the seduction of her scent clawing at him.

With great effort, he'd disentangled without waking her, and then dressed in his breeches.

He'd only popped the first berry to calm his nerves, but then the next berry went in, and the next. Before he staggered out of the cottage, she'd tried again to peel more of the markings from his body but had no luck. He should have let her continue last night. It was a sorely accepted concession on his behalf. One he kept to himself.

The mana-berry effect had worn off by the time they approached the village nestled between the Ceremonial Woods and the Seelie River. Buildings with mosaic tiled walls and thatched roofs crowded together in clusters. Smoke curled from chimneys into the overcast sky. Voices shouted as daily activity carried on—a market was being packed away or set up. Fishermen dragged their catches in great baskets from the river docks. Goats bleated as they scattered and roamed freely. A note of something familiar caught on the breeze, and he lifted his nose for a stronger scent. Wolves. Lots of them. This was a shifter village.

Ada stopped. "This is it?"

He squinted at it, then down at her pillowy lips, still taunting him, and shrugged. "I guess."

It made sense that his instincts would lead them to a shifter village.

"Any idea of where we go first?" she asked. "Or who we speak to?"

He gave another lift of his shoulder.

"Some enthusiasm would be good," she said wryly and then sighed. "I suppose we could just head in."

Slowly they approached the village entrance. There were no gates, just a path that wound past the small market and entered the cluster of buildings to become the main street. On second glance, there had been gates once, but they were recently damaged. Perhaps forced down under attack. Wariness licked down his spine. As he surveyed the buildings, more signs of battle were evident. The glass and gem mosaic walls were cracked. Wooden doors were split. Plants had been trampled and destroyed. The sound of construction rang as they drew close.

But the villagers were rallying. They repaired and washed clothing and hung them on lines strung up from building to building. There were groups of repotted plants. Decorations hung from house to house, eave to eave. Strings of paper flowers, red ribbons, and dangling glass wind chimes, shifted and swayed in a gentle breeze. There must be a festival soon.

This town was resilient. Whatever hardship had befallen them, it hadn't broken them.

Wolves were good like that.

They were scrappy. They survived. And they knew how to have fun.

As Jasper and Ada passed the first house, the smell of baked goods made his stomach rumble. Bread and berries. He moistened his lips and glanced at Ada. She'd be hungry too. Hungry, wet, and cold.

He was painfully aware he had no coin with which to procure food and lodgings. He'd have to come up with something, perhaps he could work off their board.

The first fae they walked up to was a tall female with long black hair, making half-face masks entwined with crafted flowers and red ribbon she sold on her cart. Glass beads tinkled in her hair and on her ankle jewelry. She smiled, but then her gaze snagged on Jasper's face, more precisely to the mark on his right cheekbone. Her eyes widened in fear, and she ran into her nearby house, long skirts billowing behind her, before she shut her wooden door with a loud bang.

"That was weird," Ada said. "Not a friend of yours?"

"Guess not."

A male fae further up, who was in the middle of speaking to a cluster of children, jolted upright at seeing Jasper, and hurried them away.

"You don't smell that bad," Ada joked.

"I would have thought they'd run from you, not me."

"Why's that?"

He gave her ears a look.

"Oh." She touched her hair and tugged bits over her ears. "Is this better?"

"They'll find out, eventually. Not to worry. I will keep you safe."

She snorted. "Okay, Rambo."

He stopped her and scowled. "Do you think I cannot protect you?"

"No. It's just that, like I said before, I'm fine on my own. I mean, how bad can it be? As soon as we…" Her voice trailed off as her attention caught on the growing cluster of villagers brandishing dark looks and the occasional snarl. Some held weapons in their hands—broomsticks, serrated bone swords, and glass daggers reinforced with stone.

Two black wolves trotted out from behind a mosaic building and snarled a soft warning.

Jasper's hackles rose and he tensed, gaze tracking warily around the group, waiting for the first poor buffoon to take a stab at him… or Ada. He let his claws distend from his fingertips.

A fae wearing a wide-brimmed hat pointed his finger at Jasper. "You're unwelcome here, Guardian."

Guardian? Something he'd dreamed tried to climb through the fog of his mind, but failed. He folded his arms and planted his feet.

"There are no monsters here," another said. "So you cannot claim a tax for something we've not requested assistance for."

Ada's brows lifted as she met Jasper's gaze. "Are you some kind of bounty hunter? You don't seem to be very welcome. Maybe we should go elsewhere."

She shivered against a gust of wind. They needed food, shelter, and a place to dry their clothes. His upper lip curled. "They will not run us out of town."

"You heard her, Guardian. Leave," said the fae with the hat. His dagger glinted in the light as he pointed it Jasper's way.

Ada stepped to the side, probably intending to go around, but a large male holding an ax blocked her way. He shook his head and tsked softly. "Turn back, little female."

Defeat flashed in her eyes, and she turned. The large fae pushed her between the shoulder blades. It was the last mistake he made.

Cold fury rocked through Jasper. He used his mana to throw a solid wall of air outward, not even realizing what he'd done until it was over and the fae flew backward into a row of others. Shocked shouts rose, tempers riled, and he drew more mana in preparation, letting it rise and bubble to the surface, ready for release in whichever spell he crafted. Fangs pierced his bottom lip as he partially shifted and growled, low and gravelly.

Violence and murder coursed through his veins, comforting him into believing the well-worn routine meant he'd fought before, and he'd excelled at it.

A wicked grin curved his lips. He blasted more air at the wolves daring to stalk closer. They yipped when hit and staggered back.

Well-damn, it felt good to release his mana.

He would drain his supply dry and not care because he had access to another supply—Ada's. None of these villagers were strong enough to take him. Their own personal Wells were finite, poor, and subpar. Most standard fae only had enough within them to shift, or to cast small magics. Even if there was a source of power nearby for them to replenish, he could melt them where they stood before they had the chance.

How *dare* they think to order him around?

If he had his sword, he would be invincible—his neck burned, blocking his memory before it arrived, wiping it clean from his consciousness. It annoyed him further.

"What's the matter with you people, you don't recognize one of your own?" someone shouted over the crowd. "Let me through."

Murmurs and dissent passed around, but the crowd reluctantly shifted. No, not reluctantly. He caught the relief in more than one gaze. They understood a fight picked with him could not be won.

Bodies made way for a female shifter with short brown hair. The long, loose gown she wore was a classic style in pure shifter communities such as these. It made for easy removal if the need to shift became urgent. While she appeared the same age as Jasper, that wasn't a signal of age. In fact, the older fae became, the more ageless they appeared. It was the eyes that held their secrets, and within hers, he saw fathomless experience. She smiled at him knowingly.

"The Well preserve us," she murmured, taking him in as though he were a ghost. "As I live and breathe, if it isn't Reed Darkfoot, only living heir to the Seelie Mithras throne, finally coming home to visit his roots."

"My name is Jasper." Wasn't it?

"D'arn Jasper"—she spat on the floor—"is the Guardian name forced on you by the Order of the Well when you emerged from the ceremonial lake some two hundred years ago. *Reed* is the name your Darkfoot mother gave you. It is the *only* name we will call you in Fenrysfield. Well, perhaps—" She gave him a wry smile. "Perhaps we may call you princeling, seeing as the King legitimized you a week ago."

Hushed murmurs broke out among the crowd. They spoke the word *prince* on more than one occasion. Somewhere in the middle, he also caught the word *bastard*.

Anxiety crawled up his spine, causing his heart to race. He looked for an escape, but his eyes clashed with Ada's.

The King. As in... the golden fae who'd tried to assassinate him.

"Your own father wants you dead?" she gasped.

"Bah," said the female alpha. "It's not the first time. So, you've come home to seek refuge, is that it? The Order can't do that job anymore?"

His lips parted, but he had no reply.

"He's lost his memories," Ada filled in for him and pointed to the marks around his neck. "That's doing something to him."

The alpha's gaze snapped to his marks, and then trailed down to the ones on his arms. She darted a glance to Ada, frowned, and then she clapped her hands in the air loudly. "Enough. Everyone disperse."

Reluctantly, the villagers, once keen to pry his eyes out with their pitchforks, filtered away.

"Come with me," the alpha beckoned.

Jasper surveyed the village and the way out of town. They had no choice. This woman knew him. She could help. So he strode after her.

The alpha took them to a two-story stone building plastered with a mural of mosaics. Black wolves danced and played, half-wolves battled, and naked fae—he squinted. What were they doing? Ada squinted too, with a hitched intake of breath.

"Good Lord, they're *doing it*," she whispered with a hint of humor.

He shot a sideways glance at her. Her cheeks were flushed. He sensed bashfulness coming from their bond-marks. Was his little mate a shy lover? His stomach dipped with the thrilling thought that he'd get to find out.

The alpha had seen them halt and returned. She, too, gave Ada a thoughtful look.

"You're not a wolf," she clipped. Her chin lifted as she scented. "But I can't place what you are."

"Keen nose," Jasper remarked, but he didn't feel the need to enlighten her.

"Live as long as I have, and there's not much I miss." Her gaze dipped to their matching blue arm markings. "Like the fact you're both locked into a Well-blessed union."

"A what?" Ada choked.

Jasper folded his arms. "I told you."

"We should talk inside." The alpha continued into the building, dipping to avoid the strings of glass wind chimes tinkling in the wind. They hung from the building eaves. In fact, he checked over his shoulder, the wind chimes were on most buildings, gifting his ears with a pleasant melody hard to hear beyond.

For privacy, he realized. So other shifters couldn't hear what went on in their neighbor's house. He smirked. If the mosaic murals were to be believed, plenty of battles, fun, and procreation.

Maybe he would like it here after all.

He shifted the wind chimes and followed the females inside to a large empty hall with a long table surrounded by chairs. It was either for meals or business. Perhaps both. Windows showed the village main street on one side, and a garden with a bubbling fountain on the other.

"Please, take a seat," the alpha said. "I suppose since your curse prevents you from remembering, I must take it easy on you. Not that you deserve it, Reed. Your mother would turn in her grave to know how long it's been since you've come back to us." She raised her eyes to the ceiling and made the apology hand sign against her breast. "I suppose since we're in the middle of Lupercalia preparations, perhaps she is looking after us."

He scowled at her, but took a seat. *Lupercalia...* vague recollections came to mind. Plenty of celebrations and carousing. Sounded good to him.

"I've sent for refreshments," she said.

Ada smiled and nodded. Beneath the table, she fidgeted.

"You really don't remember, do you?" The alpha asked, staring intently at him.

His only reply was a flare of his nostrils.

She sighed. "Very well. My name is Clara Darkfoot. I'm the pack matriarch. And your mother's sister."

When he kept his silence, her eyes dipped to his neck marks, then across to Ada. "How long has he been cursed?"

"Cursed?" she repeated.

A nod.

"I'm not sure," Ada continued. "We both woke up in an abandoned cottage not too far away. Neither of us knows how we got there. For me, I'm a world away from my home. And my friends. I was hoping maybe you could shed some light on my situation, too."

"I'll do my best." She shot Jasper a disapproving stare. "If only for the memory of my sister, and the hopes of her heart."

A knock came at the door, and Clara beckoned in two female fae with a pitcher of water, and a platter of cheese, and dried fruit with crackers. After filling glasses, they left. Ada made quick work of digging into her food.

"Out there they called me a Guardian," Jasper said. "What is that?"

"Guardians work for the Order of the Well," Clara explained, still with a disbelieving look in her eye. "When your mother was murdered, you went to the ceremonial lake and offered yourself as tribute." She sighed. "I suppose the Order was good for one thing, keeping you out of your father's way. They operate above the laws of Elphyne. Becoming a Guardian stripped you of any claim to the Seelie throne. That's why it surprised us all when only a week ago you were announced as the High King's heir. The abolishment of the unsanctioned breeding law also surprised us. We all assumed it was your doing considering how it came into being in the first place." She gave him a studious, long look. "Yet here you are, cursed, without your memories, and with a Well-blessed mate."

Ada patted the table. "Yeah, about that. What exactly is this Well-blessed mating thing? I feel like I should know."

Clara jerked. "There was no mating ceremony?"

Ada shook her head. "Not that we're aware of. We just woke up, and it was there."

"That cannot do. A Well-blessed mating is rare. In all of Elphyne, only two have been announced in the past few centuries."

"How do I find out who cursed me?" Jasper asked. "And how do I get it removed?"

"Casting a curse is forbidden, and irreversible. Even if it was the Order who placed that block on you, they wouldn't be able to remove it. It's simply not done. Either there is a timed deadline linked to the curse, or some unknown event has to take place, if any. It could simply hold forever."

"That's not true," Ada remarked. "I've peeled pieces from his body."

Clara stilled. Her gaze bore into Ada. "Where did you say you hailed from again?"

"I didn't."

Jasper mulled it over. If this matriarch was truly his kin, then she would be the best person to reveal Ada's heritage. Loyalty between kin ran deeper than any other bond. They might not come across help like this again. He could travel to the Order, since he seemed to have worked for them, but as Clara mentioned—it might have been the Order who'd cursed him. It was more likely the King's fault, but Jasper had to be sure.

He would rather control this information getting out than have Clara discover by surprise that she had the enemy in her midst. At least this way, it came from family.

"She's human," Jasper explained.

Clara jumped out of her seat. Blue flame licked at her hand and she glared at Ada. Jasper slowly rose. He raised his blue-marked, Well-blessed palm, reminding her of the connection.

"She's not our enemy," he intoned.

Clara's eyes dipped to his hand, then back to his eyes. She growled, "You don't understand. We barely survived the last raid. And you've invited one of them into our homes?"

"Raid?" he asked. "Please, Clara. Sit. Use your senses."

Ada made no move through it all.

Clara's flame extinguished. She took a hesitant step toward Ada and then lifted her nose. She took another step, and another, before finally meeting Jasper's eyes. Her brows lifted. "She's filled to the brim with mana. It's impossible."

"Evidently not."

"Who *are* you?" Clara asked Ada, a note of awe in her voice.

"I'm just a girl from Vegas," she murmured. "The last thing I remember is that it snowed in the city, and then—"

"Crystal City?"

"No. Las Vegas. Have you truly not heard of it?"

Clara shook her head. "There are no other human settlements but Crystal City in the wasteland."

"Then I have no idea how I got here." She bit her lip.

"No, you have some idea," Jasper prompted. "I can sense your hesitation."

"How?" She gaped at him. "How are we sensing each other's feelings?"

"It's the bond," Clara confirmed. "It links your mana with the other. You can borrow his, and he can borrow yours. You strengthen each other. That the Well paired someone so bountiful in mana as you with a Guardian seems right." She frowned. "In fact, if rumors are true, I've heard gossip that the other two Well-blessed matings happened to other Guardians."

Ada sat back and slumped. "Where I came from, there was no Well. There were no fae except in storybooks. We lived in tall skyscrapers, we had electricity and computers and cars and planes that flew in the sky. It was nothing like this. I feel like I've stepped back in time."

"No," Clara mused. "Perhaps you've stepped forward. What you describe sounds like the old world. What we call the Age of Man. The one destroyed by the greed and warring of humans."

Shock, then relief washed through the bond to Jasper.

Ada's brows puckered. "You have no idea how it feels to finally know. To be grounded. I mean, I had an inkling. I saw the remnants of my world at the cottage, and all this life bursting in nature was definitely not around when I left. At least I know now. Or some of it. I still need to figure out how I got here."

"Will you go back?" Jasper asked. *Can* she go back?

"Like you said, my time was dying."

She's from another time? How was that possible? The woman was full of surprises. Jasper didn't need his memories to see that. She could use mana. She'd bonded to him —been chosen for him. She'd somehow skipped thousands of years of history to be here. It also meant she didn't belong to the humans in the wasteland... at least, so far as she said.

Jasper looked at his hands. They were warrior's hands. If what Clara had said was true, and he was a Guardian, then he must have seen his fair share of battles.

Blood on his hands.

He blinked and shook his head. He could have sworn his hands were covered in blood when they were not.

Hot, crimson blood running down his clawed hands and furred forearms to drip on the sand below.

A crowd roared. Buzzing in his ears pierced his brain. He winced. So loud. So violent. They wanted more. Violence ripped through him. He stretched his arms wide and snarled his frustration.

They cheered more.

He would eat them. He would jump the barricade and tear into their flesh and feast on their entrails.

Pain and fire stabbed him in the lower back. He snarled through the iron mask, tried to snap and bite but the metal blocked his teeth. He whirled around, heaving lungfuls of air, ready to strike, but a small infidel shoved something electric into his side.

"Move," someone shouted. "Back to your pen. Show's over, champion."

More fire. More lightning.

A shameful whimper squeaked out of his lungs as he staggered out of the arena and toward a dark tunnel.

"That's it, nice and slow." The raspy voice—a male—held a note of sympathy.

He collapsed just inside the long, dark corridor.

580

Bloodthirsty thunder exploded around him. They wanted more blood. They called his name—Champion.

Small hands went to his neck, unclipped something, and released the iron mask. He cried out in agony as they pulled bolts from inside his flesh, but when the last of the metal was removed, he shifted forms, back to fae. The wolf was exhausted. It was ashamed. Why?

He lifted his lashes and craned his neck to peer over his shoulder.

"I wouldn't do that if I were you," came the small raspy voice.

But he had to see.

He glimpsed scattered fae bodies in a circle—a ring—as though they'd gone to their dying breath to protect something inside. Females, males, winged fae, horned fae. All with gores through their bodies, entrails stringing from their guts, and limbs torn off and thrown to the side.

"Shut the gates!" shouted the attendant. "For Crimson's sake."

But he got to his feet, one at a time. He used the stone wall to heave his body up in time to see the small childlike form at the center of corpses before the closing gates blocked the carnage from view.

"Nooo!" Jasper roared and lurched off his chair. He landed on the tiled floor. And then he vomited the water he'd drunk.

"Jasper!" Ada's chair scraped.

Footsteps came running.

A cold hand met his sweaty forehead, but he shoved her away.

"I did it," he murmured, eyes burning.

"Did what?" she asked. "Whatever it is, it's okay."

It wasn't. Flashes of what he saw hit his mind, and he retched. He couldn't breathe, couldn't hold himself upright.

"This is your doing," he growled at her.

"What?" she gasped.

"You tried to heal me. You"—he gagged—"you set memories loose."

Outside, a loud piercing howl rent the air, cutting down to his bones. His wolf sat up, alert. Another howl joined the first, and then another. It was their warning system.

Danger.

Coming in fast.

Clara jogged to the window. Screams filtered through the tinkling of wind chimes.

Clara snarled at Ada. "You lied! You brought them back."

"Who?" Jasper asked.

"The humans."

He dragged himself to the window. Panicked villagers ran through the street, rushing into homes and locking doors. Those who didn't hide brandished weapons. Some shifted to wolf form right there, tearing through clothes or stepping out of them.

"I need a weapon," he barked.

No one answered. When he turned around, Clara advanced on Ada.

"Stop." Jasper grabbed Clara as she passed him. "You don't touch her."

Clara's wild amber gaze snapped to his. "You said this was her doing."

"I was talking about my memories." He lifted Clara by the collar and narrowed his eyes. "Let me make this very clear. You hurt her, I kill you."

"Jasper," Ada admonished. "She's confused. I'm sure—"

"I'm not confused," Clara hurled back. "You turn up on the day of a second raid? It's not a coincidence."

Ada lifted her chin. "I also brought with me someone you seem to want here."

Clara's eyes slid back to Jasper.

"She may look like them, but she is not your enemy," he said.

"Why would they be back?" Clara gaped.

"What did they take last time?" Ada asked. "Maybe they want more."

Clara's eyes widened. "They came for the—" she turned to Jasper with a guilty look. "What?"

"Please don't tell the Order."

"Tell them what?"

"We should have handed over the metal, but..." A disgusted expression flitted over her face. "The Order are no friends of ours, and the King asked... well, more like demanded we stockpile. Since the Order has taxed us until we've got nothing left, we needed the coin. We can take care of our own protection. We can rid the woods of mana-warped creatures ourselves. We don't *need* the Order."

He tried to make sense of her scramble. "The humans want metal?"

"They use it to create weapons that work against fae. We thought if we simply sell the King what we scavenge from the river, then no one will know. At the very least, we thought he would protect us. But..."

"The humans found out."

She nodded.

"There must be more," he said. "Show me."

"You're going to tell the Prime, aren't you? We'll be punished."

He gritted his teeth. "I'm going to find a weapon I can use."

Clara stared at him for a long moment, then a scream and a loud crash jolted them. "Fine. Follow me."

Jasper followed her out of the room, but when Ada jogged after him, he forced her back. "Stay here. Stay safe."

"There must be something I can do," she said.

"Are you a fighter? A warrior in your time?"

She shook her head. "I guess I'm more of a carer."

"Then stay and help care for the wounded. There will be many."

CHAPTER
SIX

Ada was reeling. Hit after hit of information swam through her mind while she waited for Jasper and Clara to return.

She was from another time, long before everyone here. All her friends were probably dead. She now lived in a world where the residents had drastically changed. They could access magic—and she could, too. Except she looked like their enemy, who couldn't access magic.

And they were attacking.

The small piece of world she'd come to understand grew inexplicably tighter, like a band constricting around her chest.

Ada had magic, yet she couldn't help.

Filled to the brim with mana. That's what Clara had said.

Ada must be able to do something. When they'd arrived, Jasper had magicked a strong wind to push back a villager. He could shift into a wolf. Clara had conjured blue fire. There was so much Ada didn't understand about this world. Maybe if she tried something, she could help. She went for the door, but it opened suddenly.

Her heart leapt into her throat.

But it was only Jasper and Clara. He looked fierce with a long, metal sword dangling from his hand. Livid amber eyes scanned the room, landed on her, and frowned before darting back to Clara.

"Keep her safe," he ordered. "If I sense she is in danger, I will drop everything and come here. Do you understand?"

Clara's lips flattened, her eyes dipped to his Well-blessed arm marks, and she reluctantly tipped her chin. "As a fellow Darkfoot, you have my oath. I will keep her safe."

Jasper returned her curt nod and then left.

Ada watched through the window as he plowed through the street, barking for fae to get in their houses, and to leave the battle to him.

Just him?

Adrenaline surged, pushing blood through Ada's veins, causing her to break out into a cold sweat when a group of black clad humans encroached down the street. They wore fatigues like modern soldiers from her time. They looked so strangely familiar that a splice of doubt dipped in her stomach. Did she belong with *them*, or the wolf outside who seemed so very different from her? Then she saw the weapons the humans carried—swords, grenades, and—

"Gun," she gasped, pointing. "He's got a gun."

She slammed her palm against the window, trembling the glass. Jasper wore naught but breeches and blue glowing marks. A bullet would tear through his flesh like it was paper. A bullet would go straight through his heart.

Two fae came up behind Jasper with bone swords brandished in their fists. One had silver long hair, the other's was similar to Jasper's. These fae were ill prepared for modern warfare... or past warfare. Whatever it was, she had to warn them.

Heart galloping in her chest, she spun, intending to run out the front door, but ran straight into Clara. For a small woman, she was incredibly strong. She stopped Ada with a hand to her shoulders.

"I gave my oath to keep you safe," Clara growled, eyebrows down. "Don't make me break it."

"But you don't understand. They've got guns. I have to warn him."

"Your bond-mate is a Guardian," Clara returned, face hard. "He will endure, and he will protect. This is what he does. Now, help me prepare this room for wounded." She pointed at the long wooden table. "We can use that for operating. We need clean cloths and water. Come with me. And keep your ears hidden."

Ada gaped at her, then darted a glance back out the window.

Wind buffeted Jasper's dark hair, whipping the strands into his long-lashed, scowling eyes. Veins writhed down his hard muscles as each limb pumped full of tension. Tendons in his neck popped. Every ounce of his flesh said not to mess with him—except his face wore a wolfish grin and displayed a hint of sharp canines. Was he about to fight, or play a game?

Upon seeing his face, the humans hesitated.

Big mistake. Jasper threw his sword, point first, like a spear. It embedded in the middle of a man's head. Not waiting a second, he flicked out his hands. Sharp claws shot out from his fingertips. His guttural growl curdled Ada's stomach. She wanted to flee, just from the sound of it.

The humans balked, again.

Another mistake.

Then one with a sword lurched forward. Faster than her eye could see, Jasper ran forward, long legs gracefully eating up the street. He met the group, blocked the sword by taking the man's wrist. Ada should have been watching his other hand. It buried deep within the soldier's chest. When he pulled out, he dropped something sloppy and red on the floor.

Oh God. Ada covered her mouth and looked away. It was his heart.

Clara took her shoulder and yanked her away from the window.

"Snap out of it. I need your help."

The sounds of fighting filtered in—wet thuds, grunts, gurgles, cries—Ada wanted to look, to check on Jasper, but felt his fury vibrating down their bond like a plucked string. *He's fine. He's fine.* He's a mother-fucking, brutal warrior. Maybe *she* wasn't fine.

That wet slop as the heart landed on the ground.

She shuddered.

Jeez. She forced her attention to the back of Clara's pixie haircut and followed her into another part of the building to a kitchen and food storeroom.

Clara pointed to a pile of folded towels. "Take those."

Ada grabbed the towels, found sharp knives, and took them back into the hall. Back and forth she and Clara went, gathering supplies and bowls of water, ignoring the shouts and clashes from outside with determination. She refused to look, instead, focusing on the feeling in her arm—the sensation of energy, and the blind rage from Jasper. If he was angry, he was alive.

When the fight moved on from the front of their building, Clara went to the door and waved down a tall gray-haired fae carrying one of their wounded—a youth that couldn't have been more than fifteen years of age.

"In here!" Clara shouted.

They burst through the front and were spirited into the hall.

"Put Lake on the table, Percival," Clara ordered.

Percival put the youth down with a wince. A long, thin metal rod stuck out from the patient's stomach. His face had gone green.

"I thought maybe I could pull it out, but..." Percival's eyes watered. "It's metal. I don't know if I should. Don't worry, son. We'll get you right." To Clara, "He just wanted to help."

"I know." Clara put her hand on Percival's shoulder. "Lake needs to shift to heal. We will have to remove it. Can you hold him down?"

"Wait!" Ada blurted. "You can't. What if its hit an artery, or pierced a vital organ? What if he bleeds out before he can shift?"

Clara looked at Ada as though she'd gone mad. "Shifting is how we heal."

"Doesn't metal block the flow of mana? I'm sure Jasper mentioned that to me. What if we pull it out and metal filings are stuck in there? Can he still shift?"

Silence stretched. It appeared as though no one knew the answer to that question.

"You healed Reed," Clara noted. "You said you also removed parts of his curse."

"I did, but... did he tell you that when you were gone? I don't know *how* I did it."

"Well, we're going to find out." Clara took Ada's hand and put it on Lake's chest. He winced. "Tell me what you feel."

Ada knew enough about healing animals and first aid that she understood never to let the patient see her worry, or her incompetence. If the patient thought Ada didn't know what she was doing, then panic would set in. They could go into shock. That was the last thing anyone needed. As her friend Laurel used to always say, fake it until you make it. She forced her breathing to calm and hoped to high hell that the boy didn't see the perspiration dotting her upper lip.

"Lake, is it?"

Shaggy gray hair dipped onto his forehead as he nodded.

"We're going to get this out of you, don't worry. I have a unique gift. Apparently I'm overflowing with *mana*." She held up her arm so he could see the blue glowing marks. "See this?"

He nodded.

"They said it means the Well has blessed me. It means I'm going to do everything I can to help you live. Okay? Will you let me try?"

A glimmer of awe entered his eyes as he took in her arm before nodding.

"Okay, let's see what I can do. While I'm doing that, why don't you see if you can count the lines on my markings." Half doubting, half hoping, Ada placed her palm on Lake's chest, careful not to disturb the foot-long rod coming out of his side. He flinched, but he zeroed in on her arm. Whether or not he was counting, she couldn't tell, but it seemed her distraction worked. She didn't want him looking at the wound.

She shifted her hands an inch to see if she could feel anything but felt ridiculous. His flesh was hot. That's all she felt. Nothing happened.

Ada flared her lashes at Clara. *What now?*

"What did you do when you helped Reed?"

She cast her mind back. When he was poisoned, she did what she always did. Sucked it out. But even as the thoughts flittered in her mind, she knew in her heart it went much deeper than snake bite first aid. Jasper's wounds had turned black and purple. The venom had worked into his bloodstream. The sucking should have come too late. Part of her knew it.

So what did she do that was different?

"I imagined it happening," she murmured. "I envisioned the poison coming out of his body."

She'd done the same thing again when peeling the curse marks off.

"Connecting with your mana comes on an intrinsic level. There are six elemental affinities fae can have with the well. Earth, air, water, fire, chaos and spirit. Healing is a mixture of everything. Place both hands on him. Close your eyes. Feel the water flow through his veins. Feel the energy of his spirit. The fire of his life force. Try to listen to his mana."

Sure. Easy peasy. It made perfect sense.

Her second palm joined the first. Ada's lashes lowered, and she slowed her breathing. She blocked the sounds of battle. She ignored the chimes tinkling. She focused on the beating of her heart, of Lake's heart beneath her touch. His breathing. The clamminess of his skin. She pushed her awareness into her hands, and then she went lower.

She trusted her intuition.

Clara's voice murmured softly, "Just do what you did with Reed. What comes naturally? What needs to be done?"

The heat of Lake's body grew hotter. It scorched her palms as her awareness spread outward, to the side, up, down, and then back again. It took her a moment, but she realized this confined heat map was his body. Where it went was his life force. Elation lifted her spirits, and she lost focus for a moment, shook her head and frowned in concentration.

"I feel the limits of his body," she said without opening her eyes.

"Good. What else?"

Ada continued to search the heated area with her mind's eye. Her awareness shifted with sluggish strokes at first, but the more she flexed the muscle, the easier it became. She swam around, getting to know the sensation, until she came to a cold spot where the heat wouldn't flow.

"There's a cold spot," she whispered with a shiver. "A dark area I can't see."

"That's the metal rod," Clara said. "Look closer. Are there any other cold spots?"

Ada searched, but came up with nothing. "I don't think so."

"Good."

The cold spot suddenly burned hot. Lake screamed in pain. Ada's lashes flipped open, and she jolted back just as Lake jackknifed up, his hand to his now rod-free, wounded side. Blood flowed between his fingers and he glared at Clara with a mix of accusation and relief.

"Shift, my boy," Clara barked, the bloody rod dangling in her hand, dripping onto the floor.

Air shimmered around Lake, hair sprouted on his jaw, on the back of his hands, and his teeth elongated. He gave a long, strangled whimper. Sweat plastered his forehead, but he dropped back to the table, still in fae form, panting hard.

"I can't," he whined, thrashing his head. "I can't."

Clara's face paled. "There must still be metal in him. I thought you said there was only one cold spot."

"There was!" Ada flattened her lips, biting back a retort that she'd been right. "I didn't know you were going to just yank it out. Some must have broken off!"

She took the rod and inspected it. The metal was rusted.

"Search again," Clara said. "Find the shard."

Shit.

Ada put her palm on Lake's chest, but Clara guided her hand down to the wound. He squirmed, bottom lip and hand trembling as he made way for Ada by letting go of his wound.

"It's okay, son," Percival said, taking Lake's bloody hand.

Blood oozed from the hole. Ada slammed her palm over it. Hot, wet mess flowed onto her hand. She slammed her eyes shut and concentrated.

Feel the cold spot.

Heat. Heat, everywhere.

Vaguely she heard Clara direct Percival out of the room with orders to send the wounded here. He was reluctant to go, but when Ada found the cold spot, she knew why he'd been sent away. No father should see his son screaming in agony. And that was going to happen next.

"I found it," she said grimly to Clara, swallowed, and glanced at the puncture wound. "It seems to be in one piece."

"Do it," Clara said. She gave Lake the rod to bite down on and then took his hand. "She's going to dig it out, love. Okay?"

He nodded, eyes wild and darting.

"Good boy. Brave boy."

Clara nodded at Ada. She dug her finger into the wound and used the lack of heat she sensed as a guide. The boy screamed through the bit. His back arched, and both Ada and Clara held him down.

They should have antiseptic. They should have *anesthetic*. But this was a species like no other. They healed when they shifted. Ada had to trust Clara knew what she was talking about. Ada gritted her teeth and dug around his wound with her finger until she found it. A small sharp prick. It felt *wrong*. Never had she simply touched an inanimate object and felt something, but she wanted to throw the metal splinter into the darkest depths of the ocean and forget about it. Better yet, launch it into space.

Like the rod, her awareness wouldn't extend through the splinter. It was simply an empty void of nothing. Was this the Well's aversion to metal she sensed? Was this why metals and plastics were forbidden? She gritted her teeth and inserted her second finger to clamp onto the splinter, then pulled it out.

"Got it," she gasped.

The boy spat out the rod, and then shifted so fast that Ada had trouble seeing anything but a blur of air and fur until a gray wolf with brown feet lay on the table, panting heavily, eyes bright.

Clara made short work of checking the fur around the wolf's abdomen and then nodded. "Skin is closed. You'll be fine, lad. Scarred, but you'll live. Go find somewhere to lie low until your mana is replenished."

The wolf gave a soft whine of annoyance, but heaved himself to his paws, and hopped down from the table. He snuffled Ada's leg briefly before trotting out the door.

Ada turned to Clara. "He's okay?"

She nodded grimly. "He's lucky he had enough mana to shift. Most of us can only do so once or twice a day. Unless, of course, you're a Guardian." Her eyes skated outside. "Some won't be so lucky."

Ada looked at her hands, still tingling with heat and sticky with blood. This time, the awareness she sensed felt alive inside her own body. As though it were a buzzing, living thing. This was her power, her gift. Her eyes shifted back to Clara.

"Can you teach me more?" she asked.

"We'll soon find out." Clara lifted her chin toward the door where Percival brought another fae limping in, blood dripping from a gouge in his thigh.

Behind them, two more wounded limped, using each other as a crutch. One was the fae who'd accosted them on arrival. His wide-brimmed hat no longer on top of his head but carrying something at his stomach. As they drew closer, she noticed dark rivulets of blood streaking from it. When Ada looked into it, her stomach dipped.

His intestines.

"How are you still alive?" she gasped. Alive *and* walking, let alone helping an injured fae walk.

His glazed eyes met hers and seemed to see right through her.

Clara took one look at him and then shook her head. "Why haven't you shifted?"

"Used the last of my mana to portal us all here from the docks."

"Well-damn, you're a tough wolf." Clara swallowed, then gave Ada an almost imperceptible shake of the head. *He's not going to make it.*

He must have known because he handed his companion to Clara and stepped aside. So they were just going to leave him?

Clara pointed at the first two who'd arrived and said to Ada, "You take them."

Hardly able to breathe, she forced herself to triage the first who'd arrived with Percival. He had a gash down his calf, and one over his eye. His arm hung limply at the side.

"In there," she said and pointed into the hall. "Find somewhere to sit. You're not on death's door yet. I'll be with you in a moment."

Then she went to the man with his guts in his hat. His face had turned a paler shade of green and he leaned heavily on the wall, barely holding onto his package.

"What's your name?" she asked.

From the way he'd accosted them upon arrival, she thought he might clam up. But he either didn't recognize her or didn't care. "Moon."

"Alright, Moon. Can you come with me to the table inside the hall?"

There was no way she'd be able to carry him. She placed her hand on the hat's cap, swallowed when she felt the contents through the fabric, and whispered, "I've got you. It's okay. Let's do this together."

"Ada," Clara warned as she helped her patient.

But Ada ignored her. She knew in her soul she could help this fae. She knew her gift went beyond finding cold spots and draining poison. It had to. Even if it didn't, she would not let him die without trying. Never in her life had she abandoned a wounded animal, no matter how fierce or stubborn, and she wasn't about to start now.

"Let's go, Moon," she said and fit herself under his big arm.

He fell heavily onto her shoulder. She staggered, gained her footing, and together they shuffled into the hall. With effort, they got him onto the table. He laid back and met her eyes.

"I'm the only one in town who can create a portal," he croaked.

She wasn't sure what that meant, probably exactly what it sounded like, but nodded. "You did good. They're safe."

He nodded. His lashes drooped.

"Stay with me, Moon. Your job's not done."

But his hands fell from the hat. She caught it before everything spilled. Time was running out.

"Moon?"

No response. Ada looked at the long abdomen gash with clinical distance. She wasn't a surgeon, not even a doctor or veterinarian, but she had *something.* It was the same thing that kept her alive all those years ago when her mother left her for days on end. It was the same thing that put her in Harold's path. The same thing that brought her here to this time, and it was the same thing that gave her this ability.

Call it fate. Call it the Well. Whatever it was, she wouldn't run from it.

This time, when she focused inward, the buzzing energy of her gift rose to her call and danced within her, as though it had been waiting. She knew a little about anatomy from what she'd studied during high school, and from dissecting frogs and rats. Even what she'd learned while rehabilitating wild animals and on the flip side, hunting to keep herself fed and alive. Occasionally, she had to skin her hunt herself.

Holding her breath, she peeled back the jagged flesh of the wound and checked around, both with her eyes and her senses. No cold spots. No metal blocking what she was hoping to do next. Exhaling, then inhaling, she held her breath and tried not to think about the punctured intestinal smell that she'd just inhaled. She started putting entrails back into his body, slowly and surely. With every yard she put in, she tested it with her awareness, searching for... she wasn't sure. Just anything not right. When the heat of her gift fluctuated, she focused intently. She envisioned his wounds healing, just how she had with Jasper's wounds back at the cottage. *Get better. Heal. Knit together.* Fire in her touch burned hotter, brighter, with more power. For a moment, she was afraid she'd either burn him alive, or herself. But she kept her mind focused on willing him to become what he was before the injury struck—whole.

When the last of her heat waned, she opened her eyes and inspected the flesh beneath her hands. She swiped her thumb over the red-orange sticky mess and found clean, puckered scars beneath. Ada dropped her ear to the fae's chest, listened, and heard his heartbeat. A smile tipped her lips. She did it. She hoped.

Lifting her head, she found not only Moon's eyes on her, but everyone else's in the room.

Clara finished wrapping the leg of the fae with white hair, and came over with wide, almost fearful eyes.

"You did what the shift does," she said to Ada.

"I healed him."

"Oh, you did more than that, love." She peeked at the scarred stomach. "He was on death's door."

Moon, still staring at Ada, rasped. "You're human."

A coldness entered the room. It was as though the very air froze. Ada's fingers fluttered to her ears and found her hair had been subconsciously tucked sometime while she'd worked.

"We don't know what she is," Clara clipped, eyes narrowing. "Because a human can't do what she just did. A human can't be in a Well-blessed union with a Guardian. But she is. For now, we carry on. She is on our side."

The tension relaxed. A word from their matriarch was all they needed.

Ada washed her hands in a bowl and rushed to the one she'd told to find a seat and began to triage. He said he had no reserve mana left to shift. She was about to treat the wound with her gift, but Clara cautioned against using all of her mana for non-life threatening wounds. She felt fine, not empty, if that was such a thing, but could see the logic in Clara's warning, so treated the wound the old school way—with water, stitches, and a cloth. Behind her, Moon rolled to his side and spoke to Clara.

"They came from the dock," he rumbled. "But not by boat."

"How is that possible? Crystal City is weeks away by foot."

"I fear they portaled in."

"But that's impossible. They carried metal weapons. And they're here to collect our hidden stash. Metal won't travel through a portal. Not unless a Guardian held it or created the portal."

Neither said anything beyond that. More wounded came in and Ada became lost in treating them for the next few hours. From one fae to another, she attended the injured. By the time the room became crowded with moaning and groaning shifters, her arms had turned to lead and her legs moved like rocks.

A loud roar filled the air, somewhere outside. The building shook, wind chimes fretted as though blasted with wind, and agony sliced down the bond from Jasper.

Ada's head snapped up.

"He's been hit," she said, eyes blurring.

Fireworks went off, but that was impossible. Who would shoot fireworks? Not fireworks. Gunfire.

A draining sensation pulled through her arm. Energy tugged from her body as though she'd been hit with a tranquilizer dart that kept drugging. She dropped to her knees, gasping and holding onto the chair of the patient she'd been treating.

"What's happening?" she gasped, chest heaving.

The patient shouted. Clara jogged over, blood smeared on her face, wariness on her expression.

"Ada?" she said, and bent low to check. "What's the matter?"

"My arm," she held up the blue marked arm, but couldn't move. *Too heavy.* "It's like I feel my life draining through there."

"He's borrowing your mana."

"What?" she croaked. But then she realized the truth in those words. "Jasper's injured. I felt his pain."

Ada used Clara to push to her feet. She staggered to the door. "I have to go to him."

"You can't!" Clara urged. "I gave an oath you'd be safe."

"I'll go," Moon offered.

He'd recovered since she'd mended his stomach. While still a little green in the face, he'd been walking around the room, helping as best he could.

Before Ada could protest, or even take another step, Moon left.

"Sit down," Clara ordered. "Have a drink."

She guided Ada to the side where her aching body collapsed on a velvet covered dining chair. Her arms barely lifted to take hold of the terracotta cup Clara handed her. When the water hit her lips, she found her throat parched and guzzled it down.

"I don't understand how your bond works," Clara said. "It's been a long time since we've seen a Well-blessed union—perhaps hundreds of years—so I can't tell you why this is happening. But I can tell you that there are rumors of other Guardians bonded like you. The wolves are whispering from pack to pack. When you're finished in this town, I suggest you find them. They will teach you more about your bond."

The front door burst open. Moon and another large fae—the same one who'd pushed her when they'd arrived—carried a big, heavy, bullet riddled fae between them, his dark head hanging low.

Ada's heart clenched. *Jasper.*

CHAPTER
SEVEN

Jasper dreamed of blood and fire. Crimson on his hands, in his mouth, and on his skin. Fire in his veins, arrowing toward his heart, burrowing closer with only one end in sight—and he welcomed it. He deserved it.

He was not brave. He was not kind. He was not worthy.

He'd taken so many lives... and the worst part was, he'd liked it. Or at least, his wolf had. Who could tell the difference these days? Flashes of the carnage at the Ring swam before his eyes, taunting him with his cowardice. The crowd cheering for it. All he'd needed to do was give in and let his opponents take his life instead of the other way around. His suffering would have been over. But on the day his mother had died, he'd promised to live.

So, while in the Ring, he'd submitted control of his body to his wolf—that primordial part of him with the hunger for blood—every Well-damn time.

Tiny fingers curled and covered in blood.

"No!" he bellowed.

Tiny fingers touching his chest.

"Get off!" He shoved.

Chains held him back. He whipped his head to the side—not chains, a big hand. To the other side—a large hand, one of the guards. He *bellowed*. Another on his abdomen, moving with the rise and fall of his heaving breath, then sliding over to a bloody wound.

Tiny fingers tested the tiny wounds in his chest.

Tears burned his eyes, and he choked.

"*No!*" He thrashed his head, took gulping breaths until he had the power to shout. "*Leave it in.* I want the suffering to end."

"Jasper."

Her voice. His angel calling through the water.

"It's okay, Jasper."

"No," he grunted. "Leave it in."

The icy burn in his body arrowing toward his heart. He knew what it was. He'd felt it so many times. Usually it pierced into either side of his neck, halting his transformation, ensuring when he killed it wasn't all wolf, but part him, part the fae who was once worthy, who was once kind and fun and brave.

"I deserve it," he moaned through the agony swamping his senses, slicing his veins open as the metal reached for his heart. "Just leave it in. Let it take me."

Finally.

He dropped his head back. It clunked on something hard.

"I'm getting it out."

She's stubborn, his wicked angel.

Scorching pain in his pectoral, under his rib. She followed the flight of the bullet deep inside him. He shouted, knocked her tiny fingers away and roared his fury with great trembling fangs and dripping saliva.

Large brown eyes glistened. Blond hair. Perfect plump lips opened into the shape of an O.

"Leave me," he begged.

His limbs felt heavy. His head lolled to the side. Fog curled into his mind and, he thought, at least he'd done something right before he died. He'd put his clawed fist through every single raiding human he could find until their blood had painted the street. They would never get the metal to make more killing pellets like the ones lodged in his chest.

He would never give them an advantage over fae land. He would never let them take control of the Well. It was his job. His duty. And he'd at least done some of it. At least he remembered that.

"Jasper, look at me." Cool fingers touched his stubbled jaw.

He squeezed his eyes shut.

Then... soft pressure at his lips. Movement. Kissing. She tasted like sugar and sin, like everything his body wanted, but his soul didn't deserve. She kept pressing her lips to his, and he felt... he felt—compassion, kindness and hidden yearning scorch down their bond. It struck him deeply. It stoked the fire inside until he felt the echo of her desire become a raging furnace of want. He opened to her kiss, welcomed her with a groan full of longing and need. His tongue delved inside her mouth, tasting her life-giving flavor that frenzied every cell of his body. She pulled back, and he chased her, nipping the air between them. Beautiful. She tasted like his. Like... mana-berries and cider and everything nice.

More.

Straining to reach her, he tried to capture her lips again, but almost fell from the table he lay on. Pain stabbed his middle as he settled into a sitting position.

Her small, teasing smile. "If I'd had known that's all it took to make you fall in line, I would have kissed you a while ago."

He growled in warning.

"You want it so bad, let me get the bullets out so you can heal. Then you can have another kiss."

He licked parched lips, bit back his hunger, glanced down at the bloody mess on his torso, and saw the room for the first time. It was filled with injured fae, two of which held him down by the shoulders, and Ada... his beautiful... what was she? His mate? A distraction? A reprieve until he finally caught the oblivion he didn't deserve?

If his memories were true, then he'd committed the most heinous atrocities known to Elphyne. He'd brutalized and killed for entertainment in the gladiator pit that served as a corporal punishment in Cornucopia, the border town between the Seelie and Unseelie kingdoms.

"Jasper." She patted his chest.

He met her gaze and could feel hope trickling down their connection. She wanted to help him, to keep him alive. He didn't have the heart to disappoint her.

He may as well add cowardice to his list of failures because, when his gaze dropped to her lips, all he wanted in that moment was another taste of her sugar. The idea consumed him.

Damn, he was so weak.

Swallowing hard, he set himself down on the table and looked hard at the ceiling. He clutched the table's edge with each hand and readied himself, then nodded. Bone deep agony filled his body as she hunted the cold, killing metal, but he didn't scream, didn't cry out. This was his penance, or the beginning of it. Maybe this never-ending wretched life of shame and regret was his worth.

The notion took root in his heart, and when she stripped the last metal pellet from his body, he knew it was true. Happiness was not reserved for someone broken like him.

Feeling the connection to the Well spring to life in his blood, he siphoned Ada's mana down their bond and shifted into wolf form. A flash of guilt stabbed him at taking something she hadn't offered, at seeing her eyes flutter because he was draining her, but he was beyond shame now. What was one more act of cowardice?

The wolf took over—just like it had always managed the preservation of his life— and Jasper's consciousness faded. He lay on his side, panting heavily as his body repaired, and when tiny fingers stroked his face and scratched behind his ear, he turned away with a small whine. He retreated into the locked cage of his mind, knowing it didn't matter which part of him reigned. Whether it was the primal instincts of his wolf, or his fae logic, it was all him. There was no escaping what he'd done.

JASPER AWOKE to the sound of a crackling fire. Other strange sounds filtered in—the slow tinkling of wind chimes, the soft regular breathing of another, and the musky scent of female. The heat of a body pressed close. His lashes lifted to find a dim, softly furnished room flickering from firelight. Stone walls plastered with mosaics depicting scenes of black wolves chasing dark-haired maidens, catching them. He'd seen those images before, on the outside of the great hall… and… perhaps somewhere in his memory.

His gaze swept to the sleeping blond-haired angel nestled within the curve of his body—his furred body. He was in wolf form. The awareness settled on him with the accompanying thought that she would only sleep with him in this form, so he should stay.

Resting his head back down, he pushed his awareness around his body. No longer did he feel the sting of injury, and no longer did he feel the emptiness of having spent his mana stores. Enough time must have passed that he'd been refilled by the Cosmic Well. Usually it took the passing of the moon to soak up mana from the earth. Finding a source of power could replenish him within minutes. Maybe he'd discovered a source and had soaked in it. Or maybe it was her.

How did he know that?

His memories were seeping back into him, that's how, and he wasn't sure he wanted them to.

His lids drooped again as he languished in the comfort of his position. She might wake soon. She might try to peel more of the curse away.

But she couldn't see it through the fur covering his body.

So he stayed wolf.

And he dreamed.

"Why is he after us, Mama?" he asked and plopped another picked berry into her wicker basket as they strode from mana-berry bush to blackcurrant.

Her elegant fingers paused over an overripe berry, then she twisted it on the stem and added it to their growing collection.

"Because I did something I wasn't allowed to do," she replied.

"What?" he asked, this time, plopping the berry into his mouth, letting the tart juices explode on his tastebuds. He licked his lips. "Mmm."

Again, she held her tongue, but he wanted to know.

"Mama? Why?"

She placed her basket on the floor and crouched low to touch his cheek. She smiled warmly.

"Because, my love, I chose you over him. There's not a day that goes by that I'm not thankful for that decision. You are going to make many people very happy. You will save lives."

His skin suddenly felt tight, his body too big. "Me?"

"Yes, my love. You."

"How do you know?"

"Because the Well showed me."

"I don't want to make everyone happy, Mama. Just you."

He lifted his chin proudly and went to another bush to snap a berry off, but before it could enter his gaping mouth, she pushed it away.

"No!" she cried. "Not those berries."

Tears burned his eyes at the shock. What had he done? His bottom lip trembled as she took his hands in hers.

"I'm sorry, my love, but you must never eat those berries. They addle the mind."

"Sun said they were fun. Why is that so bad?"

"Sun's head is full of wool."

"But you said fun is good."

She sighed. "Yes, but it's a fine line between fun and wasting your life pretending it doesn't exist. Just... don't waste for too long."

CHAPTER

EIGHT

"Not a nasty cut," Ada said, inspecting Primrose's finger wound.

Like the last two patients Ada had received today, she had the sense Primrose was there to inspect Ada, not the other way around. Two twitching, pointed, and lightly furred ears poked out from beneath long wavy blond hair tied at Primrose's nape. White baker's flour dusted her form fitting dress. She appeared in her late twenties but could be as old as Clara—somewhere in the hundreds of years. Somehow, that unsettled Ada more than knowing the female shifter had come to snoop.

"I honestly don't know how I did it. It's so silly of me," Primrose said.

Sure you don't.

It had been two days since the raid, and while most injured fae had been treated, a trickle of snoops kept coming in. Ada couldn't blame them. She looked like the enemy, yet she had a gift reserved for the fae. But if they were snooping, they were curious, not angry. She could deal with that.

Ada smiled gently. "Don't worry. Accidents happen to the best of us."

"I was so busy with preparations for Lupercalia that I wasn't watching what I was doing. I'm the official baker, you know."

"Congratulations." Ada still wasn't clear about the festival, but knew the village had been preparing for weeks, and still had a few days to go before the big event.

Ada focused her awareness on the shallow finger cut, feeling it out with her sixth sense, seeing if she could coax the broken skin back together. Clara had kept up her tuition over the past few days and was keen to keep teaching all she knew about healing, which wasn't much, but it was better than nothing. Apparently Fenrysfield had no official healer. Since most of them shifted, one wasn't really needed.

"It looks pretty shallow to me. Is there a reason you're not shifting to heal it?" *Or putting up with it?*

Primrose's posture stiffened. Tension sliced through the air.

In the background, Clara's actions grew inexplicably louder as she cleaned and restocked the room. She must have heard Ada's question because she came over carrying her bowl of fresh water.

"You must be patient with Ada, Prim. She doesn't quite understand the intricacies of fae manners." To Ada, she added, "Prim is Lesser Fae, meaning she doesn't hold enough mana to shift or to harness. She was just born like that. There's nothing she can do about it, but it doesn't do to talk about it in front of her face. There are many other Lesser Fae in all races. If a fae can't shift or cast, then it's not up to us to pry." Clara looked back at Primrose's finger. "Ensure you keep going until every bit of flesh knits together. You've got time."

Ada bit back words about Clara doing exactly what she'd just told Ada not to do— talk about the Lesser Fae in front of her face.

But there was so much to learn. If no one talked about it, Ada would continue to be ignorant, and in the days since waking in this time, she'd accepted her new reality. She needed to blend in.

Ada's brain hurt. There were many new cultural idiosyncrasies she wasn't sure she'd ever learn. And this was just a shifter village. Apparently, there were different customs within different fae races all around Elphyne.

They ranged from horned and antlered fae, to pixies with dragonfly wings, to elves, vampires, and more. The list was never-ending.

Clara swapped Ada's dirty bowl with the clean one and then continued around the room, replenishing stock, as if she hadn't just dropped the most awkward bomb in the room, and then headed toward the exit.

Prim's pointed ears flattened as Clara passed. *Interesting.* Ada was fast learning that a particular pattern of ear behavior had either something to do with aggression or submission. It was much like the natural behavior of the wolves they shifted into.

Clara stopped at the door before leaving and turned to Ada. "We must be patient with you, but also remember to be patient with us too. Change takes time. For both sides."

Ada watched the empty space Clara left for a long moment, wondering if she'd said something to make Clara think Ada was impatient. But perhaps it was just a friendly warning.

"This might feel a bit warm," Ada said as she went back to the wound.

"Can you fix me?" Prim blurted. "I mean, give me the ability to shift?"

So that was why she came.

"I don't think so," Ada said slowly, thinking about it. "As far as I know, it's beyond the scope of my gift. But I'm only just learning. Clara said I should head toward the, um, Order of the Well, or one of the Elven Courts to train from the best. I don't really know what that means yet, but it's a start. Who knows what my gift could do after I receive more training."

Prim sighed. "That's okay. I thought it was worth a shot to ask. I didn't really want to ask around Clara. I know the Well is the only thing that can grant the capacity to hold mana within, and since I'm not as brave as your mate, I'll never enter the ceremonial lake. I'll just have to keep making do without it."

Ada frowned. "Did he not have mana before entering the lake? Or is that rude of me to ask too?"

"Unlike some others around here, I'm not as concerned with stuffy manners and tradition. I don't mind if you ask me. How else are you supposed to learn? You know, Reed would have been the new alpha if it wasn't for... well, it's best I don't talk about that part. That's only gossiping." Prim's eyes turned distant and dreamy, and Ada felt a brief twinge of something she couldn't decipher as Prim explained. "He's the son of the King, so he had a good amount of mana to start. We used to play together as children. He always had a bigger capacity for holding mana, but then he joined the Guardians. And now—" Her eyes snagged on Ada's Well-blessed markings. "Now I suppose he has you. I know my wound isn't big, but I wanted an excuse to meet you. If there's anything you want to know about, well, anything, I hope you ask me." She straightened. "Maybe come down to the bakery where we can talk more freely. I can show you around."

Ada finished healing the cut and stood back. Maybe Prim wasn't so uptight as she'd initially thought, and Ada needed a friend. Clara was the alpha and not exactly easy to approach. Primrose's big eyes blinked with such earnest regard that Ada couldn't help smiling.

"Sure, I'd like that. It's definitely hard being someone who looks like the enemy around here."

"I know what it feels like to be the outsider, don't worry, and I've lived here all my life." Her gaze dipped to Ada's neck, then back up to meet her eyes. "While we're being honest, if you don't mind me asking, why is it that your mate hasn't marked you?"

"Marked me?"

"Yes, well, shifters mark their mates. On the neck." She pointed to Ada's bare neck. "With their teeth."

Ada's hand fluttered to her neck. "Why would they do that?"

"It's a sign of possession. Don't humans do that?"

"No." Ada's brows lifted, derisively. "No, we don't maim each other to prove ownership."

Prim's nose crinkled. "Oh, I didn't say he owned you. Just that... well, yes, I suppose it is like ownership. But he also belongs to you. His scent and mark on you proves to all the other potential mates that you're both taken."

Ada snorted, about to make some female empowerment speech, but then realized the marking could be construed as something similar to an engagement or wedding ring. So this was some kind of arranged marriage. The very idea of having that choice taken away from her made her squirm.

"Jasper and I aren't in that kind of relationship," she explained with a tight smile.

"Oh."

Prim opened her mouth to say more, but movement at the door nabbed both their attentions. A tall shifter walked in. Messy brown hair brushed his collar. A black tattoo curled up his neck on one side. Just the hint of the hilt from his bone sword poked over a brown, leather clad shoulder. Ada remembered him as the other shifter who'd brought Jasper in to get treated during the raid.

"Sun," Prim said as she got to her feet and raised her brows, unimpressed. "I'm not done with the human. Your turn is coming."

The human?

Sun smirked and leaned his lithe body against the doorjamb. "I'll just wait here then, shall I?"

Prim made a frustrated sound and then rolled her eyes. "I suppose I am done here, then. The test cakes need to come out of the oven." She touched Ada's arm and her tone turned syrupy sweet. "Don't forget to come down to the bakery."

She left with a suspicious side-eye turned Sun's way, and an extra sway in her step. Ada got the impression those two enjoyed picking at each other's threads to see who would unravel first. There was a history there. Maybe they'd dated once. Sun pushed off the door and strode into the room. He glanced about, searching for someone, and then sat on the chair Prim had vacated.

Ada washed her hands in the bowl. "You're the last one waiting, right?"

He shrugged.

There was something so familiar about him, more so than the fact Ada had already met him a few nights ago.

"What can I help you with?" she asked, giving him a once over in case he was injured.

"I'm here because my mother is too stubborn to ask you something."

"Okay." She stood back. "Who's your mother?"

He arched his brow as if Ada should know. "Clara."

"Oh." Now it was making sense why he was so familiar. That dark hair. That devil-may-care expression. Clara was Jasper's aunt, which made Sun Jasper's cousin. And Moon. "My goodness. Moon is also Clara's son?"

Ada's mind went back to how Clara had been prepared to accept her son's initial prognosis, but Ada had saved his life.

"That's why she doesn't want to ask you this. She feels as though she's already in debt to you, and all you've asked for is a room and some training in return for the lives you saved."

"I don't want anything in return. Saving lives shouldn't come at a price."

Sun rubbed his jaw and scrutinized Ada. All fae seemed to want something in return for a good deed. Keeping track was getting tiresome, but maybe Ada could see how the cultural expectation had formed. In a ruthless post-apocalyptic world, when the economy had shut down, favors could be currency.

"So," Ada said. "She's sent you because if you ask me for the favor, then it's you who will owe me the debt? If there even is one."

He smiled, slow and pleased. "Now you're catching on."

"Okay. So what is it?"

"Lupercalia is in a few nights' time. We want you and Reed be our guests of honor."

"That's it?" she asked. "No kidney? No blood transfusion?"

When Sun stared at her blankly, she elaborated. "I was expecting some sort of mammoth quest."

"Lupercalia is a time-honored tradition that we haven't been able to follow until a recent change in the law a few weeks ago. It's been a long time since our crops were plentiful. We've been plagued with mana-warped monsters, both in the river and in the woods surrounding our village. All our coin has been taxed by the Order for the culling of these monsters. And as you've seen firsthand, we're being targeted for raids, and the High King has failed to come to our aid. Our luck is running out. During Lupercalia, we make tribute to the Well and pray for our seed to be blessed for the coming harvest. Clara believes since you're Well-blessed, and your timely arrival saved so many lives, that the Well would look favorably on us this year if you and Reed honor us as Luperci."

After that speech, how could she say no?

"Sure. Well, I can't really speak for Jasper—I mean, Reed. But I can ask him."

"We would have a better outcome if the question came from you."

"Is there something else you're not telling me?"

"One of the last traditional Lupercalia festivals was when the King set his sights on Reed's mother. She had Reed after that and hid it from the King. We used to have a Seer in the village who'd prophesied one of the King's offspring would take over his throne and be the end of him. When Mithras found out about Reed, he came for them. Reed escaped. His mother didn't." He took a deep inhale, then let the air out slowly. "Clara pretends the reason there's bad blood between us and Reed is because he left to join the Guardians. But we all know it's because she feels guilty she couldn't keep him safe. For an alpha to admit that would be akin to acknowledging a debt."

"And Fae hate to be in debt."

"Exactly."

"So, if he participates at Lupercalia, it's a bridge mended. For both sides."

"An answer tonight would be great." Sun stood and gave Ada's shoulder a lingering touch. "And if my cousin doesn't grow some balls and show his face soon, I'll be happy to take his place as one of the Luperci with you."

He shot her a smirk, and then sauntered away, leaving her confused.

"Um." Ada lifted her finger to stop him, but he'd already gone. "What's a Luperci?"

Somehow, she had the sense she would not like it. Her mind already traveled back to that cult that worshiped linen clothing.

Ugh. Come on, Ada. Get your head in the game.

She guessed she would find out on the night, or maybe Prim would tell her. The Luperci duties couldn't be too hard to fulfill, and they wouldn't put one of their own in danger. Jasper was a Darkfoot. He grew up in this town. If they wanted them as special guests, then it must be a good thing.

Maybe Jasper's memories had returned enough for him to know. With that thought, Ada packed up as best she could, and after waiting for Clara, who never showed, she decided she would head back to the inn. Night was falling and the tavern's meat stew called to her. It tasted so much like regular beef, and not wolpertinger meat, that she felt like it was a slice of home. A small smile played on her lips when she thought of what Laurel would say if Ada ordered the meal at a restaurant.

"Pretty Kitty, again? Really? You eat cow every time we get take out."

And then Clarke would pop her soda can in Laurel's face and the two of them would make extra yummy sounds as they enjoyed their "unhealthy" vices.

Ada was still smiling when she returned to the inn, a quaint two-story mosaicked stone and terracotta establishment. Before she went in, she emptied a piece of fish she'd had in her bag and put it in a small basket by the doorway. A meow and a growl later, and a cat-like creature she'd been told was a fee-lion meandered up and snatched the fish away. Apparently if Ada showed too much attention, the fee-lion wouldn't leave Ada alone, but she didn't care. The animal had looked a bit too skinny when she'd first arrived.

Once satisfied the animal had been fed, she pushed through the heavy front door, went upstairs and entered their room. After the raid, Clara had insisted she cover the cost of the room as a gesture of gratitude for their help against the humans. The assumption was that their Well-blessed marks kept Ada and Jasper together. Ada had felt awkward asking for a separate room and couldn't impose more on their hospitality, so had remained tight-lipped. As it turned out, it was a good thing she'd stayed with Jasper. He didn't seem mentally well and had remained in wolf form for much of the time.

"Honey, I'm home," she joked.

Unsurprisingly, Jasper's dark wolf form reclined by the fireplace. Since the fire had stayed alight all day, and there were no sprites—she'd politely declined when the innkeeper had offered some—to maintain the blaze, she knew he'd transformed into fae form during the day. How else would he have placed fresh wood on the hearth?

He may have kept the fire going during the day, but now it fizzled. Probably because he'd known she would return soon and stoke the flames back to life. Ada sighed and went over to a stacked pile of logs and threw one in. Sparks flew from the embers and drifted like lazy fireflies before settling down.

She watched Jasper for a few minutes until she decided he would not shift into fae form and say hello. Just like the other nights she'd arrived home, he stayed in his wolf form and would most likely stay like that until she left the following morning. It wasn't right, but she was still learning about the customs of this world. Perhaps staying in wolf form was something they did after being injured, although, she hadn't seen Moon do the same and his injuries had been debatably worse than Jasper's.

Unless Ada wanted to reveal Jasper's condition to a town already afraid to owe her a debt, she had to keep this to herself. She didn't trust them, and after the conversation with Sun, they weren't quite ready to trust her either.

Ada cleaned up and then went back downstairs to the tavern for a meal. It was still early enough that patrons were yet to crowd the room, and the scent of that stew was fresh in the air. Ada's mouth watered as she walked up to the bar. The top of a shifter's head could be seen as he, or she, tended to something beneath the bar. Upon Ada's approach, the bartender stood. He had a mop of brown hair and was long and gangly.

His ears flattened upon seeing Ada's round ears, but then his eyes tracked to the marks on her arms and the tension in his shoulders released.

"You must be Reed's lady."

"That's debatable," she replied wryly.

A confused look flitted over his expression, and Ada realized that associating herself with Reed wasn't a bad thing in this place. They felt more at ease knowing she belonged to him, whether it was true or not. And if they were at ease, then they weren't frightened or aggressive.

"I'm Ada," she said and gave a small wave.

"The name's Puck. The innkeeper's nephew."

"Nice to meet you."

"Can I help you with something?" he asked.

"I'd like some of that delicious smelling stew please. Two servings." Ada dug around in her pocket for some coin Clara had given her earlier in the day.

She placed all the glass coins onto the counter and dragged her bottom lip through her teeth. She had no idea how much each coin was worth. A few were clear, and one was blue. All had the etching of an M in the middle.

"You want anything to drink with the stew?" Puck asked.

"What do you recommend?"

Puck scratched his head and studied her. "Well, I don't know what you humans like to drink, but we don't carry no elixirs in this inn. Uncle doesn't like them. Says they cause mischief and ruckus and only attract the kind of clientele Rosebud Courtesans like to service. He don't want none of that here. We're a family establishment. If you know what I mean."

Yeah, sure. Ada knew exactly what he meant. At her blank look, Puck elaborated and pointed at three terracotta jugs. "We have cider, ale, and lemon water."

"Right. I'll take two lemon waters, please."

He gave her a short smile, then pointed at the coins on the counter. "Two clear will suffice. The blue is worth ten of the clear, then the gold is worth ten of the blue. Red coin is the most. You ever get your hands on one of those beauties and you use it wisely."

With a blush of gratitude, she separated two and slid them across to him, then touched her fingers to her lips and pushed them down and out, signing her thanks.

"Don't mention it." He gave her another thoughtful look then said, "Anyone who saved Moon's life is welcome here."

The kind words made her blush further and she felt a little more closer to home. Clarke probably would have said something about there being no such thing as free advice, but then again, if Clarke were here, maybe she'd be different too. God knew Ada was becoming a different person. Someone who wanted to belong more than she wanted isolation, and that frightened her more than anything because the moment you made friends, there was the potential for them to be ripped away.

A loud burst of chattering voices boomed into the room as a group of fae entered the tavern. Two tall males and a short, rotund female. They all stopped short upon seeing Ada.

Her cheeks heated and she turned back to Puck. "Could you make that order to-go?"

Puck's lips pinched. "Like I said, you're welcome here."

She signed her thanks again, but then shrugged. "I need to take it back to the room. For Jasper, I mean Reed."

He gave a curt nod. "I won't be long."

Ada stood awkwardly to the side, both wanting to say hello to the newcomers at the same time as wanting to run upstairs to their room. Since no one approached, or even acknowledged her, she said nothing either. By the time Puck returned with her meal on a tray, she smiled briefly at him and then bid him goodnight.

When she got back to the room and found Jasper sleeping, her shoulders drooped. That longing for friends gnawed at her and she couldn't deny she felt it more around Jasper. After eating the meal, and waiting to see if he would wake, she went to the toilet and then curled up next to him with a pillow and blanket pulled from the unused double bed. He stirred as she laid down, but just snuffled into her neck, licked her, and then went back to sleep. A flitter of relief mixed with anguish filtered down their bond. He wanted her there, but still refused to talk to her, or anyone else. If she couldn't get him down to this Lupercalia festival in a few days, then everyone would know.

Jasper didn't seem the kind to be okay with his secrets splashed about town. It must be the curse keeping him like this. If she could only get beyond his fur to the curse marks, she might ease some of his pain. Something tragic had happened in his past that he didn't want to remember, but pretending it didn't happen would only make things worse.

"Oh, Jasper. What are we going to do with you?" she murmured as her lids grew heavy.

A little whimper-sigh was her reply.

CHAPTER
NINE

After a few long days at the clinic with Clara, Ada returned to their room at the inn, carrying a bundle of clothes they were to put on for the Lupercalia festival.

It was tonight. And with most of the villagers now healed, her time at the makeshift clinic was up. After tonight, her future hung in the balance. She could either stay here or move on and find someone else to teach her.

They'd been living in the inn for the past week, and while Ada's relationship had grown with the townspeople, she hadn't the courage to let Clara know Jasper was very likely not going to make it to their all-important festival unless he trotted over in wolf form.

She stopped inside the door and closed it gently behind her. Jasper wasn't by the fire as he'd normally slept. Surprise curled through her. Maybe he'd emerged finally, after all. The fire had extinguished, and with no candles lit, it was hard to see through the dim room. The smell of wolf tickled her nose along with a hint of something sweet she couldn't place.

She went to the lone window, pulled back the drapes, and cracked the glass pane. Afternoon light and fresh air rushed in and pushed the staleness out. The wind chimes synonymous with the village tinkled outside the window. Ada glanced down at the street a level below. Fae milled about, putting the finishing touches on tonight's festival decorations, stringing garlands and bunting between buildings, and setting out bowls of floating glowing balls used as a light source. The same glowing balls would float inside glass lanterns dangling from the garlands once dusk fell.

The balls were manabeeze, the mana essence of all fae after they died. Ada had asked Clara whether they worried the manabeeze contained the fae's soul, and if they were disrespecting it by using the manabeeze as a source of energy. She'd just looked at her oddly. From what Ada had gathered, they believed mana was just part of the Well.

It resided in their bodies for a while and then returned to the cosmic energy of the Well in death. There was no personal attachment to it.

Unless, of course, you ingested a manabee. Then you relived memories of the life form it came from.

After the raid, they'd postponed the festival for as long as they could, but being a celebration of the end of winter and the start of a new life, they had to do it soon. Apparently, this was the first time they'd celebrated the traditional Lupercalia for hundreds of years. There had been some kind of law that prohibited parts of it until recently, and they were excited to have the guests of honor—a prince and his Well-blessed mate.

Now that some light had been let in, Ada searched for Jasper and found him naked and twisted in the sheets of the double bed he'd not slept in until now. He must have forgotten to shift back into a wolf.

She paused and let that fact sink in. She'd suspected he shifted into fae form during the day, but over the past week hadn't seen it once. Why today?

Did he know about their roles at the festival, or was he always like this when she left the room? A dark thought teased her—maybe he was always in wolf form when she came back because it was his friendly way of telling her to leave. After all, she had given him the kiss she thought he wanted, teased him with another, and yet he'd failed to claim more.

He either didn't care for it, or there was something else going on and, to be honest, she was thinking he didn't even want her help. If that was the truth, then it was time for her to leave. Her traveling feet were calling. Being in one place for so long wasn't really her thing. Back in Vegas, she'd had an apartment in the city, but also one near a state park where she worked with injured animals. Her time was spent between the two. Unlike Laurel and Clarke, who'd loved living in the city, and partying on the strip, Ada's idea of a good time was under the blue sky, smelling the rain on the pines, and listening to the cicadas on a warm day. Moving kept her from thinking too hard about life.

One thing was for sure, she would not stick around if she wasn't needed or wanted.

She perched herself on the edge of the bed. Jasper's even breathing continued. The moment her palm landed on the hard slab of muscle on his scarred back, her tension fled and she felt a rush of compassion. This was a brutal world. She'd learned some of its history from Prim while visiting the bakery this morning. She'd told Ada of how after the bombs went off in Ada's time, life was cutthroat for the survivors. And then the primordial Well bubbled to life, reclaiming the land and its inhabitants. When humans realized some were merging with animal and plant life, becoming fae for the sake of surviving the harsh unfamiliar landscape, they quarantined themselves in fear behind the walls of what has now become Crystal City. Because the city was on desecrated land filled with metal and plastic, the Well couldn't flow there, and no one changed to fae. They remained human, untouched by the Well.

While humans had cloistered themselves in fear, the fae had become the custodians of the new land. Food was hard to find, at first. Survival in the cold extremes of the nuclear winter was even harder. Two thousand or so years had passed since Ada's friends had breathed their last breath. Perhaps more from her time had awoken in

Elphyne, like Ada, but she wouldn't know anything unless she started searching for answers. And, unfortunately, she couldn't do that until she was sure Jasper was okay.

It had crossed her mind more than once to find the Order of the Well—the experts in all things magical—and these other rumored Well-blessed mated couples, but every time she'd convinced herself she owed no loyalty to this town or to Jasper, she found a reason to stay. Fae had opened up to her. They trusted her now. Clara wasn't the only one who'd taught her about the rules of the Well. Soon she'd feel confident to ask for more history on the humans of this time, and try to figure out how she fit into the grand scheme of things.

And Jasper was hurt. His injury might not be one of the body anymore, but his mind still healed. A person who wanted to die was someone who thought he had nothing to live for.

She couldn't leave him. At least not until she knew that he would not find another piece of metal and find a way to leave it in.

Inspecting the curse marks on his body, she felt the wrongness in them—the grimi-ness. They extended from his front to the back where more scars puckered. Some scars were great slices. Others were slashes as though he'd been whipped.

"You know," she said to his sleeping form. "Moon's brother is called Sun. Did you also know that they're Clara's children and your cousins?" She gave a soft snort. She started picking at his markings, this time feeling out the curse with her sixth sense, probing it for weaknesses. She'd learned that the Well felt pure, warm and bright. Places where it didn't flow were cold, and then there was what lay beneath these blue curse marks—the dark, grimy ink.

"I wonder if Moon or Sun have children and if they're named after stars or planets. Do people even know about the planets now? Jeez. Never thought of that. How much knowledge has been lost since our time?" She took a deep breath and exhaled. "I also learned about the King, and what he did to your mother. I'm... at a loss for words at what to say. It must have been horrible for you at that age to have thought the only way you could survive was to jump in a dangerous lake that takes more lives than it saves. You know, I didn't have a great childhood either." She peeled off a curse piece and wiped the black ooze it left with her sleeve. He made no move, so she continued with a frown. "My mother didn't care enough to feed me. She preferred to go out partying with her boyfriends. I learned from a young age to look after myself."

She picked off another strip of blue, lifting it from his skin and adding it to a growing pile at her side.

"There was this old cantankerous man who'd stumbled across me when I got lost in the woods the first time. He was the scariest thing an eleven-year-old girl could see, but the weird thing was, he was so kind. He taught me a lot about surviving in the wild. I guess, maybe he'd been avoiding people too. Harold was his name. I used to call him Har-*old* when he used to give me shit about doing something wrong." She laughed softly, a pang of affection rising at his memory. "He had hair coming out of his nose, and wrinkles that made his eyes sloped. He knew how to chop the tail off a scor-pion so you could eat the rest. He knew how to fish. And he knew how to hunt." Another blue strip came off. "And he taught me how to read, math basics, and about economics, of all things. I certainly learned never to judge a book by its cover with him."

Jasper remained still, so she kept going. She supposed she should take advantage of him sleeping through the process. The more she removed, the quicker he would regain his memories, and the sooner she could leave.

"You don't get many old people here. I mean, they're old. Clara told me she's a few hundred years of age—maybe close to five hundred, can you believe it? She also said you're a few hundred as well, but she's lost count over time. So you're all super geriatric, but none of you look it. It's so weird." More strips, more blue, more inky ooze. Her voice grew quiet. "A few days ago I saw some human corpses... what was left of them... and some of them were old and wrinkled. So, they definitely age. I asked Clara about it and she said it was the access to the Well that kept fae young. It was a reward for living in harmony with the planet. I like that idea. I can see why you're all more protective of the environment... you're actually around to see the changes bad choices cause."

A piece of blue resisted, but she gripped tight and yanked as though it was a wax strip on her leg. It ripped off.

Jasper flinched, and then went so still, his breathing stopped. Power rippled in the air and the sense of danger loomed. Her heart rate picked up speed. Suddenly, Jasper rolled from his back, captured the wrist of her hand holding the strip and bared his sharp teeth. Flushed and feverish eyes glared at her through dark lashes. Tousled hair draped over his forehead. A full dark beard covered his sharp jaw. Rose tinted his cheekbones. It was hard not to be attracted to him.

"I told you not to remove it," he growled. "I don't *want* to remember."

"Tough titties," she replied and wrested her hand from his iron grip. "You've wallowed for long enough."

"You have no idea what you're talking about."

She arched a brow. "Maybe I don't, but that's because you're not sharing with me. All I know is that wasting your life by pretending it doesn't exist is no way to survive."

All the signs pointed to him being healthy enough in body, so this was some kind of depression. Maybe this kick in the butt wouldn't be enough, but it was a start. It was all she knew how to do.

He blinked at her. Some sort of recognition ghosted in his eyes and then it went. He shoved her away, and she almost fell off the feather filled mattress. He stumbled to his feet, giving her a flash of well-muscled posterior before staggering to the bathroom door, flinging it wide open, and relieving himself in the toilet, one hand on his—*ahem*. The other hand braced on the wall.

"A hello would be nice!" she shouted, averting her gaze.

The sound of urine cascading into water made her blink, stupefied.

"Guess some things never change, no matter how much time has passed," she muttered, then huffed and straightened the bed, taking her anger out on the sheets. "Being a dickhead must be ingrained so deeply into the male psyche that it survived a holocaust and the mutation of DNA."

At least they had plumbed sewage in this town. Some places in Elphyne weren't so lucky, she'd been told.

When she moved the sheet, two berries tumbled out of a purple stained area. She picked them up and smelled them. Mana-berries? What were they doing there?

Jasper had staggered to the bathroom.

"Are you fucking kidding me?" She squished the berries. "No wonder you've been sleeping for days. You've been *high*."

His lazy-lidded glance over his shoulder made her think he was still high. Then he kicked the bathroom door closed, blocking her view.

She jumped to her feet, fuming.

"You know what?" she shouted at the door. "I don't even know why I'm sticking around. You don't want my help, fine. After this Lupercalia festival thing is over, I'm out of here."

"You're not going anywhere." His deep voice permeated the wooden door, rattling it.

The flush came, and the door flung open. He'd found a towel and had wrapped it around his waist, but the small thing barely came halfway down his thick thighs and split on one side from the lack of fabric. Still fever-eyed, he prowled toward her.

She folded her arms. "Ooh. I'm so afraid of you and your tiny towel."

He stopped before her and dipped his chin to meet her eyes. All humor dropped from his expression when he spoke. "You're not going anywhere because you belong to me, Ada."

Her fury was so sudden and strong that no logic could get through. When she finally moved her mouth, her words came out slow and steady through clenched teeth.

"I think maybe you're right. Removing those curse marks isn't a good idea because you're getting confused. I *belong* to myself."

What kind of arrogant asshole was he?

A prince. A king's son. That's who.

She was only now understanding what that meant. The Seelie High King of Elphyne. Half of the land was under his rule. He was the same king who'd instructed the town to hoard metal and then failed to protect them when humans came raiding. He'd also tried to assassinate his son. And Jasper was the guy who had been named as his heir. Maybe she'd been wrong, and there was another reason the King wanted Jasper dead. Maybe it was because he was a dickhead and the apple didn't fall far from the tree.

"Our union was chosen by the Well," Jasper declared, as though that excused everything.

"Yeah, about that," she said. "While you've been sleeping, I've been asking around, and no one has said that this union means we have to stick together. Prim said if I'm not marked on the neck by the bite of my mate's teeth, then I'm my own person."

"That's true for shifters." He blinked, shocked. "But a Well-blessed union is held in the highest regard. There is no other mating more revered. Marking you with my teeth is purely to satisfy my wolf. If I have to mark you that way, I will."

Her brows lifted. "You'll do no such thing. There's no rule that says I belong to you, and there's no rule that says we have to be together sexually, and there's no rule that says we have to stick together. Fae-kind mate in many ways, and I'm pretty sure, *any* kind of mating is consensual for both parties. This"—she held up her arm—"was *not* consensual."

"I didn't choose it either, but I'm willing to accept it."

"You shouldn't have to! It should be something we choose."

He went to the window and flicked the drapes aside to peer outside with a scowl darkening his handsome face.

Ada pinched the bridge of her nose. Honestly, this festival couldn't come sooner. It was definitely time for her to leave and find her own way.

Jasper wasn't the worst sort to be stuck with. He looked great. He was a scary warrior who could protect her in a world she was fast learning was far more ruthless than the one she left. But they weren't suited to each other. She could never be with a person who insisted he knew what was better for her than her own desires. What was next, telling her how to dress and what to eat? No, thank you.

The sooner she could get away from all of this, the better.

"We have an hour to get ready." She picked up the bundle of clothes she'd left on the bed. "Clara said that because we're the Luperci, we have to wear these. Something to do with ritual and tradition."

She shook the dress out. It was similar to what many female shifters wore—loose, bone-colored, and made of linen. She'd been instructed to wear her hair out, and to go barefoot.

Ugh. Catching herself in a spiraling mood, she rubbed her face.

"I'm having a bath," she announced, and left him brooding by the window. As she closed the bathroom door, the last thing she saw was a small, smug smile curving his lips as he watched the festive lanterns go up.

CHAPTER

TEN

Pounding on the bathroom door woke Ada with a jerk. Warm water sloshed over the bath lip and she slipped, barely grappling the edge before she dipped beneath the surface and dunked her head.

"Time to go," Jasper grumbled through the door.

Shit.

"I'll be right out," she called.

She must have fallen asleep. The water was just so warm. Heated by special mana-infused stones, it kept the temperature constant.

She pulled the plug and climbed out of the rose-scented water. She toweled off, ran her fingers through her long wavy hair and dried the damp ends as best she could. A quick check in the black-glass mirror over the wooden vanity showed her cheeks flushed from the heat. She dragged the loose dress over her head and let it drop. The bottom pooled on the floor, leaving a small train behind her. It was made for someone much taller, but it would have to do. The straps were thin, and the neck was a V-shape that dipped below her bust line, revealing more flesh. The same V left most of her back uncovered. She supposed, if a fae was to shift into a wolf, the wide neck would be easy to climb out of. Unimpressed, she plucked the fabric from her chest where it revealed the outline of her pebbled nipples. Bras and formfitting clothes just weren't a thing here. With a sigh of capitulation and a last check in the mirror, she opened the door and walked into the main room.

Jasper wore loose, cream linen pants and *no* shirt. He came right up to her, dipped his chin and looked into her eyes before saying succinctly, "Hello."

For a moment, Ada's mind muddled at his closeness. Why is he being so obvious? Then she remembered her offhand comment after he'd awoken and stormed off to the bathroom. *"A hello would be nice."*

Her lip twitched, wanting to smile. Was this his apology for being a dickhead? Instead, she pursed her lips and folded her arms.

"Do you ever wear a shirt?" she asked. "Or are you allergic?"

"No male will wear a shirt tonight," he said, and when she gave a questioning eyebrow, he added, "It's easier to shift without one."

"Of course. Makes sense."

Why shifting was involved in the festivities was beyond her, but in a town where they all turned into a wolf, maybe they howled at the moon or something. She'd not gleaned a lot from the townspeople, except that they were extremely excited. There would be much feasting, and much celebration. Sounded like a good old party. She could handle that.

Jasper itched the remaining curse marks on his neck with an agitated frown. Only half of what he'd originally had still remained. He still had a slight feverish look about him, but had found somewhere to clean up and shave his beard. His usual messy hair had been brushed, and she had a rare view of pointed ears twitching in irritation.

Ada glanced about the room and found it tidied. A used bowl of rosewater sat near the fireplace. Perhaps he'd called for some from the innkeeper. Ada tried to stifle her next words, but found she was helpless to ask. Just because he was stubborn, didn't mean she would be too.

"Have there been any ill effects from the latest curse mark removal?"

His sideways glance said there was, but when he clenched his jaw and faced the door, she knew he would never willingly confide.

"Memories?" she prompted. "Headaches?"

His fingers twitched at his side and she sensed a sliver of something she could only describe as need, or yearning, filter through their bond. It was as though he wanted to tell her something. Then he somehow clamped it down because it cut off. She narrowed her eyes at him. He'd never before hidden his *feelings*. This was new, and perhaps something he'd only just remembered how to do.

"Sit down," she said and pointed to the bed.

The look he gave her could have wilted a lesser woman, but she honestly didn't give a fuck. She meant what she'd said about leaving, and she was stubborn enough to do it. There was no way she'd stick around when she was treated like that. She raised her brow and waited.

One fur-tipped ear flicked back, and then he moved with a stiff gait to the bed. He sat down, placed his fists on his thighs and stared blankly ahead.

"I'm trying to help you, Jasper," she said, her tone clipped. "Have you got a problem accepting help?"

He squirmed.

Oh, shit. Maybe he did.

She pushed tension from her shoulders to reset her mood and then stepped up to his knees. Placing a palm on each shoulder, she pushed her awareness into his body and tried not to think about the virile, carved body staring her in the face. Damn him for being so annoyingly attractive.

She cleared her throat. "You may not know this, but while you were lazing about getting stoned on berries, I was learning how to use my gift. Clara's been teaching me, but I'm getting to the limits of her knowledge. Apparently, healers are rare among Mages, and even rarer in shifter villagers."

"I know," he grunted.

"You do?" That healers were rare or that Clara had been teaching her?

Long lashes flicked up, honeyed eyes clashed with hers, then lowered again. "I heard your stories when I was in wolf form."

So he had been listening to her nightly ramblings after all. She let go. Nothing was amiss in his body except the griminess she associated with the curse marks. Maybe a sluggishness she knew was linked to headaches, but that was most likely because of his recent habit. The effects of withdrawal weren't kind after any vice.

"So you have been ignoring me," she said.

"No… I've been—" He clamped his lips hard.

"Jasper." She sighed and looked at the ceiling. "You can't profess that we're meant to be together and then hide your feelings from me. I felt you shut them off, and to me, that feels like lying. I'm not going to stick around someone who's dishonest."

"I belong to you. Isn't that enough?"

She tensed. "Actions speak louder than words, and for the past week you've not acted like we're together."

Her shoulder lifted half-heartedly at his lack of response, but when her eyes drifted back down, she found he wasn't staring into the distance anymore, but straight ahead— at her chest. More specifically, the rise and fall of her breasts. She folded her arms and cocked a hip.

"Seriously?" she said. "I'm asking you to pour your heart out and you're drooling over my tits."

"Tits?" His gaze lifted to hers, a quirk to his full lips.

"Breasts." She waved at her own. "Whatever you call them in this time."

"I call them mine," his voice was low and raspy, and damn her, it triggered a bolt of traitorous heat straight through her core.

The cocky bastard knew it too. His eyes only grew heated as he drank in the sight of her body.

Having enough, she turned away, but he tugged her back by the hand. Dark desire washed over his features.

"You want to know why I've kept myself in wolf form? Why I've dulled my senses with mana-berries?"

"Yes!" It would be a start.

He slowly stood until he towered over her, and the impressive arousal tenting his pants jutted out, almost hitting her stomach. Down their bond, lust so raw and thick lashed at her. She staggered back until her shoulders hit the wall and her arm knocked the table holding the rosewater bowl. Her hand flew down to steady it.

Jasper prowled closer, sex written over his expression and in every line of his body.

"Since I first caught your scent, I've wanted you, pretty little human. I want to eat you, to lick you, to be inside you. Something about you calls to me. It's inexplicable, and it consumes my every waking moment. I don't need all my memories to know I've never felt this way before. I've hidden myself and dulled my senses because you're not ready for this. I can see it in your eyes."

He stopped a few inches from her. The heat of his body licked her front, scorching her skin. All she could see was his defined torso, ridged abdominals, and broad shoulders. Flashes of blue twinkled at her. Her eyes locked straight ahead.

Looking down would mean to acknowledge—she blushed. Nope. Not looking down.

Up meant being caught in the snare of his rich eyes.

To the side would be straight at the bulging biceps now caging her against the wall.

She swallowed.

He was right. She wasn't ready for what he felt. It was too real. Too soon. Too reliant on one person. A slash of pain pinged in her chest. She couldn't put all her eggs in one basket, because if it broke, she would too. She needed to find her feet in this world first. Despite her brain telling her this, her body wanted something else. It didn't care about waiting. It only wanted what was right here before her eyes.

Jasper dipped so his lips whispered hotly against her ear. "You forget, human, I sense your desire. I know what your body wants, even if your mind is still fighting it. You belong to me, but I also belong to you. I will never leave you. Never."

Her lashes fluttered closed. The smell of his sweet, rosewater-laced skin made her mouth water.

His teeth trailed along her neck. "I will protect you, feed you, pleasure you, revere you."

"We should go," she said without opening her eyes. "They're waiting for us."

A pause. His teeth rested on the tendon between her neck and shoulder. Then a rasping at her sides as his hands left the wall.

She opened her eyes and found he'd pushed back to study her with his head cocked to the side, ears pricked forward eagerly, a dark lock of brushed hair hanging across his forehead. She thought their encounter was over, but the moment she moved to leave, he said, "I'll be honest with you when you're honest with me."

Their gazes clashed, and he gave her a rakish grin full of secrets and dares. Her breath caught. It was a smile that powered a thousand stars. And then it was gone.

A wash of regret dipped in her belly as he walked to the door. She'd forgotten how his smile affected her, but her body hadn't. It made her think... what if? What if she let go and shared herself with him? What if he did the same?

I will never leave you. Never.

CHAPTER
ELEVEN

J asper walked beside Ada down the lantern-lit main street. Trapped manabeeze buzzed and cast reflections on glass mosaic squares plastered to the sides of every building. The tinkling of chimes followed them, as did the footsteps of a small crowd of villagers that followed. It was as though the fae folk had been waiting in their homes to join them on the pilgrimage to the Luperci grotto.

He should be excited.

Lupercalia was something he'd always wanted to take part in, but as a child, had been prohibited because of his age. Then the unsanctioned breeding law came in—a fact he'd remembered recently, along with many other bombarding memories he tried not to focus on. But try as he might, he couldn't stop the flashes of his childhood self running through the village streets, holding a red ribbon high and watching it cascade behind him in the air. The sound of childish laughter as his cousins ran along beside him, holding their own streaming red ribbons. His aunt's voice shouting for them to not tangle the lengths before the big ceremony...

"Come on, Clara," said Jasper's mother as she walked beside her, carrying a basket. "They're having fun. Leave them be."

Clara turned to her sister with a scowl. "Are you going to detangle the lengths?"

"If I have to."

"Of course you are," Clara replied sourly. "The fun always outweighs the bad with you, doesn't it?"

Jasper's mother's lips flattened.

Clara gave her a contrite look. "I didn't mean that."

"Yes you did."

Jasper remembered their conversation ending after that. It took him years to know why. But the older he got, the wiser he was. What seemed like fun with the King—a matching at Lupercalia—had ended in a pregnancy. And then death.

That night they ran the street with streaming ribbons was the last traditional Lupercalia. It was the one where the King returned to participate again, but discovered Jasper's heritage. It was the last one where Jasper's mother was alive.

Not tonight.

He shook his head. Tomorrow, he would face his demons.

All he wanted now was to feast, to find something delicious to numb his past, and to indulge. If memory served correctly, the purification elixir they offered at the main meal would cause the body to tingle and sweat, preparing it for the Lupercalia rite. There would be much cider and ale.

Flashes of past indulgences swam before his eyes. He flinched and tried to shake them away, but unwanted visions of elixirs and meaningless sex crowded his mind. How could he be so ashamed of it now when back then he'd reveled in it? He'd loved it so much he'd bought himself an apartment in Cornucopia, the almost lawless border town between the Seelie and Unseelie kingdoms. It was the only place fae could mingle without the laws of their kingdoms getting in the way. It felt more of a prison than a sanctuary now. It was the place Jasper had gone to forget about his shortcomings.

And they were all coming back to him now—his failure at being a Guardian, a friend, a mentor. His failure at protecting his Guardian partner and friend, Rush, and the female who bore his child. Then, as if he couldn't sink any lower, Jasper had failed to protect Rush's son, Thorne, and it was unforgivable. Jasper knew exactly how harsh life was for someone without parents in Elphyne, yet he'd hid behind his duty to the Well.

The truth was, he was a coward hiding from his father. He had been all along. He should have floated.

The glow of his blue arm markings caught his attention.

Why?

Why, after everything he'd failed to do, had the Well given him this gift? It was a gift so strong that it saved the town from complete devastation during the raid. It gave him access to her untapped mana source. It had given him *her*.

Not that she accepted their partnership.

She was... he glanced at Ada's profile as she walked. Her blond wavy hair danced down her back. Freckles dusted a small, petite nose. She had a sun-kissed tan he'd only seen on the fish-tailed fae that liked to bake on the warm rocks of Helianthus City beach. He could smell summer on her. She was the promise of something all winter fae wanted. She was the promise of effervescent life.

His human was beautiful, inside and out. And she had stayed with him. She had slept by his side. She had dug the sacrilegious metal out of his body with her own fingers. She'd healed him and his kind without judgement. And she wanted him. He knew she did.

It was something else that made little sense. He'd been nothing but despicable to her, but she'd remained loyal. A rush of desire so strong and thick coursed through him, and he had to snap his gaze to the flower petals littering the dirt street ahead.

When she had threatened to leave him, he'd felt sick. He couldn't fathom being away from her.

In one of her nightly ramblings, she'd spoken of wanting extra training at the Order. Perhaps it was time to take her there, to the place he'd spent most his life.

A vague memory of his cadre itched at the edges of his mind. He knew they had been involved in his rescue from his father—and Jasper's captivity at the Ring—but couldn't quite uncover the truth of their identities. When he tried to remember more, blurry faces entered his mind. The rest was occupied with his feelings for Ada, rage, and thirst for vengeance against his father. Sometimes, that anger occupied more space than Ada. Sometimes it was the other way around. And, occasionally, after more curse marks were removed, other dark parts of him tried to edge in. If he gave those parts space to breathe, they would consume him.

Better to focus on the thrill of the chase he knew was coming. The fact that his mate kept denying what they meant to each other thrilled him further. He would enjoy watching her realize their union was inevitable.

The walk out of town took them down by the river and along a bubbling brook that fed into the woods. Sprites flittered in the trees, chasing fireflies and squeaking. Lanterns and glass chimes swayed gently from branches of oak trees, guiding the way. Soft murmurs of excitement and anticipation came from the villagers walking behind. Jasper felt no cold, but Ada's nose was pink from the crisp twilight air. When they arrived at the sacred grotto, he would insist she sit by a bonfire stationed around the pool.

Dirt turned to soft grass underfoot as they followed the winding brook through trees growing bigger and sheltering them from the dusk sky. Ada's face tipped up. Awe washed down their bond and he couldn't stop the smile playing on his lips. Being the Luperci during this walk was the pride and joy of the Darkfoot pack. He not only got to share it with her, but to experience it as someone the pack revered and respected.

His mother would be proud.

He is ten times the fae you are, ten times the soul, and he will be ten times the—

He shut his mother's voice out with a wince. Still, after so many years, her sound was as sharp as it was the day she spoke.

Ada's soft gaze slid over to him. She raised her brow in silent question. He must have let some of his emotion slip. She kept staring, and he knew he had to give her something.

"My mother would have liked to see this," he admitted, and looked out at the glowing lights filtering through the haze of the trees. "It was her favorite time of year."

They'd come to the top of the grotto. Moss-covered stone steps led down to a grassed landing, and a waterfall feeding the sacred pool. If his vague memories were to be trusted, the Lupercal cave was hidden behind the curtain of water. The smell of roasting meat watered his tastebuds, and his ears pricked up. Voices and the low breathy melody of pan pipes filtered up. They were almost there.

"The last leg of the pilgrimage is tricky," he said to Ada and held out his hand. "Watch your step on the descent."

Ada clutched his forearm, her eyes wide and earnest as she looked up at him. "You remember?"

"Some." Again, her gaze lingered on him. She wouldn't let it go. And, if he was being honest with himself, a part of him would feel offended if she did. She wasn't some stranger. She was the one the Well had chosen for him, made more special because of her journey through time. This, in itself, was so rare a fact that he should sit up and pay attention.

She had been right; pretending his life didn't exist, didn't make it so. His mother had said something similar, long ago, and it had struck a chord deep inside. There were things he'd never atone for, but if she wanted to learn those parts of him, then so be it. How much worse could his life get?

"I will share after," he conceded quietly.

It was enough. She nodded.

He put his hand over hers on his forearm and held her gaze. A moment of connection passed between them, and then she smiled and stepped forward. He wouldn't release her hand and pulled her back to him.

"Keep hold of me," he murmured and walked them down together.

Down in the grotto beside the pool were multiple dining tables laden with food and drink. Scattered bonfires blazed, casting heat into the otherwise cool evening air. A waterfall spilled over a small cliff to finish in the pool where it churned the water emitting tendrils of steam.

Villagers and guests already mingled at the tables, drinking and carousing. Most of the females wore blood red versions of Ada's dress, and the males wore red, drawstring pants. The cream, pure color had been reserved for Jasper and Ada—the two Luperci.

He noted representatives from other fae races had come to experience the festivities, which wasn't unheard of, but rare. Perhaps it was because this was the first authentic Lupercalia in centuries. The excitement was shared with everyone.

Satyrs with curved-horned heads and cloven feet shared a table and spoke quietly with Darkfoot shifters. Stag fae with forked antlers huddled at a table, talking with a few local shifters. On the outskirts, near the trees, two Oak Men chatted. One was tall and craggy with striations of wood over his wrinkled face. His beard and hair of orange and brown leaves signaled old age. Soon his leaves would fall, and he'd enter the last stage of his life—Winter. Next to him was a young spring Oak Man, barely a sprout of green leaves on his head.

Jasper searched the grotto for females of their kind, because surely if they were to participate in Lupercalia, they wouldn't be alone. Sure enough, a group of females sat at a round table with a string of lanterns dangling overhead from branches.

When the knowledge freely sprang into Jasper's mind, he knew the cloud renting space in his head had almost cleared. With both equal parts sadness and acceptance, he understood his time for hiding from his responsibilities was almost over.

One last night of fun.

He glanced down at Ada and found her eyes like two big saucers as she took in the scene.

"I've never..." she gaped. "I mean... I've not seen..."

"This must be all very new for you." To come from a race where the major physical difference was the color of their skin, he imagined the diversity of fae would be something to behold.

Her eyes met his, and she nodded. "I don't know why, but I just didn't expect to see so many appearances."

"This is nothing," he said. "Wait until you visit Cornucopia, or the Unseelie lands."

"Will you tell me about them?" she asked. "I'd love to know more."

Her eagerness pervaded him and wrapped its way around his heart. She might not have realized it, but her question broached a future together.

"Of course." He squeezed her hand still clutching his forearm. "The night has only just begun."

His cousin, Sun, stood at the foot of the stone steps with his arms folded. He glanced warily at Jasper, but brightened his smile at Ada.

"Glad to see you made it," Sun said to her.

She returned his smile and Jasper felt that initial warmth around his heart dissipate.

"I'm honored," she said.

Their gazes held for too long.

With a repressed growl, Jasper's hackles raised. Even though no sound emitted, Ada glanced at him with a disapproving frown.

Sun tipped his chin at Jasper. "Good to finally see you out, Reed—"

"It's D'arn Jasper, now. Has been for centuries. You know that."

Both Ada and Sun gaped at him.

"What?" he scowled.

"Nothing, just... you remembered," Sun murmured.

Of course he remembered. He couldn't stand it when his cousins brushed off his commitment as a Guardian. Every time he had come back to Fenrysfield, they refused to believe he wasn't back for good. Sometimes Jasper believed this was the reason neither Sun nor Moon had stepped up to become the alpha. Both were clearly capable, and strong enough, but hadn't. Then again, perhaps it was because Clara was a force to be reckoned with.

Jasper scratched the curse marks as they flared.

Sun blanked for a moment, but then grinned. "You old dog. You do remember."

Then he launched at Jasper and punched him hard in the gut.

CHAPTER
TWELVE

Ada froze. Why on earth would Sun *hit* his cousin?

Jasper doubled over, wheezing... then he tensed, every muscle in his body going rigid. A spark of danger sizzled in the air.

Apprehension skipped over Ada's skin and she tensed, ready to break up the fight that would surely ruin the festival. She glanced around for a familiar face, for help, but found none. If this erupted, she was on her own.

Jasper straightened and glared at Sun, who stood with a stupid grin and a come-get-me expression. If he had a tail, Ada imagined it would be wagging.

"It's going to be like that, is it, Cousin?" Jasper took him by the shoulder and then planted his fist in Sun's gut. Soon, they were roughhousing on the grassy floor, tumbling and fighting like brothers. Fists flailed, knees became missiles, and ears were bitten.

"Yeah, they get like that."

Ada turned and found the youth she'd healed on her first day.

"It's a wolf thing," Lake explained with a grin. "We're a competitive lot."

"Right." She raised her brows at them. "So I should just leave them?"

Lake shrugged. "Guess so."

"So, you're participating in Lupercalia?" she asked him.

He laughed nervously, a blush hitting his cheeks. "No. I'm a few years away from being allowed. But I'm here to play in the band." He lifted a wooden musical instrument that sounded like a maraca. "Yay me."

"Well, I'm glad you're all healed. You look good."

This time, red colored his arched ears. He touched fingers to his lips and pushed them down and out to her.

"Don't mention it," she smiled warmly.

They both jumped back when Sun and Jasper rolled over, but not far enough. Lake's maraca fell to the ground.

Clara jogged in, clapping her hands loudly. Moon trailed after her with an unimpressed expression.

"Enough!" Clara shouted. She took each of her recalcitrant relatives by the twitching ears and yanked them to their feet. "I swear to the Well, you two have learned nothing. *Crimson save me.* This is a sacred festival!"

"He started it." Jasper shrugged Clara off and pointed at Sun, who only waggled his brows at his mother.

"I don't care who started it—" Clara gasped at Jasper's grass-stained pants. "What have you done? They're meant to symbolize purity, and you've soiled them!"

Jasper smirked, wiping a drop of blood from the corner of his lip with his thumb. "Let's be honest, Aunty, if you wanted someone pure as Luperci, you shouldn't have asked me."

Fury mottled Clara's expression, but it was with humor warring in her eyes. "I will skin you alive and wear your pelt as a coat. *Please* try to remain civil. We have Royal dignitaries and emissaries from other towns present." She lowered her voice so only they could hear. "If we want to gather allies so we're not beholden to the King, then we need to make an impression. Gah!" She threw up her hands and then walked back to the guests she'd been entertaining at the long table by the poolside.

Jasper mumbled something Ada couldn't hear. But Sun did. He burst out laughing. Ada tried not to join in, and she wasn't the only one. The rough, familiar play had dispelled a certain tension.

Not all were smiling. Moon still stood with his arms folded, and brows low at his brother and cousin. Long gray hair trailed over his broad, naked shoulders. Ada was glad to see his stomach wound was nothing but a faint scar.

The mood sobered. Jasper and Sun straightened themselves.

"Honestly," Prim said, arriving down the steps, carrying a tray of ceremonial sweet cakes. "You'd think the Darkfoot alpha heir apparent and the prince of, oh, I don't know, *half of Elphyne*, would be a little more responsible."

"Whatever gave you that idea?" Jasper joked.

Prim rolled her eyes and then gave Ada a curt smile before saying to Moon, "Where do you want these?"

"Give them to Halona at the banquet table."

Prim sashayed away, her red dress billowing behind her. Soft notes of the pan flute floated over the misting waterfall and echoed up the grotto rock walls and trees. The vibe was haunting... until shaking maracas joined in. Ada grinned, loving the rush of endorphins rising to greet her.

"What's so funny?" Jasper narrowed his eyes.

"Nothing. Private joke," she replied, looking at Lake doing his best to appear entertained.

Jasper's scowl deepened, but Ada only gave him a look that said, *I can hide things too.* It was stupid. It was teasing. But it gave her a small slice of satisfaction to know Jasper would understand what it felt like to be shut out.

"So..." Sun wiped his running nose and then pointed between Ada and Jasper. "What's the deal with you two?"

"*Sun*," Moon admonished.

"What? If you didn't have a mate, you'd ask too. Especially for tonight."

"Ada and I *are* mates," Jasper insisted.

"We're just friends," Ada said at the same time.

They both glanced at each other. Ada caught a flash of offense in Jasper's eyes, but she would not back down. If she let some notion of a cosmic power choose her love life for her, then what did she have left? Her friends were gone. Her world was gone. This was the last ounce of her control.

She explained, "We're not mated."

Jasper cocked his brow and raised his blue, glowing arm. "What do you call this?"

"A business relationship."

"Ooh," Sun goaded Jasper. "She has you there, Cousin."

Jasper's brows slammed together. "That's not a thing, Ada."

"It is now."

"So does that mean you're free game at the matching ceremony?" Sun's eyes lit up.

What?

"No," Jasper growled, his features twisting. He tensed and took a step toward Sun, who only smirked wider.

"Jasper, chill out." She touched him on the arm, but his eyes bored holes into his cousin. Everything in his posture said the next time he touched Sun, game time would be over. How Sun wasn't shitting his pants right now was beyond her. If Jasper ever turned that anger her way, she wasn't sure she'd be so brave. She tapped Jasper's arm for attention. "What's the matching ceremony?"

Since Jasper was consumed with violent thoughts about his cousin, Moon took his suicidal brother's shoulder and tugged him back before answering Ada. "It's when all the unmated pack members are paired up after we complete the Lupercalia rite."

Like The Bachelor, *or a romantic reality TV show? No thanks.*

"Oh, well, no, I won't be participating, but I appreciate the invitation."

"You just said you weren't mated to me."

Ada didn't like the mocking tone in Jasper's voice. "So by default, all single people must take part?"

"Well," Sun drawled. "Since the event is a symbol of health and fertility, both for our lands and ourselves, it would be disrespectful and a scandal not to. It's not like it's a lifelong commitment. Just a night of fun."

When Ada had heard they were asking for their seed to be blessed, she'd thought they meant *crop* seed. Now she realized there were two meanings.

"She is mine," Jasper said. "Whether or not I've marked her."

"Why don't we see what the Well thinks?" Sun asked Jasper. "I mean, if you're so certain that she's your true mate, you should have no problems, right?"

"This isn't a competition," Moon growled at them. "The Well has already paired them."

"It's always a competition," Sun returned.

"I'm standing right here." Not that they heard Ada anymore.

Jasper's luminous gaze narrowed on her. "You keep telling me you don't believe our matching is fated, so here's your chance. If we're not matched again, then..." His nostrils flared. "I'll back off."

"Why do I have to pair up with anyone?"

The idea of being forced into any kind of relationship was inconceivable.

Moon cleared his throat. "I regret to inform you, but when you accepted the role of one of the two honored Luperci, we assumed you would take part in the fertility rituals. Whether that's together, or with someone else, then we can't argue with that. For the record, no one will force you to mate. There are about fifty potential couples. When you match, it's up to you how you spend the night with your chosen one. But to deny it is to disrespect the rite and a sign of bad fortune for the coming harvest. We'd rather pick another Luperci to replace you." He glanced over at the banquet table. "I think Prim was interested. I could ask her."

Ada's stomach revolted at that idea, and it must have shown on her face because Jasper's eyes twinkled knowingly at her. He knew she liked him. And he knew her resistance was wearing thin. But Ada didn't do things by halves. If she entered any kind of relationship with Jasper, it was going to be deep. She feared being able to climb out of it if things got rough.

She had no support system in this world. She would be alone.

Ada opened her mouth to respond, but the music suddenly stopped. Clanging on glass silenced conversation. All they could hear for a moment was the rushing of the waterfall and the chirping of crickets. Ada was sure the beating of her heart picked up a few decibels.

Clara stepped on top of a table and addressed the hushed gathering.

"As alpha and matriarch of Fenrysfield, I officially declare Lupercalia open."

Cheering burst out. Drinks in hands chinked and sloshed. Smiles and grins were abound with infectious joy. Ada knew then that she couldn't rain on their parade any more than she already had. It was one thing to deny the bond between her and Jasper as romantic, but refusing to participate in their sacred traditions would be offensive. Moon had said no one would force her into any situation she wasn't comfortable with. She trusted that. These people had clothed, fed, and taught her their ways. It was the least she could do.

"Fine," she mumbled, knowing they'd all hear her above the noise. "I'll do the matching rite."

A grin broke out on Sun's face, but Jasper's expression remained much darker. It simmered with an intensity that brought a flush to her cheeks. A flicker of doubt tickled the edge of her mind... perhaps this rite wasn't as light-hearted as she imagined.

Another tinkling against glass, and the carousing quietened. When Ada looked over, Clara straightened regally and lifted her chin before sweeping her gaze across the crowd. In the space of a heartbeat, the mood turned serious. When Clara spoke, her clear voice traveled across the grotto, and lifted above the cascading waterfall.

"Lupercalia is a sacred, time-honored tradition—and for most wolf-shifter packs around Elphyne. Let us remember how it all began."

She dipped her head and closed her eyes.

Every fae around the grotto reverently did the same.

Ada followed suit and lowered her gaze, listening to Clara's cutting tale.

"When the humans and their insatiable greed wiped out the first world, the Well brought it back through harmonizing life and joining many forms as one. We celebrate Lupercalia to remember the birth of our race, of when the first fae changelings were born.

"When poisoned ice dropped across the world, and the Well was beaten back with a rain of fire, the human mother of the first stumbled into the Lupercal cave for refuge from a bitter snowstorm. Near death, she gave birth to twin babes but died shortly after, not knowing the cave was the den of a starving she-wolf.

"Coming in from the cold hunt, the she-wolf found the twins—one male and one female—and instead of eating them, she showed mercy and nursed them. Through this life-giving milk, the babes not only survived, but transformed into wolf. The first shifters grew to be strong. With their she-wolf mother, and from gaining sustenance from the sacred pool, they grew to hunt together. They survived together. But most importantly, they thrived together. Thank the Well."

"Thank the Well."

The chorus rippled over the gathering. Ada glanced down at the blue contour lines twining up her arm. They seemed to glow brighter tonight.

"We celebrate this first stage of Lupercalia to remember that the Well nourishes us. If we harmonize with nature, it makes us strong. Now, before we feast, it is time for the first Lupercalia rite." Clara returned her gaze to Jasper and Ada. "We are honored to have Luperci this year who reflect the first shifters. One wolf male. One human female. Both blessed by the Well."

A round of cheers echoed against the grotto wall. Fae clapped each other on the back, hugged and threw tiny glass beads into the air. They were so happy. They truly believed Ada and Jasper would bring them luck and a flourishing harvest. She met his fierce amber gaze shrouded in dark lashes. Her heart thundered against her ribcage, and a crack formed in her wall of denial. She averted her eyes, but the feeling remained, wedged between her ribs and the fluttering in her stomach.

How can this be real?

Clara lifted her arms into the sky. The crowd silenced, and then she spoke six words Ada would never forget.

"It is time for the sacrifice."

THIRTEEN

Jasper had to hold his smile when Ada's face paled, and a bolt of fear came charging down their link.

He whispered at her ear, "It's not us they're sacrificing."

"Oh." Her shoulders dropped, then her eyes met his. "But... who?"

"Not who, what," he replied with a half-hearted shrug. "Just a goat for the feast."

"Oh." She nodded to herself.

"Don't worry, Pretty. I'll keep you safe."

This time when their eyes clashed, a flicker of confusion crossed her expression.

"Did I say something wrong?" he prompted.

"It's just that my friends used to call me Pretty Kitty. It was weird you said that." She grimaced. "And for the record, I hate it. Don't call me that again."

A memory pinged in his head. Not Pretty Kitty, but something else... a small voice. Little fingers grasping his own.

"Sleeping Pretty needs a kiss to wake."

"Reed?" A sigh. "Fine, *D'arn Jasper,* are you ready?"

He lifted his gaze to Clara waiting for him, holding the skull of a wolf with curved goat's horns protruding from the head.

She held it out to him. "Your mask."

"Mask?" he repeated vacantly. Ada already had hers on—a smaller bone-dry human skull. Her brown, subdued eyes watched him closely from beneath. She lifted the chin of the skull to rest the mask on top of her head, smiling gently at him.

If either of them had a right to be apprehensive about this, it was Ada. Not only was everything about this rite so different to what she'd be used to, but she had to wear the skull of her own kind. But it was she who gave him the courage to continue.

Clara's eyes narrowed. "You remember what to do, don't you?"

"Of course I do." He mentally shook himself. *Snap out of it.* But the memory of the little girl's voice and her words picked at his mind, begging him to pay attention. With a growl, he took the horned skull and placed it over his head, at the last minute, sliding it to the top of his head so Ada could see the smirk he tossed her way, before covering his face and becoming the wolf.

A band constricted around his chest. Air stifled under the heat of the mask. His smile dropped. Everything darkened, despite the eye sockets being wide. The sound of a crowd cheering entered his mind, banging on the stadium stands. He blinked and shook his head.

I'm not there. I'm here.

He clenched his bare toes in the soft grass. It wasn't the dirt of an arena.

I'm here.

"Let's go," he grunted and started for the Lupercal cave.

Pan flute notes lifted in decibel, climbing with the beat of a drum and the shake of maracas. It sounded too much like the beating against the stadium floor—boots as they stomped with bloodlust.

The crowd of fae parted to make way for their procession. Both Ada and Jasper moved down the grassed bank, to the sandy shore, and then along its edge until they arrived at the rocky wall next to the waterfall. Behind the veil of misty water, he could see a single flame flickering in the darkness.

The Lupercal cave.

The creation place of the first shifters. Two species coming together with a single goal—survival. Throughout his life, Jasper had been reminded of this fact. You could be furred, you could be pale skinned or dark, horned or winged, but one common goal united them all—the health of the land they lived off.

The roar of the waterfall drowned out the rhythmic music. His lungs struggled to work, but he took Ada's hand, spun them to face the gathering, and then once everyone had taken their look, he walked them through the mist and into the cramped cave where a single goat stood tethered to a stake.

Outside, no one heard it bleat.

Its fate was sealed.

A flat, empty bowl lay on a stone that had been cut to create an altar. Next to it lay a crystal knife with wolves etched into the blade, and a second bowl filled with milk and bundles of wool.

Jasper pointed to the knife and the empty bowl. "We collect the blood to paint on ourselves. Then we purify with the milk."

The goat bleated.

And bleated.

He hardly heard Ada shuffling up behind him. The screams of bleating victims pierced his ears. One stood out more than the rest—a pixie. A female. A fallen queen, her harem already dispatched.

Jasper's mouth dried. *Can't breathe.* He tried to pull his collar but found he was already naked. He scratched at himself instead, needing to get it off... but unable. *Get it off.*

He shook his head.

He could do this. Almost in slow motion, as though he floated outside of his body, he watched his hand reach for the knife, grasp the hilt, and turn it over in his palm.

"It's just a goat," he mumbled.

"Jasper?" Ada's voice didn't sound right. Not sweet like it used to be, but muffled and unsteady. *Not right.*

"It's just a goat," he repeated. "We hunt them in the wild all the time. It's for the feast. Its sacrifice will feed us, just as the she-wolf hunted for the first shifters before they could hunt for her."

My responsibility.

But the words echoed sharply, causing him to flinch.

Air rasped into his lungs, hot through the mask. His chest heaved. He gripped the knife so tight his knuckles ached.

The goat bleated again, forcing the memory from the Ring into his mind.

"Please..." the black-haired pixie sobbed, her wings nothing but broken, fibrous shells dangling behind her. She raised her hands before her face. The roar of spectators chanted at her plight.

"More!"

"Finish her!"

"Make her pay!"

For what? He'd thought. What had she done?

Why was she here?

"... Plee-he-hease..."

Salty tears ran down her face, creating dirt tracks that somehow fascinated him. It thrilled his wolf more. The tang of metal was everywhere. Blood. On his clawed hands. On his body.

He hesitated.

"What is fun for some, isn't fun for others."

His neck burned like fire, clouding his mind, confusing him.

"Killing is kindness," his mother had said. Or was it "Kindness before killing?"

And then his own voice: "I want to play, too."

He buried his fist deep into the heat of the pixie's chest.

"Jasper!" Ada's voice.

"I'm fine."

"You're not fine. I can feel it. What's wrong?"

"Nothing," he gasped, panting, shutting the valve on his emotions. "I'm fine. We need to... we need to... for the rite."

But it was as though an *elfant* had sat on his chest. He struggled to breathe. He tossed the knife and ripped the skull mask off. Cool air splashed his face and dragged into his lungs. He tried to speak, but his mouth was dirt. His tongue wouldn't work.

Bleating. Pleading.

Darkness crowded his vision. His knee dropped to the rock, lancing white-hot pain up his thigh. He fell to all fours, breathing hard, flaring his eyes wide, trying desperately not to pass out.

Shame. It scorched him.

A cool palm met the searing flesh of his back.

"I can't," he gasped, shaking his head, eyes burning. "I just can't."

The weight between his shoulder blades lifted.

"Don't turn away from me," he begged. "Don't leave."

"It's okay, Jasper," she said, and then she started humming.

Not a falter in her voice. No tremble, no flaw.

Behind him, he *felt* Ada move through the shifting atmosphere. He heard the scraping as she claimed the knife. Calm filtered down their bond, washing over him. Her sweet, ethereal voice captured his attention, giving him a life raft to hold.

The bleating stopped.

In the vacuum of its cries, he felt peace.

He squeezed his eyes shut. *What was wrong with him?*

Scrambling to sit, he rested his back against the stone alter. While he captured his breath, his mate moved swiftly and clinically as she prepared what they needed to complete the rite. She'd removed her mask, and he was glad because he got to see her face. It was filled with kindness as she touched the goat, stroking it, singing to it, and ensuring it didn't suffer well after the last light left its eyes.

The crushing weight of his failure landed on his shoulders. His gaze skated away but landed on the fallen horned wolf's skull.

All he could see was that Well-damned Ring and its gladiator pit. That damned city, Cornucopia, and its inability to follow any laws. He'd thought it had been so fun. So full of life and free from responsibility, but ten years in that Ring, and he'd seen the dark side of abandonment and indulgence. Without a guiding hand to rule them, the people of the city weren't free. They'd become as corrupt as the humans that came before them.

It had to change.

Bleating.

His heart hammered. His vision blurred. Not real. His fingers clenched on the dirt floor, grounding him. *This is real.*

Ada brought the full bowl over and knelt before him to place it on the floor beside them.

"It's not your responsibility." He grimaced. "I should have done it. And, instead, I let you tarnish yourself."

She touched him on the jaw and brought his gaze to hers. A sad smile flitted over her lips before it was lost to him again. A swell in his chest urged him to chase her smile, to find where the sadness came from, because it was deep. She owned her own tragic history. He'd heard some of it when she'd confided in him while he was in wolf form.

"Unfortunately," she said, "this isn't the first time I've had to do something like that."

He searched her eyes for the truth hidden beneath the liquid brown. "Are you broken too?"

She gulped in a deep breath before lifting her glimmering eyes to the cave ceiling. Her change in posture was a physical thing. He saw her take ownership of her features until she forced the tears away.

"The first time I learned to kill an animal without making it suffer, I was eleven. And I'd only learned how to do it the right way because I'd failed at first—epically—" She cut off, eyes glistening and turning red around the rims. That she'd felt the same sort of pain as him, it cut him straight down the middle. It pierced between his ribs in a way he'd never felt before. All he knew was that her heartache was his. He took her hand. Their gazes clashed, and she inched toward him, urgency driving her voice to a higher pitch.

"I knew I had to eat," she said, eyes unfocused. "I would have died if I didn't. But I hadn't been prepared for what happened after, for what I had to do to that animal so I could live." Her sadness turned to anger. "And I shouldn't have had to. In my time, you didn't need to hunt your own food. You could go down to the corner store and buy whatever you needed. My mother should have taken care of me. I know that now. It was incomprehensible. I should have reported her to the authorities, but I was a coward. Sometimes I wonder if I'd never met Harold or Laurel, would I have stayed on that mountain my entire life?"

"Tell me about your friends."

Ada sat down on her haunches. A wistful smile brightened her face. "Laurel and I met while she was on a fishing trip with her family. I was maybe fourteen at the time but had taken over Harold's hut after he'd died. Already, I hadn't seen my mother in years. To this day, I have no idea what happened to her." She shrugged. "I don't really care, to be honest. I only care what her selfishness robbed me of. But Laurel... yeah, she knew something wasn't right with my situation. She coaxed me back to her place, fed me proper city food, and gave me clothes. But it was more than that. It was a lifeline back to humanity."

Ada wiped her nose with the back of her hand and swallowed.

"Anyway, we should probably do the next part of this, right?"

Jasper tore his gaze from her face and looked at the bowl of blood. Embarrassment washed through him. He should have been the one to prepare it, not Ada. It was his job.

Another nightmare to add to his failings.

"What do we do?" she asked.

He lifted her with him as he positioned himself on his knees, facing her. Then he dipped his fingers into the warm blood and swiped them across her forehead, leaving a streak of red. He guided her fingers to do the same to him.

Her intimate touch was a balm on his soul. He pushed into her hand. Contrary to his fear, she didn't flinch. She cupped his face and allowed him to stare into her eyes. In their depths, he saw salvation. Every cell in his body wanted to drink her up, to rub himself over her and cover her with his scent. All he wanted to do was kiss her. And he hated himself for it. Now that his memories were returning, he knew she was too good for him.

"Now we cleanse ourselves," he rasped. "With the wool dipped in milk."

She got to her feet and collected the milk, coming back and meeting him on her knees. She grasped a floating ball of wool and squeezed it out.

"What does this symbolize?" she asked.

"The blood represents how the humans came to the she-wolf, full of rage, unnecessary violence, and greed. The milk we use to purify the blood. It represents new life. The shift into fae."

"So I clean off the blood," she confirmed reverently.

He nodded with an uncharacteristic bashfulness heating his neck. His ears twitched. "And this might sound stupid, but we... um... laugh as we are cleansed."

She snorted. "Okay. Weird, but okay."

"Laughter purifies the soul."

Her expression sobered. "It does. Inside and out. Okay, here we go."

Jasper studied her as she wrung out the soaked wool and was so beguiled by her face that he forgot to laugh until she prompted him. But she wasn't laughing either, so when she lifted the wet wool to his head, he dodged. She frowned and shifted her aim to swipe at his face again. He dodged the other way, a slow curve lifting his lips.

"Stop it," she murmured breathlessly, but the smile was already forming on her face.

He bit his lip to hold his own. "I promise I'll be a good boy."

This made her smile broaden. "Maybe I'll reward you with a treat."

"Don't joke about that unless you mean it."

A buzzing of unsaid intent passed between them, and then she lifted the soaked wool to his head. He allowed her to clean some off, but on the next turn, dodged. They both burst out laughing. He continued to goad her and joke until she cleaned the last off his face.

"My turn, I guess," she mumbled, eyes still dancing from their laughter.

When she dunked her bloodstained wool into the milk, Jasper's fingers covered hers briefly. A spark jolted between them, and she withdrew her hand from the bowl. He went to clean her forehead, but she dodged, grinning at him with mischief. So he flicked milk at her face.

She squealed, laughing. He fell in love with the light igniting her eyes, illuminating all the dark places in his heart. The melody of her sweet honey voice warmed his blood.

"You're beautiful," he murmured, hand lowering after cleaning her face.

A blush stained her freckled cheeks.

Pink milk trickled from her temple, slid along her jaw, and pooled at her dimpled chin, ready to drop. He brushed it away with his thumb, then found his fingers refused to leave the velvet touch of her skin. They slid along her jaw and collected in the hair behind her ear, burying deep.

His gaze snagged on her tongue as it darted out to moisten her bottom lip.

Her lips parted.

They inched closer, their mingled breaths caressing each other's face.

"Give me this," he whispered, and then softly bit the air before her mouth, baring his teeth with painful longing. "Just one more."

From the way she struggled to catch her breath, and the low simmer of lust down their bond, he knew they were close. *Almost.*

Music burst into life outside the cave. The drums and the flute grew in crescendo.

He cursed softly. He would shatter those drums and shove the flutes—

Her hand flattened against his chest, derailing his thoughts.

And just like that, the beauty tamed the wolf. His mind shuttered. His body sang. Ada's brows puckered as she looked at him and swallowed.

The loud percussion of drums vibrated the cave walls. Or was it his heart?

"That's our cue," she whispered, sadness entering her tone... or had he imagined that too?

She stood, bringing him with her until they both straightened, eyes locked.

Someone shouted outside... possibly Clara trying to wrap things up.

Disappointment rocked through him with such violence, he shocked himself. He knew, in that moment, he would do anything to protect his time with her. When next they were alone, nothing would get in his way of claiming her kiss.

FOURTEEN

Ada let Jasper guide her out of the cave. The moment they emerged through the waterfall's mist, a deafening roar vibrated through the grotto. The crowd cheered and howled. Bashfulness froze her limbs. Jasper's grip on her hand flinched, tightening almost painfully.

He still shuttered his emotions from her. But she knew enough that his reaction inside the cave was caused by tragic memories. Perhaps the cheering crowd reminded him of something he'd rather forget.

When he'd fallen to his knees in the cave, she'd wanted to take his head in her hands and use her gift to remove his pain. She wasn't even sure if such a thing was possible for mental pain, but wanted to try. Regardless, it wasn't her choice to make. He needed to ask for help at some point, or else he wouldn't heal.

Are you broken too?

When he'd said those words and searched for a connection within her eyes, she hadn't the courage to tell him she was born broken, but had pieced herself back together, thanks to her friends. She now realized this was part of the reason she held him at arm's length. When her mother didn't care enough to keep her alive, Ada had been a child, angry and scared of the world. She knew how hard it had been to glue herself together when she didn't even know what whole looked like. She *would not* be broken again, and that's exactly what she would be if she fell for him, and then if he left or betrayed her.

So she'd done the next best thing she could think of—she'd completed the rite for him. It hadn't bothered her as much as she thought it might. The realization settled in her gut with an uncomfortable feeling.

Destiny.

She'd resented her upbringing in the old world to the point of bitterness, but how could she argue with that one pivotal moment where everything she'd learned about survival screamed in her face—*this is why*. It was as though she'd been training for this time, for a life here where sometimes you had to hunt for food, where creature comforts weren't the same, where sometimes you were so lonely you hurt.

Jasper picked his way through the crowd, leading her by the hand. Someone had taken the goat. She expected to soon see it on the roasting spit.

She knew it was normal, nothing to freak out over, but a silence had entered her mind in the cave. Something had shifted inside her. She'd given up a part of her past and embraced the fae culture as her own. And Jasper?

He may not have revealed what tortured him, but he'd allowed her to see him vulnerable. He'd shared that part of himself, and he'd allowed her to care for him. It was so unlike the exterior he projected to the rest of the world. She felt closer to him in a way she wasn't yet ready to comprehend.

Everyone wanted to touch them—the lucky Luperci—as they paraded through the gathering. But what started out as something almost reverent, ended in hands plucking, grasping, and invading her personal space. Single, male and female fae smothered Jasper. Ada almost lost her grip on his hand. But it wasn't just him they wanted, it was her. Females touched Ada's belly, tugging at the fabric of her dress, praying for fertility and the gift of new life. She thought this event was supposed to be serene, but it turned frenzied and feral, and when someone's fingers caught on her shoulder strap, almost pulling it off, she panicked.

She couldn't breathe.

Were they being like this because she was human, or was it the thrall of the festival?

For a mad minute, she panicked that there would always be a divide between them. Would they ever accept her as one of their own?

Jasper was there in a heartbeat, pushing fae back with a snarl of elongated teeth that made her knees tremble. Fae ears flattened, and they dipped their chins in submission, bowing as they backed away.

"Enough," he snapped to those still trying to touch him. Then, upon seeing the fear he'd just caused, he paused and seemed to catch himself. With a visible effort, he pulled his snarling lips into an easy grin before adding, "It's time to feast."

Cheers whooped. The air became less stifling as the crowd thinned, and a path to the banquet table cleared. There was nothing behind the table except a few feet of grass before the rocky shore dipped down into the pool. Above, tree branches leaned over the setting, dangling tinkling wind chimes and glowing lanterns swaying in the gentle breeze. The music started up again. An abundance of food and drink spread over the entire table length. Glasses filled with liquids of all sorts of colors made Ada's taste-buds water.

In the middle of the long table were two mosaicked thrones. Curved, wooden goat horns crowned the chairs. Or maybe they were actually goat horns... or some other creature she'd not seen before. Next to the thrones, and around the table, were smaller, less gaudy chairs filled with important fae from around the village. Clara, Moon and his mate, Halona. Sun sat opposite the thrones. As Ada's attention shifted to the chairs beside him, she noticed fae not from the village.

Clara had mentioned emissaries from other towns. The Satyrs were there, as were the Oak Men. Next to them were two pointy-eared fae dressed in luxurious silk clothing. Next, another two males with fur-tipped, pointed ears sat on either side of a Viking-type lady with a long silver braid trailing down her back. She glared at Jasper as though she knew him.

But he only had eyes for Ada.

"Are you okay?" he asked softly.

She nodded. "It just got a bit personal with all that touching. Anyone would think they actually wanted a piece of me."

A shiver ran down her spine as her doubt about being human crept in.

"It's because you're astonishing. They worship you."

Ada gave him a weak smile and untucked her hair from behind her ears so they weren't on display.

"Don't hide yourself. This world isn't going to change if we don't ask it." He brazenly tucked the hair behind her ears. "I would never let anyone hurt you," he promised.

And this time, it didn't feel empty. It didn't feel like something a man said just to get in a lady's pants. It was heartfelt. A rush of gratitude heated her blood, and she touched her fingers to her lips and pushed her hand down and out.

Amusement sparkled in his eyes. He brought her fingers to his lips, murmuring against them, "Are you ready for the first feast?"

"First?"

Roguishness replaced his fleeting humor, and she felt a little dip in her stomach.

Uh-oh.

She did *not* need to feel like that right now. Certainly not for him. But even as her heart tried to slam up walls, she knew she was in trouble. He made her forget her senses. His smile was more dangerous than his teeth, and if she wasn't careful, she would walk willingly toward both, happily allowing herself to be devoured body and soul.

"Come on," he said. "The fun part is just beginning."

Placing her hand in the crook of his arm, he was all the confidence she needed. It made her feel honored to have glimpsed his vulnerable side in the cave, and she fell even deeper in thrall with him.

He strode them straight to the banquet table and opened his mouth, presumably to make the introductions, but the Viking-like woman slammed down her glass and stood swiftly. Her two companions joined her.

"You have some nerve, D'arn Jasper," she said, glaring at him. "My brother and nephew are besides themselves with worry. They've been hunting all over Elphyne since you disappeared from the Twelve's house."

He frowned and cocked his head. "Kyra?"

"I'll have you know, it's now High Lady Kyra Nightstalk, Alpha of Crescent Hollow." She scoffed. "I mean, they said you'd lost your memories, but I didn't believe them. Now look at you, indulging as normal, forgetting about those who care about you. Don't ask me why they bother."

His fingers tightened around Ada's hand, and she gave him a soft squeeze of solidarity. This was *good*. More of his past was catching up with him. Only people who cared got angry like this.

The thought hit her with a jolt.

Who was this alpha who commanded respect? Why did she care for Jasper? Who were they to each other?

"Do you remember me?" Kyra asked. "Or Rush? Thorne?"

This time, recognition passed over his features but was shortly stamped out by confusion.

"I remember enough," he answered curtly.

Ada bit her lip. It was on the tip of her tongue to come to his defense, but she wasn't sure if she should reveal how far the curse marks had eroded his mind. As it turned out, she didn't need to.

Clara shifted back her chair and joined Ada and Jasper. She smiled tightly and pointed at the guests as she said their names.

"You know the Crescent Hollow representatives, and of course the Spring Court King Tian and his Queen Oleana."

"Elves," Jasper murmured to her.

They were the couple in fine silks. Were these the ones Clara had mentioned would be able to train her better?

"The Delphinian Oak Men, Lord Brand and Larch. And then the High Lord Aubrette and his son Lord Win."

The last two were directed at the satyrs. Ada raised her brows. Queens, Kings, Lords and Ladies. She truly was in another time and place.

"The pleasure is mine." Jasper regally bowed his head, then faced his aunt and lowered his voice. "I didn't know this Lupercalia would have so many foreign dignitaries as guests, Aunty."

"Well, if you weren't cloistered in your room for the past week, perhaps you'd know things are different this year."

"The breeding law is abolished."

Clara raised her brow. "That and the Darkfoot pack is proud to have one of our own, not only Well-blessed, but the High King's official heir, as the Luperci."

He narrowed his eyes. "But are you proud?"

She returned his sly stare. "The Darkfoot pack has a long memory." She forced a smile on her face and raised her voice. "Please take your seats, the meals are about to be served."

Ada wasn't sure what had passed between them, but it prompted a flash of pain in Jasper's eyes, and a nod of acknowledgment.

They took their seats on the thrones. To Ada, it was just some fun for the night, but Jasper blended with the regality as though he was destined for the spotlight. The affable grin plastered on his face looked so genuine, for a moment, Ada forgot his pain in the cave.

It unsettled her how quickly he could shift his facade.

The moment the thought entered her mind, she wondered which facade was the real Jasper. The fun one, or the serious one. Maybe neither. Maybe the one he'd been in the cave was it... *Are you broken like me?*

Servers came around to the table, placing entrees on all plates and filling glass goblets with some sort of fizzing beverage that smelled like sour apples. The pan flutes picked up again. A few beats behind, the maracas shook reluctantly. Ada would bet Lake was desperate to either join in with everyone or go home.

When guests sat at their sporadic table settings, the musicians stood down from their steps. Two gangly youths, both of them with pointed ears, and small stag horns growing out of their heads. Next to them, Lake's face was exactly how she imagined— bored and over it.

She caught his eye, waved and smiled. He perked up immediately and shook his maracas with extra fervor.

With the magical atmosphere, wistful music, and fantastical creatures, Ada truly felt as though she'd wandered into a fairytale book.

"So," Sun picked up a piece of meat from his plate, popped it into his mouth, and then looked at Jasper. "I'm going to say what everyone is thinking."

"Of course you are," Moon said drolly. "Maybe finish your mouthful first."

A chagrined glance at his brother, and then Sun leveled his stare at Jasper. "Are you going to tell your Guardian brethren about the raids?"

The small conversation hushed at the table. Jasper tensed, and then carefully took a sip of his drink before placing it back down. "You have been collecting something forbidden at the highest level. Chances are, they already know. Unless you can give a valid reason why, then it's the Prime's call what happens next."

Moon lost hold of his fork. "Are you telling me you have no loyalty to our pack, after all we've done to protect you this past week?"

"You, protect *me?*" Jasper's incredulous words burst out of a smirking mouth. "Correct me if I'm wrong, but I believe it was I who protected your town, and my mate who healed it."

The two shifters glared at each other, their ears twitching back.

"For Crimson's sake," Halona said, throwing her napkin down and then glaring at her mate. "Just tell him who made you do it. I won't have us go down for that royal floater."

Gasps chorused around the table.

Moon's nostrils flared, and his gaze darted between the table guests as though he was searching for signs of danger, but none came. There was something odd that Ada couldn't quite figure out, and then she realized Halona had referred to the floater as royal. Calling someone a floater was reference to them being spit out from the ceremonial lake. Could she have meant King Mithras? If so, that was treason.

And no one complained.

Sun and Moon glanced at their mother, who'd already paused her conversation with the King and Queen of the Spring Court. It seemed everyone at the table waited for the answer. Clara gave her sons a curt nod of approval.

Moon met Jasper's eyes. "It was your father."

The mood darkened. The air chilled. Jasper's gaze darkened in a way Ada had never seen before.

"If there is something you're trying to say, Cousin, then say it."

"Fine," Moon said and looked him directly in the eye. "The Order arrested the King's human advisor, then you—the King's heir—"

"He doesn't intend for me to wear the Glass Crown."

"If you'll let me finish," Moon ground out with a glare. "You disappear, and then you turn up with a human on your arm—"

"Well-blessed human," Jasper cut in, again.

"Doesn't matter." Moon slammed his palm on the table. "You can see how we might be cautious that you are colluding with them."

"You want to know whose side I'm on?" Jasper asked.

"I want to know if you are a Mithras, or a Darkfoot."

"I've never been a Mithras."

"Could have fooled us."

No one responded. Halona's previous comment was treasonous enough, but from what Ada gathered, everyone at the table wasn't happy with the current political climate. Nervously, she tried to assess their body language, but no one revealed a thing except the occasional uncomfortable shift in their seats.

Jasper chugged his drink down, planting the empty glass on the table with a clunk. "I'm on my own side. Always have been."

But the moment he said the words, a wash of shame trickled through their bond.

"Have you no pride?" Sun snarled. "We are your kin."

"He's not cared in centuries. Why start now," Moon added.

Ada noted Clara made no move to intercept.

"Be careful what you say, Cousin." Jasper's knuckles whitened around the glass.

Moon leaned forward. "I'm only stating the truth."

"I put my life on the line to save your village."

"But you just said, you're only in it for yourself."

Jasper clamped his lips shut, and it infuriated Ada because she knew he wasn't this selfish person he claimed to be. Why risk his life to protect the town? Why kill the wolpertinger for her instead of simply running into the woods? Why participate in this ceremony to which he had no obligation? She'd only known him a short while, but from what she'd seen, he'd do anything to protect his loved ones. Maybe no one had protected him. So she spoke up.

"His father tried to assassinate him only days ago. How can he be colluding with someone who wants to kill him?"

Sun blinked at Jasper. "But he legitimized you."

Kyra laughed harshly. "He's been trying to kill Jasper since the moment he knew he was born. You thought the assassination attempts would just stop because he suddenly named Jasper as successor? Rush and Thorne said he'd been kidnapped, tortured, and cursed into obedience. Why would Mithras do that if he had Jasper's loyalty? Why would the Guardians raid the Summer Court, arrest the King's advisor—human advisor, mind you—and then rescue the cursed prince?"

King Tian rubbed his beardless chin. "The High King has certainly been keeping secrets."

"That's an understatement," Kyra mumbled into her cup.

Tian cleared his throat. "That leads us to the reason we've come. During the celebration where the High King announced you as his heir, there were... interesting conversations among the congregation."

Ada sat down with an icky feeling crawling up her spine. She knew enough about conflict to understand when shady deals were being made, and from the stolen glances between the party at the table, there was something they wanted Jasper involved with. And she wasn't going to like it.

Queen Oleander ran her finger around the rim of her glass, then pursed her lips, agitated. "The increase in human slaves around Elphyne has always been something we never understood. The elves are not vicious, or gratuitously cruel. We devote ourselves to education and forwarding our race. But he gifts us with human artisan slaves—glamoured and spelled to perform and dance until their fingers and toes bleed."

The Satyr, High Lord Aubrette, leaned forward and projected his voice down the table. "He has petitioned our banner to follow him into the Unseelie Kingdom and claim vengeance against their monsters invading our lands. What do you say to that, Guardian? Or are you Prince?"

The more and more these people spoke, the more Ada felt Jasper's anxiety churn through their link. His control over blocking his emotions had long since evaporated.

Kyra spoke, leaning forward. "Two years ago, Mithras turned a blind eye to Lord Thaddeus's collusion with the enemy. Now we hear he's asking fae to hoard metal, only for a human raiding party to conveniently turn up. It's clear to me he has grand plans that go against the interests of Elphyne and the integrity of the Well. Surely as a Guardian, if not a prince, you have an opinion about that."

"Why don't you ask the Prime?" Jasper responded. "The leader of the Order would have more to say."

"Deflecting again?"

"It's not deflection. It's simply that I don't know. I was... indisposed... for much of the past decade," he conceded. "I'm only just learning now of what has come to pass."

The satyr slammed his fist on the table. "Much has come to pass. We are not happy with the direction Elphyne is headed. The Seelie High King talks about war with the Unseelie High Queen. He wants war, and she's brushing it off as nothing but a nuisance."

"Well, she does command the Wild Hunt," Kyra drawled.

The satyr glared at her. "Whether or not she commands the Wild Hunt makes no difference. What matters is that our High King wants to start a war with our own kind to be used as fodder while the real enemy is ignored while they pilfer dangerous resources from our land. And that's only the easily accessed metal, the parts scavenged above the land. If this human leader manages to get a stronghold, he can invade and claim our lands to mine for resources as he sees fit. The Well will die—*fae* will die— and the barren wasteland will expand."

"It will never come to that," Jasper growled, his jaw clenching, his eyes smoldering.

"And how can you be so sure?"

"Because I won't let it."

His words hung heavily in the music laden space that followed. With each passing second, the atmosphere thickened with a foreboding sense of duty. They all knew what had to be done, but no one wanted to make the first move.

Clara stood slowly and looked each of the guests at the table in the eye. "I will say it, if none of you will." Her eyes settled last on Jasper. "Word is Mithras made you his heir only to kill you and claim vengeance on the Unseelie High Queen. You skirt around the truth, but we all know what happened. Some of us were there when he unveiled you to the Court. And we see the remnants of the curse around your neck. He kidnapped and tortured you in the Ring. Yet, you somehow emerged from it all, stronger than before and with a further blessing from the Well." She jerked her chin toward Ada. "We don't need someone on the throne who is complicit in the rape and pillage of our land. We need someone who knows exactly what the Well needs to flourish. We need a Darkfoot. And a Guardian." She picked up her glass goblet and raised it into the air. "To the new Seelie High King Reed—"

"Stop!" Jasper slammed his fist on the table and lurched to his feet.

The table shook with the impact. All eyes were on him, watching.

"A Guardian has no claim to the throne..." He frowned, catching the falsity of his own words, and then mumbled to himself, as though just realizing it, "But I *am* the heir, *and* a Guardian."

Clara's voice turned softer. "Your mother's prophecy is coming true. It may have taken hundreds of years, but you're the last surviving heir of King Mithras's line to exist. There is no one else who can claim the Glass Crown but you. You have to admit, your re-emergence has come at the right time to breathe new life into the land."

No answer.

"What do you say, Jasper?"

Each Lord and Lady at the table raised their voices and started arguing over each other. They all agreed with Clara, but couldn't meet on a plan of action. Conversation became chaotic and heated, to the point Ada thought one of them would reach over the table and strangle the other.

Through it all, they'd forgotten that they had asked Jasper for his opinion. He scratched his neck, eyes darting over the place until his gaze leveled on Ada and brightened.

He stood and clinked his spoon against his glass to get their attention.

"Enough with the arguing. We're not here for that." He grinned charismatically at them and called over a server before saying. "The pack is waiting patiently for their Lupercalia matching rite. It's time to give it to them. Tonight is a celebration to honor the Well. It is a time for strangers to come together and, for one night, forget the trappings of their stations and breathe new life into the pack. Let us have fun and worry about politics tomorrow."

It was clear most of the table wanted to keep talking, but Sun took his glass, tinkled his porcelain spoon against it, and then raised his voice to be heard over the music and revelers.

"Here, here. It's time for the matching ceremony." Sun's half-mast eyes landed on Ada. "And then the hunt."

King Tian stood swiftly. Ada tensed, thinking he would start another argument, but his cheeks flushed adorably and smiled at his wife. "My wife and I have brought a gift from Delphinium to honor the rite. Enough servings of divilixir for all matching rite participants."

Cheers rang out. Fae clapped loudly. Someone whistled.

Must be a good drink, Ada thought as servers burst into action. Trays with small glasses of blue and yellow liquid emerged and were distributed among the tables.

Prim arrived at their side, holding her tray. Next to shot glasses were the same masquerade masks a woman had peddled from her market cart when they'd first arrived at the village. Designed and painted to resemble a wolf, the half-face masks had glass beads dangling from a thin red cord at the ears. Some were unadorned.

Prim placed two glasses before each of them—one blue and one yellow. She dropped a beaded mask before Ada, and an unadorned mask before Jasper. Then she picked up her glass of yellow and held it in the air. With her gaze locked on Jasper, she said, "Here's to purging impurities." She downed it in one gulp. "And then to getting even dirtier."

Sun roared out laughing. Even Moon cracked a smile. Kyra whooped along with her partners. Jasper shot it back with a tiny smile, so did a few others around the table.

"Your turn, Ada," Prim prompted, eyes on the full glass at Ada's fingers.

"What is it?" she asked.

"Everyone taking part in the rite must drink it."

She sniffed the liquid. It smelled like honeyed nectar. Everyone else drank it, so she shot it back, wincing at the burn down her throat. The blue glass remained. *Aw, fuck it.* Jasper was right. It was time to have some fun. Then, before she lost her nerve, she did the same with the blue shot and slammed it down with a grin splashed on her face.

Prim raised her brows, impressed, and nudged Ada's shoulder with her finger. "You're going to get real dirty then, huh?"

Ada snort-laughed, hand covering her mouth in a hiccup. "I don't know what that means."

She couldn't stop smiling. Her blood was fizzing. It was like her body was taking her down a path her mind couldn't travel.

"You'll find out soon enough," Prim said, and then shot her blue drink back, giving Jasper a wink.

What was that? But Ada had no time to ponder Prim's flirt, Sun drank his, and then slammed the empty glass on the table, shaking the foundations. "Bottoms up."

More laughter erupted.

A pleasant heat built in Ada's blood, firing through her system, and beating out the cool night air. She wiggled and couldn't help smiling at Jasper, but found him sitting still with his fingers around the glass of blue liquid. For some reason, he wasn't caught in the avalanche of revelry, and that small part of Ada that hadn't caught up, tried to pump the brakes. Something was wrong.

"I thought this sort of thing was your scene," she joked. "You're not drinking?"

A smoldering look ghosted his features. Confusion flitted over his expression, but he just shook his head and shifted the glass away.

Sun laughed and patted the table. Ada couldn't help thinking she was missing something.

"What's the joke?" she asked.

Prim smiled sweetly at her, a blush already tinting her cheeks. "Sweetling, I thought you knew. The yellow is to purge our impurities, but the blue will keep us virile and amorous for hours to come." She leaned close and whispered, "It's what makes the hunt a little more fun."

Oh my dear Lord.

FIFTEEN

The night was going to end in disaster, Jasper thought, as he watched Ada wade fully clothed into the sacred Lupercalia pool, her gown trailing behind her like a mermaid's tail. With every step, the bioluminescent silt stirred, coming alive. Unlike every other female submerging, Ada was clothed in cream. They wore red. But she didn't need the difference to stand out. The water made her gown cling to her skin, revealing every inch and perfect curve, stealing his breath, making his heart stutter.

When she'd walked in, he couldn't tear his eyes away. Then she submerged up to her shoulders, blond hair trailing on the surface like strings of gold mixing with the red ribbon of fate clutched in her fingers. But the true test of his resolve was when she emerged, inch by inch, on the other side. Water sluiced down her body to reveal the shape of her rear curves plastered to the translucent dress. He clenched his fists and then adjusted the damned mask on his face. At least this one allowed him to breathe. He would rip it off the moment he caught her.

The very idea of sinking his teeth into her caused his inner wolf to pace restlessly, ready for the hunt to begin.

Crimson only knew how his body would be reacting if he'd actually taken the divilixir.

Sun sidled up to him. Like most other hunters, he'd used the bioluminescent silt to paint stripes and patterns down his bare torso to mimic being Well-blessed. With his painted torso and dark hair and similar mask, Sun appeared remarkably similar to him. The only distinction was that Jasper's markings shone brighter than his cousin's. His were real.

"Still think she's yours?" Sun taunted.

A growl rumbled in the base of Jasper's throat, but he swallowed it down as he watched Ada's red ribbon trail behind her, churning in the water, sinking beneath the depths. With every step the females had made to cross the pool, blue bloomed to life and colored the water, making it impossible to see through. There was no way he'd be able to find out which ribbon belonged to her. His choice would be by random touch, just like everyone else's.

Anyone could match with Ada. Even Sun. Even... he shot a sideways glance to the other males eagerly bouncing on their toes, splashing on the shore. Each and every one had their hands on their pants, ready to strip. He wasn't sure whether they would shift for the advantage of using their wolf's nose in the hunt, or whether they simply wanted nothing impeding them for when they caught their match. But their hands didn't leave their pants. Maybe it was the divilixir amping up their hormones.

Didn't matter.

He would find Ada first. The Well would match them. He had faith.

And if it didn't... well, he pitied the poor soul who got in his way of claiming her. He would prove to her they were destined for each other. And they would forget about the politics being shoved down his throat.

He wanted none of it.

A wolf howled in the distance. Night birds took to the sky from branches. The drums beat faster behind them, and the spectators cheered.

All females had now emerged on the other side, dripping with water and smeared with bioluminescent blue. There had to be at least twenty, or so, but Jasper's eyes were only for Ada as she glanced coyly at him from over her shoulder, eyes bright through the slits of her mask.

His heart leapt into his throat at the impact of her beauty. Their Well-blessed marking twinkled up her arm. Wavy blond hair cascaded down her shoulders, shielding her wet chest from indecency. One end of the red ribbon was wrapped around her fist. The long length floated in the water before her, and then dipped beneath the depths, waiting for him.

He imagined he could already scent her unique arousal on the wind.

No longer was his inner wolf satisfied to pace. It hurled itself against the cages of his body, begging him to start the chase, unwilling to accept defeat.

Claim her. Mark her. Mine.

She had no idea what was coming for her.

After tonight, everything would change.

CHAPTER
SIXTEEN

Ada's brief dip in the water had been a balm against her feverish skin, too tight for her body, and already begging for the kind of relief only touch could bring. She shouldn't have drunk that blue liquid, but as she locked eyes with Jasper across the pool churning from the cascades, she found she didn't care.

The liquid had loosened something inside her, freed her from the constraints of propriety. Her limbs were jelly. Her body tingled. Butterflies crashed in her stomach. With each passing moment, a pleasant build of heaviness grew between her legs, and if she wasn't surrounded by the watchful eyes of the gathering, she would have pressed her thighs together to dispel the sensation. Heat flushed her cheeks, and she stifled a moan, grateful for the mask hiding most of her expression. Anticipation was an unknown visitor in the air, come to tease and entice her out of her usual self-imposed safe zone.

This is insane.

What am I doing?

She wasn't the only one on her side feeling a little turned on. The red-dressed females tried not to show their eagerness, but beneath their masks, their pupils were blown and their cheeks ruddy. Their hands clutched and flexed at their dresses or twirled about their ribbons. One or two even touched their breasts, squeezing. Feet danced from side to side, ready to... to what?

A delightful fuzziness swam in Ada's head.

What happens next?

She must have said the words aloud because the masked blond beside her turned with a smile and answered.

"Each of the hunters will pick a ribbon from the pool to see which maiden they've matched with, and then..." She wiggled and squirmed. "Then the hunt is on."

Ada recognized her voice. Her hair had been pulled back into a low ponytail. "Prim?"

She put her finger to her lips. "Shh. We're all nameless for tonight. I mean"—she giggled—"except for you two Luperci. Everyone knows who you are from your clothes, but we pretend, for one night, that we are nameless."

"Right," she laughed. "What happens at Lupercalia stays at Lupercalia."

Approved anonymity for everyone else... so this was like an organized one-night-stand. The moment the thought hit, she blushed from head to toe. Never in her life had she done something so wild and reckless, and she found she didn't care. She was too loose, too excited, too *hot*. She'd been in this world for a week and there had to come a time where she let go of the past and embraced her future. From what she'd learned about the humans of today, she did not align with their beliefs. Which meant she had to fully embrace this culture, these rules, and these traditions.

Or go back to living alone on a mountain.

That was the old Ada. The broken one Jasper had glimpsed. The one before she met Clarke and Laurel. Her heart twinged at the thought of her beloved friends. Sisters, more like it. They would be sad if Ada went back to her isolation. So, embracing these new customs had to be the path to her new future. Perhaps that was with Jasper.

Only one doubt niggled in her mind. She turned back to Prim with a frown. "What happens if someone gets... you know, knocked up?"

"Knocked up?" Prim giggled. "You mean with child?"

Ada nodded, to which Prim laughed further. "Oh, silly. Lupercalia is a fertility rite. That's the entire point!"

Shock bounced around in Ada's skull. She wasn't *that* willing to explore. *Oh my God.* Panic. *I'm not ready for that!*

Moon's words came back to her. No one will force her to do anything she didn't want. But as the heat of the elixir sparked in her pulse, igniting her blood, she wondered if she'd be powerless to stop herself.

And she wasn't the only one who would have impulse control. The male shifters on the other side of the pool paced and prowled along the shore, eyes skittering between the maidens and the red ribbons they would soon pull out of the water.

Her throat dried.

Naked male chests gleamed under the moonlight. They kept their identities hidden with similar half-wolf mask as the maidens. They all wore red loose pants, just like the females wore red dresses. But even without the change in clothing color, Ada could distinguish Jasper from the feel of him echoing down their bond, the scars on his torso, the glowing marks down his arm, and, of course, the tantalizing glimpse of dark hair trailing down from his lower abdomen to dip beneath his pants.

She'd recognize those abs anywhere.

Gosh. She patted her cheeks. What did that say about her?

Clara stepped onto some rocks by the waterfall so the gathered crowd could view her better. With her arms raised, she called for hush until the excitement dulled, and all eyes landed on her. Only the sound of the cascading water could be heard. That, and Ada's heart smashing against her ribcage.

Ada met Jasper's eyes through his mask. He watched her intently. A bolt of lust speared down their bond. Her hand fluttered to her throat, and a slow, wicked grin stretched his perfect lips. He'd done that on purpose. The bastard knew exactly how to control their bond.

Fuck. She was in trouble.

"Lupercalia is a time-honored tradition of the Darkfoot Pack, and indeed, many shifter packs around Elphyne. It is the celebration of the birth of our race. It is how we honor the Well. And for the first time in centuries, thanks to the appointment of our very own Darkfoot Prince, the unsanctioned breeding law has been abolished. We're finally celebrating Lupercalia the right way again—with a matching ceremony that won't end in execution."

A boisterous cheer rang out.

Unsanctioned breeding? Execution? Centuries? The words bounced around Ada's head. She couldn't imagine living in a world where you were terrified to get pregnant for fear of execution. The enthusiasm of this Lupercalia was completely understandable.

"We're honored to have these two Luperci participate in the hunt this year," Clara shouted. "As tradition dictates, because your identity is compromised, and you are the honored guests, you may choose your ribbon first."

She gestured for Jasper to enter the pool, but he just stood back and folded his arms with a smirk that hid a wealth of mysteries glinting in his eyes.

He shook his head, and then boomed back, "I'll go last."

Shocked murmurs rippled over the gathering. Some fae shot up from their tables, sloshing their drinks in their haste. Some dashed closer to the pool, eager expressions lighting up their faces.

Ada stared at Jasper.

His lips stretched wider, and then he added in a loud, arrogant voice, "My mate needs to be convinced that we are destined to be together, because it is the Well's will."

Oohs and *Ahhs* of agreement coursed around. Ada caught glimpses of fae nodding and smiling in understanding—*the poor ignorant human doesn't believe in the power of the Well.*

It riled Ada to no end. Maybe that was why the next words blustered out of her mouth. "I will enjoy proving you wrong!"

Wolf whistles and loud whoops of excitement. Ada couldn't help smiling as she caught Jasper's wide-eyed stare. Her words weren't all instinctive reaction. There was some truth to it. She supposed, even with all she'd learned about her connection to this mystical force that gave her power, there was still so much unknown. Faith seemed incredible. Unless she saw it with her own eyes, she would take their words with a grain of salt. The arrogant shifter honestly thought he stood a chance of claiming her ribbon, after all the other hunters had their chance.

The pool still churned from the maidens' recent journey across the water and the cascading waterfall. Blue silt mixed murkily so the red ribbons were hidden and tangled. There was no way Jasper could pick hers out on purpose when he couldn't even see where to put his hand.

That was the whole point, she supposed.

Her heart skipped a beat as the humor dropped from his expression and his eyes narrowed with a secret message—*You're going to pay for your doubt.*

Another shiver of heat pulsed through her. Immediately, the hard line of Jasper's mouth tipped up, as though he'd felt everything she'd projected. Or had scented it.

She said to Prim through the side of her mouth, "There's no magic matching spell in the water, or anything, is there? I mean, he can't cheat and *make* us match, right?"

"Isn't that what you want?"

"Maybe, but I won't make it easy on him."

A beat of silence stretched for longer than necessary. Ada glanced at her new friend, but found a ruthless glimmer in Prim's expression as she stared back. It was the flicker of something dark, and then it was gone, almost like Ada had imagined it like a cloud crossing the moon.

"Nope," Prim replied, her gaze swinging back to Jasper with a smile. "It's just plain, simple water."

Ada's pulse skittered with nerves. She bit her lip and turned back to Jasper as he stood calmly at the end of the line, still watching her.

"Hunters, find your maiden's ribbon!" Clara shouted, throwing her hands into the air.

Whoops, whistles, and drums beat loudly as the hunters launched into the water, pushing each other out of the way in a frenzy. As they submerged to waist length, they thrust their hands into the blue-silt churning liquid and fished beneath the surface until each emerged gripping the end of a maiden's red ribbon. Ada tried to ascertain if hers had been plucked, but it was impossible to sense. No extra tension on her ribbon had been pulled. The lengths were too long, and the cascading water had already shifted it.

Then, before they pulled the ribbon taut to meet their match, the hunters stood waiting. There was one last hunter remaining casually on the shore.

Jasper tossed Ada a cocky smirk and then sauntered into the water, continuing to submerge until the surface hit his muscular thighs. Without removing his smoldering gaze from Ada, he dipped his hand and fished around. How he found the remaining loose ribbon was beyond her, but he did. His smile broadened, and he straightened, slowly lifting his end into the air.

It was red. It was a ribbon. It could belong to anyone.

Ada's heart kicked against her chest.

"Maidens, hunters, gather your ribbons and meet your match."

One by one, each gathered their ribbons, tightening the length until it pulled taut. The maidens gathered and entered the pool, the hunters did the same. Stretches of red lines lifted out of the water, dripping. Some had criss-crossed on the journey over, some matched straight ahead, but with the tension between them, pairings were irrefutable. To avoid confusion, both parties gathered their ribbons, drawing themselves into the middle of the pool and toward their match, their hunters... or their prey. Ada held her breath as she drew closer, silently begging for none of them to be Jasper, and at the same time, for all of them to be him.

Her ribbon had entangled the worst. It curled and entwined in a mess that reminded her of wool in a knitter's bowl. She ducked beneath other ribbons and waded around people until she could take the anticipation no more. She stopped. Her lungs heaved, lifting her chest until her peaked nipples rasped against her wet dress.

Can't watch. She shut her eyes.

Water sloshed as someone drew close, tugging on her ribbon, levering themselves to her. And then... a butterfly touch on the top of her hand.

Her eyes flew open.

There he was—the same wry curve of his lips, the same amber eyes and blue marks twinkling behind his mask. He tilted his head. The water was waist high for Ada, but only hit his thighs. Splashes from passersby had left trickles of blue silt residue and glittering water running in rivulets down the dips and valleys of his musculature, sharpened by the light of the moon. It was impossible not to be mesmerized.

"What did I tell you?" Jasper rumbled, a hint of amusement in his voice.

"I'm yours," she breathed.

His eyes crinkled as he brought her ribbon-entwined fist to his mouth.

"And I'm yours," he said, lips moving against her knuckles.

"Hunters," Clara shouted. "Scent your maidens."

Held captive in Jasper's stare, Ada froze as he trailed the tip of his nose from her wrist up to her arm until he grazed along her sensitized shoulder. A moan escaped her lips as he reached the intimate spot beneath her ear. One simple, raspy lick of his tongue and heat rushed between her legs. He nuzzled into her hair, murmuring softly for her ears only, "Just so you know, I don't need to do this. Your scent is engraved on my heart. I'll find you wherever you run."

She licked her lips. Damn her, but she was ready for this. He nudged in closer, bringing their bodies together. "I'll even give you a sporting chance and not shift."

"How magnanimous of you." Her palm landed on his chest, and smoothed over the ridged scars, finding pleasure in the slippery and velvety tactile sensation. God, she already couldn't stop touching him. This elixir, it heightened every sense.

A peek over her shoulder showed other couples getting to know each other with barely restrained interactions. Fingers in hair, noses on skin, eyes full of restrained anticipation.

Jasper smiled against her shoulder. "It's for completely selfish reasons. I want this to last."

The nearby haunting howl of a wolf caused woodland sprites to take to the sky, creating a swirl of lights twinkling like drunken falling stars. It was magical, and it connected with that nature-loving part of Ada's soul. Yes... she could belong here.

Jasper unwound the ribbon from Ada's hand until he held it all, and then he stepped back with an impish look.

Clara spoke as the hunters tied their maiden's ribbons around their biceps.

"Maidens, your first and only warning—don't stray too far from the path, for there are lust-filled creatures in the woods, just waiting in the wings. We aren't the only fae inspired by Spring. It is wolpertinger mating season. Beware.

"Hunters, don't delay in finding your maidens, and may the grace of the Well color your way, blessing the Darkfoot pack's seed as plentiful for the body, as it is for the coming harvest."

Another wolf howled, this time closer. Slowly, wolves emerged from between the gathered spectators around the pool. Then another joined in, and another, until the chorus was deafening. Maidens fled the pool, turning and wading out as quickly as they could. Surprised, Ada looked to Jasper expectantly. He leaned forward, bared his teeth in a grin and growled, *"Run."*

Jolting with adrenaline, Ada waded as fast as she could out of the pool and in the direction the other maidens fled. It was the side opposite the dinner party and tables. There was nothing beyond but rocks, dirt paths, and tall trees reaching toward the twinkling night sky. Glowing sprites lazily danced above and darted off in all sorts of directions, like mini fireworks, perhaps to provide the maidens some guidance.

On the shore, Ada hiked up her sodden dress, then glanced over her shoulder, locked eyes with Jasper, and kissed the air in a brazen tease. The line of his jaw tightened beneath his mask, and she knew she was poking the beast, but fuck it. She was having fun. For the first time in... goodness, she couldn't remember. She may as well go all in. God knew her body was up for it.

Taking two steps at a time, she picked her way across the rocks and then ran full pelt down a hilly dirt path twining through the trees. She ran, her heart on fire, her lungs burning, until she reached a fork in the path only fifty feet away and stopped. Three paths. The red fluttering of a maiden's dress went down the left, trodden footsteps down the middle, and the dark right had smooth sand.

More howling pierced the night air. Ada's eyes widened, and she looked over her shoulder. Surely that was the signal for the hunters.

"Already?" she gasped.

Shit!

"Come with me!" Prim emerged from the shadows and took her hand. "I know a secret hiding spot."

With no time to waste, Ada allowed herself to be dragged down the third, less trodden path, and then they bolted. Wind whipped at their hair, laughter bubbled on their tongues. Ada was having such thrilling fun, and her body buzzed with too many distracting sensations, that she failed to comprehend why Prim had taken her hand in the first place. Surely this matching ceremony was a one-on-one thing with their matched partners. So why was Prim helping her?

Further down the path they ran, their feet getting dirty, their faces gathering dust. The sound of running water grew louder.

"In here," Prim panted as they came to a boulder. She rounded it and tugged Ada along with such urgency, her arm almost yanked from its socket.

Suddenly, Ada wasn't having fun. Every step and bounce cut into her bare feet as she slipped on hard rocks and burning sand. Every breath was sharp and hard to draw. Her throat closed. She tugged back her arm, but Prim kept them running.

"Where are we going, Prim?"

"Just a little further."

They burst out from the trees and onto the bank of a narrow river twinkling under the starlight. Ada snatched her hand back and doubled over to catch her breath. She yanked her mask off and threw it on the ground.

"What the hell is going on?" she gasped between breaths.

Prim bent down to pick up the mask and then straightened with a cold look in her eyes.

"It's harder to catch our scent after we cross the water," she explained, then gave a sudden grin. It didn't reach her eyes.

Warning bells went off in Ada's head.

"I'm good waiting here."

"We shouldn't wait, Ada. We should make them work for it. I thought you said you didn't want to make it easy on him."

Ada glanced at the river. It wasn't too wide. It looked easy to cross, but Clara had warned them not to stray too far from the path, and Ada had already faced one wolpertinger during mating season. She wasn't prepared to face another. Especially not on a night that was supposed to be fun. She told Prim this, but a shadow flashed before Ada's face. She raised her hands instinctively, but failed to protect herself.

Something knocked the side of her head. She staggered.

That's weird; Prim's fist dangled oddly at her side with a rock in her hand.

"Why do you have—" Ada's words cut off at the sight of blood on Prim's rock.

Confused, her fingers went to her head and came back sticky with blood. Groggily, Ada registered what had happened too late. With the awareness, pain exploded at the wound site.

Prim swung her rock at Ada's head.

Everything went dark.

SEVENTEEN

Ada rose from the darkness of her subconscious as someone jostled her body, tugging on her dress. Prim hunched over her but straightened. Blinking, Ada checked around. The moment her head moved, pain sloshed, making her woozy. She grasped her forehead. They were still on the riverbank under the moonlight. Alone.

Wolves howled in the distance and the beat of drums meant they weren't too far from the Lupercal cave. Or was that the pounding of Ada's heart, getting louder and more persistent with each passing second.

Prim had hit her over the head.

Why?

Ada glanced down and discovered something that didn't compute. She was now in the red dress, not the cream. *Prim* wore the cream Luperci dress. Her mask was off, and she was pulling a long, bone pin from her hair, unwinding the length, and fluffing out the long golden strands over her shoulders.

"What have you done, Prim?"

She jolted, only just realizing Ada was awake. With pursed lips, she scowled down.

"*Crimson*, Ada. You shouldn't be awake so soon."

Still muddled, Ada's brain hadn't caught up to what her heart knew to be true. Call her naïve, call her inexperienced, but Ada just never expected her only friend in this town to betray her. Surely there was another explanation. There had to be.

"Why?" she asked again.

Prim's face contorted. "You have no idea what it's like for someone like me, a Lesser Fae. I've been waiting for this chance for centuries. They all act like we're better than the humans, but there is still division between tribes, and division within tribes. It's every fae for themselves. Mana is power. Originally, I had hoped to match with Sun, he is the alpha heir apparent, after all. But then Reed comes back, and he's lusting after someone with the same hair as me. I can smell it on him every time you walk by. And you don't even want him!" Her eyes turned desperate. "Just let me have him. For one night."

"But it won't be one night, will it?"

Prim's lips curved. A glint flashed at her fingers as she moved closer. "Clever girl. Of course it won't be. With the child of the Mithras line growing in my womb, they'll have to take me seriously. I won't let you get in my way."

"And what, you're going to pretend you're me?" Ada laughed. "There's no way he'll—"

Prim launched at Ada, planted her hands on her front and knocked her backward down the slope of the riverbank. Ada tumbled into the slippery mud, crying out as stone daggers poked her body until she splashed to a stop, face first in the muddy silt. She gasped through a pinch in her gut.

"You fucking bitch," she spluttered. Anger bubbled to the surface. Her survival instincts kicked in, and she rolled to the side, using her knee to push herself up.

The pinch in her belly turned into a fiery sting, but she planted one foot in front of the other, glaring at the blond securing Ada's half-face mask on. Prim lifted her chin and swallowed, meeting Ada's hate-filled glare.

"You should have just stayed down, Ada."

She turned and ran away.

THE MORE ADA moved through the dark woods, the more confused she became. Her belly hurt. Her head hurt. Darkness crowded her vision. Her state of mind caused the effects of the amorous elixir to curdle. Nervous energy pulsed and dragged in her veins. She wanted to puke.

Gulping in deep breaths of cool night air, she used tree trunks to find her way back to the main path. Stumbling out, she glanced to the right and to the left. Where were they?

Horror visions of Jasper and Prim entwined in hot, naked passion flashed before her eyes.

He would know it wasn't Ada. He would know.

There was their Well-blessed markings. Her scent.

Your scent is engraved on my heart. That's what he'd said. But try as she might, she couldn't fight the rising panic stealing her sense. Prim wasn't stupid. She wouldn't risk everything if she didn't think she stood a chance. She knew if she could get Jasper to lay with her and impregnate her, she'd be safe.

Was it Ada's fault? Had she not acted so standoffish to Jasper, if she'd accepted his claim to be mates in public, would this have happened?

Had he taken the blue elixir?

She couldn't remember.

Were the drums getting further away? Or finishing?

Ada glanced up at the sky but couldn't see the moon. Where was it?

Shuffling to the right. She looked, found nothing, but strained her ears for more.

There—between the branches—a flash of skin. She ducked and winced as the pain in her stomach sliced excruciatingly. Her hand flew to the pain source and hit something hard and wobbly. With a sinking sense of dread, her fingers wrapped around a rod. *Hurts.*

She glanced down with a hitched breath. Prim's bone hairpin protruded from the side of her abdomen. Blood oozed over the red dress, darkening it further. The floor tilted. Her stomach revolted.

And then she did something she *knew* not to do. She pulled it out with a strangled cry. Warm blood gushed from the wound until she slapped her palm over it.

Dumb, dumb girl.

Could she heal herself as she healed others? She tried to call on her gift, but madness muddled her brain. The elixir. The attack. Her heart palpitating. The pain.

Focus.

I can't.

It was not the same as healing someone else. This was her body to search, and it felt too much like her own confusing mind.

Find Jasper.

She staggered onward, feet crunching over leaves and twigs, hand over her side, struggling to keep her eyes open.

There. Another flash of skin in the night. Someone. But as she shuffled closer, the skin became flesh, and the flesh became entwined. Two naked, writhing bodies, lost in the throes of passion, rolling around on a discarded cream, linen dress.

No.

The trees closed in. Ada blinked and flinched away, but forced her blurred, fever-pitched gaze back for a better look. Dark hair. A wall of broad, muscled back, ropy with exertion. Taut ass with feminine legs wrapped around, heels digging in as he thrust into her, grunting with passion. Blond hair on the woman. Eyes behind a wolfish mask that met Ada's stare over his shoulder. Her sleazy, wicked grin of triumph.

Jasper?

How could he? He'd promised. Ada swooned. Bile rose in her mouth. Madness in her mind grew with visions of her past, slamming behind her closed eyes—of her mother's abandonment, of her coming home one time, surprised to see Ada. She'd been almost thirteen. *"Oh, you're here. I forgot about you!"* Her mother's boyfriend laughed.

Ada jammed the heels of her palms to her fevered eye-sockets.

She heard her friend telling her there was more to life than hiding away from people. Laurel teaching her to read.

"What's that word say. Spell it out."

"S.I.S.T.E.R. It says sister."

Ada had learned to trust. And Clarke and Laurel had been with Ada to the end. But now, that trust seemed so empty. What did Ada get out of it? She'd opened her heart to a new friendship, and Prim had betrayed her, just as much as Jasper had.

Ada didn't care what the excuse was. Whether the blue elixir had addled their minds, or whether Jasper had lied and couldn't scent Ada so distinctly... or maybe he didn't care at all. It wouldn't be the first time someone had lied to her.

A sudden, overwhelmingly helplessness hit Ada like a tidal wave, causing the floor to shift beneath her feet.

Have to get out of here.

She spun, clutching her middle. She ran as hard as she could; the tears stinging her eyes, the pain in her side burning, until she fell. Crashing down, she hit a log, tumbled and slid to the ground. Heaving breaths turned into big wracking sobs. And every sad thought she'd ever had since awaking in this time culminated in a big, horrid cry.

She'd thought it would be different. She'd hoped people would be different. But they were all the same. Whether now, in this time, or two thousand years ago. They only cared for themselves. Like Prim had said, it was every fae for themselves. God, Ada wanted her sisters. If only she could see them one more time.

CHAPTER
EIGHTEEN

Jasper strolled through the moonlit woods, snapping twigs off branches with a lazy smirk, thinking about how Ada's air-kiss had triggered his hunter instincts. His wolf had snarled for him to start the chase early, no matter the protocol, but when the second round of howls erupted from the sidelines, and the other males dashed off—he'd stopped short and smiled. He knew what awaited for him. And it was the kiss of her plush lips, and the sinking in between her soft thighs.

A shuddering groan of anticipation rippled through him.

He would give her time to come to terms with the idea of their joining. She might be high on divilixir, but he wasn't, and he knew that once she distanced herself from the initial rush, she might think differently. *Crimson*, Jasper thought differently. The old him would have... the old him?

His thoughts stuttered.

The curse marks burned like fire around his neck, blocking his recognition. He frowned, itching with a flush of irritation. The pain of ignorance was fast becoming worse than the pain of his memories. At least if he knew the kind of fae he wasn't, then he could work toward being the kind Ada needed. The kind she'd happily accept as a mate.

Rustling sounds in the leaves stopped him. He'd been so lost in his thoughts, he hadn't noticed he'd walked in on the privacy of a matched couple, tumbling in the leaves beneath a moss-covered tree. The male sensed his approach and shot up with a territorial growl aimed Jasper's way.

Jasper gave him a casual salute and then kept walking, idly plucking another twig from a blackcurrant bush before lifting it to his nose and inhaling deeply. She'd passed this way. Satisfaction bloomed in his chest.

I'm coming, Ada.

Their bond kept them linked. He could *feel* her like a beacon of heat—an extension of himself—echoing silently somewhere to the right.

He tsked slightly as he realized she'd strayed from the path.

"Naughty, Ada," he grumbled to himself.

Hadn't she learned her lesson with the first wolpertinger? Perhaps he should play a game with her, frighten her and pretend to be the very thing they were warned against. He found a few branches shaped like antlers and held onto them, intending to use them as a wolpertinger disguise. This would be fun.

Although, in all seriousness, she needed marking, sooner rather than later. It was the only way he'd feel satisfied other males would avoid her. His teeth ached, elongating, ready for the task. His cock strained hard against his pants and he subtly adjusted himself for comfort.

Multiple scents of arousal clashed across the winds. Hunters had caught their prey. Every cell in his body cried out to catch his.

You have all night. Relax.

He forced the tension to disperse, but the scent of musk kept sending his inner wolf into a frenzy. Fae everywhere were engaged in lustful activities. As it should be on Lupercalia.

A cry caught on the wind. He stopped, tilted his head and pricked his ears.

Was that...?

Ada? No. It couldn't be. He shook his head and continued walking, but was remiss to stop his feet from moving faster. His heart rate picked up speed. He followed the *ping* of their bond connection, ensuring he followed the direction in which the link felt stronger. But the soft whimpers of a sobbing woman sent every hair on the back of his neck standing on edge.

It came from off the path, deeper into the woods, down by the river.

Alarm prickled through him. His first thought was of the mana-warped creatures known to visit the woods. He'd fought them once—*a burn at his neck*. He hissed a curse, hating that he failed to learn whether this wailing was friend or foe. Some of his memories had come back. Some stayed locked behind a gate, and it was impossible to work out how much was missing.

The Well-blessed bond link was weak. It felt further away than the crying female.

Wolpertingers didn't make that sound. Perhaps it was the White Woman? If it was, the Unseelie fae lurked out of her territory. Known to weep and cry for help, the White Woman lured men into her web, glamoured as a beautiful lost maiden, but she was a monster of disgusting bug-like proportions. She ate the heads of her mates, while still mating with them.

A dark memory from the corner of his mind tried to poke through, but his body revolted in horror. He shook his head. Not now. Not another flashback.

"Clarke... Laurel..." More sobs.

Those names sounded familiar. That voice was familiar. He pushed through the trees, urgency spurring him onward.

And then he found her. The sticks fell from his hands. His heart tore from his chest.

Ada. Injured. On the ground and covered in mud. Not wearing cream as he'd left her, but the red of a maiden.

It was definitely her. The mud-smeared Well-blessed marks on her arm called to his own. He rushed to her side, fell to his knees and felt his world break apart.

"Love," he said, and took her face. It lolled into his touch, limp, sweaty and weak. "Ada. It's me. What happened?"

She moaned and thrashed her head, squeezing her eyes shut. Sweat covered her pale skin. Why was she so pale? Had she eaten something? Was she—? His gaze snagged on her hands clutching her middle. Blood. Coppery, sweet-bitter blood oozing out of her body. How had he not smelled it?

A snarl ripped out of him when he realized how distracted the hunt had made him. He searched their surroundings for an enemy, but only heard the moans and sounds of lovers beneath the whispering wind. A crow cawed somewhere overhead. The soft trickle of running water filtered in from the nearby river.

He lifted her into his arms and carried her as fast as he could down to the river. The water flowed fresh. It would do.

He gently laid her down on the sloped bank, allowing her legs to dangle into the water, hoping the temperature would rouse her. Under the moonlight, dark blood blended into the water and carried away with the stream, reminding him of the ribbon at the start of the night.

She groaned in protest and tried to swat him away. "No... I want Laurel."

"Is that your mother?" he asked, his heart aching.

"S'not her," she mumbled, scrunching her face drunkenly. Her eyes focused on him as he splashed water onto her wound and tried to pry her fingers away. *Well-damn*, the wound was deep. He covered it with his hand. Betrayal lanced down their bond like hot spice. Her face hardened. She pushed him away.

"Don't you *dare* touch me," she hissed, and then fell back panting, as though the outburst had sapped all her energy.

His heart ripped a little further.

"What's happened, Ada?"

"*You...*" she ground out. "You were with *her!* I saw you."

"Who?"

"I should never have trusted you. I should never have let my guard down." She tried to scramble away from him. "But I'm a survivor. I don't need you, asshole. You're all the same."

"Who was it, Ada?" He couldn't hide the growl in his voice.

"You know who!" Her voice cracked as she strained to get closer and bared her teeth.

Jasper was too shocked to respond. All the effort in her body released, and she collapsed to the ground. Her head landed hard on the muddy bank. She winced, held her breath, and squeezed her eyes shut.

"I don't need you," she said. "I don't."

"I don't know who you saw, but it wasn't me. I've been taking my time getting to you. Whoever you saw wasn't me."

He reached for her again, to stanch the blood flow, but she jerked back.

"Ada," he admonished. "Your mind is playing tricks on you."

He dug into his pockets and pulled out the blackcurrants.

"See?" He offered them to her. "Blackcurrants. Not mana berries. I didn't take the divilixir either. I wanted to be clear in the head for this. For you."

A flicker of doubt entered her gaze. It was enough for her to pause. He used the opportunity to push her down gently and then put pressure on her wound. Her eyes rolled, and she visibly forced her awareness back to him.

"Why aren't you healing yourself?" he demanded, exasperated. Her skin was cold. Too much blood had leaked out.

He stilled with a realization that sent fear tracing down his spine. When he was tracking her, the link of their bond had seemed faint. He'd thought it was because she was further away than he'd supposed, but it was something else. Her light was dimming.

Ada was dying.

Panic pierced his lungs like the claws of a foe. *No.* She wasn't dying. He wouldn't allow it. He needed her. He unlocked the hold on his emotions and let her feel it.

Confusion swam across her expression—shock, awe, and... relief. Her lashes lifted as their gazes met. A tear glistened. It trickled along her lash line and then spilled over her cheek before joining the mud on the bank below.

"You're telling the truth," she mumbled. "It wasn't you. I can *feel* it."

His features hardened, and he pushed all the resolve he could muster into his gaze, hoping she could see and feel the truth of his next words. "I would *never* leave you. Do you understand? I will always find you." Silence. Nothing. Her lids fluttered low. "Ada," he choked, gently shaking her. "You're the reason I'm still breathing. Your voice calls me from the darkest places. I can't... I can't live without you. Now focus! Heal yourself." He took her hands and placed them over her wound, then covered them with his own. "Heal yourself."

"Can't focus," her head thrashed. "I'm too muddled. I tried. Need more training... not good enough."

"I refuse to believe that. You're the only person in Elphyinian history who has removed a curse. And you learned all that through intuition, through compassion. If you can do that, for me—as broken as I am—then you can heal yourself. You're perfect the way you are."

"Flattery..." she mumbled, too tired to finish.

"How do you search for a wound when you heal someone else?"

"I feel it out," she breathed. "Listen for changes... but I can't hear."

"Then use my voice," he said. "Let it guide you as yours has for me."

"Jasper—"

"You're not dying today, Ada," he decreed. "Now listen to my voice." He slowed down the tempo. "Let it calm you. Let it soothe you. Concentrate. Feel it. Feel our bond. We're the same. We're connected. Start there, then flow back into your body. You got it?"

A frown. A meeting of her delicate brows. And then, a nod.

"I feel you," she whispered, shivering.

Her lips were so blue.

"Keep going. Draw on me. Take my energy."

Her lips parted on a gasp as the first rush of his mana pushed into her. His lids lowered at the rush through their bond. He knew what it was like to take her mana, but this was the other way around. It gushed out of him with staggering force until her fingers heated beneath his touch. The drag on his mana slowed. He panicked, thinking she'd given up, but when he looked down, her skin color had returned.

He lifted trembling fingers from her wound. No more blood flow.

"Ada?"

Her lashes fluttered.

"Love?"

She opened her eyes. Stark need shone in the depths of her clear gaze, no longer clouded by injury. The change in her was remarkable. Her gaze dipped to his rosy lips, and a rush of lust chased him down their bond, winding itself around his senses, coaxing them back to life.

"Ada?"

Gone was the confused, afraid girl.

The woman who slowly climbed to her hands and knees, and then prowled toward him was all confidence, and presumably all healed. Muddy water splashed as she came closer. He washed his hands in the water.

"It worked?" he asked gingerly.

She nodded, a small smile playing on her lips as she climbed on his lap, pushing him back on his hands.

"It worked," she rasped, and then licked his bottom lip before sucking it between her teeth.

He groaned, eyes fluttering, his body turning hard with need. Everything he'd felt before he found her rushed back as though it had never left. Unable to help himself, he pushed forward with his lips, hardening their kiss.

"Ada," he warned. "You almost died."

"Then I didn't." She nipped at his jaw. Licked down his neck. Suckled on his Adam's apple.

He threw his head back to give her access. "You're covered in mud and blood."

"Who cares?"

"This is the divilixir still in your system. It can take hours to work itself out. Take it easy."

"Mm-hm." She didn't care, already grinding against his lap, making his cock swell and strain against his wet pants, demanding Jasper let go of his inhibitions.

But he wouldn't take advantage of her. She meant too much to him. He took her shoulders and gently pushed her back. She resisted, licking the air between them.

"Someone tried to kill you tonight," he growled, hating how weak-willed he sounded. *Crimson*, he wasn't that much of a hedonist, was he? That he couldn't separate sex from... she bit his ear, licking around the lobe, and he forgot. What was he thinking?

"I need you," she groaned. "It's not just the elixir. I need to *feel* you. To know you're here. That you're *mine*."

His brow puckered. When he'd found her, she'd spoken deliriously, accusing him of being with someone else.

She speared fingers into his hair and clenched tight, causing a ripple of pain to spark at the roots. Adrenaline and lust spiked through him, and now he couldn't tell whose was whose. His body hardened with want. His teeth elongated, ready to claim. To mark.

She'd said he was hers.

You're mine.

She'd said it.

It's the elixir, you bastard.

It wasn't him she wanted. It was the Lupercalia spell. Tomorrow this would all be over. But she'd been okay with it at the start, hadn't she? She'd wanted this night. She'd kissed the air in his direction. She'd agreed to this... sort of.

He gripped under her arms and shifted her back until he could meet her feverished gaze.

"I know exactly what I'm doing," she insisted, in a sultry voice that made his cock jolt eagerly.

Damn him to the Well Worms.

"You say that now..." He winced. She'd been so vulnerable before. She'd cried and sobbed. He'd never seen her break a tear in the week he'd known her. He hated to see her so upset, so broken.

She must be a witch, a mind-reader, or a Seer, because her next words came straight out of the dark places he was sure he'd kept locked.

"You want to take care of me?" she asked.

Fuck, yes, he wanted to take care of her. For the rest of their lives. She must have seen it on his face because her features softened. A wave of emotion glistened in her eyes, and then the seductress was back, with smoldering heat.

She put her fingers on her thighs and gathered the dress in an enticingly slow drag to reveal her calves, knees, then thighs, never once unlocking their gazes.

There was something else in that stare, something beyond the sexual challenge. She had been right. She needed him. This went beyond the lust. It was a primal, primitive need for connection and comfort. The same need they'd both danced around since first seeing each other. She kept dragging the dress. Higher and higher the fabric went, revealing skin so smooth his mouth watered for want of its taste. But he couldn't look down. If he did, there would be no holding him back.

"So take care of me," she dared.

NINETEEN

Amber eyes flashed gold. That's all Ada saw before Jasper grazed his palms up her thighs, removing the final constraints of her dress. He tested her healed abdomen, probing his fingers over her skin. It set her senses on fire. She moaned and arched into him. He responded with a strangled sound of frustration, and then buried his face between her legs, supping on the sensitive junction between her thighs. She squirmed and writhed, so full of feeling that she feared her skin would float away.

"Jesus," she gasped as he wrenched her panties aside and licked her straight down the middle.

He groaned against her flesh, kissed her inner thigh, and then hooked fingers into her underwear, dragging them off her legs. When he returned, he didn't come up for air. His tongue worked her with ravenous hunger, swirling and probing as though he was made of magic. It felt too divine, too worked up, too intense.

She wriggled back. He growled in disapproval, flattened his hand on her stomach and pinned her down. Then he went back to feasting on her, drawing keening whimpers of bliss, helpless moans, and gasps for air.

There was little Ada could do but thread her fingers into his hair and hold on, submitting to the force of his pleasure until everything inside her wound tight. *Too fast. Too much.* She clutched his hair, threw her head back, arched into him, and shouted her shuddering release.

Panting, trying to pull the stars into focus and figure out what the hell had just happened—she was in pieces—she became aware of the hot-blooded male crawling up her body with heavy-lidded, dark-lashed eyes. He nuzzled into her, rolling his stubbled cheek against her jaw, gently rocking his hips against hers, pushing his hardness to the sensitive flesh between her thighs. If it wasn't for his pants, he'd be inside her, she had no doubt.

"Look what you made me do," he chided, kissing her neck.

His fingers roamed over her front, slipping up her waist, thumbs brushing beneath the pillow of her breasts, coaxing more lazy sensations from her aching body.

"Ada," he murmured against her skin, a note of melancholy. "I wanted to wait until you were better, but you made me *want*." Another growl. He nipped her collarbone, and she gasped. "You make me lose all sense."

Still unable to form words, her weak fingers trailed down his head. "I'm... *Jesus*. Just give me a minute. I'm relearning how to form words."

His chuckle rumbled through him. He stilled with his sharp teeth on her neck. He stayed so silent that Ada thought, perhaps, he was asleep. Which made no sense. He hadn't... finished, had he?

"Jasper?" she whispered. "Are you going to... you know?"

Just give her a minute and she'd be good to go.

He pulled himself up and gave her a lazy, entitled grin. "No, my love. When I claim you, I'm going to mark you, and I want you to be in full control of your senses. You're going to beg me for it. And you're going to remember it with startling clarity. I refuse to do it another way."

Ada's heart stopped. She forgot to breathe. He'd said, *my love*. Was it a figure of speech? Or—?

"Beg for it?" She raised an eyebrow. "Really?"

His lips landed on hers with a guttural groan. All thoughts immediately vacated her mind. She became lost in his salty taste and the torture of his wicked tongue as he probed and drove into her mouth with proprietary intent. Oh, God. He was right. She would beg for it. Why had she waited so long for this?

When he drew back, she chased his lips and tried to claim more. He gave her a self-satisfied smirk that revealed how well he thought he'd taken care of her, and how much more he fantasized about. But then he pushed himself off the riverbank before hauling her into his arms and standing. Feeling rather like a damsel in distress, she clutched him around the neck as he held her.

He smiled down with a barely restrained smolder that promised more wicked things to come. He held her gaze while his thumb grazed her inner thigh and then brushed over the sensitive swell of her intimate flesh, teasing her. She squirmed with a gasp. With her dress bunched and dangling, and no underwear, the cool air traveled straight to her damp core, making her ache deliciously for more.

"Put me down," she insisted, her voice still husky. "Let's finish this."

Playfulness evaporated from his expression, and hard lines returned. "Someone tried to kill you. I'm carrying you."

"I'm seriously fine."

"Still carrying you."

"The entire way back? We're done?" she pouted.

"Yes."

"But I feel great."

"Don't argue," he grunted. "Or I'll swing you over my shoulder and spank you."

She squirmed at the thought, and he chuckled.

"Perhaps you would like that too much."

"Shut up," she grumbled with a smile.

A hearty laugh boomed from him, rumbling through their connection and her heart stopped at the sight. A rush of endorphins crashed through her, simply from watching him smile. He was perfect. Heartbreakingly so.

He swung her around and strode out of the riverbank with a saunter that made her think of the cat who'd caught the mouse. But behind them, back on the river, twinkling blue light caught her eye. For a moment, she thought it was just their arm markings reflected, but this was different. It came from the river. She stilled.

"What's that?" she asked.

Jasper sensed it at the same time. A lethal quiet crept into his posture. Not even the puff of his breath could be heard as he swung back around and they both stared at the blue spot.

Ada knew exactly what it was—the same thing she'd seen in the fountain on the day she'd awoken in this time. Someone was spying on them.

How much had they heard?

With his grip tightening on her, Jasper stepped closer. As the scene inside the blue light came into view, Ada gasped. It was the golden-haired King and his dark, hooded companion. Sitting, watching, and listening.

The King's jaw hardened as his gaze landed on Jasper. A bejeweled hand appeared by his jaw, fidgeting. Something dark and hate-filled flashed in his eyes before he stamped it down beneath a mask of pompous regality.

"That's quite the show you put on, my son." The King smirked as his eyes shifted to Ada. "Or was it your show, Primrose?"

Ada's breath hitched. Jasper tensed to the point of hardness. He pulled her tighter against his front.

"He couldn't see us," he murmured to Ada. "We have to be directly in front of the link."

Like now.

But he'd *heard* them? And he thought her name was Primrose? An icky feeling squirmed through her at the idea of this lewd, evil man listening to their intimate moment. Had this all been a trap? Was this why Prim had hurt Ada?

The King's eyes shifted to Ada, and that icky feeling expanded as he studied her. His gaze shifted to the blue Well-blessed markings of her arm before landing back on her face. "You're not Primrose."

Ada didn't think Jasper's grip could get tighter, but it did. The King's eyes flickered with surprise.

"I must say," he said to Jasper. "You're looking incredibly well for someone who should be dead."

The veiled displeasure in his tone made the hooded companion at his side shift uncomfortably.

"He should be dead," the hooded figure said. "No one survives the ponaturi's bite."

The King's piercing stare settled on Ada again. "Who are you?"

The hooded figure leaned closer. Ada glimpsed a crooked nose and thin lips. "She is not the same female," he confirmed, once again talking to his companion as though he cared little if they were overheard.

Only someone so cocky or drunk with power would believe he was untouchable.

"But she's not just anyone, is she?" The King pointed at Ada's Well-blessed marks, and then Jasper's neck. "Look at his curse marks."

"They're half gone."

King Mithras's lips pursed. "Another impossibility, you assured me."

"I... I don't know what to say."

"It is clear she is one of them—these mana-capable humans from the old world. I want her." Mithras slammed his palm down hard with a slap.

The jolt snapped Jasper out of his daze. He twisted them, hiding Ada from the King's eyes, and then kicked the blue water link, displacing and cutting off the connection. When Ada next looked, the glow was gone. Only the trickling river water remained and the sound of Jasper heaving lungfuls of air as he struggled to catch his breath.

"Hey." She placed her palm over his wildly beating heart. "Are you okay?"

A caged beast stared out of his amber-eyed gaze.

"He knows," Jasper growled, shocked. "He knows."

"That you're alive?"

His gaze clashed with hers. "He knows about *you*. What you mean to me. He'll come for you. It's what he does."

A pained expression crossed his features. Then Ada found herself deposited on the grassy riverbank so fast the wind knocked out of her and she crashed to her knees. Jasper landed hard beside her and placed her hands on his neck. With a jaw locked tight, he met her gaze.

"Take it all off."

"The curse marks?"

He nodded. "It's time. I need to know everything about him before he comes. I need to know how to stop him. *Now*, Ada."

"Okay, okay." Her mind swirled. Right. Forget about the unwanted thrill still thrumming in her veins from the divilixir. Forget about how he'd just had his mouth between her legs. Forget about how his father had been listening in the entire time. "Right." But... "What if he listens in again?"

Jasper scowled. "He wouldn't dare. Besides, he knows the connection can work two ways. As his blooded kin, I can seek him out. He won't be anywhere near water right now. Do it, Ada."

I can do this.

If she could focus enough while almost dying, then she could do this. With a deep exhale out, she let her breath slide over her tongue, through her lips, and thought of nothing else until the next breath dragged in. She forced herself to be calm and to concentrate on the energy brimming within her. When Jasper had told her to use their connection as an anchor, it had worked. She could sense the difference between that power compared to the sensations in the rest of her body. This was *mana*—the life-force of the Well. This was where her power came from. She reached out to it with her mind's eye. It reacted to her call, like an old friend, a separate entity. Power brimmed inside her, quicker than ever before.

She placed a palm over the ridges of the blue curse marks, slid her mana beneath, and started peeling them from his body. He tensed, the line of his jaw growing tight, but didn't complain.

It hurt, she knew it.

It always hurt him. He tried to hide the fact, even after an hour of stifled agony, but the control on his emotions slipped. His eyes pinched. His lips flattened. And a trickle of torment lanced down their bond.

Ada pulled her fingers away, but he snapped his grip around her wrist. Eyes like granite locked onto her.

The haunting howl of a distant wolf called, springing goosebumps over both Ada's and Jasper's skin. Their gazes flicked to each other. The moon had dropped. Morning birds awoke and tweeted their warning of the coming sun.

"Lupercalia is over," Jasper muttered. "That's all it means."

More howls joined the first.

"Keep going," he growled.

She placed her palm on his Well-blessed bond mark.

"Share it with me," she said. "Let me feel your pain so you're not alone."

Jasper's Adam's apple bobbed as he swallowed. His hand came to her jaw. He pressed his lips to hers, breathing deeply through his nose. When he let go, a wealth of emotion echoed in his gaze. It was her only warning before he gave a curt nod, and the floodgates opened.

A solid wall of pain knocked into her. It took all of Ada's resolve to stop herself from visibly reacting, but the shards of broken glass scraping down her insides were almost too hard to bear. After a few forced breaths, she kissed him briefly on the tip of his nose and continued picking the curse apart.

Long minutes passed by.

The entire process took almost two hours. Sometimes she pulled a piece, and he flinched, his gaze turning inward with gleaned memories unleashing from the dark recess of his mind. Sometimes the pain lessened down their bond. Sometimes he panted like Lake had when wounded and in wolf form. Sometimes the pain morphed into fleeting moments of joy, bringing a tear to her eyes. But one thing remained constant—the further she went, the more memories revealed, and a slow bubbling fury stole over him like an approaching avalanche threatening to crush them whole.

"Last one." She picked off the final blue gelatinous mark. It sloughed away with a surprising lack of resistance.

When it was done, she sat back, unsure what to say.

Jasper became a different man. Before, he'd been loose, almost carefree. But with the rise of his unfolding body, a halo of violence wrapped around his form. He flexed his hands. Muscles in his arms and back rolled and pumped. Veins wreathed in fury.

"Jasper?" she whispered hesitantly.

Dark brows drew together as he studied his hands, turning them over from back to front. Then his gaze ran up his arms, looking at them from all angles. He flexed his hands again. This time, a charge of power crackled in the air. Ada tasted electricity on her tongue, and the hairs on her arm lifted. He thrust an open palm at the river. Water sprung in a geyser straight for the sky. He dropped his hand, and the water followed, falling in a great splash.

Ada jumped back. Her heart leaped into her throat. What the hell had he done... move water?

"He took my tattoos," he mumbled, brow furrowing again. "Cloud's going to be pissed."

"Tattoos?"

"They covered most of my body. Some fae get them to enhance their connection to the Well. Cloud is the Guardian who put them on me. It took him months to craft, and he was very proud of the outcome. Mithras used that *floater* Dark Mage to—" He shook his head, body pulling taut with rage until, finally, he drew his head back and bellowed at the moon, his body shuddering with power. The roar tore through the night, waking the last of the creatures from their slumber. When the last note died on his tongue, he stalked out of the river toward her.

"What did you remember?" Ada asked.

"Everything."

CHAPTER

TWENTY

Jasper paced along the riverbank, still trying to find space in his cramped mind for the memories that had been pushed to the edges for... *Crimson*... how long? He'd been living as a husk, forced to commit despicable acts for the King's sick pleasure for at least a decade. Maybe more.

Images jammed into his mind.

"You get three sets," Jasper said to the young Guardian recruit, and pointed at his uniforms. "You're in charge of laundering them."

Thorne set his simmering glare on Jasper.

"Go away," he snapped.

Laughter roared out of Jasper. The kid had gumption, he'd give him that. His fire will serve him well when he's up against a Manticore with no mana left.

"Go float yourself," Thorne snarled again, fury welling to overtake his despair.

"Been there, done that. Didn't stick. Just like you."

"So what, you think we're the same?"

Now hang on a gosh-darn, faery minute. The boy was yet another of King Mithras's victims—as was he. Jasper's dark brow rose. "We're more alike than you think. One day, you'll get that. Until then, launder your uniform, or don't. I don't really care." The kid scowled, and he looked so much like Jasper's cousin, Moon from his mother's pack. Unlike his brother, Sun, Moon was always so serious. As children, Sun and Jasper had made it their life's mission to unnerve Moon every chance they could. A bolt of compassion hit Jasper. He removed a small package from his pocket and held it out to Thorne. "Here. It's a bit of mana-weed. Just don't smoke it before training. Preceptor in charge won't be happy if you turn up wasted."

Thorne took the package, eyes flaring wide with nervous caution as though Jasper had just handed him the keys to the Winter Court coffers. Jasper knew that smile wouldn't last. The road ahead at the Order was often thankless, brutal, and unforgiving. This was the second from the Nightstalk Pack he'd seen come up the ranks. One, he'd lost. He wouldn't lose this one, too.

"Yeah, I know you're a bit young, kid, but the training will harden you. Smoke it with some friends. We work hard here, but we play hard too." Jasper's eyes twinkled with humor, but his heart sank like lead. "You're among family now, Nightstalk. Get some rest."

Jasper shook his head. Finding his memories was like coming out of a fog and not knowing he'd been lost. He imagined it would be the way the Crystal City humans felt the first time they left their snowy wasteland and stepped into the lush verdant greenery of Elphyne.

Life was now full of so much more color, both dark and light. His brain hurt. A few hours ago, he'd been a fraction of himself with only a handful of acquaintances. He frowned as faces of friends cascaded in his mind. At least, he'd called them friends once. What would they think of him now?

The Cadre of Twelve—his fellow Guardians. Two of which were wolf-shifters, like him. Rush was alive, not dead as Jasper had feared. Rush's son, Thorne, had rallied the cadre to rescue Jasper from the King's clutches. He remembered it in patches. There had been a ball at the Summer Court. Thorne had also infiltrated the Ring, and was pitted against Jasper.

More fire. More flames. More heat. Jasper's face burned.

"Enough!" someone roared.

A female's grunt of effort, and the flames doused. For a split moment, Jasper felt reprieve, then his skin ached. But... it was a different ache. Clean. He blinked. Blue sky. Dust. A roaring crowd. Blood. A silver-haired shifter scowling down at him.

"Jasper. It's me. Fuck, what have they done to you?"

Pain everywhere. Jasper moaned and forced his eyes to lock onto the male—I know you.

"Rush?" he gasped. "Rush." A whimper. All of Jasper's sins came rushing back. All his failings. "You came. You... I don't deserve it. I don't deserve to be rescued. Not when I left you... not when—" He'd failed to save Véda.

"Hush, Jasper. It's Thorne. Not Rush."

"No. No. No. I shouldn't have let her die. Véda. She was pregnant. Not her fault. I should have said something." He'd been too afraid to make waves. A coward.

"Jasper!"

"I looked after your son, just like you asked. I kept an eye on him for you." Another moan. But was it enough to replace the kid's mother? His father? A whimper. "Please don't hate me."

Jasper struggled to breathe as shame washed over him with the memory.

After everything, Thorne had come for him. No. It wasn't just Thorne... his mate had helped too. His *Well-blessed* human mate. Laurel. Dark-haired, dusky skinned, tall and athletic.

More pieces of the puzzle slammed into place.

Laurel had a red-headed friend named Clarke.

After they rescued Jasper from the King, there was a little girl—Rush's daughter, Jasper realized, startled—*Rush has a daughter!*—who had dragged Jasper upstairs to a room where a beautiful woman had slept. Ada. The girl had told him Ada needed a kiss to wake. She'd called her *Sleeping Pretty*.

Jasper's eyes slid to Ada with surprise. She stood by a tree, a wary eye on him as he paced along the riverbank. Hadn't she called out those names when she was near death? He was sure she'd mentioned the names earlier, too. Clarke and Laurel must be close friends from Ada's time.

It was all slotting together in his mind. It made perfect sense.

Jasper stopped as another thought settled with dread.

Ada would want to know about her friends. But... the more he thought about it, the more he remembered those women had been furious when Jasper took Ada from the house of the Twelve. They'd shouted for him to get away from her. He jammed the heels of his palms into his eyes.

"Sleeping Pretty needs a kiss to wake."

He glanced down at the child, frowned, and then looked back at the sleeping female. His frown deepened. An undeniable urge to go to her swam through him. It was as though something pushed him.

He didn't know how, he didn't know anything, but he knew her.

So he went to her. Her mana called to his like a siren at sea, and like a wave rising to meet the shore, his mana called back. He touched her arm. A spark of heat zipped up his arm. Blue flames engulfed them both, and then he heard a scream.

Behind him.

A redheaded woman.

"Leave her alone!"

Footsteps thudded up the stairs. Down the hall. People he should know came barging into the room, scowling at him as though he'd done wrong. They frowned at his golden-haired female on the bed. The one inexplicably linked to him. They wanted to take her away from him.

She was his. Mine.

Something wild and feral within him growled. His fangs elongated, and a snarl ripped out of his lungs. He picked up Sleeping Pretty, carried her in his arms, and wished himself gone.

He'd portaled himself. That, in itself, was confusing. Usually fae created portals to walk through, not became one themselves. There were a rare few fae races that did. The Sluagh flickered through space. The vampires slid through shadows. But never had a wolf portaled.

And the redhead's anger... it had never made sense. But now he knew why. Ada's friends knew he was to blame for Rush's excommunication from the Order. Even if it was Rush's son who'd come to Jasper's aid, even if Rush was back at the Order, and not cursed—there would be bad blood between them. There had to be.

If Ada's closest friends disapproved of Jasper, what chance did he have of her accepting his mark? What chance did he have of her staying with him? A dark part of him shouted that it was wrong of him to think Ada was his redemption, but he couldn't stop. He latched onto the notion with obsessive, irrational greed.

He wouldn't risk her friends tainting his burgeoning relationship, not when he hadn't marked her yet. The Well-blessed union was too new. Would it be enough to keep her at his side? *Damn the curse.* What had he been thinking, leaving her unmarked? It's what shifters did. They marked their females for protection. He should have done it immediately after the wolpertinger attack, with or without her permission.

Panic bloomed in his chest.

And then she would have hated him.

He simply couldn't risk losing her. She was too important. He hadn't lied when he said she was the reason he breathed.

If her friends told her all the dark, cowardly, horrible—

"Jasper?" she prodded.

He scrubbed his face. "I need time for all this to sink in."

"You're right. I can't imagine how it would feel. We should go back to the inn, and just... you know, chill for a few days. God knows you need the break."

Ada's expression softened as she came to him and searched his eyes. A rush of warm compassion flowed through their bond. He latched onto her, drawing her into his embrace and pressing her against his chest.

He'd startled her into submission. She wrapped her arms around him and then softened against his form.

"So... what now?" she murmured.

I can't lose you.

He plastered a smile on his face and looked down at her. "Now I'm going to take you back to the inn, draw you a bath, and then I'm going to spend the next few days doing as you suggested. But it won't be cold or chilled. The inn is heated."

She blinked for a bit, then laugher burst out. It brightened her face to a beauty that stopped his heart.

She patted his chest. "*Chill* is just something we used to say instead of relax."

He gave a tight-lipped smile.

"My friends would have understood."

He tipped her chin by his finger. "I'm your friend. If you need someone to joke with, it can be me."

She brought her fingers to her lips and then pushed them to his with a sigh. It was a mix of the thank-you sign and a kiss, and the moment her touch landed on him, he knew he was in love with her.

"I miss them, that's all." she murmured.

He cleared his throat and pointed to the woods that led back to the path into town. "How would you like to return? A walk, or portal?"

"Portal?" She blinked.

"Well, not exactly a portal," he frowned, thinking back to how he'd taken Ada from the cadre house and ended up at his old family cottage. He hadn't actually stepped through a portal, he'd *become* the portal. It was the first time he'd ever teleported. But he was over three centuries old. It wasn't unheard of for the Well to gift older fae with new abilities. Did this new skill mean the Well still favored him? Or was it something he'd taken from Ada? Most likely the latter. Why would the Well keep favoring someone like him?

He shut his eyes briefly against the onslaught of blood-filled memories trying to break through. The Well *had* favored him. It made little sense.

"You know what?" he said. "Let's walk back. It's a shame to waste the last of this beautiful night. And if we stumble across a certain blond-haired Lesser Fae, then all the better for a little retribution."

"You don't mean to kill her, do you?" Ada asked.

"You're right. We should probably question her first."

Ada stopped. "She may be a nasty person, but dealing out righteous punishment is a slippery slope. Don't you have a law, or something like the police?"

"Police?" He stared at her. "I am a Guardian. I am above the law."

"But…" A small line appeared between her brows.

He used his fist to make a circular motion against his heart. "I will alert the alpha."

She took his hand, still over his heart. "Are you sure you're okay?"

"Prim stabbed you. I'm not okay." Anger swirled through his body. Maybe he wouldn't leave Primrose to Clara. Maybe he'd pay her a visit the instant Ada fell asleep.

When her grip tightened on his hand, he knew his anger must have rolled onto her, so he quietly reined back his emotions and put a clamp on the bond. It shut off with little effort. He silently marveled at how easy the action had come to him. Damn, he'd felt so impotent under the curse, and hadn't even realized it.

Shame, embarrassment, and inadequacy boiled and bubbled beneath the surface of his restraint. He darted a glance to Ada, checking to see if his hold on the bond had slipped, but she had her head tipped to the sky, astonished at the new day.

Pre-dawn colored the sky in hues of pinks and refracted through the mist curling about the moss-covered woods. The air was fresh, but he wasn't cold. A glance to see if her skin pebbled told him she wasn't cold either. The elixir must be keeping her blood warm.

Woodland sprites flittered over the top branches of gnarled oak trees while song-birds flitted between their usual morning arias and sniping at the sprites getting too close to their nests.

Nature provided the melody for their journey home, and by the time the sound of the Lupercal waterfall announced their proximity, they were both bone tired and ready for sleep.

But even beneath the dull senses of exhaustion, Jasper sensed danger. He tugged on Ada's hand for her to halt.

A coppery taint in the air.

He frowned as an understanding dawned. The howling wolves he'd heard hours ago weren't the signal of the end of Lupercalia. He'd been wrong. Lupercalia usually ran longer. The lovers might be finished, but the celebration and revelers often carried on until the early hours of the next morning. There should be more sounds above the cascading waterfall. His ears pricked, straining.

Nothing.

Even the songbirds had stopped.

He glanced down at Ada. "Something's wrong."

"Another raid?"

His blood turned cold as the King's conversation filtered back to him in fragments.

He'd confused Primrose with Ada, meaning Prim was a spy. She was probably the one who'd confirmed the stockpiled metal to Mithras and caused the raid.

When Jasper had cut the communication with Mithras at the river, his father had probably gathered his soldiers and portaled straight here.

That call had ended hours ago.

Jasper's jaw stiffened. He crept toward the waterfall, using his grip on Ada's hand to keep her behind him.

The breaking of glass sent claws springing from his fingertips. Ada's breath hitched. He thought maybe he'd hurt her, but it was only her surprise. He tightened his grip and refused to look into her eyes. With a tug, he kept them moving.

They cleared the trees and crested the path leading to the top of the waterfall where blood splattered down the rocks, blending with the sacred pool, churning the blue water and silt into dark purple. Leaning against an upturned table, picking food from his elongated teeth with a claw, was the King dressed in blood spattered finery. A bejeweled sword hung at his hip, unused and clean.

In the flesh, he was a shock to Jasper's frayed mind. Images and sensations bombarded him: Mithras's voice when he'd killed Jasper's mother; his twisted and perfectly cruel face when he'd watched the Dark Mage paint the crippling curse marks onto his body.

Jasper momentarily blacked out. Just a for a second. But it was long enough for him to delay in shielding Ada from the rest of the scene.

She cried out.

The King glanced up at them, and a slow, sinister smile spread across the disgustingly handsome face that looked too much like Jasper's own, if not for the lighter hair.

Bile burned the back of Jasper's throat.

All around them, littered throughout the grotto, were mutilated bodies of his kin—his old pack—as they lay defiled and discarded. A matched couple's ribbon of fate lay trampled in the mud, all dark with blood. The mask Helona had worn, ripped in two. The maracas and pan-flute from the band. He swallowed, eyes trailing further to find Halona's cold dead hand peeking out from beneath the table, lying in a pool of congealed blood. It had been a massacre. No one had stood a chance in their inebriated and festive state.

A final few manabeeze drifted lazily from bodies before dispersing into the sky.

If Jasper had arrived minutes earlier, he might have saved them.

"About time you joined us," Mithras shouted jovially. His voice echoed against the grotto walls. "I almost sent out a search party."

Us?

The hairs on Jasper's arms lifted as the Dark Mage strode down the stone steps leading from the village. Movement in the trees behind Jasper froze his feet to the ground. Without looking, he scented them. Soldiers everywhere surrounded them.

"Are you ready to talk now?" the King asked.

"There is no talking with you," Jasper replied. "You're insane."

The King shrugged, already bored. "If you won't come willingly, then we'll just curse you again. Or maybe it will be the iron mask."

"And I'll take it off," Ada shouted.

Reckless, brave, and beautiful mate. She attracted the King's attention, and that was a dangerous thing. He squeezed her hand, his heart thumping.

"Is that so, little human healer?" Mithras's gaze raked over her. "My, my. You're even better than the last one, aren't you?"

Every protective instinct of Jasper's flared to life. He tucked Ada beneath his arms and kept her caged at his front.

"Why would I go with you?" Jasper said to steer the King's attention away from her. "I know exactly what you're planning to do with me."

While he'd been cursed and under the King's influence at the Summer Palace, Jasper had been privy to all of his plans and sick dreams. Mithras was working with the humans, feeding them metal and mana in exchange for scientific knowledge on how to dominate Unseelie High Queen Maebh and her soul eating Sluagh. Mithras's focus had been borderline obsessive. More than once, Jasper had wondered in a haze whether the King was being influenced by the human advisor—Bones was his name. But the advisor had been captured by the Order, and the King was still embroiled with the humans.

His Seelie subjects believed their fearless leader to be the great adventurer who immigrated them from the Winter climate, but Jasper knew the truth. He was just a fae terrified to lose the power he'd amassed. Jasper had long suspected that Mithras had something over Maebh, but there was no proof.

The King pushed off the table and stepped toward the base of the waterfall. He propped his foot on a rock and leveled his stare at Ada.

"You know," he shouted up, studying her more closely. "It's a well-known fact that he's with a different female every other day. He won't be faithful to you."

Ada stiffened.

Jasper bared his teeth, unable to stop the shame heating his blood. It was true. Just like his father, Jasper had hopped from bed to bed, never settling. Until now.

"Come to me, human. Be my bride," the King offered. "I could use someone with your skills in the family."

"You haven't taken a bride for centuries," Jasper bit out. "You seduce and use every woman you meet before discarding them like chewed up second-hand meat."

Mithras's eyes narrowed at Jasper. "Your mother would know, wouldn't she?"

Anger boiled Jasper's blood, and he wondered if he had enough combined mana with Ada to smite his father where he stood. If only he commanded the elements as well as some of his Guardian brethren.

Jasper's eyes locked onto the water behind the King, bubbling away in the pool and running down the waterfall. He could move the water and drown the King... maybe. If he was fast enough.

The sound of weapons being drawn set Jasper's heart hammering against his ribs, and when the King gave an almost imperceptible nod, Jasper summoned his mana and portaled them away.

CHAPTER
TWENTY-ONE

Ada felt an incredible shifting of equilibrium. One moment, she was in the bloodstained grotto, the next she was in a high-ceilinged, empty apartment. She dropped to her knees and heaved in air, trying to get the stench of death from her nose.

It wasn't working.

"We're safe. I portaled us here." Jasper crouched beside her and placed a palm on her shoulder. "Are you well?"

She forced herself to nod and swallowed the dry lump in her throat. All she could see was Lake's blood-stained maraca lying on the dirt. "I can't believe the King did that."

This was a whole new level to this world she'd not realized. Tears burned her eyes. Was this the truth of this world—danger from within their own society, and danger without? She thought she was done with that part of her life. She thought upon seeing the green, vibrant life of Elphyne that the world had changed, but it was just as bad as before.

What was the point?

Without a word, Jasper gathered her into his lap and forced her head down against his beating heart. One big palm landed assuredly on the small of her back, and the other gently stroked her hair. When he spoke, the timbre of his smooth voice enveloped her like a blanket.

"Shh," he said, and only then did she realize tears were streaming from her eyes. "It's going to be okay."

"We should go back," she sobbed, straining against him. "Maybe someone is alive. Maybe I can help them."

"Shh, my love."

"But..."

"No one is alive."

She collapsed and squeezed her eyes shut. "I'm tired, Jasper."

Tired of missing her friends. Tired of having her hopes extinguished. Tired of everything.

"I'll get you cleaned up and then you can sleep."

There was no emotion in his voice, no energy. He was tired too. That was his family, distant as they had been. She felt them rise and walk as he carried her into another room. She wanted to open her eyes, but her strength failed her.

"Where are we?" she asked.

"My apartment in Cornucopia."

She made a non-committal sound and then the next few minutes were a blur of water, a brief bath, and then finally laying down on a soft mattress.

Sleep stole over her until she awoke with a jolt to the overwhelming mix of sadness and hatred barreling down the bond. She bolted upright in a state of confusion.

Red spattered rock.

Trodden ribbon.

Bloody maraca.

Churning water.

Manabeeze floating into the air.

So much blood mixing with the food and into the elixir glasses. She'd drunk from those glasses, and now they were filled with death.

Chest squeezing tight, she rubbed her eyes. The sheet covering her body had fallen. Her nipples peaked in the cool air. She shivered. Groggily, she lifted the sheet, covering herself.

Ada had slept for most of the day. The moon shone through the window, glancing off the hard lines of Jasper's stern face as he glared outside. His arm braced against the window, fingers curled into a fist. Hair stuck out in all directions, as though he'd obsessively tugged it. Black, buckskin breeches hung from his hips, top button popped at the fly, but he remained shirtless.

The sight of his potent masculinity shot a bolt of appreciation straight through her. She bit down on the sheet, forcing herself to relax at the steady sight of him. No matter what had transpired, she'd always felt safe around him. From the first moment she'd opened her eyes to see his annoyingly gorgeous face, there was a *knowing*... as though she were in the middle of experiencing a memory yet to happen. He felt right.

But from the way his head dipped low, the massacre had affected him as much as it had her.

Holding the sheet around her, she submitted to her instincts and went to him.

"Have you slept?"

A switch flipped and his emotions cut off, silencing their bond. It was the only sign of his awareness of her. Dark circles shadowed his eyes. So she guessed he hadn't slept. He continued to brood, eyes tracking unseen things outside the window.

Had the King found them?

Ada swept her gaze outside and saw nothing but the tops of townhouses. Some appeared in good condition, others were ramshackle and falling apart. None were more than three stories, like the building they were in. Further into the distance, an orange glow emanated from a ground spot, reminding her of a sports stadium at night.

Frustration welled, and she knew he sensed it, because unlike him, she didn't hide her emotions.

"What are you looking at?" she asked, hugging her sheet to her front.

No answer.

Her lips flattened. "Are you going to answer me at some point? Or just hide your words like you do your emotions?"

He flared his nostrils, and then gave up the next words as though they cost him a life. "It's the Ring."

The Ring. Her mind traveled back, thinking, scouring until she came up with an answer. Someone told her it was how Cornucopians solved their differences—a gladiator style battle, sometimes to the death. Had it been Jasper who'd told her? Did he know because he'd been there? Participated?

"Jasper," she said. "At some point we're going to have to talk about things. I know the Darkfoots were your family. What happened was... well it was inconceivable having to witness that." She took a deep breath. How could she handsign an apology if he stared outside. "Will you look at me?"

No.

He stayed as still as a marble statue.

In her mind, all she kept hearing was his wounded plea: *Just leave it in. Let it take me.*

An overwhelming sense of fear swamped her. He had no new visible scars. No new wounds. She couldn't fix him like last time. No curse to pick apart. No poison to drain. The lack of understanding his state of mind drove her to distraction, to the point she found herself checking him over.

She stopped.

What am I doing?

She couldn't keep fighting an uphill battle.

"I can fix your body, Jasper, but you are still broken inside, and I don't know what to do. You can't mend unless you want to."

His braced fist dragged down the window, and he turned to meet her eyes. Tension cut through the lines of his body, making muscles bulge and strain. Eyes glimmering gold revealed a story more potent than any book or bond. It was that same stare she'd come across when they first met.

Wounded animal.

Caution.

She gathered his fist and pried his fingers open, humming a tune to ease the tension. Nestled inside his palm was a small, heart-shaped, polished amulet made of amber and with a crumpled leather cord looped through the center.

"It was my mother's," he explained, voice rough.

"It's beautiful."

"It's all I have of her, apart from my memories." He turned it over in his fingers, glaring as though it would burn him.

Keep talking. Please.

She tried to quieten her breath, to still her beating heart, so nothing would distract him from speaking.

"I'm afraid that…" He stopped and clenched his fist around the heart.

She covered his hand. "Tell me."

Glimmering eyes met hers. "She died for nothing."

"What do you mean?"

"She died to protect me because she believed I would one day take over my father's reign. I still dream about the day that she put me in the dugout beneath the floorboards and willed me to stay quiet." His voice went so quiet, Ada had to strain to hear it. "I was a coward. I could have at least tried to save her. But instead, I stayed there until her blood dripped down on my face."

Oh, Jasper. Ada's heart clenched. "And then you became a Guardian?"

"My mother matched with Mithras at Lupercalia. He came, they had the festival, and he left. My mother was fine with it. Fae often became with child after Lupercalia and the village helped raise them. She kept the knowledge of her pregnancy from him. She kept me safe for over a decade, and then he found out. Some people think the unsanctioned breeding law was because the Seelie kingdom ran low on food. But it wasn't. Mithras didn't want any child of his to grow and take over his throne. He killed my mother and then hunted me. I became a Guardian so I could stop those like my mother from suffering again," he said. "But I failed at that, too. In three centuries, I've done nothing to make her proud, and now… I—" He shook his head, admonishing himself. "Now it's too late. The entire Darkfoot pack is gone. Because of me."

She thought of the King, of his snide, sick smile. "It's never too late. You can still make a stand against your father. I know you can."

"How? He's beaten me at every turn. I'm just not enough."

"Bullshit," she said. "You survived a ponaturi bite. You killed the wolpertinger—"

"No, you did. He was virtually dead by the time I got to him." He laughed.

"You saved an entire village from the humans—"

"Only to have them murdered."

"—you saved my life!"

Grave eyes settled on her and narrowed. "You *healed* yourself."

"I would never have done it without your help."

She made a frustrated sound. This wasn't the Jasper she'd gotten to know.

"You're such a hypocrite," she murmured, acid coating her tongue. "You *hounded* me, promising that we were meant to be together because some cosmic entity willed it. You didn't give up. Jesus, you made me believe in something bigger than myself. I didn't even realize until now, but the Well—this lifesaving magic—you've dedicated your life to preserving it. I think that's so incredible, I can't even put it into words. But you don't even believe in yourself."

He glared down at her, eyes blazing.

She pushed against his immovable chest. "I believed you. Believed *in* you. After Lupercalia, and the ribbon linked us, I was ready to give you everything." Her voice softened, and she touched his jaw. "Giving up is the only way to fail. It's the only way your mother's sacrifice was for nothing."

Life had been a series of moments Ada thought she'd never survive... until she did. And most of the time, she'd had help. But she'd tried to help Jasper, and there was only so much talking to a brick wall she could take.

He stared at her for so long she thought he'd slipped into a fugue state, but then something flashed luminous in his eyes. He took a step closer.

She went back, her heart already pattering.

He hesitated, eyes wide.

"Don't walk away," he murmured. "Without you, I'm nothing."

Fae couldn't lie.

He truly believed his words, and they cut her like a knife. She deflated.

"Then maybe we shouldn't be together," she declared stupidly... bravely. His hitched breath only spurred her onward. "I don't want that pressure. I can't be walking on eggshells, thinking you hold me up on a pedestal and be afraid to mess up. We have a saying from our time: I'm only human. It means, I'm not perfect. No one is. I'm going to make mistakes. I'm going to fall. But the worth of someone's character is how many times they pick themselves up and try again... do you understand? If you're nothing *without* me, then you're nothing *with* me."

She would always try to fix him. And he would always feel unworthy. He had to pick himself up. Without her. He had to find out who he was. Without her.

Her words still hung in the air between them, vibrating with tension.

This was it. Her lungs froze as she waited for his response, and when he turned back to the window, she thought she'd lost him. Back muscles flexed as he braced against the glass.

"I won't know what I'm worth unless I submit to the initiation ceremony again," he confessed. "I need to do it. For myself."

"The one where two thirds die?" She gaped. "That's not the introspection I was talking about."

"I've done it before, but when Mithras took me, he made me—" He shivered, mouth twisting with a nasty taste. "He made me feel unclean. I need to complete the initiation again."

But he could die. "Has anyone else done it twice?"

He shook his head and faced her. "But I need to know."

She blinked, shocked. "You don't even know if the Well will let you take it a second time. It's too extreme, and it's still waiting for someone else to validate you. What have I been telling you? *You need to believe in yourself.*" She thumped his chest. "And for the record, I believe in you. Even when you couldn't remember your name, I knew you were someone of worth."

The sadness that spilled from his eyes almost felled her. "I've killed children in the Ring, Ada. Children and females. Helpless victims of all fae races. And then I went up to the champion's suite and let them shower me with rewards—sex, elixirs, drugs, indulgence. I wanted to block it all out. And that's only the things I did to others. Things were done to me. Those debasing memories suffocate me so much, I feel like I'm drowning. I've been defiled in the most filthy ways." He put his forehead on the window and stared outside, jaw twitching. "How can you think me worthy?"

Oh, Jasper.

Her heart ached for him. To be held prisoner, to be forced into despicable acts, and then to live as long as he would with the horrible memories. No one should do that alone.

God, she thought she could push him away until he sorted himself out, but she was wrong. Just flirting with the idea of separating hurt too much. She'd thought, maybe, he could learn to love himself if he was on his own. But the truth was, for a moment, she'd let her own fear take over. When he'd said he was nothing without her, it frightened her because, maybe, she felt the same way. And that kind of all consuming love was devasting to lose.

The hard truth was, she was already at the place she feared—the one where she would break without him.

Her eyes brimmed with tears. He'd been cursed, coerced, and abused. Nothing would bring his victims back. Nothing would turn back time. He might always feel unclean. Unable to stop herself, she rushed forward and encircled her arms around him, blubbering her confession against his back, "You're worth it because I'm falling in love with you."

His broad back heaved with a hitched breath. He turned in her arms, eyes wild and disbelieving.

"Shut up," she said before he could speak. "I'm scared, Jasper. I'm scared of how much it will hurt if we're separated, and that's why I said you have to figure this out without me. For a fraction of a second, I thought maybe if we end things now, that I won't get hurt. I still think you need to believe in yourself, but maybe this will help. I'm already in love with you, Jasper. And I won't let you give up. If you're drowning, then I'll pick you up. I'll swim us both to the surface, and if I can't, then I'll drown with you." Tears spilled over. "I won't let you suffer alone."

She rose on her toes and reverently swiped her lips along his. His arms became marble around her while he let her explore his mouth. Her swipe turned into a press, a nibble on the bottom lip, a kiss at the corner. Their breaths mingled and his taste filled her with raw heat. She pulled back.

His molten gaze darted to her mouth.

They stood there, rock solid in each other's arms, panting with stilted breaths.

"Just kiss me," she begged.

His mouth collided with hers. She dropped the sheet and melted with a pained, guttural groan that struck every chord in her body. They kissed, devoured, and tried to touch every inch of each other. His fingers clawed into her hair and pulled her face back, exposing her neck where he licked and sucked and worshiped before coming back to her mouth. When she felt his palm on her breast, grazing over the peak of her nipple, a ragged breath shot out. She shoved her hand down his breeches, eliciting his own hiss of breath.

She smiled against his lips as she found his steely length and stroked.

"Bed," he grunted with a gasp.

"Mm."

Strong hands lifted her by the rear. She wrapped her legs around his hips and ground against his hard length until they both gasped at the sensation. Jasper all but flew across the floor until his knees hit the bed and they fell. Together. Always together, she knew that now. He rolled on top and pressed her into the mattress, holding her still until she squirmed beneath his intense stare. In the way only a lover could, his gaze roved over her body, setting her senses on fire.

Oh, what I'm going to do to you, his eyes seemed to say as they landed on her intimate body parts—her neck, her breasts, her stomach, below...

Something clicked inside Ada.

She wanted to be the one looking at him like he was her world because staring up at him like this, swathed in moonlight, he was some kind of divine perfection and she wanted to take her fill. She reared forward and pushed him down. He landed back with a huff. Displaced air gusted and blew into her face and hair.

"You're so fucking mine," he growled possessively, eyes heating, taking her hips and settling her over him.

"I think we already had this conversation." Her eyes fluttered as he drove his rock-hard erection into her softness. She whimpered, "I won't be marked. But..." He found her most sensitive spot and rubbed. She moaned, slapping her hands on his chest, hardly able to form words, hardly able to hold herself up.

"But what?" he demanded.

"But—*ooh, yes.*"

His dark brow arched as he studied her face, gauging how he hit the right spots from her expression. She was too damned strung out to even care. And then his lips found her breast, drawing her nipple into his mouth and rolling deep. He groaned around her flesh, rasping it with his teeth, wrenching another breathy whimper from her lungs.

"I love how you're so responsive," he murmured, continuing his thumb's rhythm between her legs. "You're aching for me."

"Yes," she gasped.

"You want more." Not a question. A demand.

"No."

"What?"

Panting, she pushed him back down, eyes blazing. "My turn. I want to make *you* feel good."

Defiance blazed in his expression and then softened as a splash of color hit his cheeks. His ears flattened before springing back up. God, she loved that. He might try to hide his feelings down their bond, but he could never change his body language. Her declaration had stupefied her rogue shifter, and that emboldened her.

"I won't hurt you," she teased, a mimic of the first time he'd tried to mate with her after the wolpertinger attack.

More blood rushed to his cheeks as he grappled internally with something. Choice made, his lids lowered to half-mast. He took her hands and placed them on the buttons of his breeches. The first button was already popped. Holding his gaze, she popped the rest. Every time one came loose, he gave a short groan of anticipation and she sucked in a breath. Goosebumps erupted across his lower abdomen, darkly dusted with hair.

She'd licked her lips raw by the time she cleared his pants and revealed his thick erection.

"Ada." His hand landed hesitantly on the back of her neck.

"Mm?" She raked her nails through the trail of coarse hair, causing his hips to buck involuntarily.

"Be... gentle."

Their gazes clashed, and fragility flickered back. That wounded animal.

I've been defiled in the most filthy ways.

Had he been...? She couldn't finish the thought. All that she knew was that he wanted this. Whatever pain he'd experienced, he wanted this to replace it. The thought of giving him pleasure consumed her. She touched her lips to the broad crown of his cock and butterfly kissed down the length, right along the vein.

"Shit. Not that gentle," he bit out and thrust into her, fingers catching in her hair.

But she kept herself slow and light. A feather-light lick. A little stroke. A swirling suck.

"Ada."

She tugged the breeches all the way off, and climbed on top of him, aligning her lips again with his hard, thick length. Looking up at him from beneath her lashes, satisfaction surged. She could give him a wonderful memory. They both wanted this. They needed something to wipe away the bad. Her lips parted wide. She took him inside her mouth and worked his tip with her tongue before sucking him deep. Again and again, she bobbed on him, savoring his taste.

But when she glanced up, a frown marred his brow as he concentrated on the ceiling. So she started humming, like she did around injured animals. She scraped her fingers through the coarse hair at his lower abdomen, trailed them below, fondled his testicles, and then stroked his length. She did everything she could to make him feel at peace... well, close to it.

Skin stretched taut across his stomach. Veins rippled. Abs bunched and twitched. His breath turned ragged and when she hummed a last time, he yanked her off. Suddenly, she was on the bottom and he was above, hands braced on either side of her head, panting. Smoldering eyes blinked as if he was also surprised with the swift change in position.

He was beautiful. A face she'd only ever seen crafted by an artist—mischievous devil and honorable angel at the same time. And he was flush with the passion he felt for her. The notion sparked a moan and a squirm that triggered another round of kissing so hungry, she found it hard to breathe. He was there. In her mouth. With his tongue. His teeth. Salty taste. Deft fingers trailed down her front, between her legs, testing her readiness. A swipe through her slick center.

A groan into her mouth, and his pupils expanded. "You're..."

She nodded.

"I'm going to..."

She nodded again.

He fit himself between her legs and thrust inside. Her back bowed. She gasped at the sensation of him stretching her inner walls. They fit. Just one swift move and they fit.

"You okay?" he rasped.

Another nod.

"Good. Ready?"

She smiled. "Am I ever."

Savoring thrusts began the rhythm of their dance. It was a slow, sensation-filled torment that quickly turned fast, deep, and relentless. Soon he drove into her hard, sparking her pleasure, lighting the fuse. There was nothing she could do but hold on. It was mad, sweaty, crazy lovemaking that made Ada feel alive. It was a heart pulling, vision blurring, lose your hearing, sort of orgasm that hit them both hard at the same time.

Many things had been left unsaid, but when Jasper drifted to sleep, still in her arms, she felt at peace for the first time in a long time... maybe since before... maybe forever.

And maybe that terrified her.

CHAPTER

TWENTY-TWO

Making love with Ada had shaken loose the final, dark memories from Jasper's mind. He slept restlessly. Fitfully. And full of dreams that were too visceral to be fake.

"I'm going to enjoy this," Mithras sniggered, lifting his candle to illuminate Jasper's broken and swollen face.

Jasper wrenched his wrists, metal manacles biting into him. "Fuck you."

An empty laugh. "No. Not me, son."

"The metal won't hold me for long," he warned.

"Yeah, yeah. Guardian. Special. Blah blah. But I don't need long, or rather, she doesn't need long."

Scraping. Skittering. A shadow moved in the corner as a creature came into the light. Long, black hair coated her face, sharp with insect-like bone structure.

Already, his mind shut down. This wasn't the first time he'd been tortured. And it wouldn't be the last.

"I want to hear his screams from the throne room," the King said, walking away.

The definitive sound of the dungeon door closing cast the room into darkness.

Something tugged on his pants, dragging them from his hips.

Her kiss was cold, tasting like earth.

Jasper's eyes opened. Sweat itched his head, slicked his torso, and pooled beneath him on the bed.

"You okay?"

Sweet voice. Not hissing.

He turned. Blond hair. Not black.

Ada.

Her eyes were puffy with sleep. Her lips, still swollen from his kisses. He slid his

689

fingers along her jaw and into her hair, then brought those lips to his so her taste would obliterate the earth from his memory.

She submitted with an agreeable sound, rolling back to let him climb on top of her. He found his way kissing down her body until his lips landed between her legs, to the sweetest taste of all. She was like some kind of drug. He lapped at her with addiction, hungrily tasting it all. He brought her to climax with his mouth, and then was inside her again, his new favorite place to be. He took her with slow and steady strokes, this time making it last, reveling in how each lazy, sweaty thrust made her cheeks flush and her eyes flutter.

When they were spent, and she lay pliant in his arms, he knew he couldn't pretend his life didn't exist forever. She'd been right. He had to make a stand. If he didn't, the nightmares would never end.

Snow tickled Jasper's face as he stood on the frozen shore of the Aconite Sea. The glacial waters rolled all the way to the other side, where an obsidian castle nestled between foggy mountains. Storm clouds gathered, darkening the sky. The vampires would be out early if the sun stayed hidden, and he wanted Ada well within the safety of the Queen's protection by that time.

Humans were tasty. Well-blessed humans, possibly tastier still. Ada would smell like catnip to any vampire scenting her. One of the vampires in the cadre of Twelve had once lost himself to bloodlust around humans, glutting himself on their blood and accidentally killing all. Vampires were dangerous. Not to mention the other Unseelie crawling about the wilderness.

"Is that it?" Ada asked, shielding her eyes from the glare.

"That's it," he muttered. "The Winter Palace."

With black spires dusted in snow, the castle reached high into the air and provided multiple landing points for the many winged fae among the Unseelie. The black stone foundation stood out starkly against the white. Blood red vines crawling over the facade only increased the foreboding image. Along the mountain behind the castle, dark houses from the neighboring city pushed smoke into the air from their chimneys. While it looked less crowded than Helianthus City, Aconite City was half within the mountain itself and shielded from view.

Hundreds of thousands of fae lived here.

Jasper counted on his Guardian status to give him a reprieve from immediate attack. If they chose to recognize his link to the Seelie King first, then Ada and he might be thrown straight into the dungeons.

Both of them had dressed warmly in clothes he'd found inside the Cornucopia apartment closet. None of the clothes were bought by him, which meant other Guardians had visited his place over the past ten years. Most likely Thorne, since he was the only one keyed to the blood-warded lock on the front door. A pang of guilt hit him when he remembered who'd saved him from Mithras, but Thorne and Rush would have to wait. He needed to try this first. He refused to go back to the Order empty handed, and while Ada had taken back her comment about them needing to separate until he could pick himself up, she'd still said it. And it played on his mind. She'd helped chase away his demons last night, but she was right. He had to make a stand.

Fuck Mithras.

"You're very subdued this morning," she noted.

"It's nothing."

"It's not... what happened between us last night, is it?"

"No," he said, a little too quickly. Whether she referenced their lovemaking, or the fact she still resisted his mark, he wasn't sure. But he wouldn't have her second guessing their relationship. "It's just... some dark memories stirred last night."

Concerned eyes studied him. "You were dreaming and kicking about."

He hand-signed an apology, to which she stopped with her hand before he could finish. "Never be sorry for that."

Something cracked inside his chest. He lowered his lips to hers, claiming her mouth in a passionate kiss, only pulling back because she was too cold. Also, he wasn't comfortable being near water. That was how the King had been spying on him. That type of communication could only occur between blooded kin, and Jasper had given him too much already. It was time to go on the offensive.

"Why didn't you portal us straight there?" Ada asked, tugging her fur-lined cape around her body. The icy air had turned her nose and human ears pink.

He adjusted her hood over her head, tucking her blond hair inside. When he caught her frown, he explained, "The Seelie might be more forgiving with your human status. But the Unseelie will bite first, ask questions later. Malevolence is at their core, and if they don't use you for food, they'll do their best to manipulate you for entertainment. The bleeding feet and finger human artisans the Spring Court Queen spoke of are nothing compared to what they do to humans here. If I portal us into their castle, it would cause surprise. I prefer not to kill anyone before I speak with the High Queen."

"Right."

He summoned his mana to cast a glamour over her ears, just in case. Air shimmered, and it suddenly appeared as though her ears were pointed. Although Maebh would most likely see through the child's trick, it didn't hurt to be safe.

"We landed here first out of courtesy," he elaborated on his answer to her earlier question. "To give them warning that I approach."

She scowled over the sea. "It's quite the warning. I can barely see the castle."

"They know we're here." He gave a pointed look to the crows watching from the skeletal branches of trees scattered before the mountain behind them. A crow cawed impudently and took to the sky, flapping like mad to battle the arctic winds across the water. His brethren, or sisters, followed swiftly, leaving only a handful behind to keep watch.

"We'll give them some time to fly across," he said. "Then I'll take us over."

It had crossed his mind to leave Ada behind within the secure Cornucopia apartment, but there had been too many signs that Thorne had been by. And he wasn't ready to reveal that truth to Ada yet. He needed her to believe he was strong. Someone who picked himself up. He needed a reason her friends had been wrong to shout at him.

At the very thought of them causing a divide between Ada and him, panic tightened across his chest like a writhing, thorn riddled vine. Every instinct in his body urged him to run the other way from that eventuality. Ada was his.

"I suppose while we're waiting, you can tell me about them."

He blanched, thinking she meant her friends, but then realized her eyes were on the trees behind them.

"The crow-shifters?" he asked.

"All of them. The Seelie versus the Unseelie. Back at the, um, Lupercalia rite, they talked of a brewing war."

"Mithras has been making it look like the Unseelie are sending monsters into Seelie land, and vice versa. He knows the Order will stay out of fae politics if it has nothing to do with a danger to the integrity to the Well."

"And Seelie and Unseelie used to be one nation?"

"For the beginning, after the Age of Man was over, there were no rulers. Fae were just trying to survive. If there had to be a ruler, it might have been Jackson Crimson, the founder of the Order. He discovered the link between the Well, our mana, and its resistance of metals and plastics. He led us all, but... he disappeared. The Prime took over the Order, and then Maebh took over ruling the fae. Eventually, the humans had enough of their wasteland and tried to take back control of Elphyne, but the Order, Maebh, and Mithras banded together to beat them back. Even though it was Maebh's Sluagh—"

"What are they?"

"Soul eating fae."

She shivered. "Right. Continue."

"Maebh's Sluagh and their Wild Hunt turned the tide against the humans. But somehow Mithras gained a lot of support among the fae, enough to rally backing for the split of the nation when she clearly had the power to deny him. There hasn't been a fae strong enough to match Maebh's powers in millennia. But since Mithras split and formed the Seelie, she's left everyone south of the border untouched."

"And this is the woman you're asking for help?"

"Yes." He paused. "But I can't ask for help. I just need to tell her about Mithras's plans to use me to incite a war."

"Why can't you just ask for help?"

"In this world, a crown or the title of alpha, is won by battle and blood in two ways. One, because I'm his blooded kin. Two, because I'll pry the glass crown from his bloody hands after I defeat him. If I have assistance, no one will respect me. The crown will be contested."

She chewed her lip. "I get that. Doesn't mean I like the idea of you putting yourself in danger, though."

"This is how I pick myself up, my love. This is how I glue my broken pieces back together." A small, haunted smile lifted his lips. He gathered her closer to him. "Are you worried about me, little human?"

She snorted. "I've seen you rip a heart from someone's chest. I'm not worried about you winning a battle." She frowned, letting herself fall into him. "But I am worried about the toll it will take."

He squeezed her arm and then kissed the top of her head. "It's time to go."

With a dizzying rush, they portaled through space and simply appeared at the base of the castle, their boots crunching in the snow upon landing.

"Oh my God. This is incredible," Ada breathed, shielding her eyes against the glare so she could look upon the enormous black walls.

He tried to see it from her point of view. "Your buildings were not like this?"

"Oh, ours were bigger... but not so finely detailed. It's just different, I guess."

He grunted.

What seemed like a simple stone structure from across the sea, came alive with black-coated soldiers on the ground and dark-winged fae on the turrets, their bows stretched taut with arrows nocked and aimed. The drawbridge creaked open, lowering to provide a walkway from the gatehouse and over a moat that was home to some very nasty Unseelie fae. A dark fae waltzed across the walkway, his black snow-dusted mantle billowing behind. Red lining provided a splash of color, just enough to remind them of blood, danger, and their fate if they opposed the Queen.

The guard stopped before Jasper and narrowed his eyes at Ada. Icicles tinkled in his beard. With the snow dusting his shoulders, it was clear he'd recently arrived from some time spent outdoors.

A long, jagged scar deformed one side of his craggy face. When fae appeared aged, it was usually because their mana had been forced out in such a way that it was irreplaceable. They were effectively cut from the Well, just like humans. This guard had either been tortured, or displeased the Queen... or both.

"What business do you have here, Guardian?" he asked.

"I seek an audience with the High Queen," Jasper replied.

The guard arched his dark brow. "She's busy. Go back to the Order."

Jasper pursed his lips. "It's vital I speak with her. Tell her the safety of her nation is at risk."

The guard sucked his teeth, clearly not convinced, but he knew better than to dismiss a claim of national danger from a Guardian. "You can wait in the guest suites until you are called."

Jasper forced his expression to deadpan. Guest suites meant they would be locked behind doors and seen to whenever it pleased Maebh. It could be today, it could be a week, or even a month from now. He supposed at least it wasn't the dungeon.

Jasper gave a flat smile. "Lead the way."

He took Ada's cold hand, thinking at least they'd be out of the elements. The temperature didn't bother him, but she shivered beneath her cape. They might have a long wait ahead, but he knew how to warm her up. It was the one thing he looked forward to.

TWENTY-THREE

Ada gaped the entire walk through the castle to the guest suites. Obsidian walls with glistening marbled veins surrounded them on all sides. Red decadent carpet softened their steps through the halls. After crossing the foyer, they went outside through a sunken courtyard where a crystal clear, bottomless pool sparkled. Surrounding the pool, gargoyle statues sat on a balcony and spurted water from their mouths, adding to the peaceful atmosphere which went against everything Jasper had told her about the Unseelie.

It surprised Ada the pool wasn't frozen like half the sea outside. It could be a hot spring, like the one at the Lupercal cave. If it was a source of power, it made sense a settlement was built around it.

The guard took them beyond the courtyard and up four flights of stairs to an arched, double door with two guards standing outside. Like the guard who'd greeted them, these wore black uniforms. Long coats, black breeches, and mantlets covering their shoulders. Their ears were pointed but had no fur on the tips. Ada darted a glance to Jasper to see if he would explain, but his scowling gaze was fixed on them as though he expected an attack. Probably better to ask when they had some privacy. Clara had said that it could be deemed impolite to ask someone about their race, as it was back in Ada's time. She had to remember to learn when to display her curiosity, and when to hide it.

"You may stay here until the Queen calls you," the gatehouse guard said. The icicles on his beard tinkled to the ground. "Pull the bell rope if you require sustenance."

Jasper gave a curt nod, and when the doors opened, they went inside.

"These are the *guest* suites?" Ada asked, unable to hide the awe in her voice.

The chambers were vast, featured two queen beds, and an opulent parlor with brocade cushioned settees. There were two fireplaces in the rooms, crackling with low heat. The black and red decor included a gothic stained-glass window in the parlor, refracting eery red and shadow into the room. She glimpsed a fractured view of the sea beyond the rose design on the window.

Ada startled when the doors closed behind them with a thud. The guard was gone.

"We're prisoners," Jasper explained, lashes lowering in vexation.

"Oh." She turned around. "At least the digs are nice."

Sighing, he tossed his cape onto a bed and then strode toward the parlor. The hard lines of his cleanly shaven jaw twitched.

She understood his frustration. Standing up to his father had left tiny lines carved between his brows. But something had shifted last night, both good and bad. He finally understood his troubles wouldn't disappear if he ignored them. He could stop Mithras from causing a war, and by aligning with the Queen and going public about his opposition to his father's plans, Jasper was also saving his own life. As Ada understood it, one reason the King had tried to kill Jasper was because he wanted to blame the Unseelie Queen and trigger the war. So if they took that excuse off the table, it had to make Mithras stop, right?

Of course, there were all the other reasons the King wanted Jasper dead.

"So, how long do you think we have to wait?" she asked.

"Could be hours. Could be days."

"I know it wasn't easy for you to come here," she said, meeting him at the window. "This first step in standing up to your father is the hardest, but you've done it. We're here. I'm proud of you."

"It will be done after I speak with Maebh," he grimaced. "Rather, it will be the beginning of the end."

"What will you say to her?"

He glanced warily at the door and lowered his voice. "We must be careful what we say in the castle, and in much of the city. The walls have ears."

"Literally?" She wouldn't be surprised with all the strange things she'd learned since awaking in this time.

"Could be the fire-sprites minding the hearths, or a fae actually within the walls, or advanced fae hearing. We only know that the Queen hears everything, eventually."

She made a zipping motion on her lips. "Got it." When he didn't elaborate, she asked, "You say 'we' a lot. Do you mean your friends at the Order? The ones who rescued you?"

It was another topic he'd failed to talk about, and it made little sense to her. These were his people. They'd risked life and limb to save him, yet he didn't want to go back and ask them for help.

He gave a curt nod but said nothing else. She ran her hand down his arm, fingers rasping over the wool of his sweater.

"I'm here if you want to talk."

Vibrant eyes met hers, and she had to stifle a gasp. Even knowing him as intimately as she did, when he looked at her, her heart stopped from the impact. When he smiled, she was dead.

A line appeared between his brows, and he dipped his chin.

"You'll find out about them soon enough," he muttered, cupping her jaw. "And when you do, promise not to hate me."

"Jasper," she admonished. "I could never."

His hand dropped from her jaw. "I'll cast a privacy ward about us, just in case they're listening."

"You can do that?"

He nodded and began to move about the room, placing his palm at certain points on the wall. It didn't look like he did much, but Ada felt a tingle of something in the air. When he was done, he came back to her.

"That should do it."

"Can you teach me how to do that?"

His eyes crinkled. "What will you give me if I do?"

She laughed. "Always wanting a reward. I'm sure I can find a treat around here somewhere for you."

Heated eyes lowered to her lips.

A few moments of silence passed while they stared at each other. She exhaled slowly and undid the ties on her cape, twirling to survey the room, knowing full well he watched her. Anticipation buzzed in her veins.

"Well," she said, biting her lip, praying he walked closer behind her. "What shall we do to pass the time?"

Two hands landed on her waist and she almost groaned. He kissed behind her ear. She squirmed down to her legs, shivering into him.

"I have a few ideas," he rumbled, then nipped her earlobe playfully before his teeth landed on her neck and grazed. He exerted the tiniest bit of pressure, just enough to let her know his intentions, but then drew back. "Like I said, when I mark you, Ada, you'll beg me for it."

She scoffed. "I don't beg."

He spun her to face him. "You'll want it so bad that you'll take my teeth and put them on your neck."

"Oh, really?" Who was she kidding? She probably would. She smirked, untying her blouse buttons and walked backward. When the buttons opened, the middle gaped, revealing her complete and utter lack of underwear.

He virtually simmered at the sight of her naked breasts, and then tore at his clothes —lifting his sweater and shirt in one smooth motion, unbuttoning his breeches, and then storming her until she fell back against the bed with a giggle.

ON THE THIRD day of their captivity, Ada sat in the parlor on the settee with Jasper sitting on the floor between her legs, facing the stained glass window. He toyed with the amber heart that had belonged to his mother. Her hands were in his hair, braiding little lengths as he told her stories about his life and about Elphyne and the Well.

"A source of power is where you can replenish your mana stores faster than usual," he said, leaning back into her touch until she scratched behind his ears and he all but purred.

With a smile, she ran her fingers through his hair and sectioned out another piece before splitting the hair into three and twining. "Like what?"

"Usually they're heated lakes, or bodies of water. Like the Lupercalia pool."

"And the one down stairs, right? That was a source of power?"

He nodded. "If any fae run low in mana, they can sit in the water for a few minutes and be restored."

"Cool."

"Otherwise it could take up to a few days to replenish the store from nature."

Ada paused, crinkling her nose. "I've not needed to."

He craned his neck and gave her a heart-rending smile. "That's because you're special."

"You're just saying that to get in my pants." She swatted him.

"Is it working?"

She snorted, and turned his face back to face the front. "When doesn't it work?"

He tried to twist back around but she stopped him with a tug of the hair.

"Ow," he simpered.

"You're ruining my style."

He frowned, still looking back at her. "And you're sure this is a style many males from your time wear?"

"Sure," she mumbled, biting back a smile. "Now, tell me some more stories. What about your friends at the Order?"

He settled back to face the front with a barely contained huff. "I don't know what they'd think of me now," he confessed. "But it's not good."

Ada's fingers stilled on his head. "They're your friends. They rescued you."

His broad, sweater covered shoulders shrugged. "They don't know the depraved things I did while with the King."

Neither did Ada. Not really. She held her breath, waiting for more. When his words came, they spilled out of him.

"Thorne was the angriest kid I'd ever seen come into the Order, and it was the first time I really saw how my behavior had affected someone else. He was angry because of me. I'd failed to step in and help his mother from being executed. I'd failed to stop his father from being cursed. Then I did nothing to help him as a child until he came to the Order." Jasper tensed. "Thorne only entered the ceremonial lake because his Uncle Thaddeus had forced him. Thaddeus was a cruel man, and I knew it. I could have done something... but..." He exhaled. "Sometimes I freeze."

"I get that," she murmured, and stroked his hair gently, unraveling the braids. "I get scared too. It's why I said those stupid things to you the other day. I thought I was protecting myself. Obviously, I was wrong."

He turned on his knees and slotted himself between her legs, placing a palm on each knee. His hair stood on end, making him more adorable than before.

"Ada," he said, eyes turning solemn. "There's something I've been meaning to tell you, but... I don't want you to think differently of me."

698

Pain and hurt flashed over his expression. She placed her palm on his cheek.

"Nothing you could say would make me think differently about you."

"You say that now."

"So don't," she said. "If you're not ready, tell me another time. It doesn't matter to me."

"What does matter to you?"

"Your happiness."

His brows quirked up and a playful expression crossed his features. "So if I were to tell you, this made me happy"—his hands slid up her thighs, thumbs angling inside until they hit her apex with a firm, tingling press—"then it would matter to you?"

She squirmed back as heat pooled at his touch.

"Yes," she breathed.

"And this?" He brushed his thumbs over the seam in her pants, creating friction against her sensitive junction.

She bit her lip, nodding, unable to stop her hips from rocking against him. God, she was a wanton addict around him. Since they'd been locked up, it was all they could do. Eat, sleep, talk, and make love.

"And this?" He took her hips and dragged her closer to the edge of the settee—closer to him. He placed his mouth between her thighs and bit through the fabric, making a tiny growling sound as pleasure sparked and fired in her groin.

"Jasper," she gasped, as he gave up the pretense of his game and opened the buttons on her pants. "What about the wards?" Had he set any today? She couldn't remember.

"They're fine," he said, and tugged her pants and underwear down her legs. He tossed them to the side and then pushed her knees wide until she was on display for him.

"And the window?"

They were right near the window. Anyone could see through.

"We're up too high," he grumbled and slid a finger deep into her slick center.

"But... *oh, God*." She rocked against him, chasing his touch every time he withdrew.

"This is all you need to worry about," he rasped, drugged eyes drinking in the sight of his actions. "This makes me very happy."

Seeing how he watched made Ada even hotter. Curls of heat bloomed low in her belly. Her head tipped back and she submitted to Jasper's insatiable wants.

"Ride my fingers, Ada," he demanded. "Show me how much you want this."

Unable to stop herself, she rocked against him just as he plunged into the heat of her. When he added a second finger, her pulse rabbited. She squirmed and fisted his hair, lifting his gaze to hers.

"Tell me what you want, my love," he muttered.

God... when he called her that. "You."

"Where?"

She rocked her hips. "Here."

A slow, wicked smile curved his lips.

"This makes me very happy," he said, and then replaced his fingers with his mouth.

His tongue did magical things. He sucked, licked, nipped and swirled until Ada's body broke into a million blissful pieces. And yet, he continued to feast on her until the last of her throes died, and she needed a different kind of completion.

She tugged him by the hair, dragged him up and then kissed him. He groaned into her mouth, deepening the kiss.

"Ada," he murmured.

That's all he said. She thought maybe he'd mention marking her again, but he didn't. She would have said yes. The moment hung suspended between them. She saw the hesitation in his eyes, and his words from earlier came back to haunt her.

There's something I've been meaning to tell you...

Before she could let the doubt take purchase, Jasper growled low in his throat, his expression turned intense, and he flipped her onto her stomach, maneuvering her with ease to suit himself. He kicked her legs apart so one fell off the settee, and one stayed on. Then he lifted her hips, angling her rear and positioned his cock at her swollen, sensitive entrance before driving in to the hilt and lying on top of her, savoring their connection.

He gave a shuddering groan that rumbled down her spine and tingled all the inside places of her body.

"This," he murmured into her ear, hot breath against her neck. "This right here, Ada."

She could only nod with a whimper and bite her hand. The sensation of him surrounding her, filling her, was almost too much.

He lowered his lips to her ear and whispered, "This feels like home."

SOME TIME LATER, they lay naked and sweaty on the settee. Jasper was on bottom and Ada on top, her head in the crook of his arm with the two of them entwined. Making each other happy had taken all of her energy, and the ability to snooze was all that remained.

Jasper's hand trailed idly down the length of her long hair, starting at her head and running down her back. It was so soothing, she'd nodded off on more than one occasion. She might have napped, but he hadn't. She knew something played on his mind.

"What are you thinking about?" she murmured and ran her hand over his chest.

He inhaled, hesitated, and then spoke. "Nothing."

For a moment, she considered leaving it, but wanted to know some things herself. "Is it about your father? And how we're going to take him down?"

His grip tightened in her hair. "It was actually about the Ring."

"Oh."

He went back to stroking. "I hate it. It needs to go."

"But..."

"But even if I did become king, it's not in my jurisdiction. Cornucopia is independent. Any change I make as king will be a sign of aggression against the Unseelie people. I'd need her cooperation."

Silence ticked by. Ada's lashes drifted with every stroke of Jasper's hand. Her mind traveled to other things... things that both frightened her and settled in her with a sense of purpose.

"Jasper?"

"Mm-hm?"

"When you become king—"

"If—"

"When!"

He grumbled.

She continued, "Let's just pretend for a minute you will be."

She felt his smile against her head as he kissed the top. "Fine. When."

"What will happen to me?"

"You'll be by my side. As Queen."

A frown tightened her brow. "But I'm human."

"And blessed by the Well."

"It still took the Darkfoot pack a while to get used to me."

"No it didn't. They fell in love with you by Lupercalia. If you can do that to a pack that was ravaged by humans, then you can do it to the general Seelie people. Besides," he said. "We don't even know if that's going to happen. We still need to speak with Maebh."

"I know."

"Let's not get ahead of ourselves. If it were up to me, I'd let someone else take the throne."

"Is there anyone else?"

He paused. "Not really. Not if we don't want Maebh taking the power back."

"And that's not good?"

He shook his head. "She's changed since the first time she controlled all of Elphyne. She's darker, secretive, and merciless. Perhaps even mad. She is very old."

"I'm so looking forward to meeting her," Ada said drolly.

"I can handle her."

Ada sat back and looked him in the eyes. "Just so you know, you're going to be magnificent in whatever future you choose."

His smile crinkled his eyes and Ada went all gooey inside. And then he said something that melted Ada into a puddle.

"As long as you're in it, I believe you."

TWENTY-FOUR

They waited eight days before the Queen called them. *Eight days.* Jasper could have portaled them both out, but they agreed that doing so would mean giving up. They were better than that, so they used the time to get to know one another, both between the sheets and out of them.

The more Ada learned about him, the more she fell in love.

He was a hero. He battled monsters. He stepped in front of danger daily because it was the right thing to do. He was also funny and fun. In some stories, he told of the shenanigans he would get up to with his cadre. They sounded like an interesting lot, and she looked forward to meeting them.

But then he'd been taken. Things had changed. He still refused to talk much about what happened while he'd been under the King's influence but, like she'd told him already, she could wait. As long as he was happy, she was too. She didn't need to know everything. Everyone was entitled to their secrets. Back in Vegas, when she'd finally attended the local high school, none of them knew the depths of her childhood isolation. None of them knew the only reason she could attend was because Harold and Laurel had taught her how to read.

Jasper also trained Ada more in the nuances of accessing her gift. She couldn't light a flame, but she could shift water with her power—only enough to move the faucet flow and the bathwater around in circles. Thinking of that moment brought another smile to Ada's face.

That bath had been a very happy one for both of them.

And it wasn't all about Ada making Jasper happy. He made her happy in countless of ways. On the bed... by the fireplace... back at the window.

There was a limit, though. After eight days, even her lessons grew tiring. She could heal any ache from her body, but she needed more training. The fact became evident when Jasper struggled to explain what certain elements of mana meant. Apparently, there were fire, earth, air and water, but also chaos and spirit. Each felt differently, and he wasn't proficient in all of them.

To know what spells she could cast, she needed to know her elemental affinities, and that could only be isolated at the Order of the Well. Hopefully, they would get there soon.

Jasper snoozed in an armchair by the parlor fire, and she was in the middle of the very important task of counting the corners in the gothic, arched ceiling when the knock came at the door.

Jasper's ears perked and he sat up. Their eyes met briefly before Ada scrambled off the bed and ran a palm down her front. Because of the long duration of their stay, they'd been given clothing along with food three times a day. She now wore leather pants and a simple black sweater with feathered shoulder cuffs. Her hair draped about her shoulders, concealing her ears.

Jasper was also decked in top to toe form-fitting black—leather breeches and a thin black sweater showing all his God-given talents. It seemed the Queen enjoyed her guests wearing the colors of her brand. Ada wasn't complaining.

"Enter," Jasper rumbled and joined her at the bedside.

She wasn't sure if he'd spoken loud enough to be heard, but the door opened.

The dark guard from the gatehouse strode in. They'd since learned from the servants that he was a vampire named Gastnor. Jasper had warned Ada more than once to be wary around him.

Today he wore clothing more suited to indoors—black pants and a sweater. *Well, what do you know?* Black, black, black.

He motioned for them to follow but said nothing as they walked the long thin hallways.

"If this queen isn't wearing black, I swear I'll pay you whatever you want."

Jasper's lips quirked. Ada smiled back, happy to see the strain lift from his posture, if only for a moment.

"Never make a wager with a fae, Ada," he drawled, clearly amused. "You won't like the outcome."

She snorted and waggled her brows. "You know I'll *wager* with you anytime. Just ask."

This time, a humored huff burst out of him, and by the time they arrived at the throne room, he'd draped his arm casually around her shoulders. "Ada, Ada," he chided with a twinkle in his eye.

"What?" she smiled, looking up at him.

He lowered his lips to her ear. "You're perfect for me."

She molded to him. He kissed the top of her head and then guided her through the enormous arched doorway.

Inside, she was grateful for Jasper's steady touch because she shrank beneath the attention of a room full of gawping fae.

The throne room was an enormous obsidian chamber. The sickly sweet scent of vanilla and rose permeated the air. Red banners dangled from the ceiling between a criss-cross sculpture of bones, antlers, and driftwood that reached from cornice to cornice. Up on a dais, before a stained-glass window depicting violent, deviant scenes involving fae, blood, and animals, sat the Queen on a throne made of black bone. Or maybe it was obsidian, carved to look like bone.

The Queen herself was a striking woman with big dark eyes and pouting purple lips. Long afro hair carried an antler crown crested with rubies. It reminded Ada of the thorns Jesus wore on the cross, the red rubies like blood. Her dark dress wasn't saintly. It clung to her voluptuous form until it flared at the knees and trailed down the steps of the dais where two goblin-like creatures simpered and preened against the lengths. Collars linked them to a stake wedged into the steps.

As they walked down the aisle, Ada couldn't help shivering under the weight of the watchful eyes of the members of the Court. Some fae appeared human, some weren't. Antlers on heads. Antennas. Wings. Faces that weren't human moved with unblinking eyes and slashes for mouths. Underbites with fangs. A few faces were deathly pale, and Ada could have sworn she glimpsed the outline of a skull when looking at one. It was only a flicker beneath his hauntingly beautiful face, as though someone had shone a torch over translucent skin, but then when the light switched off, the skull was gone.

When her gaze landed on two short, thickset old men with long prominent teeth, a shiver skated down her spine. Red berets sat atop their scraggly hair. Skinny, taloned fingers clicked at their thighs, and large red eyes tracked her as she walked by. Their hats were glossy, as though dipped in actual blood, and when she caught the sight of a few flies swarming about, she knew it to be true. Gross.

Jasper squeezed her shoulder as they came to a standstill at the foot of the dais. Gastnor continued up the steps and stood to the Queen's right. On her left stood a stocky man in a dark robe, his face shadowed by the cowl. He clutched a round glass globe.

"High Queen Maebh," Jasper said, and inclined his head.

"Bow, Guardian," she demanded. Her deep voice oozed confidence.

Ada swiftly curtsey-bowed, wishing that she'd at least asked Jasper about the proper protocol. Jasper deepened the incline of his head, but went no lower. She tapped her black-stained fingertips on the throne, long pointed nails ticking.

"I see the ego of your new station has already consumed you," she remarked drolly. "A Guardian *and* a prince. My how times are changing."

Jasper met her gaze.

"Speak." She gestured, barely lifting her finger as though the entire situation bored her.

He glanced around the congregation. "Perhaps we should speak about politics in private."

"This is my court," she drawled. "And these are my trusted advisors. There is nothing I won't tell them."

Ada highly doubted it. This was a power play, anyone could see it. The silence and watchful eyes intended to intimidate, to display the Queen's control of her subjects, and to show she was a woman to fear and respect. And it worked—for Ada.

But Jasper didn't flinch. He arched a regal brow. "Very well. The Seelie High King is plotting against you. He's colluding with humans to frame Unseelie as perpetrators in a rash of attacks. He wants to incite a war, a war which he planned to trigger by killing me and claiming you were responsible."

The Queen stared at him, calculations running behind her shark eyes. Not one person in the room reacted. It was as though they either already knew, didn't care, or were spelled to look statuesque.

Ada was officially spooked.

"I must admit," Maebh said, thrumming her nails. "I was suspicious when word arrived of you portaling into our territory. And curious. They said you've been missing for over a decade, and then the King suddenly announces you're his heir." Her smile failed to reach her eyes. "We've both been around for long enough to know he never intended for you to ascend to his throne. So why come to me? I care little for what happens on Seelie soil."

Jasper scowled. "He's got eyes on your kingdom. He wants to rule all of Elphyne as you once did. The only reason he acknowledged me as his heir is so that he could kill me, blame you, and claim grievance to the Seelie throne."

"If the humans failed to beat my Sluagh and their Wild Hunt, then what makes Mithras think he can?"

"Like I said, he's working with the humans. He's giving them metal in exchange for weapons that work against the fae."

More silent contemplation from the Queen. Then she made a tedious, limp hand gesture. "I care as much about the Seelie as an *elfant* cares about a mouse."

"You want to know where I was for the past decade?" Jasper growled, taking a step forward. "Mithras forced me to fight in the Ring with an iron mask embedded into my neck. Because the iron was inside my body, it halted my transformation. I got stuck halfway between wolf and fae. They stripped me of my power-enhancing tattoos. They stole my memories. If he can do that to a Guardian thought impervious to metal, what makes you think you can survive what they have in store for you?"

Her eyes flashed. A ripple of power washed about the room like a rogue wind. Ada tried not to shiver for fear the Queen would notice her and do something drastic.

Jasper stepped forward and continued talking.

"During the past one hundred years, since the last war against the humans, their warfare tactics have vastly advanced. They can now inject liquid metal into our bodies and force our mana out. Are you honestly telling me you'd say no to the offer of a metal cage if the Order allowed it? Just one? Or any metal weapon, for that matter. It might halt your use of mana while holding it, but on the flip side, you could kill any magical creature. Imagine the fae you could have under your thumb. Imagine the power you'd amass."

"Are you making me an offer, Guardian? Are you working with the humans too?"

"No," he said. "I want to kill the one who is."

Ada thought it had been silent before, but after Jasper's words dropped, the room was a virtual vacuum. The Queen's rogue wind stopped. Not a feather ruffled on her dress. Not a breath was taken by the goblins at her feet. And her eyes—cold, dark eyes—stared at Jasper so long and hard, Ada thought she was trying to read his mind.

Then the room burst into screeching laughter. Each of the Unseelie fae howled like hyenas until the Queen stopped them with a look, albeit humor-laced.

She raised her black stained fingers and said to Jasper, "Very well. Convince me."

"Convince you?"

"Yes, you want my help to defeat your king, then show me why I should care. He's no threat to me. Unless you can convince me otherwise."

Jasper looked thoughtful. Ada wasn't sure what he'd say. It seemed impossible the Queen would help them with Mithras. They should just leave. But his gaze flicked sideways to Ada, and then back to the Queen.

"How about a wager?" he asked, all smiles and charm.

Maebh's dark brow rose. "I'm listening."

Jasper became the showman once more. He lifted his arms and rotated, staring at the court before settling back on the Queen. "If I beat your best warrior, you will owe me a boon."

A chorus of gasps erupted, including Ada's.

"Very well," Maebh grinned. "But I will have no open ended boon. Name your prize. Use of my Wild Hunt to kill the King? Mana? Metal? What?"

Ada thought it was curious she offered the use of metal, meaning she had some stockpiled somewhere against the Order's mandate.

"After I kill the King, I want the Ring disbanded in Cornucopia."

"That is neutral territory," Maebh said. "Even if you become the Seelie High King, neither of us have the right to disband the Ring."

"Which is why I'm asking for your cooperation. If both of us provide a united front, then Cornucopia will have to fall in line."

"And if the Ring is gone, how do you expect Cornucopian law to work? Will you provide the resources for a guard?"

"I expect you and I to come up with a solution beneficial to everyone."

She pondered his suggestion and then nodded. "Agreed, although, I am surprised you don't simply ask for assistance to dispatch your king."

"I won't need help for that." Jasper walked up to her, held out his hand and said, "A bargain must be struck."

She clasped his hand and studied him. "If you beat my finest warrior, or if I forfeit the match, then I, High Queen Maebh, agree to parlay with you, D'arn Jasper, regarding abolishing the Ring in Cornucopia until a mutually beneficial solution can be arranged."

Jasper repeated her words but added the time limit of four seasons, much to Maebh's chagrin, but she agreed. A spark erupted between their palms, and the bargain was struck.

"Now," the Queen said, rising to her feet with a slow smile. "Who shall you battle? The vampire leader of my personal guard, Gastnor? Or perhaps one of my redcap warriors... oh, no. Of course, you said my best warrior. How silly of me."

She flicked her fingers in the air. A ghostly wind fluttered through the room. The screams of unseen prisoners screeched in Ada's ears, distant dogs barked, and then quite suddenly, a man appeared before Jasper.

Tall, pale, and hauntingly beautiful, he was almost gothic in appearance with his long dark cape—no, *wings,* they were wings—draped down from his shoulders. They shuddered and fluttered as fast as a dragonfly's. Fast enough to make Ada want to rub her eyes. He stepped closer to Jasper and Ada gasped, her heart leaping into her throat. He hadn't stepped. But he'd moved. It was like frames of the film were missing and he'd skipped ahead in the space at spooky irregular intervals.

The Queen smiled. "One of my Sluagh will be your opponent."

TWENTY-FIVE

J asper had hoped Maebh would choose a Sluagh, but hid his triumph. He would have been happy with any fae, to be honest. As long as it wasn't her. All he needed was for her to forfeit, and for that to happen, he needed to trick her just as she was trying to trick him.

The key to defeating the Sluagh was separating its soul from its body in the daylight.

"I thought you were smarter than this, Guardian," the Queen drawled. "Then again, your father captured you and forced you to battle in the Ring for years."

Sniggers tittered around the Court. No one thought he'd win.

"Jasper?" Ada whispered, her eyes wide.

He kept his expression amused and dropped the block on his emotions. For this to succeed, he would need her calm. He jogged over and whispered in her ear, "It's easier to give her some entertainment to get what I want."

He made sure she sensed he wasn't concerned. Her jaw clenched and she nodded. "Give 'em hell, honey."

He winked, loving how confident she was of him.

Perfect for me.

Ada shuffled to the side. He pulled her back to him, remembering something.

"I might have to borrow your mana," he murmured. "Is this okay?"

"Take whatever you need."

Her words hit him harder than he'd been prepared for. They'd spent the past eight days loving each other, yet, in truth, he'd taken more than she should give without giving back himself. He knew her friends were somewhere in Elphyne. On more than one occasion he had an opening to tell her. But every time he opened his mouth, nothing came out. He'd frozen. The thought of disappointing her, of her friends poisoning her against him, was the new source of his nightmares. It was irrational, but still something he couldn't let go of.

Which was why he had to find a way to tell her, or this would all backfire.

He strode back to the empty space before the throne and rolled his shoulders. "You want to do this here?"

"Here, outside—" Maebh shrugged. "Either place, you will still die. And I will enjoy supping on your human mate."

Jasper's eyes narrowed. His humor dropped. Things just got personal. Fine. He would make this end as swiftly as possible.

Making a show of it, he held out his palm and distended a claw from a fingertip. He used the point to scratch bloody symbols into his left palm and then summoned his steel weapon, Ghostmaker. It probably still sat in his room at the Order. When the spell found it, the sword would portal to him. He stared at the Queen while he waited and kept his back to the Sluagh.

"I sense your doubt, Guardian." The Sluagh's voice whispered into Jasper's mind. *"Turn around and face me."*

Jasper remained stoic. His brazen disregard for his safety baffled the crowd, but the Queen narrowed her eyes. She knew he'd just summoned a weapon.

"Metal won't kill it," she taunted. "You know that."

He gave a half shrug. "But it might slow it down."

"Not enough. You have seconds before your life is forfeit. Do you have any last words, shifter prince?" She sneered the word "prince" and he hated it.

He never thought he'd grow attached to the word, but after the King had massacred the Darkfoot pack, and then Ada's subsequent belief he could make a stand, he'd thought, perhaps, he had a chance at fixing things in the Seelie nation. He had a chance to make his mother proud. Perhaps those dignitaries who'd sat at the Lupercalia feast and had urged him to take the crown were right. Perhaps he owed his kin to protect the innocent—beyond the Order's prerogative. It was the dream that had driven him to becoming a Guardian in the first place.

Before the hour was over, Maebh would eat her words. She would see him as an equal, and when they finally entered negotiations regarding the Ring, she would come to the table with respect.

"Coward." The Sluagh's words slid into his thoughts. *"She will know the truth. She will despise you. Surrender now and save your dignity."*

Jasper tensed, knowing the Sluagh spoke about Ada. His hands clenched at his sides.

Just a little longer.

"Turn around, Guardian. Face me."

A rumbling in the atmosphere signaled his long broadsword, Ghostmaker, coming through time and space, pulled by the spell he'd carved in blood. He held out his hand, ready to claim it. The instant the hilt hit his palm, he dematerialized.

And appeared behind the Sluagh, bringing Ghostmaker's blade to his neck, ready to slice it open. The Sluagh had sensed him coming. It flickered away. Two skips and it was two feet further away. It gathered its bearings and then flickered to Jasper, but this time, Jasper portaled away. And so their game of cat and mouse began, each of them flickering or portaling across the room, trying to catch the other until eventually, the Sluagh's specter, a skull faced blur of shadow and light, appeared like a ghost within its face. Its perfect, debonair mouth twisted into a snarl, revealing sharp jagged teeth, and then it separated its soul from its body with a gust of air.

Even though he couldn't see it, Jasper had been prepared. He waited until he sensed the spirit coming, and then portaled about the room, leading the specter on a seemingly random chase. He could sense the confusion—from the Sluagh, the Queen, and the spectators. None of them had realized how much mana Jasper had access too. He should be tired by now. Spent. But he was only getting warmed up.

With a final dart about the room, he landed behind the Sluagh's physical body, gripped his arm and portaled away.

They landed on a mountaintop covered in snow. Jasper let go of the snarling and hissing Sluagh. It hated sunlight, more so than the vampires.

"My soul will find me," the Sluagh warned, twisting and lashing out with its clawed fingers. Without its soul, it couldn't speak directly into Jasper's mind. Its wings shuddered, preparing to fly. "No matter where in the world you have taken me, I will reunite with my specter, and then I will find you. And I will feast on your cowardly eternal soul."

Jasper's snarl echoed across the mountain. His blade was against the Sluagh's neck before he could blink. "I should run you through right now and be damned with the consequences."

The Sluagh grinned a shark's tooth grin. "You don't have the courage."

Ghostmaker cut the pale neck, just a sliver. Dark crimson oozed from the shallow wound. The Sluagh's eyes widened.

"Yes," Jasper whispered. "I know the blade will kill you without your soul inside."

"That's a lie."

"Is it?" Jasper returned.

His opponent said nothing because it was true. Without this ghostly presence, the body was virtually Lesser Fae. It was sheer luck no one had discovered this weakness so far.

Jasper shrugged. "I only needed a few minutes with you out of the room."

He portaled himself back to the Queen's throne room, knowing that the Sluagh's specter would already be hurtling through the world, arrowing straight back to its body, expending mana.

The Queen pretended to look bored.

"Please don't tell me you're playing a game of fetch with my Sluagh."

He bared his teeth in a grin for he knew beneath her droll countenance was a female fearing the worst. She knew nothing.

Maebh waved her hand. "You know he will be back, at any moment. And all he needs to replenish his mana is to eat a soul within this room. Perhaps it will be your mate's."

Jasper brandished his sword, twirling it around in his hand as he began a slow, steady walk toward the Queen, making sure to show the blood stain dripping down Ghostmaker.

"I think not," he said.

"Oh, really." Her eyes darted to his blade. "Enlighten me."

"You haven't fulfilled your end of the bargain. The Sluagh wasn't your best warrior. Even if it was, I can keep up a game of fetch all day."

Her expression darkened. She knew he was right, and now she knew he'd not killed the Sluagh like he could have.

"Is your best warrior too afraid to face me?" he taunted. "Is that it?"

Fury flashed in her eyes, and she stood, menace rippling from her in waves.

"You test my patience."

"And you manipulated the bargain."

The crowd sniggered and laughed. It was an Unseelie thing to do. If their queen hadn't tried to rig the contest, they would have been disappointed. But the Queen wasn't as clever as she thought.

He knew one thing gave her power among her people; it was her utter lack of fear over the metal killing strength of the humans. All Jasper needed to do was to prove metal had the power to kill her greatest warrior, and her illusion of power would be shattered. She would lose subjects in droves.

The walls shook as the Sluagh approached, coming in at such a force, it displaced sound and created thunder.

Jasper swung his sword, scrutinizing the bloody blade, thinking aloud, "I wonder what would happen if this long, thick piece of steel was portaled *inside* your strongest warrior."

He arched his brow at Maebh. She knew she would either have to admit that metal did, indeed, kill a Sluagh if done correctly. Or herself. Either way, someone would come out looking weak in front of her Court. And it wouldn't be him.

She stilled. She stared.

And the instant the Sluagh flickered into the room, she held up her hand, halting it.

It seethed in fury, but did as commanded.

"I tire of this game. I forfeit," she yawned, then scowled at the Court. "Begone! All of you."

As they scuttled out of the room, unsure of what had transpired, he smiled at the Queen.

She was her own strongest warrior. She held the greatest capacity for holding mana. By sending the Sluagh to fight in her stead meant the bargain was in breech, and Jasper had won by default. She would either have to stand up and admit she was to fight next, but with his threat lying heavy in the air, she would also be putting herself at risk.

By forfeiting, she could save face and retain the mystery.

What she failed to consider was that, in order to get the sword inside the Queen or the Sluagh, Jasper would have had to portal with it, and it was highly unlikely he would survive himself. He was solid. She was, too. Their cells would battle for supremacy in the space, and... he didn't want to risk it. It was the same thing that happened when a portal was activated and the exit on the other side was solid. Leaf had once created a portal that landed in the middle of a wall. It blew up. But the Queen didn't realize that.

Either way, her ego had been her downfall because if she'd thought long and hard enough, she would have known that to beat him, all she had needed to do was attack Ada.

CHAPTER

TWENTY-SIX

Ada's heart was still in her throat as the throne room emptied, and the Queen stepped down from her dais to meet Jasper. Ada still wasn't sure what had happened. Some kind of other battle went on, a psychological one no one understood except the Queen and Jasper.

When the last of the Unseelie left the room, the doors remained open, and the Queen gestured for someone to come in. Two well-built, silver-haired soldiers came in, dragging a prisoner between them.

Both soldiers wore black leather and had the twinkling blue Guardian tattoo beneath their eye. Great metal weapons were strapped to their backs. One had a sword, the other a battle ax. Scruff covered the long-haired Guardian's square jaw, while the short-haired Guardian was clean shaven. From the way their fur-tipped ears perked, they must be shifters. Both glared at Jasper.

Jasper paled as they dropped the prisoner at the Queen's feet.

"We've been waiting for hours," the long-haired Guardian growled.

"We don't like waiting," added the other and folded his arms.

Maebh's eyes narrowed. "You wait as long as I intend you to wait."

"You didn't tell me you had company," Jasper said to her.

"Surprise." More unsaid animosity passed between the Queen and Jasper, but neither acted on it. Instead, the Queen directed hers toward the prisoner, a wicked gleam entering her gaze. "Perfect timing. I find myself in the mood to dole out some punishment."

"Interrogation," the long-haired Guardian reminded her. "We agreed to lend you our prisoner for interrogation purposes only."

"I don't care," the short-haired Guardian mumbled. "Punish away."

The Queen smiled coyly. "Interrogation, punishment... same thing. My Sluagh is feeling a little cheated after the battle he just had, and I want to give him something to make up for it. Human souls are so very tasty."

"Just get the information."

"Oh, he'll get the information," the Queen said. "He'll hunt around this little man's mind until he finds what we need."

Ada shifted her focus to the prisoner and almost lost the contents of her stomach. He was a man—*human*—with deep-set eyes, a hook nose, and a very familiar face. But it wasn't possible. Was it?

Her reality began to slide. This prisoner was from her past. Like, deep within her past, from when she lived in Vegas. She *knew* it. Where had she seen him?

The prisoner spat blood onto the floor and lifted his head. When he saw Ada, his eyes widened a fraction before returning passive. And then it hit—he was the mercenary who'd attacked Laurel back in their time. He'd kidnapped her to force Clarke to reveal the nuclear codes. He was the same man who'd worked for the man who inevitably caused the apocalypse—the Void.

What the hell was he doing here? Now?

Panic surged, closing Ada's throat. She couldn't breathe. Could barely think. She tugged on Jasper's arm, trying to speak, but her only sound was a hiss as she tried to form words.

"Ada?"

"He's... he's...." Her jaw opened and closed.

The long-haired Guardian stalked over. "He's a dangerous man, yes, we know."

"No, you don't understand. He's from my time. He's the one who—"

"Works for the Void," rumbled the short-haired Guardian.

"You know?" The blood drained from her face. "How?"

A shuffle behind her. A waft of a scent too familiar to be real.

"I told them, Pretty Kitty."

Ada's shoulders tensed. She knew that voice, that nickname. All heads swiveled to the new arrivals at the door. Two women. One red-headed and one dark-haired. Ada's heart leaped into her throat. Her knees weakened.

The women smiled, tears in their eyes as they walked forward. Ada was too numb to move, too scared she would wake from the dream, but when Clarke turned to Jasper and nodded, everything turned pear-shaped.

He nodded back, jaw tight.

He knew them.

What?

"Clarke. Laurel," he mumbled and then shifted his gaze to the two Guardians. "Rush. Thorne."

A sharp snap tweaked in her chest. She clutched her sweater. How did he know them?

"Jasper?" she whispered. "You... know my friends?"

His eyes widened, but he said nothing.

Clarke and Laurel rushed to her. They all crashed together in one big embrace. Ada couldn't stop the tears bursting out. Her friends. They were here. Alive. They smelled the same. Even after all this time.

"Oh my God," she gasped, clutching onto them. "I missed you both so much."

Her friends were blubbering too. Tears streaming down their faces, smiling despite the torrent of emotion raging through them all. Ada pulled back and looked at Jasper. He refused to meet her eyes. But down their connection she felt everything... shame, resignation, fear.

"You know them, Jasper. How long... how... how long have you known? From the start?" Her voice cracked as the worst scenarios played in her mind.

He'd lied to her? But she thought that was impossible for a fae. *Fae can't lie.* That's exactly what a liar would say. But she'd just witnessed her lover prove he was a master manipulator. And she had never outright asked him if he knew her friends. So he'd never outright lied. She hadn't thought it was necessary. If he knew her friends were alive, any person who cared for her would have said something.

It all became too much.

"I can't breathe." She started hyperventilating.

"We're here," Laurel said.

"It's okay," Clarke added, running her palm over Ada's back. "We've got you."

"He—"

"I know. He took you about two weeks ago. We tried to find you but couldn't."

"He *took* me?"

Oh, my God. That made it worse. Now Ada couldn't look at him. Who was he? Was his amnesia real? Was the curse real?

The past eight days with him had been groundbreaking for her relationship with him. Had that been fake?

The walls closed in.

"I need air," she gasped. "Have to get out of here."

The Queen's voice rang out above everything.

"I will take her outside," she ordered, and pushed through to get to her.

Icy fingers wrapped around Ada's wrist.

"Come, human. Follow me."

"I don't think so," Jasper growled, his sword already in his hand and pointed at the Queen's throat.

The two Guardians stiffened, their eyes darting between the Queen and Jasper. Maebh rolled her eyes.

"You think I need to squirrel her away to kill her?"

"One never knows with the Unseelie." A quiet desperation brightened his eyes as they narrowed. "And you had mentioned something about supping."

"After the stunt you pulled, in *my* throne room, you owe me a moment with your mate."

"I owe you nothing. And you were the one who pulled a stunt first."

Storm clouds seemed to gather in the room. "Be careful, Guardian prince. You are in *my* home. You came to *me* for help."

Jasper's jaw clenched. The other two Guardians, and even Laurel and Clarke tensed.

Ada didn't want another battle. Not now. Not when things were already spirally out of control.

Maebh pursed her lips. "I give you my oath. No harm will come to this woman during this visit to the Winter Palace. Now let me get the poor girl some air."

Reluctantly, and probably because Ada didn't refuse—she was still too numb—Jasper stood to the side.

Clarke and Laurel remained restrained and wary.

"It's fine," Ada said to them. "I just need some air."

The Queen wouldn't harm her.

"We'll be right here," Laurel said.

Ada nodded, then followed the Queen as she glided toward the exit, commanding attention with every step.

Maebh took her to a snow dusted balcony overlooking the frozen sea. The blood vines covering the railing gave off a pleasant vanilla rose scent. An icy wind ruffled Ada's shoulder feathers and cut through the gaps in her sweater. Their breath puffed out in white clouds. She shivered and wrapped her arms around herself.

But she was outside. She could see the ocean, the snow, and the sky. Nature always made Ada feel like her problems weren't so big. How could they be under the face of the world? She felt better. Mildly. She inhaled deep breaths, feeling her wits slowly seep back into her mind with every exhale.

"This is good," she said, lifting her chin to the sea. "This feels better."

"So," the Queen drawled, giving Ada an unassuming once over. "You are human. And you are brimming with mana like the other two. What is your gift?"

And here was the real reason the Queen wanted a quiet word. To snoop. As long as she wasn't thinking about Jasper, it suited Ada fine.

"I can heal," she answered.

"A natural born healer. Interesting. We haven't had one of your kind around for a long time. Lately it's been all tinctures and salves. We could use someone of your skills in the Winter Court. Injecting some of your gift into a royal line would be even better." She tapped her lips. "I fear I have no heirs with which you can become betrothed. Perhaps Gastnor will do."

A sick feeling churned in Ada's gut. Being alone with this woman was dangerous. She had to tread carefully.

Dangerous things come in pretty packages.

The Queen had kept Jasper and Ada locked in a room for over a week, simply because it amused her. Or perhaps she'd been waiting for this opportunity the entire time—waiting until she had the Guardians and Ada's friends in the same place. Waiting to see the fireworks go off. Perhaps the Queen orchestrated it all. It couldn't be a coincidence her friends arrived on the same day—at the same time—Jasper was in the throne room.

"It's nice of you to offer," she added meekly, choosing her words wisely. She forced a smile on her face and then held up her blue marked hand. "But, Jasper is my mate."

The moment she said the words, she doubted them. *Is he?*

Would a mate keep the most precious secret from her?

He'd felt fear under all that shame when her friends had walked in. What was he afraid of?

A wry, dark brow rose as the Queen glanced at Ada's unblemished neck. "He hasn't claimed you. Besides, there is much we can teach you here. For example..." She took Ada's hand and turned it over to stroke her palm. "There are two sides to every gift. Did your Seelie prince tell you that? Or did he omit it, like so many other things?" When she didn't answer, Maebh continued. "What is the opposite of healing, Ada? Answer me that."

"Um... injury, I suppose."

The Queen's slow, wicked smile sent shivers down Ada's spine.

Ada gaped. "Are you telling me, I can make someone hurt just as I make them heal?"

Maebh stroked the back of Ada's hand. "The Well has a dark side, and contrary to what others make you believe, the Well does not punish you for using it. All nature has a destructive side. Without it, there is no life." She raised and clenched her fist. The ice in the air suddenly dissipated. "I can create ice. I can take it away."

Ada stopped rubbing her arms. Maebh had taken the coldness away, and in doing so, created warmth. Ada swiped her hand through the air, marveling at the change in temperature. But that churning feeling in her gut wouldn't leave.

"Why are you telling me this?" she asked. The Queen knew Jasper was a Guardian. The use of the dark side of the Well is forbidden. "Are you trying to put a wedge between Jasper and me?"

"Oh, Jasper doesn't need any help from me to do that."

"What?"

"Well, he's done a fine job on his own, don't you think? I mean, keeping knowledge of your friends from you. Who would do such a thing?"

Ada scowled at her. How she dealt with Jasper was her own business, and the longer she stayed out here on the balcony, the more she realized this was some sort of sick side game for the Queen. The Queen who had just lost face in front of Jasper.

"You're Unseelie," Ada said. "Manipulation is what you do."

Maebh laughed, tilting her head to the sky. "Well, my dear, it sounds like you have it all figured out then."

Ada made a frustrated sound and stepped toward the balcony railing, resting her palms on the balustrade, and stared out to sea. She scoured the icy water, looking for answers only Jasper could give her. What they shared was real... wasn't it?

But could she ever trust him again?

If he continued to hide his feelings, Ada was afraid of how that mistrust would fester.

The Queen placed her palm on the railing next to Ada, her little finger twitching out to reach Ada's. Ada jolted at the intimate connection, but froze, temporarily stupefied. Was the Queen actively *trying* to invade her personal space? What the fuck? Inches away from shouting for her friends, Ada flinched when the Queen spoke.

"Did he tell you he was Unseelie once... before, when our nations were one?"

Ada shook her head.

"And did he tell you what his father did to me?"

Frustrated, she glared at the Queen. "No."

"Let's just say I have more in common with Jasper's mother than he'll ever know."

"So why aren't you helping him to defeat Mithras? Why the game?"

"For me to align with Jasper, a Seelie, would not only look unfavorably among my own people, but it would signal to the fae who've sided with Mithras that I truly am trying to conquer their land by overthrowing their leader. I'm not ready to deal with that level of scrutiny. Besides, as I mentioned, I care little about them. There are far more interesting things happening north of Cornucopia."

"Thanks for the heart to heart, but I'm ready to rejoin my friends. If it's okay with you."

Black eyes flickered with something alive inside, and Ada had a moment to wonder what kind of fae the Queen was. Just a moment. And then Maebh grinned.

"Of course. Off you go." She shooed her.

"Just... go?" Ada checked the balcony door.

"I'm not holding you prisoner. You may leave Aconite City."

Ada bowed, then hand signed her gratitude.

Maebh watched her with calculating eyes, then inclined her head slightly before turning back to the sea and holding out her hand for a crow to land upon. When the bird settled on her fingers, the Queen whispered gently to it, and kissed its feathered head.

What the fuck?

Ada kept mumbling curses to herself on the walk back to the throne room. *What the fuck? Fuckity fuck fuck.* Her mind was awhirl, and by the time she saw the arched doors of the throne room, she broke into a jog.

Relief hit as she burst through. The only people left in the chamber were her friends, and the three Guardians: Rush, Thorne, and Jasper.

She met Jasper's gaze and felt more of his confusion come down their bond. He stepped toward her, but she couldn't help it. Her instincts slammed up and she went straight for Clarke and Laurel, taking the two into a group hug. Tears burned in her eyes.

"I can't believe it's really you!" she sobbed, feeling safe again.

All three of them became another mess of blubbers, rushed words, and teary hugs.

When Laurel patted her cheeks, a ring twinkled on her finger.

"You're engaged!" Ada squeaked.

"Married, actually." Laurel blushed and darted a glance at Thorne. Ada caught sight of a bite mark that looked suspiciously like a healed over, scarred hickey. She pointed, gaping. "Is that a mating mark? You always said you'd never settle down."

Another blush. Laurel pointed her finger at Clarke. "She's the one who's had a child."

"What?" Ada squeaked. And here she was being so protective of her own neck when her friends were dolling mating marks out like candy.

"Laurel, give her a moment to process," Clarke laughed, but also pulled her long red hair back from her neck, revealing a bite mark. "Rush and I have been together for about three years. Since I woke in this time."

Oh. Okay, three years. So, not like candy then.

"You woke? How did we get here?"

"Frozen." Clarke threw up her hands, as if it had boggled her too. "The most we've guessed is that the nuclear winter froze us, but the Well is waking us. From what I gathered, the temperature dropped so suddenly the day it snowed in Vegas that we were"— she snapped her fingers—"snap frozen like peas!"

"Holy shit."

"It's pretty far-out," Laurel agreed.

"You said the Well is waking us?"

Clarke's eyes turned bleak. "You saw Bones. The Void is in this time too. We think the Void dropped the bombs, purely to create the circumstances so he could freeze and wake in a time where the population was small enough so he could control everything."

All the blood drained from Ada's face. "Where is he now?"

"In Crystal City, locked behind walls of mana-blocking metal. We know he's planning some sort of takeover, but not when or how."

"And Bones?"

"We handed him over to the Queen's guards. The Guardians can't get enough information out of him, but Maebh has ways of extracting the truth."

I'll bet she does.

Thorne broke from his conversation and shuffled closer with a scowl pointed at Laurel. "You should have let me kill him."

Laurel smiled patiently at him. "Babe, I appreciate you want to protect me, I do, but if we want to get ahead of them, we need the information in his head. The human city is still in the middle of desecrated ground. None of us have power there."

Rush removed a smooth stone from his pocket and said, "I think it's time we portal out of here." When Jasper tentatively put his arm around Ada's shoulder, she stiffened and removed it.

"Good idea," she said, smiling tightly at her friends. "I'll go with you."

"I can take us," Jasper offered to Ada.

"I'd rather go with them." She stepped away from him and took Laurel's hand. "I need some time."

She wasn't ready to deal with his betrayal. She might never be.

TWENTY-SEVEN

Alone in his old room at the Order, Jasper stood before the door, looking over the decor as though it were foreign. It had only been ten years since he'd last been there, and in fae terms, that was a drop in the ocean. But the drink tasted like chalk. The air held no warmth. And without Ada, he wasn't sure he would stay.

Would she give him a chance to explain? But what would he say? He'd known exactly what he was doing when he kept the information from her.

The door opened and Thorne walked in.

"Kid," Jasper grunted.

"Haven't been a kid for a long time."

He shrugged. "I know that. It's still fun to call you that. I need my hits where I can take them."

Silence. There were so many things Jasper wanted to say but couldn't. He didn't know where to start.

Thorne pulled out a rolled stick of mana-weed from his pocket and offered it to Jasper, but Jasper declined with a shake of his head.

"You shitting me?" Thorne gaped. "Saying no to mana-weed? You really have changed."

Another half shrug. Ada already avoided him. If he fell back into his old habits, she might... his throat closed up.

"Ten years of torture will do that," he mumbled instead.

"I searched for you," Thorne said, shoving the roll back into his pocket. "The entire time you were missing, I didn't stop. Thought you should know that."

Jasper's gaze clashed with his. "You shouldn't have."

"Why the fuck not?" A scowl twisted Thorne's face so suddenly that Jasper had to laugh.

Still with the same temper. The sudden humor dispelled his tension, and Jasper sighed heavily, rubbing his forehead. He'd thought he'd had a win today, but the look in Ada's eyes when she'd learned he'd kept the truth from her—it cut him straight down the middle. This was the moment he'd feared, and he'd caused it himself.

A knock came at the door, and Rush entered.

Great. Another male Jasper had to apologize to. Another wave of inadequacy.

"I heard through the door," Rush grumbled, shutting the door behind. He glanced at Thorne. "Jasper thinks you should have left him because he believes he failed me."

Thorne's eyes narrowed. He reclined on the bed, putting his hands behind his head. "By not stopping Mithras's soldiers from executing Véda? Wasn't it Thaddeus's fault?"

Jasper rolled his eyes. "Just take my bed. Why not?"

But they took none of his dry humor. Like father, like son. They glared at Jasper.

Rush growled, "I admit I was pissed at you for many years. But you weren't the only one to blame. We all played our parts."

Jasper narrowed his eyes. "What do you mean?"

"He means," Thorne said, "that the Prime used us to get what she wanted."

"She never used me," Jasper replied. "Beyond the usual Guardian duties."

"Oh, yes, she fucking did." Thorne's shoulders bunched. He lit his mana-weed roll and toked, inhaling deep before exhaling.

Rush walked around Jasper's bed to stare out the window, a deep frown on his face.

Jasper asked Thorne, "What do you mean?"

"The Prime played us. She traded you to Mithras so he would keep the sanctioned breeding law active, which ensured my mother would be executed and Rush cursed, which lead to Rush finding Clarke and now the rest of the waking, powered humans before the Void does. They believe if they hadn't, then the Void would have the power to finish what he started and destroy the world. The Prime knew what she was doing the entire time."

"But they kidnapped me years after Rush was cursed."

"That delay was part of the bargain, too. She didn't want anyone figuring out her plan."

Cold, hard fury rattled Jasper's cage. His inner wolf paced about, snarling and growling. Red coated his vision. "She *sold* me to Mithras?"

"And now she wants to put you on the throne," Rush rumbled from the window, still watching something outside.

When Jasper walked over, he saw Clarke chasing after a small silver-haired girl.

The Prime *wanted* him on the throne? "She doesn't get involved with fae politics."

Rush slid his gaze to Jasper's. "We should probably let her explain. She's called a meeting with the Twelve."

"If I see her... I'll..." He flexed his fists to dispel the trembling taking root, and his wolf from surging forward. He wouldn't be able to stop himself from attacking her.

"I tried to kill her, too," Rush confessed. "Almost put Starcleaver through her neck."

"What stopped you?"

"I missed."

They all stared at each other. Then laughed. They laughed out their tension, chuckling whole heartedly over something so stupid. But it felt good to release the pressure.

Rush's eyes turned solemn. "The truth is, I realized that without her, I'd never have met Clarke. And I would never have had Willow. And the Prime may be right... the world may have ended. Still could end."

Jasper still couldn't believe Rush had a daughter, and she was the one who'd led Jasper to Ada. A stone in a pond caused so many ripples.

"And you?" Jasper asked Thorne.

Pity flashed in his eyes before a wistful smile. "I can't argue with the fact I'd never have met Laurel, and now that Ada is here, I believe the dark future the Prime has foreseen will come to pass if we don't work together to stop it."

Jasper rubbed his chest, feeling his heart thud, wishing he could go to Ada.

If you're nothing without me, then you're nothing with me.

He needed to keep picking himself up.

"You say Clarke is a psychic?" Jasper asked.

"Yes," Rush replied.

"What has she seen?"

"She knows the Void wants to take over. She sees fire and destruction in our future. And she knows we have the power to stop it. But, like the Prime said, we need to work with these Well-blessed humans waking from the Old World. We don't like that the Prime was right, but we accept it."

Jasper's gaze flicked to Thorne who clenched his jaw and gave a curt nod of agreement. Yes, Jasper wanted to throttle the Prime. He wanted to rip her limb from limb. But if two of the most ruthless and honorable Guardians he'd had the fortune of meeting believed the Prime's visions about this Void—the same one instigating raids and murdering innocent villagers—then Jasper couldn't dispute it. The Prime had the entire land to worry about. He was one fae.

Jasper knew if he could go back in time and stop the massacre of the Darkfoot pack, he would. If he'd somehow been granted a vision, then wouldn't he have acted like the Prime had? Wouldn't he have sacrificed the discomfort of one fae for the sake of hundreds? *Crimson*, he'd sacrifice his own discomfort for the sake of one: Ada.

His anger seeped out of him. A ruler couldn't be selfish and worry about one person. A ruler had to think of the many. The Prime was responsible for the fate of the world because without the Well, it died. Jasper may be in denial, he may be a coward at heart, but he would never put his own needs above the innocents.

"Let's go to this meeting," Jasper said and started walking out. He stopped, frowned and turned to his two closest friends. "Thank you. For coming to my aid."

Both of them stared at him solemnly.

"No debt acknowledged," Rush replied.

Thorne nodded the same. "You're family. We don't have debts between us."

JASPER FOLLOWED Rush and Thorne up several flights of wide stairs to the council chambers. Water trickled down the stair edges in a cascading stream, ending in a small pool at the base, that in turn, led to culverts winding around the campus. Two crow-shifters flew overhead toward the columned, open plan temple in angel form, shouting down some kind of joke about them being slow.

He flipped his middle finger with a smile. They knew he'd always whined about the wingless Guardians having to walk up the tedious steps when the winged fae could simply fly up.

When they crested the top, Jasper turned and looked over the Order campus grounds. Buildings and training fields stretched for at least a mile on either side. On the surface, nothing seemed to have changed since he'd last been there. He didn't know which was worse, that it was unchanged, or that it had remained so for most of his three-hundred years of service. But the Order wasn't interested in changing the design and architecture, only keeping it the same—just like they wanted to keep Elphyne the same.

Jasper was the longest serving Guardian. There were Mages older than him, the Prime among them, but a warrior? If they didn't lose their life in battle… well, that was it. Most didn't last. He couldn't decide if it was because he'd been a coward, or if he was good at his job.

The library and academy were to the left, and the Guardian barracks to the right. Blue-robed Mages milled about. Leather clad Guardians engaged in battle, honing their skills on the training fields. Metallic clanks from the blacksmith floated across the breeze. It was the only Elphynian smithy sanctioned to craft weapons out of steel.

Coming up the stone steps were Leaf, Aeron, and Forrest. The elves were also unchanged. Leaf was still the leader of the Cadre of Twelve. Aeron still walked with a stiff spine, and Forrest still smelled like the stables—Jasper's nose caught a whiff on the wind with a snuffle.

All so familiar, but so foreign. Still, as Jasper surveyed the unchanged place he called home, and the people he'd called family, he couldn't help thinking that it all looked different. Like he no longer fit in. Like his dreams were bigger than these campus walls.

Jasper turned and went inside the temple, feeling an errant trip of excitement at knowing he'd see the rest of his cadre, some of whom he'd worked with for over a century, maybe two. He'd lost count. When he crossed from the temple into the adjoining council chamber, he almost wished for his sword but pushed the simmering hatred for the Prime down to bearable levels deep in his belly.

With her back to him, the Prime stood between the long, carved marble pillars, staring out to the campus below. Her long white feathered wings draped onto the floor. Water trickled down the columns before running off the fenceless balcony and dripped onto the jagged rock foundation. A slight shift in the Prime's shoulder tension said she knew he'd arrived.

He could walk right up to her and run his claws through her neck. The dark fantasy swirled in his mind for a moment, and then he forced himself to take in the rest of the room. He had to get past her betrayal, even if his feelings were just.

Large human-sized vases were the only decoration. There were no tables, no chairs, just an empty marble floor. Three vampires stood to one side, two crow-shifters on the other.

Jasper nodded at the vampires. They stuck to the shadows and away from the sunny opening, all folding their arms and looking very put out for being called to a meeting during the day. While the vampire Guardians had been conditioned to survive in the sun, they were generally not pleased about it, and preferred night missions. All had shifted their leathery bat-like wings away and wore their Guardian leathers.

Haze nodded his shaved head in greeting. Shade, their unofficial leader, looked suave and slick as he leaned against a vase. He folded his arms and gave Jasper a half-smile. Next to him, Indigo broke out into a crooked grin and came over to slap Jasper on the back.

"Good to see you, wolf."

"You too, bat," Jasper replied dryly.

"Sounds like you've had an adventure or two. I'm jealous."

"Seriously?"

"Sure," he said, raising his brows. "Beats the boring shit we've been doing."

Jasper shot him a wry look. "Keep holding your breath. Maybe there's still time for you to be tortured yet."

Indigo laughed. "That's what I like about you, J. Sense of humor."

The two crow-shifters by the Prime were in angel form, their black feathered wings tucked behind them. They watched curiously, as the crows often did. River's blue-black feathers ruffled as he nodded in greeting. Ash did the same. Those two jokers were trickier and craftier than the vamps, but Jasper had gotten used to them. He even liked them. They knew how to party.

One of the Twelve was missing. As if summoned by thought, the air cracked with electricity, sparking a static residue that lifted the hairs on Jasper's arms.

Of course, Cloud would make an entrance. True to form, the heavily tattooed crow-shifter flew down, landing hard on the balcony, finding his footing with the grace of a wildcat. He snapped his wings shut but didn't shift them away. Static ruffled his feathers, an occurrence that seemed to cling to him permanently. He scowled and stalked straight to Jasper, stopping inches away.

"Where the fuck have you been?"

"You missed me?" Jasper kissed the air, his eyes crinkling.

"You wish," Cloud scoffed, his electric blue gaze traveling down to Jasper's neck scars, then to the blue marks on his right hand. When Cloud kept searching Jasper's body with a frown, Jasper realized he'd noted the missing power enhancing oil-slick tattoos. They had both been inked at the same time. Cloud's eyes darted back to Jasper's Well-blessed marks and narrowed.

"So it's true, then," he clipped.

"What?"

"Another one bites the dust." Cloud sucked his teeth and left Jasper with a judgmental glare tossed over his shoulder. "You want enhanced tatts again, come and see me."

"Don't need them anymore." Jasper couldn't help the grin forming on his face. Cloud hadn't changed a bit. Perfect.

"Pussy whipped," Cloud grumbled under his breath as he went to stand next to Shade.

Shade's lips curved. "I think that's precisely the point, Cloud."

Now that the Twelve were all there, the Prime turned around, demanding attention. Her blue dress and white-feathered wings scraped the dust along the ground. Her bare feet were dirty, a fact that always both intrigued and confused Jasper. For a female so rigid and formal, she neglected to care about tidiness and cleanliness. Sometimes he wondered if it was simply an oversight due to her perpetual busyness, but a small part of him—the part that warred with his vitriolic hate—hoped it was the last remnant of the female rumored to have been in a torrid love affair with Jackson Crimson himself. Because if it was, then it gave him a reason not to kill her. It gave another reason why she might be redeemable and not a monster like the ones he used to hunt.

The Prime's solemn gaze settled on Jasper.

Despite his best efforts, he wanted to snarl and snap at her. His wolf wanted revenge. Vengeance. Claws sprung from his fingers. His teeth elongated, ready to bite.

Play time was over.

The Prime fearlessly took in his reaction and crossed the floor to him. Her casual gait incensed him further. Leather creaked around the room as Guardians tensed. No one would be swift enough to stop Jasper's retribution, if it came to that. Then again, she was also powerful, and likely to dodge. If Rush had failed to kill her, then Jasper would struggle. Even if he did succeed, they would take him afterward. Killing the Prime would have dire consequences. Jasper might trust these eleven warriors with his life on a battlefield, but they were all loyal to the Well, first and foremost.

And the Prime was the epitome of the Well's will.

She kneeled before him, pulled her white ringlets to bare a brown, smooth neck, submitting.

Jasper startled and glanced about. Surprise rippled across the room. Shade stepped forward, but the Prime held out her palm, halting him.

"D'arn Jasper," she said, with her head hanging low. "For the crime of selling you to our enemy, I humbly apologize and accept any punishment, or bargain you wish to inflict on me."

He stared at her for a long time. No one made a sound. He wanted to rage, to rip his teeth into her neck and tear chunks from her body. He wanted her to bleed out. To die, or at least suffer the way he had for the past decade. But that was the thing... it had only been a decade. He'd suffered immeasurably, but he was here, still standing, still alive.

Rush had lost fifty years of his life to her machinations.

"Did you apologize to Rush, too?" he demanded.

She glanced up, eyes narrowing. *Ahh.* Pieces clicked together. This female bowed to no one. She submitted to no one, yet she somehow felt he was different to the others she'd played.

"You didn't," he confirmed. "Nor, I suppose, did you apologize to Thorne."

Leather uniforms creaked, especially from Jasper's two wolf-shifter brethren standing next to him. He knew, without looking up, they were hanging on every word.

He'd just pointed out something so obvious that all of them would be searching through their memories, wondering what else they had missed.

Jasper was done being manipulated. It was time he did the scheming.

"I want my bargain rights shifted to Rush," he declared.

The Prime stood swiftly, a crease deepening between her white brows.

There she is. The spitfire, prideful leader.

"You're not concerned with your current situation?" she asked. "You know there is no other way you'll be allowed to leave the Order except for using your bargain."

He smiled. "You're going to allow me to leave, anyway."

Something like respect sparked in her eyes before she clamped her expression down to unreadable. "What makes you so sure?"

"The only reason you apologized was because you want to be on my good side. You know I'll become king. You've Seen it—or someone has. Preceptress Dawn, maybe?"

Rush rumbled, "Keep the boon for yourself, Jasper. It's unnecessary to give it to me. Like I said before, we all have regrets over what's happened."

"It is necessary," Jasper insisted. "It's the least I can do. You have a daughter. I don't. You'll need a favor one day to protect her. Believe me."

"You'll have children of your own," Rush said.

"I'm three hundred. I haven't yet. I may never." His heart clenched at the fear of no future with Ada.

Jasper understood Rush was grateful for meeting his mate, and having his daughter, but Thorne had suffered too. He could give them this. A favor from the most powerful fae in Elphyne would come in handy, especially if dark times were ahead.

"Your family will need it," Jasper insisted, his eyes shifting to Thorne. "Kid, tell him I'm right."

Thorne scowled at Jasper. "You may be right, but it doesn't stop us wanting you to have it."

Jasper didn't deserve their capitulation. He deserved to grovel at their feet for the pain he'd caused them. Yes, the Prime had done everything she could to manipulate the events, but Jasper always had a choice. He could have protected Véda. He could have saved Thorne's mother. Maybe they both saw the agony in his eyes because Rush gave a curt nod, and Jasper exhaled.

Then he squared his shoulders and lifted his chin.

"That's my price," he said.

"Very well," she said. "It is done."

A whisper in the air made them all shiver as the Prime's intention became something bound by the Well. They didn't need to see the boon shifted to Rush; it was simply known. One day, so long as the Prime was alive, Rush could call on the Prime to claim the favor.

"Good," Jasper said. "Now, you didn't call this meeting to prostrate yourself before me, so what is it?"

"Careful, D'arn Jasper," the Prime warned. "You are still a Guardian, so long as that teardrop mark exists beneath your eye. Watch your tone."

Another smile crinkled Jasper's eyes. The Prime's words just proved she couldn't release him from his servitude to the Well. Only death could do that. Even if he had bargained to leave the Order, she would always hold some kind of sway over him.

"So what did your Seer see?" he asked. "How will I ascend to the throne?"

"Contrary to your belief, we have not Seen *how* you ascend, only that a future exists with you wearing the glass crown." She turned her steady gaze to the entire cadre. "And a future where all of you will find a Well-blessed mate."

Eyes flew wide. Some Guardians smiled. Others, like Cloud, scowled.

"The Order will issue new edicts that allow any Well-blessed Guardian to have certain liberties the others do not."

"Such as?" Leaf asked.

"Such as taking a mate and having a family."

"But you've never explicitly forbidden it," he replied.

"Neither have we approved it."

"What if we don't give a shit about being Well-blessed?" Cloud spat.

"Mark my words, D'arn. There is a reason only those in this cadre are being granted this sacred bond. Do you wish to deny a higher purpose?"

His hands clenched, but he said nothing. The Prime continued, "Regardless of which future becomes true, there is a war coming. One like we've never seen. Our best chance at defeating this human monster is to trust in the Well's plan, and to accept the gifts bestowed upon us. Working with humans who understand the world our enemy comes from will be integral in defeating him. We are stronger together."

Aeron stepped forward, also with a scowl on his face. "So you brought us here to tell us about the war we already know is coming?"

"I brought you here because the Seelie High King has committed grave crimes against the Well." Her gaze darkened. "I'm talking about the incidents leading to the massacre of the Darkfoot Pack. Namely, his collusion with the human enemy, and the explicit directions for fae to hoard metal. It cannot be tolerated. It is time for the Order to flex our Well-given rights."

Bitterness lanced Jasper's gut. Of course her retribution wouldn't be for the Darkfoot lives lost, but only for the blasphemy and the metal. But then, this was the very reason Jasper had to step up and take the glass crown for himself. It was *his* responsibility to seek retribution for losing his kin, not the Prime's.

Glances were shared about the room.

The Prime raised her palm before anyone could speak. "We have witness statements from reputable sources explaining how he encouraged them to hoard metal, and to deliberately hide it from the Order. This meeting was called to declare the official warrant for High King Mithras's arrest. He is now a fugitive. All of you are tasked with bringing him in."

Cloud stepped forward, a gleam in his eyes. "Alive or dead?"

"Preferably alive. Being high profile, he will need to stand trial and publicly answer for his crimes." She met them all in the eye. "You will meet resistance from his guard and loyal followers. Be mindful of innocents caught in the way. His life is not worth more than theirs. Dismissed."

One by one, the Guardians nodded and left until it was just Jasper and the Prime.

She leveled her gaze on him, and he wondered how he'd ever thought she'd submitted.

"Well played, D'arn. It seems you've the mind of a king, after all. What shall we call you now? Will you take your Darkfoot name?"

He strode to the freefall edge of the temple and looked over the campus. Wind buffeted his face and brought with it the familiar scent of his home, a home he was about to leave for good. This was the Prime's way of saying he would be free to leave the Order. Free to become king. But would that be as Reed Darkfoot, or Jasper, or as a Mithras descendent? He stifled a shudder. Never a Mithras. Perhaps Darkfoot, but he'd been D'arn Jasper for most of his life.

"Are you certain I'm going to be the Seelie High King?" he asked quietly.

"Nothing is certain, D'arn. You know that."

"Then why did you agree to shifting the bargain to Rush?"

"Because I owe him too, but, unlike with you, I'm not sorry for it. His sacrifice was worth the outcome."

"And mine wasn't?"

"You suffered," she murmured. "Yours is the one that keeps me up at night. You will understand the toll it takes when you ascend to the throne."

"You just said you weren't certain."

"I'm hopeful."

Her words drifted away on the gentle breeze, and in their absence, another realization occurred to him.

"You sent the Twelve after Mithras because you don't think I can take him on my own."

"I didn't say that."

"You didn't have to."

"I'm trying to give you the best chance at succeeding."

"I don't want your help. I don't want anything from you."

"Regardless, the warrant has been issued."

"If I have a hope of taking the glass crown uncontested, I need to do this on my own." He may already have the tentative support of other Seelie factions, but any of them could seek the throne. If he defeated the King himself, Jasper would have a stronger claim.

"Then you'd better be quick."

CHAPTER
TWENTY-EIGHT

Ada sat in the cadre house kitchen, eating a scone with berry jam, catching up with one of her two best friends—sisters—still not believing the turn of events.

"So you got married?" she asked Laurel, who showed her the ring. The jewel was like a tiny snow globe, but with sparkling stars dancing about each other.

"Only days ago. I figure, he gets the mating mark, I get a wedding."

"Days ago? You mean I just missed it?"

"Afraid so."

"Jasper's memories returned a week ago," she fumed. "He knew the entire time who you were to me while we were at the Obsidian Palace. I could have made it to your wedding!"

A high-pitched squeal came from somewhere beyond the kitchen. In came a silver-haired two-year-old, tearing a path straight for Ada. Her stubby legs moved so fast, she almost tripped over herself. Clarke chased after her, a flustered blush hitting her cheeks.

"Pretty Kitty Pretty Kitty Sleeping Kitty." The little girl's words came at Ada like a machine gun. She launched herself at Ada, climbing up her legs and into her lap. When she was at eye level in Ada's arms, she sighed heavily and made a *phew* sound.

Ada grinned. "Now don't tell me. You must be Willow."

"You want a blanket?" Willow asked, her chubby face screwed up in contemplation. "Last time you were cold."

"Last time?"

Clarke shrugged. "We might not have put enough cover on you when you slept. She sensed you were cold and, yeah. We found a blanket."

"Well, thank you very much Miss Willow."

She gasped, eyes going wide, and then darted a look between her mother and Ada. "You said somefing naughty."

"I suppose saying thank you is naughty to the wrong person, but not to you." The truth was, if Willow had never brought Jasper to Ada when she'd been sleeping, she might never have awoken. She was sure it was the trigger of the Well-blessed union that did it. "You can ask me to do anything now, apparently."

"Mmm." Willow touched her lip. "I want prickleberry jelly!"

"Willow! You've already had one serving today." Clarke made a face at Ada. "It's full of sugar."

"Oh well. I'll just have to find you some more, then." Ada put the ecstatic child down and went to the cupboards. "I don't know what I'm looking for."

"Never mind," Clarke sighed. "I'll get Jocinda to make some more."

"Jocinda?"

"One of the house brownies. You'll meet her soon. A word of wisdom? Never complain to the brownies unless you want to do all the chores yourself."

"Noted."

Ada turned back around and leaned her hips against the counter. Willow had already forgotten the deal and had run back outside again.

"She's beautiful, Clarke," Ada said. "You're very lucky."

Both of her friends sent her eyes full of pity, and she knew exactly what they were thinking. She dashed away tears.

"I don't know what to do," she said. "Am I overreacting? I mean, Jasper knew about you, and he kept it from me. You're family."

"Yeah, well..." Clarke made an awkward face. "That might have a teensy tiny bit to do with me."

"What?" Ada gaped.

"Why am I not surprised?" Laurel raised her brow and pointed her thumb at Clarke before saying to Ada, "She's been awake for three years, and already she's acting as crafty as the fae." When Ada still didn't quite understand, Laurel elaborated. "Her psychic powers have grown astronomically. You thought it was hard to beat her at poker before, now it's impossible."

"Hey," Clarke said. "That's not fair. I was terrible at poker. I cheated."

Laurel poked out her tongue. Clarke grinned, but then met Ada's stare with a loud exhale.

"Okay," she said. "Promise you won't be mad."

"Clarke," she warned. "Spit it out."

"I may have, just a little bit, shouted at Jasper when I caught him in the room with you when you were asleep."

"Why is that so bad? Isn't he some big warrior type?"

"But it frightened him so much, he poofed out of here."

"Poof. Really?" Laurel said sarcastically and then stole the half-eaten scone from Ada's plate and licked the jam.

"Whatever," Clarke replied. "The point is, he got scared. He left. If he thought your best friends hated him, it might have caused some reluctance to come home. Someone who was manipulated and tortured like him would be a little jumpy."

Ada's eyes narrowed at her friend. "Has he spoken with you?"

"No," Clarke said, biting her lip. "In fact... I... well, I've *Seen* some things he went through. So... I guess, I'm asking you to cut him some slack."

Ada pinched the bridge between her eyes. Clarke was right. Ada loved the guy. She could completely understand why he was reluctant to tell her.

A strange shuffling sound made her drop her hand. Clarke's eyes had turned completely white. She trembled on the spot. Laurel rushed to her side, and tried to hold her body upright, but Clarke's convulsing turned into a full-blown fit.

"What's happening?" Ada asked, taking Clarke's other side and helping her down to the floor.

"She's having a vision," Laurel replied, looking a lot calmer than Ada felt.

"She never used to do this, right?"

"It's something she's picked up in this time. She should be out of it soon."

They stayed with Clarke until the trembling stopped and she started gulping air. Her unfocused gaze darted about until it landed on Ada. Then she grabbed Ada's shirt.

"You need to find Jasper," she gasped, eyes wide with fear.

"What did you see?"

"Mithras, iron, and blood."

With Clarke and Laurel at her side, Ada rushed through the house of the Twelve, searching upstairs and downstairs for Jasper. When Clarke had awoken from her vision, Ada tried to locate Jasper using their link. As usual, he'd hidden his emotions from her—or he was too far away for them to register. Over the past few weeks, she'd learned that beneath the sense of emotions, she could still feel a connection. It was a little ping of awareness. And right now, that ping felt very far away.

"He's not here," Ada said, after closing Jasper's bedroom door. She hadn't explored it yet but knew the moment she had entered that she felt like an intruder at the same time as feeling like she was home. She needed him here, to explain things, to tell him she forgave him, and to talk about their future.

"They could still be at the meeting with the Prime," Laurel offered. She turned to Clarke. "Did you see any specifics in your vision?"

Clarke shook her head. "Just a lot of blood and water."

"*Jesus.*" Ada thrust her hand into her hair.

"Goddammit. I'd never thought I'd see the day I missed tracking on cell phones," Laurel mumbled.

Downstairs, the front door slammed as someone came home. All three of them jogged through the house to get to the ground floor living room, only to find it was Thorne and Rush returning from the meeting without Jasper.

Blood drained from Ada's face.

Thorne came over to Laurel and curled his hand around the back of her neck. "He gave up an open-ended boon from the Prime so Rush could have it."

"So our family could have it," Rush corrected him. "That includes you, Thorne."

Clarke blinked. "But that's... very valuable."

Still with a flummoxed look on his face, Rush shook his head. "He did it because he still feels guilty for not stepping in when Véda was executed, or when I was cursed and Thorne was orphaned."

Thorne frowned. "Rush tried to tell him it wasn't necessary, but he insisted we would need it for Willow."

Clarke stiffened. "He's not a Seer, is he? He hasn't foretold that it's warranted?"

Ada shook her head. "I don't think so..."

But no one knew for sure.

"Whatever his reasons, we'll have to thank him," Clarke said, fitting herself under Rush's arm. "I mean it."

"He won't accept your thanks," Thorne said. "Trust me."

Ada's heart surged in her chest. Why would he giveaway such an important boon?

Mithras. Blood. Iron.

She had to find him.

"Where is he?" she asked the Guardians.

Thorne shrugged. "He was with the Prime at the temple a moment ago."

"That's just on the other side of campus, right?" she asked, but already felt dread grow because their connection through the Well-blessed bond was not strong, not like it should be if they were within a mile of each other.

"I have to find him," she said, heart thumping.

"I had a vision," Clarke explained gravely to her mate. "I saw Jasper, Mithras, iron, and blood."

"*Well-dammit,*" Rush grunted, a calm determination settling over him. "Thorne, you head back to the temple and see if he told the Prime anything about his intentions."

Thorne nodded, gave Laurel a quick kiss on the cheek, and then rushed out the front door.

Laurel turned to Ada. "I'll find Preceptress Dawn. She's the Order's official Seer and might know something Clarke missed. Sometimes pooling resources will help, right?"

"I'll go with you. I speak fluent Seer," Clarke added, then turned to Ada. "You stay here. Jasper might turn up."

When the two of them had left, Ada focused her attention on Rush.

"What happened at the meeting? Anything to upset him?"

A baffled look crossed his face. "It all sounded fine. The Prime apologized for what she did to him, which was astounding but then basically alluded to the fact that she believed Jasper would take the throne."

"That's not so bad." Unless Jasper was getting nervous about it. Maybe he was just taking some time, like he had when his memories first came back. Guilt stabbed her. Maybe she'd been a bit too harsh on him. No, she definitely had. Telling someone to simply pick themselves up after falling wasn't as easy to do. It took time to heal from trauma, and she'd all but tried to force it on him when they'd had that argument in Cornucopia. Damn it. She knew those words would come back to haunt her the moment she'd let them spill out of her angst-ridden mouth.

She could understand why he didn't want to tell her about her friends. He was afraid to lose her. She didn't want to lose him either. The thought of it made her insides cramp.

"Oh," Rush added. "And the Prime declared Mithras a fugitive. All Twelve Guardians are tasked with hunting him down."

Ada frowned. "She's helping Jasper take the throne? Does she not think he can do it on his own?"

"The King has committed crimes against the Well. This is just due course."

"Is it?" Would Jasper see it that way? She knew him, whether or not he admitted it. He put so much pressure on himself. He'd already explained how he believed he should take the crown on his own—to gain the respect of his subjects, and to prove that he could pick himself up. To prove that he was something without her.

So he could be something *with* her.

Ada's throat closed up.

If Jasper construed the Prime's warrant as intentional help... he would believe it an insult to his competence.

"I have to find him," she gasped, eyes wide. "How can I find him? He can portal anywhere."

"Can you feel him through your bond?" Rush asked, folding his arms and frowning in concentration.

"Yes, but it's weak."

"What's he feeling?"

"He hides that from me."

Another frown from Rush. He shook his head.

"Stubborn bastard," he murmured. Then gestured for Ada to follow him. "We'll find a winged Guardian."

All the crows were gone, already eager to hunt down Mithras. The only winged Guardians left were the vampires, and all three were sitting around the dining table next to the living room, playing some sort of card game.

Ada frowned, wondering if they were shifters like the wolves because she couldn't see their wings. And then once she started thinking about their wings, her mind traveled to all sorts of weird places. Like, were they anything like the vampires in storybooks? Could they fry in the sun and die from a stake to the heart? Did they have a soul? A reflection?

"I'm Ada," she said, waving gingerly.

If one deigned to glance at her, she was lucky.

"I need someone to fly Ada around and track Jasper," Rush said.

"Nope." Shade played his card with a slap to the table. It was the only emotion in his countenance. The rest of him was slick, smooth and cut from diamond encrusted marble—hard, yet veined with luxury. Pointed bronze ears twitched under Ada's attention. Soft caramel tipped hair brushed back from his forehead as though he'd ran his fingers through it. She had the sense he studied her as much as she did him, yet it wasn't with his eyes. With a shiver, she turned to the other two vampires.

"Can't," Haze grunted, before she'd had a chance to ask. He scraped his hand over his shaved head, exasperated eyes ping-ponging between the card Shade had just played, and his hand.

"Yeah, I'm kinda busy," Indigo mumbled, eyes glued to his hand. He contemplated with such concentration, Ada thought the boyishly handsome fae might hurt himself. He dropped a card. "Read it and weep, sleep-feeders."

"Fuck me," Haze grumbled.

"You have the shittest poker face, my friend," Indigo snorted. "And now you owe me a feed. I'm hungry. Pay up."

Haze's dark eyes flashed and then rolled in exasperation. "Fine. I'll find a donor."

"I don't mind sharing."

"Fine."

"Guys," Rush growled. "Clarke's had a vision. This is important."

All three vampires lowered their cards and sat back, smoky eyes shifting to study Ada. They had the kind of warm skin, brown hair, and sun-kissed vibe she'd have expected to see on a race that enjoyed living in the sun, not those who hid from it. These vampires weren't the Dracula kind. They were sensual and warm-blooded.

"We've been out in the sun already today," Shade said, arrogantly arching his eyebrow. "We need our rest for the big hunt tonight."

Haze grunted his agreement. The vampire's hulking, muscular body barely fit on the chair. He stared at Ada a while before asking, "Are you in danger?"

"Not me, Jasper."

Her words had no appeal to him, and he cast his already bored gaze back to his cards.

"Fine," Rush said. "I'll find a kuturi in the stables."

"A kuturi will take too long to prepare. Indi will do it," Shade offered.

"Fine. I'll do it," Indigo said, a dimple flashing in his cheek. He scraped his chair back to stand. "You twisted my fang."

Ada exhaled in relief.

"On one condition," he added, eyes flaring in mischief.

"Not happening, Indi," Rush growled, to which Indigo grinned further and held up his palms.

"I won't go out on an empty stomach."

"What do you mean?" Ada asked. What had she missed?

Rush glared at Indigo. "He wants to feed from you. Jasper would never allow it."

"When a vamp's gotta eat, a vamp's gotta eat," Indigo drawled.

"No—" Rush said.

"I'll do it," Ada burst out.

Rush growled and took Indigo by the scruff of his collar. "I'm warning you. Jasper won't like it."

Haze and Shade stood, menace tightening their posture. The last thing Ada needed was an in-house brawl.

"It's fine, Rush. It's only once, right? I won't be sick or anything, will I?"

"You won't even notice," Indigo smirked. "Not really."

Indigo slapped Rush's hands away with a scowl. "Touch me again, wolf, and sleep with one eye open."

"Come on," Ada said. "The quicker we do this, the quicker we can find Jasper."

Still vibrating fury, Rush folded his arms and glared before snarling a warning, "I'll be watching the entire time. Don't get any ideas."

Rush's animosity would have wilted Ada, but Indigo just smiled and said, "You know we like it when we're watched."

"No, we don't," Shade said as he dealt another hand between himself and Haze. "*You* like it."

Indigo pouted. "Spoil sport."

It was clear where the power balance lay in the trio. Shade didn't even look up, but the other two vamps had fallen in line behind him.

"M'lady." Indigo gestured toward the living room where the curtains were drawn to keep the sunlight out.

What the hell was she doing? Bad vampire movie scenes kept flashing before her eyes. Horror scenarios of throats being torn out and blood gushing. How weak would she feel after this? She'd donated blood a few times when she'd been hard up for cash and had always felt tired. How much would he take?

With her fingers twisting and fretting, she sat down on a couch, eyes darting to Rush who stood by the door, shoulder resting against the jamb, arms folded, eyes like lasers pointed at Indigo as he quietly slotted himself next to her. She couldn't help but feel this was a weirdly intimate moment, despite Rush glaring. Intimate because of the way Indigo shifted himself into the seat, making himself comfortable. And the way he casually flicked lint off the backrest behind Ada. The way his breath changed and grew shallower. She could smell his unique masculine scent.

Indigo brushed fallen hair from her neck with a lover's touch, and leaned in, but she stopped him. Her heart pounded a million miles an hour.

"Not there," she said, feeling unsteady. That place was reserved for Jasper. Rush was right. If Jasper discovered she let someone else bite her where he intended, he would be furious, hurt, and betrayed. The neck was too personal.

Without skipping a beat, Indigo took her wrist and held it to his nose with a graceful touch. He pushed the hem of her sweater sleeve until it gathered along her forearm and then ran the tip of his nose along the flesh, up and down as though tracking a scent... or finding a vein. Unable to help herself, Ada shivered from his feather light touch. Hot breath tickled and goosebumps broke out on her skin. Indigo's dimple appeared in his cheek before he went back to a particular spot on her inner elbow. He licked it a few times with an extremely pointed, and long tongue. Seeing it was a shock to her system. She'd become accustomed to the pointed and arched ears. She'd even become used to the fangs and claws of a wolf-shifter. But seeing that tongue, and the glimpse of razor sharp fangs—so different to Jasper's canines—Ada sensed a dangerous predator about him.

She could barely feel his touch, he was that deft and graceful. At night time, when walking by herself on a street, she wouldn't know if a vampire attacked until it was too late.

The only warning she had was a meeting of the eyes, and then sharp fangs pierced her flesh.

She gasped at the sting, but the pain soon turned into a pleasing tingle, shooting sparks of heat zipping up her arm and then down her spine. Blood welled at the wound, and contrary to her bias, it surprised her to see he didn't suck her blood like they did in the movies. No. He lapped at it lazily, enjoying every oozing drop like it was a fine wine, making little moans of appreciation, shuffling closer.

"Back off, Indi," Rush growled.

"But she tastes so good." He hummed as he lapped, like a child eating their first round of chocolate ice-cream and unable to hide their bliss. "Why does she taste so good?"

Shade and Haze both neglected their game and came over, eyes mesmerized as Indigo laved with his lashes fluttering and eyes full of heat. With every lick of his tongue, the tingles shooting up Ada's arm turned into something more insistent, echoing the throb of her pulse everywhere in her system, especially between her legs. Good God, she was getting aroused. So was Indigo. She could see it in the flush of his cheeks and the sizable bulge straining against his leather breeches.

"Enough," Rush barked, striding over.

But Indigo wouldn't stop. He clutched her wrist tighter.

"Too good," he muttered.

"*Indi.*"

"If I stop now, she won't clot, and it will go to waste."

From the desperate lilt to his voice, Indigo's words sounded like the excuse of an addict.

Rush snarled and put his hand on Indigo's neck, letting his claws elongate until they pressed into the vampire's flesh.

Indigo went very still. The air buzzed with strife. Slowly, he lifted his palms in surrender, but then took one last lick before pulling back with a satiated look on his face, eyelids fluttering to half-mast and dopey. His pink, pointed tongue darted out and traced along his lips, relishing.

"*Bloody Well,*" he cursed. "You taste like…" He made a sound caught between a groan and a shuddering moan. "Fu-*uck* me sideways, Ada, and call it Moonsday. I'm cooked."

His gave a long, drawn out, shuddering exhale as he shifted his hips low on the couch, and rested his head back, eyes fluttering closed, smiling lazily to himself.

"Is he…" Ada clamped her hand on her wrist and healed herself, pleased to see her flesh knit together with ease at her mental directive. She didn't think Indigo had taken that much. The blood didn't gush. It oozed. She felt fine. "Is he drunk?"

Shade stalked closer to inspect Indigo. Shade's perfect bone structure pinched with restraint. He sniffed, his long lashes fluttered as though simply smelling Ada's blood gave him a high. He darted a glance to Haze.

"What do you think?"

Haze already looked scary with his bulk, neck tattoos, and shaved head, but now, as his eyes locked onto Ada with predatory intent, he was positively terrifying. There was hunger in that stare.

"Maybe because she's human."

"Do humans taste better?" she asked nervously. Jasper had mentioned something, but she didn't think it was this good.

"And she's Well-blessed," Shade surmised, ignoring Ada.

"That must be it. Two-thousand-year aged wine."

"You're discussing me like the latest vintage," she snapped. "I'm not—" Not food? Not a drug? Not what? She couldn't come up with the right word that wasn't the truth. A moment ago, the vampires had barely looked at her, probably categorizing her as simply the enemy and food at the same time. Now she could turn one of them into a melted puddle from the simple taste of her blood.

A glance at Indigo, and she knew the vampires wouldn't walk away easily. He still slouched on the couch, making little sighs of pleasure and delight as whatever was in her blood made its way through his system.

Rush's guttural growl tore through the room. "Stay away from her. Stay away from Laurel and Clarke. And especially, stay away from Willow."

"Willow's half-fae," Indigo slurred. "S-she won't taste as good. Don't worry. *Crimson*, I'm not cooked. I'm dead. Fuck. How am I going to fly?"

"You have to," Ada gaped, standing.

He tried to stand, stumbled, and took hold of the couch armrest. "I'm good."

"For fuck's sake, Indi," Rush scowled.

Shade glanced at Haze.

"I'll do it," Haze grunted with a sigh of resignation. "You'll kill yourself. And her."

Haze pushed Indigo on the chest, who then fell back on his ass with a chuckle. "Fine. You take her."

Rush pointed at each of the vampires. "This is your first and final warning. The last thing we need is for all the vamps in Elphyne hearing about this. If a word of this gets out, I'll be coming for you. So will Thorne and Jasper. Understood?"

Something dark and dangerous flitted in Shade's gaze that morphed him from model to maniac in a blink, and then it was gone. Ada had to suppress a shudder and remind herself that these cadre members weren't normal. They were all dangerous, ruthless warriors. And she was about to go flying about Elphyne with one of them.

"If you think we're the kind of fae who would put our cadre members' females in jeopardy, then you must be getting us confused with your own kind. Vampires don't sell their females out."

A snarl curled Rush's lips. "If you find Jasper, come back and get us."

Haze gestured for Ada to head outside the front exit. "Let's go."

She followed him out.

Haze materialized two leathery, bat-like wings through slits in the back of his Guardian uniform. They snapped out, twice as long as his body was high. Already, he winced at the sun and scowled.

"Let's make it fast."

He closed thickly muscled arms around her and then beat his wings until they became airborne with a whoosh. Ada's stomach dropped to her feet.

She focused on the sense of Jasper down their bond but couldn't pinpoint a location.

"Can you fly around in a circle?" she shouted up at him. "I'll see which direction the link feels strongest."

He gave a curt nod and then flew over the Order until Ada slapped her palm on his forearm.

"That way." She pointed into the forest surrounding the Order campus.

Craning her neck, she caught the frown marring his rugged features.

"What's that way?" she asked.

"The ceremonial lake."

A stone dropped in Ada's stomach. "He mentioned wanting to submit to the initiation trial again."

Haze's wings beat faster, and their speed increased. "Hold on."

It didn't take them long, only about thirty minutes or so. They broke the boundary of the trees and came to an enormous lake stretching for miles. When she saw the shadow of a figure wading into the shallow end of the lake, she knew it was him.

"There!"

Jasper's tanned, muscular back glistened under the sun as he swam toward the center of the lake, gliding through the water with ease.

"Doesn't seem to be anyone else around. He's all yours." Haze put her down on the beach, wincing at the glare of the sun, and then swiftly took off without another word.

Ada ran toward the folded shirt Jasper had left on the sand. She took a few steps into the water and waved, shouting his name. About forty feet away, he turned.

And that's when everything went to shit.

CHAPTER

TWENTY-NINE

Treading water, Jasper's gaze settled on his love. She waved erratically and shouted for him to come back, but he knew if he did, he'd lose his nerve. He'd never face the Well Worms. He'd never know if the past three hundred years had turned him into a coward or if they'd made him stronger.

Mithras knew exactly how to prey on Jasper's weaknesses. Jasper needed this before facing him.

Ada cupped her mouth and shouted. "Come back! I was wrong."

What?

"I should never have said you were nothing without me. It was a dumb figure of speech, that's all." Her voice tightened, becoming high pitched. "I'm nothing without *you*. Please come back. Don't... don't leave me."

He let himself dip beneath the surface, just a fraction, as he considered her words. She forgave him. Or was she just saying that to get him out? Irrational doubt pervaded his mind. Whatever the reason for Ada's words, they came too late. Something smooth brushed against his leg. And again. He looked down, trying to see through the water, but found only shadow. He'd taken his eyes off her for only a moment, but when he glanced back up, his world collapsed.

Mithras stood behind Ada, his fingers curling around her throat. Coming up beside him was the shriveled Dark Mage, his hunched form carrying something heavy beneath his billowing black cape.

Heart thudding in his chest, Jasper considered his options. Portal there and risk Mithras doing something drastic the instant Jasper disappeared. Or let the worms slithering around his ankles take him down into the dark depths and judge him, hopefully allowing him to return with more power, enough that even without Ada's mana, he could face down Mithras and win. Another worm slithered around Jasper's ankle and tugged. The decision was made for him. He sank beneath the water. The last thing he glimpsed was Ada's tear tracked face.

It was that sight that made him see the truth in his heart. Any decision was better than none. Sitting quietly had left him in that dugout while they slew his mother. Ignoring his identity, hiding out in wolf form at the inn after the first raid, was cowardice. He should have worked to restore his memories sooner. If he had, he wouldn't have been surprised by Mithras's attack on the Darkfoot pack. He might have saved them. And now... slowly sinking down when his heart was still with Ada, he knew inaction would be her death.

He didn't need the Well to imbue him with more power. He just needed to act. So he portaled to the shore, arriving with a splash of displaced water only yards from where Mithras's hands were wrapped around Ada's neck. Not just wrapped, but poised to snap with the slightest provocation. Jasper stilled.

"I'm sorry, I'm sorry, I'm sorry," Ada sobbed, chest heaving, desperate eyes locked onto Jasper.

His beautiful love thought this was her fault. It infuriated him that she blamed herself.

Mithras's hair was straggly. That he even wore his lopsided crown was a sign of how desperate he was to keep it. Panic in his eyes betrayed his true state. It gave Jasper confidence.

"What do you want?" Jasper asked, words slow and enunciated.

"You ruined my life," Mithras snarled, fingers tightening around Ada's neck.

"Tell me what you want," Jasper repeated.

Fire flashed in amber eyes as Mithras studied Jasper. His lips curved into a slithering smile. "All I had dreamed of was to kill you and ensure my reign went uncontested. I had the perfect plan. Name you as heir, kill you, blame Maebh, and incite a war. Simple. But since you went to her and revealed everything, I'm going to have to settle on making you suffer. I want you back in the iron mask. I want everyone to see that I control you."

Did he not know that the Order was after him? Even if he did take Jasper now, he wouldn't get away with the crimes he'd committed. The mad fae had lost touch on reality.

The Dark Mage stepped forward and revealed the package he carried; a newly forged iron mask complete with new bolts to drill into Jasper's neck.

"What did I ever do to you?" Jasper growled, aghast. "That you had to chase me for three hundred years and make my life miserable at every turn. I was no threat to you or your reign as a child, or a Guardian."

"You were a threat from the moment your mother chose to keep you."

Rage simmered in Jasper's blood. He could take out the Mage, but that would alert Mithras who would snap Ada's neck. Jasper could also portal behind Mithras and attack there. But, once again, Mithras was fast. He was powerful. He didn't get to be king by falling there. He clawed his way to the top. A tiny shift in the atmosphere, and Mithras would kill Ada.

There was no other option.

He looked at the mask, reacting with violent nausea. Not again.

But he would do anything for Ada. Anything.

He met his beloved's red-rimmed eyes. Pain aplenty echoed back at him. She tried to shake her head, but Mithras firmed his grip, choking her. A pouring of love washed down their bond from her.

In slow motion, he saw the end of his life play out. He would pick up the mask. The Mage would bore the bolts into his neck. His mana would be incapacitated, his access to the Well blocked. They might let Ada go. They might not. But the fifty-fifty chance was better than nothing. Maybe she would escape. He hoped.

He swallowed the lump in his throat and picked up the mask. He hesitated before putting it on and locked eyes with the King.

"For the record, I hope you understand that I will get this off eventually, and when I do, your reign will end when I beat you bloody with it. I never wanted the throne, but, Mithras, mark my words, you had better kill me this time, because I'll come for you. And that inevitability is of your own making."

Jasper gritted his teeth and lifted the mask again.

"No!" Ada screamed. Fury surged down their link. Her face contorted. She slapped her palms over Mithras's and... something happened. The air shimmered. Mithras started choking. Tiny black veins squirmed on his face as though his blood had turned to poison. He tried to let go of Ada, but she had a death grip on him. She was doing this to him.

Jasper lowered the mask, stupefied.

The Dark Mage gasped.

With every passing second, the King's fate worsened, and Ada's energy felt grimy. Dirty.

Jasper's breath hitched, realizing what she was doing; accessing the dark side of her gift, mana scraped from the inky side of the Well.

"Stop!" he shouted, holding his hand out. "Stop, Ada, please listen to me."

Her chest heaved in great motions as she sucked in air. Wild brown eyes held his.

"Look at him," Jasper said, pointing to the Mage. "That's what happens when you access the dark side of the Well. You wither. You shrivel."

"Maebh said it was natural," she rasped.

For Crimson's sake, her voice sounded different—slick, oily, deep.

"Ada," he tried again. "Please. Don't do it. You were right, love. We're stronger together. Fuck what we are apart, right? You and me, forever."

She stared.

He nodded and approached her with slow, cautious steps. She lowered her hands. He beckoned her. She took a step—

The iron mask slammed onto his face. He reared back. Strong hands pushed him down. Somewhere, he heard a woman scream. *Ada.* He roared, lashing out, but it was too late. In his tunnel vision focus to get to Ada, he'd missed the Dark Mage approaching from the side. The bolts were now in his neck, burrowing in like an agony filled drill. His link to the Well cut off. He felt no connection to Ada. No mana.

Gone.

Empty.

All because the metal invaded his body. Jasper's hands clutched the mask, and he howled his fury. He'd underestimated the sensation of entrapment, of being locked in a cage again. He swiped to the side where the Mage had been and then charged until his hands landed on something soft and breakable. An arm. Maybe a neck. He couldn't see properly through the iron mask's slits. He squeezed. He dug his fingers in deep until he felt the hot lifeforce running free from the Mage's frail body. He kept squeezing until that body went limp and collapsed. And then he landed on his knees, found the Dark Mage's neck, and squashed it with an irrational need to protect himself. And Ada.

Wrenching himself away, he stumbled around, growling, trying to see through the slits. Flashes of lake, beach, trees. Golden hair. Sniggering smile. Haggard face.

Panting with heated breaths against the iron, Jasper stumbled. The metal tormented him like nothing else. His body screamed for it to be removed. *Take it off! Get it off me!*

Bring back the Well. Bring back life. Love.

Looking up, gasping, he saw Mithras had recovered. He didn't go to his Mage, his faithful companion. He went straight for Ada and, with lightning quick reflexes, he put one hand on the side of Ada's head and another beneath her jaw. He met Jasper's gaze and then snapped her neck.

A sickening wet crunch. Ada's last breath, a *puh* of air. And then her lifeless body fell limp to the sand, tumbling in a dead weight to the side, her blond hair falling across her lax face.

Jasper went stone cold.

No. It can't be. He'd imagined it. He was dreaming.

No!

His every fear had come to life. He'd failed. He lost. *Her*.

Nothing mattered after that. Nothing but the firestorm raging in his blood, beating out the iron sickness. Slowly. Surely. It rumbled into an inferno.

Kill. Revenge. Die.

His mind locked onto those three words and repeated them over and over. With the absence of Ada's lifeforce, breathing compassion into him, accepting him, loving him... gone forever... those three dark words became his anchor.

Kill. Revenge. Die.

He snarled, low and guttural. What's a few more scars? He held his breath, dug his fingers into his flesh where the bolts pierced, and tore them from his flesh. A loud bellow of pain hurtled out of him. *Hurts so bad. Keep pulling. Get them out. Kill.*

Murder the fae who'd taken her life.

The mask tore clean off Jasper's face, spraying blood on the white sand. His blood gushed from his neck and he staggered. His connection to the Well hurtled back into him. Mana rose to his will, and he triggered the shift, dragging his entire capacity to pump into the wolf, building him bigger, stronger, more feral. He knew the shift would heal his neck—enough to make a final stand.

The wolf sprang free.

Black, furred paws padded beneath him, so big he'd torn through his clothes. He gave a guttural snarl, teeth snapping.

Mithras stepped backward, stark eyes on Jasper in wolf form. He was so big; he was at Mithras's eye level. One bite, and he was gone.

Options calculated in Mithras's eyes as Jasper prowled closer. He steadied his crown, gaze darting to the dead Mage. Black veins still peppered his face. Ada's attack had weakened him. He was alone, and moments away from becoming wolf food.

Would Mithras shift? *Could* he shift? Or would he run?

Jasper hoped he would flee. He wanted to feel his claws ripping into the coward's back as he chased him down.

Mithras drew a weapon and held it between them. If Jasper was in fae form, he'd have laughed at the *floater* trying to brandish a metal weapon. The Well hadn't chosen him. Hadn't blessed him. All this time Jasper had wondered if he was good enough to be king. He'd wondered why his father hated him so much.

Mithras was jealous.

The King never had the guts to enter the lake.

He never had the worth to be granted the powers of holding metal and plastic and still access the Well.

And the King never had the love of a compassionate woman.

Had.

His heart broke. Ada was gone.

For her, Jasper would do this last thing, rid the world of the coward. He would take him into the lake, feed him to the Well Worms. Let him taste rejection on a metaphysical level. Let him relive the pain he'd caused. Jasper's howl shook the trees, shattering the wilderness, sending winged wildlife fleeing for the sky. When the last note died, he transformed back to fae form, his neck partially healed, fresh scars pulling with an ache.

The wolf couldn't save him from this next task. He had to do it with his hands. The wolf was part of him, not the other way around. Jasper had to make this final stand.

He portaled behind the King, gripped his arms, and then portaled them into the middle of the lake. Even before he let go of Mithras, the worms took hold of him, hungry. They'd been waiting. Mithras tried to take Jasper down with him. He clawed at the surface of the water, scratching Jasper's arms, but Jasper pushed him away with disgust. And the worms took Mithras under.

There was nothing left but a gurgle in the water.

For long seconds, Jasper treaded water, refusing to look back at the shore. He knew what he'd find. Two lifeless bodies. One dark-haired. One blond. One his love. His reason for breathing.

He raised his eyes to the blue sky, painfully aware of what circled beneath. Their recent meal would satisfy them only for a short while. Time was running out.

Wolves howled in the distance. His sluggish heart beat a little faster.

They're coming.

Not the King's men this time. The Guardians. His cadre. His family. Too late.

His mother had bid him to be kind... to be brave. His lover had bid him to accept his faults, to pick himself up. So he'd come to the place where the bravest go. And the cowards died.

Time to end this, once and for all. His bottom lip trembled.

... kind... brave... worth it.

Slimy, thick worms wrapped around Jasper's ankles, and he plummeted.

CHAPTER
THIRTY

Ada's consciousness rose slowly from the deep. A gritty dizziness swam in her head. Apart from that she felt nothing. No pain. No sensation. Nothing. She was a prisoner within her paralyzed body.

Vaguely, sounds came at her from a distance. Someone was fighting. Snarling. Raging.

Mithras had snapped her neck!

It was why she couldn't move. A surge of fear blanked her mind.

Did Jasper know she was alive? She had to heal. Had to tell him. Had to help him. But she couldn't move.

Don't panic. Don't die. *Heal.*

So she shut her eyes, slowed her breathing, her heartbeat, everything. She filtered all her awareness into her body, focusing inward, hunting for the damage.

Mana came to her with a ferocity she'd never known before. Her gift sprung to life, aggrieved it had been almost cheated of doing all the things she'd wanted to do. She could heal the world if she tried.

Start small.

Start with yourself.

To do so, she had to filter every sound out, especially the howl of grief tearing through the sky. *You're no good to him if you're broken. Heal.*

She thought of everything that hurt, but other hurts sprang to the forefront. Flashes of her childhood. No matter how she tried to push them back, she couldn't. Her mother. Her lack of love. Of how she'd kept Jasper at a distance. All because she was terrified of how much it would hurt to lose him. It was ridiculous. Unfounded. She'd grown out of this.

She wasn't unwanted. She was loved and cherished above all. Jasper loved her so much, he'd become the bravest person she'd ever known. Putting on that iron mask had terrified him, but he did it anyway.

If that wasn't bravery, then what was?

Pick yourself up.

It was time to survive.

Ada focused on the here and the now. She sent her magic scouring through her system, hunting down every last impurity and broken cell it could find, restoring it with life, making it whole. Tingles prickled her feet. Fire lanced down her legs. Her arms twitched as blood flow restored, as her nervous system came to life. Slowly, surely, she healed herself.

And then she felt it... a flicker of life deep within her womb. So tiny it was almost not there. So new. Her hands flew to her stomach. She was pregnant?

Why wouldn't she be? They'd not used protection. She'd been having sex with Jasper since Lupercalia night—the fertility rite.

They were going to be a family.

She rolled to her side and took a deep, shuddering breath. Tears of triumph and joy burning her eyes. She did it. She had to tell Jasper. Had to... her gaze lifted, searching for him, but only found the cold dead stare of the Dark Mage. Scrambling to her feet, she scoured the beach. Nothing. Where was he?

Her bond. She focused on it, and found something close... where? She rotated, homing in on the direction. A splash in the lake, deep into the middle. Jasper's head bobbed gently as he floated, staring up at the sky. His ears were in the water.

"Jasper!" she rasped.

He shut his eyes, and he sank.

Without thinking, without understanding what the worms would do, Ada ran, launching herself through the shallows. All she knew was that she had to get to him. When she could run no more, she dove and swam, kicking her feet. She pushed herself until she could move no faster. She swam until her arms and lungs burned. She followed the sense of Jasper. He was still there, somewhere in the deep, his energy pulsing at her from the depths.

Too long. This was taking too long.

Arriving where she saw him go down, she heaved in air until her lungs protested, and dove. Jasper had said there were creatures here no one wanted to experience. Only a third of initiates emerged alive. Fear skated along her spine as she stroked through the dark water.

Down their bond she felt his eery, calm acceptance. Jasper's emotions were unblocked, probably because he thought there was no one left to hide them from. He was giving up. The knowledge spurred her onward.

A tiny blue beacon glowed gently below—his Well-blessed markings.

She kicked, stroked, and pushed herself down, urging her emotions to scream for her.

Look up. I'm coming. I won't leave you.

Her own blue marks added to the light. Murky shadows twirled around her, circling. The worms were here, but she couldn't look at them. She refused to acknowledge their existence. No time.

Dark hair floating.

Her heart swelled. She reached down, scraped his hair, but missed. Sensing her, his face lifted. Glimmering amber eyes latched onto her. He should have rejoiced. He should have smiled. But no. His face crumpled. His bottom lip trembled. His brows joined in the middle and lifted. He reached for her.

He thought she was dead. An angel.

Another stroke, and she caught hold of his grip. She tugged, trying to reverse her trajectory, but he was caught. Something had him. Dark shadows darted closer, brushing against her. Her lungs burned. She was running out of air, out of time.

But she wouldn't leave him. Never.

So she stopped struggling. She sank. Down, her body drifted, toes first into his awaiting arms. Into the writhing nest of worms wrapping themselves around his body, slithering up toward his heart. Glimmers of blue cast the hard planes of his face into soft, ghostly light. His melancholic happiness washed into her. She took his face between her palms and planted her lips on his. Bubbles exploded from his mouth as he kissed her back. And then he let go. He drifted. Dark lashes lowered lazily. He was out of air. Giving up.

No.

She refused to accept it.

Long, slithering Well Worms wrapped around her legs, squashing her against Jasper.

She took his mouth and angled it against her neck, silently begging him to mark her. To clamp down and bite. When he did nothing but lay his lips on her skin, a silent scream of impotent rage smashed about her body. It can't end like this! She wouldn't allow it.

She'd survived abandonment as a child.

She'd survived being frozen for thousands of years.

She'd survived a knife to the stomach. A broken neck.

And she'd done all those things, not from someone else's actions, but from hers. And now she had a family to fight for. Her eyes flew open. The worms wiggled up her torso, tightening, trying to squeeze the air from her abused lungs. But she knew what to do. She bit down hard on his neck, claiming him for herself.

The watery graveyard suddenly shifted. It moved. Oxygen burst into her lungs. Water splashed and cascaded. They landed hard on something soft, bouncing and sloshing in displaced water. Gaping like a fish, she breathed, heaving in air. And it came. The sweet, ever loving air surged like fire into her lungs.

Where were they?

Plain ceiling. Check-quilted bed. The cadre house. Jasper's room. Jasper?

He'd portaled them here.

Next to her, wheezing, rolling to his side, manic eyes landing on her. He reached.

She grasped his hand.

"You're alive," he croaked. "How?"

She nodded, still panting. "I healed myself." Her eyes watered. She choked. "Because of you. And me."

Pain fractured his expression. "What do you mean?"

"I don't know if you heard me when I shouted at you from the shore, but you were right. I was wrong. We're not nothing apart. We're stronger together."

They stared at each other, laying side by side on a half-soaked bed, holding hands.

More anguish clogged her throat.

"Jasper," she sobbed. "I'm sorry I was too afraid to let you in. I thought if I did, I wouldn't survive it if you left. But I..."

His voice broke. "You survived."

"Because I can't breathe without you either."

He rolled on top of her. "Ada," he whispered. "You came for me."

"I love you... and..." She took his hands and slid them down to her wet stomach. "And there's something else. Our fertility rite was a little too successful."

His eyes met hers, confused. "What?"

"We're pregnant."

His lashes widened. Shock blanked his features. "What?"

She smiled, biting her lip, letting him take it all in and then turned her head to the side and pulled back her hair, uncovering her neck. Even without seeing his face, she felt the shift in his emotions. He let her feel it all: triumph, relief, a pouring of love.

He made a sound, something caught between a groan and a pained sigh, and then he dug his long teeth into her neck, growling around her skin. It didn't hurt as much as she feared. A prick. A sting. Like fine needles. Without removing his teeth, he ripped her shirt open, tugged her pants over her hips, and only when he needed the arm room did he relinquish his hold on her neck. Tearing the last of her clothes from her body, he reared back and studied her, eyes full of self satisfied appreciation.

"What do you see?" she asked.

"A mother. A warrior. My queen."

"That queen bit is just weird."

"Get used to it." He lowered his head and laved at the bite. The small throbbing pain swiftly turned into heated desire, spreading through every limb, melting her to the core until she became a breathless, whimpering mess.

He groaned. "You're really mine."

She nodded, arching into him.

"We're going to have a child."

"A prince or a princess."

"Fuck me."

"Okay."

He pulled back, eyes bright and crinkled at the edges. "Are you ready?"

"For what?"

He grinned against her neck. "I'm going to take you rough." He kissed her throat. "I'm going to take you hard." He licked down her front. "And I'm going to cover you with my scent."

She moaned as his tongue trailed across to her breast, laved her nipple, then pulled away. Dark, smoky eyes clashed with hers as he dipped his fingers between her legs and speared into her core. Her back bowed from the sensation. Her hips moved on their own, riding his fingers as he slipped them in and out, around and—*God*. Up. Down. In.

She was a shambles of stimulation. His lips on her breasts. His fingers between her legs. He kissed her stomach reverently. And then he moved, taking himself in hand and positioning right where she needed it.

"I'm claiming you, my love."

He thrust in.

THIRTY-ONE

Still coming down from the bone demolishing high of Ada's blood, Indigo flew himself to the ceremonial lake. He could see clearly now, but his flight path tipped as though he were in the grip of a hurricane. A storm named Ada.

Human—*Well-blessed* human—tasted like potent, syrupy, pulse tingling bliss. And her blood had satisfied him in a way no other had.

He scrubbed his face, trying to shake the residue of longing from his expression. It had nothing to do with her... but how she tasted. But he'd have to get used to that being his last drop. Ada belonged to Jasper. The entire house heard him mate with her. The walls had shaken. The chandeliers rattled. That's why Indigo had to get out of there.

All he could think of was Jasper biting her neck.

He could smell her arousing blood filtering through the currents of air in the house.

So he came here. To the aftermath of Jasper's recent battle. He'd found out about it from the shifters, and they needed someone to collect the floating, bloated body of the King from the middle of the lake. Haze was halfway back to the Order when he'd heard the forest-shattering wolf's howl. He'd turned back and found Ada diving into the lake, a dead Dark Mage on the sand, and a discarded glass crown. No king.

Shielding his eyes from the sun, Indigo circled the ceremonial lake and located the other Guardians. Rush, Thorne, Leaf and Clarke. Thank Crimson, they were in the shade of a tree. It wasn't that the sun made him sick, it just sapped his energy. And after the hit of blood he'd had, he just wanted to go back to sleep and dream of more. This time with a sexy, naked human of his own.

Arcing back toward the lake, he flew until he spotted the King's body, dove, scooped the disgusting thing up, and took it back to the shore where he dumped it unceremoniously.

"What kind of lunacy happened here?" he asked, landing on the sand. Grains puffed up, stinging his eyes.

Rush narrowed his eyes at Indigo. "Why are you here?"

Indigo snorted. "Why not?"

Clearly he was still wary Indigo would attack the tasty human standing next to him.

"Don't worry, Wolfie. I've can control my bloodlust."

Another snarl, to which Clarke explained to Indigo, "Jasper killed the King. And the Dark Mage. Now we don't know where Jasper or Ada are."

He lifted his pointer finger. "I can answer that."

They all stared at him.

"They're going to Bone Town in Jasper's room."

"Lady present," Thorne warned with a glare.

Clarke waved it off. "I've heard worse. So... they're making up. Excellent."

"They're making up, hard. I could smell it from the living room." Indigo grimaced.

"Ew." Clarke punched him.

He scowled, slapping his hand on the sore spot. The sun made everything sensitive.

Leaf, who'd been inspecting the King's body, walked over. He cast a disapproving glance at Indigo.

"This shouldn't need to be said, but if I catch you sniffing about the humans living in the cadre house, you're out. No warning. You're just out."

"I wasn't sniffing her out on purpose!" He threw up his hands. "Why does everyone think I'll let bloodlust consume me?"

Leaf arched a brow. "You know why."

That shut Indigo up. He ground his teeth and stormed over to the Mage's body. He'd fucked up once, years ago. They never let him forget it. So, he had sensitive tastebuds. So, he sometimes got a little carried away when drinking. He wasn't the first vampire to kill a meal, and he wouldn't be the last.

The Mage was so shriveled with ink sickness that he must have been sampling mana from the dark side of the Well for years. Between all that viscera and gore, he smelled rotten inside.

Jasper must have been furious to do that much damage.

Footsteps next to him.

"Indigo," Clarke said, stopping.

"Better be careful," he drawled. "I might forget myself and drain you dry."

She scoffed. "You'd never do that."

"How can you be so sure?"

"I know."

Indigo slid his gaze her way and found her watching him studiously.

"What do you want?" he snapped.

Her lip twitched with a mysterious smile he'd come to learn was part of her plotting face. All the Seers had a look that revealed their secret knowledge.

"Nothing," she said, then glanced at the body. "Ew. Can we talk somewhere else?"

"You want to talk?"

"By the trees?"

He went with her, silently rejoicing in the shade, and then raised his brow. "What have you Seen? What insane mission are you about to send me on and does the Prime know about it?"

Her eyes turned to slits. "Can you read minds like the Six? Or are you just intuitive?"

"I'm lucky."

She took a deep breath and glanced over to where Rush, Thorne and Leaf discussed the glass crown.

"When Mithras died, something happened to my visions. They turned… dark. It's as though he was the catalyst for another potential future timeline. All I know is that it's got something to do with Maebh."

Indigo folded his arms. "Why are you telling me?"

"Because I need you to find the next Well-blessed human before the Void or Maebh."

"Me?"

"No one will track and covet her as you will. It has to be you."

His stomach flipped. "Are you saying she's my mate?"

"All I know is that she's already awake in this time. I thought I was the first, but I was wrong. So wrong. There are more, and like the Void, they woke before me. For all we know, she's living in Elphyne, disguised as a fae. She could be anyone."

"How are we supposed to find her?"

She cocked her head. "You've tasted one of us."

She shocked him to silence. Clarke knew exactly what the blood did to Indigo, yet she trusted him to find this human.

"What makes her so important?"

"She was a weapon's maker."

"Like a blacksmith?"

"Much worse. A nuclear physicist."

"I don't understand."

"She knows how to build the bombs that destroyed the old world, and she's out there somewhere. Alone. Hidden. And both Maebh and the Void are already hunting her."

THIRTY-TWO

A week had passed since Jasper killed Mithras. Or rather, since he'd let the Well Worms take him. He'd spent half the time cloistered in his room with his new mate, ensuring his claim was well and truly staked. The other half, he'd spent at the Summer Palace, talking to the castle staff and soldiers.

Everyone knew about the death of the King. The Prime had made sure of it. They knew it was he who'd taken down Mithras with his own hands, no assistance. Now everyone expected his answer.

He was almost ready to give it but had to do one last thing.

He took Ada's hand and, together, they walked into his mother's old cottage. They went straight toward the soggy beat-up rug in the living room. Jasper bent down and flipped the corner to reveal the loose board. He levered it up, and the one next to it.

Below was a tiny dugout.

"It's so small," he murmured.

"You were only a child, Jasper."

With all that responsibility resting on his little shoulders, he'd felt so much older. A dig around his pocket and he found the heart-shaped amber pendant. He placed it in the dirt and then boarded up the hole. He put his hand on top and closed his eyes.

His mother would be proud of him, of Ada, and of their new family.

"Are you sure you don't want to keep it?" Ada asked.

He shook his head, frowning. "Every time I look at it, I remembered the wrong things. I need to move on, to look to the future."

Touching his fingers to his lips, he then pressed them down on the boards. This all started with his mother. She'd died in this very spot. And he'd finally avenged her.

When he straightened, Ada handed him the glass crown. "Who will you be?"

He turned the crown over in his hands, watching the light twinkle off its shape. Reflections danced about the room.

Clarke had told them about her new visions. Mithras's death had set something loose in the Queen. Darkness crowded everything Clarke foresaw. There were dark times ahead. The Seelie people needed a strong king. They needed someone to make things fun. They needed someone brave.

"I'll be whatever the people need me to be, whatever my family needs me to be."

"But what name will you take?"

He thought about it. Mithras was never in the cards. But he couldn't go back to Reed. He could, however, be both. He could honor his mother and the place he'd spent most of his life. He could honor them.

"Jasper Darkfoot."

Slow clapping came from the darkness. Jasper strained his senses, trying to sniff out the interloper. But what he found made no sense.

"Clara?"

She emerged from the dark hallway, hobbling on a cane. Behind her, more bodies emerged. One of them, the youth Ada had healed. Lake.

Ada ran to Clara and took her in a hug. Then grabbed the boy. "We thought you were all dead."

Clara's eyes watered. "Some of us escaped. But we had to lie low until we were sure. The Prime had learned of our part with the hoarding." Her glimmering gaze shifted to Jasper. "But now a Darkfoot is taking the crown, we're hoping you'll grant us one more favor."

"Clara," he admonished. "I would never let the Order punish you. Mithras manipulated all of you."

Clara's shoulders dropped with relief. "You don't know how it feels to hear that." She wiped her eyes. "It will feel even better when the official announcement is out."

She gave the crown in his hand a pointed look.

As king, Jasper couldn't be a Guardian anymore—technically—and that was harder than he realized to give up. But the teardrop tattoo couldn't be removed. It couldn't even be glamoured away. It was permanent. He hadn't finished facing the Well Worms for the second time, but he didn't need to. He was already everything his mother had hoped. It had just taken a few hundred years to get here. The good, the bad, and the painful—it had all shaped the fae he was today. It was time to stop living up to old dreams and time to make new ones.

He stared at Clara. He stared at Ada. And then he put on the crown.

The End.

Of the first Fae Guardians Trilogy, Season of the Wolf. Our warm blooded vampires are coming up next in the Season of the Vampire!

EPILOGUE

Pain was his world. Never ending agony filled him from head to toe, bone to blood, flesh to mind. He peeled open his swollen eyes. Dried blood cracked in his lashes. He shook his arms, testing the rope manacles, but he was still securely tied above his head to a wall in the Obsidian Castle dungeon.

What they'd done to him.

What those *things* had done.

Filthy, vile, unnatural *things*.

"Ahh, and so he wakes."

Bones lifted his head.

She was there. The worst one of them all. The Unseelie Queen. Dressed in a revealing dress, a crow sat on her shoulder. She was depraved, wicked, and full of deranged wishes. Next to her was the vile, sickeningly pretty, ghostly creature that had violated Bones's mind. It had raped him metaphysically.

They were all the demons the Void wanted to end.

Bones laughed to himself.

The Void wanted to end them all. They all deserved to die. If they could just find a way to kill the Sluagh, the humans could take back what was rightfully theirs. All of it.

The Queen stepped up to him and placed a long, black nail under his chin. "Oh, my dear human."

"Why haven't you sent me back to the Order?" At least those feral animals were easier to stomach.

"They think you're dead," she laughed. "Whoops."

His stomach dropped. "Why am I still alive?"

"Because when my darling Sluagh ravaged your mind, we found something. A special weapon you humans are building." Her plum lips stretched into a devious smile. "And you're going to tell me all about it, and more importantly, how to make it myself."

NEED TO TALK TO OTHER READERS?

BOOKS ARE OUR LIFE!

Join Lana's Angels Facebook Group for fun chats, giveaways, and exclusive content.
https://www.facebook.com/groups/lanasangels

DOMINION ANGEL

ABOUT THE AUTHOR

OMG! How do you say my name?

Lana (straight forward enough - Lah-nah) **Pecherczyk** (this is where it gets tricky - Pe-her-chick).

I've been called Lana Price-Check, Lana Pera-Chickywack, Lana Pressed-Chicken, Lana Pech...*that girl!* You name it, they said it. So if it's so hard to spell, why on earth would I use this name instead of an easy pen name?

To put it simply, it belonged to my mother. And she was my dream champion.

For most of my life, I've been good at one thing – art. The world around me saw my work, and said I should do more of it, so I did.

But, when at the age of eight, I said I wanted to write stories, and even though we were poor, my mother came home with a blank notebook and a pencil saying I should follow my dreams, no matter where they take me for they will make me happy. I wasn't very good at it, but it didn't matter because I had her support and I liked it.

She died when I was thirteen, and left her four daughters orphaned. Suddenly, I had lost my dream champion, I was split from my youngest two sisters and had no one to talk to about the challenge of life.

So, I wrote in secret. I poured my heart out daily to a diary and sometimes imagined that she would listen. At the end of the day, even if she couldn't hear, writing kept that dream alive.

Eventually, after having my own children (two firecrackers in the guise of little boys) and ignoring my inner voice for too long, I decided to lead by example. How could I teach my children to follow their dreams if I wasn't? I became my own dream champion and the rest is history, here I am.

When I'm not writing the next great action-packed romantic novel, or wrangling the rug rats, or rescuing GI Joe from the jaws of my Kelpie, I fight evil by moonlight, win love by daylight and never run from a real fight.

I live in Australia, but I'm up for a chat anytime online. Come and find me.

Stalker Links
www.lanapecherczyk.com

facebook.com/lanapecherczykauthor
instagram.com/lana_p_author
amazon.com/-/e/B00V2TP0HG
tiktok.com/@lanapauthor
goodreads.com/lana_p_author
patreon.com/lanacreates

ALSO BY LANA PECHERCZYK

THE FAE GUARDIANS WORLD

Fae Guardians - Elphyne

(Fantasy/Paranormal Romance)

Season of the Wolf Trilogy

The Longing of Lone Wolves

The Solace of Sharp Claws

Of Kisses & Wishes Novella (free for subscribers)

The Dreams of Broken Kings

Season of the Vampire Trilogy

The Secrets in Shadow and Blood

A Labyrinth of Fangs and Thorns

A Symphony of Savage Hearts

Of Pixies and Promises Novella

Season of the Elf Trilogy

A Song of Sky and Sacrifice

A Crown of Cruel Lies

A War of Ruin and Reckoning

Season of the Crow Trilogy

The Company of Vengeful Crows

Fae Devils

(Fae Guardians Sluagh Spin-off)

Castle of Nevers and Nightmares

Trials of Dusk and Dreams

THE DEADLYVERSE

The Sinner Sisterhood

(Demon-hunting Paranormal Romance)

The Sinner and the Scholar

The Sinner and the Gunslinger

The Sinner and the Priest

The Deadly Seven
(Fated Mate Paranormal/Sci-Fi Romance)
The Deadly Seven Box Set Books 1-3
Sinner

Envy

Greed

Wrath

Sloth

Gluttony

Lust

Pride

Despair